THE LAST MAN

THE LAST MAN

Mary Wollstonecraft Shelley

Edited with an introduction by Anne McWhir

broadview literary texts

Canadian Cataloguing in Publication Data

Shelley, Mary Wollstonecraft, 1797-1851
  The last man

(Broadview literary texts)
Includes bibliographical references.
ISBN 1-55111-076-8

I. McWhir, Anne Ruth, 1947- . II. Title. III. Series..

PR5397.L3 1996 823'.7 C96-930180-4

Broadview Press
Post Office Box 1243, Peterborough, Ontario, Canada K9J 7H5

in the United States of America:
3576 California Road, Orchard Park, NY 14127

in the United Kingdom:
B.R.A.D. Book Representation & Distribution Ltd., 244a, London Road, Hadleigh, Essex SS7 2DE

Broadview Press is grateful to Professor Eugene Benson for advice on editorial matters for the Broadview Literary Texts series.

Broadview Press gratefully acknowledges the support of the Canada Council, the Ontario Arts Council, and the Ministry of Canadian Heritage.

Typesetting and assembly: True to Type Inc., Mississauga, Canada.

PRINTED IN CANADA

Mary Wollstonecraft Shelley by R. Rothwell, 1841. (Photo courtesy of
The National Portrait Gallery.)

Contents

Preface   ix

Introduction   xiii

A Note on the Text   xxxvii

Mary Wollstonecraft Shelley: A Brief Chronology   xxxix

The Last Man
   Introduction   1
   Volume 1   7
   Volume 2   129
   Volume 3   247

Map of Lionel Verney's World   368

Appendix A: Some Contemporaries of the Last Man

1. George Gordon, Lord Byron, "Darkness" (1816)   369
2. Thomas Campbell, "The Last Man" (1823)   371
3. Thomas Campbell, letter in *The Times*, 24 March 1825   373
4. Thomas Hood, from "The Last Man" (1826)   374
5. George Dibdin Pitt, from *The Last Man; or, The Miser of Eltham Green* (1833)   375
6. Thomas Love Beddoes, notes for a projected play, *The Last Man*   376

Appendix B: The Sibyl's Cave

1. Virgil, from *Aeneid* 6   377
2. Jean-Baptiste Cousin de Grainville, from *The Last Man, or Omegarus and Syderia, A Romance in Futurity* (1806)   379

Appendix C: Versions of Plague

1. Edward Gibbon, from *The Decline and Fall of the Roman Empire* (1776–88)   383
2. Daniel Defoe, from *A Journal of the Plague Year* (1722)   386
3. Charles Brockden Brown, from *Arthur Mervyn* (1799–1800)   388
4. John Wilson, from *The City of the Plague* (1816)   390
5. From "Contagion and Sanitary Laws," *Westminster Review* 3 (1825): 134-67   391

Appendix D: "The Web of Mind"

1. Constantin François de Chasseboeuf, comte de Volney, from *The Ruins* (1791)   394
2. William Godwin, from *Political Justice* (1793)   396
3. Thomas Robert Malthus, from *An Essay on Population* (1798)   398
4. Mary Wollstonecraft, from *The French Revolution* (1794)   399
5. Edmund Burke, from *A Letter to a Noble Lord* (1796)   401
6. Percy Bysshe Shelley, from Notes to *Queen Mab* (1813)   401
7. Percy Bysshe Shelley, from Preface to *The Revolt of Islam* (1818)   402
8. William Godwin, from *Essay on Sepulchres* (1809)   403

Appendix E: Mary Shelley's poems (1825)

1. "The Choice"   405
2. "On Reading Wordsworth's Lines on Peel Castle"   409
3. "To Jane— (with the 'Last Man')"   410

Appendix F: Contemporary comments on and reviews of *The Last Man*

1. From *The Literary Magnet or Monthly Journal of the Belles Lettres*, ns 1 (January 1826): 56   411
2. From *The Literary Gazette, and Journal of the Belles Letters*, 474 (Saturday 18 Feb. 1826): 103-05   411
3. From *Monthly Review* 1 (1826): 333-35   412
4. From *Blackwood's* 21 (January 1827): 54   413

Appendix G: Postscript

From Mary Shelley, *Rambles in Germany and Italy* (1844)   415

Works Cited/Recommended Reading   417

Preface

Several editions of *The Last Man* have appeared over the past few years, testifying to a growing interest in Mary Shelley's life and work. This new version of the first edition (1826) sets out to provide not only an annotated text, but sufficient intertexts to help students of Mary Shelley's fiction acquire knowledge of its intellectual and literary milieu. *The Last Man* is a deliberately and significantly allusive text, and knowledge of contexts often affects reading. Further, Mary Shelley's wide-ranging reading is an important part of the texture of this generically complex novel, which has affinities to personal journal, biography, autobiography, romantic apocalypse, fantasy, science fiction, essay, travel narrative and history as well as to the novel or, as Shelley herself preferred to call it, "romance."

As my Introduction argues, one of her own images in *The Last Man* is the "clue," the thread which enables one to explore and escape from the labyrinth of the text. The thread has more than one strand, for there are many paths to the centre and back again. Some readers may choose to get access to *The Last Man* through contemporary issues and interests—AIDS as a late twentieth-century version of plague, millennial hopes and fears, the novel as speculative fiction. Others may be more interested in the context of Shelley's other fiction, or in how she uses, and perhaps repudiates, the writings of her father, William Godwin, her husband, Percy Bysshe Shelley, or even her mother, Mary Wollstonecraft. Because of the remarkably broad swath that this novel cuts through texts and ideas, and because of its wide-ranging implications for modern readers, this edition can provide only a few clues which will, I hope, introduce readers to some of the twists of the labyrinth.

Since that labyrinth is partly geographical, I include a map. Although the world of the novel extends to Pekin, Quito, Ispahan, and Van Diemen's Land, the map is limited to Europe, the world of all Lionel Verney's adventures and the cultural centre from which he projects his final journey. Appendices include literary contexts (some classical intertexts, the "last man" as early nineteenth-century hero, reviews of Shelley's book), a political context (post-revolutionary retrospect), a sociological context (the debate initiated by T. R. Malthus in 1798 about the adequacy of the food supply to sustain population), several historical contexts (especially various accounts of outbreaks of plague), and a personal context (especially Shelley's own poems representing her feelings after the death of her husband). In framing *The Last Man* with such contemporary intertexts, I follow D. Lorne Macdonald and Kathleen Scherf's edition of the 1818 text of *Frankenstein* (Broadview, 1994), which demonstrates how appendices of this kind can engage in dialogue with Shelley's fiction.

My choice of James Beresford's blank-verse translation of the *Aeneid* (1794) is based less on its merits (Dryden's version is far livelier) than on my desire to present readers with styles of writing familiar to Mary Shelley and her contemporaries. In spite of the importance of Percy Bysshe Shelley's work, I have included only three brief selections, all from his prose. His poetry is readily available elsewhere: I hope that readers will follow hints in the footnotes to this edition and consult, among other works, *The Revolt of Islam, Hellas, Prometheus Unbound,* and "Ode to the West Wind."

I have chosen material in the Appendices less because of direct correspondence with particular passages in the novel (though such correspondences will strike some readers) than because the material illuminates Shelley's book as a whole. Working with the text of *The Last Man,* however, one recognizes a far denser and more specific intertextual structure than can be demonstrated by a few passages from other writers, no matter how carefully selected. I have therefore chosen to annotate quite thoroughly, hoping by doing so to emphasize the novel's complexity. When she wrote *The Last Man* Shelley relied pointedly and precisely on her extensive reading: she herself appears not to have written fragments of verse to suit her context, as some previous editors have suspected. Having tracked down all but a few quotations and references, I hope that readers will help me to identify those that remain.

While the material in the Appendices allows readers to explore contexts and intertexts for themselves, my Introduction suggests how I myself have put Shelley's sibylline fragments together. Texts mentioned in the notes are listed in Works Cited/Recommended Reading, a bibliography intended not just for those who want a list of articles on *The Last Man,* but especially for those who wish to extend their study of Mary Shelley and her circle, or of the literary, political, and social contexts of the novel, through further reading primarily in contemporary sources. Wherever possible, I have chosen to cite editions readily available to students and general readers; the bibliography includes all references in the notes in order to emphasize the intertextual range of Shelley's novel. Those readers who would like to trace the last man into the twentieth century, in works by such writers as M. P. Shiel (*The Purple Cloud,* 1901), Olaf W. Stapledon (*Last and First Men,* 1930), and Nevil Shute (*On the Beach,* 1957), might like to begin with the bibliography in Arthur McA. Miller, *The Last Man: A Study of the Eschatological Theme in English Poetry and Fiction from 1809 Through 1839* (diss. Duke University, 1966).

I would like to acknowledge the work of previous editors of *The Last Man,* particularly Hugh J. Luke, Jr., and Morton D. Paley, whose annotations often pointed me in useful directions. For their patience and persistence, thanks to the library staff at the University of Calgary and at the Thomas Fisher Rare Book Library, University of Toronto. I am particularly grateful to those staff members at the Bruce Peel Special Collections Library, University of Alberta, who prepared a photocopy of the first edition of *The Last Man* and who met continuing requests for photocopying cheerfully and promptly. I acknowledge the kind permission of Oxford University Press to reprint as Appendix E Mary Shelley's poems, "The Choice," "On Reading Wordsworth's Lines on Peel Castle," and "To Jane— (with the 'Last Man')," from *The Journals of Mary Shelley*, ed. Paula R. Feldman and Diana Scott-Kilvert (Clarendon, 1987) 2: 490-95, and as part of Appendix A two short selections from Thomas Lovell Beddoes' "The Last Man," from *The Works of Thomas Lovell Beddoes*, ed. R.W. Donner (Oxford UP, 1935), 520, 525-26. For help in defraying expenses, I am grateful to the English Department and to the Faculty of Humanities, University of Calgary.

Stephen Rupp, Victoria College, University of Toronto, kindly helped with translations from Calderón. Robin Poitras of the Department of Geography, University of Calgary, prepared the map. For both encouragement and practical help, many thanks to Ron Bond, John Charles, Barbara Conolly, Michael Dewar, Jeannine Green, Adrienne Kertzer, David Latane, Don LePan, Lorne Macdonald, Jay Macpherson, Donna Morrow, Mical Moser, David Oakleaf, Roger Peattie and Apollonia Steele.

Special thanks to Jay, who first introduced me to Mary Shelley; to David, as always; and to Stephen and Catherine, who without having read it themselves have helped to shape my reading of Mary Shelley's novel.

Anne McWhir
University of Calgary, Canada

Introduction

In a letter to her friend John Howard Payne shortly after *The Last Man* was published in 1826, Mary Shelley expresses considerable nervousness about its reception: "The curiosity excited by the title frightens me, because of the disappointment that must of course follow. You can form no idea of the difficulty of the subject—the necessity of making the scene universal to all mankind and of combining this with a peculiar interest which must constitute the novel."[1]

With these words, she situates her third published novel in the literary context of the early nineteenth century, where poems and stories treating the subject of the "last man"—the last survivor of humankind—were popular. At the same time, she draws attention to the problem of reconciling such visionary, prophetic writing with the expectations of novel-readers and, perhaps, with her own private agenda. *The Last Man* is at once a personal, even autobiographical and confessional meditation and a prophetic, encyclopedic, philosophical vision. Its focus is at once narrow and sweeping, for Mary Shelley's last man, the narrator Lionel Verney, leads the reader in two different directions—towards Mary Shelley's own suffering after Shelley's death (an important part of this novel's "peculiar interest" of character and feeling) and towards a literary context through which, perhaps, the novel may be made "universal to all mankind." *The Last Man* thus challenges conventional expectations of genre in ways that may surprise, but will not disappoint, the twentieth-century reader alert to generic and formal experiments.

As a literary figure, the last man has comic as well as tragic possibilities, if only because he keeps coming back like the movie-monster who won't stay dead. Mary Shelley did not invent him, for other writers had experimented with various versions of the end of things and the last survivor of humankind long before 1826. Apart from the general Romantic interest in solitary figures, the specific figure of the last man enters English literature with the 1806 translation of a French novel, *Le dernier homme*, by Jean-Baptiste Cousin de Grainville.[2] Grainville emphasizes millennial and apocalyptic vision rather than the elegiac solitude that dominates Mary Shelley's novel. His book is a peculiar mixture of romance, epic, revolutionary fantasy, operatic set-design, and quasi-reli-

---

1   *The Letters of Mary Wollstonecraft Shelley*, ed. Betty T. Bennett (Baltimore: Johns Hopkins UP, 1980) 1: 510.

2   Trans. as *The Last Man, or Omegarus and Syderia: A Romance in Futurity*, 2 vols. (London: Dutton, 1806). Henry F. Majewski gives an account of the French novel in "Grainville's *Le Dernier Homme*," *Symposium* 17.2 (1963): 114-22.

gious vision: the fate of a pair of lovers is finally less important than a divine plan according to which Death is victorious over the Genius of Earth. The structure of the story is shapeless and confusing because Grainville seems uncertain how to reconcile his human characters with his transcendent conflict—or how to link the hope of an earthly millennium with the fated victory of death. The novel's tone wavers between triumph and regret, optimism and despair, perhaps reflecting the political and philosophical mood of post-revolutionary France.

Grainville's last man is important mostly for his possible influence on other writers, among them Byron, Thomas Campbell, Thomas Lovell Beddoes, and Mary Shelley. By the time she returned to England the year after her husband drowned off the Italian coast in 1822, Mary Shelley did not have to look far for a literary subject. On 14 May 1824, the day before she learned about Byron's death in Greece, she wrote in her diary: "The last man! Yes I may well describe that solitary being's feelings, feeling myself as the last relic of a beloved race, my companions, extinct before me."[3] A subject of contemporary literature provided a way not only of coping with her own situation, but of reworking personal experience in fiction.

She had considerable experience of death and loss. Daughter of the feminist Mary Wollstonecraft, who died ten days after her birth, and of the radical philosopher William Godwin, Mary Wollstonecraft Godwin had fallen in love at sixteen with the poet Percy Bysshe Shelley. Between their elopement in 1814 and his death in 1822, she had coped with the fallout from two suicides (that of her half-sister Fanny Imlay Godwin and that of Percy's first wife, Harriet), with frequent domestic moves, with financial stress, miscarriage, family illness, and the deaths of three of her children. Forced back to England in 1823 by a need to appease her father-in-law, Sir Timothy Shelley (from whom she needed an allowance to support her only surviving child, Percy Florence), she set out to write *The Last Man* partly to raise some money. Since Sir Timothy had forbidden her to write his son's biography, *The Last Man* might also have provided an opportunity to write covertly about her relationship with Shelley. Sir Timothy must have suspected so, because he temporarily cut off Mary Shelley's allowance after its publication.[4]

Thinking about her own situation on her return to England, Mary might well have identified with the mood of Thomas Campbell's "The Last Man," published in the *New Monthly Magazine*,[5] which Campbell edited. Campbell's poem looks back in turn to Byron's "Darkness," a

---

3   *The Journals of Mary Shelley*, ed. Paula R. Feldman and Diana Scott-Kilvert (Oxford: Clarendon, 1987) 2: 476-77.

4   See *Letters of Mary Wollstonecraft Shelley*, ed. Bennett 1: 513, n 2.

5   8 (1823): 272-73.

poem written during the summer of 1816, when Mary and Percy Shelley had visited Byron frequently and when Mary had begun writing her first novel, *Frankenstein*. In choosing to identify herself with the last man in 1824, Mary Shelley deliberately chose a subject with both wide popular appeal and specific personal associations. However wretched her situation and feelings, she chose to express them within a much debated literary context involving several people in her own immediate circle.

According to Thomas Campbell, Byron's poem about the end of the world had been far from original. In a letter to the Editor of the *Edinburgh Review*, published in the *Times*, Campbell claims for himself some of Byron's ideas: "I remember my saying to [Byron], that I thought the idea of a being witnessing the extinction of his species and of the Creation, and of his looking, under the fading eye of nature, at desolate cities, ships floating at sea with the dead, would make a striking subject for a poem."[6] Campbell goes on to suggest that he is asserting his claim to originality because the subject has become trendy: "my friend Barry Cornwall informed me that an acquaintance of his intended to write a long poem, entitled the *Last Man*."

Bryan Waller Procter, who wrote poetry under the name of Barry Cornwall, visited and corresponded with Mary Shelley during this time and may well have brought the subject of the last man to her attention. Procter's "acquaintance," however, was the poet and playwright Thomas Lovell Beddoes, who claimed in February 1824 to have finished the first act of a verse play (never completed) called *The Last Man*.[7] Beddoes makes fun of Campbell's proprietary interest in the subject, remarking in a letter that "the gentleman is completely addled."[8] And after the publication of Mary Shelley's *The Last Man* in January 1826, Beddoes expresses keen interest. On 13 March 1826 he writes to Procter from Germany asking for news: "I am quite delighted at Mrs Shelley's overwhelming your charming friend of the New Monthly [Campbell]"; and on 1 April he writes to Thomas Forbes Kelsall, "Now you must tell me all about the Last Man; I am very glad that Mrs S. has taken it from the New Monthly Fellow—and I am sure that in almost every respect, she will do much better than either of us."[9] Whether or not Campbell was "overwhelmed" by the publication of Mary Shelley's novel, he chose not to review it in the *New Monthly*: it was simply tucked away in a list of Recent Publications; and, as if to emphasize this neglect, the May 1826 number included a notice of a musical setting of Campbell's "The Last Man":

---

6   Printed in *The Times*, 24 March 1825. See Appendix A.3.
7   Letter to Thomas Forbes Kelsall in *The Works of Thomas Lovell Beddoes*, ed.
     with introd. R. W. Donner (Oxford: Oxford UP, 1935) 580.
8   Letter to Kelsall, March 1825, in *Works*, ed. Donner 597.
9   Letters to Barry Cornwall and to Kelsall, in *Works*, ed. Donner 615, 618.

"The Last Man; a Scene, sung by Mr. Phillips ... the words of which, by Mr. Campbell, were taken from a former number of this Magazine."[10] This context of alleged plagiarism and personal rivalry goes some way towards explaining "the curiosity excited by the title" of *The Last Man*. The novel is deliberately public, even ostentatious, in its choice of subject. It appears the same year as magazine pieces with such titles as "The Death of the World" (*European Magazine* ns 2 [1826]: 351-53), "The City of the Dead" (*New Monthly* 16 [1826]: 404-05) and "The Last Man" (*Blackwood's* 19 [March 1826]: 284-86). Yet its subject is personal loss and its emotional focus is sometimes painfully intimate and confessional. Neither merely conventional nor merely personal, Mary Shelley's *The Last Man* eludes definition. It weaves the particular and the general together, making personal meaning out of the breadth of Shelley's reading and out of the resonance of a range of literary conventions. An extraordinarily ambitious book, its complexity is produced not primarily by narrative intensity, but by intertextuality. The plot, episodic and theatrical, proceeding to a predictable conclusion, is neither the "peculiar interest" nor the "universal" theme of *The Last Man*; the plot's pretext or framework suggests a subtler kind of interest, tightly integrated with the figurative language of the text. Not a conventional novel of plot and character, *The Last Man* is well described as Mary Shelley herself described it in a proposed subtitle that never appeared on the title-page: "a romance."[11]

* * *

This romance begins with a frame that makes explicit the relation of biography to fiction. The narrator visits the Sibyl's Cave near Naples in 1818, naming places also recorded in Mary Shelley's journals.[12] There, she[13] and

10   *New Monthly Magazine*, 18 (1826): 188-89.
11   Letter to Charles Ollier (who worked for Colburn, Shelley's publisher), 15 November 1825: "The title of my book is to be simply 'The Last Man, a Romance, by the Author of Frankenstein.' " *Letters*, ed. Bennett 1: 504.
12   "The Elysian fields—Avernus Solfatara—The Bay of Baiae is beautiful but we are disappointed by the various places we visit." *Journals*, ed. Feldman and Scott-Kilvert 1: 242.
13   The narrator's gender is unstated, but one identifies her with the "Author of Frankenstein" on the novel's title-page—also identified as Mary Shelley by contemporary readers and reviewers. Anne K. Mellor points out, however, that the quotation from Petrarch in the Author's Introduction "implicitly aligns the voice of the Author with the male gender," and goes on to ask, "Is Mary Shelley here raising the possibility of a new kind of subject in which gender is absent, or at the least, unstable, fluid, and unimportant?" Introduction to *The Last Man*, ed. Hugh J. Luke, Jr., introd. Anne K. Mellor (Lincoln: U of Nebraska P, 1993) xxv.

her companion find, in a cavern off the beaten tourist track, leaves inscribed with writing in various ancient and modern languages. Making a selection, and returning later for more, they work to decipher the Sibyl's words. Having lost her companion, the narrator continues alone, presenting the story that follows as an attempt to make a pattern out of mosaic fragments. Partly her own creative work, partly transcription and translation, the narrative within the frame is presented as therapeutic and transformative: Mary Shelley takes up the work of the Sibyl to make sense of broken fragments of truth in spite of loss and grief.

The story she tells belongs not to the remote past (as sibylline leaves might lead one to expect) but to the future. At the end of the twenty-first century, another narrator, Lionel Verney, inhabits a newly republican England which, in spite of some allusions to seventeenth-century republicanism, recalls the vaguely chivalric world of many early nineteenth-century romances. Lionel and his sister, Perdita, have grown up in obscurity and poverty after their father's death. Before the abdication of the last king, their father had been a favourite at court; but profligate habits had driven him into the obscurity of Cumberland, where he had married in poverty and died without regaining his lost status and fortune. Resentful at what he takes to be neglect by his father's friends, Lionel hates Adrian, Earl of Windsor, the son of the former king. When he meets Adrian, however, Lionel changes his mind, submits to Adrian's civilizing influence, and falls in love with his sister, Idris.

Meanwhile Lord Raymond, the English hero of the Greek people in their struggle against Turkey, returns to England planning to marry Idris. As children of the former king, Idris and Adrian become pawns in their Austrian mother's ambitious scheme to reinstate the monarchy and put Adrian on the throne. Adrian (an idealized version of Percy Shelley) is more interested in books than in politics. Lord Raymond, on the other hand, is fascinated by power; and although he secretly loves Lionel's sister Perdita, ambition prompts him to court Idris. For his part, Adrian has fallen in love with a beautiful Greek princess, Evadne, whose hopeless passion for Raymond, saviour of her people, drives her away from England in despair, leaving Adrian desolate and on the brink of madness.

After a period of uncertainty, Adrian recovers his health and resigns himself to celibacy: in a sense Lionel, Mary Shelley's alter ego, takes the place of the wife and soul-mate Adrian lacks. Raymond temporarily sets ambition aside to marry Perdita; Lionel and Idris, who have loved each other all along, also marry. A domestic idyll follows, characterized by sensibility, high-minded conversation, and idealized parenthood. Soon, however, Raymond enters politics in spite of his intention to renounce ambition, contending for and winning the highest office in the land, that of Lord Protector. When Evadne returns from the continent after complicated marital and political entanglements, she and Raymond meet again. Perdita finds out about their ensuing affair. Raymond once again leaves England for Greece, planning to lead an assault on Constantinople, which the Turks (represented as barbarians by everyone but Adrian) still hold.[14] Finding out that Raymond has been captured, Perdita and her child, Clara, follow, along with Lionel, who records Raymond's release from prison, his military successes, Evadne's death (in the guise of a soldier on the battlefield), Raymond's death at the fall of Constantinople, and Perdita's suicide by drowning.

The plague that enters the novel with Evadne's dying curse on Raymond spreads through Asia, Europe and America and eventually reaches England. From this point on, the novel is primarily peripatetic and episodic, as Lionel records stories of courage, loyalty, despair, suffering, and death. He contracts the plague but recovers, the only person to do so.[15] After Idris dies and is buried at Windsor, Lionel travels to Paris, where he attempts to rescue a young woman from a doomsday cult. He then crosses the Alps in a vain attempt to save the dwindling remnant of humanity. As everyone in the world dies one by one, the narrative becomes increasingly meditative and introspective but also increasingly broad and panoramic. Finally, having lost not only his wife but also their son, Evelyn, Lionel sets out from Venice in a small boat with Adrian and Perdita's daughter Clara, in the wild hope of reaching Greece and visiting Perdita and Raymond's grave. The boat is wrecked in a storm, and Lionel finds himself washed ashore near Ravenna, alone in the world. He makes his way through an unpeopled landscape to Rome, where he leaves behind the record of his suffering and prepares to set off, with little hope of finding a companion, down the Tiber into the open sea.

* * *

The Last Man presents a series of spatial and sometimes temporal overviews—Cumberland moors, battlefields, seas, mountains laid out as scenery and, at the end, the eternal city of Rome. In this sense it is strik-

---

14   The Shelleys' support for the revolutionary struggle of the Greeks against the Ottoman empire colours Mary Shelley's position in *The Last Man*. In *Frankenstein*, Safie's Turkish (and Moslem) father is tyrannical and treacherous. In spite of Percy Shelley's atheism, in his play *Hellas* (published 1822) he supports the "Christians" (meaning Greek freedom-lovers) against the "Mohammedans" (meaning tyrants and oppressors). In *The Last Man*, however, Adrian offers an alternative to such divisive labels when he tries to prevent the rape of a Turkish girl by two Christian soldiers (124), or comes between Irish and English armies to remind them of their common humanity (236).

15   So Lionel claims, though readers may notice an inconsistency in the text on this point: earlier, an old woman called Martha claims to have recovered from plague (212).

ingly different from Mary Shelley's best known work, *Frankenstein*—apart from, perhaps, the fields of ice at the end of that novel. In contrast to *Frankenstein*'s tightly structured interlocking narratives and detailed scrutiny of a small cast of characters, *The Last Man* is loosely structured and expansive.

A good visual analogue to *Frankenstein* is the portrait, perhaps with a doubled or mirrored subject—Caroline Beaufort mourning over her father's coffin, the miniature the creature uses to frame Justine, or the 1831 frontispiece in which creature and creator reflect each other at the moment of first recognition. However, in spite of the portraits of Byron and Shelley that readers will recognize in *The Last Man*, a better visual analogue to this novel is the apocalyptic panorama popular in the early nineteenth century and typified by John Martin's or Francis Danby's representations of scenes from the Bible: the deluge, the plagues of Egypt, the Last Judgement. As the plague moves closer to his family, Lionel Verney tells the reader, "Time and experience have placed me on a height from which I can comprehend the past as a whole; and in this way I must describe it, bringing forward the leading incidents, and disposing light and shade so as to form a picture in whose very darkness there will be harmony" (209). The "mosaic of circumstance" that Lionel puts together here is like the mosaic pattern of the sibylline leaves that Mary Shelley describes in her Introduction, clear only from sufficient distance. The material of Lionel's (and Mary Shelley's) personal memory is caught up into a pattern that includes (in addition to biography and autobiography) myth, legend, history, politics, the map of the world, the Bible, and writers in many languages (not all of them European) over more than two thousand years.

The text finally focuses not on Mary Shelley's idealized or self-justifying memory of her dead husband, but on the ways in which writers and readers are driven to make sense of the world. Lionel Verney has regarded all experience as a book in which he reads the thoughts and actions of his companions: "perusing this animated volume, I was the less surprised at the tale I read on the new-turned page" (136). Alone in Rome at the novel's end, he continues against all reason to leave written records of his experience; and his inscription in three languages—a clue to future interpreters for whom English may be as alien as "ancient Chaldee" (3)—reminds readers of the intertextual complexity of *The Last Man* and of the role of the reader as interpreter, extending the narrator's editorial task.

There are, however, differences as well as resemblances between *The Last Man* and other versions of disaster. In John Martin's watercolour, "The Last Man" (c. 1832, though a lost sketch was completed in 1826), the solitary figure stands high on a cliff overlooking the sea. The ships drift below him; bodies are piled everywhere. A later treatment in oils of the same subject (1849) focuses on a dead female figure beside the last man.[16] Byron's "Darkness" describes a charnel-house world; even Campbell's pious last man stands surrounded by "the skeletons of nations." Apart from some derivative set pieces, especially in Volume 2, Mary Shelley's *The Last Man* is comparatively restrained about representing physical death. Loss, not horror, increasingly dominates as the novel goes on. When Lionel Verney enters Rome, he enters not a city of corpses, but a depopulated city of marble statues mocking life. The setting of *The Last Man* becomes a shadow-world of neither life nor death, characterized by sadness, not sublimity, and by hauntings, not physical horrors.

This combination of restraint and allusiveness emphasizes the paradox noted earlier: *The Last Man* is both an intensely personal novel and a carefully contrived displacement of personal suffering into intertextual community. Lionel Verney is not alone in his suffering—partly because we are able to read his story (no matter how implausible the pretext), and partly because his very textual identity challenges the personal tragedy of his tale. He "is" Mary Shelley (allowing for the change of gender, to which we will return); he "is" also Percy Bysshe Shelley (who used the name Lionel to represent himself in two of his poems). Identity thus eludes the merely personal in ways that challenge simple identifications of fictional characters with people in the Shelley circle. There are several versions of Percy Bysshe Shelley: Adrian (the idealized portrait), Lionel (the narrator more obviously identified with Mary), even at times Raymond (most obviously identified with Lord Byron, but sharing certain roles and characteristics in common with Percy Shelley too). Similarly, Mary appears under various guises: Lionel the narrator, grieving survivor of a spouse and three children; the "cold and repulsive" Perdita (12); and Evadne—dark, passion-driven counterpart to the fair-haired Perdita or to the conventional Idris. Possibly a version of Mary's step-sister, Claire Clairmont, Evadne also functions as Mary's other self.

Many readers will recognize the primary portraits of Percy Shelley and Byron (disguised as Adrian and Raymond) and will trace certain connections with Mary Shelley's actual experiences. The idyllic life of Lionel's circle at Windsor Park corresponds to Mary's idealized memories of life at Bishopsgate in 1815 and Marlow in 1817. Raymond and Perdita's daughter Clara has the name of Mary's baby daughter Clara Everina, who died at Venice in 1818—and also of Clara Mary Jane (Claire) Clairmont, Mary's step-sister, whose daughter by Byron, Clara Allegra, was born in 1817. Perdita drowns herself, like Percy's first wife, Harriet—or as Mary's mother, Mary Wollstonecraft, attempted to do in 1795. Adrian perishes at

---

16   William Feaver, *The Art of John Martin* (Oxford: Clarendon, 1975) plates 67, 141.

sea, as Percy did in 1822. Raymond dies a champion of the Greeks against the Turks, in a heroic rewriting of Byron's death in 1824.[17] Nevertheless, the novel eludes the straightforward biographical interpretation such correspondences seem to suggest. Like her narrator, Lionel Verney, who begins by writing "the biography of favourite historical characters, especially those whom I believed to have been traduced, or about whom clung obscurity and doubt" (120), Mary Shelley seems to have discovered a kind of community in the process of writing: in Lionel's words, "I found another and a valuable link to enchain me to my fellow-creatures"(120), as biography is caught up into a recovery of creative imagination.

Yet, as Morton D. Paley reminds us, imagination itself is problematic.[18] Further, the "new-found web of mind" (120), associated with enthusiasm and sublimity, is in *The Last Man* also a web of language which may entangle and control those caught up in it. Lionel's verb "enchain" suggests a still darker connection, for the web of mind may be obsessive and constraining. In Lionel's words towards the end of the novel, "grief is fantastic; it weaves a web on which to trace the history of its woe from every form and change around" (348). A figure of both community and entrapment, the web of mind, like the record of loss it becomes by the novel's end, signifies both creativity and death.

"Death" becomes an alternative world of blurred and dissolving identity, a metaphor for an underworld (or innerworld) of fragmentation, assimilation, and transformation. Shortly before his death Raymond distinguishes himself from Lionel by telling him, "you do not yet divide the feeling of identity from the mortal form that shapes forth Lionel"(147). Dividing identity from the personal body, Mary Shelley engages in a paradoxical act of creation as complicity in disintegration. Like her most famous hero, Frankenstein, she puts together new versions of identity out of fragments of text, rather as her letters show her clinging through relics and monuments to fading, uncertain memories of lost physical presences. Weaving the web of mind, thereby taking on one role of the archetypal female creator, Mary Shelley blurs the boundaries between historical periods and historical persons, uses quotation associatively to create new contexts and, in effect, subsumes biography and history in myth.

* * *

---

17 Byron went to Greece in 1823 to fight for Greek independence, contributing large sums of money to the cause; he died of fever at Missolonghi on 19 April 1824 and was given full military honours before his body was shipped home to England for burial.

18 "*The Last Man*: Apocalypse without Millennium," *The Other Mary Shelley*, ed. Audrey A. Fisch, Anne K. Mellor, and Esther H. Schor (New York: Oxford UP, 1993), 113-14.

At the most powerful moments of *The Last Man,* personality and the boundaries of both body and text are lost. Shelley works at times with details, focusing obsessively on a particular expression of feeling. At other times—probably with more success—she provides intertextual clues to a meaning beyond personal pain or joy. An allusion, a quotation, a single word may unravel the textual web, so that in the scholarly tracking of sources and analogues the reader learns something about the relation between private grief and the public realm of literary fiction. Reading *The Last Man* is thus an unusually intense meeting of scholarship and personal recognition.

Speaking of love, for example, Lionel suggests, "We walk the pathless mazes of society, vacant of joy, till we hold this clue, leading us through that labyrinth to paradise" (48). By means of this figure, he reminds us of references elsewhere in the text to the story of the Cretan labyrinth. In the myth, the princess Ariadne gives Theseus a thread (or clue) by means of which to extricate himself from the den of the monstrous minotaur, half man, half bull. The story of the labyrinth, like *The Last Man* itself, is an ambivalent story of entrapment and despair on the one hand and of escape and hope on the other. Calling love the clue to the labyrinth of society, or describing life (later in the novel) as "that labyrinth of evil, that scheme of mutual torture" (171), provides a way of presenting emotional experience in terms of narrative pattern. Lionel's allusion reminds us that the text itself is a labyrinth: at its heart (as at the heart of *Frankenstein*) there is a monster, at its circumference the hope of love and renewed life.

The story of Ariadne, however, leads to a larger context. In Book 6 of Virgil's *Aeneid,* the story of the Cretan labyrinth is represented on the temple-gates of Apollo at the very entrance to the underworld.[19] Significantly, *The Last Man* begins where Aeneas begins his descent to hell—in the cave of the Sibyl. Shelley's novel is, in effect, a new version of the underworld descent, beginning in the same place, reminding us of the difficulty of retracing one's path through the labyrinth to the upper air, leading us past a series of phantoms or shadows who may or may not be true prophets, and leaving us with a vision of the future which, like Aeneas's vision in his underworld, may or may not be a false dream. The obvious guide may be a male narrator, Lionel Verney; but only half buried in the intertexts, Ariadne appears with the clue—her name a faint echo of that of Mary Shelley's more sinister Greek, Evadne, whose role is a version of the guiding Sibyl's, shedding light on the world of death.

The role of the Sibyl in *The Last Man* is thus deeply ambiguous: she brings death into the world (associated as she is with the underworld and with the power evoked in Evadne's curse on Raymond [142]); but she

---

19   *Aeneid* 6.27-30. Lines 36-41 in James Beresford's translation: see below, Appendix B.1.

also provides the clue to whatever meaning might be left in a world of disintegrating fragments. Power is found in the darkness of the Sibyl's cave rather than in the upper air of domestic happiness: an apparition of Idris appears after her death "pacing slowly towards [a] cave" (288) that signifies the commanding power of death. When at the height of the plague in London Lionel goes to a performance of *Macbeth* at Drury Lane and describes the cavern of the witches, we glimpse the Sibyl's cave from another perspective. Like the Sibyl, Shakespeare's witches offer ambiguous prophecy subject to the dangerous act of interpretation. Witchcraft and magic recur in *The Last Man* as ways of representing the power of the other as both creative and destructive.

The ambiguity of this power spreads out to include the roles of other mythical and literary figures alluded to in the novel. Evadne functions not only as the dark side of the Sibyl but as a version of Pandora (who is, in turn, a version of Eve, whose name is perhaps echoed in Evadne's). Evadne is beautiful, desirable, passionate, creative—but also destructive and wretched, consumed by the frustration of her own desire. The misery she unleashes into the world *is* its plague—which literally enters the novel with her death, replacing her as a destructive female agent. Plague functions both metaphorically and literally, as emotional misery, political and sexual intrigue, and lawless desire plant the seeds of disease.

Thus, female figures both fictional and mythical dominate the symbolic structure in spite of the dominance of male characters in the plot. Reducing *The Last Man* merely to a roman à clef obscures the significance of this. Evadne cannot simply be identified with a particular person outside the novel or with the psychological pain or guilt that Shelley expresses in her poem, "The Choice," [20] for her identity swirls out of various intertexts, only one of which is biographical. Possibly reflecting (along with Perdita) Mary Shelley's own self-blaming regret for the past, Evadne also intersects (ironically) with the faithful wife of Euripides' *The Suppliants*, who casts herself into her husband's funeral pyre (as Mary might have imagined doing when Percy's body was cremated on the beach at Viareggio). Treacherous wife and loyal mistress, she is also related to the Evadne of Beaumont and Fletcher's *The Maid's Tragedy*, whose judgement on herself and other women is relevant to Mary Shelley's novel:

> All the creatures
> Made for Heaven's honors have their ends, and good ones,
> All but the cozening crocodiles, false women:
> They reign here like those plagues, those killing sores

---

20   See Appendix E.1, reprinted from *Journals*, ed. Feldman and Scott-Kilvert 2: 490-94.

Men pray against, and when they die, like tales
Ill told and unbeliev'd, they pass away
And go to dust forgotten. (4.1.245-51)

Evadne's very name simultaneously encodes destructiveness, deception,
and devotion. Like Lionel Verney's, her identity—princess, plague, adul-
teress, artist—remains uncertain and unstable.

As if to underline this unstable identity, Evadne is the most striking of
those characters in *The Last Man* who cross gender boundaries. When she
reappears in London after Raymond (by now Lord Protector of a republican England) has married Perdita, she adopts a masculine persona, sub-
mitting an architectural drawing for a proposed national gallery. Assuming
that she is a man, Raymond visits the artist whose work has intrigued him
and discovers the woman who has continued to love him through a long
absence. Their affair undermines his marriage to Perdita and sends him
back to the Greek wars, precipitating his early death and the beginning of
the plague that destroys the world.

To the extent that Mary Shelley identifies with Perdita, Evadne is the
object of jealousy, the third party in a love triangle. This role of sexual
rival is by no means inconsistent with a masculine disguise. An early draft
of Percy Shelley's Preface to *Epipsychidion* explains that a young
Englishman "who died on his passage from Leghorn to the Levant"

> was accompanied by a lady [...] supposed to be his wife, & an effeminate
> looking youth, to whom he shewed... so [...] excessive an attachment as to
> give rise to the suspicion, that she was a woman—At his death this suspi-
> cion was confirmed; [ ] object speedily found a refuge both from the taunts
> of the brute multitude, and from the [ ] of her grief in the same grave that
> contained her lover.[21]

Whatever speculations about the relations of the Shelley circle this pas-
sage may encourage, it helps to illuminate one of Evadne's roles in *The
Last Man*. The "effeminate looking youth" corresponds to Evadne's male
disguises and, perhaps, to some real or imagined rival of Mary Shelley.
The youth who turns out to be a woman in the *Epipsychidion* preface takes
part in a triangular relationship similar to that of Raymond, Perdita, and
Evadne. The quotation that Lionel Verney uses to describe the dead
Evadne,

> Crushed and o'erworn,
> The hours had drained her blood, and filled her brow
> With lines and wrinkles,

---

21 Percy Bysshe Shelley, *Poetical Works*, ed. Thomas Hutchinson, corrected by G.
M. Matthews (Oxford UP, 1970) 425.

is adapted from one of Shakespeare's sonnets, addressed to a young man who may well be another version of Percy Shelley's "effeminate looking youth."[22] A version of the young man of the sonnets, no longer young and transformed into a woman, Evadne signifies transgressive power. An agent of mutability and destruction in a world that looks back longingly to its lost paradise, she is Mary Shelley's alter ego, both other and self, the focus of desire and power but also of guilt and self-distrust.

Yet if Evadne's feminine role as Perdita's sexual rival seems to make her Mary Shelley's rival too, her masculine role as creative artist doubles Mary Shelley's narrative disguise as Lionel Verney. Here, however, shifting gender roles emphasize uncertainty about creative authority: Verney's wildness has been tamed by Adrian's gentle certainty; Evadne's wildness, on the other hand, remains a source of destruction. It is no accident that Lionel Verney ends as he began, "as uncouth a savage, as the wolf-bred founder of old Rome" (11; cf. 362), for the tendency of the novel is towards the vindication of subversive, destructive, anti-civilizing power, most vividly symbolized first by plague and finally by the ruins of depopulated Rome.

Steven Goldsmith argues that the relation of Percy Shelley to Mary—dominant, civilizing, culturally authoritative—parallels that of Adrian to Lionel (and that of Apollo in Virgil's *Aeneid* to the Cumaean Sibyl whom he tames).[23] Evadne is, however, untameable, beyond the repressive, civilizing control of male institutions. In Goldsmith's words, she is "the Sibyl as *she* might have represented herself" (148). On the conscious, moralizing level, Shelley judges and defines Evadne conventionally. On a deeper level, as Evadne is superseded by Plague, *The Last Man* enacts the revenge of female power against control.

Lionel finds her dying in masculine disguise on the battlefield:

> Suddenly I heard a piercing shriek; a form seemed to rise from the earth; it flew swiftly towards me, sinking to the ground again as it drew near. All this passed so suddenly, that I with difficulty reined in my horse, so that it should not trample on the prostrate being. The dress of this person was that

---

22 Compare Shakespeare, Sonnet 63, 1-4: "Against my love shall be as I am now, / With Time's injurious hand crush'd and o'erworn; / When hours have drain'd his blood, and fill'd his brow / With lines and wrinkles...." Shelley changes not only the pronouns but also the verb tense, putting into the past an event that Shakespeare projects into the future. Shelley's own conflation of past and future and of subject and object is, however, underlined by knowledge of her quotation's source.

23 Steven Goldsmith, "Of Gender, Plague, and Apocalypse: Mary Shelley's *Last Man*," *The Yale Journal of Criticism* 4.1 (1990): 129-73. For Virgil's description of Apollo controlling the Sibyl, see Appendix B.1, lines 107-09.

of a soldier, but the bared neck and arms, and continued shrieks discovered a female thus disguised. (142)

The terror of the moment is conveyed as uncertainty about identity: the apparition turns out to be a human being; the soldier turns out to be a woman.[24] Yet those revelations do not solve all the mystery of the episode, the effect of which remains supernatural. Calling fire, war, and plague her "servitors," and summoning Raymond to join her in the grave (as the apparition of the bleeding nun does to another Raymond in M. G. Lewis's novel *The Monk*),[25] Evadne, like her namesake in Beaumont and Fletcher's play, allies herself with destruction, leaving first Raymond and then everyone else in a world of death.

Mary Shelley thus resists fixed or reductive interpretation of her text. The novel's supposedly male narrative voice may attempt to cover a female perspective—but may do so no more effectively than a soldier's garments disguise Evadne. Characters may be fluid enough to represent a range of biographical and literary voices: Evadne may be at once the frustrated artist (hence Mary Shelley's counterpart) and the feared erotic rival; "good" and "evil," like life and death, may transgress their conventional boundaries; guilt, self-justification, blame, and idealization can co-exist, speaking through and projected onto a range of characters. Character is thus less important than voice in *The Last Man*; or, in other words, who speaks may be less significant than what is said.

In a sense, all voices are finally subsumed by the voice of the Sibyl, which is also the narrator's voice, discovered beneath the civilized surface in "the ominous voice breathed up with pestiferous vapours from fear's dim cavern" (215). Because voices speak from no certain point of view, the effect of the novel can be like the hubbub of voices in Virgil's underworld or in the lonely mind haunted by echoes and whispers from the grave. Fictional characters (Lionel, Perdita, and so on) are entangled with biographical persons (Shelley, Byron), historical characters alluded to in the narrative (Alexander, Cleopatra, Cincinnatus, Napoleon), literary or mythical figures (Antigone, Pandora, Noah, Oedipus, Samson, Byron's Childe Harold), and thinkers and theorists (Bacon, Burke, Wollstonecraft, Godwin). The novel imposes films and veils between layers of its own reality as we look through one Perdita or Evadne to another. Prophesied

---

24   As, indeed, the Raymond-like phantom on the battlefield in PBS's *The Revolt of Islam* turns out to be the heroine, Cythna (6.19).

25   Matthew Gregory Lewis, *The Monk*, ed. Howard Anderson (Oxford: Oxford UP, 1980) 160: "*Raymond! Raymond! Thou art mine! / Raymond! Raymond! I am thine! / In thy veins while blood shall roll, / I am thine! / Thou art mine! / Mine thy body! Mine thy soul!—.*"

events such as the Greek wars of the novel do not merely reshuffle the events of the 1820s, but provide ironic perspective on history's subversions and repetitions (alluding particularly to the invasion of Constantinople by the Turks in 1453).

In this way, *The Last Man* dismantles chronology and identity to reconstruct history as a kind of visionary synchronicity. The web of mind includes all points of view and all times and places—or, at least, as many as its author can imagine. Consequently, this is a novel of ideas without a consistent or unifying viewpoint. One by one, positions are discussed, quoted, alluded to, and dismissed, leaving an ideological framework without conviction and, at the point of Lionel's deepest despair, empty temples and marble forms from which the spirit has departed.

* * *

Still, there is a monster at the centre of the labyrinth, and its name is Plague. Literally, the labyrinth of the text is mirrored by Constantinople, the maze-like city of death where Lord Raymond dies as the plague-stricken city, deserted by its defenders, explodes. After that disaster, searching for Raymond's body at the centre of the labyrinth, Lionel sees an apparition:

... my friend's shape, altered by a thousand distortions, expanded into a gigantic phantom, bearing on its brow the sign of pestilence. The growing shadow rose and rose, filling, and then seeming to endeavour to burst beyond, the adamantine vault that bent over, sustaining and enclosing the world. (158)

Raymond here embodies transgressive power, bursting beyond the boundaries of containment in an image of demonic excess. The "adamantine vault" that "enclos[es] the world" is as vulnerable as the vaults and domes of Constantinople—seemingly as permanent and unchanging as the laws and truths that bind human life, but actually affected by the bubbles and shadows of desire, power, and force and their allies, disease and death. When Lionel wakes from his nightmare and succeeds "in extricating [him]self from [the] enclosure" of the city (159), plague has already begun its work. That work is, in effect, a redefinition of categories, as life is replaced by death, and nightmares, phantoms, and shadows of the past take on greater reality than the illusion of continuing life.

Death rises up out of the vaults and tombs of Constantinople to embrace the living. In a version of the Faustian pact with the devil, Evadne claims on the battlefield to have sold her own life for power over Raymond's: "I have sold myself to death, with the sole condition that thou shouldst follow me—Fire, and war, and plague, unite for thy destruction—O my Raymond, there is no safety for thee!" (142).

Constantinople is, in effect, a demonic city into which Raymond rides as if into the mouth of hell, through the "fatal entrance" (156) into the Golden City of fire. A microcosm of the labyrinth of life-in-death that the whole world becomes later in the novel, Constantinople is one of its chief symbols of the Other as evil.

It is tempting to situate the source of that evil in the foreign and the alien, recognizing that Mary Shelley participates in the demonization of Islam by Christian Europeans that goes back to the Crusades. This is consistent with Evadne's vilification not only as uncontrollable woman and artist, but as the only foreigner among the central characters. The foreign, the alien, and the female constitute much of the meaning of "plague" in *The Last Man*,[26] associated as it is with alien races and religions and with female rebellion. The movement of plague is from east to west; as Anne K. Mellor has emphasized, Lionel Verney contracts the disease from a black man,[27] a detail that may come from one of Shelley's sources, John Wilson's play, *The City of the Plague* (1816). Here, a black man driving the death-cart is transformed for one of the characters into "a horrid demon ... / With sable visage and white-glaring eyes,"[28] a racialized devil like the "negro half clad" who winds his "naked festering arms" around Lionel Verney (265).

Reading plague as a spectre conjured up by xenophobia, sexism, and racism is consistent with Lionel's repeated longing for domestic retirement, signified most strongly by Windsor Castle and environs and thus with an English aristocratic and patriarchal tradition. In Kate Ferguson Ellis's words, "[t]he kind of harmony celebrated by the bourgeois family as an ideal can only be obtained by keeping 'the world' at a distance."[29] Thus, even more than Greece as the source of European culture and values, *The Last Man* repeatedly celebrates England, Englishness, English literature and culture. These values are, however, inadequate to withstand the invasion of plague, which demands political decisions and political action for which Verney has neither the skill nor the inclination:

---

26 This relates plague in *The Last Man* to the political discourse of disease prevalent at the end of the eighteenth century: see Lee Sterrenburg, "*The Last Man*: Anatomy of Failed Revolutions," *Nineteenth-Century Fiction* 33 (1978): 324-47, and below, Appendix D.4.ii and Appendix D.5.

27 Introduction to *The Last Man*, ed. Hugh J. Luke, Jr., xxiv.

28 *The City of the Plague, and Other Poems* (Edinburgh: Constable, 1816) 1.4, p. 49. Wilson may in turn recall Charles Brockden Brown, *Arthur Mervyn*, in which a hearse stops at a house: "Presently a coffin, borne by two men, issued from the house. The driver was a negro ..." (1: 141).

29 "Subversive Surfaces: The Limits of Domestic Affection in Mary Shelley's Later Fiction," Fisch, Mellor, and Schor 227.

Adrian, carrying Shelleyan idealism into practice, rises to the occasion that duty presents, a model of English heroism and humanity asserting civilized values as civilization crumbles.

Read like this, the assumptions about race and culture in *The Last Man* seem to prefigure those of Bram Stoker's *Dracula* (1897), where foreign ships bring from the east a plague of blood and moral decay and where good men rise reluctantly but bravely to public duty. More chillingly, as Anne K. Mellor reminds us, such assumptions prefigure modern racist fear of AIDS as a disease brought to Europe and North America by Africans and Haitians. Stories of foreign sailors and ships bearing alien infection do not belong to folklore and fiction alone; restrictive immigration policies and an emphasis on moral judgment and social exclusion result from believing them. Dangerous infection can be understood as moral and ideological, not only as biological. Thus the well-born refugees who escape to England in *The Last Man* are explicitly compared to those victims of the Reign of Terror who sought refuge there in 1794 (186): the actual *source* of disease (including the infection of foolish or dangerous foreign ideas) is understood to be alien and excluded.

Yet this is a novel of siege rather than of secure retreat, and besieged England bears the consequences of the earlier siege of Constantinople. While the labyrinth in *The Last Man* figures not only the text but the city or even the world as an enclosed space, Mary Shelley's labyrinth often turns inside out to become a map, spreading out all the continents of the world into which Lionel Verney projects himself beyond the novel's end. The map is no safer than the labyrinth: "I spread the whole earth out as a map before me. On no one spot of its surface could I put my finger and say, here is safety" (204). As an account of several journeys—the Constantinople expedition, the overland trip bearing Raymond's body to Athens, the trek of emigrants through France and Switzerland to Italy, Lionel's projected voyage beyond the limits of his world—the novel itself spreads "the whole earth out as a map" before the reader. References to the discovery of America and shipments of gold from Mexico to Spain (23, 133) hint at a subtextual critique of imperialism. Figuratively, the novel maps western culture as well as the labyrinthine windings of the mind, exploring at once the inner obsessions of grief and the outer world, almost as dangerous, of history, geography, and society.

Given this movement beyond England into the wider world, fear of contact and contagion is not the whole story of plague in *The Last Man*. Loving England, Lionel nevertheless deplores the anglocentrism of his countrymen, who speak "of Thrace and Macedonia, as they would of a lunar territory" (173). English people are not merely victims of foreign infection, for they themselves have moved out from their protected centre to carry their own infection into the world. While Englishmen deplore the superstition of foreigners—"above the dome of St. Sophia the superstitious Greek saw Pestilence, and shrunk in trepidation from her influence" (151)—they have their own version of such an apparition in Lord Raymond, that exemplar of English valour who can scarcely be distinguished from an apparition of plague, "that fiend more cruel than tempest, less tame than fire" (173). The apparition of Raymond implies troubling questions. What business did he have leading the revolution of a foreign power? What are we to make of the civilization he represents? What is the nature and appropriate direction of power? Like Evadne's misdirected love, which proceeds tragically through adultery to death, or, later, like the religious fanatic's hypocritical manipulation of his followers, Raymond's disproportionate drive for power is transgressive, self-serving, and ultimately destructive. The wild madness of the Sibyl and the civilizing control of male-dominated English culture begin as opposites (in the initial contrast between Lionel and Adrian and in the confrontation of Evadne's curse with Raymond's will-to-power), only to reveal a strange resemblance.

Corrupted by power to a selfish sense of his own invulnerability, and unwilling to consider the vulnerability of others, Raymond exposes a whole army to a disease that springs from his own wilfulness. At first a self-deluding opportunist, he accepts his role as Evadne's victim. Raymond, marked with the sign of pestilence, and Evadne, identified with the female embodiment of plague that "has invested [man's] form, is incarnate in his flesh, has entwined herself with his being, and blinds his heaven-seeking eyes" (250), haunt the novel long after their deaths near the beginning of Volume 2. As "Queen of the World" (273), plague is the embodiment of female power and transgression.[30] As a male presence (for Plague is another androgynous figure in the novel), plague is a servant of Death, sometimes even identified with death, an external evil which is *also* the sign of an inner corruption. This androgyny links Plague both to the male civilizing enterprise that besieges Constantinople and to the female power that undermines the civilized institutions that would contain it. Lionel, tamed by Adrian yet rediscovering by the novel's end his affinity with animals and the shepherd's life of his boyhood, is a more positive example of this complicity of difference.

Debates of the 1820s about whether or not plague is contagious are relevant here. If plague can be passed on (like smallpox) through contact with infected bodies or objects, then trade restrictions, quarantine laws, and other policies of exclusion will be advocated as public-health measures. If, on the other hand, plague is passed on (in some way not understood in the 1820s) through the very air itself, it becomes an arbitrary,

---

30   The identity even of this demonic queen is elusive: in an odd twist, another
     example of the novel's use of disguise to complicate questions of identity,
     Raymond and Perdita's daughter Clara becomes "little queen of the world"
     (335) shortly before the voyage during which she drowns.

insidious assailant beyond the reach of will or reason.[31] In spite of some ambivalence and inconsistency on this point, Mary Shelley explicitly adopts the second view (182). The stagnation of commerce and its economic effects on the lives of ordinary people exacerbate the effects of plague in *The Last Man*. Since Shelley's plague is not "contagious," it cannot be avoided by restricted trade and travel; consequently, its inflictions—air-borne, invisible, inescapable—seem as remote from human agency as any supernatural force. Mary's journal entries during the years in Italy are filled with descriptions of winds, perhaps after her son William's death understood to be potentially fatal. Unlike the "uncontrollable" wind that scatters autumn leaves from Percy Bysshe Shelley's "unextinguished hearth" (in his "Ode to the West Wind," 47, 66), so that they can "quicken a new birth" (64) of mind and imagination, Mary Shelley's winds stir the seeds of plague.[32]

Plague-bearing winds, like those that figure inspiration for the Romantic poets, have their correspondent breeze within.[33] Sometimes the breeze becomes a storm, "a tempest ... wilder than the winds, a tempest bred by the passions of man, nourished by his most violent impulses, unexampled and dire" (231). Uncontrollable, the wind is nevertheless infected by human choices. Thus, the wind does not chill the dead on the battlefield; on the contrary, "the rushing wind disturbed the garments of the dead, and was chilled as it passed over their icy forms" (141). Through such adaptation of familiar images, Mary Shelley demonstrates that bad political and moral decisions render human beings complicit with the external means of their destruction.

Adultery and Evadne's curse forge a causal chain that leads Raymond, defying superstition and behaving with excessive bravado, to die the victim of superstition, identified with the malignancy that destroys him. Human agency remains central to the chain of necessity in *The Last Man*, as Lionel Verney's role in the novel illustrates. It is he who reveals Evadne's dying words to Raymond, thus precipitating the entry into Constantinople that kills Raymond and perhaps unleashes plague on his

---

31 Two review articles in the *Westminster Review* 3 (1825) discuss the question of contagion, also much debated by medical visitors to Constantinople in the eighteenth and early nineteenth centuries: "Contagion and Sanitary Laws" (134-67, excerpted in Appendix C.5) and "Plague—Typhus Fever—Quarantine" (499-530). Plague is actually a disease of rodents spread to humans by contact with infected animals (usually rats) or their fleas.

32 Contrast "Ode to the West Wind" 5-10—"O thou, / Who chariotest to their dark wintry bed / The winged seeds, where they lie cold and low, / Each like a corpse within its grave, until / Thine azure sister of the Spring shall blow / Her clarion o'er the dreaming earth"—with Ryland's words in *The Last Man*: "Be assured that earth is not, nor ever shall be heaven, while the seeds of hell are natives of our soil" (172).

33 See William Wordsworth, *The Prelude* 1.33-35.

world. Later, after Raymond's body has been recovered and buried outside Athens, it is Lionel who orders that Perdita be drugged and taken back to England for her own good. The episode is a rewriting of an earlier episode, in Volume 1, where the authoritarian ex-queen tries to drug and kidnap Idris, similarly for her own good. This time, however, the story has a tragic ending: waking up and discovering Lionel's plot, Perdita drowns herself.

Moral and emotional failure, well-intentioned stupidity, thoughtless replication of past failure, unwillingness to read the lessons of history—all these collaborate with "plague" in *The Last Man*. Plague (or such a disease as typhus, closely associated with plague in the novel) does not cause every death: Idris dies of a decline brought on by exhaustion; Juliet, victim of a religious fanatic, stabs herself; Adrian and Clara drown on their way to Greece. Nor is death always horrific: the ex-queen, chastened by loss, dies peacefully in old age, lamenting not her own fate but that of others. Nevertheless, as an agent of death uncontrollable when unleashed, plague remains part of the fabric of the world. It is borne on winds that blow from the interactions of cultures, individuals, ideas, and armies, revealing much about the adequacy of human ideas, institutions, and ambitions. Not just a disembodied external force arbitrarily destroying humankind, it takes strength from choice and negligence and, inscribed on Raymond's phantom, invites a reconsideration of the role of military heroism and the will-to-power. Leaving England after Idris' death with his little band of survivors, and setting sail at the end of the novel to find a human companion wherever on earth a survivor may remain, Lionel shows how little hope remains beyond the plagues of war, betrayal, and self-delusion with which he, too, has been complicit.

* * *

Plague begins as a "word" (137) and, borne on the winds, becomes incarnate death. This demonic word made flesh grimly subverts the web of language in *The Last Man* by making intertextuality itself a pattern of potential infection. Words can be tainted, dangerous, and ambiguous. Thus the decomposition of ideas and words in *The Last Man* corresponds to the dissolution of human life, and is figured by the "thin scant" sibylline leaves in the Cumaean cave of the Introduction. Mary Shelley sets down words to show their inefficacy and futility in the face of plague and death and even to demonstrate their contribution to chaos and destruction.

One of these words, as we have seen, is love, both refuge and infection. Others are political: republic, monarchy, aristocracy, nobility. The republican passion of Ryland, Raymond's rival for the office of Lord Protector, is meaningless when he faces the ruin of his ambition and his own imminent death. Equally, the monarchical dreams of the old queen,

Adrian's mother, are mere vanity. Lionel Verney quotes several times—approvingly—from the writings of Edmund Burke, eloquent opponent of the French revolutionaries in the 1790s against whom Mary Shelley's mother, Mary Wollstonecraft, had written *A Vindication of the Rights of Men*.[34] Yet in the extreme situation Shelley describes, Burke's ideas are no more solid than Godwin's, and Wollstonecraft's disillusionment with revolutionary excess (expressed in her *Historical and Moral View of the Origin and Progress of the French Revolution*[35]) seems more reasonable than her visionary faith in reason. Even Percy Bysshe Shelley's idealism, held up through Adrian as noble and admirable, is futile—subject like everything else in the book to a particularly grim version of the triumph of life as a "labyrinth of evil"(171). If the enemy of humankind is beyond the control of human beings, pacificism and humanitarianism like Adrian's seem no more effective than militarism like Raymond's; if spring brings plague, the return of the Golden Age is the ultimate myth of despair. Tyrannical king of the world, death is also, as Ryland reminds us, the great leveller (192). All the political debates of the novel (and all those implicit in its intertexts) are demonstrated by its plot to be mere word-games, irrelevant in the face of annihilation.

As if to emphasize this subversion of ideals and convictions, Lionel continually quotes words out of context. Distinguishing between a traditional nobility based on hereditary rank and "nature's true nobility" of talent and virtue, he quotes a phrase from Burke—"the Corinthian capital of polished society"—to describe the former (174),[36] probably with mild irony at Burke's expense. A few pages later, Lionel quotes Burke again: Burke claims (in a passage from his *Reflections on the Revolution in France*) that human society is permanent because "the whole, at one time, is never old, or middle-aged, or young," although individuals grow old and die (179).[37]

This view is obviously shown to be absurd as the world's population dwindles. When Lionel later goes to Windsor to lay Idris in the vault beneath St. George's chapel, he quotes a pro-monarchical passage (once again from Burke, and once again out of context) comparing the monarchy to "the proud Keep of Windsor, rising in the majesty of proportion,

---

34   *A Vindication of the Rights of Men*, in *Political Writings*, ed. Janet Todd (Toronto: U of Toronto P, 1993) 1-65.

35   Mary Wollstonecraft, *An Historical and Moral View of the Origin and Progress of the French Revolution; and the effect it has produced in Europe*, vol. 1 [of only one completed] (London: J. Johnson, 1794), excerpted in *Political Writings*, ed. Janet Todd 299-387.

36   Edmund Burke, *Reflections on the Revolution in France*, ed. Conor Cruise O'Brien (Harmondsworth: Penguin, 1986) 245.

37   *Reflections*, ed. Conor Cruise O'Brien 120.

girt with the double belt of its kindred and coeval towers."[38] Lionel uses Burke's words (280) not to justify monarchy, but simply to describe a particular place and create a mood of rather sentimental if ironic regret: arguments about kings, nobles, republicans, tyrants, and fanatics are all equally irrelevant by this point in the narrative. Like Percy Bysshe Shelley's "Ozymandias, king of kings," whose name survives only as an inscription on a ruined statue,[39] power and the ideas that have sustained it are mere dreams and broken memories of the lost past.

In this way, *The Last Man* continually echoes the words of canonical writers, reinscribing the dominating Word: "the diminutive letters grew gigantic to the bewildered eye of fear: they seemed graven with a pen of iron, impressed by fire, woven in the clouds, stamped on the very front of the universe" (186). Yet by separating words from their writers and their original contexts, Mary Shelley subverts them even as she echoes them. While she never directly quotes from her mother's *Vindication of the Rights of Woman*, on the other hand, she repeatedly chooses to quote passages Wollstonecraft also quotes, thus indirectly echoing a book that challenges her novel's overt treatment of love. Similarly, Shelley's repeated adjectives "pestilential" and "pestiferous" echo her mother's figurative language. As all other words in *The Last Man* are displaced by a single Word, "Plague," its victory is at once vengeance pronounced on civilization and the final infliction of civilization's oppressive power. Finally, in spite of the novel's ambivalence towards female power and in spite of the dominance of men's words in quotations and allusions, Shelley's own voice survives the editorial role she has taken on, speaking through the intertextual web.

Fathers die, their exploits part of the memory of a lost world. Not only is Raymond associated with the plague, the seeds of which are stirred by violence and betrayal, but he is also indirectly responsible for the final catastrophe: drawn to his grave, Clara and Adrian are drowned. Other powerful fathers haunt the intertexts—Godwin, whose vision of the "Illustrious Dead" Mary Shelley gently mocks;[40] Prospero, whose island-world (like England in *The Last Man*) fades into a dream; and Oedipus, who succeeded in solving the Sphinx's riddle only to shrink in horror from further unthinkable knowledge. Retelling that story (with Lionel Verney in the role of Oedipus), Shelley also reminds her readers of a later stage in Oedipus' life, when, blinded by his own hand, he is guided to Colonus by his daughter, Antigone (61). Fathers are sometimes lit-

---

38 Edmund Burke, *A Letter to a Noble Lord, Writings and Speeches of Edmund Burke*, ed. R. B. McDowell et al. (Oxford: Clarendon, 1991) 9: 172.
39 "I met a traveller from an antique land," first published in the *Examiner*, January 1818.
40 See Appendix D.8.

erally blind, like the old man whose daughter plays the organ for him in a depopulated Swiss village, protecting him from knowledge of their plight. Sometimes, however, they are figuratively blind, like Merrival, deluded by his astronomical speculations, or like Ryland, incapable of surviving when ideology fails. The plague that "blinds [man's] heaven-seeking eyes" (250) may even be a demonic means of achieving patriarchal power, as in the case of the fanatic who, through "the pestilential atmosphere which adhered to his demoniac nature" (307), dispenses the plague he offers refuge from.

Ryland dies alone, in a terrified frenzy of self-protection. Merrival, unable to function without his wife and children, dies on their grave, his speculative knowledge shown to be irrelevant. The novel implies the limitations of certain kinds of knowledge and, as the Appendices to this edition may suggest, hints at connections between the convictions and delusions of its blind fathers and those of Shelley's father and even, occasionally, her husband. *The Last Man* presents as alternatives a remarkable range of heroines, including such intertextual figures of resistance and endurance as Antigone and Epicharis,[41] who help the reader to understand the role of Merrival's wife or of the Swiss girl protecting her blind father. The Countess of Windsor, the novel's one powerful mother-figure, is converted from despotic, stony self-will in an episode that is really the father-daughter paradigm turned inside out: the Countess is reconciled with her son-in-law, Lionel, over the body of her daughter, Idris—in contrast to Sir Timothy Shelley, who refused reconciliation with Mary, his daughter-in-law, after Percy Shelley's death.

The Last Man resists the very plague that is necessary to bear its plot to a conclusion of heroic resistance. Deploring the failure of men's knowledge and heroism, the novel celebrates the gaining of wisdom while it also recognizes that wisdom and plague have the same source. Representing wisdom therefore requires an alert and engaged reader who will enter the labyrinth of the text as Mary Shelley enters the Sibyl's cave and who will bring its fragments back to the upper air.[42] Presenting a narrative constructed out of infectious words from the dead that can, in turn, generate death, the narrator/editor refers not only to Lionel Verney's story, but to "writings ... expressed in various languages," to "prophecies, detailed relations of events but lately passed; names, now well known, but of modern date; and often exclamations of exultation or woe, victory or defeat" (3). The story she tells, based in turn on the Sibyl's story, could

---

41 Tacitus, *Annals* 15.51.
42 Shelley's journal entry for 25 February 1822 is relevant here: "above all let me fearlessly descend into the remotest caverns of my own mind—carry the torch of self knowledge into its dimmest recesses—but too happy if I dislodge any evil spirit or ensh[r]ine a new deity in some hitherto uninhabited nook—." *Journals*, ed. Feldman and Scott-Kilvert, 1: 400.

have been a familiar one of military heroism, romantic transcendence, or repression bursting forth with revolutionary power to destroy as well as change the world. Yet working with fragments of all learning and all literature, Shelley, like Lionel, weaves a web of words that celebrates the compulsion to make sense of the world not through replication, but through transformation.

As a reader of Percy Bysshe Shelley, William Godwin, and all the other writers she quotes and alludes to, she expresses grief, remorse, and love; but she hardly offers uncomplicated assent to the words she reads, transcribes, and recontextualizes. A particularly interested reader, Shelley writes apologetically at the end of her Introduction, as if she might be writing about the emotional and intellectual difficulties of editing her dead husband's work, "Doubtless the leaves of the Cumæan Sibyl have suffered distortion and diminution of interest and excellence in my hands. My only excuse for thus transforming them, is that they were unintelligible in their pristine condition" (4). There is perhaps self-assertion here as well as apology: the novel points not only to the original source of words but to the necessary work of transformation.

If Mary Shelley is referring in part to Percy Shelley's writings, she is also referring to a web woven out of her own experience. For her readers, the text of *The Last Man* itself becomes part of the web it unravels to weave again. Its strength is that it compels us to consider the process by which we construct and reconstruct meaning. Beyond this book, and indeed beyond the making of books at all, Lionel Verney and Shelley herself invite us to read traces of experience not for the single truth they tell but for the "web of mind" they reveal. Caught in that changing web, readers of *The Last Man* are also creators and editors, the three roles inextricable.

A Note on the Text

This edition is based on that published by Henry Colburn in 1826, the only edition with which Mary Shelley was directly involved. Some copies of the Colburn edition have the words "second edition" on their title-page; however, in every other respect, including typographical errors and occasionally broken or displaced type, they appear to be identical with the first edition.

I retain idiosyncratic spelling and punctuation: Mary Shelley frequently breaks compound words ("some times," "to-night") and uses archaic spellings ("shew," "encrease," "groupe"). I have retained characteristic spellings that may be strange to a modern reader—for example, "desart" for "desert," "herse" for "hearse" and "chesnut" for "chestnut." I have, however, corrected mistakes, substituting "recall" for "recal," "exhilarating" for "exhilirating," "mother's" for "mothers," "forth" for "forthn," and so on. While Mary Shelley prefers the spelling "Bishopgate," she also uses the more familiar "Bishopsgate": in this case and a few others, I have retained the inconsistency of the first edition. When in a couple of places I am uncertain about a particular reading, I provide a footnote rather than emending the text.

An edition of *The Last Man* (in English) was published by Galignani in Paris in March 1826. Mary Shelley seems to have given tacit approval and even assistance to this project, writing to her friend John Howard Payne in Paris in November 1825,

> Would it be of any use to you to send you over an early copy [of the Colburn edition]. I do not suppose that my name is sufficiently attractive (mind I do not want a Compliment) to raise much curiosity—but if it were a translation or republication might be a speculation to the speculative—such I am not, and it is therefore an hint quite at your service—only if I can serve you in it I shall be most happy to do so:—a circumstance I trust, my dear friend, you do not doubt. (*Letters*, 1: 505)

In spite of this interest, however, there is no evidence that Shelley had any active role in preparing the text of the Paris edition. The only other edition published during her lifetime was the two-volume Philadelphia edition of 1833, with which she was not involved.

The epigraph to *The Last Man*, quoted on the title-page of each of the three volumes of the 1826 edition, is from *Paradise Lost* 11.770-72. Two chapters in Volume 1 of the 1826 text are numbered 4; I have corrected chapter numbers in Volume 1, and I have numbered chapters consecutively throughout the novel, rather than (as in the 1826 edition) separately for each volume. There are eleven chapters in Volume 1, nine in Volume 2, and ten in Volume 3.

Mary Wollstonecraft Shelley: A Brief Chronology

In the following Chronology, as in explanatory notes to the text, MWS refers to Mary Wollstonecraft Godwin, later Shelley; PBS refers to Percy Bysshe Shelley.

1797　MWS born 30 August; her mother, Mary Wollstonecraft, dies 10 September.

1801　William Godwin, her father, marries Mary Jane Clairmont 21 December.

1812　MWS visits Dundee in June, meets PBS 11 November.

1813　ten-month visit to friend Isabel Baxter in Scotland.

1814　returns from Scotland 30 March; elopes with PBS 28 July, accompanied by her step-sister, Clara Mary Jane (Claire) Clairmont; they travel through France to Switzerland, returning to Rotterdam via the Rhine (July-August); return to London 13 September.

1815　premature daughter born 22 February; MWS writes in her journal, 6 March, "find my baby dead"; MWS and PBS tour south coast and Devon in June; move to Bishopsgate, near Windsor Park, in early August.

1816　son William born 24 January; makes second trip to the Continent with PBS and Claire, meeting with Byron in Switzerland in May; begins *Frankenstein*; returns to England 29 August; Fanny Imlay, MWS's half-sister, commits suicide 9 October; Harriet Westbrook, PBS's wife, drowns herself and is discovered 10 December; MWS and PBS marry 30 December.

1817　Alba (later Allegra) born 12 January, daughter of Claire Clairmont and Byron; MWS moves to Marlow in March; *Frankenstein* finished 14 May; daughter Clara Everina born 2 September; *History of a Six Week's Tour* published in November.

1818　*Frankenstein* published in January; the Shelley family leaves for Italy in March, moving from Milan to Pisa to Leghorn to Bagni di Lucca (June), Este, Venice (where Clara Shelley dies 24 September), Rome (November) and Naples (December).

1819　family moves to Rome in March; William dies there 7 June; moves to Livorno, then Montenero, where MWS starts *Mathilda*, in June, and to Florence in September; Percy Florence born 12 November.

1820 family moves to Pisa in January; MWS writes *Proserpine* and *Midas* (April-May); begins *Valperga*; moves to Livorno in June, to Bagni di San Giuliano in August, and to Pisa in October.

1821 returns to Bagni di San Giuliano in May and to Pisa in October.

1822 Claire Clairmont's and Byron's daughter Allegra dies 20 April; family moves to Lerici in May; MWS miscarries 16 June; PBS and Edward Williams drowned 8 July; MWS moves to Genoa in September.

1823 *Valperga* published in February; MWS writes "The Choice"; second edition of *Frankenstein* and adaptation on the London stage; MWS arrives back in London in August.

1824 Byron dies in Missolonghi, Greece, 19 April; MWS publishes her edition of PBS's *Posthumous Poems*, but soon recalls copies under pressure from Sir Timothy Shelley; allowance of £200 a year begins.

1826 *The Last Man* published by Colburn 23 January; Sir Timothy Shelley temporarily cuts off MWS's allowance; Percy and Harriet Shelley's son Charles Bysshe dies in September; Percy Florence is now heir to the baronetcy.

1830 *The Fortunes of Perkin Warbeck* published in May.

1831 revised third edition of *Frankenstein* published in November in Colburn and Bentley's Standard Novels.

1835 *Lodore* published in March. *Lives of the Most Eminent Literary and Scientific Men of Italy, Spain and Portugal*, vols. 1 and 2, published (February and October).

1836 William Godwin dies 7 April.

1837 *Falkner* published in February; Percy Florence attends Trinity College, Cambridge.

1838 *Lives of the Most Eminent Literary and Scientific Men of France*, vol. 1, published (July).

1839 PBS's *Poetical Works* published (January-May); *Essays and Letters* published (December); *Lives of the Most Eminent Literary and Scientific Men of France*, vol. 2.

1840 trip to the Continent with Percy Florence and his friends (June to November).

1842-43 another trip to the Continent.

1844 PBS's father dies 23 April, and Percy Florence inherits the estate and title; *Rambles in Germany and Italy* published in August.

1848 Sir Percy Florence Shelley marries Jane St. John.

1851 MWS dies 1 February.

Life is the Desert and the Solitude

Frontispiece to William Godwin, *Essay on Sepulchres* (London: W. Miller, 1809). See 160n, below.

THE LAST MAN.

BY

THE AUTHOR OF FRANKENSTEIN.

IN THREE VOLUMES.

Let no man seek
Henceforth to be foretold what shall befall
Him or his children.
MILTON.

VOL. I.

LONDON:

HENRY COLBURN, NEW BURLINGTON STREET.

1826.

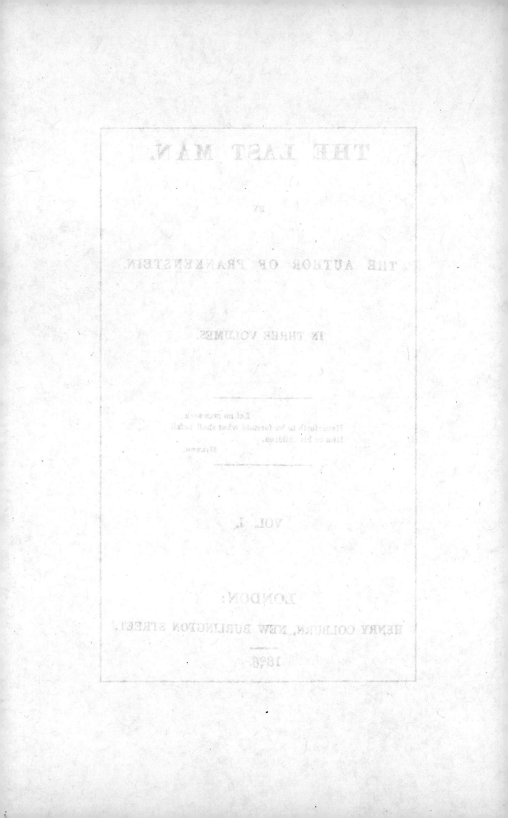

INTRODUCTION

I VISITED Naples in the year 1818. On the 8th of December of that year, my companion and I crossed the Bay, to visit the antiquities which are scattered on the shores of Baiæ.[1] The translucent and shining waters of the calm sea covered fragments of old Roman villas, which were interlaced by sea-weed, and received diamond tints from the chequering of the sun-beams; the blue and pellucid element was such as Galatea might have skimmed in her car of mother of pearl; or Cleopatra, more fitly than the Nile, have chosen as the path of her magic ship.[2] Though it was winter, the atmosphere seemed more appropriate to early spring; and its genial warmth contributed to inspire those sensations of placid delight, which are the portion of every traveller, as he lingers, loath to quit the tranquil bays and radiant promontories of Baiæ.

We visited the so called Elysian Fields and Avernus: and wandered through various ruined temples, baths, and classic spots; at length we entered the gloomy cavern of the Cumæan Sibyl.[3] Our Lazzeroni[4] bore flaring torches, which shone red, and almost dusky, in the murky subterranean passages, whose darkness thirstily surrounding them, seemed eager to imbibe more and more of the element of light. We passed by a natural archway, leading to a second gallery, and enquired, if we could not enter there also. The guides pointed to the reflection of their torches on the water that paved it, leaving us to form our own conclusion; but adding it was a pity, for it led to the Sibyl's Cave. Our curiosity and enthusiasm

---

1   MWS's Introduction begins with an actual event: in her *Journals* for the same date, 8 December 1818, she records a visit to the site of Baiae, an ancient seaside resort near Naples (ed. Paula Feldman and Diana Scott-Kilvert 1: 242). In "Ode to the West Wind" PBS describes its "old palaces and towers / Quivering within the wave's intenser day" (33-34).

2   In one version of the myth, Galatea is a Nereid or sea-maiden, in love with the Sicilian shepherd Acis and loved by the Cyclops Polyphemus; in another, she is married to Polyphemus. For Cleopatra's ship, see Enobarbus' description in Shakespeare's *Antony and Cleopatra* 2.2.195-201.

3   Names of places near Naples, the Elysian Fields and Avernus recall the fields inhabited after death by those favoured by the gods, and the underworld in Virgil's *Aeneid* 6: see MWS's journal entry for 8 December 1818 (1: 242). Virgil's Aeneas visits the Cumaean Sibyl, priestess of the ancient oracle of Apollo at Cumae (near modern Naples), to learn how to enter the underworld and return alive (see *Aeneid* 6.106-09). If the Shelleys visited the Sibyl's Cave in 1818, they were probably shown the "Crypta Romana," communications tunnels for Augustus' artificial naval harbour, the Portus Julius; the "Antro," probably Virgil's Sibyl's cave, was not discovered until 1932. See *P. Vergili Maronis Aeneidos Liber Sextus*, commentary R.G. Austin, 49-57.

4   "Lazzaroni" were beggars or casual labourers in Naples, here employed as guides.

were excited by this circumstance, and we insisted upon attempting the passage. As is usually the case in the prosecution of such enterprizes, the difficulties decreased on examination. We found, on each side of the humid pathway, "dry land for the sole of the foot."[5] At length we arrived at a large, desert, dark cavern, which the Lazzeroni assured us was the Sibyl's Cave. We were sufficiently disappointed—Yet we examined it with care, as if its blank, rocky walls could still bear trace of celestial visitant. On one side was a small opening. Whither does this lead? we asked: can we enter here?—"*Questo poi, no,*"[6]—said the wild looking savage, who held the torch; "you can advance but a short distance, and nobody visits it."

"Nevertheless, I will try it," said my companion; "it may lead to the real cavern. Shall I go alone, or will you accompany me?"

I signified my readiness to proceed, but our guides protested against such a measure. With great volubility, in their native Neapolitan dialect, with which we were not very familiar, they told us that there were spectres, that the roof would fall in, that it was too narrow to admit us, that there was a deep hole within, filled with water, and we might be drowned. My friend shortened the harangue, by taking the man's torch from him; and we proceeded alone.

The passage, which at first scarcely admitted us, quickly grew narrower and lower; we were almost bent double; yet still we persisted in making our way through it. At length we entered a wider space, and the low roof heightened; but, as we congratulated ourselves on this change, our torch was extinguished by a current of air, and we were left in utter darkness. The guides bring with them materials for renewing the light, but we had none—our only resource was to return as we came. We groped round the widened space to find the entrance, and after a time fancied that we had succeeded. This proved however to be a second passage, which evidently ascended. It terminated like the former; though something approaching to a ray, we could not tell whence, shed a very doubtful twilight in the space. By degrees, our eyes grew somewhat accustomed to this dimness, and we perceived that there was no direct passage leading us further; but that it was possible to climb one side of the cavern to a low arch at top, which promised a more easy path, from whence we now discovered that this light proceeded. With considerable difficulty we scrambled up, and came to another passage with still more of illumination, and this led to another ascent like the former.

After a succession of these, which our resolution alone permitted us to surmount, we arrived at a wide cavern with an arched dome-like roof. An

---

5   In the biblical story of the flood, Noah sends out a dove from the ark to see if the waters have subsided; "but the dove found no rest for the sole of her foot" (Genesis 8.9).

6   "That won't do!"

aperture in the midst let in the light of heaven; but this was overgrown with brambles and underwood, which acted as a veil, obscuring the day, and giving a solemn religious hue to the apartment. It was spacious, and nearly circular, with a raised seat of stone, about the size of a Grecian couch, at one end. The only sign that life had been here, was the perfect snow-white skeleton of a goat, which had probably not perceived the opening as it grazed on the hill above, and had fallen headlong. Ages perhaps had elapsed since this catastrophe; and the ruin it had made above, had been repaired by the growth of vegetation during many hundred summers.

The rest of the furniture of the cavern consisted of piles of leaves, fragments of bark, and a white filmy substance, resembling the inner part of the green hood which shelters the grain of the unripe Indian corn. We were fatigued by our struggles to attain this point, and seated ourselves on the rocky couch, while the sounds of tinkling sheep-bells, and shout of shepherd-boy, reached us from above.

At length my friend, who had taken up some of the leaves strewed about, exclaimed, "This *is* the Sibyl's cave; these are Sibylline leaves."[7] On examination, we found that all the leaves, bark, and other substances, were traced with written characters. What appeared to us more astonishing, was that these writings were expressed in various languages: some unknown to my companion, ancient Chaldee, and Egyptian hieroglyphics, old as the Pyramids.[8] Stranger still, some were in modern dialects, English and Italian. We could make out little by the dim light, but they seemed to contain prophecies, detailed relations of events but lately passed; names, now well known, but of modern date; and often exclamations of exultation or woe, of victory or defeat, were traced on their thin scant pages. This was certainly the Sibyl's Cave; not indeed exactly as Virgil describes it; but the whole of this land had been so convulsed by earthquake and volcano, that the change was not wonderful, though the traces of ruin were effaced by time; and we probably owed the preservation of these leaves, to the accident which had closed the mouth of the cavern, and the swift-growing vegetation which had rendered its sole opening impervious to the storm. We made a hasty selection of such of

---

7   Pages inscribed with the Sibyl's oracular words; cf. the title of Coleridge's
     Sibylline Leaves (1817).
8   The variety of languages might parallel Lionel's inscription in three languages
     at the end of the novel (see 355 below). Ancient Chaldee referred to the
     ancient language of Babylon, incorrectly thought in MWS's day to have been
     Aramaic; Chaldea was an ancient land in southern Babylonia (modern Iraq)
     famous for astronomical and astrological knowledge.

the leaves, whose writing one at least of us could understand; and then, laden with our treasure, we bade adieu to the dim hypæthric[9] cavern, and after much difficulty succeeded in rejoining our guides.

During our stay at Naples, we often returned to this cave, sometimes alone, skimming the sun-lit sea, and each time added to our store. Since that period, whenever the world's circumstance has not imperiously called me away, or the temper of my mind impeded such study, I have been employed in deciphering these sacred remains. Their meaning, wondrous and eloquent, has often repaid my toil, soothing me in sorrow, and exciting my imagination to daring flights, through the immensity of nature and the mind of man. For awhile my labours were not solitary; but that time is gone; and, with the selected and matchless companion of my toils, their dearest reward is also lost to me—

Di mie tenere frondi altro lavoro
Credea mostrarte; e qual fero pianeta
Ne' nvidiò insieme, o mio nobil tesoro?[10]

I present the public with my latest discoveries in the slight Sibylline pages. Scattered and unconnected as they were, I have been obliged to add links, and model the work into a consistent form. But the main substance rests on the truths contained in these poetic rhapsodies, and the divine intuition which the Cumæan damsel obtained from heaven.

I have often wondered at the subject of her verses, and at the English dress of the Latin poet. Sometimes I have thought, that, obscure and chaotic as they are, they owe their present form to me, their decipherer. As if we should give to another artist, the painted fragments which form the mosaic copy of Raphael's Transfiguration in St. Peter's;[11] he would put them together in a form, whose mode would be fashioned by his own peculiar mind and talent. Doubtless the leaves of the Cumæan Sibyl have suffered distortion and diminution of interest and excellence in my hands. My only excuse for thus transforming them, is that they were unintelligible in their pristine condition.

---

9   Roofless: in *Rhododaphne* (1818) 1, line 2, Thomas Love Peacock uses the word *hypaethric* to describe a temple open to the sky; in a letter to Peacock, 23-24 January 1819, PBS describes the Greek temples as "mostly upaithric; & the flying clouds the stars or the deep sky were seen above" (*Letters*, ed. Frederick L. Jones 2: 74-75). Cf. PBS, *The Revolt of Islam* 7.12.2935.

10   Petrarch, Sonnet 322, addressed to his patron Giacomo Colonna: "I thought to show you some other work of my young leaves; and what cruel planet was displeased to see us together, O my noble treasure?" (*Petrarch's Lyric Poems*, trans. Robert M. Durling).

11   Raphael's painting of the Transfiguration (Vatican) is copied in mosaic on the altarpiece of the Cappella Clementina in St. Peter's, Rome.

My labours have cheered long hours of solitude, and taken me out of a world, which has averted its once benignant face from me, to one glowing with imagination and power. Will my readers ask how I could find solace from the narration of misery and woeful change? This is one of the mysteries of our nature, which holds full sway over me, and from whose influence I cannot escape. I confess, that I have not been unmoved by the development of the tale; and that I have been depressed, nay, agonized, at some parts of the recital, which I have faithfully transcribed from my materials. Yet such is human nature, that the excitement of mind was dear to me, and that the imagination, painter of tempest and earthquake, or, worse, the stormy and ruin-fraught passions of man, softened my real sorrows and endless regrets, by clothing these fictitious ones in that ideality, which takes the mortal sting from pain.

I hardly know whether this apology is necessary. For the merits of my adaptation and translation must decide how far I have well bestowed my time and imperfect powers, in giving form and substance to the frail and attenuated Leaves of the Sibyl.

[VOLUME ONE]

CHAPTER I

I AM the native of a sea-surrounded nook, a cloud-enshadowed land, which, when the surface of the globe, with its shoreless ocean and track-less continents, presents itself to my mind, appears only as an inconsider-able speck in the immense whole; and yet, when balanced in the scale of mental power, far outweighed countries of larger extent and more numer-ous population. So true it is, that man's mind alone was the creator of all that was good or great to man, and that Nature herself was only his first minister. England, seated far north in the turbid sea, now visits my dreams in the semblance of a vast and well-manned ship, which mastered the winds and rode proudly over the waves. In my boyish days she was the universe to me. When I stood on my native hills, and saw plain and mountain stretch out to the utmost limits of my vision, speckled by the dwellings of my countrymen, and subdued to fertility by their labours, the earth's very centre was fixed for me in that spot, and the rest of her orb was as a fable, to have forgotten which would have cost neither my imag-ination nor understanding an effort.

My fortunes have been, from the beginning, an exemplification of the power that mutability may possess over the varied tenor of man's life.[12] With regard to myself, this came almost by inheritance. My father was one of those men on whom nature had bestowed to prodigality the envied gifts of wit and imagination, and then left his bark of life to be impelled by these winds, without adding reason as the rudder, or judg-ment as the pilot for the voyage. His extraction was obscure; but circum-stances brought him early into public notice, and his small paternal prop-erty was soon dissipated in the splendid scene of fashion and luxury in which he was an actor. During the short years of thoughtless youth, he was adored by the high-bred triflers of the day, nor least by the youthful sovereign, who escaped from the intrigues of party, and the arduous duties of kingly business, to find never-failing amusement and exhilara-tion of spirit in his society. My father's impulses, never under his own controul, perpetually led him into difficulties from which his ingenuity alone could extricate him; and the accumulating pile of debts of honour and of trade, which would have bent to earth any other, was supported by him with a light spirit and tameless hilarity; while his company was so necessary at the tables and assemblies of the rich, that his derelictions

---

12 Mutability, or changeability and impermanence, is also the explicit subject of two of PBS's poems, "We are as clouds that veil the midnight moon" (pub-lished with *Alastor*, 1816, and quoted in *Frankenstein*, 1818), and "The flower that smiles to-day" (published in *Posthumous Poems*, 1824).

were considered venial, and he himself received with intoxicating flattery.

This kind of popularity, like every other, is evanescent: and the difficulties of every kind with which he had to contend, increased in a frightful ratio compared with his small means of extricating himself. At such times the king, in his enthusiasm for him, would come to his relief, and then kindly take his friend to task; my father gave the best promises for amendment, but his social disposition, his craving for the usual diet of admiration, and more than all, the fiend of gambling, which fully possessed him, made his good resolutions transient, his promises vain. With the quick sensibility peculiar to his temperament, he perceived his power in the brilliant circle to be on the wane. The king married; and the haughty princess of Austria, who became, as queen of England, the head of fashion, looked with harsh eyes on his defects, and with contempt on the affection her royal husband entertained for him. My father felt that his fall was near; but so far from profiting by this last calm before the storm to save himself, he sought to forget anticipated evil by making still greater sacrifices to the deity of pleasure, deceitful and cruel arbiter of his destiny.

The king, who was a man of excellent dispositions, but easily led, had now become a willing disciple of his imperious consort. He was induced to look with extreme disapprobation, and at last with distaste, on my father's imprudence and follies. It is true that his presence dissipated these clouds; his warm-hearted frankness, brilliant sallies, and confiding demeanour were irresistible: it was only when at a distance, while still renewed tales of his errors were poured into his royal friend's ear, that he lost his influence. The queen's dextrous management was employed to prolong these absences, and gather together accusations. At length the king was brought to see in him a source of perpetual disquiet, knowing that he should pay for the short-lived pleasure of his society by tedious homilies, and more painful narrations of excesses, the truth of which he could not disprove. The result was, that he would make one more attempt to reclaim him, and in case of ill success, cast him off for ever.

Such a scene must have been one of deepest interest and high-wrought passion. A powerful king, conspicuous for a goodness which had heretofore made him meek, and now lofty in his admonitions, with alternate entreaty and reproof, besought his friend to attend to his real interests, resolutely to avoid those fascinations which in fact were fast deserting him, and to spend his great powers on a worthy field, in which he, his sovereign, would be his prop, his stay, and his pioneer. My father felt this kindness; for a moment ambitious dreams floated before him; and he thought that it would be well to exchange his present pursuits for nobler duties. With sincerity and fervour he gave the required promise: as a pledge of continued favour, he received from his royal master a sum of money to defray pressing debts, and enable him to enter under good auspices his new career. That very night, while yet full of gratitude and good resolves, this whole sum, and its amount doubled, was lost at the gaming-table. In his desire to repair his first losses, my father risked double stakes, and thus incurred a debt of honour he was wholly unable to pay. Ashamed to apply again to the king, he turned his back upon London, its false delights and clinging miseries; and, with poverty for his sole companion, buried himself in solitude among the hills and lakes of Cumberland.[13] His wit, his bon mots, the record of his personal attractions, fascinating manners, and social talents, were long remembered and repeated from mouth to mouth. Ask where now was this favourite of fashion, this companion of the noble, this excelling beam, which gilt with alien splendour the assemblies of the courtly and the gay—you heard that he was under a cloud, a lost man; not one thought it belonged to him to repay pleasure by real services, or that his long reign of brilliant wit deserved a pension on retiring. The king lamented his absence; he loved to repeat his sayings, relate the adventures they had had together, and exalt his talents—but here ended his reminiscence.

Meanwhile my father, forgotten, could not forget. He repined for the loss of what was more necessary to him than air or food—the excitements of pleasure, the admiration of the noble, the luxurious and polished living of the great. A nervous fever was the consequence; during which he was nursed by the daughter of a poor cottager, under whose roof he lodged. She was lovely, gentle, and, above all, kind to him; nor can it afford astonishment, that the late idol of high-bred beauty should, even in a fallen state, appear a being of an elevated and wondrous nature to the lowly cottage-girl. The attachment between them led to the ill-fated marriage, of which I was the offspring.

Notwithstanding the tenderness and sweetness of my mother, her husband still deplored his degraded state. Unaccustomed to industry, he knew not in what way to contribute to the support of his increasing family. Sometimes he thought of applying to the king; pride and shame for a while withheld him; and, before his necessities became so imperious as to compel him to some kind of exertion, he died. For one brief interval before this catastrophe, he looked forward to the future, and contemplated with anguish the desolate situation in which his wife and children would be left. His last effort was a letter to the king, full of touching eloquence, and of occasional flashes of that brilliant spirit which was an integral part of him. He bequeathed his widow and orphans to the friendship of his royal master, and felt satisfied that, by this means, their prosperity was better assured in his death than in his life. This letter was enclosed to the care of a nobleman, who, he did not doubt, would perform the last and inexpensive office of placing it in the king's own hand.

He died in debt, and his little property was seized immediately by his creditors. My mother, pennyless and burthened with two children, wait-

13   A county of the Lake District in northwest England on the Scottish border.

ed week after week, and month after month, in sickening expectation of a reply, which never came. She had no experience beyond her father's cottage; and the mansion of the lord of the manor was the chiefest type of grandeur she could conceive. During my father's life, she had been made familiar with the name of royalty and the courtly circle; but such things, ill according with her personal experience, appeared, after the loss of him who gave substance and reality to them, vague and fantastical. If, under any circumstances, she could have acquired sufficient courage to address the noble persons mentioned by her husband, the ill success of his own application caused her to banish the idea. She saw therefore no escape from dire penury: perpetual care, joined to sorrow for the loss of the wondrous being, whom she continued to contemplate with ardent admiration, hard labour, and naturally delicate health, at length released her from the sad continuity of want and misery.

The condition of her orphan children was peculiarly desolate. Her own father had been an emigrant from another part of the country, and had died long since: they had no one relation to take them by the hand; they were outcasts, paupers, unfriended beings, to whom the most scanty pittance was a matter of favour, and who were treated merely as children of peasants, yet poorer than the poorest, who, dying, had left them, a thankless bequest, to the close-handed charity of the land.

I, the elder of the two, was five years old when my mother died. A remembrance of the discourses of my parents, and the communications which my mother endeavoured to impress upon me concerning my father's friends, in slight hope that I might one day derive benefit from the knowledge, floated like an indistinct dream through my brain. I conceived that I was different and superior to my protectors and companions, but I knew not how or wherefore. The sense of injury, associated with the name of king and noble, clung to me; but I could draw no conclusions from such feelings, to serve as a guide to action. My first real knowledge of myself was as an unprotected orphan among the valleys and fells of Cumberland. I was in the service of a farmer; and with crook in hand, my dog at my side, I shepherded a numerous flock on the near uplands. I cannot say much in praise of such a life; and its pains far exceeded its pleasures. There was freedom in it, a companionship with nature, and a reckless loneliness; but these, romantic as they were, did not accord with the love of action and desire of human sympathy, characteristic of youth. Neither the care of my flock, nor the change of seasons, were sufficient to tame my eager spirit; my out-door life and unemployed time were the temptations that led me early into lawless habits. I associated with others friendless like myself; I formed them into a band, I was their chief and captain. All shepherd-boys alike, while our flocks were spread over the pastures, we schemed and executed many a mischievous prank, which drew on us the anger and revenge of the rustics. I was the leader and protector of my comrades, and as I became distinguished among them, their misdeeds were usually visited upon me. But while I endured punishment and pain in their defence with the spirit of an hero, I claimed as my reward their praise and obedience.

In such a school my disposition became rugged, but firm. The appetite for admiration and small capacity for self-controul which I inherited from my father, nursed by adversity, made me daring and reckless. I was rough as the elements, and unlearned as the animals I tended. I often compared myself to them, and finding that my chief superiority consisted in power, I soon persuaded myself that it was in power only that I was inferior to the chiefest potentates of the earth. Thus untaught in refined philosophy, and pursued by a restless feeling of degradation from my true station in society, I wandered among the hills of civilized England as uncouth a savage as the wolf-bred founder of old Rome.[14] I owned but one law, it was that of the strongest, and my greatest deed of virtue was never to submit.

Yet let me a little retract from this sentence I have passed on myself. My mother, when dying, had, in addition to her other half-forgotten and misapplied lessons, committed, with solemn exhortation, her other child to my fraternal guardianship; and this one duty I performed to the best of my ability, with all the zeal and affection of which my nature was capable. My sister was three years younger than myself; I had nursed her as an infant, and when the difference of our sexes, by giving us various occupations, in a great measure divided us, yet she continued to be the object of my careful love. Orphans, in the fullest sense of the term, we were poorest among the poor, and despised among the unhonoured. If my daring and courage obtained for me a kind of respectful aversion, her youth and sex, since they did not excite tenderness, by proving her to be weak, were the causes of numberless mortifications to her; and her own disposition was not so constituted as to diminish the evil effects of her lowly station.

She was a singular being, and, like me, inherited much of the peculiar disposition of our father. Her countenance was all expression; her eyes were not dark, but impenetrably deep; you seemed to discover space after space in their intellectual glance, and to feel that the soul which was their soul, comprehended an universe of thought in its ken. She was pale and fair, and her golden hair clustered on her temples, contrasting its rich hue with the living marble beneath. Her coarse peasant-dress, little consonant apparently with the refinement of feeling which her face expressed, yet in a strange manner accorded with it. She was like one of Guido's saints,[15] with heaven in her heart and in her look, so that when you saw her you

---

14   According to legend Romulus, the founder of Rome, was suckled by a wolf along with his twin brother Remus.

15   The paintings and portraits of Guido Reni (1574-1642) were popular among writers of the Romantic period, influencing, for example, some of the descriptions in Ann Radcliffe's *The Italian* and PBS's treatment of Beatrice Cenci in *The Cenci*.

only thought of that within, and costume and even feature were secondary to the mind that beamed in her countenance.

Yet though lovely and full of noble feeling, my poor Perdita (for this was the fanciful name my sister had received from her dying parent), was not altogether saintly in her disposition. Her manners were cold and repulsive.[16] If she had been nurtured by those who had regarded her with affection, she might have been different; but unloved and neglected, she repaid want of kindness with distrust and silence. She was submissive to those who held authority over her, but a perpetual cloud dwelt on her brow; she looked as if she expected enmity from every one who approached her, and her actions were instigated by the same feeling. All the time she could command she spent in solitude. She would ramble to the most unfrequented places, and scale dangerous heights, that in those unvisited spots she might wrap herself in loneliness. Often she passed whole hours walking up and down the paths of the woods; she wove garlands of flowers and ivy, or watched the flickering of the shadows and glancing of the leaves; sometimes she sat beside a stream, and as her thoughts paused, threw flowers or pebbles into the waters, watching how those swam and these sank; or she would set afloat boats formed of bark of trees or leaves, with a feather for a sail, and intensely watch the navigation of her craft among the rapids and shallows of the brook. Meanwhile her active fancy wove a thousand combinations; she dreamt "of moving accidents by flood and field"[17]—she lost herself delightedly in these self-created wanderings, and returned with unwilling spirit to the dull detail of common life.

Poverty was the cloud that veiled her excellencies, and all that was good in her seemed about to perish from want of the genial dew of affection. She had not even the same advantage as I in the recollection of her parents; she clung to me, her brother, as her only friend, but her alliance with me completed the distaste that her protectors felt for her; and every error was magnified by them into crimes. If she had been bred in that sphere of life to which by inheritance the delicate framework of her mind and person was adapted, she would have been the object almost of adoration, for her virtues were as eminent as her defects. All the genius that ennobled the blood of her father illustrated hers; a generous tide flowed in her veins; artifice, envy, or meanness, were at the antipodes of her nature; her countenance, when enlightened by amiable feeling, might have belonged to a queen of nations; her eyes were bright; her look fearless.

---

16   Perdita means the lost one: Shakespeare's Perdita in *A Winter's Tale* is a princess, daughter of Leontes and Hermione, raised as a shepherdess and restored to her rightful rank at the end of the play. Reserved (not unattractive, as modern usage of "repulsive" might suggest), MWS's Perdita repels attempts at intimacy.

17   *Othello* 1.3.135; Othello is recalling the stories of his adventures he has told to Desdemona and her father.

Although by our situation and dispositions we were almost equally cut off from the usual forms of social intercourse, we formed a strong contrast to each other. I always required the stimulants of companionship and applause. Perdita was all-sufficient to herself. Notwithstanding my lawless habits, my disposition was sociable, hers recluse. My life was spent among tangible realities, hers was a dream. I might be said even to love my enemies, since by exciting me they in a sort bestowed happiness upon me; Perdita almost disliked her friends, for they interfered with her visionary moods. All my feelings, even of exultation and triumph, were changed to bitterness, if unparticipated; Perdita, even in joy, fled to loneliness, and could go on from day to day, neither expressing her emotions, nor seeking a fellow-feeling in another mind. Nay, she could love and dwell with tenderness on the look and voice of her friend, while her demeanour expressed the coldest reserve. A sensation with her became a sentiment, and she never spoke until she had mingled her perceptions of outward objects with others which were the native growth of her own mind. She was like a fruitful soil that imbibed the airs and dews of heaven, and gave them forth again to light in loveliest forms of fruits and flowers; but then she was often dark and rugged as that soil, raked up, and new sown with unseen seed.

She dwelt in a cottage whose trim grass-plat sloped down to the waters of the lake of Ulswater;[18] a beech wood stretched up the hill behind, and a purling brook gently falling from the acclivity ran through poplar-shaded banks into the lake. I lived with a farmer whose house was built higher up among the hills: a dark crag rose behind it, and, exposed to the north, the snow lay in its crevices the summer through. Before dawn I led my flock to the sheep-walks, and guarded them through the day. It was a life of toil; for rain and cold were more frequent than sunshine; but it was my pride to contemn the elements. My trusty dog watched the sheep as I slipped away to the rendezvous of my comrades, and thence to the accomplishment of our schemes. At noon we met again, and we threw away in contempt our peasant fare, as we built our fire-place and kindled the cheering blaze destined to cook the game stolen from the neighbouring preserves. Then came the tale of hair-breadth escapes, combats with dogs, ambush and flight, as gipsey-like we encompassed our pot. The search after a stray lamb, or the devices by which we elude or endeavoured to elude punishment, filled up the hours of afternoon; in the evening my flock went to its fold, and I to my sister.

---

18   Ullswater, in Cumberland, is the second-largest lake in England. By associating Perdita with the Lake District, associated with William Wordsworth and Samuel Taylor Coleridge, MWS makes her a Wordsworthian heroine as well as a Shakespearean one; see also below, 40, where Lionel quotes Wordsworth to describe Perdita.

It was seldom indeed that we escaped, to use an old-fashioned phrase, scot free. Our dainty fare was often exchanged for blows and imprisonment. Once, when thirteen years of age, I was sent for a month to the county jail. I came out, my morals unimproved, my hatred to my oppressors encreased tenfold. Bread and water did not tame my blood, nor solitary confinement inspire me with gentle thoughts. I was angry, impatient, miserable; my only happy hours were those during which I devised schemes of revenge; these were perfected in my forced solitude, so that during the whole of the following season, and I was freed early in September, I never failed to provide excellent and plenteous fare for myself and my comrades. This was a glorious winter. The sharp frost and heavy snows tamed the animals, and kept the country gentlemen by their firesides; we got more game than we could eat, and my faithful dog grew sleek upon our refuse.

Thus years passed on; and years only added fresh love of freedom, and contempt for all that was not as wild and rude as myself. At the age of sixteen I had shot up in appearance to man's estate; I was tall and athletic; I was practised to feats of strength, and inured to the inclemency of the elements. My skin was embrowned by the sun; my step was firm with conscious power. I feared no man, and loved none. In after life I looked back with wonder to what I then was; how utterly worthless I should have become if I had pursued my lawless career. My life was like that of an animal, and my mind was in danger of degenerating into that which informs brute nature. Until now, my savage habits had done me no radical mischief; my physical powers had grown up and flourished under their influence, and my mind, undergoing the same discipline, was imbued with all the hardy virtues. But now my boasted independence was daily instigating me to acts of tyranny, and freedom was becoming licentiousness. I stood on the brink of manhood; passions, strong as the trees of a forest, had already taken root within me, and were about to shadow with their noxious overgrowth, my path of life.

I panted for enterprises beyond my childish exploits, and formed distempered dreams of future action. I avoided my ancient comrades, and I soon lost them. They arrived at the age when they were sent to fulfil their destined situations in life; while I, an outcast, with none to lead or drive me forward, paused. The old began to point at me as an example, the young to wonder at me as a being distinct from themselves; I hated them, and began, last and worst degradation, to hate myself. I clung to my ferocious habits, yet half despised them; I continued my war against civilization, and yet entertained a wish to belong to it.

I revolved again and again all that I remembered my mother to have told me of my father's former life; I contemplated the few relics I possessed belonging to him, which spoke of greater refinement than could be found among the mountain cottages; but nothing in all this served as a guide to lead me to another and pleasanter way of life. My father had been connected with nobles, but all I knew of such connection was subsequent neglect. The name of the king,—he to whom my dying father had addressed his latest prayers, and who had barbarously slighted them, was associated only with the ideas of unkindness, injustice, and consequent resentment. I was born for something greater than I was—and greater I would become; but greatness, at least to my distorted perceptions, was no necessary associate of goodness, and my wild thoughts were unchecked by moral considerations when they rioted in dreams of distinction. Thus I stood upon a pinnacle, a sea of evil rolled at my feet; I was about to precipitate myself into it, and rush like a torrent over all obstructions to the object of my wishes—when a stranger influence came over the current of my fortunes, and changed their boisterous course to what was in comparison like the gentle meanderings of a meadow-encircling streamlet.

CHAPTER II

I LIVED far from the busy haunts of men, and the rumour of wars or political changes came worn to a mere sound, to our mountain abodes. England had been the scene of momentous struggles, during my early boyhood. In the year 2073, the last of its kings, the ancient friend of my father, had abdicated in compliance with the gentle force of the remonstrances of his subjects, and a republic was instituted. Large estates were secured to the dethroned monarch and his family; he received the title of Earl of Windsor, and Windsor Castle, an ancient royalty, with its wide demesnes were a part of his allotted wealth. He died soon after, leaving two children, a son and a daughter.

The ex-queen, a princess of the house of Austria,[19] had long impelled her husband to withstand the necessity of the times. She was haughty and fearless; she cherished a love of power, and a bitter contempt for him who had despoiled himself of a kingdom. For her children's sake alone she consented to remain, shorn of regality, a member of the English republic. When she became a widow, she turned all her thoughts to the educating her son Adrian, second Earl of Windsor, so as to accomplish her ambitious ends; and with his mother's milk he imbibed, and was intended to grow up in the steady purpose of re-acquiring his lost crown. Adrian was now fifteen years of age. He was addicted to study, and imbued beyond his years with learning and talent: report said that he had already begun to thwart his mother's views, and to entertain republican principles. However this might be, the haughty Countess entrusted none with the

19   The ex-queen's nationality foretells her conservative views. After the
       Congress of Vienna (1814-15), the Austrian empire under Prince Klemens von
       Metternich was reactionary and anti-democratic, supporting the restoration of
       royal dynasties in France, Germany, and Italy.

secrets of her family-tuition. Adrian was bred up in solitude, and kept apart from the natural companions of his age and rank. Some unknown circumstance now induced his mother to send him from under her immediate tutelage; and we heard that he was about to visit Cumberland. A thousand tales were rife, explanatory of the Countess of Windsor's conduct; none true probably; but each day it became more certain that we should have the noble scion of the late regal house of England among us.

There was a large estate with a mansion attached to it, belonging to this family, at Ulswater. A large park was one of its appendages, laid out with great taste, and plentifully stocked with game. I had often made depredations on these preserves; and the neglected state of the property facilitated my incursions. When it was decided that the young Earl of Windsor should visit Cumberland, workmen arrived to put the house and grounds in order for his reception. The apartments were restored to their pristine splendour, and the park, all disrepairs restored, was guarded with unusual care.

I was beyond measure disturbed by this intelligence. It roused all my dormant recollections, my suspended sentiments of injury, and gave rise to the new one of revenge. I could no longer attend to my occupations; all my plans and devices were forgotten; I seemed about to begin life anew, and that under no good auspices. The tug of war, I thought, was now to begin. He would come triumphantly to the district to which my parent had fled broken-hearted; he would find the ill-fated offspring, bequeathed with such vain confidence to his royal father, miserable paupers. That he should know of our existence, and treat us, near at hand, with the same contumely which his father had practised in distance and absence, appeared to me the certain consequence of all that had gone before. Thus then I should meet this titled stripling—the son of my father's friend. He would be hedged in by servants; nobles, and the sons of nobles, were his companions; all England rang with his name; and his coming, like a thunderstorm, was heard from far: while I, unlettered and unfashioned, should, if I came in contact with him, in the judgment of his courtly followers, bear evidence in my very person to the propriety of that ingratitude which had made me the degraded being I appeared.

With my mind fully occupied by these ideas, I might be said as if fascinated, to haunt the destined abode of the young Earl. I watched the progress of the improvements, and stood by the unlading waggons, as various articles of luxury, brought from London, were taken forth and conveyed into the mansion. It was part of the Ex-Queen's plan, to surround her son with princely magnificence. I beheld rich carpets and silken hangings, ornaments of gold, richly embossed metals, emblazoned furniture, and all the appendages of high rank arranged, so that nothing but what was regal in splendour should reach the eye of one of royal descent. I looked on these; I turned my gaze to my own mean dress.—Whence sprung this difference? Whence but from ingratitude, from falsehood, from a dereliction on the part of the prince's father, of all noble sympathy

and generous feeling. Doubtless, he also, whose blood received a mingling tide from his proud mother—he, the acknowledged focus of the
kingdom's wealth and nobility, had been taught to repeat my father's
name with disdain, and to scoff at my just claims to protection. I strove to
think that all this grandeur was but more glaring infamy, and that, by
planting his gold-enwoven flag beside my tarnished and tattered banner,
he proclaimed not his superiority, but his debasement. Yet I envied him.
His stud of beautiful horses, his arms of costly workmanship, the praise
that attended him, the adoration, ready servitor, high place and high
esteem,—I considered them as forcibly wrenched from me, and envied
them all with novel and tormenting bitterness.

To crown my vexation of spirit, Perdita, the visionary Perdita, seemed
to awake to real life with transport, when she told me that the Earl of
Windsor was about to arrive.

"And this pleases you?" I observed, moodily.

"Indeed it does, Lionel," she replied; "I quite long to see him; he is
the descendant of our kings, the first noble of the land: every one admires
and loves him, and they say that his rank is his least merit; he is generous,
brave, and affable."

"You have learnt a pretty lesson, Perdita," said I, "and repeat it so literally, that you forget the while the proofs we have of the Earl's virtues;
his generosity to us is manifest in our plenty, his bravery in the protection
he affords us, his affability in the notice he takes of us. His rank his least
merit, do you say? Why, all his virtues are derived from his station only;
because he is rich, he is called generous; because he is powerful, brave;
because he is well served, he is affable. Let them call him so, let all
England believe him to be thus—we know him—he is our enemy—our
penurious, dastardly, arrogant enemy; if he were gifted with one particle
of the virtues you call his, he would do justly by us, if it were only to shew,
that if he must strike, it should not be a fallen foe. His father injured my
father—his father, unassailable on his throne, dared despise him who only
stooped beneath himself, when he deigned to associate with the royal
ingrate. We, descendants from the one and the other, must be enemies
also. He shall find that I can feel my injuries; he shall learn to dread my
revenge!"

A few days after he arrived. Every inhabitant of the most miserable
cottage, went to swell the stream of population that poured forth to meet
him: even Perdita, in spite of my late philippic, crept near the highway, to
behold this idol of all hearts. I, driven half mad, as I met party after party
of the country people, in their holiday best, descending the hills, escaped
to their cloud-veiled summits, and looking on the sterile rocks about me,
exclaimed—"*They* do not cry, long live the Earl!" Nor, when night came,
accompanied by drizzling rain and cold, would I return home; for I knew
that each cottage rang with the praises of Adrian; as I felt my limbs grow
numb and chill, my pain served as food for my insane aversion; nay, I
almost triumphed in it, since it seemed to afford me reason and excuse for

my hatred of my unheeding adversary. All was attributed to him, for I confounded so entirely the idea of father and son, that I forgot that the latter might be wholly unconscious of his parent's neglect of us; and as I struck my aching head with my hand, I cried: "He shall hear of this! I will be revenged! I will not suffer like a spaniel! He shall know, beggar and friendless as I am, that I will not tamely submit to injury!"

Each day, each hour added to these exaggerated wrongs. His praises were so many adder's stings infixed in my vulnerable breast. If I saw him at a distance, riding a beautiful horse, my blood boiled with rage; the air seemed poisoned by his presence, and my very native English was changed to a vile jargon, since every phrase I heard was coupled with his name and honour. I panted to relieve this painful heart-burning by some misdeed that should rouse him to a sense of my antipathy. It was the height of his offending, that he should occasion in me such intolerable sensations, and not deign himself to afford any demonstration that he was aware that I even lived to feel them.

It soon became known that Adrian took great delight in his park and preserves. He never sported, but spent hours in watching the tribes of lovely and almost tame animals with which it was stocked, and ordered that greater care should be taken of them than ever. Here was an opening for my plans of offence, and I made use of it with all the brute impetuosity I derived from my active mode of life. I proposed the enterprize of poaching on his demesne to my few remaining comrades, who were the most determined and lawless of the crew; but they all shrunk from the peril; so I was bent to achieve my revenge myself. At first my exploits were unperceived; I increased in daring; footsteps on the dewy grass, torn boughs, and marks of slaughter, at length betrayed me to the gamekeepers. They kept better watch; I was taken, and sent to prison. I entered its gloomy walls in a fit of triumphant extasy: "He feels me now," I cried, "and shall, again and again!"—I passed but one day in confinement; in the evening I was liberated, as I was told, by the order of the Earl himself. This news precipitated me from my self-raised pinnacle of honour. He despises me, I thought; but he shall learn that I despise him, and hold in equal contempt his punishments and his clemency. On the second night after my release, I was again taken by the gamekeepers—again imprisoned, and again released; and again, such was my pertinacity, did the fourth night find me in the forbidden park. The gamekeepers were more enraged than their lord by my obstinacy. They had received orders that if I were again taken, I should be brought to the Earl; and his lenity made them expect a conclusion which they considered ill befitting my crime. One of them, who had been from the first the leader among those who had seized me, resolved to satisfy his own resentment, before he made me over to the higher powers.

The late setting of the moon, and the extreme caution I was obliged to use in this my third expedition, consumed so much time, that something like a qualm of fear came over me when I perceived dark night yield to twilight. I crept along by the fern, on my hands and knees, seeking the shadowy coverts of the underwood, while the birds awoke with unwelcome song above, and the fresh morning wind, playing among the boughs, made me suspect a footfall at each turn. My heart beat quick as I approached the palings; my hand was on one of them, a leap would take me to the other side, when two keepers sprang from an ambush upon me: one knocked me down, and proceeded to inflict a severe horse-whipping. I started up—a knife was in my grasp; I made a plunge at his raised right arm, and inflicted a deep, wide wound in his hand. The rage and yells of the wounded man, the howling execrations of his comrade, which I answered with equal bitterness and fury, echoed through the dell; morning broke more and more, ill accordant in its celestial beauty with our brute and noisy contest. I and my enemy were still struggling, when the wounded man exclaimed, "The Earl!" I sprang out of the herculean hold of the keeper, panting from my exertions; I cast furious glances on my persecutors, and placing myself with my back to a tree, resolved to defend myself to the last. My garments were torn, and they, as well as my hands, were stained with the blood of the man I had wounded; one hand grasped the dead birds—my hard-earned prey, the other held the knife; my hair was matted; my face besmeared with the same guilty signs that bore witness against me on the dripping instrument I clenched; my whole appearance was haggard and squalid. Tall and muscular as I was in form, I must have looked like, what indeed I was, the merest ruffian that ever trod the earth.

The name of the Earl startled me, and caused all the indignant blood that warmed my heart to rush into my cheeks; I had never seen him before; I figured to myself a haughty, assuming youth, who would take me to task, if he deigned to speak to me, with all the arrogance of superiority. My reply was ready; a reproach I deemed calculated to sting his very heart. He came up the while; and his appearance blew aside, with gentle western breath, my cloudy wrath: a tall, slim, fair boy, with a physiognomy expressive of the excess of sensibility and refinement stood before me; the morning sunbeams tinged with gold his silken hair, and spread light and glory over his beaming countenance. "How is this?" he cried. The men eagerly began their defence; he put them aside, saying, "Two of you at once on a mere lad—for shame!" He came up to me: "Verney," he cried, "Lionel Verney,[20] do we meet thus for the first time? We were

---

20 Here Lionel's full name is used for the first time. In "Rosalind and Helen" (published 1819) and in "The Boat on the Serchio" (*Posthumous Poems*, 1824), PBS represents himself under the name of Lionel. While some of Lionel Verney's qualities suggest Shelleyan idealism, MWS's use of the name Verney, borrowed from a well-known seventeenth-century family, may emphasize her novel's political scepticism: like Sir Ralph Verney, who refused to take sides during the Civil War, Lionel Verney avoids commitment to a particular political cause. In *Desmond* (1792), Charlotte Smith uses the names "Lionel" and "Verney."

born to be friends to each other; and though ill fortune has divided us, will you not acknowledge the hereditary bond of friendship which I trust will hereafter unite us?"

As he spoke, his earnest eyes, fixed on me, seemed to read my very soul: my heart, my savage revengeful heart, felt the influence of sweet benignity sink upon it; while his thrilling voice, like sweetest melody, awoke a mute echo within me, stirring to its depths the life-blood in my frame. I desired to reply, to acknowledge his goodness, accept his proffered friendship; but words, fitting words, were not afforded to the rough mountaineer; I would have held out my hand, but its guilty stain restrained me. Adrian took pity on my faltering mien: "Come with me," he said, "I have much to say to you; come home with me—you know who I am?"

"Yes," I exclaimed, "I do believe that I now know you, and that you will pardon my mistakes—my crime."

Adrian smiled gently; and after giving his orders to the gamekeepers, he came up to me; putting his arm in mine, we walked together to the mansion.

It was not his rank—after all that I have said, surely it will not be suspected that it was Adrian's rank, that, from the first, subdued my heart of hearts, and laid my entire spirit prostrate before him. Nor was it I alone who felt thus intimately his perfections: his sensibility and courtesy fascinated every one. His vivacity, intelligence, and active spirit of benevolence, completed the conquest. Even at this early age, he was deep read and imbued with the spirit of high philosophy. This spirit gave a tone of irresistible persuasion to his intercourse with others, so that he seemed like an inspired musician, who struck, with unerring skill, the "lyre of mind,"[21] and produced thence divine harmony. In person, he hardly appeared of this world; his slight frame was overinformed by the soul that dwelt within; he was all mind; "Man but a rush against"[22] his breast, and it would have conquered his strength; but the might of his smile would have tamed an hungry lion, or caused a legion of armed men to lay their weapons at his feet.

I spent the day with him. At first he did not recur to the past, or indeed to any personal occurrences. He wished probably to inspire me with confidence, and give me time to gather together my scattered thoughts. He talked of general subjects, and gave me ideas I had never before conceived. We sat in his library, and he spoke of the old Greek sages, and of the power which they had acquired over the minds of men, through the force of love and wisdom only. The room was decorated with the busts of

---

21 PBS, "To the Lord Chancellor" 28; MWS published part of this poem (including this line) in *Poetical Works*, 1839.

22 Cf. *Othello* 5.2.273-74: "Man but a rush against Othello's breast, / And he retires."

many of them, and he described their characters to me. As he spoke, I felt subject to him; and all my boasted pride and strength were subdued by the honeyed accents of this blue-eyed boy. The trim and paled demesne of civilization, which I had before regarded from my wild jungle as inaccessible, had its wicket opened by him; I stepped within, and felt, as I entered, that I trod my native soil.

As evening came on, he reverted to the past. "I have a tale to relate," he said, "and much explanation to give concerning the past; perhaps you can assist me to curtail it. Do you remember your father? I had never the happiness of seeing him, but his name is one of my earliest recollections: he stands written in my mind's tablets as the type of all that was gallant, amiable, and fascinating in man. His wit was not more conspicuous than the overflowing goodness of his heart, which he poured in such full measure on his friends, as to leave, alas! small remnant for himself."

. Encouraged by this encomium, I proceeded, in answer to his inquiries, to relate what I remembered of my parent; and he gave an account of those circumstances which had brought about a neglect of my father's testamentary letter. When, in after times, Adrian's father, then king of England, felt his situation become more perilous, his line of conduct more embarrassed, again and again he wished for his early friend, who might stand a mound against the impetuous anger of his queen, a mediator between him and the parliament. From the time that he had quitted London, on the fatal night of his defeat at the gaming-table, the king had received no tidings concerning him; and when, after the lapse of years, he exerted himself to discover him, every trace was lost. With fonder regret than ever, he clung to his memory; and gave it in charge to his son, if ever he should meet this valued friend, in his name to bestow every succour, and to assure him that, to the last, his attachment survived separation and silence.

A short time before Adrian's visit to Cumberland, the heir of the nobleman to whom my father had confided his last appeal to his royal master, put this letter, its seal unbroken, into the young Earl's hands. It had been found cast aside with a mass of papers of old date, and accident alone brought it to light. Adrian read it with deep interest; and found there that living spirit of genius and wit he had so often heard commemorated. He discovered the name of the spot whither my father had retreated, and where he died; he learnt the existence of his orphan children; and during the short interval between his arrival at Ulswater and our meeting in the park, he had been occupied in making inquiries concerning us, and arranging a variety of plans for our benefit, preliminary to his introducing himself to our notice.

The mode in which he spoke of my father was gratifying to my vanity; the veil which he delicately cast over his benevolence, in alledging a duteous fulfilment of the king's latest will, was soothing to my pride. Other feelings, less ambiguous, were called into play by his conciliating manner and the generous warmth of his expressions, respect rarely before experienced, admiration, and love—he had touched my rocky heart with his magic power, and the stream of affection gushed forth, imperishable and pure. In the evening we parted; he pressed my hand: "We shall meet again; come to me to-morrow." I clasped that kind hand; I tried to answer; a fervent "God bless you!" was all my ignorance could frame of speech, and I darted away, oppressed by my new emotions.

I could not rest. I sought the hills; a west wind swept them, and the stars glittered above. I ran on, careless of outward objects, but trying to master the struggling spirit within me by means of bodily fatigue. "This," I thought, "is power! Not to be strong of limb, hard of heart, ferocious, and daring; but kind, compassionate and soft."—Stopping short, I clasped my hands, and with the fervour of a new proselyte, cried, "Doubt me not, Adrian, I also will become wise and good!" and then quite overcome, I wept aloud.

As this gust of passion passed from me, I felt more composed. I lay on the ground, and giving the reins to my thoughts, repassed in my mind my former life; and began, fold by fold, to unwind the many errors of my heart, and to discover how brutish, savage, and worthless I had hitherto been. I could not however at that time feel remorse, for methought I was born anew; my soul threw off the burthen of past sin, to commence a new career in innocence and love. Nothing harsh or rough remained to jar with the soft feelings which the transactions of the day had inspired; I was as a child lisping its devotions after its mother, and my plastic soul was remoulded by a master hand, which I neither desired nor was able to resist.

This was the first commencement of my friendship with Adrian, and I must commemorate this day as the most fortunate of my life. I now began to be human. I was admitted within that sacred boundary which divides the intellectual and moral nature of man from that which characterizes animals. My best feelings were called into play to give fitting responses to the generosity, wisdom, and amenity of my new friend. He, with a noble goodness all his own, took infinite delight in bestowing to prodigality the treasures of his mind and fortune on the long-neglected son of his father's friend, the offspring of that gifted being whose excellencies and talents he had heard commemorated from infancy.

After his abdication the late king had retreated from the sphere of politics, yet his domestic circle afforded him small content. The ex-queen had none of the virtues of domestic life, and those of courage and daring which she possessed were rendered null by the secession of her husband: she despised him, and did not care to conceal her sentiments. The king had, in compliance with her exactions, cast off his old friends, but he had acquired no new ones under her guidance. In this dearth of sympathy, he had recourse to his almost infant son; and the early development of talent and sensibility rendered Adrian no unfitting depository of his father's confidence. He was never weary of listening to the latter's often repeated accounts of old times, in which my father had played a distinguished part;

his keen remarks were repeated to the boy, and remembered by him; his wit, his fascinations, his very faults were hallowed by the regret of affection; his loss was sincerely deplored. Even the queen's dislike of the favourite was ineffectual to deprive him of his son's admiration: it was bitter, sarcastic, contemptuous—but as she bestowed her heavy censure alike on his virtues as his errors, on his devoted friendship and his ill-bestowed loves, on his disinterestedness and his prodigality, on his pre-possessing grace of manner, and the facility with which he yielded to temptation, her double shot proved too heavy, and fell short of the mark. Nor did her angry dislike prevent Adrian from imaging my father, as he had said, the type of all that was gallant, amiable, and fascinating in man. It was not strange therefore, that when he heard of the existence of the offspring of this celebrated person, he should have formed the plan of bestowing on them all the advantages his rank made him rich to afford. When he found me a vagabond shepherd of the hills, a poacher, an unlettered savage, still his kindness did not fail. In addition to the opinion he entertained that his father was to a degree culpable of neglect towards us, and that he was bound to every possible reparation, he was pleased to say that under all my ruggedness there glimmered forth an elevation of spirit, which could be distinguished from mere animal courage, and that I inherited a similarity of countenance to my father, which gave proof that all his virtues and talents had not died with him. Whatever those might be which descended to me, my noble young friend resolved should not be lost for want of culture.

Acting upon this plan in our subsequent intercourse, he led me to wish to participate in that cultivation which graced his own intellect. My active mind, when once it seized upon this new idea, fastened on it with extreme avidity. At first it was the great object of my ambition to rival the merits of my father, and render myself worthy of the friendship of Adrian. But curiosity soon awoke, and an earnest love of knowledge, which caused me to pass days and nights in reading and study. I was already well acquainted with what I may term the panorama of nature, the change of seasons, and the various appearances of heaven and earth. But I was at once startled and enchanted by my sudden extension of vision, when the curtain, which had been drawn before the intellectual world, was withdrawn, and I saw the universe, not only as it presented itself to my outward senses, but as it had appeared to the wisest among men. Poetry and its creations, philosophy and its researches and classifications, alike awoke the sleeping ideas in my mind, and gave me new ones.

I felt as the sailor, who from the topmast first discovered the shore of America; and like him I hastened to tell my companions of my discoveries in unknown regions. But I was unable to excite in any breast the same craving appetite for knowledge that existed in mine. Even Perdita was unable to understand me. I had lived in what is generally called the world of reality, and it was awakening to a new country to find that there was a deeper meaning in all I saw, besides that which my eyes conveyed to me.

The visionary Perdita beheld in all this only a new gloss upon an old reading, and her own was sufficiently inexhaustible to content her. She listened to me as she had done to the narration of my adventures, and sometimes took an interest in this species of information; but she did not, as I did, look on it as an integral part of her being, which having obtained, I could no more put off than the universal sense of touch.

We both agreed in loving Adrian: although she not having yet escaped from childhood could not appreciate as I did the extent of his merits, or feel the same sympathy in his pursuits and opinions. I was for ever with him. There was a sensibility and sweetness in his disposition, that gave a tender and unearthly tone to our converse. Then he was gay as a lark carolling from its skiey tower, soaring in thought as an eagle, innocent as the mild-eyed dove.[23] He could dispel the seriousness of Perdita, and take the sting from the torturing activity of my nature. I looked back to my restless desires and painful struggles with my fellow beings as to a troubled dream, and felt myself as much changed as if I had transmigrated into another form, whose fresh sensorium and mechanism of nerves had altered the reflection of the apparent universe in the mirror of mind. But it was not so; I was the same in strength, in earnest craving for sympathy, in my yearning for active exertion. My manly virtues did not desert me, for the witch Urania spared the locks of Sampson, while he reposed at her feet;[24] but all was softened and humanized. Nor did Adrian instruct me only in the cold truths of history and philosophy. At the same time that he taught me by their means to subdue my own reckless and uncultured spirit, he opened to my view the living page of his own heart, and gave me to feel and understand its wondrous character.

The ex-queen of England had, even during infancy, endeavoured to implant daring and ambitious designs in the mind of her son. She saw that he was endowed with genius and surpassing talent; these she cultivated for the sake of afterwards using them for the furtherance of her own views. She encouraged his craving for knowledge and his impetuous courage; she even tolerated his tameless love of freedom, under the hope that this would, as is too often the case, lead to a passion for command.

---

23 Cf. Matthew 10.16: "Behold, I send you forth as sheep in the midst of wolves: be ye therefore wise as serpents, and harmless as doves."

24 After Delilah had Samson's hair cut, he lost his strength: see Judges 16.19. MWS replaces Delilah by Urania, the classical muse of astronomy and Milton's Heavenly Muse. For the association of Urania with heavenly love (rather than the earthly love Delilah represents), see MWS's note on PBS's *Pandemos and Urania* (the first draft of his poem *Prince Athanase*, 1817), and see Thomas Love Peacock's notes to *Rhododaphne* (1818): "Uranian Love, in the mythological philosophy of Plato, is the deity or genius of pure mental passion for the good and the beautiful; and Pandemian Love, of ordinary sexual attachment." Cf. Plutarch, "The Dialogue on Love," *Moralia* 9: 397, and Plato, *Symposium*, trans. PBS 7: 181.

She endeavoured to bring him up in a sense of resentment towards, and a desire to revenge himself upon, those who had been instrumental in bringing about his father's abdication. In this she did not succeed. The accounts furnished him, however distorted, of a great and wise nation asserting its right to govern itself, excited his admiration: in early days he became a republican from principle. Still his mother did not despair. To the love of rule and haughty pride of birth she added determined ambition, patience, and self-control. She devoted herself to the study of her son's disposition. By the application of praise, censure, and exhortation, she tried to seek and strike the fitting chords; and though the melody that followed her touch seemed discord to her, she built her hopes on his talents, and felt sure that she would at last win him. The kind of banishment he now experienced arose from other causes.

The ex-queen had also a daughter, now twelve years of age; his fairy sister, Adrian was wont to call her; a lovely, animated, little thing, all sensibility and truth. With these, her children, the noble widow constantly resided at Windsor; and admitted no visitors, except her own partizans, travellers from her native Germany, and a few of the foreign ministers. Among these, and highly distinguished by her, was Prince Zaimi, ambassador to England from the free States of Greece; and his daughter, the young Princess Evadne,[25] passed much of her time at Windsor Castle. In company with this sprightly and clever Greek girl, the Countess would relax from her usual state. Her views with regard to her own children, placed all her words and actions relative to *them* under restraint: but Evadne was a plaything she could in no way fear; nor were her talents and vivacity slight alleviations to the monotony of the Countess's life.

Evadne was eighteen years of age. Although they spent much time together at Windsor, the extreme youth of Adrian prevented any suspicion as to the nature of their intercourse. But he was ardent and tender of heart beyond the common nature of man, and had already learnt to love, while the beauteous Greek smiled benignantly on the boy. It was strange to me, who, though older than Adrian, had never loved, to witness the whole heart's sacrifice of my friend. There was neither jealousy, inquietude, or mistrust in his sentiment; it was devotion and faith. His life was swallowed up in the existence of his beloved; and his heart beat only in

---

25 Evadne is ambiguously named. In Euripides' play *The Suppliants*, Evadne throws herself on the funeral pyre of her husband, Capaneus; in the *Aeneid* 6, Aeneas meets her in the Fields of Mourning. In Beaumont and Fletcher's *The Maid's Tragedy* (1610), Evadne masks her status as the king's mistress by marrying Amintor in spite of his engagement to Aspatia; caught in an ironic conflict of loyalties, she stabs the king to death. In *Evadne, or, The Statue*, a play by Richard Sheil (first produced in 1818), similar material is reworked: falsely accused of being the king's mistress, Evadne is eventually vindicated and married to her lover. The last two plays are both concerned with themes of illicit love, honour, power, and betrayal.

unison with the pulsations that vivified hers. This was the secret law of his life—he loved and was beloved. The universe was to him a dwelling, to inhabit with his chosen one; and not either a scheme of society or an enchainment of events, that could impact to him either happiness or misery. What, though life and the system of social intercourse were a wilderness, a tiger-haunted jungle! Through the midst of its errors, in the depths of its savage recesses, there was a disentangled and flowery pathway, through which they might journey in safety and delight. Their track would be like the passage of the Red Sea, which they might traverse with unwet feet, though a wall of destruction were impending on either side.[26]

Alas! why must I record the hapless delusion of this matchless specimen of humanity? What is there in our nature that is for ever urging us on towards pain and misery? We are not formed for enjoyment; and, however we may be attuned to the reception of pleasureable emotion, disappointment is the never-failing pilot of our life's bark, and ruthlessly carries us on to the shoals. Who was better framed than this highly-gifted youth to love and be beloved, and to reap unalienable joy from an unblamed passion? If his heart had slept but a few years longer, he might have been saved; but it awoke in its infancy; it had power, but no knowledge; and it was ruined, even as a too early-blowing bud is nipt by the killing frost.

I did not accuse Evadne of hypocrisy or a wish to deceive her lover; but the first letter that I saw of hers convinced me that she did not love him; it was written with elegance, and, foreigner as she was, with great command of language. The hand-writing itself was exquisitely beautiful; there was something in her very paper and its folds, which even I, who did not love, and was withal unskilled in such matters, could discern as being tasteful. There was much kindness, gratitude, and sweetness in her expression, but no love. Evadne was two years older than Adrian; and who, at eighteen, ever loved one so much their junior? I compared her placid epistles with the burning ones of Adrian. His soul seemed to distil itself into the words he wrote; and they breathed on the paper, bearing with them a portion of the life of love, which was his life. The very writing used to exhaust him; and he would weep over them, merely from the excess of emotion they awakened in his heart.

Adrian's soul was painted in his countenance, and concealment or deceit were at the antipodes to the dreadless frankness of his nature. Evadne made it her earnest request that the tale of their loves should not be revealed to his mother; and after for a while contesting the point, he yielded it to her. A vain concession; his demeanour quickly betrayed his secret to the quick eyes of the ex-queen. With the same wary prudence that characterized her whole conduct, she concealed her discovery, but hastened to remove her son from the sphere of the attractive Greek. He

---

26   For the crossing of the Red Sea, see Exodus 14.21-31.

was sent to Cumberland; but the plan of correspondence between the lovers, arranged by Evadne, was effectually hidden from her. Thus the absence of Adrian, concerted for the purpose of separating, united them in firmer bonds than ever. To me he discoursed ceaselessly of his beloved Ionian.[27] Her country, its ancient annals, its late memorable struggles, were all made to partake in her glory and excellence. He submitted to be away from her, because she commanded this submission; but for her influence, he would have declared his attachment before all England, and resisted, with unshaken constancy, his mother's opposition. Evadne's feminine prudence perceived how useless any assertion of his resolves would be, till added years gave weight to his power. Perhaps there was besides a lurking dislike to bind herself in the face of the world to one whom she did not love—not love, at least, with that passionate enthusiasm which her heart told her she might one day feel towards another. He obeyed her injunctions, and passed a year in exile in Cumberland.

CHAPTER III

HAPPY, thrice happy, were the months, and weeks, and hours of that year. Friendship, hand in hand with admiration, tenderness and respect, built a bower of delight in my heart, late rough as an untrod wild in America, as the homeless wind or herbless sea. Insatiate thirst for knowledge, and boundless affection for Adrian, combined to keep both my heart and understanding occupied, and I was consequently happy. What happiness is so true and unclouded, as the overflowing and talkative delight of young people. In our boat, upon my native lake, beside the streams and the pale bordering poplars—in valley and over hill, my crook thrown aside, a nobler flock to tend than silly sheep, even a flock of new-born ideas, I read or listened to Adrian; and his discourse, whether it concerned his love or his theories for the improvement of man, alike entranced me. Sometimes my lawless mood would return, my love of peril, my resistance to authority; but this was in his absence; under the mild sway of his dear eyes, I was obedient and good as a boy of five years old, who does his mother's bidding.

After a residence of about a year at Ulswater, Adrian visited London, and came back full of plans for our benefit. You must begin life, he said: you are seventeen, and longer delay would render the necessary apprenticeship more and more irksome. He foresaw that his own life would be one of struggle, and I must partake his labours with him. The better to fit me for this task, we must now separate. He found my name a good passport to preferment, and he had procured for me the situation of private

---

27 Ionia, where Greek literature and philosophy were principally developed, was on the west coast of Asia Minor; here, Ionian simply means Greek.

secretary to the Ambassador at Vienna, where I should enter on my career under the best auspices. In two years, I should return to my country, with a name well known and a reputation already founded.

And Perdita?—Perdita was to become the pupil, friend and younger sister of Evadne. With his usual thoughtfulness, he had provided for her independence in this situation. How refuse the offers of this generous friend?—I did not wish to refuse them; but in my heart of hearts, I made a vow to devote life, knowledge, and power, all of which, in as much as they were of any value, he had bestowed on me—all, all my capacities and hopes, to him alone I would devote.

Thus I promised myself, as I journied towards my destination with roused and ardent expectation: expectation of the fulfilment of all that in boyhood we promise ourselves of power and enjoyment in maturity. Methought the time was now arrived, when, childish occupations laid aside, I should enter into life. Even in the Elysian fields, Virgil describes the souls of the happy as eager to drink of the wave which was to restore them to this mortal coil.[28] The young are seldom in Elysium, for their desires, outstripping possibility, leave them as poor as a moneyless debtor. We are told by the wisest philosophers of the dangers of the world, the deceits of men, and the treason of our own hearts: but not the less fearlessly does each put off his frail bark from the port, spread the sail, and strain his oar, to attain the multitudinous streams of the sea of life. How few in youth's prime, moor their vessels on the "golden sands,"[29] and collect the painted shells that strew them. But all at close of day, with riven planks and rent canvas make for shore, and are either wrecked ere they reach it, or find some wave-beaten haven, some desart strand, whereon to cast themselves and die unmourned.

A truce to philosophy!—Life is before me, and I rush into possession. Hope, glory, love, and blameless ambition are my guides, and my soul knows no dread. What has been, though sweet, is gone; the present is good only because it is about to change, and the to come is all my own. Do I fear, that my heart palpitates? high aspirations cause the flow of my blood; my eyes seem to penetrate the cloudy midnight of time, and to discern within the depths of its darkness, the fruition of all my soul desires.

Now pause!—During my journey I might dream, and with buoyant wings reach the summit of life's high edifice. Now that I am arrived at its

---

28 In Virgil's *Aeneid* 6, the happiest souls dwell in Elysium. There Aeneas meets his father, Anchises, who explains that purified souls prepare to return to earth after a thousand years by drinking the water of Lethe and losing all memory of their past lives.

29 Probably an echo of Thomas Love Peacock, *Rhododaphne* (1818): PBS quotes the same phrase, "golden sands" (from the last line of canto 5), in a review of Peacock's poem (*Complete Works*, ed. Roger Ingpen and Walter E. Peck 6: 275).

base, my pinions are furled, the mighty stairs are before me, and step by step I must ascend the wondrous fane—

Speak!—What door is opened?[30]

Behold me in a new capacity. A diplomatist: one among the pleasure-seeking society of a gay city; a youth of promise; favourite of the Ambassador. All was strange and admirable to the shepherd of Cumberland. With breathless amaze I entered on the gay scene, whose actors were

—the lilies glorious as Solomon,
Who toil not, neither do they spin.[31]

Soon, too soon, I entered the giddy whirl; forgetting my studious hours, and the companionship of Adrian. Passionate desire of sympathy, and ardent pursuit for a wished-for object still characterized me. The sight of beauty entranced me, and attractive manners in man or woman won my entire confidence. I called it rapture, when a smile made my heart beat; and I felt the life's blood tingle in my frame, when I approached the idol which for awhile I worshipped. The mere flow of animal spirits was Paradise, and at night's close I only desired a renewal of the intoxicating delusion. The dazzling light of ornamented rooms; lovely forms arrayed in splendid dresses; the motions of a dance, the voluptuous tones of exquisite music, cradled my senses in one delightful dream.

And is not this in its kind happiness? I appeal to moralists and sages. I ask if in the calm of their measured reveries, if in the deep meditations which fill their hours, they feel the extasy of a youthful tyro in the school of pleasure? Can the calm beams of their heaven-seeking eyes equal the flashes of mingling passion which blind his, or does the influence of cold philosophy steep their soul in a joy equal to his, engaged

In this dear work of youthful revelry.[32]

---

30   PBS's translation of Euripides' *The Cyclops* 504; first published in *Posthumous Poems* (1824).

31   PBS, *Charles the First* 1.154-57: "Here is the pomp that strips the houseless orphan, / Here is the pride that breaks the desolate heart. / These are the lilies glorious as Solomon, / Who toil not neither do they spin." The two lines MWS quotes are a version of Matthew 6.28 and Luke 12.27.

32   PBS's translation of "Homer's Hymn to Mercury" 610; first published in *Posthumous Poems*, 1839.

But in truth, neither the lonely meditations of the hermit, nor the tumultuous raptures of the reveller, are capable of satisfying man's heart. From the one we gather unquiet speculation, from the other satiety. The mind flags beneath the weight of thought, and droops in the heartless intercourse of those whose sole aim is amusement. There is no fruition in their vacant kindness, and sharp rocks lurk beneath the smiling ripples of these shallow waters.

Thus I felt, when disappointment, weariness, and solitude drove me back upon my heart, to gather thence the joy of which it had become barren. My flagging spirits asked for something to speak to the affections; and not finding it, I drooped. Thus, notwithstanding the thoughtless delight that waited on its commencement, the impression I have of my life at Vienna is melancholy. Goëthe has said, that in youth we cannot be happy unless we love.[33] I did not love; but I was devoured by a restless wish to be something to others. I became the victim of ingratitude and cold coquetry—then I desponded, and imagined that my discontent gave me a right to hate the world. I receded to solitude; I had recourse to my books, and my desire again to enjoy the society of Adrian became a burning thirst.

Emulation, that in its excess almost assumed the venomous properties of envy, gave a sting to these feelings. At this period the name and exploits of one of my countrymen filled the world with admiration. Relations of what he had done, conjectures concerning his future actions, were the never-failing topics of the hour. I was not angry on my own account, but I felt as if the praises which this idol received were leaves torn from laurels destined for Adrian. But I must enter into some account of this darling of fame—this favourite of the wonder-loving world.

Lord Raymond was the sole remnant of a noble but impoverished family. From early youth he had considered his pedigree with complacency, and bitterly lamented his want of wealth. His first wish was aggrandisement; and the means that led towards this end were secondary considerations. Haughty, yet trembling to every demonstration of respect; ambitious, but too proud to shew his ambition; willing to achieve honour, yet a votary of pleasure,—he entered upon life. He was met on the threshold by some insult, real or imaginary; some repulse, where he least expected it; some disappointment, hard for his pride to bear. He writhed beneath an injury he was unable to revenge; and he quitted England with a vow not to return, till the good time should arrive, when she might feel the power of him she now despised.

---

33   Perhaps in *Dichtung und Wahrheit*, Part 3, book 12: "How can young people be expected to find the highest interests in life, how can they hope to arouse interest among their own kind if they are not animated by love?" (trans. Catherine Hutter 196).

He became an adventurer in the Greek wars.[34] His reckless courage and comprehensive genius brought him into notice. He became the darling hero of this rising people. His foreign birth, and he refused to throw off his allegiance to his native country, alone prevented him from filling the first offices in the state. But, though others might rank higher in title and ceremony, Lord Raymond held a station above and beyond all this. He led the Greek armies to victory; their triumphs were all his own. When he appeared, whole towns poured forth their population to meet him; new songs were adapted to their national airs, whose themes were his glory, valour, and munificence.

A truce was concluded between the Greeks and Turks. At the same time, Lord Raymond, by some unlooked-for chance, became the possessor of an immense fortune in England, whither he returned, crowned with glory, to receive the meed of honour and distinction before denied to his pretensions. His proud heart rebelled against this change. In what was the despised Raymond not the same? If the acquisition of power in the shape of wealth caused this alteration, that power should they feel as an iron yoke. Power therefore was the aim of all his endeavours; aggrandizement the mark at which he for ever shot. In open ambition or close intrigue, his end was the same—to attain the first station in his own country.

This account filled me with curiosity. The events that in succession followed his return to England, gave me keener feelings. Among his other advantages, Lord Raymond was supremely handsome; every one admired him; of women he was the idol. He was courteous, honey-tongued—an adept in fascinating arts. What could not this man achieve in the busy English world? Change succeeded to change; the entire history did not reach me; for Adrian had ceased to write, and Perdita was a laconic correspondent. The rumour went that Adrian had become—how write the fatal word—mad: that Lord Raymond was the favourite of the ex-queen, her daughter's destined husband. Nay, more, that this aspiring noble revived the claim of the house of Windsor to the crown, and that, on the event of Adrian's incurable disorder and his marriage with the sister, the brow of the ambitious Raymond might be encircled with the magic ring of regality.

Such a tale filled the trumpet of many voiced fame; such a tale rendered my longer stay at Vienna, away from the friend of my youth, intolerable. Now I must fulfil my vow; now range myself at his side, and be his

---

34   MWS bases these wars on the revolutionary struggle of the Greeks against the Ottoman (Turkish) empire that was taking place in her own day. Lord Byron, on whom Raymond is modelled, died in Missolonghi, Greece, in 1824, while aiding the Greek cause. In *The Last Man*, before Lord Raymond enters the novel Greece has successfully gained its independence under his leadership: the continuing wars aim to defend that independence and to extend Greek power.

ally and support till death. Farewell to courtly pleasures; to politic intrigue; to the maze of passion and folly! All hail, England! Native England, receive thy child! thou art the scene of all my hopes, the mighty theatre on which is acted the only drama that can, heart and soul, bear me along with it in its development. A voice most irresistible, a power omnipotent, drew me thither. After an absence of two years I landed on its shores, not daring to make any inquiries, fearful of every remark. My first visit would be to my sister, who inhabited a little cottage, a part of Adrian's gift, on the borders of Windsor Forest. From her I should learn the truth concerning our protector; I should hear why she had withdrawn from the protection of the Princess Evadne, and be instructed as to the influence which this overtopping and towering Raymond exercised over the fortunes of my friend.

I had never before been in the neighbourhood of Windsor; the fertility and beauty of the country around now struck me with admiration, which encreased as I approached the antique wood. The ruins of majestic oaks which had grown, flourished, and decayed during the progress of centuries, marked where the limits of the forest once reached, while the shattered palings and neglected underwood shewed that this part was deserted for the younger plantations, which owed their birth to the beginning of the nineteenth century, and now stood in the pride of maturity. Perdita's humble dwelling was situated on the skirts of the most ancient portion; before it was stretched Bishopgate Heath, which towards the east appeared interminable, and was bounded to the west by Chapel Wood and the grove of Virginia Water.[35] Behind, the cottage was shadowed by the venerable fathers of the forest, under which the deer came to graze, and which for the most part hollow and decayed, formed fantastic groups that contrasted with the regular beauty of the younger trees. These, the offspring of a later period, stood erect and seemed ready to advance fearlessly into coming time; while those out worn stragglers, blasted and broke, clung to each other, their weak boughs sighing as the wind buffetted them—a weather-beaten crew.

A light railing surrounded the garden of the cottage, which, low-roofed, seemed to submit to the majesty of nature, and cower amidst the venerable remains of forgotten time. Flowers, the children of the spring,

---

35   MWS and PBS moved to Bishopsgate, in the vicinity of Windsor Park, in August 1815; many places mentioned in *The Last Man* are nearby. Englefield Green is east of Windsor Park; Chapel Wood and Virginia Water, an artificial lake, are in the park. Eton, where Lionel's son Alfred later goes to school, is across the river from the town of Windsor. Staines, where Lionel rides with Adrian (66), and Egham (see 201) are further down the Thames between Windsor and Richmond; Datchet (225) is nearby. Revisiting some of these places when she was working on *The Last Man*, MWS wrote, "Windsor—Eton &c is the only spot of English ground for which I have an affection" (to John Howard Payne, 27 September 1825, *Letters* 1: 502).

adorned her garden and casements; in the midst of lowliness there was an air of elegance which spoke the graceful taste of the inmate. With a beating heart I entered the enclosure; as I stood at the entrance, I heard her voice, melodious as it had ever been, which before I saw her assured me of her welfare.

A moment more and Perdita appeared; she stood before me in the fresh bloom of youthful womanhood, different from and yet the same as the mountain girl I had left. Her eyes could not be deeper than they were in childhood, nor her countenance more expressive; but the expression was changed and improved; intelligence sat on her brow; when she smiled her face was embellished by the softest sensibility, and her low, modulated voice seemed tuned by love. Her person was formed in the most feminine proportions; she was not tall, but her mountain life had given freedom to her motions, so that her light step scarce made her foot-fall heard as she tript across the hall to meet me. When we had parted, I had clasped her to my bosom with unrestrained warmth; we met again, and new feelings were awakened; when each beheld the other, childhood passed, as full grown actors on this changeful scene. The pause was but for a moment; the flood of association and natural feeling which had been checked, again rushed in full tide upon our hearts, and with tenderest emotion we were swiftly locked in each other's embrace.

This burst of passionate feeling over, with calmed thoughts we sat together, talking of the past and present. I alluded to the coldness of her letters; but the few minutes we had spent together sufficiently explained the origin of this. New feelings had arisen within her, which she was unable to express in writing to one whom she had only known in childhood; but we saw each other again, and our intimacy was renewed as if nothing had intervened to check it. I detailed the incidents of my sojourn abroad, and then questioned her as to the changes that had taken place at home, the causes of Adrian's absence, and her secluded life.

The tears that suffused my sister's eyes when I mentioned our friend, and her heightened colour seemed to vouch for the truth of the reports that had reached me. But their import was too terrible for me to give instant credit to my suspicion. Was there indeed anarchy in the sublime universe of Adrian's thoughts, did madness scatter the well-appointed legions, and was he no longer the lord of his own soul? Beloved friend, this ill world was no clime for your gentle spirit; you delivered up its governance to false humanity, which stript it of its leaves ere winter-time, and laid bare its quivering life to the evil ministration of roughest winds. Have those gentle eyes, those "channels of the soul"[36] lost their meaning, or do they only in their glare disclose the horrible tale of its aberrations? Does that voice no longer "discourse excellent music?"[37] Horrible, most horri-

---

36 Unidentified.
37 An echo of *Hamlet* 3.2.350: "it will discourse most eloquent music."

ble! I veil my eyes in terror of the change, and gushing tears bear witness to my sympathy for this unimaginable ruin.

In obedience to my request Perdita detailed the melancholy circumstances that led to this event.

The frank and unsuspicious mind of Adrian, gifted as it was by every natural grace, endowed with transcendant powers of intellect, unblemished by the shadow of defect (unless his dreadless independence of thought was to be construed into one), was devoted, even as a victim to sacrifice, to his love for Evadne. He entrusted to her keeping the treasures of his soul, his aspirations after excellence, and his plans for the improvement of mankind. As manhood dawned upon him, his schemes and theories, far from being changed by personal and prudential motives, acquired new strength from the powers he felt arise within him; and his love for Evadne became deep-rooted, as he each day became more certain that the path he pursued was full of difficulty, and that he must seek his reward, not in the applause or gratitude of his fellow creatures, hardly in the success of his plans, but in the approbation of his own heart, and in her love and sympathy, which was to lighten every toil and recompence every sacrifice.

In solitude, and through many wanderings afar from the haunts of men, he matured his views for the reform of the English government, and the improvement of the people. It would have been well if he had concealed his sentiments, until he had come into possession of the power which would secure their practical development. But he was impatient of the years that must intervene, he was frank of heart and fearless. He gave not only a brief denial to his mother's schemes, but published his intention of using his influence to diminish the power of the aristocracy, to effect a greater equalization of wealth and privilege, and to introduce a perfect system of republican government into England. At first his mother treated his theories as the wild ravings of inexperience. But they were so systematically arranged, and his arguments so well supported, that though still in appearance incredulous, she began to fear him. She tried to reason with him, and finding him inflexible, learned to hate him.

Strange to say, this feeling was infectious. His enthusiasm for good which did not exist; his contempt for the sacredness of authority; his ardour and imprudence were all at the antipodes of the usual routine of life; the worldly feared him; the young and inexperienced did not understand the lofty severity of his moral views, and disliked him as a being different from themselves. Evadne entered but coldly into his systems. She thought he did well to assert his own will, but she wished that will to have been more intelligible to the multitude. She had none of the spirit of a martyr, and did not incline to share the shame and defeat of a fallen patriot. She was aware of the purity of his motives, the generosity of his disposition, his true and ardent attachment to her; and she entertained a great affection for him. He repaid this spirit of kindness with the fondest gratitude, and made her the treasure-house of all his hopes.

At this time Lord Raymond returned from Greece. No two persons could be more opposite than Adrian and he. With all the incongruities of his character, Raymond was emphatically a man of the world. His passions were violent; as these often obtained the mastery over him, he could not always square his conduct to the obvious line of self-interest, but self-gratification at least was the paramount object with him. He looked on the structure of society as but a part of the machinery which supported the web on which his life was traced. The earth was spread out as an highway for him; the heavens built up as a canopy for him.[38]

Adrian felt that he made a part of a great whole. He owned affinity not only with mankind, but all nature was akin to him; the mountains and sky were his friends; the winds of heaven and the offspring of earth his play-mates; while he the focus only of this mighty mirror, felt his life mingle with the universe of existence.[39] His soul was sympathy, and dedicated to the worship of beauty and excellence. Adrian and Raymond now came into contact, and a spirit of aversion rose between them. Adrian despised the narrow views of the politician, and Raymond held in supreme contempt the benevolent vision of the philanthropist.

With the coming of Raymond was formed the storm that laid waste at one fell blow the gardens of delight and sheltered paths which Adrian fancied that he had secured to himself, as a refuge from defeat and contumely. Raymond, the deliverer of Greece, the graceful soldier, who bore in his mien a tinge of all that, peculiar to her native clime, Evadne cherished as most dear—Raymond was loved by Evadne. Overpowered by her new sensations, she did not pause to examine them, or to regulate her conduct by any sentiments except the tyrannical one which suddenly usurped the empire of her heart. She yielded to its influence, and the too natural consequence in a mind unattuned to soft emotions was, that the attentions of Adrian became distasteful to her. She grew capricious; her gentle conduct towards him was exchanged for asperity and repulsive coldness. When she perceived the wild or pathetic appeal of his expressive countenance, she would relent, and for a while resume her ancient kindness. But these fluctuations shook to its depths the soul of the sensitive youth; he no longer deemed the world subject to him, because he possessed Evadne's love; he felt in every nerve that the dire storms of the mental universe were about to attack his fragile being, which quivered at the expectation of its advent.

Perdita, who then resided with Evadne, saw the torture that Adrian endured. She loved him as a kind elder brother; a relation to guide, pro-

---

38 In *Hamlet* 2.2.300, Shakespeare describes the air as "this most excellent canopy."

39 Cf. Byron, *Childe Harold's Pilgrimage*, 3.72.686-88: "the soul can flee, / And with the sky, the peak, the heaving plain / Of ocean, or the stars, mingle, and not in vain."

tect, and instruct her, without the too frequent tyranny of parental authority. She adored his virtues, and with mixed contempt and indignation she
saw Evadne pile drear sorrow on his head, for the sake of one who hardly
marked her. In his solitary despair Adrian would often seek my sister, and
in covered terms express his misery, while fortitude and agony divided
the throne of his mind. Soon, alas! was one to conquer. Anger made no
part of his emotion. With whom should he be angry? Not with Raymond,
who was unconscious of the misery he occasioned; not with Evadne, for
her his soul wept tears of blood—poor, mistaken girl, slave not tyrant was
she, and amidst his own anguish he grieved for her future destiny. Once
a writing of his fell into Perdita's hands; it was blotted with tears—well
might any blot it with the like—

   "Life"—it began thus—"is not the thing romance writers describe it;
going through the measures of a dance, and after various evolutions arriving at a conclusion, when the dancers may sit down and repose. While
there is life there is action and change. We go on, each thought linked to
the one which was its parent, each act to a previous act. No joy or sorrow
dies barren of progeny, which for ever generated and generating, weaves
the chain that make our life:

   Un dia llama à otro dia
   y ass i llama, y encadena
   llanto à llanto, y pena à pena.[40]

Truly disappointment is the guardian deity of human life; she sits at the
threshold of unborn time, and marshals the events as they come forth.
Once my heart sat lightly in my bosom; all the beauty of the world was
doubly beautiful, irradiated by the sun-light shed from my own soul. O
wherefore are love and ruin for ever joined in this our mortal dream? So
that when we make our hearts a lair for that gently seeming beast, its companion enters with it, and pitilessly lays waste what might have been an
home and a shelter."[41]

   By degrees his health was shaken by his misery, and then his intellect
yielded to the same tyranny. His manners grew wild; he was sometimes
ferocious, sometimes absorbed in speechless melancholy. Suddenly
Evadne quitted London for Paris; he followed, and overtook her when
the vessel was about to sail; none knew what passed between them,

---

40   Calderón, *El Príncipe Constante*, Act 2 [scene 4]: "One day calls to another day;
     and so it calls again and links cry to cry and pain to pain" (1129-31).
41   Contrast with PBS, *Prometheus Unbound*, where, "Though Ruin now Love's
     shadow be" (1.780), the Chorus prophesies the defeat of ruin by love and
     Earth celebrates love's victory: "Labour, and pain, and grief, in life's green
     grove / Sport like tame beasts, none knew how gentle they could be!"
     (4.404-05).

but Perdita had never seen him since; he lived in seclusion, no one knew where, attended by such persons as his mother selected for that purpose.

CHAPTER IV

THE next day Lord Raymond called at Perdita's cottage, on his way to Windsor Castle. My sister's heightened colour and sparkling eyes half revealed her secret to me. He was perfectly self-possessed; he accosted us both with courtesy, seemed immediately to enter into our feelings, and to make one with us. I scanned his physiognomy, which varied as he spoke, yet was beautiful in every change. The usual expression of his eyes was soft, though at times he could make them even glare with ferocity; his complexion was colourless; and every trait spoke predominate self-will; his smile was pleasing, though disdain too often curled his lips—lips which to female eyes were the very throne of beauty and love. His voice, usually gentle, often startled you by a sharp discordant note, which shewed that his usual low tone was rather the work of study than nature. Thus full of contradictions, unbending yet haughty, gentle yet fierce, tender and again neglectful, he by some strange art found easy entrance to the admiration and affection of women; now caressing and now tyrannizing over them according to his mood, but in every change a despot.

At the present time Raymond evidently wished to appear amiable. Wit, hilarity, and deep observation were mingled in his talk, rendering every sentence that he uttered as a flash of light. He soon conquered my latent distaste; I endeavoured to watch him and Perdita, and to keep in mind every thing I had heard to his disadvantage. But all appeared so ingenuous, and all was so fascinating, that I forgot everything except the pleasure his society afforded me. Under the idea of initiating me in the scene of English politics and society, of which I was soon to become a part, he narrated a number of anecdotes, and sketched many characters; his discourse, rich and varied, flowed on, pervading all my senses with pleasure. But for one thing he would have been completely triumphant. He alluded to Adrian, and spoke of him with that disparagement that the worldly wise always attach to enthusiasm. He perceived the cloud gathering, and tried to dissipate it; but the strength of my feelings would not permit me to pass thus lightly over this sacred subject; so I said emphatically, "Permit me to remark, that I am devotedly attached to the Earl of Windsor; he is my best friend and benefactor. I reverence his goodness, I accord with his opinions, and bitterly lament his present, and I trust temporary, illness. That illness, from its peculiarity, makes it painful to me beyond words to hear him mentioned, unless in terms of respect and affection."

Raymond replied; but there was nothing conciliatory in his reply. I saw that in his heart he despised those dedicated to any but worldly idols.

"Every man," he said, "dreams about something, love, honour, and pleasure; you dream of friendship, and devote yourself to a maniac; well, if that be your vocation, doubtless you are in the right to follow it."—

Some reflection seemed to sting him, and the spasm of pain that for a moment convulsed his countenance, checked my indignation. "Happy are dreamers," he continued, "so that they be not awakened! Would I could dream! but 'broad and garish day'[42] is the element in which I live; the dazzling glare of reality inverts the scene for me. Even the ghost of friendship has departed, and love"—He broke off; nor could I guess whether the disdain that curled his lip was directed against the passion, or against himself for being its slave.

This account may be taken as a sample of my intercourse with Lord Raymond. I became intimate with him, and each day afforded me occasion to admire more and more his powerful and versatile talents, that together with his eloquence, which was graceful and witty, and his wealth now immense, caused him to be feared, loved, and hated beyond any other man in England.

My descent, which claimed interest, if not respect, my former connection with Adrian, the favour of the ambassador, whose secretary I had been, and now my intimacy with Lord Raymond, gave me easy access to the fashionable and political circles of England. To my inexperience we at first appeared on the eve of a civil war; each party was violent, acrimonious, and unyielding. Parliament was divided by three factions, aristocrats, democrats, and royalists. After Adrian's declared predeliction to the republican form of government, the latter party had nearly died away, chiefless, guideless; but, when Lord Raymond came forward as its leader, it revived with redoubled force. Some were royalists from prejudice and ancient affection, and there were many moderately inclined who feared alike the capricious tyranny of the popular party, and the unbending despotism of the aristocrats. More than a third of the members ranged themselves under Raymond, and their number was perpetually encreasing. The aristocrats built their hopes on their preponderant wealth and influence; the reformers on the force of the nation itself; the debates were violent, more violent the discourses held by each knot of politicians as they assembled to arrange their measures. Opprobrious epithets were bandied about, resistance even to the death threatened; meetings of the populace disturbed the quiet order of the country; except in war, how could all this end? Even as the destructive flames were ready to break forth, I saw them shrink back; allayed by the absence of the military, by the aversion entertained by every one to any violence, save that of speech, and by the cordial politeness and even friendship of the hostile leaders when they met in private society. I was from a thousand motives

---

42 Cf. PBS, *The Cenci* 2.1.177: "It is a garish, broad, and peering day."

induced to attend minutely to the course of events, and watch each turn with intense anxiety.

I could not but perceive that Perdita loved Raymond; methought also that he regarded the fair daughter of Verney with admiration and tenderness. Yet I knew that he was urging forward his marriage with the presumptive heiress of the Earldom of Windsor, with keen expectation of the advantages that would thence accrue to him. All the ex-queen's friends were his friends; no week passed that he did not hold consultations with her at Windsor.

I had never seen the sister of Adrian. I had heard that she was lovely, amiable, and fascinating. Wherefore should I see her? There are times when we have an indefinable sentiment of impending change for better or for worse, to arise from an event; and, be it for better or for worse, we fear the change, and shun the event. For this reason I avoided this high-born damsel. To me she was everything and nothing; her very name mentioned by another made me start and tremble; the endless discussion concerning her union with Lord Raymond was real agony to me. Methought that, Adrian withdrawn from active life, and this beauteous Idris,[43] a victim probably to her mother's ambitious schemes, I ought to come forward to protect her from undue influence, guard her from unhappiness, and secure to her freedom of choice, the right of every human being. Yet how was I to do this? She herself would disdain my interference. Since then I must be an object of indifference or contempt to her, better, far better avoid her, nor expose myself before her and the scornful world to the chance of playing the mad game of a fond, foolish Icarus.[44]

One day, several months after my return to England, I quitted London to visit my sister. Her society was my chief solace and delight; and my spirits always rose at the expectation of seeing her. Her conversation was full of pointed remark and discernment; in her pleasant alcove, redolent with sweetest flowers, adorned by magnificent casts, antique vases, and copies of the finest pictures of Raphael, Correggio, and Claude,[45] painted by herself, I fancied myself in a fairy retreat untainted by and inaccessible to the noisy contentions of politicians and the frivolous pursuits of fashion. On this occasion, my sister was not alone; nor could I fail to recognise her companion: it was Idris, the till now unseen object of my mad idolatry.

In what fitting terms of wonder and delight, in what choice expression and soft flow of language, can I usher in the loveliest, wisest, best? How

---

43 The Greek word *idris* means "provident creature."
44 That is, the game of risking self-destruction. Wearing wings fastened with wax, Icarus flew too close to the sun and plunged into the sea; see Ovid, *Metamorphoses* 8.220-35.
45 The painters Raffaello Sanzio (1483-1520), Antonio Allegri Correggio (c. 1489-1534), and Claude Lorraine (1600-1682).

in poor assemblage of words convey the halo of glory that surrounded her, the thousand graces that waited unwearied on her. The first thing that struck you on beholding that charming countenance was its perfect goodness and frankness; candour sat upon her brow, simplicity in her eyes, heavenly benignity in her smile. Her tall slim figure bent gracefully as a poplar to the breezy west, and her gait, goddess-like, was as that of a winged angel new alit from heaven's high floor; the pearly fairness of her complexion was stained by a pure suffusion; her voice resembled the low, subdued tenor of a flute. It is easiest perhaps to describe by contrast. I have detailed the perfections of my sister; and yet she was utterly unlike Idris. Perdita, even where she loved, was reserved and timid; Idris was frank and confiding. The one recoiled to solitude, that she might there entrench herself from disappointment and injury; the other walked forth in open day, believing that none would harm her. Wordsworth has compared a beloved female to two fair objects in nature; but his lines always appeared to me rather a contrast than a similitude:

A violet by a mossy stone
    Half hidden from the eye,
Fair as a star when only one
    Is shining in the sky.[46]

Such a violet was sweet Perdita, trembling to entrust herself to the very air, cowering from observation, yet betrayed by her excellences; and repaying with a thousand graces the labour of those who sought her in her lonely bye-path. Idris was as the star, set in single splendour in the dim anadem of balmy evening; ready to enlighten and delight the subject world, shielded herself from every taint by her unimagined distance from all that was not like herself akin to heaven.

I found this vision of beauty in Perdita's alcove, in earnest conversation with its inmate. When my sister saw me, she rose, and taking my hand, said, "He is here, even at our wish; this is Lionel, my brother."

Idris arose also, and bent on me her eyes of celestial blue, and with grace peculiar said—"You hardly need an introduction; we have a picture, highly valued by my father, which declares at once your name. Verney, you will acknowledge this tie, and as my brother's friend, I feel that I may trust you."

Then, with lids humid with a tear and trembling voice, she continued—"Dear friends, do not think it strange that now, visiting you for the

---

46   The second stanza of William Wordsworth's "She dwelt among th'untrodden ways," first published in *Lyrical Ballads* (1800) and included among "Poems Founded on the Affections" in his *Poems* of 1815. MWS uses part of the first stanza of this poem to describe the heroine of her novella, *Mathilda* (unpublished until 1959).

first time, I ask your assistance, and confide my wishes and fears to you. To you alone do I dare speak; I have heard you commended by impartial spectators; you are my brother's friends, therefore you must be mine. What can I say? if you refuse to aid me, I am lost indeed!" She cast up her eyes, while wonder held her auditors mute; then, as if carried away by her feelings, she cried—"My brother! beloved, ill-fated Adrian! how speak of your misfortunes? Doubtless you have both heard the current tale; perhaps believe the slander; but he is not mad! Were an angel from the foot of God's throne to assert it, never, never would I believe it. He is wronged, betrayed, imprisoned—save him! Verney, you must do this; seek him out in whatever part of the island he is immured; find him, rescue him from his persecutors, restore him to himself, to me—on the wide earth I have none to love but only him!"

Her earnest appeal, so sweetly and passionately expressed, filled me with wonder and sympathy; and, when she added, with thrilling voice and look, "Do you consent to undertake this enterprize?" I vowed, with energy and truth, to devote myself in life and death to the restoration and welfare of Adrian. We then conversed on the plan I should pursue, and discussed the probable means of discovering his residence. While we were in earnest discourse, Lord Raymond entered unannounced: I saw Perdita tremble and grow deadly pale, and the cheeks of Idris glow with purest blushes. He must have been astonished at our conclave, disturbed by it I should have thought; but nothing of this appeared; he saluted my companions, and addressed me with a cordial greeting. Idris appeared suspended for a moment, and then with extreme sweetness, she said, "Lord Raymond, I confide in your goodness and honour."

Smiling haughtily, he bent his head, and replied, with emphasis, "Do you indeed confide, Lady Idris?"

She endeavoured to read his thought, and then answered with dignity, "As you please. It is certainly best not to compromise oneself by any concealment."

"Pardon me," he replied, "if I have offended. Whether you trust me or not, rely on my doing my utmost to further your wishes, whatever they may be."

Idris smiled her thanks, and rose to take leave. Lord Raymond requested permission to accompany her to Windsor Castle, to which she consented, and they quitted the cottage together. My sister and I were left—truly like two fools, who fancied that they had obtained a golden treasure, till daylight showed it to be lead—two silly, luckless flies, who had played in sunbeams and were caught in a spider's web. I leaned against the casement, and watched those two glorious creatures, till they disappeared in the forest-glades; and then I turned. Perdita had not moved; her eyes fixed on the ground, her cheeks pale, her very lips white, motionless and rigid, every feature stamped by woe, she sat. Half frightened, I would have taken her hand; but she shudderingly withdrew it, and strove to collect herself. I entreated her to speak to me: "Not now," she replied, "nor do you speak to me, my dear Lionel; you *can* say nothing, for you know nothing. I will see you to-morrow; in the meantime, adieu!" She rose, and walked from the room; but pausing at the door, and leaning against it, as if her over-busy thoughts had taken from her the power of supporting herself, she said, "Lord Raymond will probably return. Will you tell him that he must excuse me to-day, for I am not well. I will see him to-morrow if he wishes it, and you also. You had better return to London with him; you can there make the enquiries agreed upon, concerning the Earl of Windsor and visit me again to-morrow, before you proceed on your journey—till then, farewell!"

She spoke falteringly, and concluded with a heavy sigh. I gave my assent to her request; and she left me. I felt as if, from the order of the systematic world, I had plunged into chaos, obscure, contrary, unintelligible. That Raymond should marry Idris was more than ever intolerable; yet my passion, though a giant from its birth, was too strange, wild, and impracticable, for me to feel at once the misery I perceived in Perdita. How should I act? She had not confided in me; I could not demand an explanation from Raymond without the hazard of betraying what was perhaps her most treasured secret. I would obtain the truth from her the following day—in the mean time—But, while I was occupied by multiplying reflections, Lord Raymond returned. He asked for my sister; and I delivered her message. After musing on it for a moment, he asked me if I were about to return to London, and if I would accompany him: I consented. He was full of thought, and remained silent during a considerable part of our ride; at length he said, "I must apologize to you for my abstraction; the truth is, Ryland's motion comes on to-night, and I am considering my reply."

Ryland[47] was the leader of the popular party, a hard-headed man, and in his way eloquent; he had obtained leave to bring in a bill making it treason to endeavour to change the present state of the English government and the standing laws of the republic. This attack was directed against Raymond and his machinations for the restoration of the monarchy.

Raymond asked me if I would accompany him to the House that evening. I remembered my pursuit for intelligence concerning Adrian; and, knowing that my time would be fully occupied, I excused myself. "Nay," said my companion, "I can free you from your present impediment. You are going to make enquiries concerning the Earl of Windsor. I can answer them at once, he is at the Duke of Athol's seat at Dunkeld.[48]

---

47 Ryland is sometimes said to be modelled on the reformer and editor of the *Political Register*, William Cobbett. There are, however, some striking differences: unlike Ryland, Cobbett was neither a republican nor the son of a wealthy father.

48 Dunkeld, where the seat of the Duke of Atholl is situated, is in central Scotland, in the highlands north of Perth.

On the first approach of his disorder, he travelled about from one place to another; until, arriving at that romantic seclusion he refused to quit it, and we made arrangements with the Duke for his continuing there."

I was hurt by the careless tone with which he conveyed this information, and replied coldly: "I am obliged to you for your intelligence, and will avail myself of it."

"You shall, Verney," said he, "and if you continue of the same mind, I will facilitate your views. But first witness, I beseech you, the result of this night's contest, and the triumph I am about to achieve, if I may so call it, while I fear that victory is to me defeat. What can I do? My dearest hopes appear to be near their fulfilment. The ex-queen gives me Idris; Adrian is totally unfitted to succeed to the earldom, and that earldom in my hands becomes a kingdom. By the reigning God it is true; the paltry earldom of Windsor shall no longer content him, who will inherit the rights which must for ever appertain to the person who possesses it. The Countess can never forget that she has been a queen, and she disdains to leave a diminished inheritance to her children; her power and my wit will rebuild the throne, and this brow will be clasped by a kingly diadem.—I can do this—I can marry Idris."—

He stopped abruptly, his countenance darkened, and its expression changed again and again under the influence of internal passion. I asked, "Does Lady Idris love you?"

"What a question," replied he laughing. "She will of course, as I shall her, when we are married."

"You begin late," said I, ironically, "marriage is usually considered the grave, and not the cradle of love. So you are about to love her, but do not already?"

"Do not catechise me, Lionel; I will do my duty by her, be assured. Love! I must steel my heart against *that*; expel it from its tower of strength, barricade it out: the fountain of love must cease to play, its waters be dried up, and all passionate thoughts attendant on it die—that is to say, the love which would rule me, not that which I rule. Idris is a gentle, pretty, sweet little girl; it is impossible not to have an affection for her, and I have a very sincere one; only do not speak of love—love, the tyrant and the tyrant-queller; love, until now my conqueror, now my slave; the hungry fire, the untameable beast, the fanged snake—no—no—I will have nothing to do with that love. Tell me, Lionel, do you consent that I should marry this young lady?"

He bent his keen eyes upon me, and my uncontrollable heart swelled in my bosom. I replied in a calm voice—but how far from calm was the thought imaged by my still words—"Never! I can never consent that Lady Idris should be united to one who does not love her."

"Because you love her yourself."

"Your Lordship might have spared that taunt; I do not, dare not love her."

"At least," he continued haughtily, "she does not love you. I would not marry a reigning sovereign, were I not sure that her heart was free. But, O, Lionel! a kingdom is a word of might, and gently sounding are the terms that compose the style of royalty. Were not the mightiest men of the olden times kings? Alexander was a king; Solomon, the wisest of men, was a king; Napoleon was a king; Cæsar died in his attempt to become one, and Cromwell, the puritan and king-killer, aspired to regality.[49] The father of Adrian yielded up the already broken sceptre of England; but I will rear the fallen plant, join its dismembered frame, and exalt it above all the flowers of the field.

"You need not wonder that I freely discover Adrian's abode. Do not suppose that I am wicked or foolish enough to found my purposed sovereignty on a fraud, and one so easily discovered as the truth or falsehood of the Earl's insanity. I am just come from him. Before I decided on my marriage with Idris, I resolved to see him myself again, and to judge of the probability of his recovery.—He is irrecoverably mad."

I gasped for breath—

"I will not detail to you," continued Raymond, "the melancholy particulars. You shall see him, and judge for yourself; although I fear this visit, useless to him, will be insufferably painful to you. It has weighed on my spirits ever since. Excellent and gentle as he is even in the downfall of his reason, I do not worship him as you do, but I would give all my hopes of a crown and my right hand to boot, to see him restored to himself."

His voice expressed the deepest compassion: "Thou most unaccountable being," I cried, "whither will thy actions tend, in all this maze of purpose in which thou seemest lost?"

"Whither indeed? To a crown, a golden begemmed crown, I hope; and yet I dare not trust and though I dream of a crown and wake for one, ever and anon a busy devil whispers to me, that it is but a fool's cap that I seek, and that were I wise, I should trample on it, and take in its stead, that which is worth all the crowns of the east and presidentships of the west."

"And what is that?"

"If I do make it my choice, then you shall know; at present I dare not speak, even think of it."

Again he was silent, and after a pause turned to me laughingly. When scorn did not inspire his mirth, when it was genuine gaiety that painted his features with a joyous expression, his beauty became super-eminent, divine. "Verney," said he, "my first act when I become King of England,

---

49   Alexander the Great (356-323 BC), who extended the Greek empire as far as India; Solomon, the biblical king renowned for his wisdom; Napoleon Bonaparte (1769-1821), Emperor of France in the aftermath of the French Revolution from 1804-15; Gaius Julius Caesar (c. 102-44 BC), conqueror of Gaul and Britain, master of Rome after the first Civil War in 49 BC; Oliver Cromwell (1599-1658), Lord Protector of England from 1653-1658.

will be to unite with the Greeks, take Constantinople, and subdue all Asia. I intend to be a warrior, a conqueror; Napoleon's name shall vail to[50] mine; and enthusiasts, instead of visiting his rocky grave, and exalting the merits of the fallen, shall adore my majesty, and magnify my illustrious achievements."

I listened to Raymond with intense interest. Could I be other than all ear, to one who seemed to govern the whole earth in his grasping imagination, and who only quailed when he attempted to rule himself. Then on his word and will depended my own happiness—the fate of all dear to me. I endeavoured to divine the concealed meaning of his words. Perdita's name was not mentioned; yet I could not doubt that love for her caused the vacillation of purpose that he exhibited. And who was so worthy of love as my noble-minded sister? Who deserved the hand of this self-exalted king more than she whose glance belonged to a queen of nations? who loved him, as he did her; notwithstanding that disappointment quelled her passion, and ambition held strong combat with his.

We went together to the House in the evening. Raymond, while he knew that his plans and prospects were to be discussed and decided during the expected debate, was gay and careless. An hum, like that of ten thousand hives of swarming bees, stunned us as we entered the coffee-room. Knots of politicians were assembled with anxious brows and loud or deep voices. The aristocratical party, the richest and most influential men in England, appeared less agitated than the others, for the question was to be discussed without their interference. Near the fire was Ryland and his supporters. Ryland was a man of obscure birth and of immense wealth, inherited from his father, who had been a manufacturer. He had witnessed, when a young man, the abdication of the king, and the amalgamation of the two houses of Lords and Commons; he had sympathized with these popular encroachments, and it had been the business of his life to consolidate and encrease them. Since then, the influence of the landed proprietors had augmented; and at first Ryland was not sorry to observe the machinations of Lord Raymond, which drew off many of his opponent's partizans. But the thing was now going too far. The poorer nobility hailed the return of sovereignty, as an event which would restore them to their power and rights, now lost. The half extinct spirit of royalty roused itself in the minds of men; and they, willing slaves, self-constituted subjects, were ready to bend their necks to the yoke. Some erect and manly spirits still remained, pillars of state; but the word republic had grown stale to the vulgar ear; and many—the event would prove whether it was a majority—pined for the tinsel and show of royalty. Ryland was roused to resistance; he asserted that his sufferance alone had

---

50   Submit to.

permitted the encrease of this party; but the time for indulgence was passed, and with one motion of his arm he would sweep away the cobwebs that blinded his countrymen.

When Raymond entered the coffee-room, his presence was hailed by his friends almost with a shout. They gathered round him, counted their numbers, and detailed the reasons why they were now to receive an addition of such and such members, who had not yet declared themselves. Some trifling business of the House having been gone through, the leaders took their seats in the chamber; the clamour of voices continued, till Ryland arose to speak, and then the slightest whispered observation was audible. All eyes were fixed upon him as he stood—ponderous of frame, sonorous of voice, and with a manner which, though not graceful, was impressive. I turned from his marked, iron countenance to Raymond, whose face, veiled by a smile, would not betray his care; yet his lips quivered somewhat, and his hand clasped the bench on which he sat, with a convulsive strength that made the muscles start again.

Ryland began by praising the present state of the British empire. He recalled past years to their memory; the miserable contentions which in the time of our fathers arose almost to civil war, the abdication of the late king, and the foundation of the republic. He described this republic; shewed how it gave privilege to each individual in the state, to rise to consequence, and even to temporary sovereignty. He compared the royal and republican spirit; shewed how the one tended to enslave the minds of men; while all the institutions of the other served to raise even the meanest among us to something great and good. He shewed how England had become powerful, and its inhabitants valiant and wise, by means of the freedom they enjoyed. As he spoke, every heart swelled with pride, and every cheek glowed with delight to remember, that each one there was English, and that each supported and contributed to the happy state of things now commemorated. Ryland's fervour increased—his eyes lighted up—his voice assumed the tone of passion. There was one man, he continued, who wished to alter all this, and bring us back to our days of impotence and contention:—one man, who would dare arrogate the honour which was due to all who claimed England as their birthplace, and set his name and style above the name and style of his country. I saw at this juncture that Raymond changed colour; his eyes were withdrawn from the orator, and cast on the ground; the listeners turned from one to the other; but in the meantime the speaker's voice filled their ears—the thunder of his denunciations influenced their senses. The very boldness of his language gave him weight; each knew that he spoke truth—a truth known, but not acknowledged. He tore from reality the mask with which she had been clothed; and the purposes of Raymond, which before had crept around, ensnaring by stealth, now stood a hunted stag—even at bay—as all perceived who watched the irrepressible changes of his countenance. Ryland ended by moving, that any attempt to re-erect the kingly power should be declared treason, and he a traitor who should endeavour to change the present form of government. Cheers and loud acclamations followed the close of his speech.

After his motion had been seconded, Lord Raymond rose,—his countenance bland, his voice softly melodious, his manner soothing, his grace and sweetness came like the mild breathing of a flute, after the loud, organ-like voice of his adversary. He rose, he said, to speak in favour of the honourable member's motion, with one slight amendment subjoined. He was ready to go back to old times, and commemorate the contests of our fathers, and the monarch's abdication. Nobly and greatly, he said, had the illustrious and last sovereign of England sacrificed himself to the apparent good of his country, and divested himself of a power which could only be maintained by the blood of his subjects—these subjects named so no more, these, his friends and equals, had in gratitude conferred certain favours and distinctions on him and his family for ever. An ample estate was allotted to them, and they took the first rank among the peers of Great Britain. Yet it might be conjectured that they had not forgotten their ancient heritage; and it was hard that his heir should suffer alike with any other pretender, if he attempted to regain what by ancient right and inheritance belonged to him. He did not say that he should favour such an attempt; but he did say that such an attempt would be venial; and, if the aspirant did not go so far as to declare war, and erect a standard in the kingdom, his fault ought to be regarded with an indulgent eye. In his amendment he proposed, that an exception should be made in the bill in favour of any person who claimed the sovereign power in right of the earls of Windsor.

Nor did Raymond make an end without drawing in vivid and glowing colours, the splendour of a kingdom, in opposition to the commercial spirit of republicanism. He asserted, that each individual under the English monarchy, was then as now, capable of attaining high rank and power—with one only exception, that of the function of chief magistrate; higher and nobler rank, than a bartering, timorous commonwealth could afford. And for this one exception, to what did it amount? The nature of riches and influence forcibly confined the list of candidates to a few of the wealthiest; and it was much to be feared, that the ill-humour and contention generated by this triennial struggle, would counterbalance its advantages in impartial eyes. I can ill record the flow of language and graceful turns of expression, the wit and easy raillery that gave vigour and influence to his speech. His manner, timid at first, became firm—his changeful face was lit up to superhuman brilliancy; his voice, various as music, was like that enchanting.

It were useless to record the debate that followed this harangue. Party speeches were delivered, which clothed the question in cant, and veiled its simple meaning in a woven wind of words. The motion was lost; Ryland withdrew in rage and despair; and Raymond, gay and exulting, retired to dream of his future kingdom.

CHAPTER V

Is there such a feeling as love at first sight? And if there be, in what does its nature differ from love founded in long observation and slow growth? Perhaps its effects are not so permanent; but they are, while they last, as violent and intense. We walk the pathless mazes of society, vacant of joy, till we hold this clue, leading us through that labyrinth to paradise.[51]Our nature dim, like to an unlighted torch, sleeps in formless blank till the fire attain it; this life of life, this light to moon, and glory to the sun. What does it matter, whether the fire be struck from flint and steel, nourished with care into a flame, slowly communicated to the dark wick, or whether swiftly the radiant power of light and warmth passes from a kindred power, and shines at once the beacon and the hope. In the deepest fountain of my heart the pulses were stirred; around, above, beneath, the clinging Memory as a cloak enwrapt me. In no one moment of coming time did I feel as I had done in time gone by. The spirit of Idris hovered in the air I breathed; her eyes were ever and for ever bent on mine; her remembered smile blinded my faint gaze, and caused me to walk as one, not in eclipse, not in darkness and vacancy—but in a new and brilliant light, too novel, too dazzling for my human senses. On every leaf, on every small division of the universe, (as on the hyacinth αςͅ is engraved) was imprinted the talisman of my existence—SHE LIVES! SHE IS![52]—I had not time yet to analyze my feeling, to take myself to task, and leash in the tameless passion; all was one idea, one feeling, one knowledge—it was my life!

But the die was cast—Raymond would marry Idris. The merry marriage bells rung in my ears; I heard the nation's gratulation which followed the union; the ambitious noble uprose with swift eagle-flight, from the lowly ground to regal supremacy—and to the love of Idris. Yet, not so! She did not love him; she had called me her friend; she had smiled on me; to me she had entrusted her heart's dearest hope, the welfare of Adrian. This reflection thawed my congealing blood, and again the tide of life and

---

51 Love becomes a means of escape from joyless social entrapment; in classical mythology, Ariadne saves Theseus from the minotaur at the heart of the Cretan labyrinth by giving him a thread, or clue, by which he finds his way out.

52 The Greek word αἰαῖ ("alas") is supposed to be inscribed on the petals of a sort of iris that sprang from the blood of Hyacinthus; MWS appears to have made a mistake in the Greek here. Ovid tells the Hyacinthus story in *Metamorphoses* 10.162-219 and alludes to it in 13.394-97. Cf. PBS, translations of Bion, "A Fragment of the Elegy on the Death of Adonis," and of Moschus, "Fragment of the Elegy on the Death of Bion": "thou, O hyacinth, / Utter thy legend now—yet more, dumb flower, / Than 'Ah! alas!'—thine is no common grief—" (10-12).

love flowed impetuously onward, again to ebb as my busy thoughts changed.

The debate had ended at three in the morning. My soul was in tumults; I traversed the streets with eager rapidity. Truly, I was mad that night— love—which I have named a giant from its birth, wrestled with despair! My heart, the field of combat, was wounded by the iron heel of the one, watered by the gushing tears of the other. Day, hateful to me, dawned; I retreated to my lodgings—I threw myself on a couch—I slept—was it sleep?—for thought was still alive—love and despair struggled still, and I writhed with unendurable pain.

I awoke half stupefied; I felt a heavy oppression on me, but knew not wherefore; I entered, as it were, the council-chamber of my brain, and questioned the various ministers of thought therein assembled; too soon I remembered all; too soon my limbs quivered beneath the tormenting power; soon, too soon, I knew myself a slave!

Suddenly, unannounced, Lord Raymond entered my apartment. He came in gaily, singing the Tyrolese song of liberty; noticed me with a gracious nod, and threw himself on a sopha opposite the copy of a bust of the Apollo Belvidere.[53] After one or two trivial remarks, to which I sullenly replied, he suddenly cried, looking at the bust, "I am called like that victor! Not a bad idea; the head will serve for my new coinage, and be an omen to all dutiful subjects of my future success."

He said this in his most gay, yet benevolent manner, and smiled, not disdainfully, but in playful mockery of himself. Then his countenance suddenly darkened, and in that shrill tone peculiar to himself, he cried, "I fought a good battle last night; higher conquest the plains of Greece never saw me achieve. Now I am the first man in the state, burthen of every ballad, and object of old women's mumbled devotions. What are your meditations? You, who fancy that you can read the human soul, as your native lake reads each crevice and folding of its surrounding hills—say what you think of me; king-expectant, angel or devil, which?"

This ironical tone was discord to my bursting, over-boiling-heart; I was nettled by his insolence, and replied with bitterness; "There is a spirit, neither angel or devil, damned to limbo merely."[54] I saw his cheeks

---

53 Writing about Byron after his death, MWS asks, "Can I forget our evening visits to Diodati—our excursions of the lake when he sang the Tyrolese hymn—and his voice was harmonized with winds and waves?" (May 1824; *Journals* 2: 478); the reference is to Thomas Moore's "Tyrolese Song of Liberty," "Merrily Every Bosom Boundeth." The Apollo Belvedere is a marble copy in the Vatican of a Hellenistic bronze still admired in MWS's time as a Greek masterwork. PBS mentions it twice, admiringly, in his *Notes on Sculptures* (*Works*, ed. Ingpen and Peck 6: 321, 330), and MWS describes it in her *Rambles in Germany and Italy* (2: 217).

54 Limbo is the outmost circle of hell, where in Dante's *Inferno* virtuous pagans (including poets, philosophers, and heroes) spend eternity.

become pale, and his lips whiten and quiver; his anger served but to enkindle mine, and I answered with a determined look his eyes which glared on me; suddenly they were withdrawn, cast down, a tear, I thought, wetted the dark lashes; I was softened, and with involuntary emotion added, "Not that you are such, my dear lord."

I paused, even awed by the agitation he evinced; "Yes," he said at length, rising and biting his lip, as he strove to curb his passion; "Such am I! You do not know me, Verney; neither you, nor our audience of last night, nor does universal England know aught of me. I stand here, it would seem, an elected king; this hand is about to grasp a sceptre; these brows feel in each nerve the coming diadem. I appear to have strength, power, victory; standing as a dome-supporting column stands; and I am—a reed! I have ambition, and that attains its aim; my nightly dreams are realized, my waking hopes fulfilled; a kingdom awaits my acceptance, my enemies are overthrown. But here," and he struck his heart with violence, "here is the rebel, here the stumbling-block; this over-ruling heart, which I may drain of its living blood; but, while one fluttering pulsation remains, I am its slave."

He spoke with a broken voice, then bowed his head, and, hiding his face in his hands, wept. I was still smarting from my own disappointment; yet this scene oppressed me even to terror, nor could I interrupt his access of passion. It subsided at length; and, throwing himself on the couch, he remained silent and motionless, except that his changeful features shewed a strong internal conflict. At last he rose, and said in his usual tone of voice, "The time grows on us, Verney, I must away. Let me not forget my chiefest errand here. Will you accompany me to Windsor to-morrow? You will not be dishonoured by my society, and as this is probably the last service, or disservice you can do me, will you grant my request?"

He held out his hand with almost a bashful air. Swiftly I thought—Yes, I will witness the last scene of the drama. Beside which, his mien conquered me, and an affectionate sentiment towards him, again filled my heart—I bade him command me. "Aye, that I will," said he gaily, "that's my cue now; be with me to-morrow morning by seven; be secret and faithful; and you shall be groom of the stole[55] ere long."

So saying he hastened away, vaulted on his horse, and with a gesture as if he gave me his hand to kiss, bade me another laughing adieu. Left to myself, I strove with painful intensity to divine the motive of his request, and foresee the events of the coming day. The hours passed on

---

55   An official position in the British royal household: Raymond aspires to be king in all but name. For implicit criticism, see Thomas Paine, *The Rights of Man*: in an aristocracy, "[o]ne turns a candle-holder, or a lord in waiting; another a lord of the bed-chamber, a groom of the stole, or any insignificant nominal office, to which a salary is annexed, paid out of the public taxes, and which avoids the direct appearance of corruption" (introd. Eric Foner 228).

unperceived; my head ached with thought, the nerves seemed teeming with the over full fraught—I clasped my burning brow, as if my fevered hand could medicine its pain.

I was punctual to the appointed hour on the following day, and found Lord Raymond waiting for me. We got into his carriage, and proceeded towards Windsor. I had tutored myself, and was resolved by no outward sign to disclose my internal agitation.

"What a mistake Ryland made," said Raymond, "when he thought to overpower me the other night. He spoke well, very well; such an harangue would have succeeded better addressed to me singly, than to the fools and knaves assembled yonder. Had I been alone, I should have listened to him with a wish to hear reason, but when he endeavoured to vanquish me in my own territory, with my own weapons, he put me on my mettle, and the event was such as all might have expected."

I smiled incredulously, and replied: "I am of Ryland's way of thinking, and will, if you please, repeat all his arguments; we shall see how far you will be induced by them, to change the royal for the patriotic style."

"The repetition would be useless," said Raymond, "since I well remember them, and have many others, self-suggested, which speak with unanswerable persuasion."

He did not explain himself, nor did I make any remark on his reply. Our silence endured for some miles, till the country with open fields, or shady woods and parks, presented pleasant objects to our view. After some observations on the scenery and seats, Raymond said: "Philosophers have called man a microcosm of nature, and find a reflection in the internal mind for all this machinery visibly at work around us. This theory has often been a source of amusement to me; and many an idle hour have I spent, exercising my ingenuity in finding resemblances. Does not Lord Bacon say that, 'the falling from a discord to a concord, which maketh great sweetness in music, hath an agreement with the affections, which are re-integrated to the better after some dislikes?'[56] What a sea is the tide of passion, whose fountains are in our own nature! Our virtues are the quick-sands, which shew themselves at calm and low water; but let the waves arise and the winds buffet them, and the poor devil whose hope was in their durability, finds them sink from under him. The fashions of the world, its exigencies, educations and pursuits, are winds to drive our wills, like clouds all one way; but let a thunderstorm arise in the shape of love, hate, or ambition, and the rack goes backward, stemming the opposing air in triumph."

"Yet," replied I, "nature always presents to our eyes the appearance of a patient: while there is an active principle in man which is capable of rul-

---

56 Francis Bacon, *Sylva Sylvarum: or a Natural History* [1627], Century 2, part 113 (*Works*, ed. J. Spedding, R. L. Ellis, and D. D. Heath 2: 389).

ing fortune, and at least of tacking against the gale, till it in some mode conquers it."

"There is more of what is specious than true in your distinction," said my companion. "Did we form ourselves, choosing our dispositions, and our powers? I find myself, for one, as a stringed instrument with chords and stops—but I have no power to turn the pegs, or pitch my thoughts to a higher or lower key."

"Other men," I observed, "may be better musicians."

"I talk not of others, but myself," replied Raymond, "and I am as fair an example to go by as another. I cannot set my heart to a particular tune, or run voluntary changes on my will. We are born; we choose neither our parents, nor our stations; we are educated by others, or by the world's circumstance, and this cultivation, mingling with our innate disposition, is the soil in which our desires, passions, and motives grow."

"There is much truth in what you say," said I, "and yet no man ever acts upon this theory. Who, when he makes a choice, says, Thus I choose, because I am necessitated? Does he not on the contrary feel a freedom of will within him, which, though you may call it fallacious, still actuates him as he decides?"

"Exactly so," replied Raymond, "another link of the breakless chain. Were I now to commit an act which would annihilate my hopes, and pluck the regal garment from my mortal limbs, to clothe them in ordinary weeds, would this, think you, be an act of free-will on my part?"

As we talked thus, I perceived that we were not going the ordinary road to Windsor, but through Englefield Green, towards Bishopgate Heath. I began to divine that Idris was not the object of our journey, but that I was brought to witness the scene that was to decide the fate of Raymond—and of Perdita. Raymond had evidently vacillated during his journey, and irresolution was marked in every gesture as we entered Perdita's cottage. I watched him curiously, determined that, if this hesitation should continue, I would assist Perdita to overcome herself, and teach her to disdain the wavering love of him, who balanced between the possession of a crown, and of her, whose excellence and affection transcended the worth of a kingdom.

We found her in her flower-adorned alcove; she was reading the newspaper report of the debate in parliament, that apparently doomed her to hopelessness. That heart-sinking feeling was painted in her sunk eyes and spiritless attitude; a cloud was on her beauty, and frequent sighs were tokens of her distress. This sight had an instantaneous effect on Raymond; his eyes beamed with tenderness, and remorse clothed his manners with earnestness and truth. He sat beside her; and, taking the paper from her hand, said, "Not a word more shall my sweet Perdita read of this contention of madmen and fools. I must not permit you to be acquainted with the extent of my delusion, lest you despise me; although, believe me, a wish to appear before you, not vanquished, but as a conqueror, inspired me during my wordy war."

Perdita looked at him like one amazed; her expressive countenance shone for a moment with tenderness; to see him only was happiness. But a bitter thought swiftly shadowed her joy; she bent her eyes on the ground, endeavouring to master the passion of tears that threatened to overwhelm her. Raymond continued, "I will not act a part with you, dear girl, or appear other than what I am, weak and unworthy, more fit to excite your disdain than your love. Yet you do love me; I feel and know that you do, and thence I draw my most cherished hopes. If pride guided you, or even reason, you might well reject me. Do so; if your high heart, incapable of my infirmity of purpose, refuses to bend to the lowness of mine. Turn from me, if you will,—if you can. If your whole soul does not urge you to forgive me—if your entire heart does not open wide its door to admit me to its very centre, forsake me, never speak to me again. I, though sinning against you almost beyond remission, I also am proud; there must be no reserve in your pardon—no drawback to the gift of your affection."

Perdita looked down, confused, yet pleased. My presence embarrassed her; so that she dared not turn to meet her lover's eye, or trust her voice to assure him of her affection; while a blush mantled her cheek, and her disconsolate air was exchanged for one expressive of deep-felt joy. Raymond encircled her waist with his arm, and continued, "I do not deny that I have balanced between you and the highest hope that mortal man can entertain; but I do so no longer. Take me—mould me to your will, possess my heart and soul to all eternity. If you refuse to contribute to my happiness, I quit England to-night, and will never set foot in it again.

"Lionel, you hear: witness for me: persuade your sister to forgive the injury I have done her; persuade her to be mine."

"There needs no persuasion" said the blushing Perdita, "except your own dear promises, and my ready heart, which whispers to me that they are true."

That same evening we all three walked together in the forest, and, with the garrulity which happiness inspires, they detailed to me the history of their loves. It was pleasant to see the haughty Raymond and reserved Perdita changed through happy love into prattling, playful children, both losing their characteristic dignity in the fulness of mutual contentment. A night or two ago Lord Raymond, with a brow of care, and a heart oppressed with thought, bent all his energies to silence or persuade the legislators of England that a sceptre was not too weighty for his hand, while visions of dominion, war, and triumph floated before him; now, frolicsome as a lively boy sporting under his mother's approving eye, the hopes of his ambition were complete, when he pressed the small fair hand of Perdita to his lips; while she, radiant with delight, looked on the still pool, not truly admiring herself, but drinking in with rapture the reflection there made of the form of herself and her lover, shewn for the first time in dear conjunction.

I rambled away from them. If the rapture of assured sympathy was theirs, I enjoyed that of restored hope. I looked on the regal towers of

Windsor. High is the wall and strong the barrier that separate me from my Star of Beauty. But not impassable. She will not be his. A few more years dwell in thy native garden, sweet flower, till I by toil and time acquire a right to gather thee. Despair not, nor bid me despair! What must I do now? First I must seek Adrian, and restore him to her. Patience, gentleness, and untired affection, shall recall him, if it be true, as Raymond says, that he is mad; energy and courage shall rescue him, if he be unjustly imprisoned.

After the lovers again joined me, we supped together in the alcove. Truly it was a fairy's supper; for though the air was perfumed by the scent of fruits and wine, we none of us either ate or drank—even the beauty of the night was unobserved; their extasy could not be increased by outward objects, and I was wrapt in reverie. At about midnight Raymond and I took leave of my sister, to return to town. He was all gaiety; scraps of songs fell from his lips; every thought of his mind—every object about us, gleamed under the sunshine of his mirth. He accused me of melancholy, of ill-humour and envy.

"Not so," said I, "though I confess that my thoughts are not occupied as pleasantly as yours are. You promised to facilitate my visit to Adrian; I conjure you to perform your promise. I cannot linger here; I long to soothe—perhaps to cure the malady of my first and best friend. I shall immediately depart for Dunkeld."

"Thou bird of night," replied Raymond, "what an eclipse do you throw across my bright thoughts, forcing me to call to mind that melancholy ruin, which stands in mental desolation, more irreparable than a fragment of a carved column in a weed-grown field. You dream that you can restore him? Dædalus never wound so inextricable an error round Minotaur, as madness has woven about his imprisoned reason. Nor you, nor any other Theseus, can thread the labyrinth, to which perhaps some unkind Ariadne has the clue."[57]

"You allude to Evadne Zaimi: but she is not in England."

"And were she," said Raymond, "I would not advise her seeing him. Better to decay in absolute delirium, than to be the victim of the methodical unreason of ill-bestowed love. The long duration of his malady has probably erased from his mind all vestige of her; and it were well that it should never again be imprinted. You will find him at Dunkeld; gentle and tractable he wanders up the hills, and through the wood, or sits listening beside the waterfall. You may see him—his hair stuck with wild flowers—his eyes full of untraceable meaning—his voice broken—his

---

57   Ariadne helps Theseus to escape from the Cretan labyrinth after he kills the minotaur, half man, half bull. Daedalus the artificer designed the labyrinth and, later, escaped from Crete by flying over the sea with his son, Icarus, who plunged to his death when his waxen wings melted. These stories are mentioned by Virgil, *Aeneid* 6: see Appendix B.1.

person wasted to a shadow. He plucks flowers and weeds, and weaves chaplets of them, or sails yellow leaves and bits of bark on the stream, rejoicing in their safety, or weeping at their wreck. The very memory half unmans me. By Heaven! the first tears I have shed since boyhood rushed scalding into my eyes when I saw him."

It needed not this last account to spur me on to visit him. I only doubted whether or not I should endeavour to see Idris again, before I departed. This doubt was decided on the following day. Early in the morning Raymond came to me; intelligence had arrived that Adrian was dangerously ill, and it appeared impossible that his failing strength should surmount the disorder. "To-morrow," said Raymond, "his mother and sister set out for Scotland to see him once again."

"And I go to-day," I cried; "this very hour I will engage a sailing balloon;[58] I shall be there in forty-eight hours at furthest, perhaps in less, if the wind is fair. Farewell, Raymond; be happy in having chosen the better part in life. This turn of fortune revives me. I feared madness, not sickness—I have a presentiment that Adrian will not die; perhaps this illness is a crisis, and he may recover."

Everything favoured my journey. The balloon rose about half a mile from the earth, and with a favourable wind it hurried through the air, its feathered vans cleaving the unopposing atmosphere. Notwithstanding the melancholy object of my journey, my spirits were exhilarated by reviving hope, by the swift motion of the airy pinnace, and the balmy visitation of the sunny air. The pilot hardly moved the plumed steerage, and the slender mechanism of the wings, wide unfurled, gave forth a murmuring noise, soothing to the sense. Plain and hill, stream and corn-field, were discernible below, while we unimpeded sped on swift and secure, as a wild swan in his spring-tide flight. The machine obeyed the slightest motion of the helm; and, the wind blowing steadily, there was no let or obstacle to our course. Such was the power of man over the elements; a power long sought, and lately won; yet foretold in by-gone time by the prince of poets, whose verses I quoted much to the astonishment of my pilot, when I told him how many hundred years ago they had been written:—

Oh! human wit, thou can'st invent much ill,
Thou searchest strange arts: who would think by skill,

---

58   In 1783 the first hot-air balloon was launched at Annonay, France, by two brothers, Joseph Michel and Jacques Etienne Montgolfier. Later the same year, the physicist J.A.C. Charles supervised the launching of a hydrogen balloon from the Champs de Mars. Unlike MWS's strange machine, neither had wings. Flights had been made across the English Channel by MWS's day, but she imagines far longer (and safer) journeys, as does the Comte de Grainville in *Le Dernier homme*, translated as *The Last Man, or Omegarus and Syderia* (1806).

An heavy man like a light bird should stray,
And through the empty heavens find a way?[59]

I alighted at Perth; and, though much fatigued by a constant exposure to the air for many hours, I would not rest, but merely altering my mode of conveyance, I went by land instead of air, to Dunkeld. The sun was rising as I entered the opening of the hills. After the revolution of ages Birnam hill was again covered with a young forest,[60] while more aged pines, planted at the very commencement of the nineteenth century by the then Duke of Athol, gave solemnity and beauty to the scene. The rising sun first tinged the pine tops; and my mind, rendered through my mountain education deeply susceptible of the graces of nature, and now on the eve of again beholding my beloved and perhaps dying friend, was strangely influenced by the sight of those distant beams: surely they were ominous, and as such I regarded them, good omens for Adrian, on whose life my happiness depended.

Poor fellow! he lay stretched on a bed of sickness, his cheeks glowing with the hues of fever, his eyes half closed, his breath irregular and difficult. Yet it was less painful to see him thus, than to find him fulfilling the animal functions uninterruptedly, his mind sick the while. I established myself at his bedside; I never quitted it day or night. Bitter task was it, to behold his spirit waver between death and life: to see his warm cheek, and know that the very fire which burned too fiercely there, was consuming the vital fuel; to hear his moaning voice, which might never again articulate words of love and wisdom; to witness the ineffectual motions of his limbs, soon to be wrapt in their mortal shroud. Such for three days and nights appeared the consummation which fate had decreed for my labours, and I became haggard and spectre-like, through anxiety and watching. At length his eyes unclosed faintly, yet with a look of returning life; he became pale and weak; but the rigidity of his features was softened by approaching convalescence. He knew me. What a brimful cup of joyful agony it was, when his face first gleamed with the glance of recognition—when he pressed my hand, now more fevered than his own, and when he pronounced my name! No trace of his past insanity remained, to dash my joy with sorrow.

This same evening his mother and sister arrived. The Countess of Windsor was by nature full of energetic feeling; but she had very seldom in her life permitted the concentrated emotions of her heart to shew themselves on her features. The studied immovability of her counte-

---

59   An unidentified translation of Ovid, *Ars Amatoria* [The Art of Love] 2.43-44, part of a version of the story of Icarus: "Ingenium mala saepe movent: quis crederet umquam / Aerias hominem corpore posse vias?"

60   Birnam hill (site of the Birnam wood of *Macbeth* 5.3.59-60) is near Dunkeld in Perthshire, Scotland.

nance; her slow, equable manner, and soft but unmelodious voice, were a mask, hiding her fiery passions, and the impatience of her disposition. She did not in the least resemble either of her children; her black and sparkling eye, lit up by pride, was totally unlike the blue lustre, and frank, benignant expression of either Adrian or Idris. There was something grand and majestic in her motions, but nothing persuasive, nothing amiable. Tall, thin, and strait, her face still handsome, her raven hair hardly tinged with grey, her forehead arched and beautiful, had not the eye-brows been somewhat scattered—it was impossible not to be struck by her, almost to fear her. Idris appeared to be the only being who could resist her mother, notwithstanding the extreme mildness of her character. But there was a fearlessness and frankness about her, which said that she would not encroach on another's liberty, but held her own sacred and unassailable.

The Countess cast no look of kindness on my worn-out frame, though afterwards she thanked me coldly for my attentions. Not so Idris; her first glance was for her brother; she took his hand, she kissed his eye-lids, and hung over him with looks of compassion and love. Her eyes glistened with tears when she thanked me, and the grace of her expressions was enhanced, not diminished, by the fervour, which caused her almost to falter as she spoke. Her mother, all eyes and ears, soon interrupted us; and I saw, that she wished to dismiss me quietly, as one whose services, now that his relatives had arrived, were of no use to her son. I was harassed and ill, resolved not to give up my post, yet doubting in what way I should assert it; when Adrian called me, and clasping my hand, bade me not leave him. His mother, apparently inattentive, at once understood what was meant, and seeing the hold we had upon her, yielded the point to us.

The days that followed were full of pain to me; so that I sometimes regretted that I had not yielded at once to the haughty lady, who watched all my motions, and turned my beloved task of nursing my friend to a work of pain and irritation. Never did any woman appear so entirely made of mind, as the Countess of Windsor. Her passions had subdued her appetites, even her natural wants; she slept little, and hardly ate at all; her body was evidently considered by her as a mere machine, whose health was necessary for the accomplishment of her schemes, but whose senses formed no part of her enjoyment. There is something fearful in one who can thus conquer the animal part of our nature, if the victory be not the effect of consummate virtue; nor was it without a mixture of this feeling, that I beheld the figure of the Countess awake when others slept, fasting when I, abstemious naturally, and rendered so by the fever that preyed on me, was forced to recruit myself with food. She resolved to prevent or diminish my opportunities of acquiring influence over her children, and circumvented my plans by a hard, quiet, stubborn resolution, that seemed not to belong to flesh and blood. War was at last tacitly acknowledged between us. We had many pitched battles, during which no word was spoken, hardly a look was interchanged, but in which each resolved not to submit to the other. The Countess had the advantage of position; so I was vanquished, though I would not yield.

I became sick at heart. My countenance was painted with the hues of ill health and vexation. Adrian and Idris saw this; they attributed it to my long watching and anxiety; they urged me to rest, and take care of myself, while I most truly assured them, that my best medicine was their good wishes; those, and the assured convalescence of my friend, now daily more apparent. The faint rose again blushed on his cheek; his brow and lips lost the ashy paleness of threatened dissolution; such was the dear reward of my unremitting attention—and bounteous heaven added over-flowing recompence, when it gave me also the thanks and smiles of Idris.

After the lapse of a few weeks, we left Dunkeld. Idris and her mother returned immediately to Windsor, while Adrian and I followed by slow journies and frequent stoppages, occasioned by his continued weakness. As we traversed the various counties of fertile England, all wore an exhilarating appearance to my companion, who had been so long secluded by disease from the enjoyments of weather and scenery. We passed through busy towns and cultivated plains. The husbandmen were getting in their plenteous harvests, and the women and children, occupied by light rustic toils, formed groupes of happy, healthful persons, the very sight of whom carried cheerfulness to the heart. One evening, quitting our inn, we strolled down a shady lane, then up a grassy slope, till we came to an eminence, that commanded an extensive view of hill and dale, meandering rivers, dark woods, and shining villages. The sun was setting; and the clouds, straying, like new-shorn sheep, through the vast fields of sky, received the golden colour of his parting beams; the distant uplands shone out, and the busy hum of evening came, harmonized by distance, on our ear. Adrian, who felt all the fresh spirit infused by returning health, clasped his hands in delight, and exclaimed with transport:

"O happy earth, and happy inhabitants of earth! A stately palace has God built for you, O man! and worthy are you of your dwelling! Behold the verdant carpet spread at our feet, and the azure canopy above; the fields of earth which generate and nurture all things, and the track of heaven, which contains and clasps all things. Now, at this evening hour, at the period of repose and refection,[61] methinks all hearts breathe one hymn of love and thanksgiving, and we, like priests of old on the mountain-tops, give a voice to their sentiment.

"Assuredly a most benignant power built up the majestic fabric we inhabit, and framed the laws by which it endures. If mere existence, and not happiness, had been the final end of our being, what need of the profuse luxuries which we enjoy? Why should our dwelling place be so lovely, and why should the instincts of nature minister pleasurable sensations? The very sustaining of our animal machine is made delightful; and our

---

61   This reading in the first edition is probably an error for "reflection."

sustenance, the fruits of the field, is painted with transcendant hues, endued with grateful odours, and palatable to our taste. Why should this be, if HE were not good? We need houses to protect us from the seasons, and behold the materials with which we are provided; the growth of trees with their adornment of leaves; while rocks of stone piled above the plains variegate the prospect with their pleasant irregularity.

"Nor are outward objects alone the receptacles of the Spirit of Good. Look into the mind of man, where wisdom reigns enthroned; where imagination, the painter, sits, with his pencil dipt in hues lovelier than those of sunset, adorning familiar life with glowing tints. What a noble boon, worthy the giver, is the imagination! it takes from reality its leaden hue: it envelopes all thought and sensation in a radiant veil,[62] and with an hand of beauty beckons us from the sterile seas of life, to her gardens, and bowers, and glades of bliss. And is not love a gift of the divinity? Love, and her child, Hope, which can bestow wealth on poverty, strength on the weak, and happiness on the sorrowing.

"My lot has not been fortunate. I have consorted long with grief, entered the gloomy labyrinth of madness, and emerged, but half alive. Yet I thank God that I have lived! I thank God, that I have beheld his throne, the heavens, and earth, his footstool.[63] I am glad that I have seen the changes of his day; to behold the sun, fountain of light, and the gentle pilgrim moon; to have seen the fire bearing flowers of the sky, and the flowery stars of earth; to have witnessed the sowing and the harvest. I am glad that I have loved, and have experienced sympathetic joy and sorrow with my fellow-creatures. I am glad now to feel the current of thought flow through my mind, as the blood through the articulations of my frame; mere existence is pleasure; and I thank God that I live!

"And all ye happy nurslings of mother-earth, do ye not echo my words? Ye who are linked by the affectionate ties of nature; companions, friends, lovers! fathers, who toil with joy for their offspring; women, who while gazing on the living forms of their children, forget the pains of maternity; children, who neither toil nor spin,[64] but love and are loved!

"Oh, that death and sickness were banished from our earthly home! that hatred, tyranny, and fear could no longer make their lair in the human heart! that each man might find a brother in his fellow, and a nest of repose amid the wide plains of his inheritance! that the source of tears were dry, and that lips might no longer form expressions of sorrow. Sleeping thus under the beneficent eye of heaven, can evil visit thee, O

---

62 MWS here inverts PBS's image in *A Defence of Poetry*: "Poetry lifts the veil from the hidden beauty of the world" (*Works*, ed. Ingpen and Peck 7: 117).
63 Isaiah 66.1: "Thus saith the Lord, The heaven is my throne, and the earth is my footstool: where is the house that ye build unto me? and where is the place of my rest?"
64 Cf. 29n.

Earth, or grief cradle to their graves thy luckless children? Whisper it not, lest the dæmons hear and rejoice! The choice is with us; let us will it, and our habitation becomes a paradise.[65] For the will of man is omnipotent, blunting the arrows of death, soothing the bed of disease, and wiping away the tears of agony. And what is each human being worth, if he do not put forth his strength to aid his fellow-creatures? My soul is a fading spark, my nature frail as a spent wave;[66] but I dedicate all of intellect and strength that remains to me, to that one work, and take upon me the task, as far as I am able, of bestowing blessings on my fellow-men!"

His voice trembled, his eyes were cast up, his hands clasped, and his fragile person was bent, as it were, with excess of emotion. The spirit of life seemed to linger in his form, as a dying flame on an altar flickers on the embers of an accepted sacrifice.

CHAPTER VI

WHEN we arrived at Windsor, I found that Raymond and Perdita had departed for the continent. I took possession of my sister's cottage, and blessed myself that I lived within view of Windsor Castle. It was a curious fact, that at this period, when by the marriage of Perdita I was allied to one of the richest individuals in England, and was bound by the most intimate friendship to its chiefest noble, I experienced the greatest excess of poverty that I had ever known. My knowledge of the worldly principles of Lord Raymond, would have ever prevented me from applying to him, however deep my distress might have been. It was in vain that I repeated to myself with regard to Adrian, that his purse was open to me; that one in soul, as we were, our fortunes ought also to be common. I could never, while with him, think of his bounty as a remedy to my poverty; and I even put aside hastily his offers of supplies, assuring him of a falsehood, that I needed them not. How could I say to this generous being, "Maintain me in idleness. You who have dedicated your powers of mind and fortune to the benefit of your species, shall you so misdirect your exertions, as to support in uselessness the strong, healthy, and capable?"

---

65 In her note on *Prometheus Unbound* MWS wrote, "Shelley believed that mankind had only to will that there should be no evil, and there would be none." In PBS, *Julian and Maddalo* (1818, published in *Posthumous Poems*, 1824), Julian observes, "it is our will / That thus enchains us to permitted ill" (170-71); cf. below, 83; "men were not happy, not because they could not, but because they would not rouse themselves to vanquish self-raised obstacles."

66 Cf. PBS, "Ode to the West Wind" (1820), where the poet's words are "ashes and sparks" (66-67) and where a wave is one of the images for the poet; see also his *Defence of Poetry*, where "the mind in creation is as a fading coal" (*Works*, ed. Ingpen and Peck 7: 135).

And yet I dared not request him to use his influence that I might obtain an honourable provision for myself—for then I should have been obliged to leave Windsor. I hovered for ever around the walls of its Castle, beneath its enshadowing thickets; my sole companions were my books and my loving thoughts. I studied the wisdom of the ancients, and gazed on the happy walls that sheltered the beloved of my soul. My mind was nevertheless idle. I pored over the poetry of old times; I studied the metaphysics of Plato and Berkley;[67] I read the histories of Greece and Rome, and of England's former periods, and I watched the movements of the lady of my heart. At night I could see her shadow on the walls of her apartment; by day I viewed her in her flower-garden, or riding in the park with her usual companions. Methought the charm would be broken if I were seen, but I heard the music of her voice and was happy. I gave to each heroine of whom I read, her beauty and matchless excellences—such was Antigone, when she guided the blind Œdipus to the grove of the Eumenides, and discharged the funeral rites of Polynices; such was Miranda in the unvisited cave of Prospero; such Haidee, on the sands of the Ionian island.[68] I was mad with excess of passionate devotion; but pride, tameless as fire, invested my nature, and prevented me from betraying myself by word or look.

In the mean time, while I thus pampered myself with rich mental repasts, a peasant would have disdained my scanty fare, which I sometimes robbed from the squirrels of the forest. I was, I own, often tempted to recur to the lawless feats of my boy-hood, and knock down the almost tame pheasants that perched upon the trees, and bent their bright eyes on me. But they were the property of Adrian, the nurslings of Idris; and so, although my imagination rendered sensual by privation, made me think that they would better become the spit in my kitchen, than the green leaves of the forest,

---

67 Plato (c. 427-c. 348 BC) taught that there is a distinction between truth, or the realm of ideas, and the ordinary world of mutable opinions. George Berkeley (1685-1753) was one of the most influential philosophers of the idealist school, maintaining that nothing exists unless it perceives or is perceived.

68 MWS here refers to three literary heroines, all of whom (unlike Idris) have strong fathers. In Sophocles' *Oedipus at Colonus*, Oedipus, having blinded himself after learning that he has killed his father and married his mother, is guided by his daughter, Antigone, to Colonus, where an oracle has prophesied he will die; in *Antigone*, the heroine performs funeral rites for her brother, Polynices, in defiance of Creon, King of Crete; imprisoned in a cave, she hangs herself. In Shakespeare's *The Tempest*, Miranda is the daughter of the magician Prospero, who controls everyone on his island. Haidée is Juan's Greek lover in Byron's *Don Juan*, cantos 2-4, who dies after her father separates her from Juan.

> Nathelesse,
> I checked my haughty will, and did not eat;

but supped upon sentiment, and dreamt vainly of "such morsels sweet," as I might not waking attain.[69]

But, at this period, the whole scheme of my existence was about to change. The orphan and neglected son of Verney, was on the eve of being linked to the mechanism of society by a golden chain, and to enter into all the duties and affections of life. Miracles were to be wrought in my favour, the machine of social life pushed with vast effort backward. Attend, O reader! while I narrate this tale of wonders!

One day as Adrian and Idris were riding through the forest, with their mother and accustomed companions, Idris, drawing her brother aside from the rest of the cavalcade, suddenly asked him, "What had become of his friend, Lionel Verney?"

"Even from this spot," replied Adrian, pointing to my sister's cottage, "you can see his dwelling."

"Indeed!" said Idris, "and why, if he be so near, does he not come to see us, and make one of our society?"

"I often visit him," replied Adrian; "but you may easily guess the motives, which prevent him from coming where his presence may annoy any one among us."

"I do guess them," said Idris, "and such as they are, I would not venture to combat them. Tell me, however, in what way he passes his time; what he is doing and thinking in his cottage retreat?"

"Nay, my sweet sister," replied Adrian, "you ask me more than I can well answer; but if you feel interest in him, why not visit him? He will feel highly honoured, and thus you may repay a part of the obligation I owe him, and compensate for the injuries fortune has done him."

"I will most readily accompany you to his abode," said the lady, "not that I wish that either of us should unburthen ourselves of our debt, which, being no less than your life, must remain unpayable ever. But let us go; to-morrow we will arrange to ride out together, and proceeding towards that part of the forest, call upon him."

The next evening therefore, though the autumnal change had brought on cold and rain, Adrian and Idris entered my cottage. They found me Curius-like, feasting on sorry fruits for supper; but they brought gifts rich-

---

69 These two quotations are from PBS's translation of "Homer's Hymn to Mercury" (*Posthumous Poems*, 1824): "Natheless / He checked his haughty will and did not eat, / Though what it cost him words can scarce express, / And every wish to put such morsels sweet / Down his most sacred throat, he did repress" (167-71).

er than the golden bribes of the Sabines,[70] nor could I refuse the invaluable store of friendship and delight which they bestowed. Surely the glorious twins of Latona were not more welcome, when, in the infancy of the world, they were brought forth to beautify and enlighten this "sterile promontory," than were this angelic pair to my lowly dwelling and grateful heart.[71] We sat like one family round my hearth. Our talk was on subjects, unconnected with the emotions that evidently occupied each; but we each divined the other's thought, and as our voices spoke of indifferent matters, our eyes, in mute language, told a thousand things no tongue could have uttered.

They left me in an hour's time. They left me happy—how unspeakably happy. It did not require the measured sounds of human language to syllable the story of my extasy. Idris had visited me; Idris I should again and again see—my imagination did not wander beyond the completeness of this knowledge. I trod air; no doubt, no fear, no hope even, disturbed me; I clasped with my soul the fulness of contentment, satisfied, undesiring, beatified.

For many days Adrian and Idris continued to visit me thus. In this dear intercourse, love, in the guise of enthusiastic friendship, infused more and more of his omnipotent spirit. Idris felt it. Yes, divinity of the world, I read your characters in her looks and gesture; I heard your melodious voice echoed by her—you prepared for us a soft and flowery path, all gentle thoughts adorned it—your name, O Love, was not spoken, but you stood the Genius of the Hour, veiled, and time, but no mortal hand, might raise the curtain. Organs of articulate sound did not proclaim the union of our hearts; for untoward circumstance allowed no opportunity for the expression that hovered on our lips.

Oh my pen! haste thou to write what was, before the thought of what is, arrests the hand that guides thee. If I lift up my eyes and see the desart earth, and feel that those dear eyes have spent their mortal lustre, and that those beauteous lips are silent, their "crimson leaves"[72] faded, for ever I am mute!

But you live, my Idris, even now you move before me! There was a glade, O reader! a grassy opening in the wood; the retiring trees left its

---

70 The Sabines were an ancient Italian people, defeated by the Romans about 290 BC. After the Romans carried off the Sabine women by force, the Sabines besieged Rome; Tarpeia, daughter of the Roman commanding officer, agreed to open the citadel to the invaders in exchange for golden bracelets. In contrast to Tarpeia, Curius (third century BC), who returned to his farm having defeated the enemies of the Roman people, exemplifies incorruptible virtue.

71 Latona (or Leto) was the mother of the twins Apollo and Artemis. The phrase "sterile promontory" comes from *Hamlet* 2.2.300.

72 PBS, *The Cenci* 5.4.137-39: "Let me / Kiss those warm lips before their crimson leaves / Are blighted ... white ... cold."

velvet expanse as a temple for love; the silver Thames bounded it on one side, and a willow bending down dipt in the water its Naiad hair, dishevelled by the wind's viewless hand. The oaks around were the home of a tribe of nightingales—there am I now; Idris, in youth's dear prime, is by my side—remember, I am just twenty-two, and seventeen summers have scarcely passed over the beloved of my heart.[73] The river swollen by autumnal rains, deluged the low lands, and Adrian in his favourite boat is employed in the dangerous pastime of plucking the topmost bough from a submerged oak. Are you weary of life, O Adrian, that you thus play with danger?—

He has obtained his prize, and he pilots his boat through the flood; our eyes were fixed on him fearfully, but the stream carried him away from us; he was forced to land far lower down, and to make a considerable circuit before he could join us. "He is safe!" said Idris, as he leapt on shore, and waved the bough over his head in token of success; "we will wait for him here."

We were alone together; the sun had set; the song of the nightingales began; the evening star shone distinct in the flood of light, which was yet unfaded in the west. The blue eyes of my angelic girl were fixed on this sweet emblem of herself: "How the light palpitates," she said, "which is that star's life. Its vacillating effulgence seems to say that its state, even like ours upon earth, is wavering and inconstant; it fears, methinks, and it loves."

"Gaze not on the star, dear, generous friend," I cried, "read not love in *its* trembling rays; look not upon distant worlds; speak not of the mere imagination of a sentiment. I have long been silent; long even to sickness have I desired to speak to you, and submit my soul, my life, my entire being to you. Look not on the star, dear love, or do, and let that eternal spark plead for me; let it be my witness and my advocate, silent as it shines—love is to me as light to the star; even so long as that is uneclipsed by annihilation, so long shall I love you."

Veiled for ever to the world's callous eye must be the transport of that moment. Still do I feel her graceful form press against my full-fraught heart—still does sight, and pulse, and breath sicken and fail, at the remembrance of that first kiss. Slowly and silently we went to meet Adrian, whom we heard approaching.

I entreated Adrian to return to me after he had conducted his sister home. And that same evening, walking among the moon-lit forest paths, I poured forth my whole heart, its transport and its hope, to my friend. For a moment he looked disturbed—"I might have foreseen this," he said, "what strife will now ensue! Pardon me, Lionel, nor wonder that the expectation of contest with my mother should jar me, when else I should

---

73   MWS was not quite seventeen when on 28 July 1814 she eloped with PBS, who was just a few days short of his twenty-second birthday.

delightedly confess that my best hopes are fulfilled, in confiding my sister to your protection. If you do not already know it, you will soon learn the deep hate my mother bears to the name of Verney. I will converse with Idris; then all that a friend can do, I will do; to her it must belong to play the lover's part, if she be capable of it."

While the brother and sister were still hesitating in what manner they could best attempt to bring their mother over to their party, she, suspecting our meetings, taxed her children with them; taxed her fair daughter with deceit, and an unbecoming attachment for one whose only merit was being the son of the profligate favourite of her imprudent father; and who was doubtless as worthless as he from whom he boasted his descent. The eyes of Idris flashed at this accusation; she replied, "I do not deny that I love Verney; prove to me that he is worthless; and I will never see him more."

"Dear Madam," said Adrian, "let me entreat you to see him, to cultivate his friendship. You will wonder then, as I do, at the extent of his accomplishments, and the brilliancy of his talents." (Pardon me, gentle reader, this is not futile vanity;—not futile, since to know that Adrian felt thus, brings joy even now to my lone heart).

"Mad and foolish boy!" exclaimed the angry lady, "you have chosen with dreams and theories to overthrow my schemes for your own aggrandizement; but you shall not do the same by those I have formed for your sister. I but too well understand the fascination you both labour under; since I had the same struggle with your father, to make him cast off the parent of this youth, who hid his evil propensities with the smoothness and subtlety of a viper. In those days how often did I hear of his attractions, his wide spread conquests, his wit, his refined manners. It is well when flies only are caught by such spiders' webs; but is it for the high-born and powerful to bow their necks to the flimsy yoke of these unmeaning pretensions? Were your sister indeed the insignificant person she deserves to be, I would willingly leave her to the fate, the wretched fate, of the wife of a man, whose very person, resembling as it does his wretched father, ought to remind you of the folly and vice it typifies—but remember, Lady Idris, it is not alone the once royal blood of England that colours your veins, you are a Princess of Austria, and every life-drop is akin to emperors and kings. Are you then a fit mate for an uneducated shepherd-boy, whose only inheritance is his father's tarnished name?"

"I can make but one defence," replied Idris, "the same offered by my brother; see Lionel, converse with my shepherd-boy"—

The Countess interrupted her indignantly—"Yours!" she cried: and then, smoothing her impassioned features to a disdainful smile, she continued—"We will talk of this another time. All I now ask, all your mother, Idris, requests is, that you will not see this upstart during the interval of one month."

"I dare not comply," said Idris, "it would pain him too much. I have no right to play with his feelings, to accept his proffered love, and then sting him with neglect."

"This is going too far," her mother answered, with quivering lips, and eyes again instinct by anger.

"Nay, Madam," said Adrian, "unless my sister consent never to see him again, it is surely an useless torment to separate them for a month."

"Certainly," replied the ex-queen, with bitter scorn, "his love, and her love, and both their childish flutterings, are to be put in fit comparison with my years of hope and anxiety, with the duties of the offspring of kings, with the high and dignified conduct which one of her descent ought to pursue. But it is unworthy of me to argue and complain. Perhaps you will have the goodness to promise me not to marry during that interval?"

This was asked only half ironically; and Idris wondered why her mother should extort from her a solemn vow not to do, what she had never dreamed of doing—but the promise was required and given.

All went on cheerfully now; we met as usual, and talked without dread of our future plans. The Countess was so gentle, and even beyond her wont, amiable with her children, that they began to entertain hopes of her ultimate consent. She was too unlike them, too utterly alien to their tastes, for them to find delight in her society, or in the prospect of its continuance, but it gave them pleasure to see her conciliating and kind. Once even, Adrian ventured to propose her receiving me. She refused with a smile, reminding him that for the present his sister had promised to be patient.

One day, after the lapse of nearly a month, Adrian received a letter from a friend in London, requesting his immediate presence for the furtherance of some important object. Guileless himself, Adrian feared no deceit. I rode with him as far as Staines: he was in high spirits; and, since I could not see Idris during his absence, he promised a speedy return. His gaiety, which was extreme, had the strange effect of awakening in me contrary feelings; a presentiment of evil hung over me; I loitered on my return; I counted the hours that must elapse before I saw Idris again. Wherefore should this be? What evil might not happen in the mean time? Might not her mother take advantage of Adrian's absence to urge her beyond her sufferance, perhaps to entrap her? I resolved, let what would befall, to see and converse with her the following day. This determination soothed me. To-morrow, loveliest and best, hope and joy of my life, to-morrow I will see thee—Fool, to dream of a moment's delay!

I went to rest. At past midnight I was awaked by a violent knocking. It was now deep winter; it had snowed, and was still snowing; the wind whistled in the leafless trees, despoiling them of the white flakes as they fell; its drear moaning, and the continued knocking, mingled wildly with my dreams—at length I was wide awake; hastily dressing myself, I hurried to discover the cause of this disturbance, and to open my door to the unexpected visitor. Pale as the snow that showered about her, with clasped hands, Idris stood before me. "Save me!" she exclaimed, and would have sunk to the ground had I not supported her. In a moment however she revived, and, with energy, almost with violence, entreated me to saddle horses, to take her away, away to London—to her brother—at least to save her. I had no horses—she wrung her hands. "What can I do?" she cried, "I am lost—we are both for ever lost! But come—come with me, Lionel; here I must not stay,—we can get a chaise at the nearest post-house; yet perhaps we have time! come, O come with me to save and protect me!"

When I heard her piteous demands, while with disordered dress, dishevelled hair, and aghast looks, she wrung her hands—the idea shot across me—is she also mad?—"Sweet one," and I folded her to my heart, "better repose than wander further;—rest—my beloved, I will make a fire—you are chill."

"Rest!" she cried, "repose! you rave, Lionel! If you delay we are lost; come, I pray you, unless you would cast me off for ever."

That Idris, the princely born, nursling of wealth and luxury, should have come through the tempestuous winter-night from her regal abode, and standing at my lowly door, conjure me to fly with her through darkness and storm—was surely a dream—again her plaintive tones, the sight of her loveliness assured me that it was no vision. Looking timidly around, as if she feared to be overheard, she whispered: "I have discovered—to-morrow—that is, to-day—already the to-morrow is come—before dawn, foreigners, Austrians, my mother's hirelings, are to carry me off to Germany, to prison, to marriage—to anything, except you and my brother—take me away, or soon they will be here!"

I was frightened by her vehemence, and imagined some mistake in her incoherent tale; but I no longer hesitated to obey her. She had come by herself from the Castle, three long miles, at midnight, through the heavy snow; we must reach Englefield Green, a mile and a half further, before we could obtain a chaise. She told me, that she had kept up her strength and courage till her arrival at my cottage, and then both failed. Now she could hardly walk. Supporting her as I did, still she lagged: and at the distance of half a mile, after many stoppages, shivering fits, and half faintings, she slipt from my supporting arm on the snow, and with a torrent of tears averred that she must be taken, for that she could not proceed. I lifted her up in my arms; her light form rested on my breast.—I felt no burthen, except the internal one of contrary and contending emotions. Brimming delight now invested me. Again her chill limbs touched me as a torpedo; and I shuddered in sympathy with her pain and fright. Her head lay on my shoulder, her breath waved my hair, her heart beat near mine, transport made me tremble, blinded me, annihilated me—till a suppressed groan, bursting from her lips, the chattering of her teeth, which she strove vainly to subdue, and all the signs of suffering she evinced, recalled me to the necessity of speed and succour. At last I said to her, "There is Englefield Green; there the inn. But, if you are seen thus strangely circumstanced, dear Idris, even now your enemies may learn your flight too soon: were it not better that I hired the chaise alone? I will put you in safety meanwhile, and return to you immediately."

She answered that I was right, and might do with her as I pleased. I observed the door of a small out-house a-jar. I pushed it open; and, with some hay strewed about, I formed a couch for her, placing her exhausted frame on it, and covering her with my cloak. I feared to leave her, she looked so wan and faint—but in a moment she re-acquired animation, and, with that, fear; and again she implored me not to delay. To call up the people of the inn, and obtain a conveyance and horses, even though I harnessed them myself, was the work of many minutes; minutes, each freighted with the weight of ages. I caused the chaise to advance a little, waited till the people of the inn had retired, and then made the post-boy draw up the carriage to the spot where Idris, impatient, and now somewhat recovered, stood waiting for me. I lifted her into the chaise; I assured her that with our four horses we should arrive in London before five o'clock, the hour when she would be sought and missed. I besought her to calm herself; a kindly shower of tears relieved her, and by degrees she related her tale of fear and peril.

That same night after Adrian's departure, her mother had warmly expostulated with her on the subject of her attachment to me. Every motive, every threat, every angry taunt was urged in vain. She seemed to consider that through me she had lost Raymond; I was the evil influence of her life; I was even accused of encreasing and confirming the mad and base apostacy of Adrian from all views of advancement and grandeur; and now this miserable mountaineer was to steal her daughter. Never, Idris related, did the angry lady deign to recur to gentleness and persuasion; if she had, the task of resistance would have been exquisitely painful. As it was, the sweet girl's generous nature was roused to defend, and ally herself with, my despised cause. Her mother ended with a look of contempt and covert triumph, which for a moment awakened the suspicions of Idris. When they parted for the night, the Countess said, "To-morrow I trust your tone will be changed: be composed; I have agitated you; go to rest; and I will send you a medicine I always take when unduly restless—it will give you a quiet night."

By the time that she had with uneasy thoughts laid her fair cheek upon her pillow, her mother's servant brought a draught; a suspicion again crossed her at this novel proceeding, sufficiently alarming to determine her not to take the potion; but dislike of contention, and a wish to discover whether there was any just foundation for her conjectures, made her, she said, almost instinctively, and in contradiction to her usual frankness, pretend to swallow the medicine. Then, agitated as she had been by her mother's violence, and now by unaccustomed fears, she lay unable to sleep, starting at every sound. Soon her door opened softly, and on her springing up, she heard a whisper, "Not asleep yet," and the door again closed. With a beating heart she expected another visit, and when after an interval her chamber was again invaded, having first assured herself that the intruders were her mother and an attendant, she composed herself to feigned sleep. A step approached her bed, she dared not move, she strove to calm her palpitations, which became more violent, when she heard her mother say mutteringly, "Pretty simpleton, little do you think that your game is already at an end for ever."

For a moment the poor girl fancied that her mother believed that she had drank poison: she was on the point of springing up; when the Countess, already at a distance from the bed, spoke in a low voice to her companion, and again Idris listened: "Hasten," said she, "there is no time to lose—it is long past eleven; they will be here at five; take merely the clothes necessary for her journey, and her jewel-casket." The servant obeyed; few words were spoken on either side; but those were caught at with avidity by the intended victim. She heard the name of her own maid mentioned;—"No, no," replied her mother, "she does not go with us; Lady Idris must forget England, and all belonging to it." And again she heard, "She will not wake till late to-morrow, and we shall then be at sea."—"All is ready," at length the woman announced. The Countess again came to her daughter's bed-side: "In Austria at least," she said, "you will obey. In Austria, where obedience can be enforced, and no choice left but between an honourable prison and a fitting marriage."

Both then withdrew; though, as she went, the Countess said, "Softly; all sleep; though all have not been prepared for sleep, like her. I would not have any one suspect, or she might be roused to resistance, and per-haps escape. Come with me to my room; we will remain there till the hour agreed upon." They went. Idris, panic-struck, but animated and strength-ened even by her excessive fear, dressed herself hurriedly, and going down a flight of back-stairs, avoiding the vicinity of her mother's apart-ment, she contrived to escape from the castle by a low window, and came through snow, wind, and obscurity to my cottage; nor lost her courage, until she arrived, and, depositing her fate in my hands, gave herself up to the desperation and weariness that overwhelmed her.

I comforted her as well as I might. Joy and exultation, were mine, to possess, and to save her. Yet not to excite fresh agitation in her, *"per non turbar quel bel viso sereno,"*[74] I curbed my delight. I strove to quiet the eager dancing of my heart; I turned from her my eyes, beaming with too much tenderness, and proudly, to dark night, and the inclement atmos-phere, murmured the expressions of my transport. We reached London, methought, all too soon; and yet I could not regret our speedy arrival, when I witnessed the extasy with which my beloved girl found herself in her brother's arms, safe from every evil, under his unblamed protection.

Adrian wrote a brief note to his mother, informing her that Idris was under his care and guardianship. Several days elapsed, and at last an

74 Petrarch, Sonnet 236: "so as not to darken her clear face." The poet says he can no longer control his desire even in the face of displeasure: "you have taken the reins from my hand, and my despairing soul has acquired boldness" (*Petrarch's Lyric Poems*, trans. Robert M. Durling).

answer came, dated from Cologne. "It was useless," the haughty and disappointed lady wrote, "for the Earl of Windsor and his sister to address again the injured parent, whose only expectation of tranquillity must be derived from oblivion of their existence. Her desires had been blasted, her schemes overthrown. She did not complain; in her brother's court she would find, not compensation for their disobedience (filial unkindness admitted of none), but such a state of things and mode of life, as might best reconcile her to her fate. Under such circumstances, she positively declined any communication with them."

Such were the strange and incredible events, that finally brought about my union with the sister of my best friend, with my adored Idris. With simplicity and courage she set aside the prejudices and opposition which were obstacles to my happiness, nor scrupled to give her hand, where she had given her heart. To be worthy of her, to raise myself to her height through the exertion of talents and virtue, to repay her love with devoted, unwearied tenderness, were the only thanks I could offer for the matchless gift.

CHAPTER VII

AND now let the reader, passing over some short period of time, be introduced to our happy circle. Adrian, Idris and I, were established in Windsor Castle; Lord Raymond and my sister, inhabited a house which the former had built on the borders of the Great Park, near Perdita's cottage, as was still named the low-roofed abode, where we two, poor even in hope, had each received the assurance of our felicity. We had our separate occupations and our common amusements. Sometimes we passed whole days under the leafy covert of the forest with our books and music. This occurred during those rare days in this country, when the sun mounts his etherial throne in unclouded majesty, and the windless atmosphere is as a bath of pellucid and grateful water, wrapping the senses in tranquillity. When the clouds veiled the sky, and the wind scattered them there and here, rending their woof, and strewing its fragments through the aërial plains—then we rode out, and sought new spots of beauty and repose. When the frequent rains shut us within doors, evening recreation followed morning study, ushered in by music and song. Idris had a natural musical talent; and her voice, which had been carefully cultivated, was full and sweet. Raymond and I made a part of the concert, and Adrian and Perdita were devout listeners. Then we were as gay as summer insects, playful as children; we ever met one another with smiles, and read content and joy in each other's countenances. Our prime festivals were held in Perdita's cottage; nor were we ever weary of talking of the past or dreaming of the future. Jealousy and disquiet were unknown among us; nor did a fear or hope of change ever disturb our tranquillity. Others said, We might be happy—we said—We are.

When any separation took place between us, it generally so happened, that Idris and Perdita would ramble away together, and we remained to discuss the affairs of nations, and the philosophy of life. The very difference of our dispositions gave zest to these conversations. Adrian had the superiority in learning and eloquence; but Raymond possessed a quick penetration, and a practical knowledge of life, which usually displayed itself in opposition to Adrian, and thus kept up the ball of discussion. At other times we made excursions of many days' duration, and crossed the country to visit any spot noted for beauty or historical association. Sometimes we went up to London, and entered into the amusements of the busy throng; sometimes our retreat was invaded by visitors from among them. This change made us only the more sensible to the delights of the intimate intercourse of our own circle, the tranquillity of our divine forest, and our happy evenings in the halls of our beloved Castle.

The disposition of Idris was peculiarly frank, soft, and affectionate. Her temper was unalterably sweet; and although firm and resolute on any point that touched her heart, she was yielding to those she loved. The nature of Perdita was less perfect; but tenderness and happiness improved her temper, and softened her natural reserve. Her understanding was clear and comprehensive, her imagination vivid; she was sincere, generous, and reasonable. Adrian, the matchless brother of my soul, the sensitive and excellent Adrian, loving all, and beloved by all, yet seemed destined not to find the half of himself, which was to complete his happiness. He often left us, and wandered by himself in the woods, or sailed in his little skiff, his books his only companions. He was often the gayest of our party, at the same time that he was the only one visited by fits of despondency; his slender frame seemed overcharged with the weight of life, and his soul appeared rather to inhabit his body than unite with it. I was hardly more devoted to my Idris than to her brother, and she loved him as her teacher, her friend, the benefactor who had secured to her the fulfilment of her dearest wishes. Raymond, the ambitious, restless Raymond, reposed midway on the great high-road of life, and was content to give up all his schemes of sovereignty and fame, to make one of us, the flowers of the field. His kingdom was the heart of Perdita, his subjects her thoughts; by her he was loved, respected as a superior being, obeyed, waited on. No office, no devotion, no watching was irksome to her, as it regarded him. She would sit apart from us and watch him; she would weep for joy to think that he was hers. She erected a temple for him in the depth of her being, and each faculty was a priestess vowed to his service. Sometimes she might be wayward and capricious; but her repentance was bitter, her return entire, and even this inequality of temper suited him who was not formed by nature to float idly down the stream of life.

During the first year of their marriage, Perdita presented Raymond with a lovely girl. It was curious to trace in this miniature model the very traits of its father. The same half-disdainful lips and smile of triumph, the same intelligent eyes, the same brow and chestnut hair; her very hands and taper fingers resembled his. How very dear she was to Perdita! In progress of time, I also became a father, and our little darlings, our playthings and delights, called forth a thousand new and delicious feelings. Years passed thus,—even years. Each month brought forth its successor, each year one like to that gone by; truly, our lives were a living comment on that beautiful sentiment of Plutarch, that "our souls have a natural inclination to love, being born as much to love, as to feel, to reason, to understand and remember."[75] We talked of change and active pursuits, but still remained at Windsor, incapable of violating the charm that attached us to our secluded life.

> Pareamo aver qui tutto il ben raccolto
> Che fra mortali in più parte si rimembra.[76]

Now also that our children gave us occupation, we found excuses for our idleness, in the idea of bringing them up to a more splendid career. At length our tranquillity was disturbed, and the course of events, which for five years had flowed on in hushing tranquillity, was broken by breakers and obstacles, that woke us from our pleasant dream.

A new Lord Protector[77] of England was to be chosen; and, at Raymond's request, we removed to London, to witness, and even take a part in the election. If Raymond had been united to Idris, this post had been his stepping-stone to higher dignity; and his desire for power and fame had been crowned with fullest measure. He had exchanged a sceptre for a lute, a kingdom for Perdita.

Did he think of this as we journeyed up to town? I watched him, but could make but little of him. He was particularly gay, playing with his child, and turning to sport every word that was uttered. Perhaps he did this because he saw a cloud upon Perdita's brow. She tried to rouse herself, but her eyes every now and then filled with tears, and she looked wistfully on Raymond and her girl, as if fearful that some evil would betide them. And so she felt. A presentiment of ill hung over her. She leaned from the window looking on the forest, and the turrets of the Castle, and as these became hid by intervening objects, she passionately

---

75 Source unidentified: the passage appears not to be from Plutarch's *Dialogue on Love*.

76 Ariosto, *Orlando Furioso* 6.47.2-3: " 'The sum of all delights it seemed to be, / Such as no lovers in this world enjoy' " (trans. Barbara Reynolds). The second line should read, "che fra i mortali in più parti si smembra."

77 The title conferred on Oliver Cromwell when he took over the British government in 1653, Lord Protector could indicate republican principles or be a merely nominal substitute for "king"; William Godwin, *History of the Commonwealth*, argues that Cromwell abandoned his republican principles when he became Lord Protector (3: 598-99).

exclaimed—"Scenes of happiness! scenes sacred to devoted love, when shall I see you again! and when I see ye, shall I be still the beloved and joyous Perdita, or shall I, heart-broken and lost, wander among your groves, the ghost of what I am!"

"Why, silly one," cried Raymond, "what is your little head pondering upon, that of a sudden you have become so sublimely dismal? Cheer up, or I shall make you over to Idris, and call Adrian into the carriage, who, I see by his gesture, sympathizes with my good spirits."

Adrian was on horseback; he rode up to the carriage, and his gaiety, in addition to that of Raymond, dispelled my sister's melancholy. We entered London in the evening, and went to our several abodes near Hyde Park.

The following morning Lord Raymond visited me early. "I come to you," he said, "only half assured that you will assist me in my project, but resolved to go through with it, whether you concur with me or not. Promise me secrecy however; for if you will not contribute to my success, at least you must not baffle me."

"Well I promise. And now—"

"And now, my dear fellow, for what are we come to London? To be present at the election of a Protector, and to give our yea or nay for his shuffling Grace of —? or for that noisy Ryland? Do you believe, Verney, that I brought you to town for that? No, we will have a Protector of our own. We will set up a candidate, and ensure his success. We will nominate Adrian, and do our best to bestow on him the power to which he is entitled by his birth, and which he merits through his virtues.

"Do not answer; I know all your objections, and will reply to them in order. First, Whether he will or will not consent to become a great man? Leave the task of persuasion on that point to me; I do not ask you to assist me there. Secondly, Whether he ought to exchange his employment of plucking blackberries, and nursing wounded partridges in the forest, for the command of a nation? My dear Lionel, *we* are married men, and find employment sufficient in amusing our wives, and dancing our children. But Adrian is alone, wifeless, childless, unoccupied. I have long observed him. He pines for want of some interest in life. His heart, exhausted by his early sufferings, reposes like a new-healed limb, and shrinks from all excitement. But his understanding, his charity, his virtues, want a field for exercise and display; and we will procure it for him. Besides, is it not a shame, that the genius of Adrian should fade from the earth like a flower in an untrod mountain-path, fruitless? Do you think Nature composed his surpassing machine for no purpose? Believe me, he was destined to be the author of infinite good to his native England. Has she not bestowed on him every gift in prodigality?—birth, wealth, talent, goodness? Does not every one love and admire him? and does he not delight singly in such efforts as manifest his love to all? Come, I see that you are already persuaded, and will second me when I propose him to-night in parliament."

"You have got up all your arguments in excellent order," I replied; "and, if Adrian consent, they are unanswerable. One only condition I would make,—that you do nothing without his concurrence."

"I believe you are in the right," said Raymond; "although I had thought at first to arrange the affair differently. Be it so. I will go instantly to Adrian; and, if he inclines to consent, you will not destroy my labour by persuading him to return, and turn squirrel again in Windsor Forest. Idris, you will not act the traitor towards me?"

"Trust me," replied she, "I will preserve a strict neutrality."

"For my part," said I, "I am too well convinced of the worth of our friend, and the rich harvest of benefits that all England would reap from his Protectorship, to deprive my countrymen of such a blessing, if he consent to bestow it on them."

In the evening Adrian visited us.—"Do you cabal also against me," said he, laughing; "and will you make common cause with Raymond, in dragging a poor visionary from the clouds to surround him with the fire-works and blasts of earthly grandeur, instead of heavenly rays and airs? I thought you knew me better."

"I do know you better," I replied, "than to think that you would be happy in such a situation; but the good you would do to others may be an inducement, since the time is probably arrived when you can put your theories into practice, and you may bring about such reformation and change, as will conduce to that perfect system of government which you delight to portray."

"You speak of an almost-forgotten dream," said Adrian, his countenance slightly clouding as he spoke; "the visions of my boyhood have long since faded in the light of reality; I know now that I am not a man fitted to govern nations; sufficient for me, if I keep in wholesome rule the little kingdom of my own mortality.

"But do not you see, Lionel, the drift of our noble friend; a drift, perhaps, unknown to himself, but apparent to me. Lord Raymond was never born to be a drone in the hive, and to find content in our pastoral life. He thinks, that he ought to be satisfied; he imagines, that his present situation precludes the possibility of aggrandisement; he does not therefore, even in his own heart, plan change for himself. But do you not see, that, under the idea of exalting me, he is chalking out a new path for himself; a path of action from which he has long wandered?

"Let us assist him. He, the noble, the war-like, the great in every quality that can adorn the mind and person of man; he is fitted to be the Protector of England. If *I*—that is, if *we* propose him, he will assuredly be elected, and will find, in the functions of that high office, scope for the towering powers of his mind. Even Perdita will rejoice. Perdita, in whom ambition was a covered fire until she married Raymond, which event was for a time the fulfilment of her hopes; Perdita will rejoice in the glory and advancement of her lord—and, coyly and prettily, not be discontented with her share. In the mean time, we, the wise of the land, will return to our Castle, and, Cincinnatus-like,[78] take to our usual labours, until our friend shall require our presence and assistance here."

The more Adrian reasoned upon this scheme, the more feasible it appeared. His own determination never to enter into public life was insurmountable, and the delicacy of his health was a sufficient argument against it. The next step was to induce Raymond to confess his secret wishes for dignity and fame. He entered while we were speaking. The way in which Adrian had received his project for setting him up as a candidate for the Protectorship, and his replies, had already awakened in his mind, the view of the subject which we were now discussing. His countenance and manner betrayed irresolution and anxiety; but the anxiety arose from a fear that we should not prosecute, or not succeed in our idea; and his irresolution, from a doubt whether we should risk a defeat. A few words from us decided him, and hope and joy sparkled in his eyes; the idea of embarking in a career, so congenial to his early habits and cherished wishes, made him as before energetic and bold. We discussed his chances, the merits of the other candidates, and the dispositions of the voters.

After all we miscalculated. Raymond had lost much of his popularity, and was deserted by his peculiar partizans. Absence from the busy stage had caused him to be forgotten by the people; his former parliamentary supporters were principally composed of royalists, who had been willing to make an idol of him when he appeared as the heir of the Earldom of Windsor; but who were indifferent to him, when he came forward with no other attributes and distinctions than they conceived to be common to many among themselves. Still he had many friends, admirers of his transcendent talents; his presence in the house, his eloquence, address and imposing beauty, were calculated to produce an electric effect. Adrian also, notwithstanding his recluse habits and theories, so adverse to the spirit of party, had many friends, and they were easily induced to vote for a candidate of his selection.

The Duke of —, and Mr. Ryland, Lord Raymond's old antagonist, were the other candidates. The Duke was supported by all the aristocrats of the republic, who considered him their proper representative. Ryland was the popular candidate; when Lord Raymond was first added to the list, his chance of success appeared small. We retired from the debate which had followed on his nomination: we, his nominators, mortified; he dispirited to excess. Perdita reproached us bitterly. Her expectations had been strongly excited; she had urged nothing against our project, on the contrary, she was evidently pleased by it; but its evident ill success changed the current of her ideas. She felt, that, once awakened, Raymond would never return unrepining to Windsor. His habits were

---

78   A model of republican ideals, Cincinnatus left the plough in 458 BC to lead
     the Roman army, returning to obscurity when his public duty was done.

unhinged; his restless mind roused from its sleep, ambition must now be his companion through life; and if he did not succeed in his present attempt, she foresaw that unhappiness and cureless discontent would follow. Perhaps her own disappointment added a sting to her thoughts and words; she did not spare us, and our own reflections added to our disquietude.

It was necessary to follow up our nomination, and to persuade Raymond to present himself to the electors on the following evening. For a long time he was obstinate. He would embark in a balloon; he would sail for a distant quarter of the world, where his name and humiliation were unknown. But this was useless; his attempt was registered; his purpose published to the world; his shame could never be erased from the memories of men. It was as well to fail at last after a struggle, as to fly now at the beginning of his enterprise.

From the moment that he adopted this idea, he was changed. His depression and anxiety fled; he became all life and activity. The smile of triumph shone on his countenance; determined to pursue his object to the uttermost, his manner and expression seem ominous of the accomplishment of his wishes. Not so Perdita. She was frightened by his gaiety, for she dreaded a greater revulsion at the end. If his appearance even inspired us with hope, it only rendered the state of her mind more painful. She feared to lose sight of him; yet she dreaded to remark any change in the temper of his mind. She listened eagerly to him, yet tantalized herself by giving to his words a meaning foreign to their true interpretation, and adverse to her hopes. She dared not be present at the contest; yet she remained at home a prey to double solicitude. She wept over her little girl; she looked, she spoke, as if she dreaded the occurrence of some frightful calamity. She was half mad from the effects of uncontrollable agitation.

Lord Raymond presented himself to the house with fearless confidence and insinuating address. After the Duke of — and Mr. Ryland had finished their speeches, he commenced. Assuredly he had not conned his lesson; and at first he hesitated, pausing in his ideas, and in the choice of his expressions. By degrees he warmed; his words flowed with ease, his language was full of vigour, and his voice of persuasion. He reverted to his past life, his successes in Greece, his favour at home. Why should he lose this, now that added years, prudence, and the pledge which his marriage gave to his country, ought to encrease, rather than diminish his claims to confidence? He spoke of the state of England; the necessary measures to be taken to ensure its security, and confirm its prosperity. He drew a glowing picture of its present situation. As he spoke, every sound was hushed, every thought suspended by intense attention. His graceful elocution enchained the senses of his hearers. In some degree also he was fitted to reconcile all parties. His birth pleased the aristocracy; his being the candidate recommended by Adrian, a man intimately allied to the popular party, caused a number, who had no great reliance either on the Duke or Mr. Ryland, to range on his side.

The contest was keen and doubtful. Neither Adrian nor myself would have been so anxious, if our own success had depended on our exertions; but we had egged our friend on to the enterprise, and it became us to ensure his triumph. Idris, who entertained the highest opinion of his abilities, was warmly interested in the event: and my poor sister, who dared not hope, and to whom fear was misery, was plunged into a fever of disquietude.

Day after day passed while we discussed our projects for the evening, and each night was occupied by debates which offered no conclusion. At last the crisis came: the night when parliament, which had so long delayed its choice, must decide: as the hour of twelve passed, and the new day began, it was by virtue of the constitution dissolved, its power extinct.

We assembled at Raymond's house, we and our partizans. At half past five o'clock we proceeded to the House. Idris endeavoured to calm Perdita; but the poor girl's agitation deprived her of all power of self-command. She walked up and down the room,—gazed wildly when any one entered, fancying that they might be the announcers of her doom. I must do justice to my sweet sister: it was not for herself that she was thus agonized. She alone knew the weight which Raymond attached to his success. Even to us he assumed gaiety and hope, and assumed them so well, that we did not divine the secret workings of his mind. Sometimes a nervous trembling, a sharp dissonance of voice, and momentary fits of absence revealed to Perdita the violence he did himself; but we, intent on our plans, observed only his ready laugh, his joke intruded on all occasions, the flow of his spirits which seemed incapable of ebb. Besides, Perdita was with him in his retirement; she saw the moodiness that succeeded to this forced hilarity; she marked his disturbed sleep, his painful irritability—once she had seen his tears—hers had scarce ceased to flow, since she had beheld the big drops which disappointed pride had caused to gather in his eye, but which pride was unable to dispel. What wonder then, that her feelings were wrought to this pitch! I thus accounted to myself for her agitation; but this was not all, and the sequel revealed another excuse.

One moment we seized before our departure, to take leave of our beloved girls. I had small hope of success, and entreated Idris to watch over my sister. As I approached the latter, she seized my hand, and drew me into another apartment; she threw herself into my arms, and wept and sobbed bitterly and long. I tried to soothe her; I bade her hope; I asked what tremendous consequences would ensue even on our failure. "My brother," she cried, "protector of my childhood, dear, most dear Lionel, my fate hangs by a thread. I have you all about me now—you, the companion of my infancy; Adrian, as dear to me as if bound by the ties of blood; Idris, the sister of my heart, and her lovely offspring. This, O this may be the last time that you will surround me thus!"

Abruptly she stopped, and then cried: "What have I said?—foolish false girl that I am!" She looked wildly on me, and then suddenly calming herself, apologized for what she called her unmeaning words, saying that she must indeed be insane, for, while Raymond lived, she must be happy; and then, though she still wept, she suffered me tranquilly to depart. Raymond only took her hand when he went, and looked on her expressively; she answered by a look of intelligence and assent.

Poor girl! what she then suffered! I could never entirely forgive Raymond for the trials he imposed on her, occasioned as they were by a selfish feeling on his part. He had schemed, if he failed in his present attempt, without taking leave of any of us, to embark for Greece, and never again to revisit England. Perdita acceded to his wishes; for his contentment was the chief object of her life, the crown of her enjoyment; but to leave us all, her companions, the beloved partners of her happiest years, and in the interim to conceal this frightful determination, was a task that almost conquered her strength of mind. She had been employed in arranging for their departure; she had promised Raymond during this decisive evening, to take advantage of our absence, to go one stage of the journey, and he, after his defeat was ascertained, would slip away from us, and join her.

Although, when I was informed of this scheme, I was bitterly offended by the small attention which Raymond paid to my sister's feelings, I was led by reflection to consider, that he acted under the force of such strong excitement, as to take from him the consciousness, and, consequently, the guilt of a fault. If he had permitted us to witness his agitation, he would have been more under the guidance of reason; but his struggles for the shew of composure, acted with such violence on his nerves, as to destroy his power of self-command. I am convinced that, at the worst, he would have returned from the sea-shore to take leave of us, and to make us the partners of his council. But the task imposed on Perdita was not the less painful. He had extorted from her a vow of secrecy; and her part of the drama, since it was to be performed alone, was the most agonizing that could be devised. But to return to my narrative.

The debates had hitherto been long and loud; they had often been protracted merely for the sake of delay. But now each seemed fearful lest the fatal moment should pass, while the choice was yet undecided. Unwonted silence reigned in the house, the members spoke in whispers, and the ordinary business was transacted with celerity and quietness. During the first stage of the election, the Duke of — had been thrown out; the question therefore lay between Lord Raymond and Mr. Ryland. The latter had felt secure of victory, until the appearance of Raymond; and, since his name had been inserted as a candidate, he had canvassed with eagerness. He had appeared each evening, impatience and anger marked in his looks, scowling on us from the opposite side of St. Stephen's,[79] as if his mere frown would cast eclipse on our hopes.

Every thing in the English constitution had been regulated for the better preservation of peace. On the last day, two candidates only were allowed to remain; and to obviate, if possible, the last struggle between these, a bribe was offered to him who should voluntarily resign his pretensions; a place of great emolument and honour was given him, and his success facilitated at a future election. Strange to say however, no instance had yet occurred, where either candidate had had recourse to this expedient; in consequence the law had become obsolete, nor had been referred to by any of us in our discussions. To our extreme surprise, when it was moved that we should resolve ourselves into a committee for the election of the Lord Protector, the member who had nominated Ryland, rose and informed us that this candidate had resigned his pretensions. His information was at first received with silence; a confused murmur succeeded; and, when the chairman declared Lord Raymond duly chosen, it amounted to a shout of applause and victory. It seemed as if, far from any dread of defeat even if Mr. Ryland had not resigned, every voice would have been united in favour of our candidate. In fact, now that the idea of contest was dismissed, all hearts returned to their former respect and admiration of our accomplished friend. Each felt, that England had never seen a Protector so capable of fulfilling the arduous duties of that high office. One voice made of many voices, resounded through the chamber; it syllabled the name of Raymond.

He entered. I was on one of the highest seats, and saw him walk up the passage to the table of the speaker. The native modesty of his disposition conquered the joy of his triumph. He looked round timidly; a mist seemed before his eyes. Adrian, who was beside me, hastened to him, and jumping down the benches, was at his side in a moment. His appearance re-animated our friend; and, when he came to speak and act, his hesitation vanished, and he shone out supreme in majesty and victory. The former Protector tendered him the oaths, and presented him with the insignia of office, performing the ceremonies of installation. The house then dissolved. The chief members of the state crowded round the new magistrate, and conducted him to the palace of government. Adrian suddenly vanished; and, by the time that Raymond's supporters were reduced to our intimate friends merely, returned leading Idris to congratulate her friend on his success.

But where was Perdita? In securing solicitously an unobserved retreat

---

79   St. Stephen's is the meeting-hall of the House of Commons. Doing research
      for *The Last Man*, MWS wrote to John Cam Hobhouse (19 February 1825), "I
      hear that there is a place, over the roof of St. Stephens where you senators
      permit us to hear, not seen. Could you introduce me to this enviable post?"
      (*Letters* 1: 466).

in case of failure, Raymond had forgotten to arrange the mode by which she was to hear of his success; and she had been too much agitated to revert to this circumstance. When Idris entered, so far had Raymond forgotten himself, that he asked for my sister; one word, which told of her mysterious disappearance, recalled him. Adrian it is true had already gone to seek the fugitive, imagining that her tameless anxiety had led her to the purlieus of the House, and that some sinister event detained her. But Raymond, without explaining himself, suddenly quitted us, and in another moment we heard him gallop down the street, in spite of the wind and rain that scattered tempest over the earth. We did not know how far he had to go, and soon separated, supposing that in a short time he would return to the palace with Perdita, and that they would not be sorry to find themselves alone.

Perdita had arrived with her child at Darford,[80] weeping and inconsolable. She directed every thing to be prepared for the continuance of their journey, and placing her lovely sleeping charge on a bed, passed several hours in acute suffering. Sometimes she observed the war of elements, thinking that they also declared against her, and listened to the pattering of the rain in gloomy despair. Sometimes she hung over her child, tracing her resemblance to the father, and fearful lest in after life she should display the same passions and uncontrollable impulses, that rendered him unhappy. Again, with a gush of pride and delight, she marked in the features of her little girl, the same smile of beauty that often irradiated Raymond's countenance. The sight of it soothed her. She thought of the treasure she possessed in the affections of her lord; of his accomplishments, surpassing those of his contemporaries, his genius, his devotion to her.—Soon she thought, that all she possessed in the world, except him, might well be spared, nay, given with delight, a propitiatory offering, to secure the supreme good she retained in him. Soon she imagined, that fate demanded this sacrifice from her, as a mark she was devoted to Raymond, and that it must be made with cheerfulness. She figured to herself their life in the Greek isle he had selected for their retreat; her task of soothing him; her cares for the beauteous Clara,[81] her rides in his company, her dedication of herself to his consolation. The picture then presented itself to her in such glowing colours, that she feared the reverse, and a life of magnificence and power in London; where Raymond would no longer be hers only, nor she the sole source of happiness to him. So far as she merely was concerned, she began to hope for defeat; and it

---

80   Darford is probably an error for Dartford, south of the Thames east of
      London. See also 277, below.
81   Clara, meaning "bright," "shining," or even "illustrious," was the name of the
      Shelleys' infant daughter (who died at Venice in 1818), of MWS's stepsister,
      Clara Mary Jane Clairmont (who called herself Claire), and of Claire's daughter by Byron, Clara Allegra.

was only on his account that her feelings vacillated, as she heard him gallop into the court-yard of the inn. That he should come to her alone, wetted by the storm, careless of every thing except speed, what else could it mean, than that, vanquished and solitary, they were to take their way from native England, the scene of shame, and hide themselves in the myrtle groves of the Grecian isles?

In a moment she was in his arms. The knowledge of his success had become so much a part of himself, that he forgot that it was necessary to impart it to his companion. She only felt in his embrace a dear assurance that while he possessed her, he would not despair. "This is kind," she cried; "this is noble, my own beloved! O fear not disgrace or lowly fortune, while you have your Perdita; fear not sorrow, while our child lives and smiles. Let us go even where you will; the love that accompanies us will prevent our regrets."

Locked in his embrace, she spoke thus, and cast back her head, seeking an assent to her words in his eyes—they were sparkling with ineffable delight. "Why, my little Lady Protectress," said he, playfully, "what is this you say? And what pretty scheme have you woven of exile and obscurity, while a brighter web, a gold-enwoven tissue, is that which, in truth, you ought to contemplate?"

He kissed her brow—but the wayward girl, half sorry at his triumph, agitated by swift change of thought, hid her face in his bosom and wept. He comforted her; he instilled into her his own hopes and desires; and soon her countenance beamed with sympathy. How very happy were they that night! How full even to bursting was their sense of joy!

CHAPTER VIII

HAVING seen our friend properly installed in his new office, we turned our eyes towards Windsor. The nearness of this place to London was such, as to take away the idea of painful separation, when we quitted Raymond and Perdita. We took leave of them in the Protectoral Palace. It was pretty enough to see my sister enter as it were into the spirit of the drama, and endeavour to fill her station with becoming dignity. Her internal pride and humility of manner were now more than ever at war. Her timidity was not artificial, but arose from that fear of not being properly appreciated, that slight estimation of the neglect of the world, which also characterized Raymond. But then Perdita thought more constantly of others than he; and part of her bashfulness arose from a wish to take from those around her a sense of inferiority; a feeling which never crossed her mind. From the circumstances of her birth and education, Idris would have been better fitted for the formulæ of ceremony; but the very ease which accompanied such actions with her, arising from habit, rendered them tedious; while, with every drawback, Perdita evidently enjoyed her situation. She was too full of new ideas to feel much pain when we departed; she took an affectionate leave of us, and promised to visit us soon; but she did not regret the circumstances that caused our separation. The spirits of Raymond were unbounded; he did not know what to do with his new got power; his head was full of plans; he had as yet decided on none—but he promised himself, his friends, and the world, that the æra of his Protectorship should be signalized by some act of surpassing glory.

Thus, we talked of them, and moralized, as with diminished numbers we returned to Windsor Castle. We felt extreme delight at our escape from political turmoil, and sought our solitude with redoubled zest. We did not want for occupation; but my eager disposition was now turned to the field of intellectual exertion only; and hard study I found to be an excellent medicine to allay a fever of spirit with which in indolence, I should doubtless have been assailed. Perdita had permitted us to take Clara back with us to Windsor; and she and my two lovely infants were perpetual sources of interest and amusement.

The only circumstance that disturbed our peace, was the health of Adrian. It evidently declined, without any symptom which could lead us to suspect his disease, unless indeed his brightened eyes, animated look, and flustering cheeks, made us dread consumption; but he was without pain or fear. He betook himself to books with ardour, and reposed from study in the society he best loved, that of his sister and myself. Sometimes he went up to London to visit Raymond, and watch the progress of events. Clara often accompanied him in these excursions; partly that she might see her parents, partly because Adrian delighted in the prattle, and intelligent looks of this lovely child.

Meanwhile all went on well in London. The new elections were finished; parliament met, and Raymond was occupied in a thousand beneficial schemes. Canals, aqueducts, bridges, stately buildings, and various edifices for public utility, were entered upon; he was continually surrounded by projectors and projects,[82] which were to render England one scene of fertility and magnificence; the state of poverty was to be abolished; men were to be transported from place to place almost with the same facility as the Princes Houssain, Ali, and Ahmed, in the Arabian Nights.[83] The physical state of man would soon not yield to the beatitude of angels; disease was to be banished; labour lightened of its heaviest burden. Nor did this seem extravagant. The arts of life, and the discoveries of science had augmented in a ratio which left all calculation behind; food sprung up, so to say, spontaneously—machines existed to supply with facility every want of the population. An evil direction still survived;

---

82   The word "projector" may have negative, ironic connotations, implying a schemer, speculator, or charlatan.

83   The *Arabian Nights Entertainment* or *The Thousand and One Nights* is a collection of stories from Indian, Persian, and Arabic sources, translated into French by Antoine Galland between 1704 and 1717.

and men were not happy, not because they could not, but because they would not rouse themselves to vanquish self-raised obstacles. Raymond was to inspire them with his beneficial will, and the mechanism of society, once systematised according to faultless rules, would never again swerve into disorder. For these hopes he abandoned his long-cherished ambition of being enregistered in the annals of nations as a successful warrior; laying aside his sword, peace and its enduring glories became his aim—the title he coveted was that of the benefactor of his country.

Among other works of art in which he was engaged, he had projected the erection of a national gallery[84] for statues and pictures. He possessed many himself, which he designed to present to the Republic; and, as the edifice was to be the great ornament of his Protectorship, he was very fastidious in his choice of the plan on which it would be built. Hundreds were brought to him and rejected. He sent even to Italy and Greece for drawings; but, as the design was to be characterized by originality as well as by perfect beauty, his endeavours were for a time without avail. At length a drawing came, with an address where communications might be sent, and no artist's name affixed. The design was new and elegant, but faulty; so faulty, that although drawn with the hand and eye of taste, it was evidently the work of one who was not an architect. Raymond contemplated it with delight; the more he gazed, the more pleased he was; and yet the errors multiplied under inspection. He wrote to the address given, desiring to see the draughtsman, that such alterations might be made, as should be suggested in a consultation between him and the original conceiver.

A Greek came. A middle-aged man, with some intelligence of manner, but with so common-place a physiognomy, that Raymond could scarcely believe that he was the designer. He acknowledged that he was not an architect; but the idea of the building had struck him, though he had sent it without the smallest hope of its being accepted. He was a man of few words. Raymond questioned him; but his reserved answers soon made him turn from the man to the drawing. He pointed out the errors, and the alterations that he wished to be made; he offered the Greek a pencil that he might correct the sketch on the spot; this was refused by his visitor, who said that he perfectly understood, and would work at it at home. At length Raymond suffered him to depart.

The next day he returned. The design had been re-drawn; but many defects still remained, and several of the instructions given had been misunderstood. "Come," said Raymond, "I yielded to you yesterday, now comply with my request—take the pencil."

The Greek took it, but he handled it in no artist-like way; at length he

84   Founded in 1824, the National Gallery in London was not finished and officially opened until 1838. The competition for a design was won in 1831 by the Greek revival architect William Wilkins.

said: "I must confess to you, my Lord, that I did not make this drawing. It is impossible for you to see the real designer; your instructions must pass through me. Condescend therefore to have patience with my ignorance, and to explain your wishes to me; in time I am certain that you will be satisfied."

Raymond questioned vainly; the mysterious Greek would say no more. Would an architect be permitted to see the artist? This also was refused. Raymond repeated his instructions, and the visitor retired. Our friend resolved however not to be foiled in his wish. He suspected, that unaccustomed poverty was the cause of the mystery, and that the artist was unwilling to be seen in the garb and abode of want. Raymond was only the more excited by this consideration to discover him; impelled by the interest he took in obscure talent, he therefore ordered a person skilled in such matters, to follow the Greek the next time he came, and observe the house in which he should enter. His emissary obeyed, and brought the desired intelligence. He had traced the man to one of the most penurious streets in the metropolis. Raymond did not wonder, that, thus situated, the artist had shrunk from notice, but he did not for this alter his resolve.

On the same evening, he went alone to the house named to him. Poverty, dirt, and squalid misery characterized its appearance. Alas! thought Raymond, I have much to do before England becomes a Paradise. He knocked; the door was opened by a string from above—the broken, wretched staircase was immediately before him, but no person appeared; he knocked again, vainly—and then, impatient of further delay, he ascended the dark, creaking stairs. His main wish, more particularly now that he witnessed the abject dwelling of the artist, was to relieve one, possessed of talent, but depressed by want. He pictured to himself a youth, whose eyes sparkled with genius, whose person was attenuated by famine. He half feared to displease him; but he trusted that his generous kindness would be administered so delicately, as not to excite repulse. What human heart is shut to kindness? and though poverty, in its excess, might render the sufferer unapt to submit to the supposed degradation of a benefit, the zeal of the benefactor must at last relax him into thankfulness. These thoughts encouraged Raymond, as he stood at the door of the highest room of the house. After trying vainly to enter the other apartments, he perceived just within the threshold of this one, a pair of small Turkish slippers; the door was ajar, but all was silent within. It was probable that the inmate was absent, but secure that he had found the right person, our adventurous Protector was tempted to enter, to leave a purse on the table, and silently depart. In pursuance of this idea, he pushed open the door gently—but the room was inhabited.

Raymond had never visited the dwellings of want, and the scene that now presented itself struck him to the heart. The floor was sunk in many places; the walls ragged and bare—the ceiling weather-stained—a tattered bed stood in the corner; there were but two chairs in the room, and a rough broken table, on which was a light in a tin candlestick;—yet in the midst of such drear and heart sickening poverty, there was an air of order and cleanliness that surprised him. The thought was fleeting; for his attention was instantly drawn towards the inhabitant of this wretched abode. It was a female. She sat at the table; one small hand shaded her eyes from the candle; the other held a pencil; her looks were fixed on a drawing before her, which Raymond recognized as the design presented to him. Her whole appearance awakened his deepest interest. Her dark hair was braided and twined in thick knots like the head-dress of a Grecian statue; her garb was mean, but her attitude might have been selected as a model of grace. Raymond had a confused remembrance that he had seen such a form before; he walked across the room; she did not raise her eyes, merely asking in Romaic,[85] who is there? "A friend," replied Raymond in the same dialect. She looked up wondering, and he saw that it was Evadne Zaimi. Evadne, once the idol of Adrian's affections; and who, for the sake of her present visitor, had disdained the noble youth, and then, neglected by him she loved, with crushed hopes and a stinging sense of misery, had returned to her native Greece. What revolution of fortune could have brought her to England, and housed her thus?

Raymond recognized her; and his manner changed from polite benefi-cence to the warmest protestations of kindness and sympathy. The sight of her, in her present situation, passed like an arrow into his soul. He sat by her, he took her hand, and said a thousand things which breathed the deepest spirit of compassion and affection. Evadne did not answer; her large dark eyes were cast down, at length a tear glimmered on the lashes. "Thus," she cried, "kindness can do, what no want, no misery ever effect-ed; I weep." She shed indeed many tears; her head sunk unconsciously on the shoulder of Raymond; he held her hand: he kissed her sunken tear-stained cheek. He told her, that her sufferings were now over: no one possessed the art of consoling like Raymond; he did not reason or declaim, but his look shone with sympathy; he brought pleasant images before the sufferer; his caresses excited no distrust, for they arose purely from the feeling which leads a mother to kiss her wounded child; a desire to demonstrate in every possible way the truth of his feelings, and the keenness of his wish to pour balm into the lacerated mind of the unfortu-nate.

As Evadne regained her composure, his manner became even gay; he sported with the idea of her poverty. Something told him that it was not its real evils that lay heavily at her heart, but the debasement and disgrace attendant on it; as he talked, he divested it of these; sometimes speaking of her fortitude with energetic praise; then, alluding to her past state, he called her his Princess in disguise. He made her warm offers of service; she was too much occupied by more engrossing thoughts, either to accept

---

85   Modern Greek.

or reject them; at length he left her, making a promise to repeat his visit the next day. He returned home, full of mingled feelings, of pain excited by Evadne's wretchedness, and pleasure at the prospect of relieving it. Some motive for which he did not account, even to himself, prevented him from relating his adventure to Perdita.

The next day he threw such disguise over his person as a cloak afforded, and revisited Evadne. As he went, he bought a basket of costly fruits, such as were natives of her own country, and throwing over these various beautiful flowers, bore it himself to the miserable garret of his friend. "Behold," cried he, as he entered, "what bird's food I have brought for my sparrow on the house-top."

Evadne now related the tale of her misfortunes. Her father, though of high rank, had in the end dissipated his fortune, and even destroyed his reputation and influence through a course of dissolute indulgence. His health was impaired beyond hope of cure; and it became his earnest wish, before he died, to preserve his daughter from the poverty which would be the portion of her orphan state. He therefore accepted for her, and persuaded her to accede to, a proposal of marriage, from a wealthy Greek merchant settled at Constantinople. She quitted her native Greece; her father died; by degrees she was cut off from all the companions and ties of her youth.

The war, which about a year before the present time had broken out between Greece and Turkey, brought about many reverses of fortune. Her husband became bankrupt, and then in a tumult and threatened massacre on the part of the Turks, they were obliged to fly at midnight, and reached in an open boat an English vessel under sail, which brought them immediately to this island. The few jewels they had saved, supported them awhile. The whole strength of Evadne's mind was exerted to support the failing spirits of her husband. Loss of property, hopelessness as to his future prospects, the inoccupation to which poverty condemned him, combined to reduce him to a state bordering on insanity. Five months after their arrival in England, he committed suicide.

"You will ask me," continued Evadne, "what I have done since; why I have not applied for succour to the rich Greeks resident here; why I have not returned to my native country? My answer to these questions must needs appear to you unsatisfactory, yet they have sufficed to lead me on, day after day, enduring every wretchedness, rather than by such means to seek relief. Shall the daughter of the noble, though prodigal Zaimi, appear a beggar before her compeers or inferiors—superiors she had none. Shall I bow my head before them, and with servile gesture sell my nobility for life? Had I a child, or any tie to bind me to existence, I might descend to this—but, as it is—the world has been to me a harsh step-mother; fain would I leave the abode she seems to grudge, and in the grave forget my pride, my struggles, my despair. The time will soon come; grief and famine have already sapped the foundations of my being; a very short time, and I shall have passed away; unstained by the crime of self-destruction, unstung by the memory of degradation, my spirit will throw aside this miserable coil, and find such recompense as fortitude and resignation may deserve. This may seem madness to you, yet you also have pride and resolution; do not then wonder that my pride is tameless, my resolution unalterable."

Having thus finished her tale, and given such an account as she deemed fit, of the motives of her abstaining from all endeavour to obtain aid from her countrymen, Evadne paused; yet she seemed to have more to say, to which she was unable to give words. In the mean time Raymond was eloquent. His desire of restoring his lovely friend to her rank in society, and to her lost prosperity, animated him, and he poured forth with energy, all his wishes and intentions on that subject. But he was checked; Evadne exacted a promise, that he should conceal from all her friends her existence in England. "The relatives of the Earl of Windsor," said she haughtily, "doubtless think that I injured him; perhaps the Earl himself would be the first to acquit me, but probably I do not deserve acquittal. I acted then, as I ever must, from impulse. This abode of penury may at least prove the disinterestedness of my conduct. No matter: I do not wish to plead my cause before any of them, not even before your Lordship, had you not first discovered me. The tenor of my actions will prove that I had rather die, than be a mark for scorn—behold the proud Evadne in her tatters! look on the beggar-princess! There is aspic venom in the thought—promise me that my secret shall not be violated by you."

Raymond promised; but then a new discussion ensued. Evadne required another engagement on his part, that he would not without her concurrence enter into any project for her benefit, nor himself offer relief. "Do not degrade me in my own eyes," she said; "poverty has long been my nurse; hard-visaged she is, but honest. If dishonour, or what I conceive to be dishonour, come near me, I am lost." Raymond adduced many arguments and fervent persuasions to overcome her feeling, but she remained unconvinced; and, agitated by the discussion, she wildly and passionately made a solemn vow, to fly and hide herself where he never could discover her, where famine would soon bring death to conclude her woes, if he persisted in his to her disgracing offers. She could support herself, she said. And then she shewed him how, by executing various designs and paintings, she earned a pittance for her support. Raymond yielded for the present. He felt assured, after he had for awhile humoured her self-will, that in the end friendship and reason would gain the day.

But the feelings that actuated Evadne were rooted in the depths of her being, and were such in their growth as he had no means of understanding. Evadne loved Raymond. He was the hero of her imagination, the image carved by love in the unchanged texture of her heart. Seven years ago, in her youthful prime, she had become attached to him; he had served her country against the Turks; he had in her own land acquired that military glory peculiarly dear to the Greeks, since they were still obliged inch by inch to fight for their security. Yet when he returned thence, and first appeared in public life in England, her love did not purchase his, which then vacillated between Perdita and a crown. While he was yet undecided, she had quitted England; the news of his marriage reached her, and her hopes, poorly nurtured blossoms, withered and fell. The glory of life was gone for her; the roseate halo of love, which had imbued every object with its own colour, faded;—she was content to take life as it was, and to make the best of leaden-coloured reality. She married; and, carrying her restless energy of character with her into new scenes, she turned her thoughts to ambition, and aimed at the title and power of Princess of Wallachia;[86] while her patriotic feelings were soothed by the idea of the good she might do her country, when her husband should be chief of this principality. She lived to find ambition, as unreal a delusion as love. Her intrigues with Russia for the furtherance of her object, excited the jealousy of the Porte,[87] and the animosity of the Greek government. She was considered a traitor by both, the ruin of her husband followed; they avoided death by a timely flight, and she fell from the height of her desires to penury in England. Much of this tale she concealed from Raymond; nor did she confess, that repulse and denial, as to a criminal convicted of the worst of crimes, that of bringing the scythe of foreign despotism to cut away the new springing liberties of her country, would have followed her application to any among the Greeks.

She knew that she was the cause of her husband's utter ruin; and she strung herself to bear the consequences. The reproaches which agony extorted; or worse, cureless, uncomplaining depression, when his mind was sunk in a torpor, not the less painful because it was silent and moveless. She reproached herself with the crime of his death; guilt and its punishments appeared to surround her; in vain she endeavoured to allay remorse by the memory of her real integrity; the rest of the world, and she among them, judged of her actions, by their consequences. She prayed for her husband's soul; she conjured the Supreme to place on her head the crime of his self-destruction—she vowed to live to expiate his fault.

In the midst of such wretchedness as must soon have destroyed her, one thought only was matter of consolation. She lived in the same country, breathed the same air as Raymond. His name as Protector was the burthen of every tongue; his achievements, projects, and magnificence, the argument of every story. Nothing is so precious to a woman's heart as

---

86 Wallachia (now Romania) was administered by the Ottoman empire but claimed by the Greeks in MWS's day. MWS met Princess Ralou Argiropoulo of Wallachia, a Greek patriot, in Pisa in 1821.

87 *La sublime porte*, a French translation of the Arabic *babi-'ali*, refers to the high gate giving access to Turkish government buildings; hence, the government itself.

the glory and excellence of him she loves; thus in every horror Evadne revelled in his fame and prosperity. While her husband lived, this feeling was regarded by her as a crime, repressed, repented of. When he died, the tide of love resumed its ancient flow, it deluged her soul with its tumultuous waves, and she gave herself up a prey to its uncontrollable power.

But never, O, never, should he see her in her degraded state. Never should he behold her fallen, as she deemed, from her pride of beauty, the poverty-stricken inhabitant of a garret, with a name which had become a reproach, and a weight of guilt on her soul. But though impenetrably veiled from him, his public office permitted her to become acquainted with all his actions, his daily course of life, even his conversation. She allowed herself one luxury, she saw the newspapers every day, and feasted on the praise and actions of the Protector. Not that this indulgence was devoid of accompanying grief. Perdita's name was for ever joined with his; their conjugal felicity was celebrated even by the authentic testimony of facts. They were continually together, nor could the unfortunate Evadne read the monosyllable that designated his name, without, at the same time, being presented with the image of her who was the faithful companion of all his labours and pleasures. *They, their Excellencies*, met her eyes in each line, mingling an evil potion that poisoned her very blood.

It was in the newspaper that she saw the advertisement for the design for a national gallery. Combining with taste her remembrance of the edifices which she had seen in the east, and by an effort of genius enduing them with unity of design, she executed the plan which had been sent to the Protector. She triumphed in the idea of bestowing, unknown and forgotten as she was, a benefit upon him she loved; and with enthusiastic pride looked forward to the accomplishment of a work of hers, which, immortalized in stone, would go down to posterity stamped with the name of Raymond. She awaited with eagerness the return of her messenger from the palace; she listened insatiate to his account of each word, each look of the Protector; she felt bliss in this communication with her beloved, although he knew not to whom he addressed his instructions. The drawing itself became ineffably dear to her. He had seen it, and praised it; it was again retouched by her, each stroke of her pencil was as a chord of thrilling music, and bore to her the idea of a temple raised to celebrate the deepest and most unutterable emotions of her soul. These contemplations engaged her, when the voice of Raymond first struck her ear, a voice, once heard, never to be forgotten; she mastered her gush of feelings, and welcomed him with quiet gentleness.

Pride and tenderness now struggled, and at length made a compromise together. She would see Raymond, since destiny had led him to her, and her constancy and devotion must merit his friendship. But her rights with regard to him, and her cherished independence, should not be injured by the idea of interest, or the intervention of the complicated feelings attendant on pecuniary obligation, and the relative situations of the benefactor, and benefited. Her mind was uncommon strength; she could subdue her sensible wants to her mental wishes, and suffer cold, hunger and misery, rather than concede to fortune a contested point. Alas! that in human nature such a pitch of mental discipline, and disdainful negligence of nature itself, should not have been allied to the extreme of moral excellence! But the resolution that permitted her to resist the pains of privation, sprung from the too great energy of her passions; and the concentrated self-will of which this was a sign, was destined to destroy even the very idol, to preserve whose respect she submitted to this detail of wretchedness.

Their intercourse continued. By degrees Evadne related to her friend the whole of her story, the stain her name had received in Greece, the weight of sin which had accrued to her from the death of her husband. When Raymond offered to clear her reputation, and demonstrate to the world her real patriotism, she declared that it was only through her present sufferings that she hoped for any relief to the stings of conscience; that, in her state of mind, diseased as he might think it, the necessity of occupation was salutary medicine; she ended by extorting a promise that for the space of one month he would refrain from the discussion of her interests, engaging after that time to yield in part to his wishes. She could not disguise to herself that any change would separate her from him; now she saw him each day. His connection with Adrian and Perdita was never mentioned; he was to her a meteor, a companionless star, which at its appointed hour rose in her hemisphere, whose appearance brought felicity, and which, although it set, was never eclipsed. He came each day to her abode of penury, and his presence transformed it to a temple redolent with sweets, radiant with heaven's own light; he partook of her delirium. "They built a wall between them and the world"[88]—Without, a thousand harpies raved, remorse and misery, expecting the destined moment for their invasion. Within, was the peace as of innocence, reckless blindness, deluding joy, hope, whose still anchor rested on placid but unconstant water.

Thus, while Raymond had been wrapt in visions of power and fame, while he looked forward to entire dominion over the elements and the mind of man, the territory of his own heart escaped his notice; and from that unthought of source arose the mighty torrent that overwhelmed his will, and carried to the oblivious sea, fame, hope, and happiness.

---

88 Hesperus to Olivia, in Thomas Lovell Beddoes, *The Brides' Tragedy* 4.3.67-70: "We'll build a wall between us and the world, / And in some summer wilderness of flowers, / As though but two hearts beat beneath the sun, / Consume our days of love."

CHAPTER IX

IN the mean time what did Perdita?

During the first months of his Protectorate, Raymond and she had been inseparable; each project was discussed with her, each plan approved by her. I never beheld any one so perfectly happy as my sweet sister. Her expressive eyes were two stars whose beams were love; hope and light-heartedness sat on her cloudless brow. She fed even to tears of joy on the praise and glory of her Lord; her whole existence was one sacrifice to him, and if in the humility of her heart she felt self-complacency,' it arose from the reflection that she had won the distinguished hero of the age, and had for years preserved him, even after time had taken from love its usual nourishment. Her own feeling was as entire as at its birth. Five years had failed to destroy the dazzling unreality of passion. Most men ruthlessly destroy the sacred veil, with which the female heart is wont to adorn the idol of its affections. Not so Raymond; he was an enchanter, whose reign was for ever undiminished; a king whose power never was suspended: follow him through the details of common life, still the same charm of grace and majesty adorned him; nor could he be despoiled of the innate deification with which nature had invested him. Perdita grew in beauty and excellence under his eye; I no longer recognised my reserved abstracted sister in the fascinating and open-hearted wife of Raymond. The genius that enlightened her countenance, was now united to an expression of benevolence, which gave divine perfection to her beauty.

Happiness is in its highest degree the sister of goodness. Suffering and amiability may exist together, and writers have loved to depict their conjunction; there is a human and touching harmony in the picture. But perfect happiness is an attribute of angels; and those who possess it, appear angelic. Fear has been said to be the parent of religion:[89] even of that religion is it the generator, which leads its votaries to sacrifice human victims at its altars; but the religion which springs from happiness is a lovelier growth; the religion which makes the heart breathe forth fervent thanksgiving, and causes us to pour out the overflowings of the soul before the author of our being; that which is the parent of the imagination and the nurse of poetry; that which bestows benevolent intelligence on the visible mechanism of the world, and makes earth a temple with heaven for its cope. Such happiness, goodness, and religion inhabited the mind of Perdita.

During the five years we had spent together, a knot of happy human

---

89 Notably by Edmund Burke, *A Philosophical Enquiry into the Origin of our Ideas
   of the Sublime and Beautiful,* 2.3: "Those despotic governments, which are
   founded on the passions of men, and principally upon the passion of fear,
   keep their chief as much as may be from the public eye. The policy has been
   the same in many cases of religion" (ed. Adam Phillips 54).

beings at Windsor Castle, her blissful lot had been the frequent theme of my sister's conversation. From early habit, and natural affection, she selected me in preference to Adrian or Idris, to be the partner in her over-flowings of delight; perhaps, though apparently much unlike, some secret point of resemblance, the offspring of consanguinity, induced this prefer-ence. Often at sunset, I have walked with her, in the sober, enshadowed forest paths, and listened with joyful sympathy. Security gave dignity to her passion; the certainty of a full return, left her with no wish unfulfilled. The birth of her daughter, embryo copy of her Raymond, filled up the measure of her content, and produced a sacred and indissoluble tie between them. Sometimes she felt proud that he had preferred her to the hopes of a crown. Sometimes she remembered that she had suffered keen anguish, when he hesitated in his choice. But this memory of past dis-content only served to enhance her present joy. What had been hardly won, was now, entirely possessed, doubly dear. She would look at him at a distance with the same rapture, (O, far more exuberant rapture!) that one might feel, who after the perils of a tempest, should find himself in the desired port; she would hasten towards him, to feel more certain in his arms, the reality of her bliss. This warmth of affection, added to the depth of her understanding, and the brilliancy of her imagination, made her beyond words dear to Raymond.

If a feeling of dissatisfaction ever crossed her, it arose from the idea that he was not perfectly happy. Desire of renown, and presumptuous ambition, had characterized his youth. The one he had acquired in Greece; the other he had sacrificed to love. His intellect found sufficient field for exercise in his domestic circle, whose members, all adorned by refinement and literature, were many of them, like himself, distinguished by genius. Yet active life was the genuine soil for his virtues; and he some-times suffered tedium from the monotonous succession of events in our retirement. Pride made him recoil from complaint; and gratitude and affection to Perdita, generally acted as an opiate to all desire, save that of meriting her love. We all observed the visitation of these feelings, and none regretted them so much as Perdita. Her life consecrated to him, was a slight sacrifice to reward his choice, but was not that sufficient—Did he need any gratification that she was unable to bestow? This was the only cloud in the azure of her happiness.

His passage to power had been full of pain to both. He however attained his wish; he filled the situation for which nature seemed to have moulded him. His activity was fed in wholesome measure, without either exhaustion or satiety; his taste and genius found worthy expression in each of the modes human beings have invented to encage and manifest the spirit of beauty; the goodness of his heart made him never weary of conducing to the well-being of his fellow-creatures; his magnificent spir-it, and aspirations for the respect and love of mankind, now received fruition; true, his exaltation was temporary; perhaps it were better that it should be so. Habit would not dull his sense of the enjoyment of power;

nor struggles, disappointment and defeat await the end of that which would expire at its maturity. He determined to extract and condense all of glory, power, and achievement, which might have resulted from a long reign, into the three years of his Protectorate.

Raymond was eminently social. All that he now enjoyed would have been devoid of pleasure to him, had it been unparticipated. But in Perdita he possessed all that his heart could desire. Her love gave birth to sympathy; her intelligence made her understand him at a word; her powers of intellect enabled her to assist and guide him. He felt her worth. During the early years of their union, the inequality of her temper, and yet unsubdued self-will which tarnished her character, had been a slight drawback to the fulness of his sentiment. Now that unchanged serenity, and gentle compliance were added to her other qualifications, his respect equalled his love. Years added to the strictness of their union. They did not now guess at, and totter on the pathway, divining the mode to please, hoping, yet fearing the continuance of bliss. Five years gave a sober certainty to their emotions, though it did not rob them of their etherial nature. It had given them a child; but it had not detracted from the personal attractions of my sister. Timidity, which in her had almost amounted to awkwardness, was exchanged for a graceful decision of manner; frankness, instead of reserve, characterized her physiognomy; and her voice was attuned to thrilling softness. She was now three and twenty, in the pride of womanhood, fulfilling the precious duties of wife and mother, possessed of all her heart had ever coveted. Raymond was ten years older; to his previous beauty, noble mien, and commanding aspect, he now added gentlest benevolence, winning tenderness, graceful and unwearied attention to the wishes of another.

The first secret that had existed between them was the visits of Raymond to Evadne. He had been struck by the fortitude and beauty of the ill-fated Greek; and, when her constant tenderness towards him unfolded itself, he asked with astonishment, by what act of his he had merited this passionate and unrequited love. She was for a while the sole object of his reveries; and Perdita became aware that his thoughts and time were bestowed on a subject unparticipated by her. My sister was by nature destitute of the common feelings of anxious, petulant jealousy. The treasure which she possessed in the affections of Raymond, was more necessary to her being, than the life-blood that animated her veins—more truly than Othello she might say,

> To be once in doubt,
> Is—once to be resolved.[90]

---

90   *Othello* 3.3.181-84: "Think'st thou I'd make a life of jealousy, / To follow still the changes of the moon / With fresh suspicions? No; to be once in doubt / Is once to be resolv'd."

On the present occasion she did not suspect any alienation of affection; but she conjectured that some circumstance connected with his high place, had occasioned this mystery. She was startled and pained. She began to count the long days, and months, and years which must elapse, before he would be restored to a private station, and unreservedly to her. She was not content that, even for a time, he should practice concealment with her. She often repined; but her trust in the singleness of his affection was undisturbed; and, when they were together, unchecked by fear, she opened her heart to the fullest delight.

Time went on. Raymond, stopping mid-way in his wild career, paused suddenly to think of consequences. Two results presented themselves in the view he took of the future. That his intercourse with Evadne should continue a secret to, or that finally it should be discovered by Perdita. The destitute condition, and highly wrought feelings of his friend prevented him from adverting to the possibility of exiling himself from her. In the first event he had bidden an eternal farewell to open-hearted converse, and entire sympathy with the companion of his life. The veil must be thicker than that invented by Turkish jealousy; the wall higher than the unscaleable tower of Vathek,[91] which should conceal from her the workings of his heart and hide from her view the secret of his actions. This idea was intolerably painful to him. Frankness and social feelings were the essence of Raymond's nature; without them his qualities became common-place; without these to spread glory over his intercourse with Perdita, his vaunted exchange of a throne for her love, was as weak and empty as the rainbow hues which vanish when the sun is down. But there was no remedy. Genius, devotion, and courage; the adornments of his mind, and the energies of his soul, all exerted to their uttermost stretch, could not roll back one hair's breadth the wheel of time's chariot; that which had been was written with the adamantine pen of reality, on the everlasting volume of the past; nor could agony and tears suffice to wash out one iota from the act fulfilled.

But this was the best side of the question. What, if circumstance should lead Perdita to suspect, and suspecting to be resolved? The fibres of his frame became relaxed, and cold dew stood on his forehead, at this idea. Many men may scoff at his dread; but he read the future; and the peace of Perdita was too dear to him, her speechless agony too certain, and too fearful, not to unman him. His course was speedily decided upon.

---

91 In one of her letters (to the Countess of Bristol, written at Constantinople in 1717), Lady Mary Wortley Montagu describes the "*asmack* or Turkish veil" worn by Moslem women; she herself wore it to visit Old Constantinople, closed to foreigners in her day. In William Beckford's *Vathek* (1786), when the proud Caliph Vathek constructs a tower from which to contemplate the heavens, Mahomet sends genii to add to its height, thus encouraging Vathek's acts of self-destructive excess.

If the worst befell; if she learnt the truth, he would neither stand her reproaches, or the anguish of her altered looks. He would forsake her, England, his friends, the scenes of his youth, the hopes of coming time, he would seek another country, and in other scenes begin life again. Having resolved on this, he became calmer. He endeavoured to guide with prudence the steeds of destiny through the devious road which he had chosen, and bent all his efforts the better to conceal what he could not alter.

The perfect confidence that subsisted between Perdita and him, rendered every communication common between them. They opened each other's letters, even as, until now, the inmost fold of the heart of each was disclosed to the other. A letter came unawares, Perdita read it. Had it contained confirmation, she must have been annihilated. As it was, trembling, cold, and pale, she sought Raymond. He was alone, examining some petitions lately presented. She entered silently, sat on a sofa opposite to him, and gazed on him with a look of such despair, that wildest shrieks and dire moans would have been tame exhibitions of misery, compared to the living incarnation of the thing itself exhibited by her.

At first he did not take his eyes from the papers; when he raised them, he was struck by the wretchedness manifest on her altered cheek; for a moment he forgot his own acts and fears, and asked with consternation—"Dearest girl, what is the matter; what has happened?"

"Nothing," she replied at first; "and yet not so," she continued, hurrying on in her speech; "you have secrets, Raymond; where have you been lately, whom have you seen, what do you conceal from me?—why am I banished from your confidence? Yet this is not it—I do not intend to entrap you with questions—one will suffice—am I completely a wretch?"

With trembling hand she gave him the paper, and sat white and motionless looking at him while he read it. He recognised the hand-writing of Evadne, and the colour mounted in his cheeks. With lightning-speed he conceived the contents of the letter; all was now cast on one die; falsehood and artifice were trifles in comparison with the impending ruin. He would either entirely dispel Perdita's suspicions, or quit her for ever. "My dear girl," he said, "I have been to blame; but you must pardon me. I was in the wrong to commence a system of concealment; but I did it for the sake of sparing you pain; and each day has rendered it more difficult for me to alter my plan. Besides, I was instigated by delicacy towards the unhappy writer of these few lines."

Perdita gasped: "Well," she cried, "well, go on!"

"That is all—this paper tells all. I am placed in the most difficult circumstances. I have done my best, though perhaps I have done wrong. My love for you is inviolate."

Perdita shook her head doubtingly: "It cannot be," she cried, "I know that it is not. You would deceive me, but I will not be deceived. I have lost you, myself, my life!"

"Do you not believe me?" said Raymond haughtily.

"To believe you," she exclaimed, "I would give up all, and expire with joy, so that in death I could feel that you were true—but that cannot be!"

"Perdita," continued Raymond, "you do not see the precipice on which you stand. You may believe that I did not enter on my present line of conduct without reluctance and pain. I knew that it was possible that your suspicions might be excited; but I trusted that my simple word would cause them to disappear. I built my hope on your confidence. Do you think that I will be questioned, and my replies disdainfully set aside? Do you think that I will be suspected, perhaps watched, cross-questioned, and disbelieved? I am not yet fallen so low; my honour is not yet so tarnished. You have loved me; I adored you. But all human sentiments come to an end. Let our affection expire—but let it not be exchanged for distrust and recrimination. Heretofore we have been friends—lovers—let us not become enemies, mutual spies. I cannot live the object of suspicion—you cannot believe me—let us part!"

"Exactly so," cried Perdita, "I knew that it would come to this! Are we not already parted? Does not a stream, boundless as ocean, deep as vacuum, yawn between us?"

Raymond rose, his voice was broken, his features convulsed, his manner calm as the earthquake-cradling atmosphere, he replied: "I am rejoiced that you take my decision so philosophically. Doubtless you will play the part of the injured wife to admiration. Sometimes you may be stung with the feeling that you have wronged me, but the condolence of your relatives, the pity of the world, the complacency which the consciousness of your own immaculate innocence will bestow, will be excellent balm;—me you will never see more!"

Raymond moved towards the door. He forgot that each word he spoke was false. He personated his assumption of innocence even to self-deception. Have not actors wept, as they pourtrayed imagined passion? A more intense feeling of the reality of fiction possessed Raymond. He spoke with pride; he felt injured. Perdita looked up; she saw his angry glance; his hand was on the lock of the door. She started up, she threw herself on his neck, she gasped and sobbed; he took her hand, and leading her to the sofa, sat down near her. Her head fell on his shoulder, she trembled, alternate changes of fire and ice ran through her limbs: observing her emotion he spoke with softened accents:

"The blow is given. I will not part from you in anger;—I owe you too much. I owe you six years of unalloyed happiness. But they are passed. I will not live the mark of suspicion, the object of jealousy. I love you too well. In an eternal separation only can either of us hope for dignity and propriety of action. We shall not then be degraded from our true characters. Faith and devotion have hitherto been the essence of our intercourse;—these lost, let us not cling to the seedless husk of life, the unkernelled shell. You have your child, your brother, Idris, Adrian"—

"And you," cried Perdita, "the writer of that letter."

Uncontrollable indignation flashed from the eyes of Raymond. He knew that this accusation at least was false. "Entertain this belief," he cried, "hug it to your heart—make it a pillow to your head, an opiate for your eyes—I am content. But, by the God that made me, hell is not more false than the word you have spoken!"

Perdita was struck by the impassioned seriousness of his asseverations. She replied with earnestness, "I do not refuse to believe you, Raymond; on the contrary I promise to put implicit faith in your simple word. Only assure me that your love and faith towards me have never been violated; and suspicion, and doubt, and jealousy will at once be dispersed. We shall continue as we have ever done, one heart, one hope, one life."

"I have already assured you of my fidelity," said Raymond with disdainful coldness, "triple assertions will avail nothing where one is despised. I will say no more; for I can add nothing to what I have already said, to what you before contemptuously set aside. This contention is unworthy of both of us; and I confess that I am weary of replying to charges at once unfounded and unkind."

Perdita tried to read his countenance, which he angrily averted. There was so much of truth and nature in his resentment, that her doubts were dispelled. Her countenance, which for years had not expressed a feeling unallied to affection, became again radiant and satisfied. She found it however no easy task to soften and reconcile Raymond. At first he refused to stay to hear her. But she would not be put off; secure of his unaltered love, she was willing to undertake any labour, use any entreaty, to dispel his anger. She obtained an hearing, he sat in haughty silence, but he listened. She first assured him of her boundless confidence; of this he must be conscious, since but for that she would not seek to detain him. She enumerated their years of happiness; she brought before him past scenes of intimacy and happiness; she pictured their future life, she mentioned their child—tears unbidden now filled her eyes. She tried to disperse them, but they refused to be checked—her utterance was choaked. She had not wept before. Raymond could not resist these signs of distress: he felt perhaps somewhat ashamed of the part he acted of the injured man, he who was in truth the injurer. And then he devoutly loved Perdita; the bend of her head, her glossy ringlets, the turn of her form were to him subjects of deep tenderness and admiration; as she spoke, her melodious tones entered his soul; he soon softened towards her, comforting and caressing her, and endeavouring to cheat himself into the belief that he had never wronged her.

Raymond staggered forth from this scene, as a man might do, who had been just put to the torture, and looked forward to when it would be again inflicted. He had sinned against his own honour, by affirming, swearing to, a direct falsehood; true this he had palmed on a woman, and it might therefore be deemed less base—by others—not by him;—for whom had he deceived?—his own trusting, devoted, affectionate Perdita, whose generous belief galled him doubly, when he remembered the parade of innocence with which it had been exacted. The mind of Raymond was not so rough cast, nor had been so rudely handled, in the circumstance of life, as to make him proof to these considerations—on the contrary, he was all nerve; his spirit was as a pure fire, which fades and shrinks from every contagion of foul atmosphere: but now the contagion had become incorporated with its essence, and the change was the more painful. Truth and falsehood, love and hate lost their eternal boundaries, heaven rushed in to mingle with hell; while his sensitive mind, turned to a field for such battle, was stung to madness. He heartily despised himself, he was angry with Perdita, and the idea of Evadne was attended by all that was hideous and cruel. His passions, always his masters, acquired fresh strength, from the long sleep in which love had cradled them, the clinging weight of destiny bent him down; he was goaded, tortured, fiercely impatient of that worst of miseries, the sense of remorse. This troubled state yielded by degrees, to sullen animosity, and depression of spirits. His dependants, even his equals, if in his present post he had any, were startled to find anger, derision, and bitterness in one, before distinguished for suavity and benevolence of manner. He transacted public business with distaste, and hastened from it to the solitude which was at once his bane and relief. He mounted a fiery horse, that which had borne him forward to victory in Greece; he fatigued himself with deadening exercise, losing the pangs of a troubled mind in animal sensation.

He slowly recovered himself; yet, at last, as one might from the effects of poison, he lifted his head from above the vapours of fever and passion into the still atmosphere of calm reflection. He meditated on what was best to be done. He was first struck by the space of time that had elapsed, since madness, rather than any reasonable impulse, had regulated his actions. A month had gone by, and during that time he had not seen Evadne. Her power, which was linked to few of the enduring emotions of his heart, had greatly decayed. He was no longer her slave—no longer her lover: he would never see her more, and by the completeness of his return, deserve the confidence of Perdita.

Yet, as he thus determined, fancy conjured up the miserable abode of the Greek girl. An abode, which from noble and lofty principle, she had refused to exchange for one of greater luxury. He thought of the splendour of her situation and appearance when he first knew her; he thought of her life at Constantinople, attended by every circumstance of oriental magnificence; of her present penury, her daily task of industry, her lorn state, her faded, famine-struck cheek. Compassion swelled his breast; he would see her once again; he would devise some plan for restoring her to society, and the enjoyment of her rank; their separation would then follow, as a matter of course.

Again he thought, how during this long month, he had avoided Perdita, flying from her as from the stings of his own conscience. But he was awake now; all this should be remedied; and future devotion erase the memory of this only blot on the serenity of their life. He became cheerful, as he thought of this, and soberly and resolutely marked out the line of conduct he would adopt. He remembered that he had promised Perdita to be present this very evening (the 19th of October, anniversary of his election as Protector) at a festival given in his honour. Good augury should this festival be of the happiness of future years. First, he would look in on Evadne; he would not stay; but he owed her some account, some compensation for his long and unannounced absence; and then to Perdita, to the forgotten world, to the duties of society, the splendour of rank, the enjoyment of power.

After the scene sketched in the preceding pages, Perdita had contemplated an entire change in the manners and conduct of Raymond. She expected freedom of communication, and a return to those habits of affectionate intercourse which had formed the delight of her life. But Raymond did not join her in any of her avocations. He transacted the business of the day apart from her; he went out, she knew not whither. The pain inflicted by this disappointment was tormenting and keen. She looked on it as a deceitful dream, and tried to throw off the consciousness of it; but like the shirt of Nessus,[92] it clung to her very flesh, and ate with sharp agony into her vital principle. She possessed that (though such an assertion may appear a paradox) which belongs to few, a capacity of happiness. Her delicate organization and creative imagination rendered her peculiarly susceptible of pleasurable emotion. The overflowing warmth of her heart, by making love a plant of deep root and stately growth, had attuned her whole soul to the reception of happiness, when she found in Raymond all that could adorn love and satisfy her imagination. But if the sentiment on which the fabric of her existence was founded, became common place through participation, the endless succession of attentions and graceful action snapt by transfer, his universe of love wrested from her, happiness must depart, and then be exchanged for its opposite. The same peculiarities of character rendered her sorrows agonies; her fancy magnified them, her sensibility made her for ever open to their renewed impression; love envenomed the heart-piercing sting. There was neither submission, patience, nor self-abandonment in her grief; she fought with it, struggled beneath it, and rendered every pang more sharp by resistance. Again and again the idea recurred, that he loved another. She did him justice; she believed that he felt a tender affection for her; but give a paltry prize to him who in some life-pending lottery has calculated on the possession of tens of thousands, and it will disappoint him more than a blank. The affection and amity of a Raymond might be inestimable; but, beyond that affection, embosomed deeper than friendship, was the indivisible treasure of love. Take the sum in its completeness, and no arithmetic can calculate its price; take from it the smallest portion, give it but the name of parts, separate it into degrees and sections, and like the magi-

---

92   In Greek mythology, the centaur Nessus killed Heracles with a poisoned shirt; see also MWS's *Journals*, 23 November 1833 (2: 533).

cian's coin, the valuless gold of the mine, is turned to vilest substance.[93] There is a meaning in the eye of love; a cadence in its voice, an irradiation in its smile, the talisman of whose enchantments one only can possess; its spirit is elemental, its essence single, its divinity an unit. The very heart and soul of Raymond and Perdita had mingled, even as two mountain brooks that join in their descent, and murmuring and sparkling flow over shining pebbles, beside starry flowers; but let one desert its primal course, or be dammed up by choaking obstruction, and the other shrinks in its altered banks. Perdita was sensible of the failing of the tide that fed her life. Unable to support the slow withering of her hopes, she suddenly formed a plan, resolving to terminate at once the period of misery, and to bring to an happy conclusion the late disastrous events.

The anniversary was at hand of the exaltation of Raymond to the office of Protector; and it was customary to celebrate this day by a splendid festival. A variety of feelings urged Perdita to shed double magnificence over the scene; yet, as she arrayed herself for the evening gala, she wondered herself at the pains she took, to render sumptuous the celebration of an event which appeared to her the beginning of her sufferings. Woe befall the day, she thought, woe, tears, and mourning betide the hour, that gave Raymond another hope than love, another wish than my devotion; and thrice joyful the moment when he shall be restored to me! God knows, I put my trust in his vows, and believe his asserted faith—but for that, I would not seek what I am now resolved to attain. Shall two years more be thus passed, each day adding to our alienation, each act being another stone piled on the barrier which separates us? No, my Raymond, my only beloved, sole possession of Perdita! This night, this splendid assembly, these sumptuous apartments, and this adornment of your tearful girl, are all united to celebrate your abdication. Once for me, you relinquished the prospect of a crown. That was in days of early love, when I could only hold out the hope, not the assurance of happiness. Now you have the experience of all that I can give, the heart's devotion, taintless love, and unhesitating subjection to you. You must choose between these and your protectorate. This, proud noble, is your last night! Perdita has bestowed on it all of magnificent and dazzling that your heart best loves—but, from these gorgeous rooms, from this princely attendance, from power and elevation, you must return with to-morrow's sun to our rural abode; for I would not buy an immortality of joy, by the endurance of one more week sister to the last.

Brooding over this plan, resolved when the hour should come, to propose, and insist upon its accomplishment, secure of his consent, the heart of Perdita was lightened, or rather exalted. Her cheek was flushed by the

---

93 Ernest W. Baughman, *Type and Motif-Index of the Folktales of England and North America*, notes a New Jersey tale of money transformed into dung, which may be related to the story MWS alludes to here.

expectation of struggle; her eyes sparkled with the hope of triumph. Having cast her fate upon a die, and feeling secure of winning, she, whom I have named as bearing the stamp of queen of nations on her noble brow, now rose superior to humanity, and seemed in calm power, to arrest with her finger, the wheel of destiny. She had never before looked so supremely lovely.

We, the Arcadian shepherds of the tale, had intended to be present at this festivity, but Perdita wrote to entreat us not to come, or to absent ourselves from Windsor; for she (though she did not reveal her scheme to us) resolved the next morning to return with Raymond to our dear circle, there to renew a course of life in which she had found entire felicity. Late in the evening she entered the apartments appropriated to the festival. Raymond had quitted the palace the night before; he had promised to grace the assembly, but he had not yet returned. Still she felt sure that he would come at last; and the wider the breach might appear at this crisis, the more secure she was of closing it for ever.

It was as I said, the nineteenth of October; the autumn was far advanced and dreary. The wind howled; the half bare trees were despoiled of the remainder of their summer ornament; the state of the air which induced the decay of vegetation, was hostile to cheerfulness or hope. Raymond had been exalted by the determination he had made; but with the declining day his spirits declined. First he was to visit Evadne, and then to hasten to the palace of the Protectorate. As he walked through the wretched streets in the neighbourhood of the luckless Greek's abode, his heart smote him for the whole course of his conduct towards her. First, his having entered into any engagement that should permit her to remain in such a state of degradation; and then, after a short wild dream, having left her to drear solitude, anxious conjecture, and bitter, still-disappointed expectation. What had she done the while, how supported his absence and neglect? Light grew dim in these close streets, and when the well known door was opened, the staircase was shrouded in perfect night. He groped his way up, he entered the garret, he found Evadne stretched speechless, almost lifeless on her wretched bed. He called for the people of the house, but could learn nothing from them, except that they knew nothing. Her story was plain to him, plain and distinct as the remorse and horror that darted their fangs into him. When she found herself forsaken by him, she lost the heart to pursue her usual avocations; pride forbade every application to him; famine was welcomed as the kind porter to the gates of death, within whose opening folds she should now, without sin, quickly repose. No creature came near her, as her strength failed.

If she died, where could there be found on record a murderer, whose cruel act might compare with his? What fiend more wanton in his mischief, what damned soul more worthy of perdition! But he was not reserved for this agony of self-reproach. He sent for medical assistance; the hours passed, spun by suspense into ages; the darkness of the long autumnal night yielded to day, before her life was secure. He had her then removed to a more commodious dwelling, and hovered about her, again and again to assure himself that she was safe.

In the midst of his greatest suspense and fear as to the event, he remembered the festival given in his honour, by Perdita; in his honour then, when misery and death were affixing indelible disgrace to his name, honour to him whose crimes deserved a scaffold; this was the worst mockery. Still Perdita would expect him; he wrote a few incoherent words on a scrap of paper, testifying that he was well, and bade the woman of the house take it to the palace, and deliver it into the hands of the wife of the Lord Protector. The woman, who did not know him, contemptuously asked, how he thought she should gain admittance, particularly on a festal night, to that lady's presence? Raymond gave her his ring to ensure the respect of the menials. Thus, while Perdita was entertaining her guests, and anxiously awaiting the arrival of her lord, his ring was brought her; and she was told that a poor woman had a note to deliver to her from its wearer.

The vanity of the old gossip was raised by her commission, which, after all, she did not understand, since she had no suspicion, even now that Evadne's visitor was Lord Raymond. Perdita dreaded a fall from his horse, or some similar accident—till the woman's answers woke other fears. From a feeling of cunning blindly exercised, the officious, if not malignant messenger, did not speak of Evadne's illness; but she garrulously gave an account of Raymond's frequent visits, adding to her narration such circumstances, as, while they convinced Perdita of its truth, exaggerated the unkindness and perfidy of Raymond. Worst of all, his absence now from the festival, his message wholly unaccounted for, except by the disgraceful hints of the woman, appeared the deadliest insult. Again she looked at the ring, it was a small ruby, almost heart-shaped, which she had herself given him. She looked at the hand-writing, which she could not mistake, and repeated to herself the words—"Do not, I charge you, I entreat you, permit your guests to wonder at my absence:" the while the old crone going on with her talk, filled her ear with a strange medley of truth and falsehood. At length Perdita dismissed her.

The poor girl returned to the assembly, where her presence had not been missed. She glided into a recess somewhat obscured, and leaning against an ornamental column there placed, tried to recover herself. Her faculties were palsied. She gazed on some flowers that stood near in a carved vase: that morning she had arranged them, they were rare and lovely plants; even now all aghast as she was, she observed their brilliant colours and starry shapes.—"Divine infoliations of the spirit of beauty," she exclaimed, "Ye droop not, neither do ye mourn; the despair that clasps my heart, has not spread contagion over you!—Why am I not a partner of your insensibility, a sharer in your calm!"

She paused. "To my task," she continued mentally, "my guests must not perceive the reality, either as it regards him or me. I obey; they shall not, though I die the moment they are gone. They shall behold the antipodes of what is real—for I will appear to live—while I am—dead." It required all her self-command, to suppress the gush of tears self-pity caused at this idea. After many struggles, she succeeded, and turned to join the company.

All her efforts were now directed to the dissembling her internal conflict. She had to play the part of a courteous hostess; to attend to all; to shine the focus of enjoyment and grace. She had to do this, while in deep woe she sighed for loneliness, and would gladly have exchanged her crowded rooms for dark forest depths, or a drear, night-enshadowed heath. But she became gay. She could not keep in the medium, nor be, as was usual with her, placidly content. Every one remarked her exhilaration of spirits; as all actions appear graceful in the eye of rank, her guests surrounded her applaudingly, although there was a sharpness in her laugh, and an abruptness in her sallies, which might have betrayed her secret to an attentive observer. She went on, feeling that, if she had paused for a moment, the checked waters of misery would have deluged her soul, that her wrecked hopes would raise their wailing voices, and that those who now echoed her mirth, and provoked her repartees, would have shrunk in fear from her convulsive despair. Her only consolation during the violence which she did herself, was to watch the motions of an illuminated clock, and internally count the moments which must elapse before she could be alone.

At length the rooms began to thin. Mocking her own desires, she rallied her guests on their early departure. One by one they left her—at length she pressed the hand of her last visitor. "How cold and damp your hand is," said her friend; "you are over fatigued, pray hasten to rest." Perdita smiled faintly—her guest left her; the carriage rolling down the street assured the final departure. Then, as if pursued by an enemy, as if wings had been at her feet, she flew to her own apartment, she dismissed her attendants, she locked the doors, she threw herself wildly on the floor, she bit her lips even to blood to suppress her shrieks, and lay long a prey to the vulture of despair, striving not to think, while multitudinous ideas made a home of her heart; and ideas, horrid as furies, cruel as vipers, and poured in with such swift succession, that they seemed to jostle and wound each other, while they worked her up to madness.

At length she rose, more composed, not less miserable. She stood before a large mirror—she gazed on her reflected image; her light and graceful dress, the jewels that studded her hair, and encircled her beauteous arms and neck, her small feet shod in satin, her profuse and glossy tresses, all were to her clouded brow and woe-begone countenance like a gorgeous frame to a dark tempest-pourtraying picture. "Vase am I," she thought, "vase brimful of despair's direst essence. Farewell, Perdita! farewell, poor girl! never again will you see yourself thus; luxury and wealth are no longer yours; in the excess of your poverty you may envy the homeless beggar; most truly am I without a home! I live on a barren desart, which, wide and interminable, brings forth neither fruit or flower; in the midst is a solitary rock, to which thou, Perdita, art chained, and thou seest the dreary level stretch far away."

She threw open her window, which looked on the palace-garden. Light and darkness were struggling together, and the orient was streaked by roseate and golden rays. One star only trembled in the depth of the kindling atmosphere. The morning air blowing freshly over the dewy plants, rushed into the heated room. "All things go on," thought Perdita, "all things proceed, decay, and perish! When noontide has passed, and the weary day has driven her team to their western stalls, the fires of heaven rise from the East, moving in their accustomed path, they ascend and descend the skiey hill. When their course is fulfilled, the dial begins to cast westward an uncertain shadow; the eye-lids of day are opened, and birds and flowers, the startled vegetation, and fresh breeze awaken; the sun at length appears, and in majestic procession climbs the capitol of heaven. All proceeds, changes and dies, except the sense of misery in my bursting heart.

"Ay, all proceeds and changes: what wonder then, that love has journied on to its setting, and that the lord of my life has changed? We call the supernal lights fixed, yet they wander about yonder plain, and if I look again where I looked an hour ago, the race of the eternal heavens is altered. The silly moon and inconstant planets vary nightly their erratic dance; the sun itself, sovereign of the sky, ever and anon deserts his throne, and leaves his dominion to night and winter. Nature grows old,[94] and shakes in her decaying limbs,—creation has become bankrupt! What wonder then, that eclipse and death have led to destruction the light of thy life, O Perdita!"

CHAPTER X

THUS sad and disarranged were the thoughts of my poor sister, when she became assured of the infidelity of Raymond. All her virtues and all her defects tended to make the blow incurable. Her affection for me, her brother, for Adrian and Idris, was subject as it were to the reigning pas-

---

94   The narrator of "The Last Man," a story in *Blackwood's* 19 (March 1826), observes "universal nature ... worn out and exhausted—thus perishing from old age, and expiring from the sheer want of renewing materials" (286). Cf. below 252. In 1823 Leigh Hunt published a translation of a Latin poem by John Milton ("Naturam Non Pati Senium" ["That Nature is Not Subject to Old Age"], 1628) challenging this controversial and persistent idea. A related notion that human life loses its vigour with the passage of time forms part of the early nineteenth-century Malthusian debate about the adequacy of food supply to sustain a growing population.

sion of her heart; even her maternal tenderness borrowed half its force from the delight she had in tracing Raymond's features and expression in the infant's countenance. She had been reserved and even stern in childhood; but love had softened the asperities of her character, and her union with Raymond had caused her talents and affections to unfold themselves; the one betrayed, and the other lost, she in some degree returned to her ancient disposition. The concentrated pride of her nature, forgotten during her blissful dream, awoke, and with its adder's sting pierced her heart; her humility of spirit augmented the power of the venom; she had been exalted in her own estimation, while distinguished by his love: of what worth was she, now that he thrust her from this preferment? She had been proud of having won and preserved him—but another had won him from her, and her exultation was as cold as a water quenched ember.

We, in our retirement, remained long in ignorance of her misfortune. Soon after the festival she had sent for her child, and then she seemed to have forgotten us. Adrian observed a change during a visit that he afterward paid them; but he could not tell its extent, or divine the cause. They still appeared in public together, and lived under the same roof. Raymond was as usual courteous, though there was, on occasions, an unbidden haughtiness, or painful abruptness in his manners, which startled his gentle friend; his brow was not clouded but disdain sat on his lips, and his voice was harsh. Perdita was all kindness and attention to her lord; but she was silent, and beyond words sad. She had grown thin and pale; and her eyes often filled with tears. Sometimes she looked at Raymond, as if to say—That it should be so! At others her countenance expressed—I will still do all I can to make you happy. But Adrian read with uncertain aim the charactery of her face, and might mistake.—Clara was always with her, and she seemed most at ease, when, in an obscure corner, she could sit holding her child's hand, silent and lonely. Still Adrian was unable to guess the truth; he entreated them to visit us at Windsor, and they promised to come during the following month.

It was May before they arrived: the season had decked the forest trees with leaves, and its paths with a thousand flowers. We had notice of their intention the day before; and, early in the morning, Perdita arrived with her daughter. Raymond would follow soon, she said; he had been detained by business. According to Adrian's account, I had expected to find her sad; but, on the contrary, she appeared in the highest spirits: true, she had grown thin, her eyes were somewhat hollow, and her cheeks sunk, though tinged by a bright glow. She was delighted to see us; caressed our children, praised their growth and improvement; Clara also was pleased to meet again her young friend Alfred; all kinds of childish games were entered into, in which Perdita joined. She communicated her gaiety to us, and as we amused ourselves on the Castle Terrace, it appeared that a happier, less care-worn party could not have been assembled. "This is better, Mamma," said Clara, "than being in that dismal

London, where you often cry, and never laugh as you do now."—"Silence, little foolish thing," replied her mother, "and remember any one that mentions London is sent to Coventry for an hour."

Soon after, Raymond arrived. He did not join as usual in the playful spirit of the rest; but, entering into conversation with Adrian and myself, by degrees we seceded from our companions, and Idris and Perdita only remained with the children. Raymond talked of his new buildings; of his plan for an establishment for the better education of the poor; as usual Adrian and he entered into argument, and the time slipped away unperceived.

We assembled again towards evening, and Perdita insisted on our having recourse to music. She wanted, she said, to give us a specimen of her new accomplishment; for since she had been in London, she had applied herself to music, and sang, without much power, but with a great deal of sweetness. We were not permitted by her to select any but light-hearted melodies; and all the Operas of Mozart were called into service, that we might choose the most exhilarating of his airs.[95] Among the other transcendant attributes of Mozart's music, it possesses more than any other that of appearing to come from the heart; you enter into the passions expressed by him, and are transported with grief, joy, anger, or confusion, as he, our soul's master, chooses to inspire. For some time, the spirit of hilarity was kept up; but, at length, Perdita receded from the piano, for Raymond had joined in the trio of "*Taci ingiusto core,*" in Don Giovanni, whose arch entreaty was softened by him into tenderness, and thrilled her heart with memories of the changed past; it was the same voice, the same tone, the self-same sounds and words, which often before she had received, as the homage of love to her—no longer was it that; and this concord of sound with its dissonance of expression penetrated her with regret and despair. Soon after Idris, who was at the harp, turned to that passionate and sorrowful air in Figaro, "*Porgi, amor, qualche ristoro,*" in which the deserted Countess laments the change of the faithless Almaviva.[96] The soul of tender sorrow is breathed forth in this strain; and the sweet voice of Idris, sustained by the mournful chords of her instrument, added to the expression of the words. During the pathetic appeal with which it concludes, a stifled sob attracted our attention to Perdita, the cessation of the music recalled her to herself, she hastened out of the

---

95 MWS was a fan of Mozart's operas; in her letters she mentions attending performances of *Le nozze di Figaro, Don Giovanni, Cosi fan tutte, La clemenza di Tito* and *Die Zauberflöte.*

96 *Taci ingiusto core*: "Ah, silence unjust heart! Do not palpitate in my bosom! He is a villain, he is a traitor. It is a sin to have pity" (trans. Marie-Thérèse Paquin); *Porgi, amor, qualche ristoro*: "Bestow, love, some consolation on my sorrow, on my sighs! Either restore to me my treasure, or at least allow me to die" (trans. adapted from Arthur Schoep and Daniel Harris).

hall—I followed her. At first, she seemed to wish to shun me; and then, yielding to my earnest questioning, she threw herself on my neck, and wept aloud:—"Once more," she cried, "once more on your friendly breast, my beloved brother, can the lost Perdita pour forth her sorrows. I had imposed a law of silence on myself; and for months I have kept it. I do wrong in weeping now, and greater wrong in giving words to my grief. I will not speak! Be [it] enough for you to know that I am miserable [—] be it enough for you to know, that the painted veil of life is rent,[97] that I sit for ever shrouded in darkness and gloom, that grief is my sister, ever-lasting lamentation my mate!"

I endeavoured to console her; I did not question her! but I caressed her, assured her of my deepest affection and my intense interest in the changes of her fortune:—"Dear words," she cried, "expressions of love come upon my ear, like the remembered sounds of forgotten music, that had been dear to me. They are vain, I know; how very vain in their attempt to soothe or comfort me. Dearest Lionel, you cannot guess what I have suffered during these long months. I have read of mourners in ancient days, who clothed themselves in sackcloth, scattered dust upon their heads, ate their bread mingled with ashes, and took up their abode on the bleak mountain tops, reproaching heaven and earth aloud with their misfortunes. Why this is the very luxury of sorrow! thus one might go on from day to day contriving new extravagances, revelling in the para-phernalia of woe, wedded to all the appurtenances of despair. Alas! I must for ever conceal the wretchedness that consumes me. I must weave a veil of dazzling falsehood to hide my grief from vulgar eyes, smoothe my brow, and paint my lips in deceitful smiles—even in solitude I dare not think how lost I am, lest I become insane and rave."

The tears and agitation of my poor sister had rendered her unfit to return to the circle we had left—so I persuaded her to let me drive her through the park; and, during the ride, I induced her to confide the tale of her unhappiness to me, fancying that talking of it would lighten the burthen, and certain that, if there were a remedy, it should be found and secured to her.

Several weeks had elapsed since the festival of the anniversary, and she had been unable to calm her mind, or to subdue her thoughts to any regular train. Sometimes she reproached herself for taking too bitterly to heart, that which many would esteem an imaginary evil; but this was no subject for reason; and, ignorant as she was of the motives and true con-duct of Raymond, things assumed for her even a worse appearance, than the reality warranted. He was seldom at the palace; never, but when he was assured that his public duties would prevent his remaining alone with

---

97   Square brackets indicate omissions in the 1826 edition. Cf. PBS, "Lift not the painted veil which those who live / Call life" (*Posthumous Poems*, 1824); see also MWS's *Journals* 2: 446, 485, where she quotes from the same passage.

Perdita. They seldom addressed each other, shunning explanation, each fearing any communication the other might make. Suddenly, however, the manners of Raymond changed; he appeared to desire to find opportunities of bringing about a return to kindness and intimacy with my sister. The tide of love towards her appeared to flow again; he could never forget, how once he had been devoted to her, making her the shrine and storehouse wherein to place every thought and every sentiment. Shame seemed to hold him back; yet he evidently wished to establish a renewal of confidence and affection. From the moment Perdita had sufficiently recovered herself to form any plan of action, she had laid one down, which now she prepared to follow. She received these tokens of returning love with gentleness; she did not shun his company; but she endeavoured to place a barrier in the way of familiar intercourse or painful discussion, which mingled pride and shame prevented Raymond from surmounting. He began at last to shew signs of angry impatience, and Perdita became aware that the system she had adopted could not continue; she must explain herself to him; she could not summon courage to speak—she wrote thus:—

"Read this letter with patience, I entreat you. It will contain no reproaches. Reproach is indeed an idle word: for what should I reproach you?

"Allow me in some degree to explain my feeling; without that, we shall both grope in the dark, mistaking one another; erring from the path which may conduct, one of us at least, to a more eligible mode of life than that led by either during the last few weeks.

"I loved you—I love you—neither anger nor pride dictates these lines; but a feeling beyond, deeper, and more unalterable than either. My affections are wounded; it is impossible to heal them:—cease then the vain endeavour, if indeed that way your endeavours tend. Forgiveness! Return! Idle words are these! I forgive the pain I endure; but the trodden path cannot be retraced.

"Common affection might have been satisfied with common usages. I believed that you read my heart, and knew its devotion, its unalienable fidelity towards you. I never loved any but you. You came the embodied image of my fondest dreams. The praise of men, power and high aspirations attended your career. Love for you invested the world for me in enchanted light; it was no longer the earth I trod—the earth common mother, yielding only trite and stale repetition of objects and circumstances old and worn out. I lived in a temple glorified by intensest sense of devotion and rapture; I walked, a consecrated being, contemplating only your power, your excellence;

> For O, you stood beside me, like my youth,
> Transformed for me the real to a dream,
> Cloathing the palpable and familiar
> With golden exhalations of the dawn.

'The bloom has vanished from my life'[98]—there is no morning to this all investing night; no rising to the set-sun of love. In those days the rest of the world was nothing to me: all other men—I never considered nor felt what they were; nor did I look on you as one of them. Separated from them; exalted in my heart; sole possessor of my affections; single object of my hopes, the best half of myself.

"Ah, Raymond, were we not happy? Did the sun shine on any, who could enjoy its light with purer and more intense bliss? It was not—it is not a common infidelity at which I repine. It is the disunion of an whole which may not have parts; it is the carelessness with which you have shaken off the mantle of election with which to me you were invested, and have become one among the many. Dream not to alter this. Is not love a divinity, because it is immortal? Did not I appear sanctified, even to myself, because this love had for its temple my heart? I have gazed on you as you slept, melted even to tears, as the idea filled my mind, that all I possessed lay cradled in those idolized, but mortal lineaments before me. Yet, even then, I have checked thick-coming fears with one thought; I would not fear death, for the emotions that linked us must be immortal.

"And now I do not fear death. I should be well pleased to close my eyes, never more to open them again. And yet I fear it; even as I fear all things; for in any state of being linked by the chain of memory with this, happiness would not return—even in Paradise, I must feel that your love was less enduring than the mortal beatings of my fragile heart, every pulse of which knells audibly,

> The funeral note
> Of love, deep buried, without resurrection.[99]

No—no—me miserable; for love extinct there is no resurrection!

"Yet I love you. Yet, and for ever, would I contribute all I possess to your welfare. On account of a tattling world; for the sake of my—of our child, I would remain by you, Raymond, share your fortunes, partake your counsel. Shall it be thus? We are no longer lovers; nor can I call myself a friend to any; since, lost as I am, I have no thought to spare from my own wretched, engrossing self. But it will please me to see you each day! to lis-

---

98 This quotation, like the longer one that precedes it, is from S. T. Coleridge's translation of Schiller's *The Death of Wallenstein* 5.1.62-66. Claire Clairmont quotes the German text of this same passage in a journal entry for June 1825, commenting that it is "very descriptive of our lost friend" (*Journals*, ed. Marion Kingston Stocking 329). The reference is probably to PBS.

99 Byron, *Werner* 3.3.6-10: " 'Tis a perpetual knell, / Though for a marriage feast it rings: each stroke / Peals for a hope the less; the funeral note / Of Love deep-buried without resurrection / In the grave of Possession."

ten to the public voice praising you; to keep up your paternal love for our girl; to hear your voice; to know that I am near you, though you are no longer mine.

"If you wish to break the chains that bind us, say the word, and it shall be done—I will take all the blame on myself, of harshness or unkindness, in the world's eye.

"Yet, as I have said, I should be best pleased, at least for the present, to live under the same roof with you. When the fever of my young life is spent; when placid age shall tame the vulture that devours me, friendship may come, love and hope being dead. May this be true? Can my soul, inextricably linked to this perishable frame, become lethargic and cold, even as this sensitive mechanism shall lose its youthful elasticity? Then, with lack-lustre eyes, grey hairs, and wrinkled brow, though now the words sound hollow and meaningless, then, tottering on the grave's extreme edge, I may be—your affectionate and true friend,

"PERDITA."

Raymond's answer was brief. What indeed could he reply to her complaints, to her griefs which she jealously paled round, keeping out all thought of remedy. "Notwithstanding your bitter letter," he wrote, "for bitter I must call it, you are the chief person in my estimation, and it is your happiness that I would principally consult. Do that which seems best to you: and if you can receive gratification from one mode of life in preference to another, do not let me be any obstacle. I foresee that the plan which you mark out in your letter will not endure long; but you are mistress of yourself, and it is my sincere wish to contribute as far as you will permit me to your happiness."

"Raymond has prophesied well," said Perdita, "alas, that it should be so! our present mode of life cannot continue long, yet I will not be the first to propose alteration. He beholds in me one whom he has injured even unto death; and I derive no hope from his kindness; no change can possibly be brought about even by his best intentions. As well might Cleopatra have worn as an ornament the vinegar which contained her dissolved pearl,[100] as I be content with the love that Raymond can now offer me."

I own that I did not see her misfortune with the same eyes as Perdita. At all events methought that the wound could be healed; and, if they remained together, it would be so. I endeavoured therefore to sooth and soften her mind; and it was not until after many endeavours that I gave up the task as impracticable. Perdita listened to me impatiently, and answered with some asperity:—"Do you think that any of your arguments

---

100 Having impressed Antony with lavish feasts, Cleopatra outdid herself by dissolving a pearl in acid wine and drinking it (Pliny, *Natural History* 9.58.119-21).

are new to me? or that my own burning wishes and intense anguish have not suggested them all a thousand times, with far more eagerness and subtlety than you can put into them? Lionel, you cannot understand what woman's love is. In days of happiness I have often repeated to myself, with a grateful heart and exulting spirit, all that Raymond sacrificed for me. I was a poor, uneducated, unbefriended, mountain girl, raised from nothingness by him. All that I possessed of the luxuries of life came from him. He gave me an illustrious name and noble station; the world's respect reflected from his own glory: all this joined to his own undying love, inspired me with sensations towards him, akin to those with which we regard the Giver of life. I gave him love only. I devoted myself to him: imperfect creature that I was I took myself to task, that I might become worthy of him. I watched over my hasty temper, subdued my burning impatience of character, schooled my self-engrossing thoughts, educating myself to the best perfection I might attain, that the fruit of my exertions might be his happiness. I took no merit to myself for this. He deserved it all—all labour, all devotion, all sacrifice; I would have toiled up a scaleless Alp, to pluck a flower that would please him. I was ready to quit you all, my beloved and gifted companions, and to live only with him, for him. I could not do otherwise, even if I had wished; for if we are said to have two souls,[101] he was my better soul, to which the other was a perpetual slave. One only return did he owe me, even fidelity. I earned that; I deserved it. Because I was mountain bred, unallied to the noble and wealthy, shall he think to repay me by an empty name and station? Let him take them back; without his love they are nothing to me. Their only merit in my eyes was that they were his."

Thus passionately Perdita ran on. When I adverted to the question of their entire separation, she replied: "Be it so! One day the period will arrive; I know it, and feel it. But in this I am a coward. This imperfect companionship, and our masquerade of union, are strangely dear to me. It is painful, I allow, destructive, impracticable. It keeps up a perpetual fever in my veins; it frets my immedicable wound; it is instinct with poison. Yet I must cling to it; perhaps it will kill me soon, and thus perform a thankful office."

In the mean time, Raymond had remained with Adrian and Idris. He was naturally frank; the continued absence of Perdita and myself became remarkable; and Raymond soon found relief from the constraint of months, by an unreserved confidence with his two friends. He related to them the situation in which he had found Evadne. At first, from delicacy to Adrian he concealed her name; but it was divulged in the course of his

---

101 Goethe's Faust (*Faust* Part 1, "Vor dem Tor" 1112-17) claims, "As for myself, there are two of me ('Zwei Seelen'), unreconciled. The one clings to the earth with its whole body sensually, while the other soars with all its might to the abodes of the blest" (trans. Barker Fairley).

narrative, and her former lover heard with the most acute agitation the history of her sufferings. Idris had shared Perdita's ill opinion of the Greek; but Raymond's account softened and interested her. Evadne's constancy, fortitude, even her ill-fated and ill-regulated love, were matter of admiration and pity; especially when, from the detail of the events of the nineteenth of October, it was apparent that she preferred suffering and death to any in her eyes degrading application for the pity and assistance of her lover. Her subsequent conduct did not diminish this interest. At first, relieved from famine and the grave, watched over by Raymond with the tenderest assiduity, with that feeling of repose peculiar to convalescence, Evadne gave herself up to rapturous gratitude and love. But reflection returned with health. She questioned him with regard to the motives which had occasioned his critical absence. She framed her enquiries with Greek subtlety; she formed her conclusions with the decision and firmness peculiar to her disposition. She could not divine, that the breach which she had occasioned between Raymond and Perdita was already irreparable: but she knew, that under the present system it would be widened each day, and that its result must be to destroy her lover's happiness, and to implant the fangs of remorse in his heart. From the moment that she perceived the right line of conduct, she resolved to adopt it, and to part from Raymond for ever. Conflicting passions, long-cherished love, and self-inflicted disappointment, made her regard death alone as sufficient refuge for her woe. But the same feelings and opinions which had before restrained her, acted with redoubled force; for she knew that the reflection that he had occasioned her death, would pursue Raymond through life, poisoning every enjoyment, clouding every prospect. Besides, though the violence of her anguish made life hateful, it had not yet produced that monotonous, lethargic sense of changeless misery which for the most part produces suicide. Her energy of character induced her still to combat with the ills of life; even those attendant on hopeless love presented themselves, rather in the shape of an adversary to be overcome, than of a victor to whom she must submit. Besides, she had memories of past tenderness to cherish, smiles, words, and even tears, to con over, which, though remembered in desertion and sorrow, were to be preferred to the forgetfulness of the grave. It was impossible to guess at the whole of her plan. Her letter to Raymond gave no clue for discovery; it assured him, that she was in no danger of wanting the means of life; she promised in it to preserve herself, and some future day perhaps to present herself to him in a station not unworthy of her. She then bade him, with the eloquence of despair and of unalterable love, a last farewell.

All these circumstances were now related to Adrian and Idris. Raymond then lamented the cureless evil of his situation with Perdita. He declared, notwithstanding her harshness, he even called it coldness, that he loved her. He had been ready once with the humility of a penitent, and the duty of a vassal, to surrender himself to her; giving up his very soul to her tutelage, to become her pupil, her slave, her bondsman.

She had rejected these advances; and the time for such exuberant submission, which must be founded on love and nourished by it, was now passed. Still all his wishes and endeavours were directed towards her peace, and his chief discomfort arose from the perception that he exerted himself in vain. If she were to continue inflexible in the line of conduct she now pursued, they must part. The combinations and occurrences of this senseless mode of intercourse were maddening to him. Yet he would not propose the separation. He was haunted by the fear of causing the death of one or other of the beings implicated in these events; and he could not persuade himself to undertake to direct the course of events, lest, ignorant of the land he traversed, he should lead those attached to the car into irremediable ruin.

After a discussion on this subject, which lasted for many hours, he took leave of his friends, and returned to town, unwilling to meet Perdita before us, conscious, as we all must be, of the thoughts uppermost in the minds of both. Perdita prepared to follow him with her child. Idris endeavoured to persuade her to remain. My poor sister looked at the counsellor with affright. She knew that Raymond had conversed with her, had he instigated this request?—was this to be the prelude to their eternal separation?—I have said, that the defects of her character awoke and acquired vigour from her unnatural position. She regarded with suspicion the invitation of Idris; she embraced me, as if she were about to be deprived of my affection also: calling me her more than brother, her only friend, her last hope, she pathetically conjured me not to cease to love her; and with encreased anxiety she departed for London, the scene and cause of all her misery.

The scenes that followed, convinced her that she had not yet fathomed the obscure gulph into which she had plunged. Her unhappiness assumed every day a new shape; every day some unexpected event seemed to close, while in fact it led onward, the train of calamities which now befell her.

The selected passion of the soul of Raymond was ambition. Readiness of talent, a capacity of entering into, and leading the dispositions of men; earnest desire of distinction were the awakeners and nurses of his ambition. But other ingredients mingled with these, and prevented him from becoming the calculating, determined character, which alone forms a successful hero. He was obstinate, but not firm; benevolent in his first movements; harsh and reckless when provoked. Above all, he was remorseless and unyielding in the pursuit of any object of desire, however lawless. Love of pleasure, and the softer sensibilities of our nature, made a prominent part of his character, conquering the conqueror; holding him in at the moment of acquisition; sweeping away ambition's web; making him forget the toil of weeks, for the sake of one moment's indulgence of the new and actual object of his wishes. Obeying these impulses, he had become the husband of Perdita: egged on by them, he found himself the lover of Evadne. He had now lost both. He had neither the ennobling self-gratulation, which constancy inspires, to console him, nor the voluptuous sense of abandonment to a forbidden, but intoxicating passion. His heart was exhausted by the recent events; his enjoyment of life was destroyed by the resentment of Perdita, and the flight of Evadne; and the inflexibility of the former, set the last seal upon the annihilation of his hopes. As long as their disunion remained a secret, he cherished an expectation of re-awakening past tenderness in her bosom; now that we were all made acquainted with these occurrences, and that Perdita, by declaring her resolves to others, in a manner pledged herself to their accomplishment, he gave up the idea of re-union as futile, and sought only, since he was unable to influence her to change, to reconcile himself to the present state of things. He made a vow against love and its train of struggles, disappointment and remorse, and sought in mere sensual enjoyment, a remedy for the injurious inroads of passion.

Debasement of character is the certain follower of such pursuits. Yet this consequence would not have been immediately remarkable, if Raymond had continued to apply himself to the execution of his plans for the public benefit, and the fulfilling his duties as Protector. But, extreme in all things, given up to immediate impressions, he entered with ardour into this new pursuit of pleasure, and followed up the incongruous intimacies occasioned by it without reflection or foresight. The council-chamber was deserted; the crowds which attended on him as agents to his various projects were neglected. Festivity, and even libertinism, became the order of the day.

Perdita beheld with affright the encreasing disorder. For a moment she thought that she could stem the torrent, and that Raymond could be induced to hear reason from her.—Vain hope! The moment of her influence was passed. He listened with haughtiness, replied disdainfully; and, if in truth, she succeeded in awakening his conscience, the sole effect was that he sought an opiate for the pang in oblivious riot. With the energy natural to her, Perdita then endeavoured to supply his place. Their still apparent union permitted her to do much; but no woman could, in the end, present a remedy to the encreasing negligence of the Protector; who, as if seized with a paroxysm of insanity, trampled on all ceremony, all order, all duty, and gave himself up to license.

Reports of these strange proceedings reached us, and we were undecided what method to adopt to restore our friend to himself and his country, when Perdita suddenly appeared among us. She detailed the progress of the mournful change, and entreated Adrian and myself to go up to London, and endeavour to remedy the encreasing evil:—"Tell him," she cried, "tell Lord Raymond, that my presence shall no longer annoy him. That he need not plunge into this destructive dissipation for the sake of disgusting me, and causing me to fly. This purpose is now accomplished; he will never see me more. But let me, it is my last entreaty, let me in the praises of his countrymen and the prosperity of England, find the choice of my youth justified."

During our ride up to town, Adrian and I discussed and argued upon Raymond's conduct, and his falling off from the hopes of permanent excellence on his part, which he had before given us cause to entertain. My friend and I had both been educated in one school, or rather I was his pupil in the opinion, that steady adherence to principle was the only road to honour; a ceaseless observance of the laws of general utility,[102] the only conscientious aim of human ambition. But though we both entertained these ideas, we differed in their application. Resentment added also a sting to my censure; and I reprobated Raymond's conduct in severe terms. Adrian was more benign, more considerate. He admitted that the principles that I laid down were the best; but he denied that they were the only ones. Quoting the text, *there are many mansions in my father's house*,[103] he insisted that the modes of becoming good or great, varied as much as the dispositions of men, of whom it might be said, as of the leaves of the forest, there were no two alike.

We arrived in London at about eleven at night. We conjectured, notwithstanding what we had heard, that we should find Raymond in St. Stephen's: thither we sped. The chamber was full—but there was no Protector; and there was an austere discontent manifest on the countenances of the leaders, and a whispering and busy tattle among the underlings, not less ominous. We hastened to the palace of the Protectorate. We found Raymond in his dining room with six others: the bottle was being pushed about merrily, and had made considerable inroads on the understanding of one or two. He who sat near Raymond was telling a story, which convulsed the rest with laughter.

Raymond sat among them, though while he entered into the spirit of the hour, his natural dignity never forsook him. He was gay, playful, fascinating—but never did he overstep the modesty of nature, or the respect due to himself, in his wildest sallies. Yet I own, that considering the task which Raymond had taken on himself as Protector of England, and the cares to which it became him to attend, I was exceedingly provoked to observe the worthless fellows on whom his time was wasted, and the jovial if not drunken spirit which seemed on the point of robbing him of his better self. I stood watching the scene, while Adrian flitted like a shadow in among them, and, by a word and look of sobriety, endeavoured to restore order in the assembly. Raymond expressed himself delighted to see him, declaring that he should make one in the festivity of the night.

This action of Adrian provoked me. I was indignant that he should sit at the same table with the companions of Raymond—men of abandoned characters, or rather without any, the refuse of high-bred luxury, the dis-

---

102 Those principles according to which an action is right or good if it increases general happiness and reduces general suffering.
103 Cf. John 14.2: "In my Father's house are many mansions: if it were not so, I would have told you. I go to prepare a place for you."

grace of their country. "Let me entreat Adrian," I cried, "not to comply: rather join with me in endeavouring to withdraw Lord Raymond from this scene, and restore him to other society."

"My good fellow," said Raymond, "this is neither the time nor place for the delivery of a moral lecture: take my word for it that my amusements and society are not so bad as you imagine. We are neither hypocrites or fools—for the rest, 'Dost thou think because thou art virtuous, there shall be no more cakes and ale?' "[104]

I turned angrily away: "Verney," said Adrian, "you are very cynical: sit down; or if you will not, perhaps, as you are not a frequent visitor, Lord Raymond will humour you, and accompany us, as we had previously agreed upon, to parliament."

Raymond looked keenly at him; he could read benignity only in his gentle lineaments; he turned to me, observing with scorn my moody and stern demeanour. "Come," said Adrian, "I have promised for you, enable me to keep my engagement. Come with us."—Raymond made an uneasy movement, and laconically replied—"I won't!"

The party in the mean time had broken up. They looked at the pictures, strolled into the other apartments, talked of billiards, and one by one vanished. Raymond strode angrily up and down the room. I stood ready to receive and reply to his reproaches. Adrian leaned against the wall. "This is infinitely ridiculous," he cried, "if you were school-boys, you could not conduct yourselves more unreasonably."

"You do not understand," said Raymond. "This is only part of a system:—a scheme of tyranny to which I will never submit. Because I am Protector of England, am I to be the only slave in its empire? My privacy invaded, my actions censured, my friends insulted? But I will get rid of the whole together.—Be you witnesses," and he took the star, insignia of office, from his breast, and threw it on the table. "I renounce my office, I abdicate my power—assume it who will!"—

"Let him assume it," exclaimed Adrian, "who can pronounce himself, or whom the world will pronounce to be your superior. There does not exist the man in England with adequate presumption. Know yourself, Raymond and your indignation will cease; your complacency return. A few months ago, whenever we prayed for the prosperity of our country, or our own, we at the same time prayed for the life and welfare of the Protector, as indissolubly linked to it. Your hours were devoted to our benefit, your ambition was to obtain our commendation. You decorated our towns with edifices, you bestowed on us useful establishments, you gifted the soil with abundant fertility. The powerful and unjust cowered at the steps of your judgment-seat, and the poor and oppressed arose like morn-awakened flowers under the sunshine of your protection.

"Can you wonder that we are all aghast and mourn, when this appears

---

104 *Twelfth Night* 2.3.109-110.

changed? But, come, this splenetic fit is already passed; resume your functions; your partizans will hail you; your enemies be silenced; our love, honour, and duty will again be manifested towards you. Master yourself, Raymond, and the world is subject to you."

"All this would be very good sense, if addressed to another," replied Raymond, moodily, "con the lesson yourself, and you, the first peer of the land, may become its sovereign. You the good, the wise, the just, may rule all hearts. But I perceive, too soon for my own happiness, too late for England's good, that I undertook a task to which I am unequal. I cannot rule myself. My passions are my masters; my smallest impulse my tyrant. Do you think that I renounced the Protectorate (and I have renounced it) in a fit of spleen? By the God that lives, I swear never to take up that bauble again; never again to burthen myself with the weight of care and misery, of which that is the visible sign.

"Once I desired to be a king. It was in the hey-day of youth, in the pride of boyish folly. I knew myself when I renounced it. I renounced it to gain—no matter what—for that also I have lost. For many months I have submitted to this mock majesty—this solemn jest. I am its dupe no longer. I will be free.

"I have lost that which adorned and dignified my life; that which linked me to other men. Again I am a solitary man; and I will become again, as in my early years, a wanderer, a soldier of fortune. My friends, for Verney, I feel that you are my friend, do not endeavour to shake my resolve. Perdita, wedded to an imagination, careless of what is behind the veil, whose charactery is in truth faulty and vile, Perdita has renounced me. With her it was pretty enough to play a sovereign's part; and, as in the recesses of your beloved forest we acted masques, and imagined ourselves Arcadian shepherds, to please the fancy of the moment—so was I content, more for Perdita's sake than my own, to take on me the character of one of the great ones of the earth; to lead her behind the scenes of grandeur, to vary her life with a short act of magnificence and power. This was to be the colour; love and confidence the substance of our existence. But we must live, and not act our lives; pursuing the shadow, I lost the reality—now I renounce both.

"Adrian, I am about to return to Greece, to become again a soldier, perhaps a conqueror. Will you accompany me? You will behold new scenes; see a new people; witness the mighty struggle there going forward between civilization and barbarism; behold, and perhaps direct the efforts of a young and vigorous population, for liberty and order. Come with me. I have expected you. I waited for this moment; all is prepared;—will you accompany me?"

"I will," replied Adrian.

"Immediately?"

"To-morrow if you will."

"Reflect!" I cried.

"Wherefore?" asked Raymond—"My dear fellow, I have done nothing else than reflect on this step the live-long summer; and be assured that Adrian has condensed an age of reflection into this little moment. Do not talk of reflection; from this moment I abjure it; this is my only happy moment during a long interval of time. I must go, Lionel—the Gods will it; and I must. Do not endeavour to deprive me of my companion, the out-cast's friend.

"One word more concerning unkind, unjust Perdita. For a time, I thought that, by watching a complying moment, fostering the still warm ashes, I might relume in her the flame of love. It is more cold within her, than a fire left by gypsies in winter-time, the spent embers crowned by a pyramid of snow. Then, in endeavouring to do violence to my own disposition, I made all worse than before. Still I think, that time, and even absence, may restore her to me. Remember, that I love her still, that my dearest hope is that she will again be mine. I know, though she does not, how false the veil is which she has spread over the reality—do not endeavour to rend this deceptive covering, but by degrees withdraw it. Present her with a mirror, in which she may know herself; and, when she is an adept in that necessary but difficult science, she will wonder at her present mistake, and hasten to restore to me, what is by right mine, her forgiveness, her kind thoughts, her love."

CHAPTER XI

AFTER these events, it was long before we were able to attain any degree of composure. A moral tempest had wrecked our richly freighted vessel, and we, remnants of the diminished crew, were aghast at the losses and changes which we had undergone. Idris passionately loved her brother, and could ill brook an absence whose duration was uncertain; his society was dear and necessary to me—I had followed up my chosen literary occupations with delight under his tutorship and assistance; his mild philosophy, unerring reason, and enthusiastic friendship were the best ingredient, the exalted spirit of our circle; even the children bitterly regretted the loss of their kind playfellow. Deeper grief oppressed Perdita. In spite of resentment, by day and night she figured to herself the toils and dangers of the wanderers. Raymond absent, struggling with difficulties, lost to the power and rank of the Protectorate, exposed to the perils of war, became an object of anxious interest; not that she felt any inclination to recall him, if recall must imply a return to their former union. Such return she felt to be impossible; and while she believed it to be thus, and with anguish regretted that so it should be, she continued angry and impatient with him, who occasioned her misery. These perplexities and regrets caused her to bathe her pillow with nightly tears, and to reduce her in person and in mind to the shadow of what she had been. She sought solitude, and avoided us when in gaiety and unrestrained affection we met in a family circle. Lonely musings, interminable wanderings, and solemn music were her only pastimes. She neglected even her child; shutting her heart against all tenderness, she grew reserved towards me, her first and fast friend.

I could not see her thus lost, without exerting myself to remedy the evil—remediless I knew, if I could not in the end bring her to reconcile herself to Raymond. Before he went I used every argument, every persuasion to induce her to stop his journey. She answered the one with a gush of tears— telling me that to be persuaded—life and the goods of life were a cheap exchange. It was not will that she wanted, but the capacity; again and again she declared, it were as easy to enchain the sea, to put reins on the wind's viewless courses, as for her to take truth for falsehood, deceit for honesty, heartless communion for sincere, confiding love. She answered my reasonings more briefly, declaring with disdain, that the reason was hers; and, until I could persuade her that the past could be unacted, that maturity could go back to the cradle, and that all that was could become as though it had never been, it was useless to assure her that no real change had taken place in her fate. And thus with stern pride she suffered him to go, though her very heart-strings cracked at the fulfilling of the act, which rent from her all that made life valuable.

To change the scene for her, and even for ourselves, all unhinged by the cloud that had come over us, I persuaded my two remaining companions that it were better that we should absent ourselves for a time from Windsor. We visited the north of England, my native Ulswater, and lingered in scenes dear from a thousand associations. We lengthened our tour into Scotland, that we might see Loch Katrine and Loch Lomond; thence we crossed to Ireland, and passed several weeks in the neighbourhood of Killarney.[105] The change of scene operated to a great degree as I expected; after a year's absence, Perdita returned in gentler and more docile mood to Windsor. The first sight of this place for a time unhinged her. Here every spot was distinct with associations now grown bitter. The forest glades, the ferny dells, and lawny uplands, the cultivated and cheerful country spread around the silver pathway of ancient Thames, all earth, air, and wave, took up one choral voice, inspired by memory, instinct with plaintive regret.

But my essay towards bringing her to a saner view of her own situation, did not end here. Perdita was still to a great degree uneducated. When first she left her peasant life, and resided with the elegant and cultivated Evadne, the only accomplishment she brought to any perfection was that of painting, for which she had a taste almost amounting to genius. This had occupied her in her lonely cottage, when she quitted her Greek friend's protection. Her pallet and easel were now thrown aside; did she try to paint, thronging recollections made her hand tremble, her eyes fill

---

105 A town in County Kerry, Ireland; Loch Katrine and Loch Lomond are in southwest Scotland.

with tears. With this occupation she gave up almost every other; and her mind preyed upon itself almost to madness.

For my own part, since Adrian had first withdrawn me from my selvatic[106] wilderness to his own paradise of order and beauty, I had been wedded to literature. I felt convinced that however it might have been in former times, in the present stage of the world, no man's faculties could be developed, no man's moral principle be enlarged and liberal, without an extensive acquaintance with books. To me they stood in the place of an active career, of ambition, and those palpable excitements necessary to the multitude. The collation of philosophical opinions, the study of historical facts, the acquirement of languages, were at once my recreation, and the serious aim of my life. I turned author myself. My productions however were sufficiently unpretending; they were confined to the biography of favourite historical characters, especially those whom I believed to have been traduced, or about whom clung obscurity and doubt.

As my authorship increased, I acquired new sympathies and pleasures. I found another and a valuable link to enchain me to my fellow-creatures; my point of sight was extended, and the inclinations and capacities of all human beings became deeply interesting to me. Kings have been called the fathers of their people. Suddenly I became as it were the father of all mankind. Posterity became my heirs. My thoughts were gems to enrich the treasure house of man's intellectual possessions; each sentiment was a precious gift I bestowed on them. Let not these aspirations be attributed to vanity. They were not expressed in words, nor even reduced to form in my own mind; but they filled my soul, exalting my thoughts, raising a glow of enthusiasm, and led me out of the obscure path in which I before walked, into the bright noon-enlightened highway of mankind, making me, citizen of the world, a candidate for immortal honors, an eager aspirant to the praise and sympathy of my fellow men.

No one certainly ever enjoyed the pleasures of composition more intensely than I. If I left the woods, the solemn music of the waving branches, and the majestic temple of nature, I sought the vast halls of the Castle, and looked over wide, fertile England, spread beneath our regal mount, and listened the while to inspiring strains of music. At such times solemn harmonies or spirit-stirring airs gave wings to my lagging thoughts, permitting them, methought, to penetrate the last veil of nature and her God, and to display the highest beauty in visible expression to the understandings of men. As the music went on, my ideas seemed to quit their mortal dwelling house; they shook their pinions and began a flight, sailing on the placid current of thought, filling the creation with new glory, and rousing sublime imagery that else had slept voiceless. Then I would hasten to my desk, weave the new-found web of mind in firm texture and

---

106 Wooded (from Latin *silva*); the word does not appear in the *OED*.

brilliant colours, leaving the fashioning of the material to a calmer moment.

But this account, which might as properly belong to a former period of my life as to the present moment, leads me far afield. It was the pleasure I took in literature, the discipline of mind I found arise from it, that made me eager to lead Perdita to the same pursuits. I began with light hand and gentle allurement; first exciting her curiosity, and then satisfying it in such a way as might occasion her, at the same time that she half forgot her sorrows in occupation, to find in the hours that succeeded a reaction of benevolence and toleration.

Intellectual activity, though not directed towards books, had always been my sister's characteristic. It had been displayed early in life, leading her out to solitary musing among her native mountains, causing her to form innumerous combinations from common objects, giving strength to her perceptions, and swiftness to their arrangement. Love had come, as the rod of the master-prophet,[107] to swallow up every minor propensity. Love had doubled all her excellencies, and placed a diadem on her genius. Was she to cease to love? Take the colours and odour from the rose, change the sweet nutriment of mother's milk to gall and poison; as easily might you wean Perdita from love. She grieved for the loss of Raymond with an anguish, that exiled all smile from her lips, and trenched sad lines on her brow of beauty. But each day seemed to change the nature of her suffering, and every succeeding hour forced her to alter (if so I may style it) the fashion of her soul's mourning garb. For a time music was able to satisfy the cravings of her mental hunger, and her melancholy thoughts renewed themselves in each change of key, and varied with every alteration in the strain. My schooling first impelled her towards books; and, if music had been the food of sorrow, the productions of the wise became its medicine.

The acquisition of unknown languages was too tedious an occupation, for one who referred every expression to the universe within, and read not, as many do, for the mere sake of filling up time; but who was still questioning herself and her author, moulding every idea in a thousand ways, ardently desirous for the discovery of truth in every sentence. She sought to improve her understanding; mechanically her heart and dispositions became soft and gentle under this benign discipline. After awhile she discovered, that amidst all her newly acquired knowledge, her own character, which formerly she fancied that she thoroughly understood, became the first in rank among the terræ incognitæ, the pathless wilds of a country that had no chart. Erringly and strangely she began the task of

---

107 Before the story of the exodus from Egypt in the Bible, Aaron shows his power by competing with Pharoah's magicians: "For they cast down every man his rod, and they became serpents: but Aaron's rod swallowed up their rods" (Exodus 7.12).

self-examination with self-condemnation. And then again she became aware of her own excellencies, and began to balance with juster scales the shades of good and evil. I, who longed beyond words, to restore her to the happiness it was still in her power to enjoy, watched with anxiety the result of these internal proceedings.

But man is a strange animal. We cannot calculate on his forces like that of an engine; and, though an impulse draw with a forty-horse power[108]at what appears willing to yield to one, yet in contempt of calculation the movement is not effected. Neither grief, philosophy, nor love could make Perdita think with mildness of the dereliction of Raymond. She now took pleasure in my society; towards Idris she felt and displayed a full and affectionate sense of her worth—she restored to her child in abundant measure her tenderness and care. But I could discover, amidst all her repinings, deep resentment towards Raymond, and an unfading sense of injury, that plucked from me my hope, when I appeared nearest to its fulfilment. Among other painful restrictions, she has occasioned it to become a law among us, never to mention Raymond's name before her. She refused to read any communications from Greece, desiring me only to mention when any arrived, and whether the wanderers were well. It was curious that even little Clara observed this law towards her mother. This lovely child was nearly eight years of age. Formerly she had been a light-hearted infant, fanciful, but gay and childish. After the departure of her father, thought became impressed on her young brow. Children, unadepts in language, seldom find words to express their thoughts, nor could we tell in what manner the late events had impressed themselves on her mind. But certainly she had made deep observations while she noted in silence the changes that passed around her. She never mentioned her father to Perdita, she appeared half afraid when she spoke of him to me, and though I tried to draw her out on the subject, and to dispel the gloom that hung about her ideas concerning him, I could not succeed. Yet each foreign post-day she watched for the arrival of letters—knew the post mark, and watched me as I read. I found her often poring over the article of Greek intelligence in the newspaper.

There is no more painful sight than that of untimely care in children, and it was particularly observable in one whose disposition had heretofore been mirthful. Yet there was so much sweetness and docility about Clara, that your admiration was excited; and if the moods of mind are calculated to paint the cheek with beauty, and endow motions with grace, surely her contemplations must have been celestial; since every lineament was moulded into loveliness, and her motions were more harmonious than the elegant boundings of the fawns of her native forest. I sometimes expostulated with Perdita on the subject of her reserve; but she rejected my

---

108 That is, considerable force: Byron refers in 1823 to the "forty-horse-power" of a steam-engine (notes to *Don Juan* 10.34.1).

counsels, while her daughter's sensibility excited in her a tenderness still more passionate.

After the lapse of more than a year, Adrian returned from Greece.

When our exiles had first arrived, a truce was in existence between the Turks and Greeks; a truce that was as sleep to the mortal frame, signal of renewed activity on waking. With the numerous soldiers of Asia, with all of warlike stores, ships, and military engines, that wealth and power could command, the Turks at once resolved to crush an enemy, which creeping on by degrees, had from their stronghold in the Morea,[109] acquired Thrace and Macedonia, and had led their armies even to the gates of Constantinople, while their extensive commercial relations gave every European nation an interest in their success. Greece prepared for a vigorous resistance; it rose to a man; and the women, sacrificing their costly ornaments, accoutred their sons for the war, and bade them conquer or die with the spirit of the Spartan mother. The talents and courage of Raymond were highly esteemed among the Greeks. Born at Athens, that city claimed him for her own, and by giving him the command of her peculiar division in the army, the commander-in-chief only possessed superior power. He was numbered among her citizens, his name was added to the list of Grecian heroes. His judgment, activity, and consummate bravery, justified their choice. The Earl of Windsor became a volunteer under his friend.

"It is well," said Adrian, "to prate of war in these pleasant shades, and with much ill-spent oil make a show of joy, because many thousand of our fellow-creatures leave with pain this sweet air and natal earth. I shall not be suspected of being averse to the Greek cause; I know and feel its necessity; it is beyond every other a good cause. I have defended it with my sword, and was willing that my spirit should be breathed out in its defence; freedom is of more worth than life, and the Greeks do well to defend their privilege unto death. But let us not deceive ourselves. The Turks are men; each fibre, each limb is as feeling as our own, and every spasm, be it mental or bodily, is as truly felt in a Turk's heart or brain, as in a Greek's. The last action at which I was present was the taking of —. The Turks resisted to the last, the garrison perished on the ramparts, and we entered by assault. Every breathing creature within the walls was massacred. Think you, amidst the shrieks of violated innocence and helpless infancy, I did not feel in every nerve the cry of a fellow being? They were men and women, the sufferers, before they were Mahometans, and when they rise turbanless from the grave,[110] in what except their good or evil

---

109 The Morea (or the Peloponnesus) is the large peninsula in southern Greece; this was one of the six military divisions of Greece under the Ottoman Empire (1453-1829).

110 That is, when differences of rank, denoted by different colours of turbans, are no longer relevant.

actions will they be the better or worse than we? Two soldiers contended for a girl, whose rich dress and extreme beauty excited the brutal appetites of these wretches, who, perhaps good men among their families, were changed by the fury of the moment into incarnated evils. An old man, with a silver beard, decrepid and bald, he might be her grandfather, interposed to save her; the battle axe of one of them clove his skull. I rushed to her defence, but rage made them blind and deaf; they did not distinguish my Christian garb or heed my words—words were blunt weapons then, for while war cried "havoc," and murder gave fit echo, how could I—

.Turn back the tide of ills, relieving wrong
With mild accost of soothing eloquence?[111]

One of the fellows, enraged at my interference, struck me with his bayonet in the side, and I fell senseless.

"This wound will probably shorten my life, having shattered a frame, weak of itself. But I am content to die. I have learnt in Greece that one man, more or less, is of small import, while human bodies remain to fill up the thinned ranks of the soldiery; and that the identity of an individual may be overlooked, so that the muster roll contain its full numbers. All this has a different effect upon Raymond. He is able to contemplate the ideal of war, while I am sensible only to its realities. He is a soldier, a general. He can influence the blood-thirsty war-dogs, while I resist their propensities vainly. The cause is simple. Burke has said that, 'in all bodies those who would lead, must also, in a considerable degree, follow.'[112]—I cannot follow; for I do not sympathize in their dreams of massacre and glory—to follow and to lead in such a career, is the natural bent of Raymond's mind. He is always successful, and bids fair, at the same time that he acquires high name and station for himself, to secure liberty, probably extended empire, to the Greeks."

Perdita's mind was not softened by this account. He, she thought, can be great and happy without me. Would that I also had a career! Would that I could freight some untried bark with all my hopes, energies, and desires, and launch it forth into the ocean of life—bound for some attainable point, with ambition or pleasure at the helm! But adverse winds detain me on shore; like Ulysses, I sit at the water's edge and weep.[113] But my nerveless hands can neither fell the trees, nor smooth the planks. Under

---

111 From Charles Abraham Elton's translation of Hesiod's *Theogony* (2nd ed. 1815). The first lines should read "retrieving wrongs"; MWS adds the question mark to suit her own context.

112 In his *Reflections on the Revolution in France*, ed. Conor Cruise O'Brien 128.

113 In the *Odyssey*, Odysseus (Ulysses) is distracted on his way home to Ithaca by the nymph Calypso. When Calypso, urged by Hermes, is persuaded to let

the influence of these melancholy thoughts, she became more than ever in love with sorrow. Yet Adrian's presence did some good; he at once broke through the law of silence observed concerning Raymond. At first she started from the unaccustomed sound; soon she got used to it and to love it, and she listened with avidity to the account of his achievements. Clara got rid also of her restraint; Adrian and she had been old playfellows; and now, as they walked or rode together, he yielded to her earnest entreaty, and repeated, for the hundredth time, some tale of her father's bravery, munificence, or justice.

Each vessel in the mean time brought exhilarating tidings from Greece. The presence of a friend in its armies and councils made us enter into the details with enthusiasm; and a short letter now and then from Raymond told us how he was engrossed by the interests of his adopted country. The Greeks were strongly attached to their commercial pursuits, and would have been satisfied with their present acquisitions, had not the Turks roused them by invasion. The patriots were victorious; a spirit of conquest was instilled; and already they looked on Constantinople as their own. Raymond rose perpetually in their estimation; but one man held a superior command to him in their armies. He was conspicuous for his conduct and choice of position in a battle fought in the plains of Thrace, on the banks of the Hebrus, which was to decide the fate of Islam. The Mahometans were defeated, and driven entirely from the country west of this river. The battle was sanguinary, the loss of the Turks apparently irreparable; the Greeks, in losing one man, forgot the nameless crowd strewed upon the bloody field, and they ceased to value themselves on a victory, which cost them—Raymond.

At the battle of Makri he had led the charge of cavalry, and pursued the fugitives even to the banks of the Hebrus.[114] His favourite horse was found grazing by the margin of the tranquil river. It became a question whether he had fallen among the unrecognized; but no broken ornament or stained trapping betrayed his fate. It was suspected that the Turks, finding themselves possessed of so illustrious a captive, resolved to satisfy their cruelty rather than their avarice, and fearful of the interference of England, had come to the determination of concealing for ever the cold-blooded murder of the soldier they most hated and feared in the squadrons of their enemy.

Raymond was not forgotten in England. His abdication of the Protectorate had caused an unexampled sensation; and, when his magnificent

---

him leave, "She found him sitting on the shore; his eyes / Were never dried from weeping, his sweet life / With longings of return pined slow away" (from C. A. Elton, ed. *Specimens* 1: 43).

114 Makri is a town on the coast of Thrace, north of the Aegean Sea. Captured by the Turks, Raymond is sent to prison in Constantinople. The river Hebrus (Evros) flows into the Aegean west of Kishan (Keşan), where the Greek invaders of Constantinople and their allies gather later (132).

and manly system was contrasted with the narrow views of succeeding politicians, the period of his elevation was referred to with sorrow. The perpetual recurrence of his name, joined to most honourable testimonials, in the Greek gazettes,[115] kept up the interest he had excited. He seemed the favourite child of fortune, and his untimely loss eclipsed the world, and shewed forth the remnant of mankind with diminished lustre. They clung with eagerness to the hope held out that he might yet be alive. Their minister at Constantinople was urged to make the necessary perquisitions, and should his existence be ascertained, to demand his release. It was to be hoped that their efforts would succeed, and that though now a prisoner, the sport of cruelty and the mark of hate, he would be rescued from danger and restored to the happiness, power, and honour which he deserved.

The effect of this intelligence upon my sister was striking. She never for a moment credited the story of his death; she resolved instantly to go to Greece. Reasoning and persuasion were thrown away upon her; she would endure no hindrance, no delay. It may be advanced for a truth, that, if argument or entreaty can turn any one from a desperate purpose, whose motive and end depends on the strength of the affections only, then it is right so to turn them, since their docility shews, that neither the motive nor the end were of sufficient force to bear them through the obstacles attendant on their undertaking. If, on the contrary, they are proof against expostulation, this very steadiness is an omen of success; and it becomes the duty of those who love them, to assist in smoothing the obstructions in their path. Such sentiments actuated our little circle. Finding Perdita immoveable, we consulted as to the best means of furthering her purpose. She could not go alone to a country where she had no friends, where she might arrive only to hear the dreadful news, which must overwhelm her with grief and remorse. Adrian, whose health had always been weak, now suffered considerable aggravation of suffering from the effects of his wound. Idris could not endure to leave him in this state; nor was it right either to quit or take with us a young family for a journey of this description. I resolved at length to accompany Perdita. The separation from my Idris was painful—but necessity reconciled us to it in some degree: necessity and the hope of saving Raymond, and restoring him again to happiness and Perdita. No delay was to ensue. Two days after we came to our determination, we set out for Portsmouth, and embarked. The season was May, the weather stormless; we were promised a prosperous voyage. Cherishing the most fervent hopes, embarked on the waste ocean, we saw with delight the receding shore of Britain, and on the wings of desire outspeeded our well filled sails towards the South. The light curling waves bore us onward, and old ocean smiled at the freight of love and hope com-

---

115 Newspapers; here, official government papers or bulletins.

mitted to his charge; it stroked gently its tempestuous plains, and the path was smoothed for us. Day and night the wind right aft, gave steady impulse to our keel—nor did rough gale, or treacherous sand, or destructive rock interpose an obstacle between my sister and the land which was to restore her to her first beloved,

Her dear heart's confessor—a heart within that heart.[116]

---

116 The words *cor cordium* (heart of hearts), suggested by Leigh Hunt, appear on PBS's gravestone. In her *Journals*, 3 June 1823, MWS addresses PBS as "Meum cordium cor!" Cf. *The Last Man* 20, above, where Adrian "subdued [Lionel's] heart of hearts" and 267, below, where Idris addresses Lionel as "heart of my heart."

VOLUME TWO

CHAPTER XII

DURING this voyage, when on calm evenings we conversed on deck, watching the glancing of the waves and the changeful appearances of the sky, I discovered the total revolution that the disasters of Raymond had wrought in the mind of my sister. Were they the same waters of love, which, lately cold and cutting as ice, repelling as that, now loosened from their frozen chains, flowed through the regions of her soul in gushing and grateful exuberance? She did not believe that he was dead, but she knew that he was in danger, and the hope of assisting in his liberation, and the idea of soothing by tenderness the ills that he might have undergone, elevated and harmonized the late jarring element of her being. I was not so sanguine as she as to the result of our voyage. She was not sanguine, but secure; and the expectation of seeing the lover she had banished, the husband, friend, heart's companion from whom she had long been alienated, wrapt her senses in delight, her mind in placidity. It was beginning life again; it was leaving barren sands for an abode of fertile beauty; it was a harbour after a tempest, an opiate after sleepless nights, a happy waking from a terrible dream.

Little Clara accompanied us; the poor child did not well understand what was going forward. She heard that we were bound for Greece, that she would see her father, and now, for the first time, she prattled of him to her mother.

On landing at Athens we found difficulties encrease upon us: nor could the storied earth or balmy atmosphere inspire us with enthusiasm or pleasure, while the fate of Raymond was in jeopardy. No man had ever excited so strong an interest in the public mind; this was apparent even among the phlegmatic English, from whom he had long been absent. The Athenians had expected their hero to return in triumph; the women had taught their children to lisp his name joined to thanksgiving; his manly beauty, his courage, his devotion to their cause, made him appear in their eyes almost as one of the ancient deities of the soil descended from their native Olympus to defend them. When they spoke of his probable death and certain captivity, tears streamed from their eyes; even as the women of Syria sorrowed for Adonis,[1] did the wives and mothers of Greece lament our English Raymond—Athens was a city of mourning.

---

1   Adonis, a god of vegetation and fertility loved by Aphrodite the goddess of love, was killed by a boar when hunting; from his blood or her tears, the anemone sprung. In ancient times his death and survival were mourned and celebrated annually: see PBS's translation of Bion's "Elegy on the Death of Adonis," and cf. 48 above.

All these shews of despair struck Perdita with affright. With that sanguine but confused expectation, which desire engendered while she was at a distance from reality, she had formed an image in her mind of instantaneous change, when she should set her foot on Grecian shores. She fancied that Raymond would already be free, and that her tender attentions would come to entirely obliterate even the memory of his mischance. But his fate was still uncertain; she began to fear the worst, and to feel that her soul's hope was cast on a chance that might prove a blank. The wife and lovely child of Lord Raymond became objects of intense interest in Athens. The gates of their abode were besieged, audible prayers were breathed for his restoration; all these circumstances added to the dismay and fears of Perdita.

My exertions were unremitted: after a time I left Athens, and joined the army stationed at Kishan in Thrace.[2] Bribery, threats, and intrigue, soon discovered the secret that Raymond was alive, a prisoner, suffering the most rigorous confinement and wanton cruelties. We put in movement every impulse of policy and money to redeem him from their hands.

The impatience of my sister's disposition now returned on her, awakened by repentance, sharpened by remorse. The very beauty of the Grecian climate, during the season of spring, added torture to her sensations. The unexampled loveliness of the flower-clad earth—the genial sunshine and grateful shade—the melody of the birds—the majesty of the woods—the splendour of the marble ruins—the clear effulgence of the stars by night—the combination of all that was exciting and voluptuous in this transcending land, by inspiring a quicker spirit of life and an added sensitiveness to every articulation of her frame, only gave edge to the poignancy of her grief. Each long hour was counted, and *"He suffers"* was the burthen of all her thoughts. She abstained from food; she lay on the bare earth, and, by such mimickry of his enforced torments, endeavoured to hold communion with his distant pain. I remembered in one of her harshest moments a quotation of mine had roused her to anger and disdain. "Perdita," I had said, "some day you will discover that you have done wrong in again casting Raymond on the thorns of life. When disappointment has sullied his beauty, when a soldier's hardships have bent his manly form, and loneliness made even triumph bitter to him, then you will repent; and regret for the irreparable change

"will move
In hearts all rocky now, the late remorse of love."[3]

---

2   Thrace is north of the Aegean Sea; Kishan (Keşan), in the far east of this region, is in modern Turkey.

3   Lord Byron's Fourth Canto of Childe Harolde [MWS's note]; Lionel has actually quoted twice: first (a few lines above the set-down quotation) from PBS, "Ode to the West Wind"—"I fall upon the thorns of life! I bleed!" (54); and here from Bryron, *Childe Harold's Pilgrimage* 4. 1232-33.

The stinging "remorse of love" now pierced her heart. She accused herself of his journey to Greece—his dangers—his imprisonment. She pictured to herself the anguish of his solitude; she remembered with what eager delight he had in former days made her the partner of his joyful hopes—with what grateful affection he received her sympathy in his cares. She called to mind how often he had declared that solitude was to him the greatest of all evils, and how death itself was to him more full of fear and pain when he pictured to himself a lonely grave. "My best girl," he had said, "relieves me from these phantasies. United to her, cherished in her dear heart, never again shall I know the misery of finding myself alone. Even if I die before you, my Perdita, treasure up my ashes till yours may mingle with mine. It is a foolish sentiment for one who is not a materialist, yet, methinks, even in that dark cell, I may feel that my inanimate dust mingles with yours, and thus have a companion in decay." In her resentful mood, these expressions had been remembered with acrimony and disdain; they visited her in her softened hour, taking sleep from her eyes, all hope of rest from her uneasy mind.

Two months passed thus, when at last we obtained a promise of Raymond's release. Confinement and hardship had undermined his health; the Turks feared an accomplishment of the threats of the English government, if he died under their hands; they looked upon his recovery as impossible; they delivered him up as a dying man, willingly making over to us the rites of burial.

He came by sea from Constantinople to Athens. The wind, favourable to him, blew so strongly in shore, that we were unable, as we had at first intended, to meet him on his watery road. The watchtower of Athens was beseiged by inquirers, each sail eagerly looked out for; till on the first of May the gallant frigate bore in sight, freighted with treasure more invaluable than the wealth which, piloted from Mexico, the vexed Pacific swallowed, or that was conveyed over its tranquil bosom to enrich the crown of Spain.[4] At early dawn the vessel was discovered bearing in shore; it was conjectured that it would cast anchor about five miles from land. The news spread through Athens, and the whole city poured out at the gate of the Piræus,[5] down the roads, through the vineyards, the olive woods and plantations of fig-trees, towards the harbour. The noisy joy of the populace, the gaudy colours of their dress, the tumult of carriages and horses, the march of soldiers intermixed, the waving of banners and sound of martial music added to the high excitement of the scene; while round us reposed in solemn majesty the relics of antient time. To our right the Acropolis[6] rose high, spectatress of a thousand changes, of ancient glory,

---

4   One of several references in the novel to imperial conquest: Hernando Cortéz led an expedition to Mexico in 1519, conquering the Aztecs and sending their gold back to Spain.
5   The port of Athens.
6   The citadel of Athens, site of the Parthenon, temple of Athena.

Turkish slavery, and the restoration of dear-bought liberty; tombs and cenotaphs were strewed thick around, adorned by ever renewing vegetation; the mighty dead hovered over their monuments, and beheld in our enthusiasm and congregated numbers a renewal of the scenes in which they had been the actors. Perdita and Clara rode in a close carriage; I attended them on horseback. At length we arrived at the harbour; it was agitated by the outward swell of the sea; the beach, as far could be discerned, was covered by a moving multitude, which, urged by those behind toward the sea, again rushed back as the heavy waves with sullen roar burst close to them. I applied my glass, and could discern that the frigate had already cast anchor, fearful of the danger of approaching nearer to a lee shore: a boat was lowered; with a pang I saw that Raymond was unable to descend the vessel's side; he was let down in a chair, and lay wrapt in cloaks at the bottom of the boat.

I dismounted, and called to some sailors who were rowing about the harbour to pull up, and take me into their skiff; Perdita at the same moment alighted from her carriage—she seized my arm—"Take me with you," she cried; she was trembling and pale; Clara clung to her—"You must not," I said, "the sea is rough—he will soon be here—do you not see his boat?" The little bark to which I had beckoned had now pulled up; before I could stop her, Perdita, assisted by the sailors, was in it—Clara followed her mother—a loud shout echoed from the crowd as we pulled out of the inner harbour; while my sister at the prow, had caught hold of one of the men who was using a glass, asking a thousand questions, careless of the spray that broke over her, deaf, sightless to all, except the little speck that, just visible on the top of the waves, evidently neared. We approached with all the speed six rowers could give; the orderly and picturesque dress of the soldiers on the beach, the sounds of exulting music, the stirring breeze and waving flags, the unchecked exclamations of the eager crowd, whose dark looks and foreign garb were purely eastern; the sight of temple-crowned rock, the white marble of the buildings glittering in the sun, and standing in bright relief against the dark ridge of lofty mountains beyond; the near roar of the sea, the splash of oars, and dash of spray, all steeped my soul in a delirium, unfelt, unimagined in the common course of common life. Trembling, I was unable to continue to look through the glass with which I had watched the motion of the crew, when the frigate's boat had first been launched. We rapidly drew near, so that at length the number and forms of those within could be discerned; its dark sides grew big, and the splash of its oars became audible: I could distinguish the languid form of my friend, as he half raised himself at our approach.

Perdita's questions had ceased; she leaned on my arm, panting with emotions too acute for tears—our men pulled alongside the other boat. As a last effort, my sister mustered her strength, her firmness; she stepped from one boat to the other, and then with a shriek she sprang towards Raymond, knelt at his side, and glueing her lips to the hand she seized, her face shrouded by her long hair, gave herself up to tears.

Raymond had somewhat raised himself at our approach, but it was with difficulty that he exerted himself even thus much. With sunken cheek and hollow eyes, pale and gaunt, how could I recognize the beloved of Perdita? I continued awe-struck and mute—he looked smilingly on the poor girl; the smile was his. A day of sunshine falling on a dark valley, displays its before hidden characteristics; and now this smile, the same with which he first spoke love to Perdita, with which he had welcomed the protectorate, playing on his altered countenance, made me in my heart's core feel that this was Raymond.

He stretched out to me his other hand; I discerned the trace of manacles on his bared wrist. I heard my sister's sobs, and thought, happy are women who can weep, and in a passionate caress disburthen the oppression of their feelings; shame and habitual restraint hold back a man. I would have given worlds to have acted as in days of boyhood, have strained him to my breast, pressed his hand to my lips, and wept over him; my swelling heart choked me; the natural current would not be checked; the big rebellious tears gathered in my eyes; I turned aside, and they dropped in the sea—they came fast and faster;—yet I could hardly be ashamed, for I saw that the rough sailors were not unmoved, and Raymond's eyes alone were dry from among our crew. He lay in that blessed calm which convalescence always induces, enjoying in secure tranquillity his liberty and re-union with her whom he adored. Perdita at length subdued her burst of passion, and rose,—she looked round for Clara; the child frightened, not recognizing her father, and neglected by us, had crept to the other end of the boat; she came at her mother's call. Perdita presented her to Raymond; her first words were: "Beloved, embrace our child:" "Come hither, sweet one," said her father, "do you not know me?" she knew his voice, and cast herself in his arms with half bashful but uncontrollable emotion.

Perceiving the weakness of Raymond, I was afraid of ill consequences from the pressure of the crowd on his landing. But they were awed as I had been, at the change of his appearance. The music died away, the shouts abruptly ended; the soldiers had cleared a space in which a carriage was drawn up. He was placed in it; Perdita and Clara entered with him, and his escort closed round it; a hollow murmur, akin to the roaring of the near waves, went through the multitude; they fell back as the carriage advanced, and fearful of injuring him they had come to welcome, by loud testimonies of joy, they satisfied themselves with bending in a low salaam[7] as the carriage passed; it went slowly along the road of the Piraeus; passed by antique temple and heroic tomb, beneath the craggy rock of the citadel. The sound of the waves was left behind; that of the multitude continued at intervals, suppressed and hoarse; and though, in the city, the houses, churches, and public buildings were decorated with tapestry and

---

7   A ceremonial bow.

banners—though the soldiery lined the streets, and the inhabitants in thousands were assembled to give him hail, the same solemn silence prevailed, the soldiery presented arms, the banners vailed, many a white hand waved a streamer, and vainly sought to discern the hero in the vehicle, which, closed and encompassed by the city guards, drew him to the palace allotted for his abode.

Raymond was weak and exhausted, yet the interest he perceived to be excited on his account, filled him with proud pleasure. He was nearly killed with kindness. It is true, the populace restrained themselves; but there arose a perpetual hum and bustle from the throng round the palace, which added to the noise of fireworks, the frequent explosion of arms, the tramp to and fro of horsemen and carriages, to which effervescence he was the focus, retarded his recovery. So we retired awhile to Eleusis,[8] and here rest and tender care added each day to the strength of our invalid. The zealous attention of Perdita claimed the first rank in the causes which induced his rapid recovery; but the second was surely the delight he felt in the affection and good will of the Greeks. We are said to love much those whom we greatly benefit. Raymond had fought and conquered for the Athenians; he had suffered, on their account, peril, imprisonment, and hardship; their gratitude affected him deeply, and he inly vowed to unite his fate for ever to that of a people so enthusiastically devoted to him.

Social feeling and sympathy constituted a marked feature in my disposition. In early youth, the living drama acted around me, drew me heart and soul into its vortex. I was now conscious of a change. I loved, I hoped, I enjoyed; but there was something besides this. I was inquisitive as to the internal principles of action of those around me: anxious to read their thoughts justly, and for ever occupied in divining their inmost mind. All events, at the same time that they deeply interested me, arranged themselves in pictures before me. I gave the right place to every personage in the groupe, the just balance to every sentiment. This undercurrent of thought, often soothed me amidst distress, and even agony. It gave ideality to that, from which, taken in naked truth, the soul would have revolted: it bestowed pictorial colours on misery and disease, and not unfrequently relieved me from despair in deplorable changes. This faculty, or instinct, was now rouzed. I watched the re-awakened devotion of my sister; Clara's timid, but concentrated admiration of her father, and Raymond's appetite for renown, and sensitiveness to the demonstrations of affection of the Athenians. Attentively perusing this animated volume, I was the less surprised at the tale I read on the new-turned page.

The Turkish army were at this time besieging Rodosto;[9] and the

---

8   A city in Attica, famed in ancient times for religious rites performed in honour of Demeter and Persephone.

9   Known today as Tekirdağ, Rodosto is west of Istanbul on the Sea of Marmara.

Greeks, hastening their preparations, and sending each day reinforcements, were on the eve of forcing the enemy to battle. Each people looked on the coming struggle as that which would be to a great degree decisive; as, in case of victory, the next step would be the siege of Constantinople by the Greeks. Raymond, being somewhat recovered, prepared to re-assume his command in the army.

Perdita did not oppose herself to his determination. She only stipulated to be permitted to accompany him. She had set down no rule of conduct for herself; but for her life she could not have opposed his slightest wish, or do other than acquiesce cheerfully in all his projects. One word, in truth, had alarmed her more than battles or sieges, during which she trusted Raymond's high command would exempt him from danger. That word, as yet it was no more to her, was PLAGUE.[10] This enemy to the human race had begun early in June to raise its serpent-head on the shores of the Nile; parts of Asia, not usually subject to this evil, were infected. It was in Constantinople; but as each year that city experienced a like visitation, small attention was paid to those accounts which declared more people to have died there already, than usually made up the accustomed prey of the whole of the hotter months. However it might be, neither plague nor war could prevent Perdita from following her lord, or induce her to utter one objection to the plans which he proposed. To be near him, to be loved by him, to feel him again her own, was the limit of her desires. The object of her life was to do him pleasure: it had been so before, but with a difference. In past times, without thought or foresight she had made him happy, being so herself, and in any question of choice, consulted her own wishes, as being one with his. Now she sedulously put herself out of the question, sacrificing even her anxiety for his health and welfare to her resolve not to oppose any of his desires. Love of the Greek people, appetite for glory, and hatred of the barbarian government under which he had suffered even to the approach of death, stimulated him. He wished to repay the kindness of the Athenians, to keep alive the splendid associations connected with his name, and to eradicate from Europe a power which, while every other nation advanced in civilization, stood still, a monument of antique barbarism. Having effected the reunion of Raymond and Perdita, I was eager to return to England; but his earnest request, added to awakening curiosity, and an indefinable anxiety to behold the catastrophe, now apparently at hand, in the long drawn history of Grecian and Turkish warfare, induced me to consent to prolong until the autumn, the period of my residence in Greece.

As soon as the health of Raymond was sufficiently re-established, he

---

10 The word "plague" has been applied to any epidemic disease with a high
     death-rate: see headnote to Appendix C. For contemporary opinion about
     bubonic plague, including its seasonal ravages in Constantinople, see
     Appendix C.5.ii.

prepared to join the Grecian camp, near Kishan, a town of some importance, situated to the east of the Hebrus; in which Perdita and Clara were to remain until the event of the expected battle. We quitted Athens on the 2nd of June. Raymond had recovered from the gaunt and pallid looks of fever. If I no longer saw the fresh glow of youth on his matured countenance, if care had besieged his brow,

"And dug deep trenches in his beauty's field," [11]

if his hair, slightly mingled with grey, and his look, considerate even in its eagerness, gave signs of added years and past sufferings, yet there was something irresistibly affecting in the sight of one, lately snatched from the grave, renewing his career, untamed by sickness or disaster. The Athenians saw in him, not as heretofore, the heroic boy or desperate man, who was ready to die for them; but the prudent commander, who for their sakes was careful of his life, and could make his own warrior-propensities second to the scheme of conduct policy might point out.

All Athens accompanied us for several miles. When he had landed a month ago, the noisy populace had been hushed by sorrow and fear; but this was a festival day to all. The air resounded with their shouts; their picturesque costume, and the gay colours of which it was composed, flaunted in the sunshine; their eager gestures and rapid utterance accorded with their wild appearance. Raymond was the theme of every tongue, the hope of each wife, mother or betrothed bride, whose husband, child, or lover, making a part of the Greek army, were to be conducted to victory by him.

Notwithstanding the hazardous object of our journey, it was full of romantic interest, as we passed through the vallies, and over the hills, of this divine country. Raymond was inspirited by the intense sensations of recovered health; he felt that in being general of the Athenians, he filled a post worthy of his ambition; and, in his hope of the conquest of Constantinople, he counted on an event which would be as a landmark in the waste of ages, an exploit unequalled in the annals of man; when a city of grand historic association, the beauty of whose site was the wonder of the world, which for many hundred years had been the strong hold of the Moslems, should be rescued from slavery and barbarism, and restored to a people illustrious for genius, civilization, and a spirit of liberty. Perdita rested on his restored society, on his love, his hopes and fame, even as a Sybarite[12] on a luxurious couch; every thought was transport, each emotion bathed as it were in a congenial and balmy element.

---

11 Shakspeare's Sonnets [MWS's note]; cf. Shakespeare, Sonnet 2, line 2: "And dig deep trenches in thy beauty's field."

12 An inhabitant of Sybaris, an ancient city noted for pleasure, luxury and self-indulgence; hence, a pleasure-loving person.

We arrived at Kishan on the 7th of July. The weather during our journey had been serene. Each day, before dawn, we left our night's encampment, and watched the shadows as they retreated from hill and valley, and the golden splendour of the sun's approach. The accompanying soldiers received, with national vivacity, enthusiastic pleasure from the sight of beautiful nature. The uprising of the star of day was hailed by triumphant strains, while the birds, heard by snatches, filled up the intervals of the music. At noon, we pitched our tents in some shady valley, or embowering wood among the mountains, while a stream prattling over pebbles induced grateful sleep. Our evening march, more calm, was yet more delightful than the morning restlessness of spirit. If the band played, involuntarily they chose airs of moderated passion; the farewell of love, or lament at absence, was followed and closed by some solemn hymn, which harmonized with the tranquil loveliness of evening, and elevated the soul to grand and religious thought. Often all sounds were suspended, that we might listen to the nightingale, while the fire-flies danced in bright measure, and the soft cooing of the aziolo[13] spoke of fair weather to the travellers. Did we pass a valley? Soft shades encompassed us, and rocks tinged with beauteous hues. If we traversed a mountain, Greece, a living map, was spread beneath, her renowned pinnacles cleaving the ether; her rivers threading in silver line the fertile land. Afraid almost to breathe, we English travellers surveyed with extasy this splendid landscape, so different from the sober hues and melancholy graces of our native scenery. When we quitted Macedonia, the fertile but low plains of Thrace afforded fewer beauties; yet our journey continued to be interesting. An advanced guard gave information of our approach, and the country people were quickly in motion to do honour to Lord Raymond. The villages were decorated by triumphal arches of greenery by day, and lamps by night; tapestry waved from the windows, the ground was strewed with flowers, and the name of Raymond, joined to that of Greece, was echoed in the *Evive* of the peasant crowd.[14]

When we arrived at Kishan, we learnt, that on hearing of the advance of Lord Raymond and his detachment, the Turkish army had retreated from Rodosto; but meeting with a reinforcement, they had re-trod their steps. In the meantime, Argyropylo,[15] the Greek commander-in-chief, had advanced, so as to be between the Turks and Rodosto; a battle, it was said, was inevitable. Perdita and her child were to remain at Kishan. Raymond asked me, if I would not continue with them. "Now by the fells

---

13 In PBS's poem, "The Aziola," published by MWS in *The Keepsake* in 1829, one of the speakers, Mary, explains, " 'Tis nothing but a little downy owl" (12). In MWS's poem, "The Choice" (132), she associates "the aziolo's cry" with her memories of PBS; see Appendix E.1.
14 Cf. Italian *evviva*, which means "hurrah!"
15 See 88, above.

of Cumberland," I cried, "by all of the vagabond and poacher that appertains to me, I will stand at your side, draw my sword in the Greek cause, and be hailed as a victor along with you!"

All the plain, from Kishan to Rodosto, a distance of sixteen leagues,[16] was alive with troops, or with the camp-followers, all in motion at the approach of a battle. The small garrisons were drawn from the various towns and fortresses, and went to swell the main army. We met baggage waggons, and many females of high and low rank returning to Fairy[17] or Kishan, there to wait the issue of the expected day. When we arrived at Rodosto, we found that the field had been taken, and the scheme of the battle arranged. The sound of firing, early on the following morning, informed us that advanced posts of the armies were engaged. Regiment after regiment advanced, their colours flying and bands playing. They planted the cannon on the tumuli, sole elevations in this level country, and formed themselves into column and hollow square; while the pioneers threw up small mounds for their protection.

These then were the preparations for a battle, nay, the battle itself; far different from any thing the imagination had pictured. We read of centre and wing in Greek and Roman history; we fancy a spot, plain as a table, and soldiers small as chessmen; and drawn forth, so that the most ignorant of the game can discover science and order in the disposition of the forces. When I came to the reality, and saw regiments file off to the left far out of sight, fields intervening between the battalions, but a few troops sufficiently near me to observe their motions, I gave up all idea of understanding, even of seeing a battle, but attaching myself to Raymond attended with intense interest to his actions. He shewed himself collected, gallant and imperial; his commands were prompt, his intuition of the events of the day to me miraculous. In the mean time the cannon roared; the music lifted up its enlivening voice at intervals; and we on the highest of the mounds I mentioned, too far off to observe the fallen sheaves which death gathered into his storehouse, beheld the regiments, now lost in smoke, now banners and staves peering above the cloud, while shout and clamour drowned every sound.

Early in the day, Argyropylo was wounded dangerously, and Raymond assumed the command of the whole army. He made few remarks, till, on observing through his glass the sequel of an order he had given, his face, clouded for awhile with doubt, became radiant. "The day is ours," he cried, "the Turks fly from the bayonet." And then swiftly he dispatched his aides-de-camp to command the horse to fall on the routed enemy. The defeat became total; the cannon ceased to roar; the infantry rallied, and horse pursued the flying Turks along the dreary plain; the

---

16 A league is roughly three miles.
17 Ferrai is about twenty miles from Keşan (MWS's Kishan), just west of the Evros river.

staff of Raymond was dispersed in various directions, to make observations, and bear commands. Even I was dispatched to a distant part of the field.

The ground on which the battle was fought, was a level plain—so level, that from the tumuli you saw the waving line of mountains on the wide-stretched horizon; yet the intervening space was unvaried by the least irregularity, save such undulations as resembled the waves of the sea. The whole of this part of Thrace had been so long a scene of contest, that it had remained uncultivated, and presented a dreary, barren appearance. The order I had received, was to make an observation of the direction which a detachment of the enemy might have taken, from a northern tumulus; the whole Turkish army, followed by the Greek, had poured eastward; none but the dead remained in the direction of my side. From the top of the mound, I looked far round—all was silent and deserted.

The last beams of the nearly sunken sun shot up from behind the far summit of Mount Athos; the sea of Marmora still glittered beneath its rays, while the Asiatic coast beyond was half hid in a haze of low cloud.[18] Many a casque, and bayonet, and sword, fallen from unnerved arms, reflected the departing ray; they lay scattered far and near. From the east, a band of ravens, old inhabitants of the Turkish cemeteries, came sailing along towards their harvest; the sun disappeared. This hour, melancholy yet sweet, has always seemed to me the time when we are most naturally led to commune with higher powers; our mortal sternness departs, and gentle complacency invests the soul. But now, in the midst of the dying and the dead, how could a thought of heaven or a sensation of tranquillity possess one of the murderers? During the busy day, my mind had yielded itself a willing slave to the state of things presented to it by its fellow-beings; historical association, hatred of the foe, and military enthusiasm had held dominion over me. Now, I looked on the evening star, as softly and calmly it hung pendulous in the orange hues of sunset. I turned to the corse-strewn earth; and felt ashamed of my species. So perhaps were the placid skies; for they quickly veiled themselves in mist, and in this change assisted the swift disappearance of twilight usual in the south; heavy masses of cloud floated up from the south east, and red and turbid lightning shot from their dark edges; the rushing wind disturbed the garments of the dead, and was chilled as it passed over their icy forms. Darkness gathered round; the objects about me became indistinct, I

---

18   Mount Athos is a headland in the peninsula of Chalcidice in northern Greece;
      the Sea of Marmara (Propontis) is south of Constantinople ("the city of
      Constantine," called Istanbul today), between the Mediterranean and the
      Bosphorus, which leads into the Black Sea. From his tumulus at Rodosto
      Lionel enjoys an extensive prospect.

descended from my station, and with difficulty guided my horse, so as to avoid the slain.

Suddenly I heard a piercing shriek; a form seemed to rise from the earth; it flew swiftly towards me, sinking to the ground again as it drew near. All this passed so suddenly, that I with difficulty reined in my horse, so that it should not trample on the prostrate being. The dress of this person was that of a soldier, but the bared neck and arms, and the continued shrieks discovered a female thus disguised. I dismounted to her aid, while she, with heavy groans, and her hand placed on her side, resisted my attempt to lead her on. In the hurry of the moment I forgot that I was in Greece, and in my native accents endeavoured to soothe the sufferer. With wild and terrific exclamations did the lost, dying Evadne (for it was she) recognize the language of her lover; pain and fever from her wound had deranged her intellects, while her piteous cries and feeble efforts to escape, penetrated me with compassion. In wild delirium she called upon the name of Raymond; she exclaimed that I was keeping him from her, while the Turks with fearful instruments of torture were about to take his life. Then again she sadly lamented her hard fate; that a woman, with a woman's heart and sensibility, should be driven by hopeless love and vacant hopes to take up the trade of arms, and suffer beyond the endurance of man privation, labour, and pain—the while her dry, hot hand pressed mine, and her brow and lips burned with consuming fire.

As her strength grew less, I lifted her from the ground; her emaciated form hung over my arm, her sunken cheek rested on my breast; in a sepulchral voice she murmured:—"This is the end of love!—Yet not the end!"—and frenzy lent her strength as she cast her arm up to heaven: "there is the end! there we meet again. Many living deaths have I borne for thee, O Raymond, and now I expire, thy victim!—By my death I purchase thee—lo! the instruments of war, fire, the plague are my servitors. I dared, I conquered them all, till now! I have sold myself to death, with the sole condition that thou shouldst follow me—Fire, and war, and plague, unite for thy destruction—O my Raymond, there is no safety for thee!"

With an heavy heart I listened to the changes of her delirium; I made her a bed of cloaks; her violence decreased and a clammy dew stood on her brow as the paleness of death succeeded to the crimson of fever, I placed her on the cloaks. She continued to rave of her speedy meeting with her beloved in the grave, of his death nigh at hand; sometimes she solemnly declared that he was summoned; sometimes she bewailed his hard destiny. Her voice grew feebler, her speech interrupted; a few convulsive movements, and her muscles relaxed, the limbs fell, no more to be sustained, one deep sigh, and life was gone.

I bore her from the near neighbourhood of the dead; wrapt in cloaks, I placed her beneath a tree. Once more I looked on her altered face; the last time I saw her she was eighteen; beautiful as poet's vision, splendid as a Sultana of the East—Twelve years had past; twelve years of change, sorrow and hardship; her brilliant complexion had become worn and dark, her limbs had lost the roundness of youth and womanhood; her eyes had sunk deep,

> Crushed and o'erworn,
> The hours had drained her blood, and filled her brow
> With lines and wrinkles.[19]

With shuddering horror I veiled this monument of human passion and human misery; I heaped over her all of flags and heavy accoutrements I could find, to guard her from birds and beasts of prey, until I could bestow on her a fitting grave. Sadly and slowly I stemmed my course from among the heaps of slain, and, guided by the twinkling lights of the town, at length reached Rodosto.

CHAPTER XIII

ON my arrival, I found that an order had already gone forth for the army to proceed immediately towards Constantinople; and the troops which had suffered least in the battle were already on their way. The town was full of tumult. The wound, and consequent inability of Argyropylo, caused Raymond to be the first in command. He rode through the town, visiting the wounded, and giving such orders as were necessary for the siege he meditated. Early in the morning the whole army was in motion. In the hurry I could hardly find an opportunity to bestow the last offices on Evadne. Attended only by my servant, I dug a deep grave for her at the foot of the tree, and without disturbing her warrior shroud, I placed her in it, heaping stones upon the grave. The dazzling sun and glare of daylight, deprived the scene of solemnity; from Evadne's low tomb, I joined Raymond and his staff, now on their way to the Golden City.[20]

Constantinople was invested, trenches dug, and advances made. The whole Greek fleet blockaded it by sea; on land from the river Kyat Kbanah, near the Sweet Waters, to the Tower of Marmora, on the shores of the Propontis, along the whole line of the ancient walls, the trenches of the siege were drawn. We already possessed Pera; the Golden Horn itself, the city, bastioned by the sea, and the ivy-mantled walls of the Greek

---

19   This passage is adapted from Shakespeare, Sonnet 63, 1-4: "Against my love shall be as I am now, / With Time's injurious hand crush'd and o'erworn; / When hours have drain'd his blood, and fill'd his brow / With lines and wrinkles ...."

20   Cf. PBS, *The Revolt of Islam* 4.14.1531.

emperors was all of Europe that the Mahometans could call theirs.[21] Our army looked on her as certain prey. They counted the garrison; it was impossible that it should be relieved; each sally was a victory; for, even when the Turks were triumphant, the loss of men they sustained was an irreparable injury.

I rode one morning with Raymond to the lofty mound, not far from the Top Kapou, (Cannon-gate), on which Mahmoud planted his standard, and first saw the city. Still the same lofty domes and minarets towered above the verdurous walls, where Constantine had died, and the Turk had entered the city.[22] The plain around was interspersed with cemeteries, Turk, Greek, and Armenian, with their growth of cypress trees; and other woods of more cheerful aspect, diversified the scene. Among them the Greek army was encamped, and their squadrons moved to and fro—now in regular march, now in swift career.

Raymond's eyes were fixed on the city. "I have counted the hours of her life," said he; "one month, and she falls. Remain with me till then; wait till you see the cross on St. Sophia;[23] and then return to your peaceful glades."

"You then," I asked, "still remain in Greece?"

"Assuredly," replied Raymond. "Yet Lionel, when I say this, believe me I look back with regret to our tranquil life at Windsor. I am but half a soldier; I love the renown, but not the trade of war. Before the battle of Rodosto I was full of hope and spirit; to conquer there, and afterwards to take Constantinople, was the hope, the bourne, the fulfilment of my

---

21 The Turks control the old city of Constantinople, which the Greek fleet and army surround in a rough triangle. Pera, the European and Christian quarter to the northeast, is across the Golden Horn (an inlet of the Bosphorus) from Old Constantinople. To the south, the fleet occupies the Sea of Marmara, or the Propontis. The "Tower of Marmora" is the *Mermerkule* or Marble Tower, near the junction of the walls along the Sea of Marmara and the landward walls of Istanbul. The Sweet Waters of Europe, where Perdita stays, were in Ottoman times two streams feeding the Golden Horn, an inlet of the Bosphorus forming one border of the old city of Stamboul; in MWS's time this was the site of palaces and gardens outside the fortified city.

22 *Top Kapi* or Cannon-gate was known in Byzantine times as the Gate of St. Romanus. Through this gate in 1453 Sultan Mohammed II (MWS's "Mahmoud") entered the city as conqueror. "Constantine" refers not to the Emperor who founded Constantinople in AD 330, but to Constantine Paleologus (1404-53), who defended the city against Mohammed II. Edward Gibbon tells the story of the fall of Constantinople in chapter 68 of *The Decline and Fall of the Roman Empire* 6: 506; see also PBS's note 6 to his verse play, *Hellas* (1822).

23 The Church of Santa Sophia (in Greek *Hagia Sophia*, Holy Wisdom) became a mosque after the Turkish conquest of Constantinople.

ambition. This enthusiasm is now spent, I know not why; I seem to myself to be entering a darksome gulph; the ardent spirit of the army is irksome to me, the rapture of triumph null."

He paused, and was lost in thought. His serious mien recalled, by some association, the half-forgotten Evadne to my mind, and I seized this opportunity to make enquiries from him concerning her strange lot. I asked him, if he had ever seen among the troops any one resembling her; if since he had returned to Greece he had heard of her?

He started at her name,—he looked uneasily on me. "Even so," he cried, "I knew you would speak of her. Long, long I had forgotten her. Since our encampment here, she daily, hourly visits my thoughts. When I am addressed, her name is the sound I expect: in every communication, I imagine that she will form a part. At length you have broken the spell; tell me what you know of her."

I related my meeting with her; the story of her death was told and re-told. With painful earnestness he questioned me concerning her prophecies with regard to him. I treated them as the ravings of a maniac. "No, no," he said, "do not deceive yourself,—me you cannot. She has said nothing but what I knew before—though this is confirmation. Fire, the sword, and plague! They may all be found in yonder city; on my head alone may they fall!"

From this day Raymond's melancholy increased. He secluded himself as much as the duties of his station permitted. When in company, sadness would in spite of every effort steal over his features, and he sat absent and mute among the busy crowd that thronged about him. Perdita rejoined him, and before her he forced himself to appear cheerful, for she, even as a mirror, changed as he changed, and if he were silent and anxious, she solicitously inquired concerning, and endeavoured to remove the cause of his seriousness. She resided at the palace of Sweet Waters, a summer seraglio of the Sultan; the beauty of the surrounding scenery, undefiled by war, and the freshness of the river, made this spot doubly delightful. Raymond felt no relief, received no pleasure from any show of heaven or earth. He often left Perdita, to wander in the grounds alone; or in a light shallop he floated idly on the pure waters, musing deeply. Sometimes I joined him; at such times his countenance was invariably solemn, his air dejected. He seemed relieved on seeing me, and would talk with some degree of interest on the affairs of the day. There was evidently something behind all this; yet, when he appeared about to speak of that which was nearest his heart, he would abruptly turn away, and with a sigh endeavour to deliver the painful idea to the winds.

It had often occurred, that, when, as I said, Raymond quitted Perdita's drawing-room, Clara came up to me, and gently drawing me aside, said, "Papa is gone; shall we go to him? I dare say he will be glad to see you." And, as accident permitted, I complied with or refused her request. One evening a numerous assembly of Greek chieftains were gathered together in the palace. The intriguing Palli, the accomplished Karazza, the warlike Ypsilanti, were among the principal.[24] They talked of the events of the day; the skirmish at noon; the diminished numbers of the Infidels; their defeat and flight: they contemplated, after a short interval of time, the capture of the Golden City. They endeavoured to picture forth what would then happen, and spoke in lofty terms of the prosperity of Greece, when Constantinople should become its capital. The conversation then reverted to Asiatic intelligence, and the ravages the plague made in its chief cities; conjectures were hazarded as to the progress that disease might have made in the besieged city.

Raymond had joined in the former part of the discussion. In lively terms he demonstrated the extremities to which Constantinople was reduced; the wasted and haggard, though ferocious appearance of the troops; famine and pestilence was at work for them, he observed, and the infidels would soon be obliged to take refuge in their only hope—submission. Suddenly in the midst of his harangue he broke off, as if stung by some painful thought; he rose uneasily, and I perceived him at length quit the hall, and through the long corridor seek the open air. He did not return; and soon Clara crept round to me, making the accustomed invitation. I consented to her request, and taking her little hand, followed Raymond. We found him just about to embark in his boat, and he readily agreed to receive us as companions. After the heats of the day, the cooling land-breeze ruffled the river, and filled our little sail. The city looked dark to the south, while numerous lights along the near shores, and the beautiful aspect of the banks reposing in placid night, the waters keenly reflecting the heavenly lights, gave to this beauteous river a dower of loveliness that might have characterized a retreat in Paradise. Our single boatman attended to the sail; Raymond steered; Clara sat at his feet, clasping his knees with her arms, and laying her head on them. Raymond began the conversation somewhat abruptly.

"This, my friend, is probably the last time we shall have an opportunity of conversing freely; my plans are now in full operation, and my time will become more and more occupied. Besides, I wish at once to tell you my wishes and expectations, and then never again to revert to so painful a subject. First, I must thank you, Lionel, for having remained here at my request. Vanity first prompted me to ask you: vanity, I call it; yet even in this I see the hand of fate—your presence will soon be necessary; you will become the last resource of Perdita, her protector and consoler. You will take her back to Windsor."—

"Not without you," I said. "You do not mean to separate again?"

"Do not deceive yourself," replied Raymond, "the separation at hand

---

24 Here MWS borrows the name of Prince Alexandros Ypsilanti, a former aide-de-camp of Czar Alexander I who led an unsuccessful revolt against the Turks in Wallachia (now Romania) in 1821, launching the uprisings that eventually led to Greek independence.

is one over which I have no control; most near at hand is it; the days are already counted. May I trust you? For many days I have longed to disclose the mysterious presentiments that weigh on me, although I fear that you will ridicule them. Yet do not, my gentle friend; for, all childish and unwise as they are, they have become a part of me, and I dare not expect to shake them off.

"Yet how can I expect you to sympathize with me? You are of this world; I am not. You hold forth your hand; it is even as a part of yourself; and you do not yet divide the feeling of identity from the mortal form that shapes forth Lionel. How then can you understand me? Earth is to me a tomb, the firmament a vault, shrouding mere corruption. Time is no more, for I have stepped within the threshold of eternity; each man I meet appears a corse, which will soon be deserted of its animating spark, on the eve of decay and corruption.

> Cada piedra un piramide levanta,
> y cada flor costruye un monumento,
> cada edificio es un sepulcro altivo,
> cada soldado un esqueleto vivo."[25]

His accent was mournful,—he sighed deeply. "A few months ago," he continued, "I was thought to be dying; but life was strong within me. My affections were human; hope and love were the day-stars of my life. Now—they dream that the brows of the conqueror of the infidel faith are about to be encircled by triumphant laurel; they talk of honourable reward, of title, power, and wealth—all I ask of Greece is a grave. Let them raise a mound above my lifeless body, which may stand even when the dome of St. Sophia has fallen.

"Wherefore do I feel thus? At Rodosto I was full of hope; but when first I saw Constantinople, that feeling, with every other joyful one, departed. The last words of Evadne were the seal upon the warrant of my death. Yet I do not pretend to account for my mood by any particular event. All I can say is, that it is so. The plague I am told is in Constantinople, perhaps I have imbibed its effluvia—perhaps disease is the real cause of my prognostications. It matters little why or wherefore I am affected, no power can avert the stroke, and the shadow of Fate's uplifted hand already darkens me.

"To you, Lionel, I entrust your sister and her child. Never mention to her the fatal name of Evadne. She would doubly sorrow over the strange

---

25   Calderon de la Barca [MWS's note]; the passage is from *La Vida es Sueño* 3 [scene 6]: "Each stone raises a pyramid and each flower builds a monument; each building is a proud sepulchre and each soldier a living skeleton" (2472-75).

link that enchains me to her, making my spirit obey her dying voice, following her, as it is about to do, to the unknown country."

I listened to him with wonder; but that his sad demeanour and solemn utterance assured me of the truth and intensity of his feelings, I should with light derision have attempted to dissipate his fears. Whatever I was about to reply, was interrupted by the powerful emotions of Clara. Raymond had spoken, thoughtless of her presence, and she, poor child, heard with terror and faith the prophecy of his death. Her father was moved by her violent grief; he took her in his arms and soothed her, but his very soothings were solemn and fearful. "Weep not, sweet child," said he, "the coming death of one you have hardly known. I may die, but in death I can never forget or desert my own Clara. In after sorrow or joy, believe that your father's spirit is near, to save or sympathize with you. Be proud of me, and cherish your infant remembrance of me. Thus, sweetest, I shall not appear to die. One thing you must promise,—not to speak to any one but your uncle, of the conversation you have just overheard. When I am gone, you will console your mother, and tell her that death was only bitter because it divided me from her; that my last thoughts will be spent on her. But while I live, promise not to betray me; promise, my child."

With faltering accents Clara promised, while she still clung to her father in a transport of sorrow. Soon we returned to shore, and I endeavoured to obviate the impression made on the child's mind, by treating Raymond's fears lightly. We heard no more of them; for, as he had said, the siege, now drawing to a conclusion, became paramount in interest, engaging all his time and attention.

The empire of the Mahometans in Europe was at its close. The Greek fleet blockading every port of Stamboul,[26] prevented the arrival of succour from Asia; all egress on the side towards land had become impracticable, except to such desperate sallies, as reduced the numbers of the enemy without making any impression on our lines. The garrison was now so much diminished, that it was evident that the city could easily have been carried by storm; but both humanity and policy dictated a slower mode of proceeding. We could hardly doubt that, if pursued to the utmost, its palaces, its temples and store of wealth would be destroyed in the fury of contending triumph and defeat. Already the defenceless citizens had suffered through the barbarity of the Janisaries;[27] and, in time of

---

26 Stamboul refers here to the fortified old city of Constantinople, bounded by walls on the west, by the Sea of Marmara on the south, and by the Golden Horn on the northeast. Stamboul, which gives rise to the modern name, Istanbul, is derived from the Greek expression, "εἰς τὴν πόλιν," to (or in) the city.

27 An elite corps of the Ottoman army, originally recruited forcibly from among non-Moslems, the Janissaries were abolished after a massacre in 1826, the year *The Last Man* was published.

storm, tumult and massacre, beauty, infancy and decrepitude, would have alike been sacrificed to the brutal ferocity of the soldiers. Famine and blockade were certain means of conquest; and on these we founded our hopes of victory.

Each day the soldiers of the garrison assaulted our advanced posts, and impeded the accomplishment of our works. Fire-boats were launched from the various ports, while our troops sometimes recoiled from the devoted courage of men who did not seek to live, but to sell their lives dearly. These contests were aggravated by the season: they took place during summer, when the southern Asiatic wind[28] came laden with intolerable heat, when the streams were dried up in their shallow beds, and the vast basin of the sea appeared to glow under the unmitigated rays of the solsticial sun. Nor did night refresh the earth. Dew was denied; herbage and flowers there were none; the very trees drooped; and summer assumed the blighted appearance of winter, as it went forth in silence and flame to abridge the means of sustenance to man. In vain did the eye strive to find the wreck of some northern cloud in the stainless empyrean, which might bring hope of change and moisture to the oppressive and windless atmosphere. All was serene, burning, annihilating. We the besiegers were in the comparison little affected by these evils. The woods around afforded us shade,—the river secured to us a constant supply of water; nay, detachments were employed in furnishing the army with ice, which had been laid up on Hæmus,[29] and Athos, and the mountains of Macedonia, while cooling fruits and wholesome food renovated the strength of the labourers, and made us bear with less impatience the weight of the unrefreshing air. But in the city things wore a different face. The sun's rays were refracted from the pavement and buildings—the stoppage of the public fountains—the bad quality of the food, and scarcity even of that, produced a state of suffering, which was aggravated by the scourge of disease; while the garrison arrogated every superfluity to themselves, adding by waste and riot to the necessary evils of the time. Still they would not capitulate.

Suddenly the system of warfare was changed. We experienced no more assaults; and by night and day we continued our labours unimpeded. Stranger still, when the troops advanced near the city, the walls were vacant, and no cannon was pointed against the intruders. When these circumstances were reported to Raymond, he caused minute observations to be made as to what was doing within the walls, and when his scouts returned, reporting only the continued silence and desolation of the city, he commanded the army to be drawn out before the gates. No one

---

28 The simoom, described by Mary Wollstonecraft as "that destructive blast which desolates Turkey" (*A Vindication of the Rights of Woman*, ed. Carol H. Poston 44).

29 A mountain in northern Thrace.

appeared on the walls; the very portals, though locked and barred, seemed unguarded; above, the many domes and glittering crescents pierced heaven; while the old walls, survivors of ages, with ivy-crowned tower and weed-tangled buttress, stood as rocks in an uninhabited waste. From within the city neither shout nor cry, nor aught except the casual howling of a dog, broke the noon-day stillness. Even our soldiers were awed to silence; the music paused; the clang of arms was hushed. Each man asked his fellow in whispers, the meaning of this sudden peace; while Raymond from an height endeavoured, by means of glasses, to discover and observe the stratagem of the enemy. No form could be discerned on the terraces of the houses; in the higher parts of the town no moving shadow bespoke the presence of any living being: the very trees waved not, and mocked the stability of architecture with like immovability.

The tramp of horses, distinctly heard in the silence, was at length discerned. It was a troop sent by Karazza, the Admiral; they bore dispatches to the Lord General. The contents of these papers were important. The night before, the watch, on board one of the smaller vessels anchored near the seraglio wall, was roused by a slight splashing as of muffled oars; the alarm was given: twelve small boats, each containing three Janizaries, were descried endeavouring to make their way through the fleet to the opposite shore of Scutari.[30] When they found themselves discovered they discharged their muskets, and some came to the front to cover the others, whose crews, exerting all their strength, endeavoured to escape with their light barks from among the dark hulls that environed them. They were in the end all sunk, and, with the exception of two or three prisoners, the crews drowned. Little could be got from the survivors; but their cautious answers caused it to be surmised that several expeditions had preceded this last, and that several Turks of rank and importance had been conveyed to Asia. The men disdainfully repelled the idea of having deserted the defence of their city; and one, the youngest among them, in answer to the taunt of a sailor, exclaimed, "Take it, Christian dogs! take the palaces, the gardens, the mosques, the abode of our fathers—take plague with them; pestilence is the enemy we fly; if she be your friend, hug her to your bosoms. The curse of Allah is on Stamboul, share ye her fate."

Such was the account sent by Karazza to Raymond: but a tale full of monstrous exaggerations, though founded on this, was spread by the accompanying troop among our soldiers. A murmur arose, the city was the prey of pestilence; already had a mighty power subjugated the inhabitants; Death had become lord of Constantinople.

---

30   Scutari or Üsküdar, well known later as the site of Florence Nightingale's field
      hospital during the Crimean War, is on the Asian side of the Bosphorus across
      from Istanbul (Constantinople).

I have heard a picture described, wherein all the inhabitants of earth were drawn out in fear to stand the encounter of Death.[31] The feeble and decrepid fled; the warriors retreated, though they threatened even in flight. Wolves and lions, and various monsters of the desert roared against him; while the grim Unreality hovered shaking his spectral dart, a solitary but invincible assailant. Even so was it with the army of Greece. I am convinced, that had the myriad troops of Asia come from over the Propontis, and stood defenders of the Golden City, each and every Greek would have marched against the overwhelming numbers, and have devoted himself with patriotic fury for his country. But here no hedge of bayonets opposed itself, no death-dealing artillery, no formidable array of brave soldiers—the unguarded walls afforded easy entrance—the vacant palaces luxurious dwellings; but above the dome of St. Sophia the superstitious Greek saw Pestilence, and shrunk in trepidation from her influence.

Raymond was actuated by far other feelings. He descended the hill with a face beaming with triumph, and pointing with his sword to the gates, commanded his troops to—down with those barricades—the only obstacles now to completest victory. The soldiers answered his cheerful words with aghast and awe-struck looks; instinctively they drew back, and Raymond rode in the front of the lines:—"By my sword I swear," he cried, "that no ambush or stratagem endangers you. The enemy is already vanquished; the pleasant places, the noble dwellings and spoil of the city are already yours; force the gate; enter and possess the seats of your ancestors, your own inheritance!"

An universal shudder and fearful whispering passed through the lines; not a soldier moved. "Cowards!" exclaimed their general, exasperated, "give me an hatchet! I alone will enter! I will plant your standard; and when you see it wave from yon highest minaret, you may gain courage, and rally round it!"

One of the officers now came forward: "General," he said, "we neither fear the courage, nor arms, the open attack, nor secret ambush of the Moslems. We are ready to expose our breasts, exposed ten thousand times before, to the balls and scymetars of the infidels, and to fall gloriously for Greece. But we will not die in heaps, like dogs poisoned in summer-time, by the pestilential air of that city—we dare not go against the Plague!"

A multitude of men are feeble and inert, without a voice, a leader; give

---

31 Writing of S.T. Coleridge, William Hazlitt remarks in *The Liberal*, a periodical founded by PBS, Byron, and Leigh Hunt, "He sometimes gives a striking account at present of the Cartoons at Pisa, by Buffamalco [Buffalmacco] and others; of one in particular, where Death is seen in the air brandishing his scythe, and the great and mighty of the earth shudder at his approach, while the beggars and the wretched kneel to him as their deliverer" ("My First Acquaintance with Poets," *The Liberal* 2 [1823]: 44n-45n). While MWS's description is significantly different, she may have the same picture in mind.

them that, and they regain the strength belonging to their numbers. Shouts from a thousand voices now rent the air—the cry of applause became universal. Raymond saw the danger; he was willing to save his troops from the crime of disobedience; for he knew, that contention once begun between the commander and his army, each act and word added to the weakness of the former, and bestowed power on the latter. He gave orders for the retreat to be sounded, and the regiments repaired in good order to the camp.

I hastened to carry the intelligence of these strange proceedings to Perdita; and we were soon joined by Raymond. He looked gloomy and perturbed. My sister was struck by my narrative: "How beyond the imagination of man," she exclaimed, "are the decrees of heaven, wondrous and inexplicable!"

"Foolish girl," cried Raymond angrily, "are you like my valiant soldiers, panic-struck? What is there inexplicable, pray, tell me, in so very natural an occurrence? Does not the plague rage each year in Stamboul? What wonder, that this year, when as we are told, its virulence is unexampled in Asia, that it should have occasioned double havoc in that city? What wonder then, in time of siege, want, extreme heat, and drought, that it should make unaccustomed ravages? Less wonder far is it, that the garrison, despairing of being able to hold out longer, should take advantage of the negligence of our fleet to escape at once from siege and capture. It is not pestilence—by the God that lives! it is not either plague or impending danger that makes us, like birds in harvest-time, terrified by a scarecrow, abstain from the ready prey—it is base superstition—And thus the aim of the valiant is made the shuttlecock of fools; the worthy ambition of the high-souled, the plaything of these tamed hares! But yet Stamboul shall be ours! By my past labours, by torture and imprisonment suffered for them, by my victories, by my sword, I swear—by my hopes of fame, by my former deserts now awaiting their reward, I deeply vow, with these hands to plant the cross on yonder mosque!"

"Dearest Raymond!" interrupted Perdita, in a supplicating accent.

He had been walking to and fro in the marble hall of the seraglio; his very lips were pale with rage, while, quivering, they shaped his angry words—his eyes shot fire—his gestures seemed restrained by their very vehemence. "Perdita," he continued, impatiently, "I know what you would say; I know that you love me, that you are good and gentle; but this is no woman's work—nor can a female heart guess at the hurricane which tears me!"

He seemed half afraid of his own violence, and suddenly quitted the hall: a look from Perdita shewed me her distress, and I followed him. He was pacing the garden: his passions were in a state of inconceivable turbulence. "Am I for ever," he cried, "to be the sport of fortune! Must man, the heaven-climber, be for ever the victim of the crawling reptiles of his species! Were I as you, Lionel, looking forward to many years of life, to a succession of love-enlightened days, to refined enjoyments and fresh-springing hopes, I might yield, and breaking my General's staff, seek repose in the glades of Windsor. But I am about to die!—nay, interrupt me not—soon I shall die. From the many-peopled earth, from the sympathies of man, from the loved resorts of my youth, from the kindness of my friends, from the affection of my only beloved Perdita, I am about to be removed. Such is the will of fate! Such the decree of the High Ruler from whom there is no appeal: to whom I submit. But to lose all—to lose with life and love, glory also! It shall not be!

"I, and in a few brief years, all you,—this panic-struck army, and all the population of fair Greece, will no longer be. But other generations will arise, and ever and for ever will continue, to be made happier by our present acts, to be glorified by our valour. The prayer of my youth was to be one among those who render the pages of earth's history splendid; who exalt the race of man, and make this little globe a dwelling of the mighty. Alas, for Raymond! the prayer of his youth is wasted—the hopes of his manhood are null!

"From my dungeon in yonder city I cried, soon I will be thy lord! When Evadne pronounced my death, I thought that the title of Victor of Constantinople would be written on my tomb, and I subdued all moral fear. I stand before its vanquished walls, and dare not call myself a conqueror. So shall it not be! Did not Alexander leap from the walls of the city of the Oxydracæ, to shew his coward troops the way to victory, encountering alone the swords of its defenders?[32] Even so will I brave the plague—and though no man follow, I will plant the Grecian standard on the height of St. Sophia."

Reason came unavailing to such high-wrought feelings. In vain I shewed him, that when winter came, the cold would dissipate the pestilential air, and restore courage to the Greeks. "Talk not of other season than this!" he cried. "I have lived my last winter, and the date of this year, 2092,[33] will be carved upon my tomb. Already do I see," he continued, looking up mournfully, "the bourne and precipitate edge of my existence, over which I plunge into the gloomy mystery of the life to come. I am prepared, so that I leave behind a trail of light so radiant, that my worst enemies cannot cloud it. I owe this to Greece, to you, to my surviving Perdita, and to myself, the victim of ambition."

We were interrupted by an attendant, who announced, that the staff of Raymond was assembled in the council-chamber. He requested me in the meantime to ride through the camp, and to observe and report to him the dispositions of the soldiers; he then left me. I had been excited to the

---

32   This story suggests a connection between Alexander's foolhardy courage and Raymond's. In 325 BC Alexander conquered the Oxydraces in the Punjab. At the siege of Sangala, he leapt from the wall into the midst of the enemy; thinking him dead, his soldiers slaughtered everyone in the citadel where the defeated Indians had taken refuge.

33   Three hundred years after PBS's birth in 1792.

utmost by the proceedings of the day, and now more than ever by the passionate language of Raymond. Alas! for human reason! He accused the Greeks of superstition: what name did he give to the faith he lent to the predictions of Evadne? I passed from the palace of Sweet Waters to the plain on which the encampment lay, and found its inhabitants in commotion. The arrival of several with fresh stories of marvels, from the fleet; the exaggerations bestowed on what was already known; tales of old prophecies, of fearful histories of whole regions which had been laid waste during the present year by pestilence, alarmed and occupied the troops. Discipline was lost; the army disbanded itself. Each individual, before a part of a great whole moving only in unison with others, now became resolved into the unit nature had made him, and thought of himself only. They stole off at first by ones and twos, then in larger companies, until, unimpeded by the officers, whole battalions sought the road that led to Macedonia.

About midnight I returned to the palace and sought Raymond; he was alone, and apparently composed; such composure, at least, was his as is inspired by a resolve to adhere to a certain line of conduct. He heard my account of the self-dissolution of the army with calmness, and then said, "You know, Verney, my fixed determination not to quit this place, until in the light of day Stamboul is confessedly ours. If the men I have about me shrink from following me, others, more courageous, are to be found. Go you before break of day, bear these dispatches to Karazza, add to them your own entreaties that he send me his marines and naval force; if I can get but one regiment to second me, the rest would follow of course. Let him send me this regiment. I shall expect your return by to-morrow noon."

Methought this was but a poor expedient; but I assured him of my obedience and zeal. I quitted him to take a few hours rest. With the breaking of morning I was accoutred for my ride. I lingered awhile, desirous of taking leave of Perdita, and from my window observed the approach of the sun. The golden splendour arose, and weary nature awoke to suffer yet another day of heat and thirsty decay. No flowers lifted up their dew-laden cups to meet the dawn; the dry grass had withered on the plains; the burning fields of air were vacant of birds; the cicale[34] alone, children of the sun, began their shrill and deafening song among the cypresses and olives. I saw Raymond's coal-black charger brought to the palace gate; a small company of officers arrived soon after; care and fear was painted on each cheek, and in each eye, unrefreshed by sleep. I found Raymond and Perdita together. He was watching the rising sun, while with one arm he encircled his beloved's waist; she looked on him,

---

34 The cicala (pl. *cicale*) is the cicada; in a letter to Marianne Hunt (28 August 1819), MWS defines this as "a kind of little beetle that makes a noise with its tail as loud as Johnny [John Hunt] can sing."

the sun of her life, with earnest gaze of mingled anxiety and tenderness. Raymond started angrily when he saw me. "Here still?" he cried. "Is this your promised zeal?"

"Pardon me," I said, "but even as you speak, I am gone."

"Nay, pardon me," he replied; "I have no right to command or reproach; but my life hangs on your departure and speedy return. Farewell!"

His voice had recovered its bland tone, but a dark cloud still hung on his features. I would have delayed; I wished to recommend watchfulness to Perdita, but his presence restrained me. I had no pretence for my hesitation; and on his repeating his farewell, I clasped his outstretched hand; it was cold and clammy. "Take care of yourself, my dear Lord," I said.

"Nay," said Perdita, "that task shall be mine. Return speedily, Lionel."

With an air of absence he was playing with her auburn locks, while she leaned on him; twice I turned back, only to look again on this matchless pair. At last, with slow and heavy steps, I had paced out of the hall, and sprung upon my horse. At that moment Clara flew towards me; clasping my knee she cried, "Make haste back, uncle! Dear uncle, I have such fearful dreams; I dare not tell my mother. Do not be long away!" I assured her of my impatience to return, and then, with a small escort rode along the plain towards the tower of Marmora.

I fulfilled my commission; I saw Karazza. He was somewhat surprised; he would see, he said, what could be done; but it required time; and Raymond had ordered me to return by noon. It was impossible to effect any thing in so short a time. I must stay till the next day; or come back, after having reported the present state of things to the general. My choice was easily made. A restlessness, a fear of what was about to betide, a doubt as to Raymond's purposes, urged me to return without delay to his quarters. Quitting the Seven Towers,[35] I rode eastward towards the Sweet Waters. I took a circuitous path, principally for the sake of going to the top of the mount before mentioned, which commanded a view of the city. I had my glass with me. The city basked under the noon-day sun, and the venerable walls formed its picturesque boundary. Immediately before me was the Top Kapou, the gate near which Mahomet had made the breach by which he entered the city. Trees gigantic and aged grew near; before the gate I discerned a crowd of moving human figures—with intense curiosity I lifted my glass to my eye. I saw Lord Raymond on his charger; a small company of officers had gathered about him; and behind was a promiscuous concourse of soldiers and subalterns, their discipline lost, their arms thrown aside; no music sounded, no banners streamed. The only flag among them was one which Raymond carried; he pointed with

---

35   The Castle of the Seven Towers (*Yedi kule*), built by Mohammed II near the sea at the southern termination of the walls of Constantinople.

it to the gate of the city. The circle round him fell back. With angry gestures he leapt from his horse, and seizing a hatchet that hung from his saddle-bow, went with the apparent intention of battering down the opposing gate. A few men came to aid him; their numbers increased; under their united blows the obstacle was vanquished, gate, portcullis, and fence were demolished; and the wide sun-lit way, leading to the heart of the city, now lay open before them. The men shrank back; they seemed afraid of what they had already done, and stood as if they expected some Mighty Phantom to stalk in offended majesty from the opening. Raymond sprung lightly on his horse, grasped the standard, and with words which I could not hear (but his gestures, being their fit accompaniment, were marked by passionate energy,) he seemed to adjure their assistance and companionship; even as he spoke, the crowd receded from him. Indignation now transported him; his words I guessed were fraught with disdain—then turning from his coward followers, he addressed himself to enter the city alone. His very horse seemed to back from the fatal entrance; his dog, his faithful dog, lay moaning and supplicating in his path—in a moment more, he had plunged the rowels[36] into the sides of the stung animal, who bounded forward, and he, the gateway passed, was galloping up the broad and desart street.

Until this moment my soul had been in my eyes only. I had gazed with wonder, mixed with fear and enthusiasm. The latter feeling now predominated. I forgot the distance between us: "I will go with thee, Raymond!" I cried; but, my eye removed from the glass, I could scarce discern the pigmy forms of the crowd, which about a mile from me surrounded the gate; the form of Raymond was lost. Stung with impatience, I urged my horse with force of spur and loosened reins down the acclivity, that, before danger could arrive, I might be at the side of my noble, godlike friend. A number of buildings and trees intervened, when I had reached the plain, hiding the city from my view. But at that moment a crash was heard. Thunderlike it reverberated through the sky, while the air was darkened. A moment more and the old walls again met my sight, while over them hovered a murky cloud; fragments of buildings whirled above, half seen in smoke, while flames burst out beneath, and continued explosions filled the air with terrific thunders. Flying from the mass of falling ruin which leapt over the high walls, and shook the ivy towers, a crowd of soldiers made for the road by which I came; I was surrounded, hemmed in by them, unable to get forward. My impatience rose to its utmost; I stretched out my hands to the men; I conjured them to turn back and save their General, the conqueror of Stamboul, the liberator of Greece; tears, aye tears, in warm flow gushed from my eyes—I would not believe in his destruction; yet every mass that darkened the air seemed to bear with it a portion of the martyred Raymond. Horrible sights were

---

36   Revolving disks on spurs.

shaped to me in the turbid cloud that hovered over the city; and my only relief was derived from the struggles I made to approach the gate. Yet when I effected my purpose, all I could discern within the precincts of the massive walls was a city of fire: the open way through which Raymond had ridden was enveloped in smoke and flame. After an interval the explosions ceased, but the flames still shot up from various quarters; the dome of St. Sophia had disappeared. Strange to say (the result perhaps of the concussion of air occasioned by the blowing up of the city) huge, white thunder clouds lifted themselves up from the southern horizon, and gathered over-head; they were the first blots on the blue expanse that I had seen for months, and amidst this havoc and despair they inspired pleasure. The vault above became obscured, lightning flashed from the heavy masses, followed instantaneously by crashing thunder; then the big rain fell. The flames of the city bent beneath it; and the smoke and dust arising from the ruins was dissipated.

I no sooner perceived an abatement of the flames than, hurried on by an irresistible impulse, I endeavoured to penetrate the town. I could only do this on foot, as the mass of ruin was impracticable for a horse. I had never entered the city before, and its ways were unknown to me. The streets were blocked up, the ruins smoking; I climbed up one heap, only to view others in succession; and nothing told me where the centre of the town might be, or towards what point Raymond might have directed his course. The rain ceased; the clouds sunk behind the horizon; it was now evening, and the sun descended swiftly the western sky. I scrambled on, until I came to a street, whose wooden houses, half-burnt, had been cooled by the rain, and were fortunately uninjured by the gunpowder. Up this I hurried—until now I had not seen a vestige of man. Yet none of the defaced human forms which I distinguished, could be Raymond; so I turned my eyes away, while my heart sickened within me. I came to an open space—a mountain of ruin in the midst, announced that some large mosque had occupied the space—and here, scattered about, I saw various articles of luxury and wealth, singed, destroyed—but shewing what they had been in their ruin—jewels, strings of pearls, embroidered robes, rich furs, glittering tapestries, and oriental ornaments, seemed to have been collected here in a pile destined for destruction; but the rain had stopped the havoc midway.

Hours passed, while in this scene of ruin I sought for Raymond. Insurmountable heaps sometimes opposed themselves; the still burning fires scorched me. The sun set; the atmosphere grew dim—and the evening star no longer shone companionless. The glare of flames attested the progress of destruction, while, during mingled light and obscurity, the piles around me took gigantic proportions and weird shapes. For a moment I could yield to the creative power of the imagination, and for a moment was soothed by the sublime fictions it presented to me. The beatings of my human heart drew me back to blank reality. Where, in this wilderness of death, art thou, O Raymond—ornament of England, deliverer of Greece, "hero of unwritten story,"[37] where in this burning chaos are thy dear relics strewed? I called aloud for him—through the darkness of night, over the scorching ruins of fallen Constantinople, his name was heard; no voice replied—echo even was mute.

I was overcome by weariness; the solitude depressed my spirits. The sultry air impregnated with dust, the heat and smoke of burning palaces, palsied my limbs. Hunger suddenly came acutely upon me. The excitement which had hitherto sustained me was lost; as a building, whose props are loosened, and whose foundations rock, totters and falls, so when enthusiasm and hope deserted me, did my strength fail. I sat on the sole remaining step of an edifice, which even in its downfall, was huge and magnificent; a few broken walls, not dislodged by gunpowder, stood in fantastic groupes, and a flame glimmered at intervals on the summit of the pile. For a time hunger and sleep contended, till the constellations reeled before my eyes and then were lost. I strove to rise, but my heavy lids closed, my limbs over-wearied, claimed repose—I rested my head on the stone, I yielded to the grateful sensation of utter forgetfulness; and in that scene of desolation, on that night of despair—I slept.

CHAPTER XIV

THE stars still shone brightly when I awoke, and Taurus high in the southern heaven shewed that it was midnight. I awoke from disturbed dreams. Methought I had been invited to Timon's last feast;[38] I came with keen appetite, the covers were removed, the hot water sent up its unsatisfying steams, while I fled before the anger of the host, who assumed the form of Raymond; while to my diseased fancy, the vessels hurled by him after me, were surcharged with fetid vapour, and my friend's shape, altered by a thousand distortions, expanded into a gigantic phantom, bearing on its brow the sign of pestilence. The growing shadow rose and rose, filling, and then seeming to endeavour to burst beyond, the adamantine vault that bent over, sustaining and enclosing the world. The night-mare became torture; with a strong effort I threw off sleep, and recalled reason to her wonted functions. My first thought was Perdita; to her I must return; her I must support, drawing such food from despair as might best sustain her wounded heart; recalling her from the

---

37   Cf. PBS, *The Mask of Anarchy*, where Hope addresses the "'Men of England, heirs of Glory, / Heroes of unwritten story, / Nurslings of one mighty Mother, / Hopes of her, and one another'" (147-50).

38   In Shakespeare's *Timon of Athens*, the hero is deserted by his friends when he falls into difficulties. Having invited them all to a banquet at which the covers on the dishes hide only warm water, he throws the water in their faces and leaves Athens forever.

wild excesses of grief, by the austere laws of duty, and the soft tenderness of regret.

The position of the stars was my only guide. I turned from the awful ruin of the Golden City, and, after great exertion, succeeded in extricating myself from its enclosure. I met a company of soldiers outside the walls; I borrowed a horse from one of them, and hastened to my sister. The appearance of the plain was changed during this short interval; the encampment was broken up; the relics of the disbanded army met in small companies here and there; each face was clouded; every gesture spoke astonishment and dismay.

With an heavy heart I entered the palace, and stood fearful to advance, to speak, to look. In the midst of the hall was Perdita; she sat on the marble pavement, her head fallen on her bosom, her hair dishevelled, her fingers twined busily one within the other; she was pale as marble, and every feature was contracted by agony. She perceived me, and looked up enquiringly; her half glance of hope was misery; the words died before I could articulate them; I felt a ghastly smile wrinkle my lips. She understood my gesture; again her head fell; again her fingers worked restlessly. At last I recovered speech, but my voice terrified her; the hapless girl had understood my look, and for worlds she would not that the tale of her heavy misery should have been shaped out and confirmed by hard, irrevocable words. Nay, she seemed to wish to distract my thoughts from the subject: she rose from the floor: "Hush!" she said, whisperingly; "after much weeping, Clara sleeps; we must not disturb her." She seated herself then on the same ottoman where I had left her in the morning resting on the beating heart of her Raymond; I dared not approach her, but sat at a distant corner, watching her starting and nervous gestures. At length, in an abrupt manner she asked, "Where is he?"

"O, fear not," she continued, "fear not that I should entertain hope! Yet tell me, have you found him? To have him once more in my arms, to see him, however changed, is all I desire. Though Constantinople be heaped above him as a tomb, yet I must find him—then cover us with the city's weight, with a mountain piled above—I care not, so that one grave hold Raymond and his Perdita." Then weeping, she clung to me: "Take me to him," she cried, "unkind Lionel, why do you keep me here? Of myself I cannot find him—but you know where he lies—lead me thither."

At first these agonizing plaints filled me with intolerable compassion. But soon I endeavoured to extract patience for her from the ideas she suggested. I related my adventures of the night, my endeavours to find our lost one, and my disappointment. Turning her thoughts this way, I gave them an object which rescued them from insanity. With apparent calmness she discussed with me the probable spot where he might be found, and planned the means we should use for that purpose. Then hearing of my fatigue and abstinence, she herself brought me food. I seized the favourable moment, and endeavoured to awaken in her something beyond the killing torpor of grief. As I spoke, my subject carried me away; deep admiration; grief, the offspring of truest affection, the overflowing of a heart bursting with sympathy for all that had been great and sublime in the career of my friend, inspired me as I poured forth the praises of Raymond.

"Alas, for us," I cried, "who have lost this latest honour of the world! Beloved Raymond! He is gone to the nations of the dead;[39] he has become one of those, who render the dark abode of the obscure grave illustrious by dwelling there. He has journied on the road that leads to it, and joined the mighty of soul who went before him. When the world was in its infancy death must have been terrible, and man left his friends and kindred to dwell, a solitary stranger, in an unknown country. But now, he who dies finds many companions gone before to prepare for his reception. The great of past ages people it, the exalted hero of our own days is counted among its inhabitants, while life becomes doubly 'the desart and the solitude.'[40]

"What a noble creature was Raymond, the first among the men of our time. By the grandeur of his conceptions, the graceful daring of his actions, by his wit and beauty, he won and ruled the minds of all. Of one only fault he might have been accused; but his death has cancelled that. I have heard him called inconstant of purpose—when he deserted, for the sake of love, the hope of sovereignty, and when he abdicated the protectorship of England, men blamed his infirmity of purpose. Now his death has crowned his life, and to the end of time it will be remembered, that he devoted himself, a willing victim, to the glory of Greece. Such was his choice: he expected to die. He foresaw that he should leave this cheerful earth, the lightsome sky, and thy love, Perdita; yet he neither hesitated or turned back, going right onward to his mark of fame. While the earth lasts, his actions will be recorded with praise. Grecian maidens will in devotion strew flowers on his tomb, and make the air around it resonant with patriotic hymns, in which his name will find high record."

---

39 A recollection of Sir Thomas Browne, *Hydriotaphia*, chapter 5, from which MWS quotes elsewhere in *The Last Man*: "What time the persons of these Ossuaries entred the famous Nations of the dead, and slept with Princes and Counsellours, might admit a wide solution" (*Works*, ed. Geoffrey Keynes 1: 165).

40 See Edward Young, *Night Thoughts* 1.115-16: "This is the Desart, this the solitude: / How populous, how vital is the grave!" and *The Revenge* 4: "Life is the desert, life the solitude; / Death joins us to the great majority." William Godwin uses the second version on the frontispiece to his *Essay on Sepulchres* (1809): "Life is the Desert and the Solitude!" MWS alludes to it in her journal entry for 15 May 1824 (2: 478) and in her notes to PBS's poems of 1821 (*Posthumous Poems*, 1824): "when those we love have passed into eternity, 'life is the desert and the solitude' in which we are forced to linger—but never find comfort more."

I saw the features of Perdita soften; the sternness of grief yielded to tenderness—I continued:—"Thus to honour him, is the sacred duty of his survivors. To make his name even as an holy spot of ground, enclosing it from all hostile attacks by our praise, shedding on it the blossoms of love and regret, guarding it from decay, and bequeathing it untainted to posterity. Such is the duty of his friends. A dearer one belongs to you, Perdita, mother of his child. Do you remember in her infancy, with what transport you beheld Clara, recognizing in her the united being of yourself and Raymond; joying to view in this living temple a manifestation of your eternal loves. Even such is she still. You say that you have lost Raymond. O, no!—yet he lives with you and in you there. From him she sprung, flesh of his flesh, bone of his bone—and not, as heretofore, are you content to trace in her downy cheek and delicate limbs, an affinity to Raymond, but in her enthusiastic affections, in the sweet qualities of her mind, you may still find him living, the good, the great, the beloved. Be it your care to foster this similarity—be it your care to render her worthy of him, so that, when she glory in her origin, she take not shame for what she is."

I could perceive that, when I recalled my sister's thoughts to her duties in life, she did not listen with the same patience as before. She appeared to suspect a plan of consolation on my part, from which she, cherishing her new-born grief, revolted. "You talk of the future," she said, "while the present is all to me. Let me find the earthly dwelling of my beloved; let us rescue that from common dust, so that in times to come men may point to the sacred tomb, and name it his—then to other thoughts, and a new course of life, or what else fate, in her cruel tyranny, may have marked out for me."

After a short repose I prepared to leave her, that I might endeavour to accomplish her wish. In the mean time we were joined by Clara, whose pallid cheek and scared look shewed the deep impression grief had made on her young mind. She seemed to be full of something to which she could not give words; but, seizing an opportunity afforded by Perdita's absence, she preferred to me an earnest prayer, that I would take her within view of the gate at which her father had entered Constantinople. She promised to commit no extravagance, to be docile, and immediately to return. I could not refuse; for Clara was not an ordinary child; her sensibility and intelligence seemed already to have endowed her with the rights of womanhood. With her therefore, before me on my horse, attended only by the servant who was to re-conduct her, we rode to the Top Kapou. We found a party of soldiers gathered round it. They were listening. "They are human cries," said one: "More like the howling of a dog," replied another; and again they bent to catch the sound of regular distant moans, which issued from the precincts of the ruined city. "That, Clara," I said, "is the gate, that the street which yestermorn your father rode up." Whatever Clara's intention had been in asking to be brought hither, it was balked by the presence of the soldiers. With earnest gaze she looked on the labyrinth of smoking piles which had been a city, and then expressed her readiness to return home. At this moment a melancholy howl struck on our ears; it was repeated; "Hark!" cried Clara, "he is there; that is Florio, my father's dog." It seemed to me impossible that she could recognise the sound, but she persisted in her assertion till she gained credit with the crowd about. At least it would be a benevolent action to rescue the sufferer, whether human or brute, from the desolation of the town; so, sending Clara back to her home, I again entered Constantinople. Encouraged by the impunity attendant on my former visit, several soldiers who had made a part of Raymond's body guard, who had loved him, and sincerely mourned his loss, accompanied me.

It is impossible to conjecture the strange enchainment of events which restored the lifeless form of my friend to our hands. In that part of the town where the fire had most raged the night before, and which now lay quenched, black and cold, the dying dog of Raymond crouched beside the mutilated form of its lord. At such a time sorrow has no voice; affliction, tamed by its very vehemence, is mute. The poor animal recognised me, licked my hand, crept close to its lord, and died.[41] He had been evidently thrown from his horse by some falling ruin, which had crushed his head, and defaced his whole person. I bent over the body, and took in my hand the edge of his cloak, less altered in appearance than the human frame it clothed. I pressed it to my lips, while the rough soldiers gathered around, mourning over this worthiest prey of death, as if regret and endless lamentation could re-illumine the extinguished spark, or call to its shattered prison-house of flesh the liberated spirit. Yesterday those limbs were worth an universe; they then enshrined a transcendant power, whose intents, words, and actions were worthy to be recorded in letters of gold; now the superstition of affection alone could give value to the shattered mechanism, which, incapable and clod-like, no more resembled Raymond, than the fallen rain is like the former mansion of cloud in which it climbed the highest skies, and gilded by the sun, attracted all eyes, and satiated the sense by its excess of beauty.

Such as he had now become, such as was his terrene vesture, defaced and spoiled, we wrapt it in our cloaks, and lifting the burthen in our arms, bore it from this city of the dead. The question arose as to where we should deposit him. In our road to the palace, we passed through the Greek cemetery; here on a tablet of black marble I caused him to be laid; the cypresses waved high above, their death-like gloom accorded with his state of nothingness. We cut branches of the funereal trees and placed them over him, and on these again his sword. I left a guard to protect this treasure of dust; and ordered perpetual torches to be burned around.

When I returned to Perdita, I found that she had already been informed of the success of my undertaking. He, her beloved, the sole and

41 Cf. Byron, "Darkness," 46-54; see Appendix A.1.

eternal object of her passionate tenderness, was restored her. Such was the maniac language of her enthusiasm. What though those limbs moved not, and those lips could no more frame modulated accents of wisdom and love! What though like a weed flung from the fruitless sea, he lay the prey of corruption—still that was the form she had caressed, those the lips that meeting hers, had drank the spirit of love from the commingling breath; that was the earthly mechanism of dissoluble clay she had called her own. True, she looked forward to another life; true, the burning spirit of love seemed to her unextinguishable throughout eternity. Yet at this time, with human fondness, she clung to all that her human senses permitted her to see and feel to be a part of Raymond.

Pale as marble, clear and beaming as that, she heard my tale, and enquired concerning the spot where he had been deposited. Her features had lost the distortion of grief; her eyes were brightened, her very person seemed dilated; while the excessive whiteness and even transparency of her skin, and something hollow in her voice, bore witness that not tranquillity, but excess of excitement, occasioned the treacherous calm that settled on her countenance. I asked her where he should be buried. She replied, "At Athens; even at the Athens which he loved. Without the town, on the acclivity of Hymettus,[42] there is a rocky recess which he pointed out to me as the spot where he would wish to repose."

My own desire certainly was that he should not be removed from the spot where he now lay. But her wish was of course to be complied with; and I entreated her to prepare without delay for our departure.

Behold now the melancholy train cross the flats of Thrace, and wind through the defiles, and over the mountains of Macedonia, coast the clear waves of the Peneus, cross the Larissean plain, pass the straits of Thermopylæ, and ascending in succession Œrta and Parnassus, descend to the fertile plain of Athens.[43] Women bear with resignation these long drawn ills, but to a man's impatient spirit, the slow motion of our cavalcade, the melancholy repose we took at noon, the perpetual presence of the pall, gorgeous though it was, that wrapt the rifled casket which had contained Raymond, the monotonous recurrence of day and night, unvaried by hope or change, all the circumstances of our march were intolerable. Perdita shut up in herself, spoke little. Her carriage was closed; and, when we rested, she sat leaning her pale cheek on her white cold hand, with eyes fixed on the ground, indulging thoughts which refused communication or sympathy.

We descended from Parnassus, emerging from its many folds, and

---

42   A thyme-covered mountain near Athens, famous for marble and honey.

43   They take an overland route from Constantinople to Athens: Macedonia is in
       northern Greece; the river Peneus flows through the Larissean plain in
       Thessaly; Thermopylae ("the hot gates") is further south; Parnassus (the classical
       mountain of the muses) is in the Attic peninsula.

passed through Livadia on our road to Attica. Perdita would not enter Athens; but reposing at Marathon[44] on the night of our arrival, conducted me on the following day, to the spot selected by her as the treasure house of Raymond's dear remains. It was in a recess near the head of the ravine to the south of Hymettus. The chasm, deep, black, and hoary, swept from the summit to the base; in the fissures of the rock myrtle underwood grew and wild thyme, the food of many nations of bees; enormous crags protruded into the cleft, some beetling over, others rising perpendicularly from it. At the foot of this sublime chasm, a fertile laughing valley reached from sea to sea, and beyond was spread the blue Ægean, sprinkled with islands, the light waves glancing beneath the sun. Close to the spot on which we stood, was a solitary rock, high and conical, which, divided on every side from the mountain, seemed a nature-hewn pyramid; with little labour this block was reduced to a perfect shape; the narrow cell was scooped out beneath in which Raymond was placed, and a short inscription, carved in the living stone, recorded the name of its tenant, the cause and æra of his death.

Every thing was accomplished with speed under my directions. I agreed to leave the finishing and guardianship of the tomb to the head of the religious establishment at Athens, and by the end of October prepared for my return to England. I mentioned this to Perdita. It was painful to appear to drag her from the last scene that spoke of her lost one; but to linger here was vain, and my very soul was sick with its yearning to rejoin my Idris and her babes. In reply, my sister requested me to accompany her the following evening to the tomb of Raymond. Some days had passed since I had visited the spot. The path to it had been enlarged, and steps hewn in the rock led us less circuitously than before, to the spot itself; the platform on which the pyramid stood was enlarged, and looking towards the south, in a recess overshadowed by the straggling branches of a wild fig-tree, I saw foundations dug, and props and rafters fixed, evidently the commencement of a cottage; standing on its unfinished threshold, the tomb was at our right-hand, the whole ravine, and plain, and azure sea immediately before us; the dark rocks received a glow from the descending sun, which glanced along the cultivated valley, and dyed in purple and orange the placid waves; we sat on a rocky elevation, and I gazed with rapture on the beauteous panorama of living and changeful colours, which varied and enhanced the graces of earth and ocean.

"Did I not do right," said Perdita, "in having my loved one conveyed hither? Hereafter this will be the cynosure of Greece. In such a spot death loses half its terrors, and even the inanimate dust appears to partake of the spirit of beauty which hallows this region. Lionel, he sleeps there; that is the grave of Raymond, he whom in my youth I first loved; whom my heart

---

44   Livadia is in the Attic peninsula; Marathon is near the coast, northeast of Athens.

accompanied in days of separation and anger; to whom I am now joined for ever. Never—mark me—never will I leave this spot. Methinks his spirit remains here as well as that dust, which, uncommunicable though it be, is more precious in its nothingness than aught else widowed earth clasps to her sorrowing bosom. The myrtle bushes, the thyme, the little cyclamen, which peep from the fissures of the rock, all the produce of the place, bear affinity to him; the light that invests the hills participates in his essence, and sky and mountains, sea and valley, are imbued by the presence of his spirit. I will live and die here!

"Go you to England, Lionel; return to sweet Idris and dearest Adrian; return, and let my orphan girl be as a child of your own in your house. Look on me as dead; and truly if death be a mere change of state, I am dead. This is another world, from that which late I inhabited, from that which is now your home. Here I hold communion only with the has been, and to come. Go you to England, and leave me where alone I can consent to drag out the miserable days which I must still live."

A shower of tears terminated her sad harangue. I had expected some extravagant proposition, and remained silent awhile, collecting my thoughts that I might the better combat her fanciful scheme. "You cherish dreary thoughts, my dear Perdita," I said, "nor do I wonder that for a time your better reason should be influenced by passionate grief and a disturbed imagination. Even I am in love with this last home of Raymond's; nevertheless we must quit it."

"I expected this," cried Perdita; "I supposed that you would treat me as a mad, foolish girl. But do not deceive yourself; this cottage is built by my order; and here I shall remain, until the hour arrives when I may share his happier dwelling."

"My dearest girl!"

"And what is there so strange in my design? I might have deceived you; I might have talked of remaining here only a few months; in your anxiety to reach Windsor you would have left me, and without reproach or contention, I might have pursued my plan. But I disdained the artifice; or rather in my wretchedness it was my only consolation to pour out my heart to you, my brother, my only friend. You will not dispute with me? You know how wilful your poor, misery-stricken sister is. Take my girl with you; wean her from sights and thoughts of sorrow; let infantine hilarity revisit her heart, and animate her eyes; so could it never be, were she near me; it is far better for all of you that you should never see me again. For myself, I will not voluntarily seek death, that is, I will not, while I can command myself; and I can here. But drag me from this country; and my power of self control vanishes, nor can I answer for the violence my agony of grief may lead me to commit."

"You clothe your meaning, Perdita," I replied, "in powerful words, yet that meaning is selfish and unworthy of you. You have often agreed with me that there is but one solution to the intricate riddle of life; to improve ourselves, and contribute to the happiness of others: and now, in the very prime of life, you desert your principles, and shut yourself up in useless solitude. Will you think of Raymond less at Windsor, the scene of your early happiness? Will you commune less with his departed spirit, while you watch over and cultivate the rare excellence of his child? You have been sadly visited; nor do I wonder that a feeling akin to insanity should drive you to bitter and unreasonable imaginings. But a home of love awaits you in your native England. My tenderness and affection must soothe you; the society of Raymond's friends will be of more solace than these dreary speculations. We will all make it our first care, our dearest task, to contribute to your happiness."

Perdita shook her head; "If it could be so," she replied, "I were much in the wrong to disdain your offers. But it is not a matter of choice; I can live here only. I am a part of this scene; each and all its properties are a part of me. This is no sudden fancy; I live by it. The knowledge that I am here, rises with me in the morning, and enables me to endure the light; it is mingled with my food, which else were poison; it walks, it sleeps with me, for ever it accompanies me. Here I may even cease to repine, and may add my tardy consent to the decree which has taken him from me. He would rather have died such a death, which will be recorded in history to endless time, than have lived to old age unknown, unhonoured. Nor can I desire better, than, having been the chosen and beloved of his heart, here, in youth's prime, before added years can tarnish the best feelings of my nature, to watch his tomb, and speedily rejoin him in his blessed repose.

"So much, my dearest Lionel, I have said, wishing to persuade you that I do right. If you are unconvinced, I can add nothing further by way of argument, and I can only declare my fixed resolve. I stay here; force only can remove me. Be it so; drag me away—I return; confine me, imprison me, still I escape, and come here. Or would my brother rather devote the heart-broken Perdita to the straw and chains of a maniac, than suffer her to rest in peace beneath the shadow of His society, in this my own selected and beloved recess?"—

All this appeared to me, I own, methodized madness. I imagined, that it was my imperative duty to take her from scenes that thus forcibly reminded her of her loss. Nor did I doubt, that in the tranquillity of our family circle at Windsor, she would recover some degree of composure, and in the end, of happiness. My affection for Clara also led me to oppose these fond dreams of cherished grief; her sensibility had already been too much excited; her infant heedlessness too soon exchanged for deep and anxious thought. The strange and romantic scheme of her mother, might confirm and perpetuate the painful view of life, which had intruded itself thus early on her contemplation.

On returning home, the captain of the steam packet[45] with whom I had

---

45   A steamship carrying mail and passengers in a regular service.

agreed to sail, came to tell me, that accidental circumstances hastened his departure, and that, if I went with him, I must come on board at five on the following morning. I hastily gave my consent to this arrangement, and as hastily formed a plan through which Perdita should be forced to become my companion. I believe that most people in my situation would have acted in the same manner. Yet this consideration does not, or rather did not in after time, diminish the reproaches of my conscience. At the moment, I felt convinced that I was acting for the best, and that all I did was right and even necessary.

I sat with Perdita and soothed her, by my seeming assent to her wild scheme. She received my concurrence with pleasure, and a thousand times over thanked her deceiving, deceitful brother. As night came on, her spirits, enlivened by my unexpected concession, regained an almost forgotten vivacity. I pretended to be alarmed by the feverish glow in her cheek; I entreated her to take a composing draught; I poured out the medicine, which she took docilely from me. I watched her as she drank it. Falsehood and artifice are in themselves so hateful, that, though I still thought I did right, a feeling of shame and guilt came painfully upon me. I left her, and soon heard that she slept soundly under the influence of the opiate I had administered. She was carried thus unconscious on board; the anchor weighed, and the wind being favourable, we stood far out to sea; with all the canvas spread, and the power of the engine to assist, we scudded swiftly and steadily through the chafed element.

It was late in the day before Perdita awoke, and a longer time elapsed before recovering from the torpor occasioned by the laudanum, she perceived her change of situation. She started wildly from her couch, and flew to the cabin window. The blue and troubled sea sped past the vessel, and was spread shoreless around: the sky was covered by a rack, which in its swift motion shewed how speedily she was borne away. The creaking of the masts, the clang of the wheels, the tramp above, all persuaded her that she was already far from the shores of Greece. —"Where are we?" she cried, "where are we going?"—

The attendant whom I had stationed to watch her, replied, "to England."—

"And my brother?"—

"Is on deck, Madam."

"Unkind! unkind!" exclaimed the poor victim, as with a deep sigh she looked on the waste of waters. Then without further remark, she threw herself on her couch, and closing her eyes remained motionless; so that but for the deep sighs that burst from her, it would have seemed that she slept.

As soon as I heard that she had spoken, I sent Clara to her, that the sight of the lovely innocent might inspire gentle and affectionate thoughts. But neither the presence of her child, nor a subsequent visit from me, could rouse my sister. She looked on Clara with a countenance of woful meaning, but she did not speak. When I appeared, she turned away, and in reply to my enquiries, only said, "You know not what you have done!"—I trusted that this sullenness betokened merely the struggle between disappointment and natural affection, and that in a few days she would be reconciled to her fate.

When night came on, she begged that Clara might sleep in a separate cabin. Her servant, however, remained with her. About midnight she spoke to the latter, saying that she had had a bad dream, and bade her go to her daughter, and bring word whether she rested quietly. The woman obeyed.

The breeze, that had flagged since sunset, now rose again. I was on deck, enjoying our swift progress. The quiet was disturbed only by the rush of waters as they divided before the steady keel, the murmur of the moveless and full sails, the wind whistling in the shrouds, and the regular motion of the engine. The sea was gently agitated, now shewing a white crest, and now resuming an uniform hue; the clouds had disappeared; and dark ether clipt the broad ocean, in which the constellations vainly sought their accustomed mirror. Our rate could not have been less than eight knots.

Suddenly I heard a splash in the sea. The sailors on watch rushed to the side of the vessel, with the cry—some one gone overboard. "It is not from deck," said the man at the helm, "something has been thrown from the aft cabin." A call for the boat to be lowered was echoed from the deck. I rushed into my sister's cabin; it was empty.

With sails abaft, the engine stopt, the vessel remained unwillingly stationary, until, after an hour's search, my poor Perdita was brought on board. But no care could re-animate her, no medicine cause her dear eyes to open, and the blood to flow again from her pulseless heart. One clenched hand contained a slip of paper, on which was written, "To Athens." To ensure her removal thither, and prevent the irrecoverable loss of her body in the wide sea, she had had the precaution to fasten a long shawl round her waist, and again to the staunchions of the cabin window. She had drifted somewhat under the keel of the vessel, and her being out of sight occasioned the delay in finding her. And thus the ill-starred girl died a victim to my senseless rashness. Thus, in early day, she left us for the company of the dead, and preferred to share the rocky grave of Raymond, before the animated scene this cheerful earth afforded, and the society of loving friends. Thus in her twenty-ninth year she died;[46] having enjoyed some few years of the happiness of paradise, and sustaining a reverse to which her impatient spirit and affectionate disposition were unable to submit. As I marked the placid expression that had settled on her countenance in death, I felt, in spite of the pangs of

---

46   MWS was in her twenty-ninth year when *The Last Man* was published in 1826.

remorse, in spite of heart-rending regret, that it was better to die so, than to drag on long, miserable years of repining and inconsolable grief.

Stress of weather drove us up the Adriatic Gulph; and, our vessel being hardly fitted to weather a storm, we took refuge in the port of Ancona.[47] Here I met Georgio Palli, the vice-admiral of the Greek fleet, a former friend and warm partizan of Raymond. I committed the remains of my lost Perdita to his care, for the purpose of having them transported to Hymettus, and placed in the cell her Raymond already occupied beneath the pyramid. This was all accomplished even as I wished. She reposed beside her beloved, and the tomb above was inscribed with the united names of Raymond and Perdita.

I then came to a resolution of pursuing our journey to England over-land. My own heart was racked by regrets and remorse. The apprehension, that Raymond had departed for ever, that his name, blended eternally with the past, must be erased from every anticipation of the future, had come slowly upon me. I had always admired his talents; his noble aspirations; his grand conceptions of the glory and majesty of his ambition: his utter want of mean passions; his fortitude and daring. In Greece I had learnt to love him; his very waywardness, and self-abandonment to the impulses of superstition, attached me to him doubly; it might be weakness, but it was the antipodes of all that was grovelling and selfish. To these pangs were added the loss of Perdita, lost through my own accursed self-will and conceit. This dear one, my sole relation; whose progress I had marked from tender childhood through the varied path of life, and seen her throughout conspicuous for integrity, devotion, and true affection; for all that constitutes the peculiar graces of the female character, and beheld her at last the victim of too much loving, too constant an attachment to the perishable and lost, she, in her pride of beauty and life, had thrown aside the pleasant perception of the apparent world for the unreality of the grave, and had left poor Clara quite an orphan. I concealed from this beloved child that her mother's death was voluntary, and tried every means to awaken cheerfulness in her sorrow-stricken spirit.

One of my first acts for the recovery even of my own composure, was to bid farewell to the sea. Its hateful splash renewed again and again to my sense the death of my sister; its roar was a dirge; in every dark hull that was tossed on its inconstant bosom, I imaged a bier, that would convey to death all who trusted to its treacherous smiles. Farewell to the sea! Come, my Clara, sit beside me in this aerial bark;[48] quickly and gently it cleaves the azure serene, and with soft undulation glides upon the current of the air; or, if storm shake its fragile mechanism, the green earth is below; we can descend, and take shelter on the stable continent. Here aloft, the companions of the swift-winged birds, we skim through the unresisting

---

47   A city about halfway up the Adriatic coast of Italy.
48   This is, of course, another balloon. Cf. 55n, above.

element, fleetly and fearlessly. The light boat heaves not, nor is opposed by death-bearing waves; the ether opens before the prow, and the shadow of the globe that upholds it, shelters us from the noon-day sun. Beneath are the plains of Italy, or the vast undulations of the wave-like Apennines: fertility reposes in their many folds, and woods crown the summits. The free and happy peasant, unshackled by the Austrian,[49] bears the double harvest to the garner; and the refined citizens rear without dread the long blighted tree of knowledge in this garden of the world. We were lifted above the Alpine peaks, and from their deep and brawling ravines entered the plain of fair France, and after an airy journey of six days, we landed at Dieppe, furled the feathered wings, and closed the silken globe of our little pinnace. A heavy rain made this mode of travelling now incommodious; so we embarked in a steam-packet, and after a short passage landed at Portsmouth.

A strange story was rife here. A few days before, a tempest-struck vessel had appeared off the town:[50] the hull was parched-looking and cracked, the sails rent, and bent in a careless, unseamanlike manner, the shrouds tangled and broken. She drifted towards the harbour, and was stranded on the sands at the entrance. In the morning the custom-house officers, together with a crowd of idlers, visited her. One only of the crew appeared to have arrived with her. He had got to shore, and had walked a few paces towards the town, and then, vanquished by malady and approaching death, had fallen on the inhospitable beach. He was found stiff, his hands clenched, and pressed against his breast. His skin, nearly black, his matted hair and bristly beard, were signs of a long protracted misery. It was whispered that he had died of the plague. No one ventured on board the vessel, and strange sights were averred to be seen at night, walking the deck, and hanging on the masts and shrouds. She soon went to pieces; I was shewn where she had been, and saw her disjoined timbers tossed on the waves. The body of the man who had landed, had been buried deep in the sands; and none could tell more, than that the vessel was American built, and that several months before the Fortunatus had sailed from Philadelphia, of which no tidings were afterwards received.

CHAPTER XV

I RETURNED to my family estate in the autumn of the year 2092. My heart had long been with them; and I felt sick with the hope and delight of seeing them again. The district which contained them appeared the abode of

---

49 Another hint of revolutionary sympathies: in MWS's day Italy was divided into small states, largely under Austrian rule.

50 Cf. Thomas Campbell, "The Last Man" (1823): "And ships were drifting with the dead / To shores where all were dumb!" (19-20). See Appendix A.2.

every kindly spirit. Happiness, love and peace, walked the forest paths, and tempered the atmosphere. After all the agitation and sorrow I had endured in Greece, I sought Windsor, as the storm-driven bird does the nest in which it may fold its wings in tranquillity.

How unwise had the wanderers been, who had deserted its shelter, entangled themselves in the web of society, and entered on what men of the world call "life,"[51]—that labyrinth of evil, that scheme of mutual torture. To live, according to this sense of the word, we must not only observe and learn, we must also feel; we must not be mere spectators of action, we must act; we must not describe, but be subjects of description. Deep sorrow must have been the inmate of our bosoms; fraud must have lain in wait for us; the artful must have deceived us; sickening doubt and false hope must have chequered our days; hilarity and joy, that lap the soul in ecstasy, must at times have possessed us. Who that knows what "life" is, would pine for this feverish species of existence? I have lived. I have spent days and nights of festivity; I have joined in ambitious hopes, and exulted in victory: now,—shut the door on the world, and build high the wall that is to separate me from the troubled scene enacted within its precincts. Let us live for each other and for happiness; let us seek peace in our dear home, near the inland murmur of streams, and the gracious waving of trees, the beauteous vesture of earth, and sublime pageantry of the skies. Let us leave "life," that we may live.

Idris was well content with this resolve of mine. Her native sprightliness needed no undue excitement, and her placid heart reposed contented on my love, the well-being of her children, and the beauty of surrounding nature. Her pride and blameless ambition was to create smiles in all around her, and to shed repose on the fragile existence of her brother. In spite of her tender nursing, the health of Adrian perceptibly declined. Walking, riding, the common occupations of life, overcame him: he felt no pain, but seemed to tremble for ever on the verge of annihilation. Yet, as he had lived on for months nearly in the same state, he did not inspire us with any immediate fear; and, though he talked of death as an event most familiar to his thoughts, he did not cease to exert himself to render others happy, or to cultivate his own astonishing powers of mind.

Winter passed away; and spring, led by the months, awakened life in all nature. The forest was dressed in green; the young calves frisked on the new-sprung grass; the wind-winged shadows of light clouds sped over

---

51   That is, public life as opposed to domestic retirement. The word "life" echoes ironically throughout *The Last Man*, sometimes with the connotations it has in PBS's "The Triumph of Life," the poem he was working on at the time of his death (published in *Posthumous Poems*, 1824). There, it signifies an oppressive, dreary enslavement of the mind, heart, imagination, and moral vision.

the green cornfields; the hermit cuckoo repeated his monotonous all-hail to the season; the nightingale, bird of love and minion of the evening star, filled the woods with song; while Venus lingered in the warm sunset, and the young green of the trees lay in gentle relief along the clear horizon.

Delight awoke in every heart, delight and exultation; for there was peace through all the world; the temple of Universal Janus was shut,[52] and man died not that year by the hand of man.

"Let this last but twelve months," said Adrian; "and earth will become a Paradise. The energies of man were before directed to the destruction of his species: they now aim at its liberation and preservation. Man cannot repose, and his restless aspirations will now bring forth good instead of evil. The favoured countries of the south will throw off the iron yoke of servitude; poverty will quit us, and with that, sickness. What may not the forces, never before united, of liberty and peace achieve in this dwelling of man?"

"Dreaming, for ever dreaming, Windsor!" said Ryland, the old adversary of Raymond, and candidate for the Protectorate at the ensuing election. "Be assured that earth is not, nor ever can be heaven, while the seeds of hell are natives of her soil. When the seasons have become equal, when the air breeds no disorders, when its surface is no longer liable to blights and droughts, then sickness will cease; when men's passions are dead, poverty will depart. When love is no longer akin to hate, then brotherhood will exist: we are very far from that state at present."

"Not so far as you may suppose," observed a little old astronomer, by name Merrival, "the poles precede slowly, but securely; in an hundred thousand years—"

"We shall all be underground," said Ryland.

"The pole of the earth will coincide with the pole of the ecliptic," continued the astronomer, "an universal spring will be produced, and earth become a paradise."[53]

"And we shall of course enjoy the benefit of the change," said Ryland, contemptuously.

"We have strange news here," I observed. I had the newspaper in my hand, and, as usual, had turned to the intelligence from Greece. "It seems that the total destruction of Constantinople, and the supposition that winter had purified the air of the fallen city, gave the Greeks courage to visit its site, and begin to rebuild it. But they tell us that the curse of God is on

---

52 Represented with two faces, Janus was the Roman god of beginnings and endings, entrances and exits, past and future. The doors of his principal temple near the forum in Rome were open in wartime and closed in peacetime.

53 Merrival is the most critical version of William Godwin and perhaps also of PBS in the novel. With Merrival's theories of the changing relation of ecliptic and equator, and of the effect of such astronomical changes on human happiness, cf. PBS's Note to *Queen Mab* (1813), Appendix D.6.

the place, for every one who has ventured within the walls has been taint-ed by the plague; that this disease has spread in Thrace and Macedonia; and now, fearing the virulence of infection during the coming heats, a cor-don has been drawn on the frontiers of Thessaly,[54] and a strict quarantine exacted."

This intelligence brought us back from the prospect of paradise, held out after the lapse of an hundred thousand years, to the pain and misery at present existent upon earth. We talked of the ravages made last year by pestilence in every quarter of the world; and of the dreadful conse-quences of a second visitation. We discussed the best means of prevent-ing infection, and of preserving health and activity in a large city thus afflicted—London, for instance. Merrival did not join in this conversation; drawing near Idris, he proceeded to assure her that the joyful prospect of an earthly paradise after an hundred thousand years, was clouded to him by the knowledge that in a certain period of time after, an earthly hell or purgatory, would occur, when the ecliptic and equator would be at right angles.[55] Our party at length broke up; "We are all dreaming this morn-ing," said Ryland, "it is as wise to discuss the probability of a visitation of the plague in our well-governed metropolis, as to calculate the centuries which must escape before we can grow pine-apples here in the open air."

But, though it seemed absurd to calculate upon the arrival of the plague in London, I could not reflect without extreme pain on the deso-lation this evil would cause in Greece. The English for the most part talked of Thrace and Macedonia, as they would of a lunar territory, which, unknown to them, presented no distinct idea or interest to the mind. I had trod the soil. The faces of many of the inhabitants were familiar to me; in the towns, plains, hills, and defiles of these countries, I had enjoyed unspeakable delight, as I journied through them the year before. Some romantic village, some cottage, or elegant abode there situated, inhabited by the lovely and the good, rose before my mental sight, and the question haunted me, is the plague there also?—That same invinci-ble monster, which hovered over and devoured Constantinople—that fiend more cruel than tempest, less tame than fire, is, alas, unchained in that beautiful country—these reflections would not allow me to rest.

The political state of England became agitated as the time drew near when the new Protector was to be elected. This event excited the more interest, since it was the current report, that if the popular candidate

---

54   In northern Greece: the plague follows the route of the Greek army down from Thrace towards Athens.

55   See an ingenious Essay, entitled, "The Mythological Astronomy of the Ancients Demonstrated," by Mackey, a shoemaker, of Norwich printed in 1822 [MWS's note]; basing his conclusions on reading the monuments of antiquity as astronomical allegories, Sampson Arnold Mackey claims that "the Poles have been three times within the plane of the Ecliptic."

(Ryland) should be chosen, the question of the abolition of hereditary rank, and other feudal relics, would come under the consideration of par-. liament. Not a word had been spoken during the present session on any of these topics. Every thing would depend upon the choice of a Protector, and the elections of the ensuing year. Yet this very silence was awful, shewing the deep weight attributed to the question; the fear of either party to hazard an ill-timed attack, and the expectation of a furious contention when it should begin.

But although St. Stephen's did not echo with the voice which filled each heart, the newspapers teemed with nothing else; and in private companies the conversation however remotely begun, soon verged towards this central point, while voices were lowered and chairs drawn closer. The nobles did not hesitate to express their fear; the other party endeavoured to treat the matter lightly. "Shame on the country," said Ryland, "to lay so much stress upon words and frippery; it is a question of nothing; of the new painting of carriage-pannels and the embroidery of footmen's coats."

Yet could England indeed doff her lordly trappings, and be content with the democratic style of America? Were the pride of ancestry, the patrician spirit, the gentle courtesies and refined pursuits, splendid attributes of rank, to be erased among us? We were told that this would not be the case; that we were by nature a poetical people, a nation easily duped by words, ready to array clouds in splendour, and bestow honour on the dust. This spirit we could never lose; and it was to diffuse this concentrated spirit of birth, that the new law was to be brought forward. We were assured that, when the name and title of Englishman was the sole patent of nobility, we should all be noble; that when no man born under English sway, felt another his superior in rank, courtesy and refinement would become the birth-right of all our countrymen. Let not England be so far disgraced, as to have it imagined that it can be without nobles, nature's true nobility, who bear their patent in their mien, who are from their cradle elevated above the rest of their species, because they are better than the rest. Among a race of independent, and generous, and well educated men, in a country where the imagination is empress of men's minds, there needs be no fear that we should want a perpetual succession of the high-born and lordly. That party, however, could hardly yet be considered a minority in the kingdom, who extolled the ornament of the column, "the Corinthian capital of polished society;" [56] they appealed to prejudices without number, to old attachments and young hopes; to the expec-

---

56   Edmund Burke, *Reflections on the Revolution in France*, ed. Conor Cruise
     O'Brien 245. In the original context, Burke is celebrating nobility. PBS quotes
     the same passage in "An Address to the People, on the Death of Princess
     Charlotte" (*Works*, ed. Ingpen and Peck 6: 78).

tation of thousands who might one day become peers; they set up as a scarecrow, the spectre of all that was sordid, mechanic and base in the commercial republics.

The plague had come to Athens. Hundreds of English residents returned to their own country. Raymond's beloved Athenians, the free, the noble people of the divinest town in Greece, fell like ripe corn before the merciless sickle of the adversary. Its pleasant places were deserted; its temples and palaces were converted into tombs; its energies, bent before towards the highest objects of human ambition, were now forced to converge to one point, the guarding against the innumerous arrows of the plague.

At any other time this disaster would have excited extreme compassion among us; but it was now passed over, while each mind was engaged by the coming controversy. It was not so with me; and the question of rank and right dwindled to insignificance in my eyes, when I pictured the scene of suffering Athens. I heard of the death of only sons; of wives and husbands most devoted; of the rending of ties twisted with the heart's fibres, of friend losing friend, and young mothers mourning for their first born; and these moving incidents were grouped and painted in my mind by the knowledge of the persons, by my esteem and affection for the sufferers. It was the admirers, friends, fellow soldiers of Raymond, families that had welcomed Perdita to Greece, and lamented with her the loss of her lord, that were swept away, and went to dwell with them in the undistinguishing tomb.

The plague at Athens had been preceded and caused by the contagion from the East; and the scene of havoc and death continued to be acted there, on a scale of fearful magnitude. A hope that the visitation of the present year would prove the last, kept up the spirits of the merchants connected with these countries; but the inhabitants were driven to despair, or to a resignation which, arising from fanaticism, assumed the same dark hue. America had also received the taint;[57] and, were it yellow fever or plague, the epidemic was gifted with a virulence before unfelt. The devastation was not confined to the towns, but spread throughout the country; the hunter died in the woods, the peasant in the corn-fields, and the fisher on his native waters.

A strange story was brought to us from the East, to which little credit would have been given, had not the fact been attested by a multitude of witnesses, in various parts of the world. On the twenty-first of June, it was

---

57 Charles Brockden Brown described in *Arthur Mervyn* (1799-1800) the epidemic at Philadelphia in 1793. This "pestilence" was yellow fever, an intestinal hemorrhagic disease now known to be caused by a virus and transmitted by mosquitoes.

said that an hour before noon, a black sun[58] arose: an orb, the size of that luminary, but dark, defined, whose beams were shadows, ascended from the west; in about an hour it had reached the meridian, and eclipsed the bright parent of day. Night fell upon every country, night, sudden, rayless, entire. The stars came out, shedding their ineffectual glimmerings on the light-widowed earth. But soon the dim orb passed from over the sun, and lingered down the eastern heaven. As it descended, its dusky rays crossed the brilliant ones of the sun, and deadened or distorted them. The shadows of things assumed strange and ghastly shapes. The wild animals in the woods took fright at the unknown shapes figured on the ground. They fled they knew not whither; and the citizens were filled with greater dread, at the convulsion which "shook lions into civil streets;"[59]—birds, strong-winged eagles, suddenly blinded, fell in the market-places, while owls and bats shewed themselves welcoming the early night. Gradually the object of fear sank beneath the horizon, and to the last shot up shadowy beams into the otherwise radiant air. Such was the tale sent us from Asia, from the eastern extremity of Europe, and from Africa as far west as the Golden Coast.

Whether this story were true or not, the effects were certain. Through Asia, from the banks of the Nile to the shores of the Caspian, from the Hellespont even to the sea of Omar, a sudden panic was driven.[60] The men filled the mosques; the women, veiled, hastened to the tombs, and carried offerings to the dead, thus to preserve the living. The plague was forgotten, in this new fear which the black sun had spread; and, though the dead multiplied, and the streets of Ispahan,[61] of Pekin, and of Delhi were strewed with pestilence-struck corpses, men passed on, gazing on the ominous sky, regardless of the death beneath their feet. The christians sought their churches,—christian maidens, even at the feast of roses,[62] clad in white, with shining veils, sought, in long procession, the places consecrated to their religion, filling the air with their hymns; while, ever and anon, from the lips of some poor mourner in the crowd, a voice

---

58   See Rev. 6.12: "And I beheld when he had opened the sixth seal; and, lo, there was a great earthquake; and the sun became black as sackcloth of hair, and the moon became as blood."

59   *Antony and Cleopatra* 5.1.15-19: "The round world / Should have shook lions into civil streets, / And citizens to their dens. The death of Antony / Is not a single doom: in the name lay / A moiety of the world."

60   Throughout the Middle East: the Hellespont is the strait between the Aegean Sea and the Sea of Marmara; the Sea of Omar is perhaps the Gulf of Oman between the Persian Gulf and the Arabian Sea.

61   Ispahan (modern Isfahan) was the capital of Persia under Shah Abbas the Great, c. 1600.

62   In his prose introduction to *Lalla Rookh* (1817), Thomas Moore refers to "that Persian festival called the Scattering of the Roses," which he identifies in his footnote as "*Gul Reazee*" (*Poetical Works* 356).

of wailing burst, and the rest looked up, fancying they could discern the sweeping wings of angels, who passed over the earth, lamenting the disasters about to fall on man.[63]

In the sunny clime of Persia, in the crowded cities of China, amidst the aromatic groves of Cashmere,[64] and along the southern shores of the Mediterranean, such scenes had place. Even in Greece the tale of the sun of darkness encreased the fears and despair of the dying multitude. We, in our cloudy isle, were far removed from danger, and the only circumstance that brought these disasters at all home to us, was the daily arrival of vessels from the east, crowded with emigrants, mostly English; for the Moslems, though the fear of death was spread keenly among them, still clung together; that, if they were to die (and if they were, death would as readily meet them on the homeless sea, or in far England, as in Persia,)—if they were to die, their bones might rest in earth made sacred by the relics of true believers. Mecca had never before been so crowded with pilgrims; yet the Arabs neglected to pillage the caravans, but, humble and weaponless, they joined the procession, praying Mahomet to avert plague from their tents and deserts.

I cannot describe the rapturous delight with which I turned from political brawls at home, and the physical evils of distant countries, to my own dear home, to the selected abode of goodness and love; to peace, and the interchange of every sacred sympathy. Had I never quitted Windsor, these emotions would not have been so intense; but I had in Greece been the prey of fear and deplorable change; in Greece, after a period of anxiety and sorrow, I had seen depart two, whose very names were the symbol of greatness and virtue. But such miseries could never intrude upon the domestic circle left to me, while, secluded in our beloved forest, we passed our lives in tranquillity. Some small change indeed the progress of years brought here; and time, as it is wont, stamped the traces of mortality on our pleasures and expectations.

Idris, the most affectionate wife, sister and friend, was a tender and loving mother. The feeling was not with her as with many, a pastime; it was a passion. We had had three children; one, the second in age, died while I was in Greece. This had dashed the triumphant and rapturous emotions of maternity with grief and fear. Before this event, the little beings, sprung from herself, the young heirs of her transient life, seemed

---

63   Cf. Daniel Defoe, *A Journal of the Plague Year* (1722); see Appendix C.2.ii.
64   Cashmere (Kashmir) in the mountains of northwest India, thought to be
      where human life originated, was a popular literary setting in this period. In
      Lady Morgan's novel *The Missionary* (1811), the heroine, Luxima, is the
      "Prophetess of Cashmire." The "vale of Cashmire" (145) is the site of the
      Poet's dream in PBS's poem Alastor (1816) and is identical with the "lovely
      vale in the Indian Caucasus" of *Prometheus Unbound* 2.1. Thomas Moore uses
      the same setting in *Lalla Rookh* (1817).

to have a sure lease of existence; now she dreaded that the pitiless destroyer might snatch her remaining darlings, as it had snatched their brother. The least illness caused throes of terror; she was miserable if she were at all absent from them; her treasure of happiness she had garnered in their fragile being, and kept forever on the watch, lest the insidious thief should as before steal these valued gems. She had fortunately small cause for fear. Alfred, now nine years old, was an upright, manly little fellow, with radiant brow, soft eyes, and gentle, though independent disposition. Our youngest was yet in infancy; but his downy cheek was sprinkled with the roses of health, and his unwearied vivacity filled our halls with innocent laughter.

Clara had passed the age which, from its mute ignorance, was the source of the fears of Idris. Clara was dear to her, to all. There was so much intelligence combined with innocence, sensibility with forbearance, and seriousness with perfect good-humour, a beauty so transcendant, united to such endearing simplicity, that she hung like a pearl in the shrine of our possessions, a treasure of wonder and excellence.

At the beginning of winter our Alfred, now nine years of age, first went to school at Eton.[65] This appeared to him the primary step towards manhood, and he was proportionably pleased. Community of study and amusement developed the best parts of his character, his steady perseverance, generosity, and well-governed firmness. What deep and sacred emotions are excited in a father's bosom, when he first becomes convinced that his love for his child is not a mere instinct, but worthily bestowed, and that others, less akin, participate his approbation! It was supreme happiness to Idris and myself, to find that the frankness which Alfred's open brow indicated, the intelligence of his eyes, the tempered sensibility of his tones, were not delusions, but indications of talents and virtues, which would "grow with his growth, and strengthen with his strength."[66] At this period, the termination of an animal's love for its offspring,—the true affection of the human parent commences. We no longer look on this dearest part of ourselves, as a tender plant which we must cherish, or a plaything for an idle hour. We build now on his intellectual faculties, we establish our hopes on his moral propensities. His weakness still imparts anxiety to this feeling, his ignorance prevents entire intimacy; but we begin to respect the future man, and to endeav-

---

65   MWS wanted to send Percy Florence to Eton College, near Windsor, his father's school from 1804 to 1810; but when PBS's father Sir Timothy Shelley objected, Percy went to Byron's public school, Harrow, instead.

66   See Alexander Pope, *An Essay on Man* 2.133-36: "Man, perhaps, the moment of his breath, / Receives the lurking principle of death; / The young disease, that must subdue at length, / Grows with his growth, and strengthens with his strength." Mary Wollstonecraft adapts the same passage in *A Vindication of the Rights of Woman*, ed. Carol H. Poston 116.

our to secure his esteem, even as if he were our equal. What can a parent have more at heart than the good opinion of his child? In all our transactions with him our honour must be inviolate, the integrity of our relations untainted: fate and circumstance may, when he arrives at maturity, separate us for ever—but, as his ægis[67] in danger, his consolation in hardship, let the ardent youth for ever bear with him through the rough path of life, love and honour for his parents.

We had lived so long in the vicinity of Eton, that its population of young folks was well known to us. Many of them had been Alfred's playmates, before they became his school-fellows. We now watched this youthful congregation with redoubled interest. We marked the difference of character among the boys, and endeavoured to read the future man in the stripling. There is nothing more lovely, to which the heart more yearns than a free-spirited boy, gentle, brave, and generous. Several of the Etonians had these characteristics; all were distinguished by a sense of honour, and spirit of enterprize; in some, as they verged towards manhood, this degenerated into presumption; but the younger ones, lads a little older than our own, were conspicuous for their gallant and sweet dispositions.

Here were the future governors of England; the men, who, when our ardour was cold, and our projects completed or destroyed for ever, when, our drama acted, we doffed the garb of the hour, and assumed the uniform of age, or of more equalizing death; here were the beings who were to carry on the vast machine of society; here were the lovers, husbands, fathers; here the landlord, the politician, the soldier; some fancied that they were even now ready to appear on the stage, eager to make one among the dramatis personæ of active life. It was not long since I was like one of these beardless aspirants; when my boy shall have obtained the place I now hold, I shall have tottered into a grey-headed, wrinkled old man. Strange system! riddle of the Sphynx,[68] most awe-striking! that thus man remains, while we the individuals pass away. Such is, to borrow the words of an eloquent and philosophic writer, "the mode of existence decreed to a permanent body composed of transitory parts; wherein, by the disposition of a stupendous wisdom, moulding together the great mysterious incorporation of the human race, the whole, at one time, is never old, or middle-aged, or young, but, in a condition of unchangeable

---

67 Shield.
68 Elton, *Remains of Hesiod*, quotes a version of this riddle from Diodorus: "What is that, which is two-footed, and four-footed, yet one and the same? Œdipus declared that the thing propounded to him was man: for that a man, while an infant, went on four: when grown up, on two; and when old, on three: as using a staff through feebleness" (65n).

constancy, moves on through the varied tenour of perpetual decay, fall, renovation, and progression." [69]

Willingly do I give place to thee, dear Alfred! advance, offspring of tender love, child of our hopes; advance a soldier on the road to which I have been the pioneer! I will make way for thee. I have already put off the carelessness of childhood, the unlined brow, and springy gait of early years, that they may adorn thee. Advance; and I will despoil myself still further for thy advantage. Time shall rob me of the graces of maturity, shall take the fire from my eyes, and agility from my limbs, shall steal the better part of life, eager expectation and passionate love, and shower them in double portion on thy dear head. Advance! avail thyself of the gift, thou and thy comrades; and in the drama you are about to act, do not disgrace those who taught you to enter on the stage, and to pronounce becomingly the parts assigned to you! May your progress be uninterrupted and secure; born during the spring-tide of the hopes of man, may you lead up the summer to which no winter may succeed!

CHAPTER XVI

SOME disorder had surely crept into the course of the elements, destroying their benignant influence. The wind, prince of air, raged through his kingdom, lashing the sea into fury, and subduing the rebel earth into some sort of obedience.

> The God sends down his angry plagues from high,
> Famine and pestilence in heaps they die.
> Again in vengeance of his wrath he falls
> On their great hosts, and breaks their tottering walls;
> Arrests their navies on the ocean's plain,
> And whelms their strength with mountains of the main. [70]

Their deadly power shook the flourishing countries of the south, and during winter, even, we, in our northern retreat, began to quake under their ill effects.

That fable is unjust, which gives the superiority to the sun over the

---

69 Burke's Reflections on the French Revolution [MWS's note]; Burke, *Reflections*, ed. Conor Cruise O'Brien 120.

70 Elton's translation of Hesiod's Works [MWS's note]; the passage comes from Charles Abraham Elton, trans., *The Works and Days*, in *Remains of Hesiod*, 2nd ed. (1815) 32. Perhaps significantly, MWS omits the second couplet: "He smites with barrenness the marriage-bed, / And generations moulder with the dead."

wind.[71] Who has not seen the lightsome earth, the balmy atmosphere, and basking nature become dark, cold and ungenial, when the sleeping wind has awoke in the east? Or, when the dun clouds thickly veil the sky, while exhaustless stores of rain are poured down, until, the dank earth refusing to imbibe the superabundant moisture, it lies in pools on the surface; when the torch of day seems like a meteor, to be quenched; who has not seen the cloud-stirring north arise, the streaked blue appear, and soon an opening made in the vapours in the eye of the wind, through which the bright azure shines? The clouds become thin; an arch is formed for ever rising upwards, till, the universal cope being unveiled, the sun pours forth its rays, re-animated and fed by the breeze.

Then mighty art thou, O wind, to be throned above all other vice-regents of nature's power; whether thou comest destroying from the east, or pregnant with elementary life from the west; thee the clouds obey; the sun is subservient to thee; the shoreless ocean is thy slave! Thou sweepest over the earth, and oaks, the growth of centuries, submit to thy viewless axe; the snow-drift is scattered on the pinnacles of the Alps, the avalanche thunders down their vallies. Thou holdest the keys of the frost, and canst first chain and then set free the streams; under thy gentle governance the buds and leaves are born, they flourish nursed by thee.

Why dost thou howl thus, O wind? By day and by night for four long months thy roarings have not ceased—the shores of the sea are strewn with wrecks, its keel-welcoming surface has become impassable, the earth has shed her beauty in obedience to thy command; the frail balloon dares no longer sail on the agitated air; thy ministers, the clouds, deluge the land with rain; rivers forsake their banks; the wild torrent tears up the mountain path; plain and wood, and verdant dell are despoiled of their loveliness; our very cities are wasted by thee. Alas, what will become of us? It seems as if the giant waves of ocean, and vast arms of the sea, were about to wrench the deep-rooted island from its centre; and cast it, a ruin and a wreck, upon the fields of the Atlantic.

What are we, the inhabitants of this globe, least among the many that people infinite space?[72] Our minds embrace infinity; the visible mechanism of our being is subject to merest accident. Day by day we are forced to believe this. He whom a scratch has disorganized, he who disappears from apparent life under the influence of the hostile agency at work around us, had the same powers as I—I also am subject to the same laws. In the face of all this we call ourselves lords of the creation, wielders of the elements, masters of life and death, and we allege in excuse of this

71   See William Godwin, "The Sun and the Wind," *Fables Ancient and Modern* 1: 168-72.
72   Perhaps another echo of *Hamlet*: "O God, I could be bounded in a nutshell and count myself a king of infinite space, were it not that I have bad dreams" (2.2.253-56).

arrogance, that though the individual is destroyed, man continues for ever.

Thus, losing our identity, that of which we are chiefly conscious, we glory in the continuity of our species, and learn to regard death without terror. But when any whole nation becomes the victim of the destructive powers of exterior agents, then indeed man shrinks into insignificance, he feels his tenure of life insecure, his inheritance on earth cut off.

I remember, after having witnessed the destructive effects of a fire, I could not even behold a small one in a stove, without a sensation of fear. The mounting flames had curled round the building, as it fell, and was destroyed. They insinuated themselves into the substances about them, and the impediments to their progress yielded at their touch. Could we take integral parts of this power, and not be subject to its operation? Could we domesticate a cub of this wild beast, and not fear its growth and maturity?

Thus we began to feel, with regard to many-visaged death let loose on the chosen districts of our fair habitation, and above all, with regard to the plague. We feared the coming summer. Nations, bordering on the already infected countries, began to enter upon serious plans for the better keeping out of the enemy. We, a commercial people, were obliged to bring such schemes under consideration; and the question of contagion became matter of earnest disquisition.

That the plague was not what is commonly called contagious, like the scarlet fever, or extinct small-pox,[73] was proved. It was called an epidemic. But the grand question was still unsettled of how this epidemic was generated and increased. If infection depended upon the air, the air was subject to infection. As for instance, a typhus fever[74] has been brought by ships to one sea-port town; yet the very people who brought it there, were incapable of communicating it in a town more fortunately situated. But how are we to judge of airs, and pronounce—in such a city plague will die unproductive; in such another, nature has provided for it a plentiful harvest? In the same way, individuals may escape ninety-nine times, and receive the death-blow at the hundredth; because bodies are

---

73 Scarlet fever is a highly contagious streptococcal infection, easily treated today with penicillin but at one time a dangerous disease with severe complications. Smallpox, from which MWS herself suffered in 1828, is a contagious viral disease leaving survivors with disfiguring scars. It was eradicated only in the late 1970s: MWS's prophecy that it will be extinct in the twenty-first century is accurate. For the contemporary debate about contagious and epidemic diseases, and about whether outbreaks of plague should stop trade with affected regions, see Appendix C.5.

74 A frequently fatal disease, transmitted through the bite of a body louse or flea and common in crowded cities or insanitary institutions. Allegra, Claire Clairmont's and Byron's daughter, died in a convent of typhus in 1822.

sometimes in a state to reject the infection of malady, and at others, thirsty to imbibe it. These reflections made our legislators pause, before they could decide on the laws to be put in force. The evil was so wide-spreading, so violent and immedicable,[75] that no care, no prevention could be judged superfluous, which even added a chance to our escape.

These were questions of prudence; there was no immediate necessity for an earnest caution. England was still secure. France, Germany, Italy and Spain, were interposed, walls yet without a breach, between us and the plague. Our vessels truly were the sport of winds and waves, even as Gulliver was the toy of the Brobdignagians;[76] but we on our stable abode could not be hurt in life or limb by these eruptions of nature. We could not fear—we did not. Yet a feeling of awe, a breathless sentiment of wonder, a painful sense of the degradation of humanity, was introduced into every heart. Nature, our mother, and our friend, had turned on us a brow of menace. She shewed us plainly, that, though she permitted us to assign her laws and subdue her apparent powers, yet, if she put forth but a finger, we must quake. She could take our globe, fringed with mountains, girded by the atmosphere, containing the condition of our being, and all that man's mind could invent or his force achieve; she could take the ball in her hand, and cast it into space, where life would be drunk up, and man and all his efforts for ever annihilated.

These speculations were rife among us; yet not the less we proceeded in our daily occupations, and our plans, whose accomplishment demanded the lapse of many years. No voice was heard telling us to hold! When foreign distresses came to be felt by us through the channels of commerce, we set ourselves to apply remedies. Subscriptions were made for the emigrants, and merchants bankrupt by the failure of trade. The English spirit awoke to its full activity, and, as it had ever done, set itself to resist the evil, and to stand in the breach which diseased nature had suffered chaos and death to make in the bounds and banks which had hitherto kept them out.

At the commencement of summer, we began to feel, that the mischief which had taken place in distant countries was greater than we had at first suspected. Quito was destroyed by an earthquake.[77] Mexico laid waste by the united effects of storm, pestilence and famine. Crowds of emigrants

---

75   Cf. PBS, *Prometheus Unbound*: "who rains down / Evil, the immedicable plague, which, while / Man looks on his creation like a God / And sees that it is glorious, drives him on, / The wreck of his own will, the scorn of earth, / The outcast, the abandoned, the alone?" (2.4.100-05).

76   In Book 2 of *Gulliver's Travels* the giant inhabitants of Brobdingnag treat Gulliver like an animated doll, providing him with a water-filled trough in which he rows and sails for their amusement (Jonathan Swift, *Writings* 96-97).

77   Quito, the capital of Ecuador, was badly damaged by an earthquake in 1797.

inundated the west of Europe; and our island had become the refuge of thousands. In the mean time Ryland had been chosen Protector. He had sought this office with eagerness, under the idea of turning his whole forces to the suppression of the privileged orders of our community. His measures were thwarted, and his schemes interrupted by this new state of things. Many of the foreigners were utterly destitute; and their increasing numbers at length forbade a recourse to the usual modes of relief. Trade was stopped by the failure of the interchange of cargoes usual between us, and America, India, Egypt and Greece. A sudden break was made in the routine of our lives. In vain our Protector and his partizans sought to conceal this truth; in vain, day after day, he appointed a period for the discussion of the new laws concerning hereditary rank and privilege; in vain he endeavoured to represent the evil as partial and temporary. These disasters came home to so many bosoms, and, through the various channels of commerce, were carried so entirely into every class and division of the community, that of necessity they became the first question in the state, the chief subjects to which we must turn our attention.

Can it be true, each asked the other with wonder and dismay, that whole countries are laid waste, whole nations annihilated, by these disorders in nature? The vast cities of America, the fertile plains of Hindostan, the crowded abodes of the Chinese, are menaced with utter ruin. Where late the busy multitudes assembled for pleasure or profit, now only the sound of wailing and misery is heard. The air is empoisoned, and each human being inhales death, even while in youth and health, their hopes are in the flower. We called to mind the plague of 1348,[78] when it was calculated that a third of mankind had been destroyed. As yet western Europe was uninfected; would it always be so?

O, yes, it would—Countrymen, fear not! In the still uncultivated wilds of America, what wonder that among its other giant destroyers, Plague should be numbered! It is of old a native of the East, sister of the tornado, the earthquake, and the simoom. Child of the sun, and nursling of the tropics, it would expire in these climes. It drinks the dark blood of the inhabitant of the south, but it never feasts on the pale-faced Celt. If perchance some stricken Asiatic come among us, plague dies with him, uncommunicated and innoxious. Let us weep for our brethren, though we can never experience their reverse. Let us lament over and assist the children of the garden of the earth. Late we envied their abodes, their spicy groves, fertile plains, and abundant loveliness. But in this mortal life extremes are always matched; the thorn grows with the rose, the poison tree and the cinnamon mingle their boughs. Persia, with its cloth of gold, marble halls, and infinite wealth, is now a tomb. The tent of the Arab is fallen in the sands, and his horse spurns the ground unbridled and unsad-

---

78   The epidemic of bubonic plague known as the Black Death arrived in England from the Continent in 1348.

dled. The voice of lamentation fills the valley of Cashmere; its dells and woods, its cool fountains, and gardens of roses, are polluted by the dead; in Circassia and Georgia[79] the spirit of beauty weeps over the ruin of its favourite temple—the form of woman.

Our own distresses, though they were occasioned by the fictitious reciprocity of commerce, encreased in due proportion. Bankers, merchants, and manufacturers, whose trade depended on exports and interchange of wealth, became bankrupt. Such things, when they happen singly, affect only the immediate parties; but the prosperity of the nation was now shaken by frequent and extensive losses. Families, bred in opulence and luxury, were reduced to beggary. The very state of peace in which we gloried was injurious; there were no means of employing the idle, or of sending any overplus of population out of the country. Even the source of colonies was dried up, for in New Holland, Van Diemen's Land,[80] and the Cape of Good Hope, plague raged. O, for some medicinal vial to purge unwholesome nature, and bring back the earth to its accustomed health!

Ryland was a man of strong intellects and quick and sound decision in the usual course of things, but he stood aghast at the multitude of evils that gathered round us. Must he tax the landed interest to assist our commercial population? To do this, he must gain the favour of the chief land-holders, the nobility of the country; and these were his vowed enemies—he must conciliate them by abandoning his favourite scheme of equalization; he must confirm them in their manorial rights; he must sell his cherished plans for the permanent good of his country, for temporary relief. He must aim no more at the dear object of his ambition; throwing his arms aside, he must for present ends give up the ultimate object of his endeavours. He came to Windsor to consult with us. Every day added to his difficulties; the arrival of fresh vessels with emigrants, the total cessation of commerce, the starving multitude that thronged around the palace of the Protectorate, were circumstances not to be tampered with. The blow was struck; the aristocracy obtained all they wished, and they subscribed to a twelvemonths' bill, which levied twenty per cent on all the rent-rolls of the country.

Calm was now restored to the metropolis, and to the populous cities, before driven to desperation; and we returned to the consideration of distant calamities, wondering if the future would bring any alleviation to their excess. It was August; so there could be small hope of relief during the heats. On the contrary, the disease gained virulence, while starvation did its accustomed work. Thousands died unlamented; for beside the yet warm corpse the mourner was stretched, made mute by death.

---

79 Circassia was once the name of the northwest Caucasus; Georgia is the region in the south of the Caucasus, southeast of the Black Sea.

80 New Holland is Australia; Van Diemen's Land is Tasmania.

On the eighteenth of this month news arrived in London that the plague was in France and Italy. These tidings were at first whispered about town; but no one dared express aloud the soul-quailing intelligence. When any one met a friend in the street, he only cried as he hurried on, "You know!"—while the other, with an ejaculation of fear and horror, would answer,—"What will become of us?" At length it was mentioned in the newspapers. The paragraph was inserted in an obscure part: "We regret to state that there can be no longer a doubt of the plague having been introduced at Leghorn, Genoa, and Marseilles." [81] No word of comment followed; each reader made his own fearful one. We were as a man who hears that his house is burning, and yet hurries through the streets, borne along by a lurking hope of a mistake, till he turns the corner, and sees his sheltering roof enveloped in a flame. Before it had been a rumour; but now in words uneraseable, in definite and undeniable print, the knowledge went forth. Its obscurity of situation rendered it the more conspicuous: the diminutive letters grew gigantic to the bewildered eye of fear: they seemed graven with a pen of iron, impressed by fire, woven in the clouds, stamped on the very front of the universe.

The English, whether travellers or residents, came pouring in one great revulsive stream, back on their own country; and with them crowds of Italians and Spaniards. Our little island was filled even to bursting. At first an unusual quantity of specie made its appearance with the emigrants; but these people had no means of receiving back into their hands what they spent among us. With the advance of summer, and the increase of the distemper, rents were unpaid, and their remittances failed them. It was impossible to see these crowds of wretched, perishing creatures, late nurslings of luxury, and not stretch out a hand to save them. As at the conclusion of the eighteenth century, the English unlocked their hospitable store, for the relief of those driven from their homes by political revolution;[82] so now they were not backward in affording aid to the victims of a more wide-spreading calamity. We had many foreign friends whom we eagerly sought out, and relieved from dreadful penury. Our Castle became an asylum for the unhappy. A little population occupied its halls. The revenue of its possessor, which had always found a mode of expenditure congenial to his generous nature, was now attended to more parsimoniously, that it might embrace a wider portion of utility. It was not however money, except partially, but the necessaries of life, that became scarce. It was difficult to find an immediate remedy. The usual one of

---

81 All are cities on the Mediterranean, as the plague spreads along the coastal trade route: Livorno (Leghorn) is on the northwest coast of Italy; Genoa (or Genova) is further north and west; Marseilles is still farther west, on the south coast of France.

82 Like those opponents and victims of the French Revolution who took refuge in England in 1794.

imports was entirely cut off. In this emergency, to feed the very people to whom we had given refuge, we were obliged to yield to the plough and the mattock our pleasure-grounds and parks. Live stock diminished sensibly in the country, from the effects of the great demand in the market. Even the poor deer, our antlered protégés, were obliged to fall for the sake of worthier pensioners. The labour necessary to bring the lands to this sort of culture, employed and fed the offcasts of the diminished manufactories.

Adrian did not rest only with the exertions he could make with regard to his own possessions. He addressed himself to the wealthy of the land; he made proposals in parliament little adapted to please the rich; but his earnest pleadings and benevolent eloquence were irresistible. To give up their pleasure-grounds to the agriculturist, to diminish sensibly the number of horses kept for the purposes of luxury throughout the country, were means obvious, but unpleasing. Yet, to the honour of the English be it recorded, that, although natural disinclination made them delay awhile, yet when the misery of their fellow-creatures became glaring, an enthusiastic generosity inspired their decrees. The most luxurious were often the first to part with their indulgencies. As is common in communities, a fashion was set. The high-born ladies of the country would have deemed themselves disgraced if they had now enjoyed, what they before called a necessary, the ease of a carriage. Chairs, as in olden time, and Indian palanquins[83] were introduced for the infirm; but else it was nothing singular to see females of rank going on foot to places of fashionable resort. It was more common, for all who possessed landed property to secede to their estates, attended by whole troops of the indigent, to cut down their woods to erect temporary dwellings, and to portion out their parks, parterres[84] and flower-gardens, to necessitous families. Many of these, of high rank in their own countries, now, with hoe in hand, turned up the soil. It was found necessary at last to check the spirit of sacrifice, and to remind those whose generosity proceeded to lavish waste, that, until the present state of things became permanent, of which there was no likelihood, it was wrong to carry change so far as to make a reaction difficult. Experience demonstrated that in a year or two pestilence would cease; it were well that in the mean time we should not have destroyed our fine breeds of horses, or have utterly changed the face of the ornamented portion of the country.

It may be imagined that things were in a bad state indeed, before this spirit of benevolence could have struck such deep roots. The infection had now spread in the southern provinces of France. But that country had so many resources in the way of agriculture, that the rush of population from one part of it to another, and its increase through foreign emigration,

---

83 Covered litters carried by means of poles.
84 Ornamental gardens of symmetrical flower-beds arranged in patterns.

was less felt than with us. The panic struck appeared of more injury, than disease and its natural concomitants.

Winter was hailed, a general and never-failing physician. The embrowning woods, and swollen rivers, the evening mists, and morning frosts, were welcomed with gratitude. The effects of purifying cold were immediately felt; and the lists of mortality abroad were curtailed each week. Many of our visitors left us: those whose homes were far in the south, fled delightedly from our northern winter, and sought their native land, secure of plenty even after their fearful visitation. We breathed again. What the coming summer would bring, we knew not; but the present months were our own, and our hopes of a cessation of pestilence were high.

CHAPTER XVII

I HAVE lingered thus long on the extreme bank, the wasting shoal that stretched into the stream of life, dallying with the shadow of death. Thus long, I have cradled my heart in retrospection of past happiness, when hope was. Why not for ever thus? I am not immortal; and the thread of my history might be spun out to the limits of my existence. But the same sentiment that first led me to pourtray scenes replete with tender recollections, now bids me hurry on. The same yearning of this warm, panting heart, that has made me in written words record my vagabond youth, my serene manhood, and the passions of my soul, makes me now recoil from further delay. I must complete my work.

Here then I stand, as I said, beside the fleet waters of the flowing years, and now away! Spread the sail, and strain with oar, hurrying by dark impending crags, adown steep rapids, even to the sea of desolation I have reached. Yet one moment, one brief interval before I put from shore— once, once again let me fancy myself as I was in 2094 in my abode at Windsor, let me close my eyes, and imagine that the immeasurable boughs of its oaks still shadow me, its castle walls anear. Let fancy pourtray the joyous scene of the twentieth of June, such as even now my aching heart recalls it.

Circumstances had called me to London; here I heard talk that symptoms of the plague had occurred in hospitals of that city. I returned to Windsor; my brow was clouded, my heart heavy; I entered the Little Park, as was my custom, at the Frogmore gate, on my way to the Castle.[85] A great part of these grounds had been given to cultivation, and strips of potatoe-land and corn were scattered here and there. The rooks cawed loudly in the trees above; mixed with their hoarse cries I heard a lively

---

85   The Home Park or Little Park, site of Frogmore House, is south of Windsor Castle.

strain of music. It was Alfred's birthday. The young people, the Etonians, and children of the neighbouring gentry, held a mock fair, to which all the country people were invited. The park was speckled by tents, whose flaunting colours and gaudy flags, waving in the sunshine, added to the gaiety of the scene. On a platform erected beneath the terrace, a number of the younger part of the assembly were dancing. I leaned against a tree to observe them. The band played the wild eastern air of Weber intro-duced in Abon Hassan;[86] its volatile notes gave wings to the feet of the dancers, while the lookers-on unconsciously beat time. At first the trip-ping measure lifted my spirit with it, and for a moment my eyes gladly fol-lowed the mazes of the dance. The revulsion of thought passed like keen steel to my heart. Ye are all going to die, I thought; already your tomb is built up around you. Awhile, because you are gifted with agility and strength, you fancy that you live: but frail is the "bower of flesh"[87] that encaskets life; dissoluble the silver cord[88] that binds you to it. The joyous soul, charioted from pleasure to pleasure by the graceful mechanism of well-formed limbs, will suddenly feel the axle-tree give way, and spring and wheel dissolve in dust. Not one of you, O! fated crowd, can escape—not one! not my own ones! not my Idris and her babes! Horror and misery! Already the gay dance vanished, the green sward was strewn with corpses, the blue air above became fetid with deathly exhalations. Shriek, ye clarions! ye loud trumpets, howl! Pile dirge on dirge; rouse the funereal chords; let the air ring with dire wailing; let wild discord rush on the wings of the wind! Already I hear it, while guardian angels, attendant on humanity, their task achieved, hasten away, and their departure is announced by melancholy strains; faces all unseemly with weeping, forced open my lids; faster and faster many groups of these woe-begone countenances thronged around, exhibiting every variety of wretchedness—well known faces mingled with the distorted creations of fancy. Ashy pale, Raymond and Perdita sat apart, looking on with sad smiles. Adrian's countenance flitted across, tainted by death—Idris, with eyes languidly closed and livid lips, was about to slide into the wide grave. The confusion grew—their looks of sorrow changed to mockery; they nodded their heads in time to the music, whose clang became maddening.

---

86 In 1823, Carl Maria von Weber added Fatima's air to his one-act *Singspiel, Abu Hassan*, first performed in Munich in 1811. John Genest (who spells Weber's title as MWS does) notes that a production of the opera, "founded on a story in the Arabian Nights," opened at Drury Lane on 4 April 1825 (*Some Account of the English Stage from the Restoration in 1660 to 1830* 9: 292-93).

87 Cf. *Romeo and Juliet* 3.2.80-82: "O nature, what hadst thou to do in hell, / When thou didst bower the spirit of a fiend / In mortal paradise of such sweet flesh?"

88 Ecclesiastes 12.6. Matthew Prior's *Solomon*, from which MWS quotes on [2: 113], alludes to this passage: "Loos'd by devouring Time the Silver Cord / Dissever'd lies ..." (3.174-75).

I felt that this was insanity—I sprang forward to throw it off; I rushed into the midst of the crowd. Idris saw me: with light step she advanced; as I folded her in my arms, feeling, as I did, that I thus enclosed what was to me a world, yet frail as the waterdrop which the noon-day sun will drink from the water lily's cup; tears filled my eyes, unwont to be thus moistened. The joyful welcome of my boys, the soft gratulation of Clara, the pressure of Adrian's hand, contributed to unman me. I felt that they were near, that they were safe, yet methought this was all deceit;—the earth reeled, the firm-enrooted trees moved—dizziness came over me—I sank to the ground.

My beloved friends were alarmed—nay, they expressed their alarm so anxiously, that I dared not pronounce the word *plague*, that hovered on my lips, lest they should construe my perturbed looks into a symptom, and see infection in my languor. I had scarcely recovered, and with feigned hilarity had brought back smiles into my little circle, when we saw Ryland approach.

Ryland had something the appearance of a farmer; of a man whose muscles and full grown stature had been developed under the influence of vigorous exercise and exposure to the elements. This was to a great degree the case: for, though a large landed proprietor, yet, being a projector, and of an ardent and industrious disposition, he had on his own estate given himself up to agricultural labours. When he went as ambassador to the Northern States of America, he, for some time, planned his entire migration; and went so far as to make several journies far westward on that immense continent, for the purpose of choosing the site of his new abode. Ambition turned his thoughts from these designs—ambition, which labouring through various lets and hindrances, had now led him to the summit of his hopes, in making him Lord Protector of England.

His countenance was rough but intelligent—his ample brow and quick grey eyes seemed to look out, over his own plans, and the opposition of his enemies. His voice was stentorian: his hand stretched out in debate, seemed by its gigantic and muscular form, to warn his hearers that words were not his only weapons. Few people had discovered some cowardice and much infirmity of purpose under this imposing exterior. No man could crush a "butterfly on the wheel" [89] with better effect; no man better cover a speedy retreat from a powerful adversary. This had been the secret of his secession at the time of Lord Raymond's election. In the unsteady glance of his eye, in his extreme desire to learn the opinions of all, in the feebleness of his hand-writing, these qualities might be obscurely traced, but they were not generally known. He was now our Lord Protector. He had canvassed eagerly for this post. His protectorate was to be distinguished by every kind of innovation on the aristocracy.

---

89 Alexander Pope, "An Epistle to Dr. Arbuthnot" 308.

Thus his selected task was exchanged for the far different one of encountering the ruin caused by the convulsions of physical nature. He was incapable of meeting these evils by any comprehensive system; he had resorted to expedient after expedient, and could never be induced to put a remedy in force, till it came too late to be of use.

Certainly the Ryland that advanced towards us now, bore small resemblance to the powerful, ironical, seemingly fearless canvasser for the first rank among Englishmen. Our native oak, as his partisans called him, was visited truly by a nipping winter. He scarcely appeared half his usual height; his joints were unknit, his limbs would not support him; his face was contracted, his eye wandering; debility of purpose and dastard fear were expressed in every gesture.

In answer to our eager questions, one word alone fell, as it were involuntarily, from his convulsed lips: *The Plague.*—"Where?"—"Every where—we must fly—all fly—but whither? No man can tell—there is no refuge on earth, it comes on us like a thousand packs of wolves—we must all fly—where shall you go? Where can any of us go?"

These words were syllabled trembling by the iron man. Adrian replied, "Whither indeed would you fly? We must all remain; and do our best to help our suffering fellow-creatures."

"Help!" said Ryland, "there is no help!—great God, who talks of help! All the world has the plague!"

"Then to avoid it, we must quit the world," observed Adrian, with a gentle smile.

Ryland groaned; cold drops stood on his brow. It was useless to oppose his paroxysm of terror: but we soothed and encouraged him, so that after an interval he was better able to explain to us the ground of his alarm. It had come sufficiently home to him. One of his servants, while waiting on him, had suddenly fallen down dead. The physician declared that he died of the plague. We endeavoured to calm him—but our own hearts were not calm. I saw the eye of Idris wander from me to her children, with an anxious appeal to my judgment. Adrian was absorbed in meditation. For myself, I own that Ryland's words rang in my ears; all the world was infected;—in what uncontaminated seclusion could I save my beloved treasures, until the shadow of death had passed from over the earth? We sunk into silence: a silence that drank in the doleful accounts and prognostications of our guest.

We had receded from the crowd; and ascending the steps of the terrace, sought the Castle. Our change of cheer struck those nearest to us; and, by means of Ryland's servants, the report soon spread that he had fled from the plague in London. The sprightly parties broke up—they assembled in whispering groups. The spirit of gaiety was eclipsed; the music ceased; the young people left their occupations and gathered together. The lightness of heart which had dressed them in masquerade habits, had decorated their tents, and assembled them in fantastic groups, appeared a sin against, and a provocative to, the awful destiny that had laid its palsying hand upon hope and life. The merriment of the hour was an unholy mockery of the sorrows of man. The foreigners whom we had among us, who had fled from the plague in their own country, now saw their last asylum invaded; and, fear making them garrulous, they described to eager listeners the miseries they had beheld in cities visited by the calamity, and gave fearful accounts of the insidious and irremediable nature of the disease.

We had entered the Castle. Idris stood at a window that over-looked the park; her maternal eyes sought her own children among the young crowd. An Italian lad had got an audience about him, and with animated gestures was describing some scene of horror. Alfred stood immoveable before him, his whole attention absorbed. Little Evelyn had endeavoured to draw Clara away to play with him; but the Italian's tale arrested her, she crept near, her lustrous eyes fixed on the speaker. Either watching the crowd in the park, or occupied by painful reflection, we were all silent; Ryland stood by himself in an embrasure of the window; Adrian paced the hall, revolving some new and overpowering idea—suddenly he stopped and said: "I have long expected this; could we in reason expect that this island should be exempt from the universal visitation? The evil is come home to us, and we must not shrink from our fate. What are your plans, my Lord Protector, for the benefit of our country?"

"For heaven's love! Windsor," cried Ryland, "do not mock me with that title. Death and disease level all men. I neither pretend to protect nor govern an hospital—such will England quickly become."

"Do you then intend, now in time of peril, to recede from your duties?"

"Duties! speak rationally, my Lord!—when I am a plague-spotted corpse, where will my duties be? Every man for himself! the devil take the protectorship, say I, if it expose me to danger!"

"Faint-hearted man!" cried Adrian indignantly—"Your countrymen put their trust in you, and you betray them!"

"I betray them!" said Ryland, "the plague betrays me. Faint-hearted! It is well, shut up in your castle, out of danger, to boast yourself out of fear. Take the Protectorship who will; before God I renounce it!"

"And before God," replied his opponent, fervently, "do I receive it! No one will canvass for this honour now—none envy my danger or labours. Deposit your powers in my hands. Long have I fought with death, and much" (he stretched out his thin hand) "much have I suffered in the struggle. It is not by flying, but by facing the enemy, that we can conquer. If my last combat is now about to be fought, and I am to be worsted—so let it be!"

"But come, Ryland, recollect yourself! Men have hitherto thought you magnanimous and wise, will you cast aside these titles? Consider the panic your departure will occasion. Return to London. I will go with you. Encourage the people by your presence. I will incur all the danger.

Shame! shame! if the first magistrate of England be foremost to renounce his duties."

Meanwhile among our guests in the park, all thoughts of festivity had faded. As summer-flies are scattered by rain, so did this congregation, late noisy and happy, in sadness and melancholy murmurs break up, dwindling away apace. With the set sun and the deepening twilight the park became nearly empty. Adrian and Ryland were still in earnest discussion. We had prepared a banquet for our guests in the lower hall of the castle; and thither Idris and I repaired to receive and entertain the few that remained. There is nothing more melancholy than a merry-meeting thus turned to sorrow: the gala dresses—the decorations, gay as they might otherwise be, receive a solemn and funereal appearance. If such change be painful from lighter causes, it weighed with intolerable heaviness from the knowledge that the earth's desolator had at last, even as an arch-fiend, lightly over-leaped the boundaries our precautions raised,[90] and at once enthroned himself in the full and beating heart of our country. Idris sat at the top of the half-empty hall. Pale and tearful, she almost forgot her duties as hostess; her eyes were fixed on her children. Alfred's serious air shewed that he still revolved the tragic story related by the Italian boy. Evelyn was the only mirthful creature present: he sat on Clara's lap; and, making matter of glee from his own fancies, laughed aloud. The vaulted roof echoed again his infant tone. The poor mother who had brooded long over, and suppressed the expression of her anguish, now burst into tears, and folding her babe in her arms, hurried from the hall. Clara and Alfred followed. While the rest of the company, in confused murmur, which grew louder and louder, gave voice to their many fears.

The younger part gathered round me to ask my advice; and those who had friends in London were anxious beyond the rest, to ascertain the present extent of disease in the metropolis. I encouraged them with such thoughts of cheer as presented themselves. I told them exceedingly few deaths had yet been occasioned by pestilence, and gave them hopes, as we were the last visited, so the calamity might have lost its most venomous power before it had reached us. The cleanliness, habits of order, and the manner in which our cities were built, were all in our favour. As it was an epidemic, its chief force was derived from pernicious qualities in the air, and it would probably do little harm where this was naturally salubrious. At first, I had spoken only to those nearest me; but the whole assembly gathered about me, and I found that I was listened to by all. "My friends," I said, "our risk is common; our precautions and exertions shall be common also. If manly courage and resistance can save us, we will be saved. We will fight the enemy to the last. Plague shall not find us a ready prey; we will dispute every inch of ground; and, by methodical and

---

90   Cf. *Paradise Lost* 4.179-83.

inflexible laws, pile invincible barriers to the progress of our foe. Perhaps in no part of the world has she met with so systematic and determined an opposition. Perhaps no country is naturally so well protected against our invader; nor has nature anywhere been so well assisted by the hand of man. We will not despair. We are neither cowards nor fatalists; but, believing that God has placed the means for our preservation in our own hands, we will use those means to our utmost. Remember that cleanliness, sobriety, and even good-humour and benevolence, are our best medicines."

There was little I could add to this general exhortation; for the plague, though in London, was not among us. I dismissed the guests therefore; and they went thoughtful, more than sad, to await the events in store for them.

I now sought Adrian, anxious to hear the result of his discussion with Ryland. He had in part prevailed; the Lord Protector consented to return to London for a few weeks; during which time things should be so arranged, as to occasion less consternation at his departure. Adrian and Idris were together. The sadness with which the former had first heard that the plague was in London had vanished; the energy of his purpose informed his body with strength, the solemn joy of enthusiasm and self-devotion illuminated his countenance; and the weakness of his physical nature seemed to pass from him, as the cloud of humanity did, in the ancient fable, from the divine lover of Semele.[91] He was endeavouring to encourage his sister, and to bring her to look on his intent in a less tragic light than she was prepared to do; and with passionate eloquence he unfolded his designs to her.

"Let me, at the first word," he said, "relieve your mind from all fear on my account. I will not task myself beyond my powers, nor will I needlessly seek danger. I feel that I know what ought to be done, and as my presence is necessary for the accomplishment of my plans, I will take especial care to preserve my life.

"I am now going to undertake an office fitted for me. I cannot intrigue, or work a tortuous path through the labyrinth of men's vices and passions; but I can bring patience, and sympathy, and such aid as art affords, to the bed of disease; I can raise from earth the miserable orphan, and awaken to new hopes the shut heart of the mourner. I can enchain the plague in limits, and set a term to the misery it would occasion; courage, forbearance, and watchfulness, are the forces I bring towards this great work.

"O, I shall be something now! From my birth I have aspired like the eagle—but, unlike the eagle, my wings have failed, and my vision has been blinded. Disappointment and sickness have hitherto held dominion over me; twin born with me, my *would*, was for ever enchained by the *shall not*, of these my tyrants. A shepherd-boy that tends a silly flock on the mountains, was more in the scale of society than I. Congratulate me then

---

91   Zeus.

that I have found fitting scope for my powers. I have often thought of offering my services to the pestilence-stricken towns of France and Italy; but fear of paining you, and expectation of this catastrophe, withheld me. To England and to Englishmen I dedicate myself. If I can save one of her mighty spirits from the deadly shaft; if I can ward disease from one of her smiling cottages, I shall not have lived in vain."

Strange ambition this! Yet such was Adrian. He appeared given up to contemplation, averse to excitement, a lowly student, a man of visions—but afford him worthy theme, and—

Like to the lark at break of day arising
From sullen earth, sings hymns at heaven's gate.[92]

so did he spring up from listlessness and unproductive thought, to the highest pitch of virtuous action.

With him went enthusiasm, the high-wrought resolve, the eye that without blenching could look at death. With us remained sorrow, anxiety, and unendurable expectation of evil. The man, says Lord Bacon, who hath wife and children, has given hostages to fortune.[93] Vain was all philosophical reasoning—vain all fortitude—vain, vain, a reliance on probable good. I might heap high the scale with logic, courage, and resignation—but let one fear for Idris and our children enter the opposite one, and, over-weighed, it kicked the beam.

The plague was in London! Fools that we were not long ago to have foreseen this. We wept over the ruin of the boundless continents of the east, and the desolation of the western world; while we fancied that the little channel between our island and the rest of the earth was to preserve us alive among the dead. It were no mighty leap methinks from Calais to Dover. The eye easily discerns the sister land; they were united once; and the little path that runs between looks in a map but as a trodden footway through high grass. Yet this small interval was to save us: the sea was to rise a wall of adamant—without, disease and misery—within, a shelter from evil, a nook of the garden of paradise—a particle of celestial soil, which no evil could invade—truly we were wise in our generation,[94] to imagine all these things!

But we are awake now. The plague is in London; the air of England is tainted, and her sons and daughters strew the unwholesome earth. And

---

92 Shakespeare's Sonnets [MWS's note]: Sonnet 29, lines 11-12.
93 Francis Bacon, "Of Marriage and Single Life," *Essays* 22; Mary Wollstonecraft quotes the same phrase in *A Vindication of the Rights of Woman*, ed. Carol H. Poston 63-64.
94 Cf. Luke 16.8: "for the children of this world are in their generation wiser than the children of light." Mary Wollstonecraft also quotes this passage in *A Vindication of the Rights of Woman*, ed. Carol H. Poston 6.

now, the sea, late our defence, seems our prison bound; hemmed in by its gulphs, we shall die like the famished inhabitants of a besieged town. Other nations have a fellowship in death; but we, shut out from all neighbourhood, must bury our own dead, and little England become a wide, wide tomb.

This feeling of universal misery assumed concentration and shape, when I looked on my wife and children; and the thought of danger to them possessed my whole being with fear. How could I save them? I revolved a thousand and a thousand plans. They should not die—first I would be gathered to nothingness, ere infection should come anear these idols of my soul. I would walk barefoot through the world, to find an uninfected spot; I would build my home on some wave-tossed plank, drifted about on the barren, shoreless ocean. I would betake me with them to some wild beast's den, where a tyger's cubs, which I would slay, had been reared in health. I would seek the mountain eagle's eirie, and live years suspended in some inaccessible recess of a sea-bounding cliff—no labour too great, no scheme too wild, if it promised life to them. O! ye heartstrings of mine, could ye be torn asunder, and my soul not spend itself in tears of blood for sorrow!

Idris, after the first shock, regained a portion of fortitude. She studiously shut out all prospect of the future, and cradled her heart in present blessings. She never for a moment lost sight of her children. But while they in health sported about her, she could cherish contentment and hope. A strange and wild restlessness came over me—the more intolerable, because I was forced to conceal it. My fears for Adrian were ceaseless; August had come; and the symptoms of plague encreased rapidly in London. It was deserted by all who possessed the power of removing; and he, the brother of my soul, was exposed to the perils from which all but slaves enchained by circumstance fled. He remained to combat the fiend—his side unguarded, his toils unshared—infection might even reach him, and he die unattended and alone. By day and night these thoughts pursued me. I resolved to visit London, to see him; to quiet these agonizing throes by the sweet medicine of hope, or the opiate of despair.

It was not until I arrived at Brentford,[95] that I perceived much change in the face of the country. The better sort of houses were shut up; the busy trade of the town palsied; there was an air of anxiety among the few passengers I met, and they looked wonderingly at my carriage—the first they had seen pass towards London, since pestilence sat on its high places, and possessed its busy streets. I met several funerals; they were slenderly attended by mourners, and were regarded by the spectators as omens of direst import. Some gazed on these processions with wild eagerness—others fled timidly—some wept aloud.

---

95 An old market town, now a suburb of London.

Adrian's chief endeavour, after the immediate succour of the sick, had been to disguise the symptoms and progress of the plague from the inhabitants of London. He knew that fear and melancholy forebodings were powerful assistants to disease; that desponding and brooding care rendered the physical nature of man peculiarly susceptible of infection. No unseemly sights were therefore discernible: the shops were in general open, the concourse of passengers in some degree kept up. But although the appearance of an infected town was avoided, to me, who had not beheld it since the commencement of the visitation, London appeared sufficiently changed. There were no carriages, and grass had sprung high in the streets; the houses had a desolate look; most of the shutters were closed; and there was a ghast and frightened stare in the persons I met, very different from the usual business-like demeanour of the Londoners. My solitary carriage attracted notice, as it rattled along towards the Protectoral Palace—and the fashionable streets leading to it wore a still more dreary and deserted appearance. I found Adrian's anti-chamber crowded—it was his hour for giving audience. I was unwilling to disturb his labours, and waited, watching the ingress and egress of the petitioners. They consisted of people of the middling and lower classes of society, whose means of subsistence failed with the cessation of trade, and of the busy spirit of money-making in all its branches, peculiar to our country. There was an air of anxiety, sometimes of terror in the new-comers, strongly contrasted with the resigned and even satisfied mien of those who had had audience. I could read the influence of my friend in their quickened motions and cheerful faces. Two o'clock struck, after which none were admitted; those who had been disappointed went sullenly or sorrowfully away, while I entered the audience-chamber.

I was struck by the improvement that appeared in the health of Adrian. He was no longer bent to the ground, like an over-nursed flower of spring, that, shooting up beyond its strength, is weighed down even by its own coronal of blossoms. His eyes were bright, his countenance composed, an air of concentrated energy was diffused over his whole person, much unlike its former languor. He sat at a table with several secretaries, who were arranging petitions, or registering the notes made during that day's audience. Two or three petitioners were still in attendance. I admired his justice and patience. Those who possessed a power of living out of London, he advised immediately to quit it, affording them the means of so doing. Others, whose trade was beneficial to the city, or who possessed no other refuge, he provided with advice for better avoiding the epidemic; relieving overloaded families, supplying the gaps made in others by death. Order, comfort, and even health, rose under his influence, as from the touch of a magician's wand.

"I am glad you are come," he said to me, when we were at last alone; "I can only spare a few minutes, and must tell you much in that time. The plague is now in progress—it is useless closing one's eyes to the fact—the deaths encrease each week. What will come I cannot guess. As yet, thank

God, I am equal to the government of the town; and I look only to the present. Ryland, whom I have so long detained, has stipulated that I shall suffer him to depart before the end of this month. The deputy appointed by parliament is dead; another therefore must be named; I have advanced my claim, and I believe that I shall have no competitor. To-night the question is to be decided, as there is a call of the house for the purpose. You must nominate me, Lionel; Ryland, for shame, cannot shew himself; but you, my friend, will do me this service?"

How lovely is devotion! Here was a youth, royally sprung, bred in luxury, by nature averse to the usual struggles of a public life, and now, in time of danger, at a period when to live was the utmost scope of the ambitious, he, the beloved and heroic Adrian, made, in sweet simplicity, an offer to sacrifice himself for the public good. The very idea was generous and noble,—but, beyond this, his unpretending manner, his entire want of the assumption of a virtue, rendered his act ten times more touching. I would have withstood his request; but I had seen the good he diffused; I felt that his resolves were not to be shaken, so, with an heavy heart, I consented to do as he asked. He grasped my hand affectionately:—"Thank you," he said, "you have relieved me from a painful dilemma, and are, as you ever were, the best of my friends. Farewell—I must now leave you for a few hours. Go you and converse with Ryland. Although he deserts his post in London, he may be of the greatest service in the north of England, by receiving and assisting travellers, and contributing to supply the metropolis with food. Awaken him, I entreat you, to some sense of duty."

Adrian left me, as I afterwards learnt, upon his daily task of visiting the hospitals, and inspecting the crowded parts of London. I found Ryland much altered, even from what he had been when he visited Windsor. Perpetual fear had jaundiced his complexion, and shrivelled his whole person. I told him of the business of the evening, and a smile relaxed the contracted muscles. He desired to go; each day he expected to be infected by pestilence, each day he was unable to resist the gentle violence of Adrian's detention. The moment Adrian should be legally elected his deputy, he would escape to safety. Under this impression he listened to all I said; and, elevated almost to joy by the near prospect of his departure, he entered into a discussion concerning the plans he should adopt in his own county, forgetting, for the moment, his cherished resolution of shutting himself up from all communication in the mansion and grounds of his estate.

In the evening, Adrian and I proceeded to Westminster. As we went he reminded me of what I was to say and do, yet, strange to say, I entered the chamber without having once reflected on my purpose. Adrian remained in the coffee-room, while I, in compliance with his desire, took my seat in St. Stephen's. There reigned unusual silence in the chamber. I had not visited it since Raymond's protectorate; a period conspicuous for a numerous attendance of members, for the eloquence of the speakers, and the warmth of the debate. The benches were very empty, those by custom occupied by the hereditary members were vacant; the city members were there—the members for the commercial towns, few landed proprietors, and not many of those who entered parliament for the sake of a career. The first subject that occupied the attention of the house was an address from the Lord Protector, praying them to appoint a deputy during a necessary absence on his part.

A silence prevailed, till one of the members coming to me, whispered that the Earl of Windsor had sent him word that I was to move his election, in the absence of the person who had been first chosen for this office. Now for the first time I saw the full extent of my task, and I was overwhelmed by what I had brought on myself. Ryland had deserted his post through fear of the plague: from the same fear Adrian had no competitor. And I, the nearest kinsman of the Earl of Windsor, was to propose his election. I was to thrust this selected and matchless friend into the post of danger—impossible! the die was cast—I would offer myself as candidate.

The few members who were present, had come more for the sake of terminating the business by securing a legal attendance, than under the idea of a debate. I had risen mechanically—my knees trembled; irresolution hung on my voice, as I uttered a few words on the necessity of choosing a person adequate to the dangerous task in hand. But, when the idea of presenting myself in the room of my friend intruded, the load of doubt and pain was taken from off me. My words flowed spontaneously—my utterance was firm and quick. I adverted to what Adrian had already done—I promised the same vigilance in furthering all his views. I drew a touching picture of his vacillating health; I boasted of my own strength. I prayed them to save even from himself this scion of the noblest family in England. My alliance with him was the pledge of my sincerity, my union with his sister, my children, his presumptive heirs, were the hostages of my truth.

This unexpected turn in the debate was quickly communicated to Adrian. He hurried in, and witnessed the termination of my impassioned harangue. I did not see him: my soul was in my words,—my eyes could not perceive that which was; while a vision of Adrian's form, tainted by pestilence, and sinking in death, floated before them. He seized my hand, as I concluded—"Unkind!" he cried, "you have betrayed me!" then, springing forwards, with the air of one who had a right to command, he claimed the place of deputy as his own. He had bought it, he said, with danger, and paid for it with toil. His ambition rested there; and, after an interval devoted to the interests of his country, was I to step in, and reap the profit? Let them remember what London had been when he arrived: the panic that prevailed brought famine, while every moral and legal tie was loosened. He had restored order—this had been a work which required perseverance, patience, and energy; and he had neither slept nor waked but for the good of his country.—Would they dare wrong him thus? Would they wrest his hard-earned reward from him, to bestow it on one, who, never having mingled in public life, would come a tyro to the craft, in which he was an adept. He demanded the place of deputy as his right. Ryland had shewn that he preferred him. Never before had he, who was born even to the inheritance of the throne of England, never had he asked favour or honour from those now his equals, but who might have been his subjects. Would they refuse him? Could they thrust back from the path of distinction and laudable ambition, the heir of their ancient kings, and heap another disappointment on a fallen house.

No one had ever before heard Adrian allude to the rights of his ancestors. None had ever before suspected, that power, or the suffrage of the many, could in any manner become dear to him. He had begun his speech with vehemence; he ended with unassuming gentleness, making his appeal with the same humility, as if he had asked to be the first in wealth, honour, and power among Englishmen, and not, as was the truth, to be the foremost in the ranks of loathsome toils and inevitable death. A murmur of approbation rose after his speech. "Oh, do not listen to him," I cried, "he speaks false—false to himself,"—I was interrupted: and, silence being restored, we were ordered, as was the custom, to retire during the decision of the house. I fancied that they hesitated, and that there was some hope for me—I was mistaken—hardly had we quitted the chamber, before Adrian was recalled, and installed in his office of Lord Deputy to the Protector.

We returned together to the palace. "Why, Lionel," said Adrian, "what did you intend? you could not hope to conquer, and yet you gave me the pain of a triumph over my dearest friend."

"This is mockery," I replied, "you devote yourself,—you, the adored brother of Idris, the being, of all the world contains, dearest to our hearts—you devote yourself to an early death. I would have prevented this; my death would be a small evil—or rather I should not die; while you cannot hope to escape."

"As to the likelihood of escaping," said Adrian, "ten years hence the cold stars may shine on the graves of all of us; but as to my peculiar liability to infection, I could easily prove, both logically and physically, that in the midst of contagion I have a better chance of life than you.

"This is my post: I was born for this—to rule England in anarchy, to save her in danger—to devote myself for her. The blood of my forefathers cries aloud in my veins, and bids me be first among my countrymen. Or, if this mode of speech offend you, let me say, that my mother, the proud queen, instilled early into me a love of distinction, and all that, if the weakness of my physical nature and my peculiar opinions had not prevented such a design, might have made me long since struggle for the lost inheritance of my race. But now my mother, or, if you will, my mother's lessons, awaken within me. I cannot lead on to battle; I cannot, through intrigue and faithlessness rear again the throne upon the wreck of English public spirit. But I can be the first to support and guard my country, now that terrific disasters and ruin have laid strong hands upon her.

"That country and my beloved sister are all I have. I will protect the first—the latter I commit to your charge. If I survive, and she be lost, I were far better dead. Preserve her—for her own sake I know that you will—if you require any other spur, think that, in preserving her, you preserve me. Her faultless nature, one sum of perfections, is wrapt up in her affections—if they were hurt, she would droop like an unwatered floweret, and the slightest injury they receive is a nipping frost to her. Already she fears for us. She fears for the children she adores, and for you, the father of these, her lover, husband, protector; and you must be near her to support and encourage her. Return to Windsor then, my brother; for such you are by every tie—fill the double place my absence imposes on you, and let me, in all my sufferings here, turn my eyes towards that dear seclusion, and say—There is peace."

CHAPTER XVIII

I DID proceed to Windsor, but not with the intention of remaining there. I went but to obtain the consent of Idris, and then to return and take my station beside my unequalled friend; to share his labours, and save him, if it must be, at the expence of my life. Yet I dreaded to witness the anguish which my resolve might excite in Idris. I had vowed to my own heart never to shadow her countenance even with transient grief, and should I prove recreant at the hour of greatest need? I had begun my journey with anxious haste; now I desired to draw it out through the course of days and months. I longed to avoid the necessity of action; I strove to escape from thought—vainly—futurity, like a dark image in a phantasmagoria,[96] came nearer and more near, till it clasped the whole earth in its shadow.

A slight circumstance induced me to alter my usual route, and to return home by Egham and Bishopgate.[97] I alighted at Perdita's ancient abode, her cottage; and, sending forward the carriage, determined to walk across the park to the castle. This spot, dedicated to sweetest recollections, the deserted house and neglected garden were well adapted to nurse my melancholy. In our happiest days, Perdita had adorned her cottage with every aid art might bring, to that which nature had selected to favour. In the same spirit of exaggeration she had, on the event of her separation from Raymond, caused it to be entirely neglected. It was now in ruin: the deer had climbed the broken palings, and reposed among the flowers; grass grew on the threshold, and the swinging lattice creaking to the wind, gave signal of utter desertion. The sky was blue above, and the air impregnated with fragrance by the rare flowers that grew among the

96 A magic lantern show: see *Journals* 1: 56 and note.
97 See 32n, above.

weeds. The trees moved overhead, awakening nature's favourite melody—but the melancholy appearance of the choaked paths, and weed-grown flower-beds, dimmed even this gay summer scene. The time when in proud and happy security we assembled at this cottage, was gone—soon the present hours would join those past, and shadows of future ones rose dark and menacing from the womb of time, their cradle and their bier. For the first time in my life I envied the sleep of the dead, and thought with pleasure of one's bed under the sod, where grief and fear have no power. I passed through the gap of the broken paling—I felt, while I disdained, the choaking tears—I rushed into the depths of the forest. O death and change, rulers of our life, where are ye, that I may grapple with you! What was there in our tranquillity, that excited your envy—in our happiness, that ye should destroy it? We were happy, loving, and beloved; the horn of Amalthea[98] contained no blessing unshowered upon us, but, alas!

> la fortuna
> deidad barbara importuna,
> oy cadaver y ayer flor,
> no permanece jamas![99]

As I wandered on thus ruminating, a number of country people passed me. They seemed full of careful thought, and a few words of their conversation that reached me, induced me to approach and make further enquiries. A party of people flying from London, as was frequent in those days, had come up the Thames in a boat. No one at Windsor would afford them shelter; so, going a little further up, they remained all night in a deserted hut near Bolter's Lock.[100] They pursued their way the following morning, leaving one of their company behind them, sick of the plague. This circumstance once spread abroad, none dared approach within half a mile of the infected neighbourhood, and the deserted wretch was left to fight with disease and death in solitude, as he best might. I was urged by compassion to hasten to the hut, for the purpose of ascertaining his situation, and administering to his wants.

---

98 After Amalthea fed Zeus goat's milk, Zeus gave her the goat's horn—the *cornucopia* or horn of plenty—which had the power of producing whatever its owner desired. See 256n.

99 Calderon de la Barca [MWS's note]; in context, the passage reads, "Sufrid con ella el rigor / del tiempo y de la fortuna: / deidad barbara, importuna, / hoy cadaver y ayer flor, / no permanece jamas / y asi os mudara de estado"; Suffer with her the hardship of time and fortune: barbaric, importunate deity, today a corpse, yesterday a flower, moves, never permanent, from one state to another (*El Príncipe Constante*, Act 2 [scene 3], lines 1081-86).

100 Boulter's Lock is northwest of Windsor near Maidenhead.

As I advanced I met knots of country-people talking earnestly of this event: distant as they were from the apprehended contagion, fear was impressed on every countenance. I passed by a group of these terrorists, in a lane in the direct road to the hut. One of them stopped me, and, conjecturing that I was ignorant of the circumstance, told me not to go on, for that an infected person lay but at a short distance.

"I know it," I replied, "and I am going to see in what condition the poor fellow is."

A murmur of surprise and horror ran through the assembly. I continued:—"This poor wretch is deserted, dying, succourless; in these unhappy times, God knows how soon any or all of us may be in like want. I am going to do, as I would be done by."

"But you will never be able to return to the Castle—Lady Idris—his children—" in confused speech were the words that struck my ear.

"Do you not know, my friends," I said, "that the Earl himself, now Lord Protector, visits daily, not only those probably infected by this disease, but the hospitals and pest houses, going near, and even touching the sick? yet he was never in better health. You labour under an entire mistake as to the nature of the plague; but do not fear, I do not ask any of you to accompany me, nor to believe me, until I return safe and sound from my patient."

So I left them, and hurried on. I soon arrived at the hut: the door was ajar. I entered, and one glance assured me that its former inhabitant was no more—he lay on a heap of straw, cold and stiff; while a pernicious effluvia filled the room, and various stains and marks served to shew the virulence of the disorder.

I had never before beheld one killed by pestilence. While every mind was full of dismay at its effects, a craving for excitement had led us to peruse De Foe's account, and the masterly delineations of the author of Arthur Mervyn.[101] The pictures drawn in these books were so vivid, that we seemed to have experienced the results depicted by them. But cold were the sensations excited by words, burning though they were, and describing the death and misery of thousands, compared to what I felt in looking on the corpse of this unhappy stranger. This indeed was the plague. I raised his rigid limbs, I marked the distortion of his face, and the stony eyes lost to perception. As I was thus occupied, chill horror congealed my blood, making my flesh quiver and my hair to stand on end. Half insanely I spoke to the dead. So the plague killed you, I muttered. How came this? Was the coming painful? You look as if the enemy had

101 Daniel Defoe's *Journal of the Plague Year* (an account of the Great Plague of London of 1664-65) was published in 1722; Charles Brockden Brown's novel *Arthur Mervyn* (containing a vivid account of the yellow fever epidemic in Philadelphia in 1793) appeared in 1799. MWS read both in 1817, along with *The City of the Plague* (1816), a play by John Wilson (Christopher North).

tortured, before he murdered you. And now I leapt up precipitately, and escaped from the hut, before nature could revoke her laws, and inorganic words be breathed in answer from the lips of the departed.

On returning through the lane, I saw at a distance the same assemblage of persons which I had left. They hurried away, as soon as they saw me; my agitated mien added to their fear of coming near one who had entered within the verge of contagion.

At a distance from facts one draws conclusions which appear infallible, which yet when put to the test of reality, vanish like unreal dreams. I had ridiculed the fears of my countrymen, when they related to others; now that they came home to myself, I paused. The Rubicon, I felt, was passed;[102] and it behoved me well to reflect what I should do on this hither side of disease and danger. According to the vulgar superstition, my dress, my person, the air I breathed, bore in it mortal danger to myself and others. Should I return to the Castle, to my wife and children, with this taint upon me? Not surely if I were infected; but I felt certain that I was not—a few hours would determine the question—I would spend these in the forest, in reflection on what was to come, and what my future actions were to be. In the feeling communicated to me by the sight of one struck by the plague, I forgot the events that had excited me so strongly in London; new and more painful prospects, by degrees were cleared of the mist which had hitherto veiled them. The question was no longer whether I should share Adrian's toils and danger; but in what manner I could, in Windsor and the neighbourhood, imitate the prudence and zeal which, under his government, produced order and plenty in London, and how, now pestilence had spread more widely, I could secure the health of my own family.

I spread the whole earth out as a map before me. On no one spot of its surface could I put my finger and say, here is safety. In the south, the disease, virulent and immedicable, had nearly annihilated the race of man; storm and inundation, poisonous winds and blights, filled up the measure of suffering. In the north it was worse—the lesser population gradually declined, and famine and plague kept watch on the survivors, who, helpless and feeble, were ready to fall an easy prey into their hands.

I contracted my view to England. The overgrown metropolis, the great heart of mighty Britain, was pulseless. Commerce had ceased. All resort for ambition or pleasure was cut off—the streets were grass-grown—the houses empty—the few, that from necessity remained, seemed already branded with the taint of inevitable pestilence. In the larger manufacturing towns the same tragedy was acted on a smaller, yet more disastrous

102 Crossing the Rubicon means reaching a point of no return. When in 49 BC
   Caesar crossed this small river in northeast Italy, he effectively declared war
   on the Republic.

scale. There was no Adrian to superintend and direct, while whole flocks of the poor were struck and killed.

Yet we were not all to die. No truly, though thinned, the race of man would continue, and the great plague would, in after years, become matter of history and wonder. Doubtless this visitation was for extent unexampled— more need that we should work hard to dispute its progress; ere this men have gone out in sport, and slain their thousands and tens of thousands; but now man had become a creature of price; the life of one of them was of more worth than the so called treasures of kings. Look at his thought-endued countenance, his graceful limbs, his majestic brow, his wondrous mechanism—the type and model of this best work of God is not to be cast aside as a broken vessel—he shall be preserved, and his children and his children's children carry down the name and form of man to latest time.

Above all I must guard those entrusted by nature and fate to my especial care. And surely, if among all my fellow-creatures I were to select those who might stand forth examples of the greatness and goodness of man, I could choose no other than those allied to me by the most sacred ties. Some from among the family of man must survive, and these should be among the survivors; that should be my task—to accomplish it my own life were a small sacrifice. There then in that castle—in Windsor Castle, birth-place of Idris and my babes, should be the haven and retreat for the wrecked bark of human society. Its forest should be our world—its garden afford us food; within its walls I would establish the shaken throne of health. I was an outcast and a vagabond, when Adrian gently threw over me the silver net of love and civilization, and linked me inextricably to human charities and human excellence. I was one, who, though an aspirant after good, and an ardent lover of wisdom, was yet unenrolled in any list of worth, when Idris, the princely born, who was herself the personification of all that was divine in woman, she who walked the earth like a poet's dream, as a carved goddess enduced with sense, or pictured saint stepping from the canvas—she, the most worthy, chose me, and gave me herself—a priceless gift.

During several hours I continued thus to meditate, till hunger and fatigue brought me back to the passing hour, then marked by long shadows cast from the descending sun. I had wandered towards Bracknel, far to the west of Windsor. The feeling of perfect health which I enjoyed, assured me that I was free from contagion. I remembered that Idris had been kept in ignorance of my proceedings. She might have heard of my return from London, and my visit to Bolter's Lock, which, connected with my continued absence, might tend greatly to alarm her. I returned to Windsor by the Long Walk, and passing through the town towards the Castle, I found it in a state of agitation and disturbance.

"It is too late to be ambitious," says Sir Thomas Browne. "We cannot hope to live so long in our names as some have done in their persons; one face of Janus holds no proportion to the other." [103] Upon this text many fanatics arose, who prophesied that the end of time was come. The spirit of superstition had birth, from the wreck of our hopes, and antics wild and dangerous were played on the great theatre, while the remaining particle of futurity dwindled into a point in the eyes of the prognosticators. Weak-spirited women died of fear as they listened to their denunciations; men of robust form and seeming strength fell into idiotcy and madness, racked by the dread of coming eternity. A man of this kind was now pouring forth his eloquent despair among the inhabitants of Windsor. The scene of the morning, and my visit to the dead, which had been spread abroad, had alarmed the country-people, so they had become fit instruments to be played upon by a maniac.

The poor wretch had lost his young wife and lovely infant by the plague. He was a mechanic; [104] and, rendered unable to attend to the occupation which supplied his necessities, famine was added to his other miseries. He left the chamber which contained his wife and child—wife and child no more, but "dead earth upon the earth" [105]—wild with hunger, watching and grief, his diseased fancy made him believe himself sent by heaven to preach the end of time to the world. He entered the churches, and foretold to the congregations their speedy removal to the vaults below. He appeared like the forgotten spirit of the time in the theatres, and bade the spectators go home and die. He had been seized and confined; he had escaped and wandered from London among the neighbouring towns, and, with frantic gestures and thrilling words, he unveiled to each their hidden fears, and gave voice to the soundless thought they dared not syllable. He stood under the arcade of the town-hall of Windsor, and from this elevation harangued a trembling crowd.

"Hear, O ye inhabitants of the earth," he cried, "hear thou, all seeing, but most pitiless Heaven! hear thou too, O tempest-tossed heart, which breathes out these words, yet faints beneath their meaning! Death is among us! The earth is beautiful and flower-bedecked, but she is our grave! The clouds of heaven weep for us—the pageantry of the stars is but our funeral torch-light. Grey headed men, ye hoped for yet a few years in your long-known abode—but the lease is up, you must remove—children, ye will never reach maturity, even now the small grave is dug for ye—mothers, clasp them in your arms, one death embraces you!"

Shuddering, he stretched out his hands, his eyes cast up, seemed bursting from their sockets, while he appeared to follow shapes, to us

---

103 MWS reverses the order of the sentences in her source, Sir Thomas Browne's *Hydriotaphia*, chapter 5 (*Works*, ed. Geoffrey Keynes 1: 166).
104 Someone who works with tools or machines, hence a working man.
105 PBS, *Hellas* 398.

invisible, in the yielding air—"There they are," he cried, "the dead! They rise in their shrouds, and pass in silent procession towards the far land of their doom— their bloodless lips move not—their shadowy limbs are void of motion, while still they glide onwards. "We come," he exclaimed, springing forwards, "for what should we wait? Haste, my friends, apparel yourselves in the court-dress of death. Pestilence will usher you to his presence. Why thus long? they, the good, the wise, and the beloved, are gone before. Mothers, kiss your last—husbands, protectors no more, lead on the partners of your death! Come, O come! while the dear ones are yet in sight, for soon they will pass away, and we never never shall join them more."

From such ravings as these, he would suddenly become collected, and with unexaggerated but terrific words, paint the horrors of the time; describe with minute detail, the effects of the plague on the human frame, and tell heart-breaking tales of the snapping of dear affinities—the gasping horror of despair over the death-bed of the last beloved—so that groans and even shrieks burst from the crowd. One man in particular stood in front, his eyes fixt on the prophet, his mouth open, his limbs rigid, while his face changed to various colours, yellow, blue, and green, through intense fear. The maniac caught his glance, and turned his eye on him—one has heard of the gaze of the rattle-snake, which allures the trembling victim till he falls within his jaws.[106] The maniac became composed; his person rose higher; authority beamed from his countenance. He looked on the peasant, who began to tremble, while he still gazed; his knees knocked together; his teeth chattered. He at last fell down in convulsions. "That man has the plague," said the maniac calmly. A shriek burst from the lips of the poor wretch; and then sudden motionlessness came over him; it was manifest to all that he was dead.

Cries of horror filled the place—every one endeavoured to effect his escape—in a few minutes the market place was cleared—the corpse lay on the ground; and the maniac, subdued and exhausted, sat beside it, leaning his gaunt cheek upon his thin hand. Soon some people, deputed by the magistrates, came to remove the body; the unfortunate being saw a jailor in each—he fled precipitately, while I passed onwards to the Castle.

Death, cruel and relentless, had entered these beloved walls. An old servant, who had nursed Idris in infancy, and who lived with us more on the footing of a revered relative than a domestic, had gone a few days before to visit a daughter, married, and settled in the neighbourhood of London. On the night of her return she sickened of the plague. From the

---

106   The ability to kill with a look is usually attributed not to the rattlesnake but to the legendary basilisk, hatched by a serpent from a cock's egg; cf. PBS, "Ode to Naples," *Posthumous Poems*, 1824.

haughty and unbending nature of the Countess of Windsor, Idris had few tender filial associations with her. This good woman had stood in the place of a mother, and her very deficiencies of education and knowledge, by rendering her humble and defenceless, endeared her to us—she was the especial favourite of the children. I found my poor girl, there is no exaggeration in the expression, wild with grief and dread. She hung over the patient in agony, which was not mitigated when her thoughts wandered towards her babes, for whom she feared infection. My arrival was like the newly discovered lamp of a lighthouse to sailors, who are weathering some dangerous point. She deposited her appalling doubts in my hands; she relied on my judgment, and was comforted by my participation in her sorrow. Soon our poor nurse expired; and the anguish of suspense was changed to deep regret, which though at first more painful, yet yielded with greater readiness to my consolations. Sleep, the sovereign balm, at length steeped her tearful eyes in forgetfulness.

She slept; and quiet prevailed in the Castle, whose inhabitants were hushed to repose. I was awake, and during the long hours of dead night, my busy thoughts worked in my brain, like ten thousand mill-wheels, rapid, acute, untameable. All slept—all England slept; and from my window, commanding a wide prospect of the star-illumined country, I saw the land stretched out in placid rest. I was awake, alive, while the brother of death possessed my race. What, if the more potent of these fraternal deities should obtain dominion over it? The silence of midnight, to speak truly, though apparently a paradox, rung in my ears. The solitude became intolerable—I placed my hand on the beating heart of Idris, I bent my head to catch the sound of her breath, to assure myself that she still existed—for a moment I doubted whether I should not awake her; so effeminate an horror ran through my frame.—Great God! would it one day be thus? One day all extinct, save myself, should I walk the earth alone? Were these warning voices, whose inarticulate and oracular sense forced belief upon me?

Yet I would not call them
Voices of warning, that announce to us
Only the inevitable. As the sun,
Ere it is risen, sometimes paints its image
In the atmosphere—so often do the spirits
Of great events stride on before the events,
And in to-day already walks to-morrow.[107]

---

107 Coleridge's Translation of Schiller's Wallenstein [MWS's note]; the passage is
from Friedrich Schiller, *The Death of Wallenstein*, trans. S. T. Coleridge
5.1.96-102.

CHAPTER XIX

AFTER a long interval, I am again impelled by the restless spirit within me to continue my narration; but I must alter the mode which I have hitherto adopted. The details contained in the foregoing pages, apparently trivial, yet each slightest one weighing like lead in the depressed scale of human afflictions; this tedious dwelling on the sorrows of others, while my own were only in apprehension; this slowly laying bare of my soul's wounds: this journal of death; this long drawn and tortuous path, leading to the ocean of countless tears, awakens me again to keen grief. I had used this history as an opiate; while it described my beloved friends, fresh with life and glowing with hope, active assistants on the scene, I was soothed; there will be a more melancholy pleasure in painting the end of all. But the intermediate steps, the climbing the wall, raised up between what was and is, while I still looked back nor saw the concealed desert beyond, is a labour past my strength. Time and experience have placed me on an height from which I can comprehend the past as a whole; and in this way I must describe it, bringing forward the leading incidents, and disposing light and shade so as to form a picture in whose very darkness there will be harmony.

It would be needless to narrate those disastrous occurrences, for which a parallel might be found in any slighter visitation of our gigantic calamity. Does the reader wish to hear of the pest-houses, where death is the comforter—of the mournful passage of the death-cart—of the insensibility of the worthless, and the anguish of the loving heart—of harrowing shrieks and silence dire—of the variety of disease, desertion, famine, despair, and death? There are many books which can feed the appetite craving for these things; let them turn to the accounts of Boccaccio, De Foe, and Browne.[108] The vast annihilation that has swallowed all things—the voiceless solitude of the once busy earth—the lonely state of singleness which hems me in, has deprived even such details of their stinging reality, and mellowing the lurid tints of past anguish with poetic hues, I am able to escape from the mosaic of circumstance, by perceiving and reflecting back the grouping and combined colouring of the past.

I had returned from London possessed by the idea, with the intimate feeling that it was my first duty to secure, as well as I was able, the well-being of my family, and then to return and take my post beside Adrian. The events that immediately followed on my arrival at Windsor changed this view of things. The plague was not in London alone, it was every where—it came on us, as Ryland had said, like a thousand packs of

---

108 All writers who describe plague or plague-like disease—Giovanni Boccaccio in the *Decameron* (1351-53), Daniel Defoe in *A Journal of the Plague Year* (1722), and Charles Brockden Brown in *Arthur Mervyn* (1799-1800).

wolves, howling through the winter night, gaunt and fierce. When once disease was introduced into the rural districts, its effects appeared more horrible, more exigent, and more difficult to cure, than in towns. There was a companionship in suffering there, and, the neighbours keeping constant watch on each other, and inspired by the active benevolence of Adrian, succour was afforded, and the path of destruction smoothed. But in the country, among the scattered farm-houses, in lone cottages, in fields, and barns, tragedies were acted harrowing to the soul, unseen, unheard, unnoticed. Medical aid was less easily procured, food was more difficult to obtain, and human beings, unwithheld by shame, for they were unbeheld of their fellows, ventured on deeds of greater wickedness, or gave way more readily to their abject fears.

Deeds of heroism also occurred, whose very mention swells the heart and brings tears into the eyes. Such is human nature, that beauty and deformity are often closely linked. In reading history we are chiefly struck by the generosity and self-devotion that follow close on the heels of crime, veiling with supernal flowers the stain of blood. Such acts were not wanting to adorn the grim train that waited on the progress of the plague.

The inhabitants of Berkshire and Bucks had been long aware that the plague was in London, in Liverpool, Bristol, Manchester, York, in short, in all the more populous towns of England.[109] They were not however the less astonished and dismayed when it appeared among themselves. They were impatient and angry in the midst of terror. They would do something to throw off the clinging evil, and, while in action, they fancied that a remedy was applied. The inhabitants of the smaller towns left their houses, pitched tents in the fields, wandering separate from each other careless of hunger or the sky's inclemency, while they imagined that they avoided the death-dealing disease. The farmers and cottagers, on the contrary, struck with the fear of solitude, and madly desirous of medical assistance, flocked into the towns.

But winter was coming, and with winter, hope. In August, the plague had appeared in the country of England, and during September it made its ravages. Towards the end of October it dwindled away, and was in some degree replaced by a typhus, of hardly less virulence. The autumn was warm and rainy: the infirm and sickly died off—happier they: many young people flushed with health and prosperity, made pale by wasting malady, became the inhabitants of the grave. The crop had failed, the bad corn, and want of foreign wines, added vigour to disease. Before Christmas half England was under water. The storms of the last winter were renewed; but the diminished shipping of this year caused us to feel less the tempests of the sea. The flood and storms did more harm to conti-

---

109 The counties of Berkshire (where Windsor is located) and Buckinghamshire are still unaffected by plague, which now approaches from the east (London), from the west (Liverpool, Bristol), and from the north (Manchester, York).

nental Europe than to us—giving, as it were, the last blow to the calamities which destroyed it. In Italy the rivers were unwatched by the diminished peasantry; and, like wild beasts from their lair when the hunters and dogs are afar, did Tiber, Arno, and Po, rush upon and destroy the fertility of the plains. Whole villages were carried away. Rome, and Florence, and Pisa were overflowed, and their marble palaces, late mirrored in tranquil streams, had their foundations shaken by their winter-gifted power. In Germany and Russia the injury was still more momentous.

But frost would come at last, and with it a renewal of our lease of earth. Frost would blunt the arrows of pestilence, and enchain the furious elements; and the land would in spring throw off her garment of snow, released from her menace of destruction. It was not until February that the desired signs of winter appeared. For three days the snow fell, ice stopped the current of the rivers, and the birds flew out from crackling branches of the frost- whitened trees. On the fourth morning all vanished. A south-west wind brought up rain—the sun came out, and mocking the usual laws of nature, seemed even at this early season to burn with solsticial force. It was no consolation, that with the first winds of March the lanes were filled with violets, the fruit trees covered with blossoms, that the corn sprung up, and the leaves came out, forced by the unseasonable heat. We feared the balmy air—we feared the cloudless sky, the flower-covered earth, and delightful woods, for we looked on the fabric of the universe no longer as our dwelling, but our tomb, and the fragrant land smelled to the apprehension of fear like a wide church-yard.

Pisando la tierra dura
de continuo el hombre està
y cada passo que dà
es sobre su sepultura.[110]

Yet notwithstanding these disadvantages winter was breathing time; and we exerted ourselves to make the best of it. Plague might not revive with the summer; but if it did, it should find us prepared. It is a part of man's nature to adapt itself through habit even to pain and sorrow. Pestilence had become a part of our future, our existence; it was to be guarded against, like the flooding of rivers, the encroachments of ocean, or the inclemency of the sky. After long suffering and bitter experience, some panacea might be discovered; as it was, all that received infection died—all however were not infected; and it became our part to fix deep the foundations, and raise high the barrier between contagion and the sane; to introduce such order as would conduce to the well-being of the

---

110 Calderon de la Barca [MWS's note]: from *El Príncipe Constante*, Act 3 [scene 8], lines 2517-20: "Man is continually stepping on the hard ground, and each step that he takes is on his grave."

survivors, and as would preserve hope and some portion of happiness to those who were spectators of the still renewed tragedy. Adrian had introduced systematic modes of proceeding in the metropolis, which, while they were unable to stop the progress of death, yet prevented other evils, vice and folly, from rendering the awful fate of the hour still more tremendous. I wished to imitate his example, but men are used to

—move all together, if they move at all,[111]

and I could find no means of leading the inhabitants of scattered towns and villages, who forgot my words as soon as they heard them not, and veered with every baffling wind, that might arise from an apparent change of circumstance.

I adopted another plan. Those writers who have imagined a reign of peace and happiness on earth, have generally described a rural country, where each small township was directed by the elders and wise men. This was the key of my design. Each village, however small, usually contains a leader, one among themselves whom they venerate, whose advice they seek in difficulty, and whose good opinion they chiefly value. I was immediately drawn to make this observation by occurrences that presented themselves to my personal experience.

In the village of Little Marlow[112] an old woman ruled the community. She had lived for some years in an alms-house, and on fine Sundays her threshold was constantly beset by a crowd, seeking her advice and listening to her admonitions. She had been a soldier's wife, and had seen the world; infirmity, induced by fevers caught in unwholesome quarters, had come on her before its time, and she seldom moved from her little cot. The plague entered the village; and, while fright and grief deprived the inhabitants of the little wisdom they possessed, old Martha stepped forward and said—"Before now I have been in a town where there was the plague."—"And you escaped?"—"No, but I recovered."—After this Martha was seated more firmly than ever on the regal seat, elevated by reverence and love. She entered the cottages of the sick; she relieved their wants with her own hand; she betrayed no fear, and inspired all who saw her with some portion of her own native courage. She attended the markets—she insisted upon being supplied with food for those who were too poor to purchase it. She shewed them how the well-being of each included the prosperity of all. She would not permit the gardens to be neglected, nor the very flowers in the cottage lattices to droop from want of care. Hope, she said, was better than a doctor's prescription, and every

111 Wordsworth [MWS's note]; MWS quotes the same line, *Resolution and Independence* 77, in a letter of 5 March 1822 (*Letters* 1: 220).
112 A village on the Thames west of London, two miles northeast of Great Marlow where the Shelleys lived in 1817.

thing that could sustain and enliven the spirits, of more worth than drugs and mixtures.

It was the sight of Little Marlow, and my conversations with Martha, that led me to the plan I formed. I had before visited the manor houses and gentlemen's seats, and often found the inhabitants actuated by the purest benevolence, ready to lend their utmost aid for the welfare of their tenants. But this was not enough. The intimate sympathy generated by similar hopes and fears, similar experience and pursuits, was wanting here. The poor perceived that the rich possessed other means of preservation than those which could be partaken of by themselves, seclusion, and, as far as circumstances permitted, freedom from care. They could not place reliance on them, but turned with tenfold dependence to the succour and advice of their equals. I resolved therefore to go from village to village, seeking out the rustic archon[113] of the place, and by systematizing their exertions, and enlightening their views, encrease both their power and their use among their fellow-cottagers. Many changes also now occurred in these spontaneous regal elections: depositions and abdications were frequent, while, in the place of the old and prudent, the ardent youth would step forward, eager for action, regardless of danger. Often too, the voice to which all listened was suddenly silenced, the helping hand cold, the sympathetic eye closed, and the villagers feared still more the death that had selected a choice victim, shivering in dust the heart that had beat for them, reducing to incommunicable annihilation the mind for ever occupied with projects for their welfare.

Whoever labours for man must often find ingratitude, watered by vice and folly, spring from the grain which he has sown. Death, which had in our younger days walked the earth like "a thief that comes in the night,"[114] now, rising from his subterranean vault, girt with power, with dark banner floating, came a conqueror. Many saw, seated above his vice-regal throne, a supreme Providence, who directed his shafts, and guided his progress, and they bowed their heads in resignation, or at least in obedience. Others perceived only a passing casualty; they endeavoured to exchange terror for heedlessness, and plunged into licentiousness, to avoid the agonizing throes of worst apprehension. Thus, while the wise, the good, and the prudent were occupied by the labours of benevolence, the truce of winter produced other effects among the young, the thoughtless, and the vicious. During the colder months there was a general rush to London in search of amusement—the ties of public opinion were loosened; many were rich, heretofore poor—many had lost father and mother, the guardians of their morals, their mentors and restraints. It would

---

113 Ruler, from Greek *archein*, to be first, to rule.
114 Cf. Job 24.14: "The murderer rising with the light killeth the poor and needy, and in the night is as a thief"; 1 Thessalonians 5.2: "the day of the Lord so cometh as a thief in the night."

have been useless to have opposed these impulses by barriers, which would only have driven those actuated by them to more pernicious indulgencies. The theatres were open and thronged; dance and midnight festival were frequented—in many of these decorum was violated, and the evils, which hitherto adhered to an advanced state of civilization, were doubled. The student left his books, the artist his study: the occupations of life were gone, but the amusements remained; enjoyment might be protracted to the verge of the grave. All factitious colouring disappeared—death rose like night, and, protected by its murky shadows the blush of modesty, the reserve of pride, the decorum of prudery were frequently thrown aside as useless veils.

This was not universal. Among better natures, anguish and dread, the fear of eternal separation, and the awful wonder produced by unprecedented calamity, drew closer the ties of kindred and friendship. Philosophers opposed their principles, as barriers to the inundation of profligacy or despair, and the only ramparts to protect the invaded territory of human life; the religious, hoping now for their reward, clung fast to their creeds, as the rafts and planks which over the tempest-vexed sea of suffering, would bear them in safety to the harbour of the Unknown Continent. The loving heart, obliged to contract its view, bestowed its overflow of affection in triple portion on the few that remained. Yet, even among these, the present, as an unalienable possession, became all of time to which they dared commit the precious freight of their hopes.

The experience of immemorial time had taught us formerly to count our enjoyments by years, and extend our prospect of life through a lengthened period of progression and decay; the long road threaded a vast labyrinth, and the Valley of the Shadow of Death,[115] in which it terminated, was hid by intervening objects. But an earthquake had changed the scene—under our very feet the earth yawned—deep and precipitous the gulph below opened to receive us, while the hours charioted us towards the chasm. But it was winter now, and months must elapse before we are hurled from our security. We became ephemera, to whom the interval between the rising and setting sun was as a long drawn year of common time. We should never see our children ripen into maturity, nor behold their downy cheeks roughen, their blithe hearts subdued by passion or care; but we had them now—they lived, and we lived—what more could we desire? With such schooling did my poor Idris try to hush thronging fears, and in some measure succeeded. It was not as in summer-time, when each hour might bring the dreaded fate—until summer, we felt sure; and this certainty, short lived as it must be, yet for awhile satisfied her maternal tenderness. I know not how to express or communicate the

---

115 Psalm 23.4: "Yea, though I walk through the valley of the shadow of death, I will fear no evil: for thou art with me; thy rod and thy staff they comfort me"; cf. *Journals* 2: 435.

sense of concentrated, intense, though evanescent transport, that impara-dized us in the present hour. Our joys were dearer because we saw their end; they were keener because we felt, to its fullest extent, their value; they were purer because their essence was sympathy—as a meteor is brighter than a star, did the felicity of this winter contain in itself the extracted delights of a long, long life.

How lovely is spring! As we looked from Windsor Terrace on the six-teen fertile counties spread beneath, speckled by happy cottages and wealthier towns, all looked as in former years, heart-cheering and fair. The land was ploughed, the slender blades of wheat broke through the dark soil, the fruit trees were covered with buds, the husbandman was abroad in the fields, the milk-maid tripped home with well-filled pails, the swallows and martins struck the sunny pools with their long, pointed wings, the new dropped lambs reposed on the young grass, the tender growth of leaves—

Lifts its sweet head into the air, and feeds
A silent space with ever sprouting green.[116]

Man himself seemed to regenerate, and feel the frost of winter yield to an elastic and warm renewal of life—reason told us that care and sorrow would grow with the opening year—but how to believe the ominous voice breathed up with pestiferous vapours from fear's dim cavern, while nature, laughing and scattering from her green lap flowers, and fruits, and sparkling waters, invited us to join the gay masque of young life she led upon the scene?

Where was the plague? "Here—every where!" one voice of horror and dismay exclaimed, when in the pleasant days of a sunny May the Destroyer of man brooded again over the earth, forcing the spirit to leave its organic chrysalis, and to enter upon an untried life. With one mighty sweep of its potent weapon, all caution, all care, all prudence were lev-elled low: death sat at the tables of the great, stretched itself on the cot-tager's pallet, seized the dastard who fled, quelled the brave man who resisted: despondency entered every heart, sorrow dimmed every eye.

Sights of woe now became familiar to me, and were I to tell all of anguish and pain that I witnessed, of the despairing moans of age, and the more terrible smiles of infancy in the bosom of horror, my reader, his limbs quivering and his hair on end, would wonder how I did not, seized with sudden frenzy, dash myself from some precipice, and so close my eyes for ever on the sad end of the world. But the powers of love, poetry, and creative fancy will dwell even beside the sick of the plague, with the squalid, and with the dying. A feeling of devotion, of duty, of a high and steady purpose, elevated me; a strange joy filled my heart. In the midst of

---

116 Keats [MWS's note]: *Sleep and Poetry* 251-52.

saddest grief I seemed to tread air, while the spirit of good shed round me an ambrosial atmosphere, which blunted the sting of sympathy, and purified the air of sighs. If my wearied soul flagged in its career, I thought of my loved home, of the casket that contained my treasures, of the kiss of love and the filial caress, while my eyes were moistened by purest dew, and my heart was at once softened and refreshed by thrilling tenderness.

Maternal affection had not rendered Idris selfish; at the beginning of our calamity she had, with thoughtless enthusiasm, devoted herself to the care of the sick and helpless. I checked her; and she submitted to my rule. I told her how the fear of her danger palsied my exertions, how the knowledge of her safety strung my nerves to endurance. I shewed her the dangers which her children incurred during her absence; and she at length agreed not to go beyond the inclosure of the forest. Indeed, within the walls of the Castle we had a colony of the unhappy, deserted by their relatives, and in themselves helpless, sufficient to occupy her time and attention, while ceaseless anxiety for my welfare and the health of her children, however she strove to curb or conceal it, absorbed all her thoughts, and undermined the vital principle. After watching over and providing for their safety, her second care was to hide from me her anguish and tears. Each night I returned to the Castle, and found there repose and love awaiting me. Often I waited beside the bed of death till midnight, and through the obscurity of rainy, cloudy nights rode many miles, sustained by one circumstance only, the safety and sheltered repose of those I loved. If some scene of tremendous agony shook my frame and fevered my brow, I would lay my head on the lap of Idris, and the tumultuous pulses subsided into a temperate flow—her smile could raise me from hopelessness, her embrace bathe my sorrowing heart in calm peace.

Summer advanced, and, crowned with the sun's potent rays, plague shot her unerring shafts over the earth. The nations beneath their influence bowed their heads, and died. The corn that sprung up in plenty, lay in autumn rotting on the ground, while the melancholy wretch who had gone out to gather bread for his children, lay stiff and plague-struck in the furrow. The green woods waved their boughs majestically, while the dying were spread beneath their shade, answering the solemn melody with inharmonious cries. The painted birds flitted through the shades; the careless deer reposed unhurt upon the fern—the oxen and the horses strayed from their unguarded stables, and grazed among the wheat, for death fell on man alone.

With summer and mortality grew our fears. My poor love and I looked at each other, and our babes.—"We will save them, Idris," I said, "I will save them. Years hence we shall recount to them our fears, then passed away with their occasion. Though they only should remain on the earth, still they shall live, nor shall their cheeks become pale nor their sweet voices languish." Our eldest in some degree understood the scenes passing around, and at times, he with serious looks questioned me concerning the reason of so vast a desolation. But he was only ten years old; and the hilarity of youth soon chased unreasonable care from his brow. Evelyn, a laughing cherub, a gamesome infant, without idea of pain or sorrow, would, shaking back his light curls from his eyes, make the halls re-echo with his merriment, and in a thousand artless ways attract our attention to his play. Clara, our lovely gentle Clara, was our stay, our solace, our delight. She made it her task to attend the sick, comfort the sorrowing, assist the aged, and partake the sports and awaken the gaiety of the young. She flitted through the rooms, like a good spirit, dispatched from the celestial kingdom, to illumine our dark hour with alien splendour. Gratitude and praise marked where her footsteps had been. Yet, when she stood in unassuming simplicity before us, playing with our children, or with girlish assiduity performing little kind offices for Idris, one wondered in what fair lineament of her pure loveliness, in what soft tone of her thrilling voice, so much of heroism, sagacity and active goodness resided.

The summer passed tediously, for we trusted that winter would at least check the disease. That it would vanish altogether was an hope too dear—too heartfelt, to be expressed. When such a thought was heedlessly uttered, the hearers, with a gush of tears and passionate sobs, bore witness how deep their fears were, how small their hopes. For my own part, my exertions for the public good permitted me to observe more closely than most others, the virulence and extensive ravages of our sightless enemy. A short month has destroyed a village, and where in May the first person sickened, in June the paths were deformed by unburied corpses—the houses tenantless, no smoke arising from the chimneys; and the housewife's clock marked only the hour when death had been triumphant. From such scenes I have sometimes saved a deserted infant—sometimes led a young and grieving mother from the lifeless image of her first born, or drawn the sturdy labourer from childish weeping over his extinct family.

July is gone. August must pass, and by the middle of September we may hope. Each day was eagerly counted; and the inhabitants of towns, desirous to leap this dangerous interval, plunged into dissipation, and strove, by riot, and what they wished to imagine to be pleasure, to banish thought and opiate despair. None but Adrian could have tamed the motley population of London, which, like a troop of unbitted steeds rushing to their pastures, had thrown aside all minor fears, through the operation of the fear paramount. Even Adrian was obliged in part to yield, that he might be able, if not to guide, at least to set bounds to the license of the times. The theatres were kept open; every place of public resort was frequented; though he endeavoured so to modify them, as might best quiet the agitation of the spectators, and at the same time prevent a reaction of misery when the excitement was over. Tragedies deep and dire were the chief favourites. Comedy brought with it too great a contrast to the inner despair: when such were attempted, it was not unfrequent for a comedian, in the midst of the laughter occasioned by his disproportioned buffoonery, to find a word or thought in his part that jarred with his own sense of wretchedness, and burst from mimic merriment into sobs and tears, while the spectators, seized with irresistible sympathy, wept, and the pantomimic revelry was changed to a real exhibition of tragic passion.

It was not in my nature to derive consolation from such scenes; from theatres, whose buffoon laughter and discordant mirth awakened distempered sympathy, or where fictitious tears and wailings mocked the heart-felt grief within; from festival or crowded meeting, where hilarity sprung from the worst feelings of our nature, or such enthralment of the better ones, as impressed it with garish and false varnish; from assemblies of mourners in the guise of revellers. Once however I witnessed a scene of singular interest at one of the theatres, where nature overpowered art, as an overflowing cataract will tear away the puny manufacture of a mock cascade, which had before been fed by a small portion of its waters.

I had come to London to see Adrian. He was not at the palace; and, though the attendants did not know whither he had gone, they did not expect him till late at night. It was between six and seven o'clock, a fine summer afternoon, and I spent my leisure hours in a ramble through the empty streets of London; now turning to avoid an approaching funeral, now urged by curiosity to observe the state of a particular spot; my wanderings were instinct with pain, for silence and desertion characterized every place I visited, and the few beings I met were so pale and woe-begone, so marked with care and depressed by fear, that weary of encountering only signs of misery, I began to retread my steps towards home.

I was now in Holborn, and passed by a public house filled with uproarious companions, whose songs, laughter, and shouts were more sorrowful than the pale looks and silence of the mourner. Such an one was near, hovering round this house. The sorry plight of her dress displayed her poverty, she was ghastly pale, and continued approaching, first the window and then the door of the house, as if fearful, yet longing to enter. A sudden burst of song and merriment seemed to sting her to the heart; she murmured, "Can he have the heart?" and then mustering her courage, she stepped within the threshold. The landlady met her in the passage; the poor creature asked, "Is my husband here? Can I see George?"

"See him," cried the woman, "yes, if you go to him; last night he was taken with the plague, and we sent him to the hospital."

The unfortunate inquirer staggered against a wall, a faint cry escaped her—"O! were you cruel enough," she exclaimed, "to send him there?"

The landlady meanwhile hurried away; but a more compassionate bar-maid gave her a detailed account, the sum of which was, that her husband had been taken ill, after a night of riot, and sent by his boon companions with all expedition to St. Bartholomew's Hospital.[117] I had

117 The oldest hospital in London, located in Smithfield.

watched this scene, for there was a gentleness about the poor woman that interested me; she now tottered away from the door, walking as well as she could down Holborn Hill; but her strength soon failed her; she leaned against a wall, and her head sunk on her bosom, while her pallid cheek became still more white. I went up to her and offered my services. She hardly looked up—"You can do me no good," she replied; "I must go to the hospital; if I do not die before I get there."

There were still a few hackney-coaches accustomed to stand about the streets, more truly from habit than for use. I put her in one of these, and entered with her that I might secure her entrance into the hospital. Our way was short, and she said little; except interrupted ejaculations of reproach that he had left her, exclamations on the unkindness of some of his friends, and hope that she would find him alive. There was a simple, natural earnestness about her that interested me in her fate, especially when she assured me that her husband was the best of men,—had been so, till want of business during these unhappy times had thrown him into bad company. "He could not bear to come home," she said, "only to see our children die. A man cannot have the patience a mother has, with her own flesh and blood."

We were set down at St. Bartholomew's, and entered the wretched precincts of the house of disease. The poor creature clung closer to me, as she saw with what heartless haste they bore the dead from the wards, and took them into a room, whose half-opened door displayed a number of corpses, horrible to behold by one unaccustomed to such scenes. We were directed to the ward where her husband had been first taken, and still was, the nurse said, if alive. My companion looked eagerly from one bed to the other, till at the end of the ward she espied, on a wretched bed, a squalid, haggard creature, writhing under the torture of disease. She rushed towards him, she embraced him, blessing God for his preservation.

The enthusiasm that inspired her with this strange joy, blinded her to the horrors about her; but they were intolerably agonizing to me. The ward was filled with an effluvia that caused my heart to heave with painful qualms. The dead were carried out, and the sick brought in, with like indifference; some were screaming with pain, others laughing from the influence of more terrible delirium; some were attended by weeping, despairing relations, others called aloud with thrilling tenderness or reproach on the friends who had deserted them, while the nurses went from bed to bed, incarnate images of despair, neglect, and death. I gave gold to my luckless companion; I recommended her to the care of the attendants; I then hastened away; while the tormentor, the imagination, busied itself in picturing my own loved ones, stretched on such beds, attended thus. The country afforded no such mass of horrors; solitary wretches died in the open fields; and I have found a survivor in a vacant village, contending at once with famine and disease; but the assembly of pestilence, the banqueting hall of death, was spread only in London.

I rambled on, oppressed, distracted by painful emotions—suddenly I

THE LAST MAN 219

found myself before Drury Lane Theatre. The play was Macbeth—the first actor of the age was there to exert his powers to drug with irreflection the auditors;[118] such a medicine I yearned for, so I entered. The theatre was tolerably well filled. Shakspeare, whose popularity was established by the approval of four centuries, had not lost his influence even at this dread period; but was still "Ut magus,"[119] the wizard to rule our hearts and govern our imaginations. I came in during the interval between the third and fourth act. I looked round on the audience; the females were mostly of the lower classes, but the men were of all ranks, come hither to forget awhile the protracted scenes of wretchedness, which awaited them at their miserable homes. The curtain drew up, and the stage presented the scene of the witches' cave. The wildness and supernatural machinery of Macbeth, was a pledge that it could contain little directly connected with our present circumstances. Great pains had been taken in the scenery to give the semblance of reality to the impossible. The extreme darkness of the stage, whose only light was received from the fire under the cauldron, joined to a kind of mist that floated about it, rendered the unearthly shapes of the witches obscure and shadowy. It was not three decrepid old hags that bent over their pot throwing in the grim ingredients of the magic charm, but forms frightful, unreal, and fanciful. The entrance of Hecate, and the wild music that followed, took us out of this world. The cavern shape the stage assumed, the beetling rocks, the glare of the fire, the misty shades that crossed the scene at times, the music in harmony with all witch-like fancies, permitted the imagination to revel, without fear of contradiction, or reproof from reason or the heart. The entrance of Macbeth did not destroy the illusion, for he was actuated by the same feelings that inspired us, and while the work of magic proceeded we sympathized in his wonder and his daring, and gave ourselves up with our whole souls to the influence of scenic delusion. I felt the beneficial result of such excitement, in a renewal of those pleasing flights of fancy to which I had long been a stranger. The effect of this scene of incantation communicated a portion of its power to that which followed. We forgot that Malcolm and Macduff were mere human beings, acted upon by such simple passions as warmed our own breasts. By slow degrees however we were drawn to the real interest of the scene. A shudder like the swift passing of an electric shock ran through the house, when Rosse exclaimed, in answer to "Stands Scotland where it did?"

Alas, poor country;
Almost afraid to know itself! It cannot
Be called our mother, but our grave: where nothing,

---

118 MWS is thinking of Edmund Kean, whose version of *Macbeth* may influence
     the description that follows.
119 Like a magician.

But who knows nothing, is once seen to smile;
Where sighs, and groans, and shrieks that rent the air,
Are made, not marked; where violent sorrow seems
A modern extasy: the dead man's knell
Is there scarce asked, for who; and good men's lives
Expire before the flowers in their caps,
Dying, or ere they sicken.[120]

Each word struck the sense, as our life's passing bell; we feared to look at each other, but bent our gaze on the stage, as if our eyes could fall innocuous on that alone. The person who played the part of Rosse, suddenly became aware of the dangerous ground he trod. He was an inferior actor, but truth now made him excellent; as he went on to announce to Macduff the slaughter of his family, he was afraid to speak, trembling from apprehension of a burst of grief from the audience, not from his fellow-mime. Each word was drawn out with difficulty; real anguish painted his features; his eyes were now lifted in sudden horror, now fixed in dread upon the ground. This shew of terror encreased ours, we gasped with him, each neck was stretched out, each face changed with the actor's changes—at length while Macduff, who, attending to his part, was unobservant of the high wrought sympathy of the house, cried with well acted passion:

> All my pretty ones?
> Did you say all?—O hell kite! All?
> What! all my pretty chickens, and their dam,
> At one fell swoop![121]

A pang of tameless grief wrenched every heart, a burst of despair was echoed from every lip—I had entered into the universal feeling—I had been absorbed by the terrors of Rosse—I re-echoed the cry of Macduff, and then rushed out as from an hell of torture, to find calm in the free air and silent street.

Free the air was not, or the street silent. Oh, how I longed then for the dear soothings of maternal Nature, as my wounded heart was still further stung by the roar of heartless merriment from the public-house, by the sight of the drunkard reeling home, having lost the memory of what he would find there in oblivious debauch, and by the more appalling salutations of those melancholy beings to whom the name of home was a mockery. I ran on at my utmost speed until I found myself I knew not how, close to Westminster Abbey, and was attracted by the deep and swelling tone of the organ. I entered with soothing awe the lighted chancel, and

120 *Macbeth* 4.3.164-73.
121 4.3.216-19.

listened to the solemn religious chaunt, which spoke peace and hope to the unhappy. The notes, freighted with man's dearest prayers, re-echoed through the dim aisles, and the bleeding of the soul's wounds was staunched by heavenly balm. In spite of the misery I deprecated, and could not understand; in spite of the cold hearths of wide London, and the corpse-strewn fields of my native land; in spite of all the variety of agonizing emotions I had that evening experienced, I thought that in reply to our melodious adjurations, the Creator looked down in compassion and promise of relief; the awful peal of the heaven-winged music seemed fitting voice wherewith to commune with the Supreme; calm was produced by its sound, and by the sight of many other human creatures offering up prayers and submission with me. A sentiment approaching happiness followed the total resignation of one's being to the guardianship of the world's ruler. Alas! with the failing of this solemn strain, the elevated spirit sank again to earth. Suddenly one of the choristers died—he was lifted from his desk, the vaults below were hastily opened—he was consigned with a few muttered prayers to the darksome cavern, abode of thousands who had gone before—now wide yawning to receive even all who fulfilled the funeral rites. In vain I would then have turned from this scene, to darkened aisle or lofty dome, echoing with melodious praise. In the open air alone I found relief; among nature's beauteous works, her God reassumed his attribute of benevolence, and again I could trust that he who built up the mountains, planted the forests, and poured out the rivers, would erect another state for lost humanity, where we might awaken again to our affections, our happiness, and our faith.

Fortunately for me those circumstances were of rare occurrence that obliged me to visit London, and my duties were confined to the rural district which our lofty castle overlooked; and here labour stood in the place of pastime, to occupy such of the country people as were sufficiently exempt from sorrow or disease. My endeavours were directed towards urging them to their usual attention to their crops, and to the acting as if pestilence did not exist. The mower's scythe was at times heard; yet the joyless haymakers, after they had listlessly turned the grass, forgot to cart it; the shepherd, when he had sheared his sheep, would let the wool lie to be scattered by the winds, deeming it useless to provide clothing for another winter. At times however the spirit of life was awakened by these employments; the sun, the refreshing breeze, the sweet smell of the hay, the rustling leaves and prattling rivulets brought repose to the agitated bosom, and bestowed a feeling akin to happiness on the apprehensive. Nor, strange to say, was the time without its pleasures. Young couples, who had loved long and hopelessly, suddenly found every impediment removed, and wealth pour in from the death of relatives. The very danger drew them closer. The immediate peril urged them to seize the immediate opportunity; wildly and passionately they sought to know what delights existence afforded, before they yielded to death, and

Snatching their pleasures with rough strife
Through the iron gates of life,[122]

they defied the conquering pestilence to destroy what had been, or to erase even from their death-bed thoughts the sentiment of happiness which had been theirs.

One instance of this kind came immediately under our notice, where a high-born girl had in early youth given her heart to one of meaner extraction. He was a schoolfellow and friend of her brother's, and usually spent a part of the holidays at the mansion of the duke her father. They had played together as children, been the confidants of each other's little secrets, mutual aids and consolers in difficulty and sorrow. Love had crept in, noiseless, terrorless at first, till each felt their life bound up in the other, and at the same time knew that they must part. Their extreme youth, and the purity of their attachment, made them yield with less resistance to the tyranny of circumstances. The father of the fair Juliet separated them; but not until the young lover had promised to remain absent only till he had rendered himself worthy of her, and she had vowed to preserve her virgin heart, his treasure, till he returned to claim and possess it.

Plague came, threatening to destroy at once the aim of the ambitious and the hopes of love. Long the Duke of L — derided the idea that there could be danger while he pursued his plans of cautious seclusion; and he so far succeeded, that it was not till this second summer, that the destroyer, at one fell stroke, overthrew his precautions, his security, and his life. Poor Juliet saw one by one, father, mother, brothers, and sisters, sicken and die. Most of the servants fled on the first appearance of disease, those who remained were infected mortally; no neighbour or rustic ventured within the verge of contagion. By a strange fatality Juliet alone escaped, and she to the last waited on her relatives, and smoothed the pillow of death. The moment at length came, when the last blow was given to the last of the house: the youthful survivor of her race sat alone among the dead. There was no living being near to soothe her, or withdraw her from this hideous company. With the declining heat of a September night, a whirlwind of storm, thunder, and hail, rattled round the house, and with ghastly harmony sung the dirge of her family. She sat upon the ground absorbed in wordless despair, when through the gusty wind and bickering rain she thought she heard her name called. Whose could that familiar voice be? Not one of her relations, for they lay glaring on her with stony eyes. Again her name was syllabled, and she shuddered as she asked herself, am I becoming mad, or am I dying, that I hear the voices of the

---

122 Andrew Marvell [MWS's note]: "And tear our pleasures with rough strife / Thorough the iron gates of life" ("To His Coy Mistress" 43-44).

departed? A second thought passed, swift as an arrow, into her brain; she rushed to the window; and a flash of lightning shewed to her the expected vision, her lover in the shrubbery beneath; joy lent her strength to descend the stairs, to open the door, and then she fainted in his supporting arms.

A thousand times she reproached herself, as with a crime, that she should revive to happiness with him. The natural clinging of the human mind to life and joy was in its full energy in her young heart; she gave herself impetuously up to the enchantment: they were married; and in their radiant features I saw incarnate, for the last time, the spirit of love, of rapturous sympathy, which once had been the life of the world.

I envied them, but felt how impossible it was to imbibe the same feeling, now that years had multiplied my ties in the world. Above all, the anxious mother, my own beloved and drooping Idris, claimed my earnest care; I could not reproach the anxiety that never for a moment slept in her heart, but I exerted myself to distract her attention from too keen an observation of the truth of things, of the near and nearer approaches of disease, misery, and death, of the wild look of our attendants as intelligence of another and yet another death reached us; for to the last something new occurred that seemed to transcend in horror all that had gone before. Wretched beings crawled to die under our succouring roof; the inhabitants of the Castle decreased daily, while the survivors huddled together in fear, and, as in a famine-struck boat, the sport of the wild, interminable waves, each looked in the other's face, to guess on whom the death-lot would next fall. All this I endeavoured to veil, so that it might least impress my Idris; yet, as I have said, my courage survived even despair: I might be vanquished, but I would not yield.

One day, it was the ninth of September, seemed devoted to every disaster, to every harrowing incident. Early in the day, I heard of the arrival of the aged grandmother of one of our servants at the Castle. This old woman had reached her hundredth year; her skin was shrivelled, her form was bent and lost in extreme decrepitude; but as still from year to year she continued in existence, out-living many younger and stronger, she began to feel as if she were to live for ever. The plague came, and the inhabitants of her village died. Clinging, with the dastard feeling of the aged, to the remnant of her spent life, she had, on hearing that the pestilence had come into her neighbourhood, barred her door, and closed her casement, refusing to communicate with any. She would wander out at night to get food, and returned home, pleased that she had met no one, that she was in no danger from the plague. As the earth became more desolate, her difficulty in acquiring sustenance increased; at first, her son, who lived near, had humoured her by placing articles of food in her way: at last he died. But, even though threatened by famine, her fear of the plague was paramount; and her greatest care was to avoid her fellow creatures. She grew weaker each day, and each day she had further to go. The night before, she had reached Datchet;[123] and, prowling about, had found a baker's shop open and deserted. Laden with spoil, she hastened to return, and lost her way. The night was windless, hot, and cloudy; her load became too heavy for her; and one by one she threw away her loaves, still endeavouring to get along, though her hobbling fell into lameness, and her weakness at last into inability to move.

She lay down among the tall corn, and fell asleep. Deep in midnight, she was awaked by a rustling near her; she would have started up, but her stiff joints refused to obey her will. A low moan close to her ear followed, and the rustling increased; she heard a smothered voice breathe out, Water, Water! several times; and then again a sigh heaved from the heart of the sufferer. The old woman shuddered, she contrived at length to sit upright; but her teeth chattered, and her knees knocked together—close, very close, lay a half-naked figure, just discernible in the gloom, and the cry for water and the stifled moan were again uttered. Her motions at length attracted the attention of her unknown companion; her hand was seized with a convulsive violence that made the grasp feel like iron, the fingers like the keen teeth of a trap.—"At last you are come!" were the words given forth—but this exertion was the last effort of the dying—the joints relaxed, the figure fell prostrate, one low moan, the last, marked the moment of death. Morning broke; and the old woman saw the corpse, marked with the fatal disease, close to her; her wrist was livid with the hold loosened by death. She felt struck by the plague; her aged frame was unable to bear her away with sufficient speed; and now, believing herself infected, she no longer dreaded the association of others; but, as swiftly as she might, came to her grand-daughter, at Windsor Castle, there to lament and die. The sight was horrible; still she clung to life, and lamented her mischance with cries and hideous groans; while the swift advance of the disease shewed, what proved to be the fact, that she could not survive many hours.

While I was directing that the necessary care should be taken of her, Clara came in; she was trembling and pale; and, when I anxiously asked her the cause of her agitation, she threw herself into my arms weeping and exclaiming—"Uncle, dearest uncle, do not hate me for ever! I must tell you, for you must know, that Evelyn, poor little Evelyn"—her voice was choked by sobs. The fear of so mighty a calamity as the loss of our adored infant made the current of my blood pause with chilly horror; but the remembrance of the mother restored my presence of mind. I sought the little bed of my darling; he was oppressed by fever; but I trusted, I fondly and fearfully trusted, that there were no symptoms of the plague.

---

123 A village on the Thames two miles east of Windsor.

He was not three years old, and his illness appeared only one of those attacks incident to infancy. I watched him long—his heavy half-closed lids, his burning cheeks and restless twining of his small fingers—the fever was violent, the torpor complete—enough, without the greater fear of pestilence, to awaken alarm. Idris must not see him in this state. Clara, though only twelve years old, was rendered, through extreme sensibility, so prudent and careful, that I felt secure in entrusting the charge of him to her, and it was my task to prevent Idris from observing their absence. I administered the fitting remedies, and left my sweet niece to watch beside him, and bring me notice of any change she should observe.

I then went to Idris, contriving in my way, plausible excuses for remaining all day in the Castle, and endeavouring to disperse the traces of care from my brow. Fortunately she was not alone. I found Merrival, the astronomer, with her. He was far too long sighted in his view of humanity to heed the casualties of the day, and lived in the midst of contagion unconscious of its existence. This poor man, learned as La Place,[124] guileless and unforeseeing as a child, had often been on the point of starvation, he, his pale wife and numerous offspring, while he neither felt hunger, nor observed distress. His astronomical theories absorbed him; calculations were scrawled with coal on the bare walls of his garret: a hard-earned guinea, or an article of dress, was exchanged for a book without remorse; he neither heard his children cry, nor observed his companion's emaciated form, and the excess of calamity was merely to him as the occurrence of a cloudy night, when he would have given his right hand to observe a celestial phenomenon. His wife was one of those wondrous beings, to be found only among women, with affections not to be diminished by misfortune. Her mind was divided between boundless admiration for her husband, and tender anxiety for her children—she waited on him, worked for them, and never complained, though care rendered her life one long-drawn, melancholy dream.

He had introduced himself to Adrian, by a request he made to observe some planetary motions from his glass. His poverty was easily detected and relieved. He often thanked us for the books we lent him, and for the use of our instruments, but never spoke of his altered abode or change of

---

124   The French mathematician and astronomer, Pierre Simon de Laplace
        (1749-1827), who proposed the nebular origin of the solar system, perhaps also
        interested MWS (and PBS) because of his determinism; he "frequently pre-
        sented the figure of a superhuman intelligence, to whom the entire state of
        nature at a time is known, and who can therefore compute the way it will
        evolve through subsequent times" (Simon Blackburn, *Oxford Dictionary of
        Philosophy*). See also Appendix D.6, 402n.

circumstances. His wife assured us, that he had not observed any difference, except in the absence of the children from his study, and to her infinite surprise he complained of this unaccustomed quiet.

He came now to announce to us the completion of his Essay on the Pericyclical Motions of the Earth's Axis, and the precession of the equinoctial points.[125] If an old Roman of the period of the Republic had returned to life, and talked of the impending election of some laurel-crowned consul, or of the last battle with Mithridates,[126] his ideas would not have been more alien to the times, than the conversation of Merrival. Man, no longer with an appetite for sympathy, clothed his thoughts in visible signs; nor were there any readers left: while each one, having thrown away his sword with opposing shield alone, awaited the plague, Merrival talked of the state of mankind six thousand years hence. He might with equal interest to us, have added a commentary, to describe the unknown and unimaginable lineaments of the creatures, who would then occupy the vacated dwelling of mankind. We had not the heart to undeceive the poor old man; and at the moment I came in, he was reading parts of his book to Idris, asking what answer could be given to this or that position.

Idris could not refrain from a smile, as she listened; she had already gathered from him that his family was alive and in health; though not apt to forget the precipice of time on which she stood, yet I could perceive that she was amused for a moment, by the contrast between the contracted view we had so long taken of human life, and the seven league strides with which Merrival paced a coming eternity. I was glad to see her smile, because it assured me of her total ignorance of her infant's danger: but I shuddered to think of the revulsion that would be occasioned by a discovery of the truth. While Merrival was talking, Clara softly opened a door behind Idris, and beckoned me to come with a gesture and look of grief. A mirror betrayed the sign to Idris—she started up. To suspect evil, to perceive that, Alfred being with us, the danger must regard her youngest darling, to fly across the long chambers into his apartment, was the work but of a moment. There she beheld her Evelyn lying fever-stricken and motionless. I followed her, and strove to inspire more hope than I could myself entertain; but she shook her head mournfully. Anguish deprived her of presence of mind; she gave up to me and Clara

---

125 The title perhaps recalls PBS's interest in Laplace, whose works included the *Théorie du mouvement et de la figure elliptique des planètes, Mécanique céleste*, and *Système du monde*; for Laplace's relation to PBS, however, cf. Appendix D.6, and 402n.

126 Mithridates VI, king of Pontus in northeast Asia Minor on the Black Sea, was defeated by the Romans in 63 BC.

the physician's and nurse's parts; she sat by the bed, holding one little burning hand, and, with glazed eyes fixed on her babe, passed the long day in one unvaried agony. It was not the plague that visited our little boy so roughly; but she could not listen to my assurances; apprehension deprived her of judgment and reflection; every slight convulsion of her child's features shook her frame—if he moved, she dreaded the instant crisis; if he remained still, she saw death in his torpor, and the cloud on her brow darkened.

The poor little thing's fever encreased towards night. The sensation is most dreary, to use no stronger term, with which one looks forward to passing the long hours of night beside a sick bed, especially if the patient be an infant, who cannot explain its pain, and whose flickering life resembles the wasting flame of the watch-light,

> Whose narrow fire
> Is shaken by the wind, and on whose edge
> Devouring darkness hovers.[127]

With eagerness one turns toward the east, with angry impatience one marks the unchequered darkness; the crowing of a cock, that sound of glee during day-time, comes wailing and untuneable—the creaking of rafters, and slight stir of invisible insect is heard and felt as the signal and type of desolation. Clara, overcome by weariness, had seated herself at the foot of her cousin's bed, and in spite of her efforts slumber weighed down her lids; twice or thrice she shook it off; but at length she was conquered and slept. Idris sat at the bedside, holding Evelyn's hand; we were afraid to speak to each other; I watched the stars—I hung over my child—I felt his little pulse—I drew near the mother—again I receded. At the turn of morning a gentle sigh from the patient attracted me, the burning spot on his cheek faded—his pulse beat softly and regularly—torpor yielded to sleep. For a long time I dared not hope; but when his unobstructed breathing and the moisture that suffused his forehead, were tokens no longer to be mistaken for the departure of mortal malady, I ventured to whisper the news of the change to Idris, and at length succeeded in persuading her that I spoke truth.

But neither this assurance, nor the speedy convalescence of our child could restore her, even to the portion of peace she before enjoyed. Her fear had been too deep, too absorbing, too entire, to be changed to security. She felt as if during her past calm she had dreamed, but was now awake; she was

---

127 The Cenci [MWS's note]: PBS, *The Cenci* 3.2.9-11.

As one

In some lone watch-tower on the deep, awakened
From soothing visions of the home he loves,
Trembling to hear the wrathful billows roar;[128]

as one who has been cradled by a storm, and awakes to find the vessel sinking. Before, she had been visited by pangs of fear—now, she never enjoyed an interval of hope. No smile of the heart ever irradiated her fair countenance; sometimes she forced one, and then gushing tears would flow, and the sea of grief close above these wrecks of past happiness. Still while I was near her, she could not be in utter despair—she fully confided herself to me—she did not seem to fear my death, or revert to its possibility; to my guardianship she consigned the full freight of her anxieties, reposing on my love, as a wind-nipped fawn by the side of a doe, as a wounded nestling under its mother's wing, as a tiny, shattered boat, quivering still, beneath some protecting willow-tree. While I, not proudly as in days of joy, yet tenderly, and with glad consciousness of the comfort I afforded, drew my trembling girl close to my heart, and tried to ward every painful thought or rough circumstance from her sensitive nature.

One other incident occurred at the end of this summer. The Countess of Windsor, Ex-Queen of England, returned from Germany. She had at the beginning of the season quitted the vacant city of Vienna; and, unable to tame her haughty mind to anything like submission, she had delayed at Hamburgh, and, when at last she came to London, many weeks elapsed before she gave Adrian notice of her arrival. In spite of her coldness and long absence, he welcomed her with sensibility, displaying such affection as sought to heal the wounds of pride and sorrow, and was repulsed only by her total apparent want of sympathy. Idris heard of her mother's return with pleasure. Her own maternal feelings were so ardent, that she imagined her parent must now, in this waste world, have lost pride and harshness, and would receive with delight her filial attentions. The first check to her duteous demonstrations was a formal intimation from the fallen majesty of England, that I was in no manner to be intruded upon her. She consented, she said, to forgive her daughter, and acknowledge her grandchildren; larger concessions must not be expected.

To me this proceeding appeared (if so light a term may be permitted) extremely whimsical. Now that the race of man had lost in fact all dis-

---

128 The Brides' Tragedy, by T. L. Beddoes, Esq. [MWS's note]; in Thomas Lovell Beddoes, *The Brides' Tragedy* 5.4.16-19, Hesperus, on the point of execution, describes himself as "one / In some lone watch-tower on the deep, awakened / From soothing visions of the home he loves; / Trembling he hears the wrathful billows whoop, / And feels the little chamber of his life / Torn from its vale of clouds ...." Cf. MWS, 15 December 1823, *Journals* 2: 468.

tinction of rank, this pride was doubly fatuitous; now that we felt a kindred, fraternal nature with all who bore the stamp of humanity, this angry reminiscence of times for ever gone, was worse than foolish. Idris was too much taken up by her own dreadful fears, to be angry, hardly grieved; for she judged that insensibility must be the source of this continued rancour. This was not altogether the fact: but predominant self-will assumed the arms and masque of callous feeling; and the haughty lady disdained to exhibit any token of the struggle she endured; while the slave of pride, she fancied that she sacrificed her happiness to immutable principle.

False was all this—false all but the affections of our nature, and the links of sympathy with pleasure or pain. There was but one good and one evil in the world—life and death. The pomp of rank, the assumption of power, the possessions of wealth vanished like morning mist. One living beggar had become of more worth than a national peerage of dead lords—alas the day!—than of dead heroes, patriots, or men of genius. There was much of degradation in this: for even vice and virtue had lost their attributes—life—life—the continuation of our animal mechanism—was the Alpha and Omega[129] of the desires, the prayers, the prostrate ambition of human race.

CHAPTER XX

HALF England was desolate, when October came, and the equinoctial winds swept over the earth, chilling the ardours of the unhealthy season. The summer, which was uncommonly hot, had been protracted into the beginning of this month, when on the eighteenth a sudden change was brought about from summer temperature to winter frost. Pestilence then made a pause in her death-dealing career. Gasping, not daring to name our hopes, yet full even to the brim with intense expectation, we stood, as a ship-wrecked sailor stands on a barren rock islanded by the ocean, watching a distant vessel, fancying that now it nears, and then again that it is bearing from sight. This promise of a renewed lease of life turned rugged natures to melting tenderness, and by contrast filled the soft with harsh and unnatural sentiments. When it seemed destined that all were to die, we were reckless of the how and when—now that the virulence of the disease was mitigated, and it appeared willing to spare some, each was eager to be among the elect, and clung to life with dastard tenacity. Instances of desertion became more frequent; and even murders, which made the hearer sick with horror, where the fear of contagion had armed

---

129 The first and last letters of the Greek alphabet, signifying the beginning and
the end. See Revelation 1.8, and cf. MWS's journal entries for 3 Feb.
1823—"suffering is my Alpha and Omega"—and for 26 Oct. 1824: "Such is
the alpha & omega of my tale" (2: 451, 485).

those nearest in blood against each other. But these smaller and separate tragedies were about to yield to a mightier interest—and, while we were promised calm from infectious influences, a tempest arose wilder than the winds, a tempest bred by the passions of man, nourished by his most violent impulses, unexampled and dire.

A number of people from North America, the relics of that populous continent, had set sail for the East with mad desire of change, leaving their native plains for lands not less afflicted than their own. Several hundreds landed in Ireland, about the first of November, and took possession of such vacant habitations as they could find; seizing upon the superabundant food, and the stray cattle. As they exhausted the produce of one spot, they went on to another. At length they began to interfere with the inhabitants, and strong in their concentrated numbers, ejected the natives from their dwellings, and robbed them of their winter store. A few events of this kind roused the fiery nature of the Irish; and they attacked the invaders. Some were destroyed; the major part escaped by quick and well ordered movements; and danger made them careful. Their numbers ably arranged; the very deaths among them concealed; moving on in good order, and apparently given up to enjoyment, they excited the envy of the Irish. The Americans permitted a few to join their band, and presently the recruits outnumbered the strangers—nor did they join with them, nor imitate the admirable order which, preserved by the Trans-Atlantic chiefs, rendered them at once secure and formidable. The Irish followed their track in disorganized multitudes; each day encreasing; each day becoming more lawless. The Americans were eager to escape from the spirit they had roused, and, reaching the eastern shores of the island, embarked for England. Their incursion would hardly have been felt had they come alone; but the Irish, collected in unnatural numbers, began to feel the inroads of famine, and they followed in the wake of the Americans for England also. The crossing of the sea could not arrest their progress. The harbours of the desolate sea-ports of the west of Ireland were filled with vessels of all sizes, from the man of war to the small fishers' boat, which lay sailorless, and rotting on the lazy deep.[130] The emigrants embarked by hundreds, and unfurling their sails with rude hands, made strange havoc of buoy and cordage. Those who modestly betook themselves to the smaller craft, for the most part achieved their watery journey in safety. Some, in the true spirit of reckless enterprise, went on board a ship of an hundred and twenty guns; the vast hull drifted with the tide out of the bay, and after many hours its crew of landsmen contrived to spread a great part of her enormous canvass—the wind took it, and while a thousand mistakes of the helmsman made her present her head

---

130 Cf. Byron, "Darkness"—"Ships sailorless lay rotting on the sea" (75)—which in turn recalls the dead men and rotting decks of Coleridge's "The Rime of the Ancient Mariner." See Appendix A.1.

now to one point, and now to another, the vast fields of canvass that formed her sails flapped with a sound like that of a huge cataract; or such as a sea-like forest may give forth when buffeted by an equinoctial north-wind. The port-holes were open, and with every sea, which as she lurched, washed her decks, they received whole tons of water. The difficulties were increased by a fresh breeze which began to blow, whistling among the shrowds, dashing the sails this way and that, and rending them with horrid split, and such whir as may have visited the dreams of Milton, when he imagined the winnowing of the arch-fiend's van-like wings, which encreased the uproar of wild chaos.[131] These sounds were mingled with the roaring of the sea, the splash of the chafed billows round the vessel's sides, and the gurgling up of the water in the hold. The crew, many of whom had never seen the sea before, felt indeed as if heaven and earth came ruining together, as the vessel dipped her bows in the waves, or rose high upon them. Their yells were drowned in the clamour of elements, and the thunder rivings of their unwieldy habitation—they discovered at last that the water gained on them, and they betook themselves to their pumps; they might as well have laboured to empty the ocean by bucketfuls. As the sun went down, the gale encreased; the ship seemed to feel her danger, she was now completely water-logged, and presented other indications of settling before she went down. The bay was crowded with vessels, whose crews, for the most part, were observing the uncouth sportings of this huge unwieldy machine—they saw her gradually sink; the waters now rising above her lower decks—they could hardly wink before she had utterly disappeared, nor could the place where the sea had closed over her be at all discerned. Some few of her crew were saved, but the greater part clinging to her cordage and masts went down with her, to rise only when death loosened their hold.

This event caused many of those who were about to sail, to put foot again on firm land, ready to encounter any evil rather than to rush into the yawning jaws of the pitiless ocean. But these were few, in comparison to the numbers who actually crossed. Many went up as high as Belfast to ensure a shorter passage, and then journeying south through Scotland, they were joined by the poorer natives of that country, and all poured with one consent into England.

Such incursions struck the English with affright, in all those towns where there was still sufficient population to feel the change. There was room enough indeed in our hapless country for twice the number of invaders; but their lawless spirit instigated them to violence; they took a delight in thrusting the possessors from their houses; in seizing on some mansion of luxury, where the noble dwellers secluded themselves in fear of the plague; in forcing these of either sex to become their servants and

---

131 Cf. *Paradise Lost* 2.927-29: "At last his Sail-broad Vans / He spreads for flight, and in the surging smoke / Uplifted spurns the ground."

purveyors; till, the ruin complete in one place, they removed their locust visitation to another. When unopposed they spread their ravages wide; in cases of danger they clustered, and by dint of numbers overthrew their weak and despairing foes. They came from the east and the north, and directed their course without apparent motive, but unanimously towards our unhappy metropolis.

Communication had been to a great degree cut off through the paralyzing effects of pestilence, so that the van of our invaders had proceeded as far as Manchester and Derby,[132] before we received notice of their arrival. They swept the country like a conquering army, burning—laying waste—murdering. The lower and vagabond English joined with them. Some few of the Lords Lieutenant[133] who remained, endeavoured to collect the militia—but the ranks were vacant, panic seized on all, and the opposition that was made only served to increase the audacity and cruelty of the enemy. They talked of taking London, conquering England—calling to mind the long detail of injuries which had for many years been forgotten. Such vaunts displayed their weakness, rather than their strength—yet still they might do extreme mischief, which, ending in their destruction, would render them at last objects of compassion and remorse.

We were now taught how, in the beginning of the world, mankind clothed their enemies in impossible attributes—and how details proceeding from mouth to mouth, might, like Virgil's ever-growing Rumour, reach the heavens with her brow, and clasp Hesperus and Lucifer with her outstretched hands. Gorgon and Centaur, dragon and iron-hoofed lion, vast sea-monster and gigantic hydra,[134] were but types of the strange and appalling accounts brought to London concerning our invaders. Their landing was long unknown, but having now advanced within an hundred miles of London, the country people flying before them arrived in successive troops, each exaggerating the numbers, fury, and cruelty of the assailants. Tumult filled the before quiet streets—women and children deserted their homes, escaping they knew not whither—fathers, husbands, and sons, stood trembling, not for themselves, but for their loved and defenceless relations. As the country people poured into London, the citizens fled southwards—they climbed the higher edifices of the town, fancying that they could discern the smoke and flames the enemy spread

---

132 Manufacturing towns in the English midlands.
133 Principal officers of counties.
134 For Virgil's Rumour (*Fama*) see *Aeneid* 4.173-97; Hesperus and Lucifer are the evening and morning stars. The Gorgon's head turned anyone who looked at her to stone; Centaurs had human heads and upper bodies, but the lower bodies of horses. The sea-monster is probably Scylla: see 366 and 367n; the hydra, which Heracles killed, was a poisonous water-snake with many heads.

around them. As Windsor lay, to a great degree, in the line of march from the west, I removed my family to London, assigning the Tower[135] for their sojourn, and joining Adrian, acted as his Lieutenant in the coming struggle.

We employed only two days in our preparations, and made good use of them. Artillery and arms were collected; the remnants of such regiments, as could be brought through many losses into any show of muster, were put under arms, with that appearance of military discipline which might encourage our own party, and seem most formidable to the disorganized multitude of our enemies. Even music was not wanting: banners floated in the air, and the shrill fife and loud trumpet breathed forth sounds of encouragement and victory. A practised ear might trace an undue faltering in the step of the soldiers; but this was not occasioned so much by fear of the adversary, as by disease, by sorrow, and by fatal prognostications, which often weighed most potently on the brave, and quelled the manly heart to abject subjection.

Adrian led the troops. He was full of care. It was small relief to him that our discipline should gain us success in such a conflict; while plague still hovered to equalize the conqueror and the conquered, it was not victory that he desired, but bloodless peace. As we advanced, we were met by bands of peasantry, whose almost naked condition, whose despair and horror, told at once the fierce nature of the coming enemy. The senseless spirit of conquest and thirst of spoil blinded them, while with insane fury they deluged the country in ruin. The sight of the military restored hope to those who fled, and revenge took place of fear. They inspired the soldiers with the same sentiment. Languor was changed to ardour, the slow step converted to a speedy pace, while the hollow murmur of the multitude, inspired by one feeling, and that deadly, filled the air, drowning the clang of arms and sound of music. Adrian perceived the change, and feared that it would be difficult to prevent them from wreaking their utmost fury on the Irish. He rode through the lines, charging the officers to restrain the troops, exhorting the soldiers, restoring order, and quieting in some degree the violent agitation that swelled every bosom.

We first came upon a few stragglers of the Irish at St. Albans. They retreated, and, joining others of their companions, still fell back, till they reached the main body. Tidings of an armed and regular opposition recalled them to a sort of order. They made Buckingham their head-quarters, and scouts were sent out to ascertain our situation. We remained for the night at Luton.[136] In the morning a simultaneous movement caused us each to advance. It was early dawn, and the air, impregnated with

---

135 A castle on the Thames in London, used for centuries as a prison.
136 St. Alban's is an ancient cathedral town about twenty miles northwest of London; Buckingham is a county between Oxford and Bedford; Luton in Bedfordshire, now an industrial city, was a market town in MWS's day.

freshest odour, seemed in idle mockery to play with our banners, and bore onwards towards the enemy the music of the bands, the neighings of the horses, and regular step of the infantry. The first sound of martial instruments that came upon our undisciplined foe, inspired surprise, not unmingled with dread. It spoke of other days, of days of concord and order; it was associated with times when plague was not, and man lived beyond the shadow of imminent fate. The pause was momentary. Soon we heard their disorderly clamour, the barbarian shouts, the untimed step of thousands coming on in disarray. Their troops now came pouring on us from the open country or narrow lanes; a large extent of unenclosed fields lay between us; we advanced to the middle of this, and then made a halt: being somewhat on superior ground, we could discern the space they covered. When their leaders perceived us drawn out in opposition, they also gave the word to halt, and endeavoured to form their men into some imitation of military discipline. The first ranks had muskets; some were mounted, but their arms were such as they had seized during their advance, their horses those they had taken from the peasantry; there was no uniformity, and little obedience, but their shouts and wild gestures showed the untamed spirit that inspired them. Our soldiers received the word, and advanced to quickest time, but in perfect order: their uniform dresses, the gleam of their polished arms, their silence, and looks of sullen hate, were more appalling than the savage clamour of our innumerous foe. Thus coming nearer and nearer each other, the howls and shouts of the Irish increased; the English proceeded in obedience to their officers, until they came near enough to distinguish the faces of their enemies; the sight inspired them with fury: with one cry, that rent heaven and was re-echoed by the furthest lines, they rushed on; they disdained the use of the bullet, but with fixed bayonet dashed among the opposing foe, while the ranks opening at intervals, the match-men lighted the cannon, whose deafening roar and blinding smoke filled up the horror of the scene.

I was beside Adrian; a moment before he had again given the word to halt, and had remained a few yards distant from us in deep meditation: he was forming swiftly his plan of action, to prevent the effusion of blood; the noise of cannon, the sudden rush of the troops, and yell of the foe, startled him: with flashing eyes he exclaimed, "Not one of these must perish!" and plunging the rowels into his horse's sides, he dashed between the conflicting bands. We, his staff, followed him to surround and protect him; obeying his signal, however, we fell back somewhat. The soldiery perceiving him, paused in their onset; he did not swerve from the bullets that passed near him, but rode immediately between the opposing lines. Silence succeeded to clamour; about fifty men lay on the ground dying or dead. Adrian raised his sword in act to speak: "By whose command," he cried, addressing his own troops, "do you advance? Who ordered your attack? Fall back; these misguided men shall not be slaughtered, while I am your general. Sheath your weapons; these are your brothers, commit not fratricide; soon the plague will not leave one for you to glut your revenge upon: will you be more pitiless than pestilence? As you honour me—as you worship God, in whose image those also are created—as your children and friends are dear to you,—shed not a drop of precious human blood."

He spoke with outstretched hand and winning voice, and then turning to our invaders, with a severe brow, he commanded them to lay down their arms: "Do you think," he said, "that because we are wasted by plague, you can overcome us; the plague is also among you, and when ye are vanquished by famine and disease, the ghosts of those you have murdered will arise to bid you not hope in death. Lay down your arms, barbarous and cruel men—men whose hands are stained with the blood of the innocent, whose souls are weighed down by the orphan's cry! We shall conquer, for the right is on our side; already your cheeks are pale—the weapons fall from your nerveless grasp. Lay down your arms, fellow men! brethren! Pardon, succour, and brotherly love await your repentance. You are dear to us, because you wear the frail shape of humanity; each one among you will find a friend and host among these forces. Shall man be the enemy of man, while plague, the foe to all, even now is above us, triumphing in our butchery, more cruel than her own?"

Each army paused. On our side the soldiers grasped their arms firmly, and looked with stern glances on the foe. These had not thrown down their weapons, more from fear than the spirit of contest; they looked at each other, each wishing to follow some example given him,—but they had no leader. Adrian threw himself from his horse, and approaching one of those just slain: "He was a man," he cried, "and he is dead. O quickly bind up the wounds of the fallen—let not one die; let not one more soul escape through your merciless gashes, to relate before the throne of God the tale of fratricide; bind up their wounds—restore them to their friends. Cast away the hearts of tigers that burn in your breasts; throw down those tools of cruelty and hate; in this pause of exterminating destiny, let each man be brother, guardian, and stay to the other. Away with those blood-stained arms, and hasten some of you to bind up these wounds."

As he spoke, he knelt on the ground, and raised in his arms a man from whose side the warm tide of life gushed—the poor wretch gasped—so still had either host become, that his moans were distinctly heard, and every heart, late fiercely bent on universal massacre, now beat anxiously in hope and fear for the fate of this one man. Adrian tore off his military scarf and bound it round the sufferer—it was too late—the man heaved a deep sigh, his head fell back, his limbs lost their sustaining power.—"He is dead!" said Adrian, as the corpse fell from his arms on the ground, and he bowed his head in sorrow and awe. The fate of the world seemed bound up in the death of this single man. On either side the bands threw down their arms, even the veterans wept, and our party held out their hands to their foes, while a gush of love and deepest amity filled every heart. The two forces mingling, unarmed and hand in hand, talking only how each might assist the other, the adversaries conjoined; each repenting, the one side their former cruelties, the other their late violence, they obeyed the orders of the General to proceed towards London.

Adrian was obliged to exert his utmost prudence, first to allay the discord, and then to provide for the multitude of the invaders. They were marched to various parts of the southern counties, quartered in deserted villages,—a part were sent back to their own island, while the season of winter so far revived our energy, that the passes of the country were defended, and any increase of numbers prohibited.

On this occasion Adrian and Idris met after a separation of nearly a year. Adrian had been occupied in fulfilling a laborious and painful task. He had been familiar with every species of human misery, and had for ever found his powers inadequate, his aid of small avail. Yet the purpose of his soul, his energy and ardent resolution, prevented any re-action of sorrow. He seemed born anew, and virtue, more potent than Medean alchemy,[137] endued him with health and strength. Idris hardly recognized the fragile being, whose form had seemed to bend even to the summer breeze, in the energetic man, whose very excess of sensibility rendered him more capable of fulfilling his station of pilot in storm-tossed England.

It was not thus with Idris. She was uncomplaining; but the very soul of fear had taken its seat in her heart. She had grown thin and pale, her eyes filled with involuntary tears, her voice was broken and low. She tried to throw a veil over the change which she knew her brother must observe in her, but the effort was ineffectual; and when alone with him, with a burst of irrepressible grief she gave vent to her apprehensions and sorrow. She described in vivid terms the ceaseless care that with still renewing hunger ate into her soul; she compared this gnawing of sleepless expectation of evil, to the vulture that fed on the heart of Prometheus;[138] under the influence of this eternal excitement, and of the interminable struggles she endured to combat and conceal it, she felt, she said, as if all the wheels and springs of the animal machine worked at double rate, and were fast consuming themselves. Sleep was not sleep, for her waking thoughts, bridled by some remains of reason, and by the sight of her children happy and in health, were then transformed to wild dreams, all her terrors were realized, all her fears received their dread fulfilment. To this state there was no hope, no alleviation, unless the grave should quickly receive its

---

137 The enchantress Medea restored Aeson to youth by boiling him in a cauldron with magic herbs; cf. PBS, *Alastor*, "O, for Medea's wondrous alchemy, / Which wheresoe'er it fell made the earth gleam / With bright flowers, and the wintry boughs exhale / From vernal blooms fresh fragrance!" (672-75).

138 In punishment for rebellion, Zeus has Prometheus chained to a rock where (in Elton's version of Hesiod's *Theogony*, 158) an eagle "gorged his liver"; MWS's "vulture" and "heart" recur in her note on PBS's *Prometheus Unbound*.

destined prey, and she be permitted to die, before she experienced a thousand living deaths in the loss of those she loved. Fearing to give me pain, she hid as best she could the excess of her wretchedness, but meeting thus her brother after a long absence, she could not restrain the expression of her woe, but with all the vividness of imagination with which misery is always replete, she poured out the emotions of her heart to her beloved and sympathizing Adrian.

Her present visit to London tended to augment her state of inquietude, by shewing in its utmost extent the ravages occasioned by pestilence. It hardly preserved the appearance of an inhabited city; grass sprung up thick in the streets; the squares were weed-grown, the houses were shut up, while silence and loneliness characterized the busiest parts of the town. Yet in the midst of desolation Adrian had preserved order; and each one continued to live according to law and custom—human institutions thus surviving as it were divine ones, and while the decree of population was abrogated, property continued sacred. It was a melancholy reflection; and in spite of the diminution of evil produced, it struck on the heart as a wretched mockery. All idea of resort for pleasure, of theatres and festivals had passed away. "Next summer," said Adrian as we parted on our return to Windsor, "will decide the fate of the human race. I shall not pause in my exertions until that time; but, if plague revives with the coming year, all contest with her must cease, and our only occupation be the choice of a grave."

I must not forget one incident that occurred during this visit to London. The visits of Merrival to Windsor, before frequent, had suddenly ceased. At this time where but a hair's line separated the living from the dead, I feared that our friend had become a victim to the all-embracing evil. On this occasion I went, dreading the worst, to his dwelling, to see if I could be of any service to those of his family who might have survived. The house was deserted, and had been one of those assigned to the invading strangers quartered in London. I saw his astronomical instruments put to strange uses, his globes defaced, his papers covered with abstruse calculations destroyed. The neighbours could tell me little, till I lighted on a poor woman who acted as nurse in these perilous times. She told me that all the family were dead, except Merrival himself, who had gone mad—mad, she called it, yet on questioning her further, it appeared that he was possessed only by the delirium of excessive grief. This old man, tottering on the edge of the grave, and prolonging his prospect through millions of calculated years,—this visionary who had not seen starvation in the wasted forms of his wife and children, or plague in the horrible sights and sounds that surrounded him—this astronomer, apparently dead on earth, and living only in the motion of the spheres—loved his family with unapparent but intense affection. Through long habit they had become a part of himself; his want of worldly knowledge, his absence of mind and infant guilelessness, made him utterly dependent on them. It was not till one of them died that he perceived their danger; one by one they were carried off by pestilence; and his wife, his helpmate and supporter, more necessary to him than his own limbs and frame, which had hardly been taught the lesson of self-preservation, the kind companion whose voice always spoke peace to him, closed her eyes in death. The old man felt the system of universal nature which he had so long studied and adored, slide from under him, and he stood among the dead, and lifted his voice in curses.—No wonder that the attendant should interpret as phrensy the harrowing maledictions of the grief-struck old man.

I had commenced my search late in the day, a November day, that closed in early with pattering rain and melancholy wind. As I turned from the door, I saw Merrival, or rather the shadow of Merrival, attenuated and wild, pass me, and sit on the steps of his home. The breeze scattered the grey locks on his temples, the rain drenched his uncovered head, he sat hiding his face in his withered hands. I pressed his shoulder to awaken his attention, but he did not alter his position. "Merrival," I said, "it is long since we have seen you—you must return to Windsor with me—Lady Idris desires to see you, you will not refuse her request—come home with me."

He replied in a hollow voice, "Why deceive a helpless old man, why talk hypocritically to one half crazed? Windsor is not my home; my true home I have found; the home that the Creator has prepared for me."

His accent of bitter scorn thrilled me—"Do not tempt me to speak," he continued, "my words would scare you—in an universe of cowards I dare think—among the church-yard tombs—among the victims of His merciless tyranny I dare reproach the Supreme Evil. How can he punish me? Let him bare his arm and transfix me with lightning—this is also one of his attributes"—and the old man laughed.

He rose, and I followed him through the rain to a neighbouring church-yard—he threw himself on the wet earth. "Here they are," he cried, "beautiful creatures—breathing, speaking, loving creatures. She who by day and night cherished the age-worn lover of her youth—they, parts of my flesh, my children—here they are: call them, scream their names through the night; they will not answer!" He clung to the little heaps that marked the graves. "I ask but one thing; I do not fear His hell, for I have it here; I do not desire His heaven, let me but die and be laid beside them; let me but, when I lie dead, feel my flesh as it moulders, mingle with theirs. Promise," and he raised himself painfully, and seized my arm, "promise to bury me with them."

"So God help me and mine as I promise," I replied, "on one condition: return with me to Windsor."

"To Windsor!" he cried with a shriek, "Never!—from this place I never go—my bones, my flesh, I myself, are already buried here, and what you see of me is corrupted clay like them. I will lie here, and cling here, till rain, and hail, and lightning and storm, ruining on me, make me one in substance with them below."

In a few words I must conclude this tragedy. I was obliged to leave London, and Adrian undertook to watch over him; the task was soon fulfilled; age, grief, and inclement weather, all united to hush his sorrows, and bring repose to his heart, whose beats were agony. He died embracing the sod, which was piled above his breast, when he was placed beside the beings whom he regretted with such wild despair.

I returned to Windsor at the wish of Idris, who seemed to think that there was greater safety for her children at that spot; and because, once having taken on me the guardianship of the district, I would not desert it while an inhabitant survived. I went also to act in conformity with Adrian's plans, which was to congregate in masses what remained of the population; for he possessed the conviction that it was only through the benevolent and social virtues that any safety was to be hoped for the remnant of mankind.

It was a melancholy thing to return to this spot so dear to us, as the scene of a happiness rarely before enjoyed, here to mark the extinction of our species, and trace the deep uneraseable footsteps of disease over the fertile and cherished soil. The aspect of the country had so far changed, that it had been impossible to enter on the task of sowing seed, and other autumnal labours. That season was now gone; and winter had set in with sudden and unusual severity. Alternate frosts and thaws succeeding to floods, rendered the country impassable. Heavy falls of snow gave an arctic appearance to the scenery; the roofs of the houses peeped from the white mass; the lowly cot and stately mansion, alike deserted, were blocked up, their thresholds uncleared; the windows were broken by the hail, while the prevalence of a north-east wind rendered out-door exertions extremely painful. The altered state of society made these accidents of nature, sources of real misery. The luxury of command and the attentions of servitude were lost. It is true that the necessaries of life were assembled in such quantities, as to supply to superfluity the wants of the diminished population; but still much labour was required to arrange these, as it were, raw materials; and depressed by sickness, and fearful of the future, we had not energy to enter boldly and decidedly on any system.

I can speak for myself—want of energy was not my failing. The intense life that quickened my pulses, and animated my frame, had the effect, not of drawing me into the mazes of active life, but of exalting my lowliness, and of bestowing majestic proportions on insignificant objects—I could have lived the life of a peasant in the same way—my trifling occupations were swelled into important pursuits; my affections were impetuous and engrossing passions, and nature with all her changes was invested in divine attributes. The very spirit of the Greek mythology inhabited my heart; I deified the uplands, glades, and streams, I

Had sight of Proteus coming from the sea;
And heard old Triton blow his wreathed horn.[139]

---

139 Wordsworth [MWS's note]; from "The World is Too Much With Us" 13–14.

Strange, that while the earth preserved her monotonous course, I dwelt with ever-renewing wonder on her antique laws, and now that with excentric wheel she rushed into an untried path, I should feel this spirit fade; I struggled with despondency and weariness, but like a fog, they choked me. Perhaps, after the labours and stupendous excitement of the past summer, the calm of winter and the almost menial toils it brought with it, were by natural re-action doubly irksome. It was not the grasping passion of the preceding year, which gave life and individuality to each moment—it was not the aching pangs induced by the distresses of the times. The utter inutility that had attended all my exertions took from them their usual effects of exhilaration, and despair rendered abortive the balm of self applause—I longed to return to my old occupations, but of what use were they? To read were futile—to write, vanity indeed. The earth, late wide circus for the display of dignified exploits, vast theatre for a magnificent drama, now presented a vacant space, an empty stage—for actor or spectator there was no longer aught to say or hear.

Our little town of Windsor, in which the survivors from the neighbouring counties were chiefly assembled, wore a melancholy aspect. Its streets were blocked up with snow—the few passengers seemed palsied, and frozen by the ungenial visitation of winter. To escape these evils was the aim and scope of all our exertions. Families late devoted to exalting and refined pursuits, rich, blooming, and young, with diminished numbers and care-fraught hearts, huddled over a fire, grown selfish and grovelling through suffering. Without the aid of servants, it was necessary to discharge all household duties; hands unused to such labour must knead the bread, or in the absence of flour, the statesmen or perfumed courtier must undertake the butcher's office. Poor and rich were now equal, or rather the poor were the superior, since they entered on such tasks with alacrity and experience; while ignorance, inaptitude, and habits of repose, rendered them fatiguing to the luxurious, galling to the proud, disgustful to all whose minds, bent on intellectual improvement, held it their dearest privilege to be exempt from attending to mere animal wants.

But in every change goodness and affection can find field for exertion and display. Among some these changes produced a devotion and sacrifice of self at once graceful and heroic. It was a sight for the lovers of the human race to enjoy; to behold, as in ancient times, the patriarchal modes in which the variety of kindred and friendship fulfilled their duteous and kindly offices. Youths, nobles of the land, performed for the sake of mother or sister, the services of menials with amiable cheerfulness. They went to the river to break the ice, and draw water: they assembled on foraging expeditions, or axe in hand felled the trees for fuel. The females received them on their return with the simple and affectionate welcome known before only to the lowly cottage—a clean hearth and bright fire; the supper ready cooked by beloved hands; gratitude for the provision for to-morrow's meal: strange enjoyments for the high-born English, yet they were now their sole, hard earned, and dearly prized luxuries.

None was more conspicuous for this graceful submission to circumstances, noble humility, and ingenious fancy to adorn such acts with romantic colouring, than our own Clara. She saw my despondency, and the aching cares of Idris. Her perpetual study was to relieve us from labour and to spread ease and even elegance over our altered mode of life. We still had some attendants spared by disease, and warmly attached to us. But Clara was jealous of their services; she would be sole handmaid of Idris, sole minister to the wants of her little cousins; nothing gave her so much pleasure as our employing her in this way; she went beyond our desires, earnest, diligent, and unwearied,—

> Abra was ready ere we called her name,
> And though we called another, Abra came.[140]

It was my task each day to visit the various families assembled in our town, and when the weather permitted, I was glad to prolong my ride, and to muse in solitude over every changeful appearance of our destiny, endeavouring to gather lessons for the future from the experience of the past. The impatience with which, while in society, the ills that afflicted my species inspired me, were softened by loneliness, when individual suffering was merged in the general calamity, strange to say, less afflicting to contemplate. Thus often, pushing my way with difficulty through the narrow snow-blocked town, I crossed the bridge and passed through Eton. No youthful congregation of gallant-hearted boys thronged the portal of the college; sad silence pervaded the busy school-room and noisy playground. I extended my ride towards Salt Hill,[141] on every side impeded by the snow. Were those the fertile fields I loved—was that the interchange of gentle upland and cultivated dale, once covered with waving corn, diversified by stately trees, watered by the meandering Thames? One sheet of white covered it, while bitter recollection told me that cold as the winter-clothed earth, were the hearts of the inhabitants. I met troops of horses, herds of cattle, flocks of sheep, wandering at will; here throwing down a hay-rick, and nestling from cold in its heart, which afforded them shelter and food—there having taken possession of a vacant cottage.

Once on a frosty day, pushed on by restless unsatisfying reflections, I sought a favourite haunt, a little wood not far distant from Salt Hill. A bubbling spring prattles over stones on one side, and a plantation of a few elms and beeches, hardly deserve, and yet continue the name of wood. This spot had for me peculiar charms. It had been a favourite resort of Adrian; it was secluded; and he often said that in boyhood, his happiest

---

140 Prior's "Solomon" [MWS's note]; from Samuel Prior, *Solomon on the Vanity of the World* 2.362-63.
141 North of Windsor and Eton, near Slough.

hours were spent here; having escaped the stately bondage of his mother, he sat on the rough hewn steps that led to the spring, now reading a favourite book, now musing, with speculation beyond his years, on the still unravelled skein of morals or metaphysics.[142] A melancholy foreboding assured me that I should never see this place more; so with careful thought, I noted each tree, every winding of the streamlet and irregularity of the soil, that I might better call up its idea in absence. A robin red-breast dropt from the frosty branches of the trees, upon the congealed rivulet; its panting breast and half-closed eyes shewed that it was dying: a hawk appeared in the air; sudden fear seized the little creature; it exerted its last strength, throwing itself on its back, raising its talons in impotent defence against its powerful enemy. I took it up and placed it in my breast. I fed it with a few crumbs from a biscuit; by degrees it revived; its warm fluttering heart beat against me; I cannot tell why I detail this trifling incident—but the scene is still before me; the snow-clad fields seen through the silvered trunks of the beeches,—the brook, in days of happiness alive with sparkling waters, now choked by ice—the leafless trees fantastically dressed in hoar frost—the shapes of summer leaves imaged by winter's frozen hand on the hard ground—the dusky sky, drear cold, and unbroken silence—while close in my bosom, my feathered nursling lay warm, and safe, speaking its content with a light chirp—painful reflections thronged, stirring my brain with wild commotion—cold and death-like as the snowy fields was all earth—misery-stricken the life-tide of the inhabitants—why should I oppose the cataract of destruction that swept us away?—why string my nerves and renew my wearied efforts—ah, why? But that my firm courage and cheerful exertions might shelter the dear mate, whom I chose in the spring of my life; though the throbbings of my heart be replete with pain, though my hopes for the future are chill, still while your dear head, my gentlest love, can repose in peace on that heart, and while you derive from its fostering care, comfort, and hope, my struggles shall not cease,—I will not call myself altogether vanquished.

One fine February day, when the sun had reassumed some of its genial power, I walked in the forest with my family. It was one of those lovely winter-days which assert the capacity of nature to bestow beauty on barrenness. The leafless trees spread their fibrous branches against the pure sky; their intricate and pervious tracery resembled delicate sea-weed; the deer were turning up the snow in search of the hidden grass; the white was made intensely dazzling by the sun, and trunks of the trees, rendered more conspicuous by the loss of preponderating foliage, gathered around like the labyrinthine columns of a vast temple; it was impossible not to

---

142 PBS wrote essays on both morals and metaphysics; MWS remarks in her Note on *The Revolt of Islam*, "he said that he deliberated at one time whether he should dedicate himself to poetry or metaphysics."

receive pleasure from the sight of these things. Our children, freed from the bondage of winter, bounded before us; pursuing the deer, or rousing the pheasants and partridges from their coverts. Idris leant on my arm; her sadness yielded to the present sense of pleasure. We met other families on the Long Walk,[143] enjoying like ourselves the return of the genial season. At once, I seemed to awake; I cast off the clinging sloth of the past months; earth assumed a new appearance, and my view of the future was suddenly made clear. I exclaimed, "I have now found out the secret!"

"What secret?"

In answer to this question, I described our gloomy winter-life, our sordid cares, our menial labours:—"This northern country," I said, "is no place for our diminished race. When mankind were few, it was not here that they battled with the powerful agents of nature, and were enabled to cover the globe with offspring. We must seek some natural Paradise, some garden of the earth, where our simple wants may be easily supplied, and the enjoyment of a delicious climate compensate for the social pleasures we have lost. If we survive this coming summer, I will not spend the ensuing winter in England; neither I nor any of us."

I spoke without much heed, and the very conclusion of what I said brought with it other thoughts. Should we, any of us, survive the coming summer? I saw the brow of Idris clouded; I again felt, that we were enchained to the car of fate, over whose coursers we had no control. We could no longer say, This we will do, and this we will leave undone. A mightier power than the human was at hand to destroy our plans or to achieve the work we avoided. It were madness to calculate upon another winter. This was our last. The coming summer was the extreme end of our vista; and, when we arrived there, instead of a continuation of the long road, a gulph yawned, into which we must of force be precipitated. The last blessing of humanity was wrested from us; we might no longer hope. Can the madman, as he clanks his chains, hope? Can the wretch, led to the scaffold, who when he lays his head on the block, marks the double shadow of himself and the executioner, whose uplifted arm bears the axe, hope? Can the ship-wrecked mariner, who spent with swimming, hears close behind the splashing waters divided by a shark which pursues him through the Atlantic, hope? Such hope as theirs, we also may entertain!

Old fable tells us, that this gentle spirit sprung from the box of Pandora,[144] else crammed with evils; but these were unseen and null, while all admired the inspiriting loveliness of young Hope; each man's heart became her home; she was enthroned sovereign of our lives, here and hereafter; she was deified and worshipped, declared incorruptible and everlasting. But like all other gifts of the Creator to Man, she is mor-

---

143 Between Windsor Castle and the heart of Windsor Great Park.
144 Pandora's box, which contained all the world's afflictions, also contained the palliative, hope.

tal; her life has attained its last hour. We have watched over her; nursed her flickering existence; now she has fallen at once from youth to decrepitude, from health to immedicinable disease; even as we spend ourselves in struggles for her recovery, she dies; to all nations the voice goes forth, Hope is dead! We are but mourners in the funeral train, and what immortal essence or perishable creation will refuse to make one in the sad procession that attends to its grave the dead comforter of humanity?

Does not the sun call in his light? and day
Like a thin exhalation melt away—
Both wrapping up their beams in clouds to be
Themselves close mourners at this obsequie.[145]

---

145 Cleveland's Poems [MWS's note]; from "An Elegie on the best of Men, And meekest of Martyrs, Charles the I," in *Poems by J[ohn] C[leveland] with Additions, never before Printed* (1653). The poem is no longer ascribed to Cleveland.

VOLUME THREE

VOLUME THREE

CHAPTER XXI

HEAR you not the rushing sound of the coming tempest? Do you not behold the clouds open, and destruction lurid and dire pour down on the blasted earth? See you not the thunderbolt fall, and are deafened by the shout of heaven that follows its descent? Feel you not the earth quake and open with agonizing groans, while the air is pregnant with shrieks and wailings,—all announcing the last days of man?

No! none of these things accompanied our fall! The balmy air of spring, breathed from nature's ambrosial home, invested the lovely earth, which wakened as a young mother about to lead forth in pride her beauteous offspring to meet their sire who had been long absent. The buds decked the trees, the flowers adorned the land: the dark branches, swollen with seasonable juices, expanded into leaves, and the variegated foliage of spring, bending and singing in the breeze, rejoiced in the genial warmth of the unclouded empyrean: the brooks flowed murmuring, the sea was waveless, and the promontories that over-hung it were reflected in the placid waters; birds awoke in the woods, while abundant food for man and beast sprung up from the dark ground. Where was pain and evil? Not in the calm air or weltering ocean; not in the woods or fertile fields, nor among the birds that made the woods resonant with song, nor the animals that in the midst of plenty basked in the sunshine. Our enemy, like the Calamity of Homer,[1] trod our hearts, and no sound was echoed from her steps—

> With ills the land is rife, with ills the sea,
> Diseases haunt our frail humanity,
> Through noon, through night, on casual wing they glide,
> Silent,—a voice the power all-wise denied.[2]

Once man was a favourite of the Creator, as the royal psalmist sang, "God had made him a little lower than the angels, and had crowned him with glory and honour. God made him to have dominion over the works

---

1   Homer's Ate or Discord: *Iliad* 19. Plato quotes *Iliad* 19.92-93 in the
     Symposium; MWS seems to be using PBS's version of Plato, which translates
     Ate as "Calamity" (*Works*, ed. Ingpen and Peck 7: 189).
2   Elton's translation of Hesiod [MWS's note]; this quotation from *The Works and
     Days* is a comment on the ills that escape from Pandora's box: see above, 244n.
     Morton D. Paley gives a variant reading from the first edition (1812); however,
     MWS appears to have used Elton's "revised and enlarged" *Remains of Hesiod*,
     2nd ed. (1815) 16.

of his hands, and put all things under his feet."[3] Once it was so; now is man lord of the creation? Look at him—ha! I see plague! She has invested his form, is incarnate in his flesh, has entwined herself with his being, and blinds his heaven-seeking eyes. Lie down, O man, on the flower-strown earth; give up all claim to your inheritance, all you can ever possess of it is the small cell which the dead require.

Plague is the companion of spring, of sunshine, and plenty. We no longer struggle with her. We have forgotten what we did when she was not. Of old navies used to stem the giant ocean-waves betwixt Indus and the Pole for slight articles of luxury. Men made perilous journies to possess themselves of earth's splendid trifles, gems and gold. Human labour was wasted—human life set at nought. Now life is all that we covet; that this automaton of flesh should, with joints and springs in order, perform its functions, that this dwelling of the soul should be capable of containing its dweller. Our minds, late spread abroad through countless spheres and endless combinations of thought, now retrenched themselves behind this wall of flesh, eager to preserve its well-being only. We were surely sufficiently degraded.

At first the increase of sickness in spring brought increase of toil to such of us, who, as yet spared to life, bestowed our time and thoughts on our fellow creatures. We nerved ourselves to the task: "in the midst of despair we performed the tasks of hope."[4] We went out with the resolution of disputing with our foe. We aided the sick, and comforted the sorrowing; turning from the multitudinous dead to the rare survivors, with an energy of desire that bore the resemblance of power, we bade them—live. Plague sat paramount the while, and laughed us to scorn.

Have any of you, my readers, observed the ruins of an anthill immediately after its destruction? At first it appears entirely deserted of its former inhabitants; in a little time you see an ant struggling through the upturned mould; they reappear by twos and threes, running hither and thither in search of their lost companions. Such were we upon earth, wondering aghast at the effects of pestilence. Our empty habitations remained, but the dwellers were gathered to the shades of the tomb.

As the rules of order and pressure of laws were lost, some began with hesitation and wonder to transgress the accustomed uses of society. Palaces were deserted, and the poor man dared at length, unreproved, intrude into the splendid apartments, whose very furniture and decorations were an unknown world to him. It was found, that, though at first

---

3   Cf. Psalm 8.5-6: "For thou hast made [man] a little lower than the angels, and hast crowned him with glory and honour. Thou madest him to have dominion over the works of thy hands; thou hast put all things under his feet." The royal psalmist is King David.
4   Unidentified.

the stop put to all circulation of property, had reduced those before supported by the factitious wants of society to sudden and hideous poverty, yet when the boundaries of private possession were thrown down, the products of human labour at present existing were more, far more, than the thinned generation could possibly consume. To some among the poor this was matter of exultation. We were all equal now; magnificent dwellings, luxurious carpets, and beds of down, were afforded to all. Carriages and horses, gardens, pictures, statues, and princely libraries, there were enough of these even to superfluity; and there was nothing to prevent each from assuming possession of his share. We were all equal now; but near at hand was an equality still more levelling, a state where beauty and strength, and wisdom, would be as vain as riches and birth. The grave yawned beneath us all, and its prospect prevented any of us from enjoying the ease and plenty which in so awful a manner was presented to us.

Still the bloom did not fade on the cheeks of my babes; and Clara sprung up in years and growth, unsullied by disease. We had no reason to think the site of Windsor Castle peculiarly healthy, for many other families had expired beneath its roof; we lived therefore without any particular precaution; but we lived, it seemed, in safety. If Idris became thin and pale, it was anxiety that occasioned the change; an anxiety I could in no way alleviate. She never complained, but sleep and appetite fled from her, a slow fever preyed on her veins, her colour was hectic, and she often wept in secret; gloomy prognostications, care, and agonizing dread, ate up the principle of life within her. I could not fail to perceive this change. I often wished that I had permitted her to take her own course, and engage herself in such labours for the welfare of others as might have distracted her thoughts. But it was too late now. Besides that, with the nearly extinct race of man, all our toils grew near a conclusion, she was too weak; consumption, if so it might be called, or rather the over active life within her, which, as with Adrian, spent the vital oil in the early morning hours, deprived her limbs of strength. At night, when she could leave me unperceived, she wandered through the house, or hung over the couches of her children; and in the day time would sink into a perturbed sleep, while her murmurs and starts betrayed the unquiet dreams that vexed her. As this state of wretchedness became more confirmed, and, in spite of her endeavours at concealment more apparent, I strove, though vainly, to awaken in her courage and hope. I could not wonder at the vehemence of her care; her very soul was tenderness; she trusted indeed that she should not outlive me if I became the prey of the vast calamity, and this thought sometimes relieved her. We had for many years trod the highway of life hand in hand, and still thus linked, we might step within the shades of death; but her children, her lovely, playful, animated children—beings sprung from her own dear side—portions of her own being—depositories of our loves—even if we died, it would be comfort to know that they ran man's accustomed course. But it would not be so; young and blooming as they were, they would die, and from the hopes of maturity, from the proud name of attained manhood, they were cut off for ever. Often with maternal affection she had figured their merits and talents exerted on life's wide stage. Alas for these latter days! The world had grown old, and all its inmates partook of the decrepitude. Why talk of infancy, manhood, and old age? We all stood equal sharers of the last throes of time-worn nature. Arrived at the same point of the world's age—there was no difference in us; the name of parent and child had lost their meaning; young boys and girls were level now with men. This was all true; but it was not less agonizing to take the admonition home.

Where could we turn, and not find a desolation pregnant with the dire lesson of example? The fields had been left uncultivated, weeds and gaudy flowers sprung up,—or where a few wheat-fields shewed signs of the living hopes of the husbandman, the work had been left half-way, the ploughman had died beside the plough; the horses had deserted the furrow, and no seedsman had approached the dead; the cattle unattended wandered over the fields and through the lanes; the tame inhabitants of the poultry yard, baulked of their daily food, had become wild—young lambs were dropt in flower-gardens, and the cow stalled in the hall of pleasure. Sickly and few, the country people neither went out to sow nor reap; but sauntered about the meadows, or lay under the hedges, when the inclement sky did not drive them to take shelter under the nearest roof. Many of those who remained, secluded themselves; some had laid up stores which should prevent the necessity of leaving their homes;—some deserted wife and child, and imagined that they secured their safety in utter solitude. Such had been Ryland's plan, and he was discovered dead and half-devoured by insects, in a house many miles from any other, with piles of food laid up in useless superfluity. Others made long journies to unite themselves to those they loved, and arrived to find them dead.

London did not contain above a thousand inhabitants; and this number was continually diminishing. Most of them were country people, come up for the sake of change; the Londoners had sought the country. The busy eastern part of the town was silent, or at most you saw only where, half from cupidity, half from curiosity, the warehouses had been more ransacked than pillaged: bales of rich India goods, shawls of price, jewels, and spices, unpacked, strewed the floors. In some places the possessor had to the last kept watch on his store, and died before the barred gates. The massy portals of the churches swung creaking on their hinges; and some few lay dead on the pavement. The wretched female, loveless victim of vulgar brutality, had wandered to the toilet of high-born beauty, and, arraying herself in the garb of splendour, had died before the mirror which reflected to herself alone her altered appearance. Women whose delicate feet had seldom touched the earth in their luxury, had fled in fright and horror from their homes, till, losing themselves in the squalid streets of the metropolis, they had died on the threshold of poverty. The heart sickened at the variety of misery presented; and, when I saw a specimen of this gloomy change, my soul ached with the fear of what might befall my beloved Idris and my babes. Were they, surviving Adrian and myself, to find themselves protectorless in the world? As yet the mind alone had suffered—could I for ever put off the time, when the delicate frame and shrinking nerves of my child of prosperity, the nursling of rank and wealth, who was my companion, should be invaded by famine, hardship, and disease? Better die at once—better plunge a poinard in her bosom, still untouched by drear adversity, and then again sheathe it in my own! But, no; in times of misery we must fight against our destinies, and strive not to be overcome by them. I would not yield, but to the last gasp resolutely defended my dear ones against sorrow and pain; and if I were vanquished at last, it should not be ingloriously. I stood in the gap, resisting the enemy—the impalpable, invisible foe, who had so long beseiged us—as yet he had made no breach: it must be my care that he should not, secretly undermining, burst up within the very threshold of the temple of love, at whose altar I daily sacrificed.

The hunger of Death was now stung more sharply by the diminution of his food: or was it that before, the survivors being many, the dead were less eagerly counted? Now each life was a gem, each human breathing form of far, O! far more worth than subtlest imagery of sculptured stone; and the daily, nay, hourly decrease visible in our numbers, visited the heart with sickening misery. This summer extinguished our hopes, the vessel of society was wrecked, and the shattered raft, which carried the few survivors over the sea of misery, was riven and tempest tost. Man existed by twos and threes; man, the individual who might sleep, and wake, and perform the animal functions; but man, in himself weak, yet more powerful in congregated numbers than wind or ocean; man, the queller of the elements, the lord of created nature, the peer of demi-gods, existed no longer.

Farewell to the patriotic scene, to the love of liberty and well earned meed of virtuous aspiration!—farewell to crowded senate, vocal with the councils of the wise, whose laws were keener than the sword blade tempered at Damascus!—farewell to kingly pomp and warlike pageantry; the crowns are in the dust, and the wearers are in their graves!—farewell to the desire of rule, and the hope of victory; to high vaulting ambition, to the appetite for praise, and the craving for the suffrage of their fellows! The nations are no longer! No senate sits in council for the dead; no scion of a time honoured dynasty pants to rule over the inhabitants of a charnel house; the general's hand is cold, and the soldier has his untimely grave dug in his native fields, unhonoured, though in youth. The market-place is empty, the candidate for popular favour finds none whom he can represent. To chambers of painted state farewell!—To midnight revelry, and the panting emulation of beauty, to costly dress and birth-day shew,[5] to title and the gilded coronet, farewell!

Farewell to the giant powers of man,—to knowledge that could pilot the deep-drawing bark through the opposing waters of shoreless ocean,—to science that directed the silken balloon through the pathless air,—to the power that could put a barrier to mighty waters, and set in motion wheels, and beams, and vast machinery, that could divide rocks of granite or marble, and make the mountains plain!

Farewell to the arts,—to eloquence, which is to the human mind as the winds to the sea, stirring, and then allaying it;—farewell to poetry and deep philosophy, for man's imagination is cold, and his enquiring mind can no longer expatiate on the wonders of life, for "there is no work, nor device, nor knowledge, nor wisdom in the grave, whither thou goest!"[6]—to the graceful building, which in its perfect proportion transcended the rude forms of nature, the fretted gothic and massy saracenic pile, to the stupendous arch and glorious dome, the fluted column with its capital, Corinthian, Ionic, or Doric, the peristyle and fair entablature,[7] whose harmony of form is to the eye as musical concord to the ear!—farewell to sculpture, where the pure marble mocks human flesh, and in the plastic expression of the culled excellencies of the human shape, shines forth the god!—farewell to painting, the high wrought sentiment and deep knowledge of the artist's mind in pictured canvas—to paradisaical scenes, where trees are ever vernal, and the ambrosial air rests in perpetual glow:—to the stamped form of tempest, and wildest uproar of universal nature encaged in the narrow frame, O farewell! Farewell to music, and the sound of song; to the marriage of instruments, where the concord of soft and harsh unites in sweet harmony, and gives wings to the panting listeners, whereby to climb heaven, and learn the hidden pleasures of the eternals!—Farewell to the well-trod stage; a truer tragedy is enacted on the world's ample scene, that puts to shame mimic grief: to high-bred comedy, and the low buffoon, farewell!—Man may laugh no more.

Alas! to enumerate the adornments of humanity, shews, by what we have lost, how supremely great man was. It is all over now. He is solitary; like our first parents expelled from Paradise, he looks back towards the scene he has quitted. The high walls of the tomb, and the flaming sword of plague, lie between it and him. Like to our first parents, the whole

---

5 The splendid clothes courtiers wore to celebrate a monarch's birthday.
6 Ecclesiastes 9.10: "Whatsoever thy hand findeth to do, do it with thy might; for there is no work, nor device, nor knowledge, nor wisdom, in the grave, whither thou goest."
7 Corinthian, Ionic and Doric are the three orders of classical architecture, distinguished by the designs on the capitals of columns. An entablature is a horizontal superstructure supported by a row of columns called a peristyle.

earth is before him, a wide desart.[8] Unsupported and weak, let him wander through fields where the unreaped corn stands in barren plenty, through copses planted by his fathers, through towns built for his use. Posterity is no more; fame, and ambition, and love, are words void of meaning; even as the cattle that grazes in the field, do thou, O deserted one, lie down at evening-tide, unknowing of the past, careless of the future, for from such fond ignorance alone canst thou hope for ease!

Joy paints with its own colours every act and thought. The happy do not feel poverty—for delight is as a gold-tissued robe, and crowns them with priceless gems. Enjoyment plays the cook to their homely fare, and mingles intoxication with their simple drink. Joy strews the hard couch with roses, and makes labour ease.

Sorrow doubles the burthen to the bent-down back; plants thorns in the unyielding pillow; mingles gall with water; adds saltness to their bitter bread; cloathing them in rags, and strewing ashes on their bare heads. To our irremediable distress every small and pelting inconvenience came with added force; we had strung our frames to endure the Atlean weight thrown on us; we sank beneath the added feather chance threw on us, "the grasshopper was a burthen."[9] Many of the survivors had been bred in luxury—their servants were gone, their powers of command vanished like unreal shadows: the poor even suffered various privations; and the idea of another winter like the last, brought affright to our minds. Was it not enough that we must die, but toil must be added?—must we prepare our funeral repast with labour, and with unseemly drudgery heap fuel on our deserted hearths—must we with servile hands fabricate the garments, soon to be our shroud?

Not so! We are presently to die, let us then enjoy to its full relish the remnant of our lives. Sordid care, avaunt! menial labours, and pains, slight in themselves, but too gigantic for our exhausted strength, shall make no part of our ephemeral existences. In the beginning of time, when, as now, man lived by families, and not by tribes or nations, they were placed in a genial clime, where earth fed them untilled, and the balmy air enwrapt their reposing limbs with warmth more pleasant than beds of down. The south is the native place of the human race; the land of fruits, more grateful to man than the hard-earned Ceres[10] of the north,—of trees, whose boughs are as a palace-roof, of couches of roses, and of the thirst-appeasing grape. We need not there fear cold and hunger.

Look at England! the grass shoots up high in the meadows; but they

---

8   Cf. *Paradise Lost* 12.646-49 and the use of this passage in *Frankenstein*, ed. D. L. Macdonald and Kathleen Scherf 166.

9   Ecclesiastes 12.5: "the grasshopper shall be a burden, and desire shall fail; because man goeth to his long home; and the mourners go about the streets"; see also below, 326n. The "Atlean weight" is the weight of the sky, which Atlas holds up.

10 A Roman goddess identified with the Greek Demeter, goddess of the harvest.

are dank and cold, unfit bed for us. Corn we have none, and the crude fruits cannot support us. We must seek firing in the bowels of the earth, or the unkind atmosphere will fill us with rheums and aches. The labour of hundreds of thousands alone could make this inclement nook fit habitation for one man. To the south then, to the sun!—where nature is kind, where Jove has showered forth the contents of Amalthea's horn,[11] and earth is a garden.

England, late birth-place of excellence and school of the wise, thy children are gone, thy glory faded! Thou, England, wert the triumph of man! Small favour was shewn thee by thy Creator, thou Isle of the North; a ragged canvas naturally, painted by man with alien colours; but the hues he gave are faded, never more to be renewed. So we must leave thee, thou marvel of the world; we must bid farewell to thy clouds, and cold, and scarcity for ever! Thy manly hearts are still; thy tale of power and liberty at its close! Bereft of man, O little isle! the ocean waves will buffet thee, and the raven flap his wings over thee; thy soil will be birth-place of weeds, thy sky will canopy barrenness. It was not for the rose of Persia thou wert famous, nor the banana of the east; not for the spicy gales of India, nor the sugar groves of America; not for thy vines nor thy double harvests, nor for thy vernal airs, nor solstitial sun—but for thy children, their unwearied industry and lofty aspiration. They are gone, and thou goest with them the oft trodden path that leads to oblivion,—

> Farewell, sad Isle, farewell, thy fatal glory
> Is summed, cast up, and cancelled in this story.[12]

CHAPTER XXII

IN the autumn of this year 2096, the spirit of emigration crept in among the few survivors, who, congregating from various parts of England, met in London. This spirit existed as a breath, a wish, a far off thought, until communicated to Adrian, who imbibed it with ardour, and instantly engaged himself in plans for its execution. The fear of immediate death vanished with the heats of September. Another winter was before us, and we might elect our mode of passing it to the best advantage. Perhaps in rational philosophy none could be better chosen than this scheme of migration, which would draw us from the immediate scene of our woe,

---

11   With this passage cf. the following from MWS's *Proserpine*: "[Not] Crete which boasts fair Amalthea's horn / Can be compared with the bright golden fields / Of Ceres, Queen of plenteous Sicily."

12   Cleveland's Poems [MWS's note]; from "Chronosticon Decollationis Caroli Regis," in John Cleveland, *Poems* (1653). This poem, like the "Elegie" quoted above, 245, is no longer ascribed to Cleveland.

and, leading us through pleasant and picturesque countries, amuse for a time our despair. The idea once broached, all were impatient to put it in execution.

We were still at Windsor; our renewed hopes medicined the anguish we had suffered from the late tragedies. The death of many of our inmates had weaned us from the fond idea, that Windsor Castle was a spot sacred from the plague; but our lease of life was renewed for some months, and even Idris lifted her head, as a lily after a storm, when a last sunbeam tinges its silver cup. Just at this time Adrian came down to us; his eager looks shewed us that he was full of some scheme. He hastened to take me aside, and disclosed to me with rapidity his plan of emigration from England.

To leave England for ever! to turn from its polluted fields and groves, and, placing the sea between us, to quit it, as a sailor quits the rock on which he has been wrecked, when the saving ship rides by. Such was his plan.

To leave the country of our fathers, made holy by their graves!—We could not feel even as a voluntary exile of old, who might for pleasure or convenience forsake his native soil; though thousands of miles might divide him, England was still a part of him, as he of her. He heard of the passing events of the day; he knew that, if he returned, and resumed his place in society, the entrance was still open, and it required but the will, to surround himself at once with the associations and habits of boyhood. Not so with us, the remnant. We left none to represent us, none to repeople the desart land, and the name of England died, when we left her,

In vagabond pursuit of dreadful safety.[13]

Yet let us go! England is in her shroud,—we may not enchain ourselves to a corpse. Let us go—the world is our country now, and we will choose for our residence its most fertile spot. Shall we, in these desart halls, under this wintry sky, sit with closed eyes and folded hands, expecting death? Let us rather go out to meet it gallantly:—or perhaps—for all this pendulous orb,[14] this fair gem in the sky's diadem, is not surely plague-stricken—perhaps, in some secluded nook, amidst eternal spring, and waving trees, and purling streams, we may find Life. The world is vast, and England, though her many fields and wide spread woods seem interminable, is but a small part of her. At the close of a day's march over high mountains and through snowy vallies, we may come upon health, and committing our loved ones to its charge, replant the uprooted tree of

---

13 Unidentified.
14 Cf. *Paradise Lost* 2.1052-53, where earth is described as "This pendant world, in bigness as a Star / Of smallest Magnitude close by the Moon."

humanity, and send to late posterity the tale of the ante-pestilential race, the heroes and sages of the lost state of things.

Hope beckons and sorrow urges us, the heart beats high with expectation, and this eager desire of change must be an omen of success. O come! Farewell to the dead! farewell to the tombs of those we loved!—farewell to giant London and the placid Thames, to river and mountain or fair district, birth-place of the wise and good, to Windsor Forest and its antique castle, farewell! themes for story alone are they,—we must live elsewhere.

Such were in part the arguments of Adrian, uttered with enthusiasm and unanswerable rapidity. Something more was in his heart, to which he dared not give words. He felt that the end of time was come; he knew that one by one we should dwindle into nothingness. It was not adviseable to wait this sad consummation in our native country; but travelling would give us our object for each day, that would distract our thoughts from the swift-approaching end of things. If we went to Italy, to sacred and eternal Rome, we might with greater patience submit to the decree, which had laid her mighty towers low. We might lose our selfish grief in the sublime aspect of its desolation. All this was in the mind of Adrian; but he thought of my children, and, instead of communicating to me these resources of despair, he called up the image of health and life to be found, where we knew not—when we knew not; but if never to be found, for ever and for ever to be sought. He won me over to his party, heart and soul.

It devolved on me to disclose our plan to Idris. The images of health and hope which I presented to her, made her with a smile consent. With a smile she agreed to leave her country, from which she had never before been absent, and the spot she had inhabited from infancy; the forest and its mighty trees, the woodland paths and green recesses, where she had played in childhood, and had lived so happily through youth; she would leave them without regret, for she hoped to purchase thus the lives of her children. They were her life; dearer than a spot consecrated to love, dearer than all else the earth contained. The boys heard with childish glee of our removal. Clara asked if we were to go to Athens. "It is possible," I replied; and her countenance became radiant with pleasure. There she would behold the tomb of her parents, and the territory filled with recollections of her father's glory. In silence, but without respite, she had brooded over these scenes. It was the recollection of them that had turned her infant gaiety to seriousness, and had impressed her with high and restless thoughts.

There were many dear friends whom we must not leave behind, humble though they were. There was the spirited and obedient steed which Lord Raymond had given his daughter; there was Alfred's dog and a pet eagle, whose sight was dimmed through age. But this catalogue of favourites to be taken with us, could not be made without grief to think of our heavy losses, and a deep sigh for the many things we must leave behind. The tears rushed into the eyes of Idris, while Alfred and Evelyn brought now a favourite rose tree, now a marble vase beautifully carved, insisting that these must go, and exclaiming on the pity that we could not take the castle and the forest, the deer and the birds, and all accustomed and cherished objects along with us. "Fond and foolish ones," I said, "we have lost for ever treasures far more precious than these; and we desert them, to preserve treasures to which in comparison they are nothing. Let us not for a moment forget our object and our hope; and they will form a resistless mound to stop the overflowing of our regret for trifles."

The children were easily distracted, and again returned to their prospect of future amusement. Idris had disappeared. She had gone to hide her weakness; escaping from the castle, she had descended to the little park, and sought solitude, that she might there indulge her tears; I found her clinging round an old oak, pressing its rough trunk with her roseate lips, as her tears fell plenteously, and her sobs and broken exclamations could not be suppressed; with surpassing grief I beheld this loved one of my heart thus lost in sorrow! I drew her towards me; and, as she felt my kisses on her eyelids, as she felt my arms press her, she revived to the knowledge of what remained to her. "You are very kind not to reproach me," she said: "I weep, and a bitter pang of intolerable sorrow tears my heart. And yet I am happy; mothers lament their children, wives lose their husbands, while you and my children are left to me. Yes, I am happy, most happy, that I can weep thus for imaginary sorrows, and that the slight loss of my adored country is not dwindled and annihilated in mightier misery. Take me where you will; where you and my children are, there shall be Windsor, and every country will be England to me. Let these tears flow not for myself, happy and ungrateful as I am, but for the dead world—for our lost country—for all of love, and life, and joy, now choked in the dusty chambers of death."

She spoke quickly, as if to convince herself; she turned her eyes from the trees and forest-paths she loved; she hid her face in my bosom, and we—yes, *my* masculine firmness dissolved—we wept together consolatory tears, and then calm—nay, almost cheerful, we returned to the castle.

The first cold weather of an English October, made us hasten our preparations. I persuaded Idris to go up to London, where she might better attend to necessary arrangements. I did not tell her, that to spare her the pang of parting from inanimate objects, now the only things left, I had resolved that we should none of us return to Windsor. For the last time we looked on the wide extent of country visible from the terrace, and saw the last rays of the sun tinge the dark masses of wood variegated by autumnal tints; the uncultivated fields and smokeless cottages lay in shadow below; the Thames wound through the wide plain, and the venerable pile of Eton college, stood in dark relief, a prominent object; the cawing of the myriad rooks which inhabited the trees of the little park, as in column or thick wedge they speeded to their nests, disturbed the silence of evening. Nature was the same, as when she was the kind mother of the human race; now, childless and forlorn, her fertility was a mockery; her loveliness a mask for deformity. Why should the breeze gently stir the trees, man felt not its refreshment? Why did dark night adorn herself with stars—man saw them not? Why are there or fruits, or flowers, or streams,[15] man is not here to enjoy them?

Idris stood beside me, her dear hand locked in mine. Her face was radiant with a smile.—"The sun is alone," she said, "but we are not. A strange star, my Lionel, ruled our birth; sadly and with dismay we may look upon the annihilation of man; but we remain for each other. Did I ever in the wide world seek other than thee? And since in the wide world thou remainest, why should I complain? Thou and nature are still true to me. Beneath the shades of night, and through the day, whose garish light displays our solitude, thou wilt still be at my side, and even Windsor will not be regretted."

I had chosen night time for our journey to London, that the change and desolation of the country might be the less observable. Our only surviving servant drove us. We past down the steep hill, and entered the dusky avenue of the Long Walk. At times like these, minute circumstances assume giant and majestic proportions; the very swinging open of the white gate that admitted us into the forest, arrested my thoughts as matter of interest; it was an every day act, never to occur again! The setting crescent of the moon glittered through the massy trees to our right, and when we entered the park, we scared a troop of deer, that fled bounding away in the forest shades. Our two boys quietly slept; once, before our road turned from the view, I looked back on the castle. Its windows glistened in the moonshine, and its heavy outline lay in a dark mass against the sky—the trees near us waved a solemn dirge to the midnight breeze. Idris leaned back in the carriage; her two hands pressed mine, her countenance was placid, she seemed to lose the sense of what she now left, in the memory of what she still possessed.

My thoughts were sad and solemn, yet not of unmingled pain. The very excess of our misery carried a relief with it, giving sublimity and elevation to sorrow. I felt that I carried with me those I best loved; I was pleased, after a long separation to rejoin Adrian; never again to part. I felt that I quitted what I loved, not what loved me. The castle walls, and long familiar trees, did not hear the parting sound of our carriage-wheels with regret. And, while I felt Idris to be near, and heard the regular breathing of my children, I could not be unhappy. Clara was greatly moved; with streaming eyes, suppressing her sobs, she leaned from the window, watching the last glimpse of her native Windsor.

Adrian welcomed us on our arrival. He was all animation; you could no longer trace in his look of health, the suffering valetudinarian; from his smile and sprightly tones you could not guess that he was about to lead

---

15 That is, *either* fruits or flowers or streams.

forth from their native country, the numbered remnant of the English nation, into the tenantless realms of the south, there to die, one by one, till the LAST MAN should remain in a voiceless, empty world.

Adrian was impatient for our departure, and had advanced far in his preparations. His wisdom guided all. His care was the soul, to move the luckless crowd, who relied wholly on him. It was useless to provide many things, for we should find abundant provision in every town. It was Adrian's wish to prevent all labour; to bestow a festive appearance on this funeral train. Our numbers amounted to not quite two thousand persons. These were not all assembled in London, but each day witnessed the arrival of fresh numbers, and those who resided in the neighbouring towns, had received orders to assemble at one place, on the twentieth of November. Carriages and horses were provided for all; captains and under officers chosen, and the whole assemblage wisely organized. All obeyed the Lord Protector of dying England; all looked up to him. His council was chosen, it consisted of about fifty persons. Distinction and station were not the qualifications of their election. We had no station among us, but that which benevolence and prudence gave; no distinction save between the living and the dead. Although we were anxious to leave England before the depth of winter, yet we were detained. Small parties had been dispatched to various parts of England, in search of stragglers; we would not go, until we had assured ourselves that in all human probability we did not leave behind a single human being.

On our arrival in London, we found that the aged Countess of Windsor was residing with her son in the palace of the Protectorate; we repaired to our accustomed abode near Hyde Park. Idris now for the first time for many years saw her mother, anxious to assure herself that the childishness of old age did not mingle with unforgotten pride, to make this high-born dame still so inveterate against me. Age and care had furrowed her cheeks, and bent her form; but her eye was still bright, her manners authoritative and unchanged; she received her daughter coldly, but displayed more feeling as she folded her grand-children in her arms. It is our nature to wish to continue our systems and thoughts to posterity through our own offspring. The Countess had failed in this design with regard to her children; perhaps she hoped to find the next remove in birth more tractable. Once Idris named me casually—a frown, a convulsive gesture of anger, shook her mother, and, with voice trembling with hate, she said—"I am of little worth in this world; the young are impatient to push the old off the scene; but, Idris, if you do not wish to see your mother expire at your feet, never again name that person to me; all else I can bear; and now I am resigned to the destruction of my cherished hopes: but it is too much to require that I should love the instrument that providence gifted with murderous properties for my destruction."

This was a strange speech, now that, on the empty stage, each might play his part without impediment from the other. But the haughty Ex-Queen thought as Octavius Caesar and Mark Antony,

We could not stall together
In the whole world.[16]

The period of our departure was fixed for the twenty-fifth of November. The weather was temperate; soft rains fell at night, and by day the wintry sun shone out. Our numbers were to move forward in separate parties, and to go by different routes, all to unite at last at Paris. Adrian and his division, consisting in all of five hundred persons, were to take the direction of Dover and Calais.

On the twentieth of November, Adrian and I rode for the last time through the streets of London. They were grass-grown and desert. The open doors of the empty mansions creaked upon their hinges; rank herbage, and deforming dirt, had swiftly accumulated on the steps of the houses; the voiceless steeples of the churches pierced the smokeless air: the churches were open, but no prayer was offered at the altars; mildew and damp had already defaced their ornaments; birds, and tame animals, now homeless, had built nests, and made their lairs in consecrated spots. We passed St. Paul's. London, which had extended so far in suburbs in all direction, had been somewhat deserted in the midst, and much of what had in former days obscured this vast building was removed. Its ponderous mass, blackened stone, and high dome, made it look, not like a temple, but a tomb. Methought above the portico was engraved the *Hic jacet*[17] of England. We passed on eastwards, engaged in such solemn talk as the times inspired. No human step was heard, nor human form discerned. Troops of dogs, deserted of their masters, passed us; and now and then a horse, unbridled and unsaddled, trotted towards us, and tried to attract the attention of those which we rode, as if to allure them to seek like liberty. An unwieldy ox, who had fed in an abandoned granary, suddenly lowed, and shewed his shapeless form in a narrow door-way; every thing was desert; but nothing was in ruin. And this medley of undamaged buildings, and luxurious accommodation, in trim and fresh youth, was contrasted with the lonely silence of the unpeopled streets.

Night closed in, and it began to rain. We were about to return homewards, when a voice, a human voice, strange now to hear, attracted our attention. It was a child singing a merry, lightsome air; there was no other sound. We had traversed London from Hyde Park even to where we now were in the Minories, and had met no person, heard no voice nor footstep. The singing was interrupted by laughing and talking; never was merry ditty so sadly timed, never laughter more akin to tears. The door of the house from which these sounds proceeded was open, the upper rooms were illuminated as for a feast. It was a large magnificent house, in which doubtless some rich merchant had lived. The singing again commenced,

---

16   Caesar says this on learning of Antony's death, *Antony and Cleopatra* 5.1.39-40.
17   Here lies ....

and rang through the high-roofed rooms, while we silently ascended the staircase. Lights now appeared to guide us; and a long suite of splendid rooms illuminated, made us still more wonder. Their only inhabitant, a little girl, was dancing, waltzing, and singing about them, followed by a large Newfoundland dog,[18] who boisterously jumping on her, and interrupting her, made her now scold, now laugh, now throw herself on the carpet to play with him. She was dressed grotesquely, in glittering robes and shawls fit for a woman; she appeared about ten years of age. We stood at the door looking on this strange scene, till the dog perceiving us barked loudly; the child turned and saw us: her face, losing its gaiety, assumed a sullen expression: she slunk back, apparently meditating an escape. I came up to her, and held her hand; she did not resist, but with a stern brow, so strange in childhood, so different from her former hilarity, she stood still, her eyes fixed on the ground. "What do you do here?" I said gently; "Who are you?"—she was silent, but trembled violently. "My poor child," asked Adrian, "are you alone?" There was a winning softness in his voice, that went to the heart of the little girl; she looked at him, then snatching her hand from me, threw herself into his arms, clinging round his neck, ejaculating—"Save me! save me!" while her unnatural sullenness dissolved in tears.

"I will save you," he replied, "of what are you afraid? you need not fear my friend, he will do you no harm. Are you alone?"

"No, Lion is with me."

"And your father and mother?—"

"I never had any; I am a charity girl. Every body is gone, gone for a great, great many days; but if they come back and find me out, they will beat me so!"

Her unhappy story was told in these few words: an orphan, taken on pretended charity, ill-treated and reviled, her oppressors had died: unknowing of what had passed around her, she found herself alone; she had not dared venture out, but by the continuance of her solitude her courage revived, her childish vivacity caused her to play a thousand freaks, and with her brute companion she passed a long holiday, fearing nothing but the return of the harsh voices and cruel usage of her protectors. She readily consented to go with Adrian.

In the mean time, while we descanted on alien sorrows, and on a solitude which struck our eyes and not our hearts, while we imagined all of change and suffering that had intervened in these once thronged streets, before, tenantless and abandoned, they became mere kennels for dogs, and stables for cattle:—while we read the death of the world upon the

---

18 See Byron's poem, "Inscription on the Monument of a Newfoundland Dog" (1808); the child's dog, as we find out a little later, is named for the Newfoundland dog, Lyon, that accompanied Byron to Greece in 1823 and was sent to England with his body.

dark fane, and hugged ourselves in the remembrance that we possessed that which was all the world to us—in the meanwhile—

We had arrived from Windsor early in October, and had now been in London about six weeks. Day by day, during that time, the health of my Idris declined: her heart was broken; neither sleep nor appetite, the chosen servants of health, waited on her wasted form. To watch her children hour by hour, to sit by me, drinking deep the dear persuasion that I remained to her, was all her pastime. Her vivacity, so long assumed, her affectionate display of cheerfulness, her light-hearted tone and springy gait were gone. I could not disguise to myself, nor could she conceal, her life-consuming sorrow. Still change of scene, and reviving hopes might restore her; I feared the plague only, and she was untouched by that.

I had left her this evening, reposing after the fatigues of her preparations. Clara sat beside her, relating a story to the two boys. The eyes of Idris were closed: but Clara perceived a sudden change in the appearance of our eldest darling; his heavy lids veiled his eyes, an unnatural colour burnt in his cheeks, his breath became short. Clara looked at the mother; she slept, yet started at the pause the narrator made—Fear of awakening and alarming her, caused Clara to go on at the eager call of Evelyn, who was unaware of what was passing. Her eyes turned alternately from Alfred to Idris; with trembling accents she continued her tale, till she saw the child about to fall: starting forward she caught him, and her cry roused Idris. She looked on her son. She saw death stealing across his features; she laid him on a bed, she held drink to his parched lips.

Yet he might be saved. If I were there, he might be saved; perhaps it was not the plague. Without a counsellor, what could she do? stay and behold him die! Why at that moment was I away? "Look to him, Clara," she exclaimed, "I will return immediately."

She inquired among those who, selected as the companions of our journey, had taken up their residence in our house; she heard from them merely that I had gone out with Adrian. She entreated them to seek me: she returned to her child, he was plunged in a frightful state of torpor; again she rushed down stairs; all was dark, desert, and silent; she lost all self-possession; she ran into the street; she called on my name. The pattering rain and howling wind alone replied to her. Wild fear gave wings to her feet; she darted forward to seek me, she knew not where; but, putting all her thoughts, all her energy, all her being in speed only, most misdirected speed, she neither felt, nor feared, nor paused, but ran right on, till her strength suddenly deserted her so suddenly, that she had not thought to save herself. Her knees failed her, and she fell heavily on the pavement.

She was stunned for a time; but at length rose, and though sorely hurt, still walked on, shedding a fountain of tears, stumbling at times, going she knew not whither, only now and then with feeble voice she called my name, adding with heart-piercing exclamations, that I was cruel and unkind. Human being there was none to reply; and the inclemency of the night had driven the wandering animals to the habitations they had usurped. Her thin dress was drenched with rain; her wet hair clung round her neck; she tottered through the dark streets; till, striking her foot against an unseen impediment, she again fell; she could not rise; she hardly strove; but, gathering up her limbs, she resigned herself to the fury of the elements, and the bitter grief of her own heart. She breathed an earnest prayer to die speedily, for there was no relief but death. While hopeless of safety for herself, she ceased to lament for her dying child, but shed kindly, bitter tears for the grief I should experience in losing her.

While she lay, life almost suspended, she felt a warm, soft hand on her brow, and a gentle female voice asked her, with expressions of tender compassion, if she could not rise? That another human being, sympathetic and kind, should exist near, roused her; half rising, with clasped hands, and fresh springing tears, she entreated her companion to seek for me, to bid me hasten to my dying child, to save him, for the love of heaven, to save him!

The woman raised her; she led her under shelter, she entreated her to return to her home, whither perhaps I had already returned. Idris easily yielded to her persuasions, she leaned on the arm of her friend, she endeavoured to walk on, but irresistible faintness made her pause again and again.

Quickened by the encreasing storm, we had hastened our return, our little charge was placed before Adrian on his horse. There was an assemblage of persons under the portico of our house, in whose gestures I instinctively read some heavy change, some new misfortune. With swift alarm, afraid to ask a single question, I leapt from my horse; the spectators saw me, knew me, and in awful silence divided to make way for me. I snatched a light, and rushing up stairs, and hearing a groan, without reflection I threw open the door of the first room that presented itself. It was quite dark; but, as I stept within, a pernicious scent assailed my senses, producing sickening qualms, which made their way to my very heart, while I felt my leg clasped, and a groan repeated by the person that held me. I lowered my lamp, and saw a negro half clad, writhing under the agony of disease, while he held me with a convulsive grasp. With mixed horror and impatience I strove to disengage myself, and fell on the sufferer; he wound his naked festering arms round me, his face was close to mine, and his breath, death-laden, entered my vitals. For a moment I was overcome, my head was bowed by aching nausea; till, reflection returning, I sprung up, threw the wretch from me, and darting up the staircase, entered the chamber usually inhabited by my family.[19] A dim light shewed me Alfred on a couch; Clara trembling, and paler than whitest snow, had raised him on her arm, holding a cup of water to his lips. I saw

---

19   This first-person account of illness is probably indebted to Charles Brockden Brown's *Arthur Mervyn*: see Appendix C.3.i.

full well that no spark of life existed in that ruined form, his features were rigid, his eyes glazed, his head had fallen back. I took him from her, I laid him softly down, kissed his cold little mouth, and turned to speak in a vain whisper, when loudest sound of thunderlike cannon could not have reached him in his immaterial abode.

And where was Idris? That she had gone out to seek me, and had not returned, were fearful tidings, while the rain and driving wind clattered against the window, and roared round the house. Added to this, the sickening sensation of disease gained upon me; no time was to be lost, if ever I would see her again. I mounted my horse and rode out to seek her, fancying that I heard her voice in every gust, oppressed by fever and aching pain.

I rode in the dark and rain through the labyrinthine streets of unpeopled London. My child lay dead at home; the seeds of mortal disease had taken root in my bosom; I went to seek Idris, my adored, now wandering alone, while the waters were rushing from heaven like a cataract to bathe her dear head in chill damp, her fair limbs in numbing cold. A female stood on the step of a door, and called to me as I gallopped past. It was not Idris; so I rode swiftly on, until a kind of second sight, a reflection back again on my senses of what I had seen but not marked, made me feel sure that another figure, thin, graceful and tall, stood clinging to the foremost person who supported her. In a minute I was beside the suppliant, in a minute I received the sinking Idris in my arms. Lifting her up, I placed her on the horse; she had not strength to support herself; so I mounted behind her, and held her close to my bosom, wrapping my riding-cloak round her, while her companion, whose well known, but changed countenance, (it was Juliet, daughter of the Duke of L ——) could at this moment of horror obtain from me no more than a passing glance of compassion. She took the abandoned rein, and conducted our obedient steed homewards. Dare I avouch it? That was the last moment of my happiness; but I was happy. Idris must die, for her heart was broken: I must die, for I had caught the plague; earth was a scene of desolation; hope was madness; life had married death; they were one; but, thus supporting my fainting love, thus feeling that I must soon die, I revelled in the delight of possessing her once more; again and again I kissed her, and pressed her to my heart.

We arrived at our home. I assisted her to dismount, I carried her up stairs, and gave her into Clara's care, that her wet garments might be changed. Briefly I assured Adrian of her safety, and requested that we might be left to repose. As the miser, who with trembling caution visits his treasure to count it again and again, so I numbered each moment, and grudged every one that was not spent with Idris. I returned swiftly to the chamber where the life of my life reposed; before I entered the room I paused for a few seconds; for a few seconds I tried to examine my state; sickness and shuddering ever and anon came over me; my head was heavy, my chest oppressed, my legs bent under me; but I threw off resolutely the swift growing symptoms of my disorder, and met Idris with placid and even joyous looks. She was lying on a couch; carefully fastening the door to prevent all intrusion; I sat by her, we embraced, and our lips met in a kiss long drawn and breathless—would that moment had been my last!

Maternal feeling now awoke in my poor girl's bosom, and she asked: "And Alfred?" "Idris," I replied, "we are spared to each other, we are together; do not let any other idea intrude. I am happy; even on this fatal night, I declare myself happy, beyond all name, all thought—what would you more, sweet one?"

Idris understood me: she bowed her head on my shoulder and wept. "Why," she again asked, "do you tremble, Lionel, what shakes you thus?"

"Well may I be shaken," I replied, "happy as I am. Our child is dead, and the present hour is dark and ominous. Well may I tremble! but, I am happy, mine own Idris, most happy."

"I understand thee, my kind love," said Idris, "thus—pale as thou art with sorrow at our loss; trembling and aghast, though wouldest assuage my grief by thy dear assurances. I am not happy," (and the tears flashed and fell from under her down-cast lids), "for we are inmates of a miserable prison, and there is no joy for us; but the true love I bear you will render this and every other loss endurable."

"We have been happy together, at least," I said; "no future misery can deprive us of the past. We have been true to each other for years, ever since my sweet princess-love came through the snow to the lowly cottage of the poverty-stricken heir of the ruined Verney. Even now, that eternity is before us, we take hope only from the presence of each other. Idris, do you think, that when we die, we shall be divided?"

"Die! when we die! what mean you? What secret lies hid from me in those dreadful words?"

"Must we not all die, dearest?" I asked with a sad smile.

"Gracious God! are you ill, Lionel, that you speak of death? My only friend, heart of my heart, speak!"

"I do not think," replied I, "that we have any of us long to live; and when the curtain drops on this mortal scene, where, think you, we shall find ourselves?"

Idris was calmed by my unembarrassed tone and look; she answered:—"You may easily believe that during this long progress of the plague, I have thought much on death, and asked myself, now that all mankind is dead to this life, to what other life they may have been borne. Hour after hour, I have dwelt on these thoughts, and strove to form a rational conclusion concerning the mystery of a future state. What a scare-crow, indeed, would death be, if we were merely to cast aside the shadow in which we now walk, and, stepping forth into the unclouded sunshine of knowledge and love, revived with the same companions, the same affections, and reached the fulfilment of our hopes, leaving our fears with our earthly vesture in the grave. Alas! the same strong feeling which makes me sure that I shall not wholly die, makes me refuse to believe that I shall live wholly as I do now. Yet, Lionel, never, never, can I love any but you; through eternity I must desire your society; and, as I am innocent of harm to others, and as relying and confident as my mortal nature permits, I trust that the Ruler of the world will never tear us asunder."

"Your remarks are like yourself, dear love," replied I, "gentle and good; let us cherish such a belief, and dismiss anxiety from our minds. But, sweet, we are so formed, (and there is no sin, if God made our nature, to yield to what he ordains), we are so formed, that we must love life, and cling to it; we must love the living smile, the sympathetic touch, and thrilling voice, peculiar to our mortal mechanism. Let us not, through security in hereafter, neglect the present. This present moment, short as it is, is a part of eternity, and the dearest part, since it is our own unalienably. Thou, the hope of my futurity, art my present joy. Let me then look on thy dear eyes, and, reading love in them, drink intoxicating pleasure."

Timidly, for my vehemence somewhat terrified her, Idris looked on me. My eyes were bloodshot, starting from my head; every artery beat, methought, audibly, every muscle throbbed, each single nerve felt. Her look of wild affright told me, that I could no longer keep my secret:—"So it is, mine own beloved," I said, "the last hour of many happy ones is arrived, nor can we shun any longer the inevitable destiny. I cannot live long—but, again and again, I say, this moment is ours!"

Paler than marble, with white lips and convulsed features, Idris became aware of my situation. My arm, as I sat, encircled her waist, she felt the palm burn with fever, even on the heart it pressed:—"One moment," she murmured, scarce audibly, "only one moment."—

She knelt, and hiding her face in her hands, uttered a brief, but earnest prayer, that she might fulfil her duty, and watch over me to the last. While there was hope, the agony had been unendurable;—all was now concluded; her feelings became solemn and calm. Even as Epicharis,[20] unperturbed and firm, submitted to the instruments of torture, did Idris, suppressing every sigh and sign of grief, enter upon the endurance of torments, of which the rack and the wheel are but faint and metaphysical symbols.

I was changed; the tight-drawn cord that sounded so harshly was loosened, the moment that Idris participated in my knowledge of our real situation. The perturbed and passion-tossed waves of thought subsided, leaving only the heavy swell that kept right on without any outward man-

---

20 Accused of conspiracy against Nero, the slave-woman Epicharis endured torture without naming her associates (Tacitus, *Annals* 15.51). PBS alludes to the story in "A Philosophical View of Reform" and in "Speculations on Morals" (*Works*, ed. Ingpen and Peck 7: 17, 76); in a letter to Byron (12 January 1818) Claire Clairmont pointedly compares Epicharis to MWS herself (*The Clairmont Correspondence* 111).

ifestation of its disturbance, till it should break on the remote shore towards which I rapidly advanced:—"It is true that I am sick," I said, "and your society, my Idris, is my only medicine; come, and sit beside me."

She made me lie down on the couch, and, drawing a low ottoman near, sat close to my pillow, pressing my burning hands in her cold palms. She yielded to my feverish restlessness, and let me talk, and talked to me, on subjects strange indeed to beings, who thus looked the last, and heard the last, of what they loved alone in the world. We talked of times gone by; of the happy period of our early love; of Raymond, Perdita, and Evadne. We talked of what might arise on this desert earth, if, two or three being saved, it were slowly re-peopled.—We talked of what was beyond the tomb; and, man in his human shape being nearly extinct, we felt with certainty of faith, that other spirits, other minds, other perceptive beings, sightless to us, must people with thought and love this beauteous and imperishable universe.

We talked—I know not how long—but, in the morning I awoke from a painful heavy slumber; the pale cheek of Idris rested on my pillow; the large orbs of her eyes half raised the lids, and shewed the deep blue lights beneath; her lips were unclosed, and the slight murmurs they formed told that, even while asleep, she suffered. "If she were dead," I thought, "what difference? now that form is the temple of a residing deity; those eyes are the windows of her soul; all grace, love, and intelligence are throned on that lovely bosom—were she dead, where would this mind, the dearer half of mine, be? For quickly the fair proportion of this edifice would be more defaced, than are the sand-choked ruins of the desert temples of Palmyra."[21]

CHAPTER XXIII

IDRIS stirred and awoke; alas! she awoke to misery. She saw the signs of disease on my countenance, and wondered how she could permit the long night to pass without her having sought, not cure, that was impossible, but alleviation to my sufferings. She called Adrian; my couch was quickly sur-

---

21 Palmyra, the ancient city of Tadmor in the desert of Syria, once ruled by the famous Queen Zenobia. Like Volney's *The Ruins*, *The Last Man, or Omegarus and Syderia* (1806) starts here, in a cave "near the ruins of Palmyra": see below, Appendix B.2 and Appendix D.1. PBS refers in Queen Mab to "Palmyra's ruined palaces" (2.110); see also Thomas Love Peacock, *Palmyra*, which describes "The wanderer of the distant days" marking "with sorrow-clouded gaze, / The mighty wilderness of sand, / While not a sound should meet his ear, / Save of the desert-gales, that sweep, / In modulated murmurs deep, / The wasted graves above / Of those, who once had revelled here / In happiness and love."

rounded by friends and assistants, and such medicines as were judged fitting were administered. It was the peculiar and dreadful distinction of our visitation, that none who had been attacked by the pestilence had recovered.[22] The first symptom of the disease was the death-warrant, which in no single instance had been followed by pardon or reprieve. No gleam of hope therefore cheered my friends.

While fever producing torpor, heavy pains, sitting like lead on my limbs, and making my breast heave, were upon me; I continued insensible to every thing but pain, and at last even to that. I awoke on the fourth morning as from a dreamless sleep. An irritating sense of thirst, and, when I strove to speak or move, an entire dereliction of power, was all I felt.

For three days and nights Idris had not moved from my side. She administered to all my wants, and never slept nor rested. She did not hope; and therefore she neither endeavoured to read the physician's countenance, nor to watch for symptoms of recovery. All her thought was to attend on me to the last, and then to lie down and die beside me. On the third night animation was suspended; to the eye and touch of all I was dead. With earnest prayer, almost with force, Adrian tried to draw Idris from me. He exhausted every adjuration, her child's welfare and his own. She shook her head, and wiped a stealing tear from her sunk cheek, but would not yield; she entreated to be allowed to watch me that one night only, with such affliction and meek earnestness, that she gained her point, and sat silent and motionless, except when, stung by intolerable remembrance, she kissed my closed eyes and pallid lips, and pressed my stiffening hands to her beating heart.

At dead of night, when, though it was mid winter, the cock crowed at three o'clock, as herald of the morning change, while hanging over me, and mourning in silent, bitter thought for the loss of all of love towards her that had been enshrined in my heart; her dishevelled hair hung over her face, and the long tresses fell on the bed; she saw one ringlet in motion, and the scattered hair slightly stirred, as by a breath. It is not so, she thought, for he will never breathe more. Several times the same thing occurred, and she only marked it by the same reflection; till the whole ringlet waved back, and she thought she saw my breast heave. Her first emotion was deadly fear, cold dew stood on her brow; my eyes half opened; and, re-assured, she would have exclaimed, "He lives!" but the words were choked by a spasm, and she fell with a groan on the floor.

Adrian was in the chamber. After long watching, he had unwillingly fallen into a sleep. He started up, and beheld his sister senseless on the earth, weltering in a stream of blood that gushed from her mouth. Encreasing signs of life in me in some degree explained her state; the surprise, the burst of joy, the revulsion of every sentiment, had been too much for her frame, worn by long months of care, late shattered by every

---

22   Lionel (or MWS) makes a mistake here: cf. 212, above.

species of woe and toil. She was now in far greater danger than I, the wheels and springs of my life, once again set in motion, acquired elasticity from their short suspension. For a long time, no one believed that I should indeed continue to live; during the reign of the plague upon earth, not one person, attacked by the grim disease, had recovered. My restoration was looked on as a deception; every moment it was expected that the evil symptoms would recur with redoubled violence, until confirmed convalescence, absence of all fever or pain, and encreasing strength, brought slow conviction that I had recovered from the plague.

The restoration of Idris was more problematical. When I had been attacked by illness, her cheeks were sunk, her form emaciated; but now, the vessel, which had broken from the effects of extreme agitation, did not entirely heal, but was as a channel that drop by drop drew from her the ruddy stream that vivified her heart. Her hollow eyes and worn countenance had a ghastly appearance; her cheek-bones, her open fair brow, the projection of the mouth, stood fearfully prominent; you might tell each bone in the thin anatomy of her frame. Her hand hung powerless; each joint lay bare, so that the light penetrated through and through. It was strange that life could exist in what was wasted and worn into a very type of death.

To take her from these heart-breaking scenes, to lead her to forget the world's desolation in the variety of objects presented by travelling, and to nurse her failing strength in the mild climate towards which we had resolved to journey, was my last hope for her preservation. The preparations for our departure, which had been suspended during my illness, were renewed. I did not revive to doubtful convalescence; health spent her treasures upon me; as the tree in spring may feel from its wrinkled limbs the fresh green break forth, and the living sap rise and circulate, so did the renewed vigour of my frame, the cheerful current of my blood, the new-born elasticity of my limbs, influence my mind to cheerful endurance and pleasurable thoughts. My body, late the heavy weight that bound me to the tomb, was exuberant with health; mere common exercises were insufficient for my reviving strength; methought I could emulate the speed of the race-horse, discern through the air objects at a blinding distance, hear the operations of nature in her mute abodes; my senses had become so refined and susceptible after my recovery from mortal disease.

Hope, among my other blessings, was not denied to me; and I did fondly trust that my unwearied attentions would restore my adored girl. I was therefore eager to forward our preparations. According to the plan first laid down, we were to have quitted London on the twenty-fifth of November; and, in pursuance of this scheme, two-thirds of our people—*the* people—all that remained of England, had gone forward, and had already been some weeks in Paris. First my illness, and subsequently that of Idris, had detained Adrian with his division, which consisted of three hundred persons, so that we now departed on the first of January,

2098. It was my wish to keep Idris as distant as possible from the hurry and clamour of the crowd, and to hide from her those appearances that would remind her most forcibly of our real situation. We separated ourselves to a great degree from Adrian, who was obliged to give his whole time to public business. The Countess of Windsor travelled with her son. Clara, Evelyn, and a female who acted as our attendant, were the only persons with whom we had contact. We occupied a commodious carriage, our servant officiated as coachman. A party of about twenty persons preceded us at a small distance. They had it in charge to prepare our halting places and our nightly abode. They had been selected for this service out of a great number that offered, on account of the superior sagacity of the man who had been appointed their leader.

Immediately on our departure, I was delighted to find a change in Idris, which I fondly hoped prognosticated the happiest results. All the cheerfulness and gentle gaiety natural to her revived. She was weak, and this alteration was rather displayed in looks and voice than in acts; but it was permanent and real. My recovery from the plague and confirmed health instilled into her a firm belief that I was now secure from this dread enemy. She told me that she was sure she should recover. That she had a presentiment, that the tide of calamity which deluged our unhappy race had now turned. That the remnant would be preserved, and among them the dear objects of her tender affection; and that in some selected spot we should wear out our lives together in pleasant society. "Do not let my state of feebleness deceive you," she said; "I feel that I am better; there is a quick life within me, and a spirit of anticipation that assures me, that I shall continue long to make a part of this world. I shall throw off this degrading weakness of body, which infects even my mind with debility, and I shall enter again on the performance of my duties. I was sorry to leave Windsor: but now I am weaned from this local attachment; I am content to remove to a mild climate, which will complete my recovery. Trust me, dearest, I shall neither leave you, nor my brother, nor these dear children; my firm determination to remain with you to the last, and to continue to contribute to your happiness and welfare, would keep me alive, even if grim death were nearer at hand than he really is."

I was only half re-assured by these expressions; I could not believe that the over-quick flow of her blood was a sign of health, or that her burning cheeks denoted convalescence. But I had no fears of an immediate catastrophe; nay, I persuaded myself that she would ultimately recover. And thus cheerfulness reigned in our little society. Idris conversed with animation on a thousand topics. Her chief desire was to lead our thoughts from melancholy reflections; so she drew charming pictures of a tranquil solitude, of a beauteous retreat, of the simple manners of our little tribe, and of the patriarchal brotherhood of love, which would survive the ruins of the populous nations which had lately existed. We shut out from our thoughts the present, and withdrew our eyes from the dreary landscape we traversed. Winter reigned in all its gloom. The leafless trees lay without motion against the dun sky; the forms of frost, mimicking the foliage of summer, strewed the ground; the paths were overgrown; the unploughed cornfields were patched with grass and weeds; the sheep congregated at the threshold of the cottage, the horned ox thrust his head from the window. The wind was bleak, and frequent sleet or snow-storms, added to the melancholy appearance wintry nature assumed.

We arrived at Rochester, and an accident caused us to be detained there a day. During that time, a circumstance occurred that changed our plans, and which, alas! in its result changed the eternal course of events, turning me from the pleasant new sprung hope I enjoyed, to an obscure and gloomy desert. But I must give some little explanation before I proceed with the final cause of our temporary alteration of plan, and refer again to those times when man walked the earth fearless, before Plague had become Queen of the World.

There resided a family in the neighbourhood of Windsor, of very humble pretensions, but which had been an object of interest to us on account of one of the persons of whom it was composed. The family of the Claytons had known better days; but, after a series of reverses, the father died a bankrupt, and the mother heart-broken, and a confirmed invalid, retired with her five children to a little cottage between Eton and Salt Hill. The eldest of these children, who was thirteen years old, seemed at once from the influence of adversity, to acquire the sagacity and principle belonging to a more mature age. Her mother grew worse and worse in health, but Lucy attended on her, and was as a tender parent to her younger brothers and sisters, and in the meantime shewed herself so good-humoured, social, and benevolent, that she was beloved as well as honoured, in her little neighbourhood.

Lucy was besides extremely pretty; so when she grew to be sixteen, it was to be supposed, notwithstanding her poverty, that she should have admirers. One of these was the son of a country-curate; he was a generous, frank-hearted youth, with an ardent love of knowledge, and no mean acquirements. Though Lucy was untaught, her mother's conversation and manners gave her a taste for refinements superior to her present situation. She loved the youth even without knowing it, except that in any difficulty she naturally turned to him for aid, and awoke with a lighter heart every Sunday, because she knew that she would be met and accompanied by him in her evening walk with her sisters. She had another admirer, one of the head-waiters at the inn at Salt Hill. He also was not without pretensions to urbane superiority, such as he learnt from gentlemen's servants and waiting-maids, who initiating him in all the slang of high life below stairs, rendered his arrogant temper ten times more intrusive. Lucy did not disclaim him—she was incapable of that feeling; but she was sorry when she saw him approach, and quietly resisted all his endeavours to establish an intimacy. The fellow soon discovered that his rival was preferred to him; and this changed what was at first a chance admiration into a passion, whose main springs were envy, and a base desire to deprive his competitor of the advantage he enjoyed over himself.

Poor Lucy's sad story was but a common one. Her lover's father died; and he was left destitute. He accepted the offer of a gentleman to go to India with him, feeling secure that he should soon acquire an independence, and return to claim the hand of his beloved. He became involved in the war carried on there, was taken prisoner, and years elapsed before tidings of his existence were received in his native land. In the meantime disastrous poverty came on Lucy. Her little cottage, which stood looking from its trellice, covered with woodbine and jessamine, was burnt down; and the whole of their little property was included in the destruction. Whither betake them? By what exertion of industry could Lucy procure them another abode? Her mother nearly bed-rid, could not survive any extreme of famine-struck poverty. At this time her other admirer stept forward, and renewed his offer of marriage. He had saved money, and was going to set up a little inn at Datchet. There was nothing alluring to Lucy in this offer, except the home it secured to her mother; and she felt more sure of this, since she was struck by the apparent generosity which occasioned the present offer. She accepted it; thus sacrificing herself for the comfort and welfare of her parent.

It was some years after her marriage that we became acquainted with her. The accident of a storm caused us to take refuge in the inn, where we witnessed the brutal and quarrelsome behaviour of her husband, and her patient endurance. Her lot was not a fortunate one. Her first lover had returned with the hope of making her his own, and met her by accident, for the first time, as the mistress of this country inn, and the wife of another. He withdrew despairingly to foreign parts; nothing went well with him; at last he enlisted, and came back again wounded and sick, and yet Lucy was debarred from nursing him. Her husband's brutal disposition was aggravated by his yielding to the many temptations held out by his situation, and the consequent disarrangement of his affairs. Fortunately she had no children; but her heart was bound up in her brothers and sisters, and these his avarice and ill temper soon drove from the house; they were dispersed about the country, earning their livelihood with toil and care. He even shewed an inclination to get rid of her mother—but Lucy was firm here—she had sacrificed herself for her; she lived for her—she would not part with her—if the mother went, she would also go—beg bread for her, die with her, but never desert her. The presence of Lucy was too necessary in keeping up the order of the house, and in preventing the whole establishment from going to wreck, for him to permit her to leave him. He yielded the point; but in all accesses of anger, or in his drunken fits, he recurred to the old topic, and stung poor Lucy's heart by opprobrious epithets bestowed on her parent.

A passion however, if it be wholly pure, entire, and reciprocal, brings with it its own solace. Lucy was truly, and from the depth of heart, devoted to her mother; the sole end she proposed to herself in life, was the comfort and preservation of this parent. Though she grieved for the result, yet she did not repent of her marriage, even when her lover returned to bestow competence on her. Three years had intervened, and how, in their pennyless state, could her mother have existed during this time? This excellent woman was worthy of her child's devotion. A perfect confidence and friendship existed between them; besides, she was by no means illiterate; and Lucy, whose mind had been in some degree culti- vated by her former lover, now found in her the only person who could understand and appreciate her. Thus, though suffering, she was by no means desolate, and when, during fine summer days, she led her mother into the flowery and shady lanes near their abode, a gleam of unmixed joy enlightened her countenance; she saw that her parent was happy, and she knew that this happiness was of her sole creating.

Meanwhile her husband's affairs grew more and more involved; ruin was near at hand, and she was about to lose the fruit of all her labours, when pestilence came to change the aspect of the world. Her husband reaped benefit from the universal misery; but, as the disaster encreased, the spirit of lawlessness seized him; he deserted his home to revel in the luxuries promised him in London, and found there a grave. Her former lover had been one of the first victims of the disease. But Lucy continued to live for and in her mother. Her courage only failed when she dreaded peril for her parent, or feared that death might prevent her from perform- ing those duties to which she was unalterably devoted.

When we had quitted Windsor for London, as the previous step to our final emigration, we visited Lucy, and arranged with her the plan of her own and her mother's removal. Lucy was sorry at the necessity which forced her to quit her native lanes and village, and to drag an infirm par- ent from her comforts at home, to the homeless waste of depopulate earth; but she was too well disciplined by adversity, and of too sweet a temper, to indulge in repinings at what was inevitable.

Subsequent circumstances, my illness and that of Idris, drove her from our remembrance; and we called her to mind at last, only to conclude that she made one of the few who came from Windsor to join the emigrants, and that she was already in Paris. When we arrived at Rochester therefore, we were surprised to receive, by a man just come from Slough, a letter from this exemplary sufferer. His account was, that, journeying from his home, and passing through Datchet, he was surprised to see smoke issue from the chimney of the inn, and supposing that he should find comrades for his journey assembled there, he knocked and was admitted. There was no one in the house but Lucy, and her mother; the latter had been deprived of the use of her limbs by an attack of rheumatism, and so, one by one, all the remaining inhabitants of the country set forward, leaving them alone. Lucy intreated the man to stay with her; in a week or two her mother would be better, and they would then set out; but they must per- ish, if they were left thus helpless and forlorn. The man said, that his wife and children were already among the emigrants, and it was therefore, according to his notion, impossible for him to remain. Lucy, as a last resource, gave him a letter for Idris, to be delivered to her wherever he should meet us. This commission at least he fulfilled, and Idris received with emotion the following letter:—

"HONOURED LADY,

"I am sure that you will remember and pity me, and I dare hope that you will assist me; what other hope have I? Pardon my manner of writing, I am so bewildered. A month ago my dear mother was deprived of the use of her limbs. She is already better, and in another month would I am sure be able to travel, in the way you were so kind as to say you would arrange for us. But now everybody is gone—everybody—as they went away, each said, that perhaps my mother would be better, before we were quite deserted. But three days ago I went to Samuel Woods, who, on account of his newborn child, remained to the last; and there being a large family of them, I thought I could persuade them to wait a little longer for us; but I found the house deserted. I have not seen a soul since, till this good man came.—What will become of us? My mother does not know our state; she is so ill, that I have hidden it from her.

"Will you not send some one to us? I am sure we must perish miserably as we are. If I were to try to move my mother now, she would die on the road; and if, when she gets better, I were able, I cannot guess how, to find out the roads, and get on so many many miles to the sea, you would all be in France, and the great ocean would be between us, which is so terrible even to sailors. What would it be to me, a woman, who never saw it? We should be imprisoned by it in this country, all, all alone, with no help; better die where we are. I can hardly write—I cannot stop my tears—it is not for myself; I could put my trust in God; and let the worst come, I think I could bear it, if I were alone. But my mother, my sick, my dear, dear mother, who never, since I was born, spoke a harsh word to me, who has been patient in many sufferings; pity her, dear Lady, she must die a miserable death if you do not pity her. People speak carelessly of her, because she is old and infirm, as if we must not all, if we are spared, become so; and then, when the young are old themselves, they will think that they ought to be taken care of. It is very silly of me to write in this way to you; but, when I hear her trying not to groan, and see her look smiling on me to comfort me, when I know she is in pain; and when I think that she does not know the worst, but she soon must; and then she will not complain; but I shall sit guessing at all that she is dwelling upon, of famine and misery—I feel as if my heart must break, and I do not know what I say or do; my mother—mother for whom I have borne much, God preserve you from this fate! Preserve her, Lady, and He will bless you; and I, poor miserable creature as I am, will thank you and pray for you while I live.

"Your unhappy and dutiful servant,

Dec. 30th, 2097.   LUCY MARTIN."

This letter deeply affected Idris, and she instantly proposed, that we should return to Datchet, to assist Lucy and her mother. I said that I would without delay set out for that place, but entreated her to join her brother, and there await my return with the children. But Idris was in high spirits, and full of hope. She declared that she could not consent even to a temporary separation from me, but that there was no need of this, the motion of the carriage did her good, and the distance was too trifling to be considered. We could dispatch messengers to Adrian, to inform him of our deviation from the original plan. She spoke with vivacity, and drew a picture after her own dear heart, of the pleasure we should bestow upon Lucy, and declared, if I went, she must accompany me, and that she should very much dislike to entrust the charge of rescuing them to others, who might fulfil it with coldness or inhumanity. Lucy's life had been one act of devotion and virtue; let her now reap the small reward of finding her excellence appreciated, and her necessity assisted, by those whom she respected and honoured.

These, and many other arguments, were urged with gentle pertinacity, and the ardour of a wish to do all the good in her power, by her whose simple expression of a desire and slightest request had ever been a law with me. I, of course, consented, the moment that I saw that she had set her heart upon this step. We sent half our attendant troop on to Adrian; and with the other half our carriage took a retrograde course back to Windsor.

I wonder now how I could be so blind and senseless, as thus to risk the safety of Idris; for, if I had eyes, surely I could see the sure, though deceitful, advance of death in her burning cheek and encreasing weakness. But she said she was better; and I believed her. Extinction could not be near a being, whose vivacity and intelligence hourly encreased, and whose frame was endowed with an intense, and I fondly thought, a strong and permanent spirit of life. Who, after a great disaster, has not looked back with wonder at his inconceivable obtuseness of understanding, that could not perceive the many minute threads with which fate weaves the inextricable net of our destinies, until he is inmeshed completely in it?

The cross roads which we now entered upon, were even in a worse state than the long neglected high-ways; and the inconvenience seemed to menace the perishing frame of Idris with destruction. Passing through Dartford, we arrived at Hampton on the second day. Even in this short interval my beloved companion grew sensibly worse in health, though her spirits were still light, and she cheered my growing anxiety with gay sallies; sometimes the thought pierced my brain—Is she dying?—as I saw her fair fleshless hand rest on mine, or observed the feebleness with which she performed the accustomed acts of life. I drove away the idea, as if it had been suggested by insanity; but it occurred again and again, only to be dispelled by the continued liveliness of her manner.

About mid-day, after quitting Hampton, our carriage broke down: the shock caused Idris to faint, but on her reviving no other ill consequence ensued; our party of attendants had as usual gone on before us, and our coachman went in search of another vehicle, our former one being rendered by this accident unfit for service. The only place near us was a poor village, in which he found a kind of caravan, able to hold four people, but it was clumsy and ill hung; besides this he found a very excellent cabriolet:[23] our plan was soon arranged; I would drive Idris in the latter; while the children were conveyed by the servant in the former. But these arrangements cost time; we had agreed to proceed that night to Windsor, and thither our purveyors had gone: we should find considerable difficulty in getting accommodation, before we reached this place; after all, the distance was only ten miles; my horse was a good one; I would go forward at a good pace with Idris, leaving the children to follow at a rate more consonant to the uses of their cumberous machine.

Evening closed in quickly, far more quickly than I was prepared to expect. At the going down of the sun it began to snow heavily. I attempted in vain to defend my beloved companion from the storm; the wind drove the snow in our faces; and it lay so high on the ground, that we made but small way; while the night was so dark, that but for the white covering on the ground we should not have been able to see a yard before us. We had left our accompanying caravan far behind us; and now I perceived that the storm had made me unconsciously deviate from my intended route. I had gone some miles out of my way. My knowledge of the country enabled me to regain the right road; but, instead of going, as at first agreed upon, by a cross road through Stanwell to Datchet, I was obliged to take the way of Egham and Bishopsgate. It was certain therefore that I should not be rejoined by the other vehicle, that I should not meet a single fellow-creature till we arrived at Windsor.

The back of our carriage was drawn up, and I hung a pelisse before it, thus to curtain the beloved sufferer from the pelting sleet. She leaned on my shoulder, growing every moment more languid and feeble; at first she replied to my words of cheer with affectionate thanks; but by degrees she sunk into silence; her head lay heavily upon me; I only knew that she lived by her irregular breathing and frequent sighs. For a moment I resolved to stop, and, opposing the back of the cabriolet to the force of the tempest, to expect morning as well as I might. But the wind was bleak and piercing, while the occasional shudderings of my poor Idris, and the intense cold I felt myself, demonstrated that this would be a dangerous experiment. At length methought she slept—fatal sleep, induced by frost: at this moment I saw the heavy outline of a cottage traced on the dark horizon close to us: "Dearest love," I said, "support yourself but one moment, and we shall have shelter; let us stop here, that I may open the door of this blessed dwelling."

As I spoke, my heart was transported, and my senses swam with exces-

---

23   A light, two-wheeled, hooded carriage, drawn by one horse.

sive delight and thankfulness; I placed the head of Idris against the carriage, and, leaping out, scrambled through the snow to the cottage, whose door was open. I had apparatus about me for procuring light, and that shewed me a comfortable room, with a pile of wood in one corner, and no appearance of disorder, except that, the door having been left partly open, the snow, drifting in, had blocked up the threshold. I returned to the carriage, and the sudden change from light to darkness at first blinded me. When I recovered my sight—eternal God of this lawless world! O supreme Death! I will not disturb thy silent reign, or mar my tale with fruitless exclamations of horror—I saw Idris, who had fallen from the seat to the bottom of the carriage; her head, its long hair pendent, with one arm, hung over the side.—Struck by a spasm of horror, I lifted her up; her heart was pulseless, her faded lips unfanned by the slightest breath.

I carried her into the cottage; I placed her on the bed. Lighting a fire, I chafed her stiffening limbs; for two long hours I sought to restore departed life; and, when hope was as dead as my beloved, I closed with trembling hands her glazed eyes. I did not doubt what I should now do. In the confusion attendant on my illness, the task of interring our darling Alfred had devolved on his grandmother, the Ex-Queen, and she, true to her ruling passion, had caused him to be carried to Windsor, and buried in the family vault, in St. George's Chapel.[24] I must proceed to Windsor, to calm the anxiety of Clara, who would wait anxiously for us—yet I would fain spare her the heart-breaking spectacle of Idris, brought in by me lifeless from the journey. So first I would place my beloved beside her child in the vault, and then seek the poor children who would be expecting me.

I lighted the lamps of my carriage; I wrapt her in furs, and placed her along the seat; then taking the reins, made the horses go forward. We proceeded through the snow, which lay in masses impeding the way, while the descending flakes, driving against me with redoubled fury, blinded me. The pain occasioned by the angry elements, and the cold iron of the shafts of frost which buffetted me, and entered my aching flesh, were a relief to me; blunting my mental suffering. The horses staggered on, and the reins hung loosely in my hands. I often thought I would lay my head close to the sweet, cold face of my lost angel, and thus resign myself to conquering torpor. Yet I must not leave her a prey to the fowls of the air; but, in pursuance of my determination place her in the tomb of her forefathers, where a merciful God might permit me to rest also.

The road we passed through Egham was familiar to me; but the wind and snow caused the horses to drag their load slowly and heavily. Suddenly the wind veered from south-west to west, and then again to north-west. As Sampson with tug and strain stirred from their bases the

---

24 The royal chapel at Windsor; William Godwin, *History of the Commonwealth* (2: 684), reminds readers that both Henry VIII and Charles I are buried in a vault beneath.

columns that supported the Philistine temple,[25] so did the gale shake the dense vapours propped on the horizon, while the massy dome of clouds fell to the south, disclosing through the scattered web the clear empyrean, and the little stars, which were set at an immeasurable distance in the crystalline fields, showered their small rays on the glittering snow. Even the horses were cheered, and moved on with renovated strength. We entered the forest at Bishopgate, and at the end of the Long Walk I saw the Castle, "the proud Keep of Windsor, rising in the majesty of proportion, girt with the double belt of its kindred and coeval towers."[26] I looked with reverence on a structure, ancient almost as the rock on which it stood, abode of kings, theme of admiration for the wise. With greater reverence and tearful affection I beheld it as the asylum of the long lease of love I had enjoyed there with the perishable, unmatchable treasure of dust, which now lay cold beside me. Now indeed, I could have yielded to all the softness of my nature, and wept; and, womanlike, have uttered bitter plaints; while the familiar trees, the herds of living deer, the sward oft prest by her fairy-feet, one by one with sad association presented themselves. The white gate at the end of the Long Walk was wide open, and I rode up the empty town through the first gate of the feudal tower; and now St. George's Chapel, with its blackened fretted sides, was right before me. I halted at its door, which was open; I entered, and placed my lighted lamp on the altar; then I returned, and with tender caution I bore Idris up the aisle into the chancel, and laid her softly down on the carpet which covered the step leading to the communion table. The banners of the knights of the garter, and their half drawn swords, were hung in vain emblazonry above the stalls. The banner of her family hung there, still surmounted by its regal crown. Farewell to the glory and heraldry of England!—I turned from such vanity with a slight feeling of wonder, at how mankind could have ever been interested in such things. I bent over the lifeless corpse of my beloved; and, while looking on her uncovered face, the features already contracted by the rigidity of death, I felt as if all the visible universe had grown as soulless, inane, and comfortless as the clay-cold image beneath me. I felt for a moment the intolerable sense of struggle with, and detestation for, the laws which govern the world; till the calm still visible on the face of my dead love recalled me to a more soothing tone of mind, and I proceeded to fulfil the last office that could now be paid her. For her I could not lament, so much I envied her enjoyment of "the sad immunities of the grave."[27]

---

25 See Judges 16.29-30.

26 Edmund Burke, *A Letter to a Noble Lord*, offers this as a comparison to the monarchy (*Writings and Speeches of Edmund Burke* 9: 172).

27 According to Burke, the French revolutionaries "pursue, even such as me, into the obscurest retreats, and haul them before their revolutionary tribunals. Neither sex, nor age—not the sanctuary of the tomb is sacred to them. They

The vault had been lately opened to place our Alfred therein. The ceremony customary in these latter days had been cursorily performed, and the pavement of the chapel, which was its entrance, having been removed, had not been replaced. I descended the steps, and walked through the long passage to the large vault which contained the kindred dust of my Idris. I distinguished the small coffin of my babe. With hasty, trembling hands I constructed a bier beside it, spreading it with the furs and Indian shawls, which had wrapt Idris in her journey thither. I lighted the glimmering lamp, which flickered in this damp abode of the dead; then I bore my lost one to her last bed, decently composing her limbs, and covering them with a mantle, veiling all except her face, which remained lovely and placid. She appeared to rest like one over-wearied, her beauteous eyes steeped in sweet slumber. Yet, so it was not—she was dead! How intensely I then longed to lie down beside her, to gaze till death should gather me to the same repose.

But death does not come at the bidding of the miserable. I had lately recovered from mortal illness, and my blood had never flowed with such an even current, nor had my limbs ever been so instinct with quick life, as now. I felt that my death must be voluntary. Yet what more natural than famine, as I watched in this chamber of mortality, placed in a world of the dead, beside the lost hope of my life? Meanwhile as I looked on her, the features, which bore a sisterly resemblance to Adrian, brought my thoughts back again to the living, to this dear friend, to Clara, and to Evelyn, who were probably now in Windsor, waiting anxiously for our arrival.

Methought I heard a noise, a step in the far chapel, which was re-echoed by its vaulted roof, and borne to me through the hollow passages. Had Clara seen my carriage pass up the town, and did she seek me here? I must save her at least from the horrible scene the vault presented. I sprung up the steps, and then saw a female figure, bent with age, and clad in long mourning robes, advance through the dusky chapel, supported by a slender cane, yet tottering even with this support. She heard me, and looked up; the lamp I held illuminated my figure, and the moon-beams, struggling through the painted glass, fell upon her face, wrinkled and gaunt, yet with a piercing eye and commanding brow—I recognized the Countess of Windsor. With a hollow voice she asked, "Where is the princess?"

I pointed to the torn up pavement: she walked to the spot, and looked down into the palpable darkness; for the vault was too distant for the rays of the small lamp I had left there to be discernible.

"Your light," she said. I gave it her; and she regarded the now visible, but precipitous steps, as if calculating her capacity to descend.

---

have so determined a hatred to all privileged orders, that they deny even to the departed, the sad immunities of the grave" (*A Letter to a Noble Lord, Writings and Speeches of Edmund Burke* 9: 147).

Instinctively I made a silent offer of my assistance. She motioned me away with a look of scorn, saying in an harsh voice, as she pointed downwards, "There at least I may have her undisturbed."

She walked deliberately down, while I, overcome, miserable beyond words, or tears, or groans, threw myself on the pavement near—the stiffening form of Idris was before me, the death-struck countenance hushed in eternal repose beneath. That was to me the end of all! The day before, I had figured to my self various adventures, and communion with my friends in after time—now I had leapt the interval, and reached the utmost edge and bourne of life. Thus wrapt in gloom, enclosed, walled up, vaulted over by the omnipotent present, I was startled by the sound of feet on the steps of the tomb, and I remembered her whom I had utterly forgotten, my angry visitant; her tall form slowly rose upwards from the vault, a living statue, instinct with hate, and human, passionate strife: she seemed to me as having reached the pavement of the aisle; she stood motionless, seeking with her eyes alone, some desired object—till, perceiving me close to her, she placed her wrinkled hand on my arm, exclaiming with tremulous accents, "Lionel Verney, my son!" This name, applied at such a moment by my angel's mother, instilled into me more respect than I had ever before felt for this disdainful lady. I bowed my head, and kissed her shrivelled hand, and, remarking that she trembled violently, supported her to the end of the chancel, where she sat on the steps that led to the regal stall. She suffered herself to be led, and still holding my hand, she leaned her head back against the stall, while the moon beams, tinged with various colours by the painted glass, fell on her glistening eyes; aware of her weakness, again calling to mind her long cherished dignity, she dashed the tears away; yet they fell fast, as she said, for excuse, "She is so beautiful and placid, even in death. No harsh feeling ever clouded her serene brow; how did I treat her? wounding her gentle heart with savage coldness; I had no compassion on her in past years, does she forgive me now? Little, little does it boot to talk of repentance and forgiveness to the dead, had I during her life once consulted her gentle wishes, and curbed my rugged nature to do her pleasure, I should not feel thus."

Idris and her mother were unlike in person. The dark hair, deep-set black eyes, and prominent features of the Ex-Queen were in entire contrast to the golden tresses, the full blue orbs, and the soft lines and contour of her daughter's countenance. Yet, in latter days, illness had taken from my poor girl the full outline of her face, and reduced it to the inflexible shape of the bone beneath. In the form of her brow, in her oval chin, there was to be found a resemblance to her mother; nay in some moods, their gestures were not unlike; nor, having lived so long together, was this wonderful.

There is a magic power in resemblance. When one we love dies, we hope to see them in another state, and half expect that the agency of mind will inform its new garb in imitation of its decayed earthly vesture. But these are ideas of the mind only. We know that the instrument is shivered, the sensible image lies in miserable fragments, dissolved to dusty nothingness; a look, a gesture, or a fashioning of the limbs similar to the dead in a living person, touches a thrilling chord, whose sacred harmony is felt in the heart's dearest recess. Strangely moved, prostrate before this spectral image, and enslaved by the force of blood manifested in likeness of look and movement, I remained trembling in the presence of the harsh, proud, and till now unloved mother of Idris.

Poor, mistaken woman! in her tenderest mood before, she had cherished the idea, that a word, a look of reconciliation from her, would be received with joy, and repay long years of severity. Now that the time was gone for the exercise of such power, she fell at once upon the thorny truth of things, and felt that neither smile nor caress could penetrate to the unconscious state, or influence the happiness of her who lay in the vault beneath. This conviction, together with the remembrance of soft replies to bitter speeches, of gentle looks repaying angry glances; the perception of the falsehood, paltryness and futility of her cherished dreams of birth and power; the overpowering knowledge, that love and life were the true emperors of our mortal state; all, as a tide, rose, and filled her soul with stormy and bewildering confusion. It fell to my lot, to come as the influential power, to allay the fierce tossing of these tumultuous waves. I spoke to her; I led her to reflect how happy Idris had really been, and how her virtues and numerous excellencies had found scope and estimation in her past career. I praised her, the idol of my heart's dear worship, the admired type of feminine perfection. With ardent and overflowing eloquence, I relieved my heart from its burthen, and awoke to the sense of a new pleasure in life, as I poured forth the funeral eulogy. Then I referred to Adrian, her loved brother, and to her surviving child. I declared, which I had before almost forgotten, what my duties were with regard to these valued portions of herself, and bade the melancholy repentant mother reflect, how she could best expiate unkindness towards the dead, by redoubled love of the survivors. Consoling her, my own sorrows were assuaged; my sincerity won her entire conviction.

She turned to me. The hard, inflexible, persecuting woman, turned with a mild expression of face, and said, "If our beloved angel sees us now, it will delight her to find that I do you even tardy justice. You were worthy of her; and from my heart I am glad that you won her away from me. Pardon, my son, the many wrongs I have done you; forget my bitter words and unkind treatment—take me, and govern me as you will."

I seized this docile moment to propose our departure from the church. "First," she said, "let us replace the pavement above the vault."

We drew near to it; "Shall we look on her again?" I asked.

"I cannot," she replied, "and, I pray you, neither do you. We need not torture ourselves by gazing on the soulless body, while her living spirit is buried quick in our hearts, and her surpassing loveliness is so deeply carved there, that sleeping or waking she must ever be present to us."

For a few moments, we bent in solemn silence over the open vault. I consecrated my future life, to the embalming of her dear memory; I vowed to serve her brother and her child till death. The convulsive sob of my companion made me break off my internal orisons. I next dragged the stones over the entrance of the tomb, and closed the gulph that contained the life of my life. Then, supporting my decrepid fellow-mourner, we slowly left the chapel. I felt, as I stepped into the open air, as if I had quitted an happy nest of repose, for a dreary wilderness, a tortuous path, a bitter, joyless, hopeless pilgrimage.

CHAPTER XXIV

OUR escort had been directed to prepare our abode for the night at the inn, opposite the ascent to the Castle. We could not again visit the halls and familiar chambers of our home, on a mere visit. We had already left for ever the glades of Windsor, and all of coppice, flowery hedgerow, and murmuring stream, which gave shape and intensity to the love of our country, and the almost superstitious attachment with which we regarded native England. It had been our intention to have called at Lucy's dwelling in Datchet, and to have re-assured her with promises of aid and protection before we repaired to our quarters for the night. Now, as the Countess of Windsor and I turned down the steep hill that led from the Castle, we saw the children, who had just stopped in their caravan, at the inn-door. They had passed through Datchet without halting. I dreaded to meet them, and to be the bearer of my tragic story, so while they were still occupied in the hurry of arrival, I suddenly left them, and through the snow and clear moon-light air, hastened along the well known road to Datchet.

Well known indeed it was. Each cottage stood on its accustomed site, each tree wore its familiar appearance. Habit had graven uneraseably on my memory, every turn and change of object on the road. At a short distance beyond the Little Park, was an elm half blown down by a storm, some ten years ago; and still, with leafless snow-laden branches, it stretched across the pathway, which wound through a meadow, beside a shallow brook, whose brawling was silenced by frost—that stile, that white gate, that hollow oak tree, which doubtless once belonged to the forest, and which now shewed in the moonlight its gaping rent; to whose fanciful appearance, tricked out by the dusk into a resemblance of the human form, the children had given the name of Falstaff;[28]—all these

---

28   Falstaff, Shakespeare's most famous comic character, appears in *1* and *2 Henry IV* and *The Merry Wives of Windsor*, and is mentioned in *Henry V*. Many of the places around Windsor mentioned in *The Last Man*—Windsor Park, Datchet, Eton, Frogmore—are also associated with Falstaff in *Merry Wives*.

objects were as well known to me as the cold hearth of my deserted home, and every moss-grown wall and plot of orchard ground, alike as twin lambs are to each other in a stranger's eye, yet to my accustomed gaze bore differences, distinction, and a name. England remained, though England was dead—it was the ghost of merry England that I beheld, under those greenwood shade passing generations had sported in security and ease. To this painful recognition of familiar places, was added a feeling experienced by all, understood by none—a feeling as if in some state, less visionary than a dream, in some past real existence, I had seen all I saw, with precisely the same feelings as I now beheld them—as if all my sensations were a duplex mirror of a former revelation. To get rid of this oppressive sense I strove to imagine change in this tranquil spot—this augmented my mood, by causing me to bestow more attention on the objects which occasioned me pain.

I reached Datchet and Lucy's humble abode—once noisy with Saturday night revellers, or trim and neat on Sunday morning it had borne testimony to the labours and orderly habits of the housewife. The snow lay high about the door, as if it had remained unclosed for many days.

"What scene of death hath Roscius now to act?"[29]

I muttered to myself as I looked at the dark casements. At first I thought I saw a light in one of them, but it proved to be merely the refraction of the moon-beams, while the only sound was the crackling branches as the breeze whirred the snow flakes from them—the moon sailed high and unclouded in the interminable ether, while the shadow of the cottage lay black on the garden behind. I entered this by the open wicket, and anxiously examined each window. At length I detected a ray of light struggling through a closed shutter in one of the upper rooms—it was a novel feeling, alas! to look at any house and say there dwells its usual inmate—the door of the house was merely on the latch: so I entered and ascended the moon-lit staircase. The door of the inhabited room was ajar: looking in, I saw Lucy sitting as at work at the table on which the light stood; the implements of needlework were about her, but her hand had fallen on her lap, and her eyes, fixed on the ground, shewed by their vacancy that her thoughts wandered. Traces of care and watching had diminished her former attractions—but her simple dress and cap, her desponding attitude, and the single candle that cast its light upon her, gave for a moment a picturesque grouping to the whole. A fearful reality recalled me from the thought—a figure lay stretched on the bed covered by a sheet—her mother was dead, and Lucy, apart from all the world,

---

29   *3 Henry VI* 5.6.10; Roscius was a famous comic actor in ancient Rome. William Godwin's *Caleb Williams* also quotes this line after his master, Falkland, has caught him in the act of opening the secret chest.

deserted and alone, watched beside the corpse during the weary night. I entered the room, and my unexpected appearance at first drew a scream from the lone survivor of a dead nation; but she recognised me, and recovered herself, with the quick exercise of self-control habitual to her. "Did you not expect me?" I asked, in that low voice which the presence of the dead makes us as it were instinctively assume.

"You are very good," replied she, "to have come yourself; I can never thank you sufficiently; but it is too late."

"Too late," cried I, "what do you mean? It is not too late to take you from this deserted place, and conduct you to—"

My own loss, which I had forgotten as I spoke, now made me turn away, while choking grief impeded my speech. I threw open the window, and looked on the cold, waning, ghastly, misshaped circle on high, and the chill white earth beneath—did the spirit of sweet Idris sail along the moon-frozen crystal air?—No, no, a more genial atmosphere, a lovelier habitation was surely hers!

I indulged in this meditation for a moment, and then again addressed the mourner, who stood leaning against the bed with that expression of resigned despair, of complete misery, and a patient sufferance of it, which is far more touching than any of the insane ravings or wild gesticulation of untamed sorrow. I desired to draw her from this spot; but she opposed my wish. That class of persons whose imagination and sensibility have never been taken out of the narrow circle immediately in view, if they possess these qualities to any extent, are apt to pour their influence into the very realities which appear to destroy them, and to cling to these with double tenacity from not being able to comprehend any thing beyond. Thus Lucy, in desert England, in a dead world, wished to fulfil the usual ceremonies of the dead, such as were customary to the English country people, when death was a rare visitant, and gave us time to receive his dreaded usurpation with pomp and circumstance—going forth in procession to deliver the keys of the tomb into his conquering hand. She had already, alone as she was, accomplished some of these, and the work on which I found her employed, was her mother's shroud. My heart sickened at such detail of woe, which a female can endure, but which is more painful to the masculine spirit than deadliest struggle, or throes of unutterable but transient agony.

This must not be, I told her; and then, as further inducement, I communicated to her my recent loss, and gave her the idea that she must come with me to take charge of the orphan children, whom the death of Idris had deprived of a mother's care. Lucy never resisted the call of a duty, so she yielded, and closing the casements and doors with care, she accompanied me back to Windsor. As we went she communicated to me the occasion of her mother's death. Either by some mischance she had got sight of Lucy's letter to Idris, or she had overheard her conversation with the countryman who bore it; however it might be, she obtained a knowledge of the appalling situation of herself and her daughter, her aged frame could not sustain the anxiety and horror this discovery instilled—she concealed her knowledge from Lucy, but brooded over it through sleepless nights, till fever and delirium, swift forerunners of death, disclosed the secret. Her life, which had long been hovering on its extinction, now yielded at once to the united effects of misery and sickness, and that same morning she had died.

After the tumultuous emotions of the day, I was glad to find on my arrival at the inn that my companions had retired to rest. I gave Lucy in charge to the Countess's attendant, and then sought repose from my various struggles and impatient regrets. For a few moments the events of the day floated in disastrous pageant through my brain, till sleep bathed it in forgetfulness; when morning dawned and I awoke, it seemed as if my slumber had endured for years.

My companions had not shared my oblivion. Clara's swollen eyes shewed that she had passed the night in weeping. The Countess looked haggard and wan. Her firm spirit had not found relief in tears, and she suffered the more from all the painful retrospect and agonizing regret that now occupied her. We departed from Windsor, as soon as the burial rites had been performed for Lucy's mother, and, urged on by an impatient desire to change the scene, went forward towards Dover with speed, our escort having gone before to provide horses; finding them either in the warm stables they instinctively sought during the cold weather, or standing shivering in the bleak fields ready to surrender their liberty in exchange for offered corn.

During our ride the Countess recounted to me the extraordinary circumstances which had brought her so strangely to my side in the chancel of St. George's chapel. When last she had taken leave of Idris, as she looked anxiously on her faded person and pallid countenance, she had suddenly been visited by a conviction that she saw her for the last time. It was hard to part with her while under the dominion of this sentiment, and for the last time she endeavoured to persuade her daughter to commit herself to her nursing, permitting me to join Adrian. Idris mildly refused, and thus they separated. The idea that they should never again meet grew on the Countess's mind, and haunted her perpetually; a thousand times she had resolved to turn back and join us, and was again and again restrained by the pride and anger of which she was the slave. Proud of heart as she was, she bathed her pillow with nightly tears, and through the day was subdued by nervous agitation and expectation of the dreaded event, which she was wholly incapable of curbing. She confessed that at this period her hatred of me knew no bounds, since she considered me as the sole obstacle to the fulfilment of her dearest wish, that of attending upon her daughter in her last moments. She desired to express her fears to her son, and to seek consolation from his sympathy with, or courage from his rejection of, her auguries.

On the first day of her arrival at Dover she walked with him on the sea beach, and with the timidity characteristic of passionate and exaggerated feeling was by degrees bringing the conversation to the desired point, when she could communicate her fears to him, when the messenger who bore my letter announcing our temporary return to Windsor, came riding down to them. He gave some oral account of how he had left us, and added, that notwithstanding the cheerfulness and good courage of Lady Idris, he was afraid that she would hardly reach Windsor alive.

"True," said the Countess, "your fears are just, she is about to expire!"

As she spoke, her eyes were fixed on a tomb-like hollow of the cliff, and she saw, she averred the same to me with solemnity, Idris pacing slowly towards this cave. She was turned from her, her head was bent down, her white dress was such as she was accustomed to wear, except that a thin crape-like veil covered her golden tresses, and concealed her as a dim transparent mist. She looked dejected, as docilely yielding to a commanding power; she submissively entered, and was lost in the dark recess.

"Were I subject to visionary moods," said the venerable lady, as she continued her narrative, "I might doubt my eyes, and condemn my credulity; but reality is the world I live in, and what I saw I doubt not had existence beyond myself. From that moment I could not rest; it was worth my existence to see her once again before she died; I knew that I should not accomplish this, yet I must endeavour. I immediately departed for Windsor; and, though I was assured that we travelled speedily, it seemed to me that our progress was snail-like, and that delays were created solely for my annoyance. Still I accused you, and heaped on your head the fiery ashes of my burning impatience. It was no disappointment, though an agonizing pang, when you pointed to her last abode; and words would ill express the abhorrence I that moment felt towards you, the triumphant impediment to my dearest wishes. I saw her, and anger, and hate, and injustice died at her bier, giving place at their departure to a remorse (Great God, that I should feel it!) which must last while memory and feeling endure."

To medicine such remorse, to prevent awakening love and new-born mildness from producing the same bitter fruit that hate and harshness had done, I devoted all my endeavours to soothe the venerable penitent. Our party was a melancholy one; each was possessed by regret for what was remediless; for the absence of his mother shadowed even the infant gaiety of Evelyn. Added to this was the prospect of the uncertain future. Before the final accomplishment of any great voluntary change the mind vacillates, now soothing itself by fervent expectation, now recoiling from obstacles which seem never to have presented themselves before with so frightful an aspect. An involuntary tremor ran through me when I thought that in another day we might have crossed the watery barrier, and have set forward on that hopeless, interminable, sad wandering, which but a short time before I regarded as the only relief to sorrow that our situation afforded.

Our approach to Dover was announced by the loud roarings of the wintry sea. They were borne miles inland by the sound-laden blast, and by their unaccustomed uproar, imparted a feeling of insecurity and peril to our stable abode. At first we hardly permitted ourselves to think that any unusual eruption of nature caused this tremendous war of air and water, but rather fancied that we merely listened to what we had heard a thousand times before, when we had watched the flocks of fleece-crowned waves, driven by the winds, come to lament and die on the barren sands and pointed rocks. But we found upon advancing farther, that Dover was overflowed—many of the houses were overthrown by the surges which filled the streets, and with hideous brawlings sometimes retreated leaving the pavement of the town bare, till again hurried forward by the influx of ocean, they returned with thunder-sound to their usurped station.

Hardly less disturbed than the tempestuous world of waters was the assembly of human beings, that from the cliff fearfully watched its ravings. On the morning of the arrival of the emigrants under the conduct of Adrian, the sea had been serene and glassy, the slight ripples refracted the sunbeams, which shed their radiance through the clear blue frosty air. This placid appearance of nature was hailed as a good augury for the voyage, and the chief immediately repaired to the harbour to examine two steam-boats which were moored there. On the following midnight, when all were at rest, a frightful storm of wind and clattering rain and hail first disturbed them, and the voice of one shrieking in the streets, that the sleepers must awake or they would be drowned; and when they rushed out, half clothed, to discover the meaning of this alarm, they found that the tide, rising above every mark, was rushing into the town. They ascended the cliff, but the darkness permitted only the white crest of waves to be seen, while the roaring wind mingled its howlings in dire accord with the wild surges. The awful hour of night, the utter inexperience of many who had never seen the sea before, the wailing of women and cries of children added to the horror of the tumult.

All the following day the same scene continued. When the tide ebbed, the town was left dry; but on its flow, it rose even higher than on the preceding night. The vast ships that lay rotting in the roads were whirled from their anchorage, and driven and jammed against the cliff, the vessels in the harbour were flung on land like sea-weed, and there battered to pieces by the breakers. The waves dashed against the cliff, which if in any place it had been before loosened, now gave way, and the affrighted crowd saw vast fragments of the near earth fall with crash and roar into the deep. This sight operated differently on different persons. The greater part thought it a judgment of God, to prevent or punish our emigration from our native land. Many were doubly eager to quit a nook of ground now become their prison, which appeared unable to resist the inroads of ocean's giant waves.

When we arrived at Dover, after a fatiguing day's journey, we all required rest and sleep; but the scene acting around us soon drove away such ideas. We were drawn, along with the greater part of our companions, to the edge of the cliff, there to listen to and make a thousand conjectures. A fog narrowed our horizon to about a quarter of a mile, and the misty veil, cold and dense, enveloped sky and sea in equal obscurity. What added to our inquietude was the circumstance that two-thirds of our original number were now waiting for us in Paris, and clinging, as we now did most painfully, to any addition to our melancholy remnant, this division, with the tameless impassable ocean between, struck us with affright. At length, after loitering for several hours on the cliff, we retired to Dover Castle, whose roof sheltered all who breathed the English air, and sought the sleep necessary to restore strength and courage to our worn frames and languid spirits.

Early in the morning Adrian brought me the welcome intelligence that the wind had changed: it had been south-west; it was now north-east. The sky was stripped bare of clouds by the increasing gale, while the tide at its ebb seceded entirely from the town. The change of wind rather increased the fury of the sea, but it altered its late dusky hue to a bright green; and in spite of its unmitigated clamour, its more cheerful appearance instilled hope and pleasure. All day we watched the raging of the mountainous waves, and towards sunset a desire to decypher the promise for the morrow at its setting, made us all gather with one accord on the edge of the cliff. When the mighty luminary approached within a few degrees of the tempest-tossed horizon, suddenly, a wonder! three other suns,[30] alike burning and brilliant, rushed from various quarters of the heavens towards the great orb; they whirled round it. The glare of light was intense to our dazzled eyes; the sun itself seemed to join in the dance, while the sea burned like a furnace, like all Vesuvius a-light, with flowing lava beneath. The horses broke loose from their stalls in terror—a herd of cattle, panic struck, raced down to the brink of the cliff, and blinded by light, plunged down with frightful yells in the waves below. The time occupied by the apparition of these meteors was comparatively short; suddenly the three mock suns united in one, and plunged into the sea. A few seconds afterwards, a deafening watery sound came up with awful peal from the spot where they had disappeared.

Meanwhile the sun, disencumbered from his strange satellites, paced with its accustomed majesty towards its western home. When—we dared not trust our eyes late dazzled, but it seemed that—the sea rose to meet it—it mounted higher and higher, till the fiery globe was obscured, and the wall of water still ascended the horizon; it appeared as if suddenly the motion of earth was revealed to us—as if no longer we were ruled by ancient laws, but were turned adrift in an unknown region of space. Many cried aloud, that these were no meteors, but globes of burning matter, which had set fire to the earth, and caused the vast cauldron at our feet to

---

30 These meteors recall those that presage the plague in Daniel Defoe's *A Journal of the Plague Year* 40-42. See below, Appendix C.2.i.

bubble up with its measureless waves; the day of judgment was come they averred, and a few moments would transport us before the awful countenance of the omnipotent judge; while those less given to visionary terrors, declared that two conflicting gales had occasioned the last phænomenon. In support of this opinion they pointed out the fact that the east wind died away, while the rushing of the coming west mingled its wild howl with the roar of the advancing waters. Would the cliff resist this new battery? Was not the giant wave far higher than the precipice? Would not our little island be deluged by its approach? The crowd of spectators fled. They were dispersed over the fields, stopping now and then, and looking back in terror. A sublime sense of awe calmed the swift pulsations of my heart—I awaited the approach of the destruction menaced, with that solemn resignation which an unavoidable necessity instils. The ocean every moment assumed a more terrific aspect, while the twilight was dimmed by the rack which the west wind spread over the sky. By slow degrees however, as the wave advanced, it took a more mild appearance; some under current of air, or obstruction in the bed of the waters, checked its progress, and it sank gradually; while the surface of the sea became uniformly higher as it dissolved into it. This change took from us the fear of an immediate catastrophe, although we were still anxious as to the final result. We continued during the whole night to watch the fury of the sea and the pace of the driving clouds, through whose openings the rare stars rushed impetuously; the thunder of conflicting elements deprived us of all power to sleep.

This endured ceaselessly for three days and nights. The stoutest hearts quailed before the savage enmity of nature; provisions began to fail us, though every day foraging parties were dispersed to the nearer towns. In vain we schooled ourselves into the belief, that there was nothing out of the common order of nature in the strife we witnessed; our disasterous and overwhelming destiny turned the best of us to cowards. Death had hunted us through the course of many months, even to the narrow strip of time on which we now stood; narrow indeed, and buffeted by storms, was our footway overhanging the great sea of calamity—

> As an unsheltered northern shore
> Is shaken by the wintry wave—
> And frequent storms for evermore,
> (While from the west the loud winds rave,
> Or from the east, or mountains hoar)
> The struck and tott'ring sand-bank lave.[31]

It required more than human energy to bear up against the menaces of destruction that every where surrounded us.

---

31   Chorus in Œdipus Coloneus [MWS's note]; unidentified translation.

After the lapse of three days, the gale died away, the sea-gull sailed upon the calm bosom of the windless atmosphere, and the last yellow leaf on the topmost branch of the oak hung without motion. The sea no longer broke with fury; but a swell setting in steadily for shore, with long sweep and sullen burst replaced the roar of the breakers. Yet we derived hope from the change, and we did not doubt that after the interval of a few days the sea would resume its tranquillity. The sunset of the fourth day favoured this idea; it was clear and golden. As we gazed on the purple sea, radiant beneath, we were attracted by a novel spectacle; a dark speck—as it neared, visibly a boat, rode on the top of the waves, every now and then lost in the steep vallies between. We marked its course with eager questionings; and, when we saw that it evidently made for shore, we descended to the only practicable landing place, and hoisted a signal to direct them. By the help of glasses we distinguished her crew; it consisted of nine men, Englishmen, belonging in truth to the two divisions of our people, who had preceded us, and had been for several weeks at Paris. As countryman was wont to meet countryman in distant lands, did we greet our visitors on their landing, with outstretched hands and gladsome welcome. They were slow to reciprocate our gratulations. They looked angry and resentful; not less than the chafed sea which they had traversed with imminent peril, though apparently more displeased with each other than with us. It was strange to see these human beings, who appeared to be given forth by the earth like rare and inestimable plants, full of towering passion, and the spirit of angry contest. Their first demand was to be conducted to the Lord Protector of England, so they called Adrian, though he had long discarded the empty title, as a bitter mockery of the shadow to which the Protectorship was now reduced. They were speedily led to Dover Castle, from whose keep Adrian had watched the movements of the boat. He received them with the interest and wonder so strange a visitation created. In the confusion occasioned by their angry demands for precedence, it was long before we could discover the secret meaning of this strange scene. By degrees, from the furious declamations of one, the fierce interruptions of another, and the bitter scoffs of a third, we found that they were deputies from our colony at Paris, from three parties there formed, who, each with angry rivalry, tried to attain a superiority over the other two. These deputies had been dispatched by them to Adrian, who had been selected arbiter; and they had journied from Paris to Calais, through the vacant towns and desolate country, indulging the while violent hatred against each other; and now they pleaded their several causes with unmitigated party-spirit.

By examining the deputies apart, and after much investigation, we learnt the true state of things at Paris. Since parliament had elected him Ryland's deputy, all the surviving English had submitted to Adrian. He was our captain to lead us from our native soil to unknown lands, our lawgiver and our preserver. On the first arrangement of our scheme of emigration, no continued separation of our members was contemplated, and the command of the whole body in gradual ascent of power had its apex in the Earl of Windsor. But unforeseen circumstances changed our plans for us, and occasioned the greater part of our numbers to be divided for the space of nearly two months, from the supreme chief. They had gone over in two distinct bodies; and on their arrival at Paris dissension arose between them.

They had found Paris a desert. When first the plague had appeared, the return of travellers and merchants, and communications by letter, informed us regularly of the ravages made by disease on the continent. But with the encreased mortality this intercourse declined and ceased. Even in England itself communication from one part of the island to the other became slow and rare. No vessel stemmed the flood that divided Calais from Dover; or if some melancholy voyager, wishing to assure himself of the life or death of his relatives, put from the French shore to return among us, often the greedy ocean swallowed his little craft, or after a day or two he was infected by the disorder, and died before he could tell the tale of the desolation of France. We were therefore to a great degree ignorant of the state of things on the continent, and were not without some vague hope of finding numerous companions in its wide track. But the same causes that had so fearfully diminished the English nation had had even greater scope for mischief in the sister land. France was a blank; during the long line of road from Calais to Paris not one human being was found. In Paris there were a few, perhaps a hundred, who, resigned to their coming fate, flitted about the streets of the capital and assembled to converse of past times, with that vivacity and even gaiety that seldom deserts the individuals of this nation.

The English took uncontested possession of Paris. Its high houses and narrow streets were lifeless. A few pale figures were to be distinguished at the accustomed resort at the Tuileries; they wondered wherefore the islanders should approach their ill-fated city—for in the excess of wretchedness, the sufferers always imagine, that their part of the calamity is the bitterest, as, when enduring intense pain, we would exchange the particular torture we writhe under, for any other which should visit a different part of the frame. They listened to the account the emigrants gave of their motives for leaving their native land, with a shrug almost of disdain—"Return," they said, "return to your island, whose sea breezes, and division from the continent gives some promise of health; if Pestilence among you has slain its hundreds, with us it has slain its thousands. Are you not even now more numerous than we are?—A year ago you would have found only the sick burying the dead; now we are happier; for the pang of struggle has passed away, and the few you find here are patiently waiting the final blow. But you, who are not content to die, breathe no longer the air of France, or soon you will only be a part of her soil."

Thus, by menaces of the sword, they would have driven back those who had escaped from fire. But the peril left behind was deemed imminent by my countrymen; that before them doubtful and distant; and soon other feelings arose to obliterate fear, or to replace it by passions, that ought to have had no place among a brotherhood of unhappy survivors of the expiring world.

The more numerous division of emigrants, which arrived first at Paris, assumed a superiority of rank and power; the second party asserted their independence. A third was formed by a sectarian, a self-erected prophet, who, while he attributed all power and rule to God, strove to get the real command of his comrades into his own hands. This third division consisted of fewest individuals, but their purpose was more one, their obedience to their leader more entire, their fortitude and courage more unyielding and active.

During the whole progress of the plague, the teachers of religion were in possession of great power; a power of good, if rightly directed, or of incalculable mischief, if fanaticism or intolerance guided their efforts. In the present instance, a worse feeling than either of these actuated the leader. He was an impostor in the most determined sense of the term. A man who had in early life lost, through the indulgence of vicious propensities, all sense of rectitude or self-esteem; and who, when ambition was awakened in him, gave himself up to its influence unbridled by any scruple. His father had been a methodist preacher, an enthusiastic man with simple intentions; but whose pernicious doctrines of election and special grace had contributed to destroy all conscientious feeling in his son.[32] During the progress of the pestilence he had entered upon various schemes, by which to acquire adherents and power. Adrian had discovered and defeated these attempts; but Adrian was absent; the wolf assumed the shepherd's garb, and the flock admitted the deception: he had formed a party during the few weeks he had been in Paris, who zealously propagated the creed of his divine mission, and believed that safety and salvation were to be afforded only to those who put their trust in him.

When once the spirit of dissension had arisen, the most frivolous causes gave it activity. The first party, on arriving at Paris, had taken possession of the Tuileries; chance and friendly feeling had induced the second to lodge near to them. A contest arose concerning the distribution of the pillage; the chiefs of the first division demanded that the whole should be

---

32 Originally, a Methodist was a member of an evangelical Christian group formed in 1729 by John and Charles Wesley and George Whitefield; MWS uses the term loosely and negatively to refer to a stern religious fanatic. The impostor teaches that God has chosen his flock for special favour and therefore for salvation: they are, therefore, the "elect" or the chosen ones—as, in a very different sense, PBS and Edward Williams were, too (see *Letters* 1: 450). For a discussion of the relation between religious hypocrites and their victims, see Mary Wollstonecraft, *A Vindication of the Rights of Woman*, ed. Carol H. Poston 179-83.

placed at their disposal; with this assumption the opposite party refused to comply. When next the latter went to forage, the gates of Paris were shut on them. After overcoming this difficulty, they marched in a body to the Tuileries. They found that their enemies had been already expelled thence by the Elect, as the fanatical party designated themselves, who refused to admit any into the palace who did not first abjure obedience to all except God, and his delegate on earth, their chief. Such was the beginning of the strife, which at length proceeded so far, that the three divisions, armed, met in the Place Vendome, each resolved to subdue by force the resistance of its adversaries.[33] They assembled, their muskets were loaded, and even pointed at the breasts of their so called enemies. One word had been sufficient; and there the last of mankind would have burthened their souls with the crime of murder, and dipt their hands in each other's blood. A sense of shame, a recollection that not only their cause, but the existence of the whole human race was at stake, entered the breast of the leader of the more numerous party. He was aware, that if the ranks were thinned, no other recruits could fill them up; that each man was as a priceless gem in a kingly crown, which if destroyed, the earth's deep entrails could yield no paragon. He was a young man, and had been hurried on by presumption, and the notion of his high rank and superiority to all other pretenders; now he repented his work, he felt that all the blood about to be shed would be on his head; with sudden impulse therefore he spurred his horse between the bands, and, having fixed a white handkerchief on the point of his uplifted sword, thus demanded parley; the opposite leaders obeyed the signal. He spoke with warmth; he reminded them of the oath all the chiefs had taken to submit to the Lord Protector; he declared their present meeting to be an act of treason and mutiny; he allowed that he had been hurried away by passion, but that a cooler moment had arrived; and he proposed that each party should send deputies to the Earl of Windsor, inviting his interference and offering submission to his decision. His offer was accepted so far, that each leader consented to command a retreat, and moreover agreed, that after the approbation of their several parties had been consulted, they should meet that night on some neutral spot to ratify the truce. At the meeting of the chiefs, this plan was finally concluded upon. The leader of the fanatics indeed refused to admit the arbitration of Adrian; he sent ambassadors, rather than deputies, to assert his claim, not plead his cause.

The truce was to continue until the first of February, when the bands were again to assemble on the Place Vendome; it was of the utmost consequence therefore that Adrian should arrive in Paris by that day, since an

---

33   The Tuileries refers not to the gardens visitors see today, but to the Palais des Tuileries (destroyed during the Commune in 1871); Place Vendôme is notable for the column (modelled on Trajan's column in Rome) commemorating Napoleon's victories.

hair might turn the scale, and peace, scared away by intestine broils, might only return to watch by the silent dead. It was now the twenty-eighth of January; every vessel stationed near Dover had been beaten to pieces and destroyed by the furious storms I have commemorated. Our journey however would admit of no delay. That very night, Adrian, and I, and twelve others, either friends or attendants, put off from the English shore, in the boat that had brought over the deputies. We all took our turn at the oar; and the immediate occasion of our departure affording us abundant matter for conjecture and discourse, prevented the feeling that we left our native country, depopulate England, for the last time, to enter deeply into the minds of the greater part of our number. It was a serene starlight night, and the dark line of the English coast continued for some time visible at intervals, as we rose on the broad back of the waves. I exerted myself with my long oar to give swift impulse to our skiff; and, while the waters splashed with melancholy sound against its sides, I looked with sad affection on this last glimpse of sea-girt England, and strained my eyes not too soon to lose sight of the castellated cliff, which rose to protect the land of heroism and beauty from the inroads of ocean, that, turbulent as I had lately seen it, required such cyclopean walls[34] for its repulsion. A solitary sea-gull winged its flight over our heads, to seek its nest in a cleft of the precipice. Yes, thou shalt revisit the land of thy birth, I thought, as I looked invidiously on the airy voyager; but we shall, never more! Tomb of Idris, farewell! Grave, in which my heart lies sepultured, farewell for ever!

We were twelve hours at sea, and the heavy swell obliged us to exert all our strength. At length, by mere dint of rowing, we reached the French coast. The stars faded, and the grey morning cast a dim veil over the silver horns of the waning moon—the sun rose broad and red from the sea, as we walked over the sands to Calais. Our first care was to procure horses, and although wearied by our night of watching and toil, some of our party immediately went in quest of these in the wide fields of the unenclosed and now barren plain round Calais. We divided ourselves, like seamen, into watches, and some reposed, while others prepared the morning's repast. Our foragers returned at noon with only six horses—on these, Adrian and I, and four others, proceeded on our journey towards the great city, which its inhabitants had fondly named the capital of the civilized world. Our horses had become, through their long holiday, almost wild, and we crossed the plain round Calais with impetuous speed. From the height near Boulogne, I turned again to look on England; nature had cast a misty pall over her, her cliff was hidden—there was spread the watery barrier that divided us, never again to be crossed; she lay on the ocean plain,

---

34 Gigantic walls, from the Cyclops or one-eyed giant Odysseus encounters on his journey; MWS uses the same phrase below, 327.

In the great pool a swan's nest.[35]

Ruined the nest, alas! the swans of Albion had passed away for ever—an uninhabited rock in the wide Pacific, which had remained since the creation uninhabited, unnamed, unmarked, would be of as much account in the world's future history, as desert England.

Our journey was impeded by a thousand obstacles. As our horses grew tired, we had to seek for others; and hours were wasted, while we exhausted our artifices to allure some of these enfranchised slaves of man to resume the yoke; or as we went from stable to stable through the towns, hoping to find some who had not forgotten the shelter of their native stalls. Our ill success in procuring them, obliged us continually to leave some one of our companions behind; and on the first of February, Adrian and I entered Paris, wholly unaccompanied. The serene morning had dawned when we arrived at Saint Denis, and the sun was high, when the clamour of voices, and the clash, as we feared, of weapons, guided us to where our countrymen had assembled on the Place Vendome. We passed a knot of Frenchmen, who were talking earnestly of the madness of the insular invaders, and then coming by a sudden turn upon the Place, we saw the sun glitter on drawn swords and fixed bayonets, while yells and clamours rent the air. It was a scene of unaccustomed confusion in these days of depopulation. Roused by fancied wrongs, and insulting scoffs, the opposite parties had rushed to attack each other; while the elect, drawn up apart, seemed to wait an opportunity to fall with better advantage on their foes, when they should have mutually weakened each other. A merciful power interposed, and no blood was shed; for, while the insane mob were in the very act of attack, the females, wives, mothers and daughters, rushed between; they seized the bridles; they embraced the knees of the horsemen, and hung on the necks, or enweaponed arms of their enraged relatives; the shrill female scream was mingled with the manly shout, and formed the wild clamour that welcomed us on our arrival.

Our voices could not be heard in the tumult; Adrian however was eminent for the white charger he rode; spurring him, he dashed into the midst of the throng: he was recognized, and a loud cry raised for England and the Protector. The late adversaries, warmed to affection at the sight of him, joined in heedless confusion, and surrounded him; the women kissed his hands, and the edges of his garments; nay, his horse received tribute of their embraces; some wept their welcome; he appeared an angel of peace descended among them; and the only danger was, that his mortal nature would be demonstrated, by his suffocation from the kindness of his friends. His voice was at length heard, and obeyed; the crowd fell back; the chiefs alone rallied round him. I had seen Lord Raymond ride through his lines; his look of victory, and majestic mien obtained the

---

35 Shakespeare, *Cymbeline* 3.4.138.

respect and obedience of all: such was not the appearance or influence of Adrian. His slight figure, his fervent look, his gesture, more of deprecation than rule, were proofs that love, unmingled with fear, gave him dominion over the hearts of a multitude, who knew that he never flinched from danger, nor was actuated by other motives than care for the general welfare. No distinction was now visible between the two parties, late ready to shed each other's blood, for, though neither would submit to the other, they both yielded ready obedience to the Earl of Windsor.

One party however remained, cut off from the rest, which did not sympathize in the joy exhibited on Adrian's arrival, or imbibe the spirit of peace, which fell like dew upon the softened hearts of their countrymen. At the head of this assembly was a ponderous, dark-looking man, whose malign eye surveyed with gloating delight the stern looks of his followers. They had hitherto been inactive, but now, perceiving themselves to be forgotten in the universal jubilee, they advanced with threatening gestures: our friends had, as it were in wanton contention, attacked each other; they wanted but to be told that their cause was one, for it to become so: their mutual anger had been a fire of straw, compared to the slow-burning hatred they both entertained for these seceders, who seized a portion of the world to come, there to entrench and incastellate themselves, and to issue with fearful sally, and appalling denunciations, on the mere common children of the earth. The first advance of the little army of the elect reawakened their rage; they grasped their arms, and waited but their leader's signal to commence the attack, when the clear tones of Adrian's voice were heard, commanding them to fall back; with confused murmur and hurried retreat, as the wave ebbs clamorously from the sands it lately covered, our friends obeyed. Adrian rode singly into the space between the opposing bands; he approached the hostile leader, as requesting him to imitate his example, but his look was not obeyed, and the chief advanced, followed by his whole troop. There were many women among them, who seemed more eager and resolute than their male companions. They pressed round their leader, as if to shield him, while they loudly bestowed on him every sacred denomination and epithet of worship. Adrian met them half way; they halted: "What," he said, "do you seek? Do you require any thing of us that we refuse to give, and that you are forced to acquire by arms and warfare?"

His questions were answered by a general cry, in which the words election, sin, and red right arm of God, could alone be heard.

Adrian looked expressly at their leader, saying, "Can you not silence your followers? Mine, you perceive, obey me."

The fellow answered by a scowl; and then, perhaps fearful that his people should become auditors of the debate he expected to ensue, he commanded them to fall back, and advanced by himself. "What, I again ask," said Adrian, "do you require of us?"

"Repentance," replied the man, whose sinister brow gathered clouds as he spoke. "Obedience to the will of the Most High, made manifest to these his Elected People. Do we not all die through your sins, O generation of unbelief, and have we not a right to demand of you repentance and obedience?"

"And if we refuse them, what then?" his opponent inquired mildly.

"Beware," cried the man, "God hears you, and will smite your stony heart in his wrath; his poisoned arrows fly, his dogs of death are unleashed! We will not perish unrevenged—and mighty will our avenger be, when he descends in visible majesty, and scatters destruction among you."

"My good fellow," said Adrian, with quiet scorn, "I wish that you were ignorant only, and I think it would be no difficult task to prove to you, that you speak of what you do not understand. On the present occasion however, it is enough for me to know that you seek nothing of us; and, heaven is our witness, we seek nothing of you. I should be sorry to embitter by strife the few days that we any of us may have here to live; when there," he pointed downwards, "we shall not be able to contend, while here we need not. Go home, or stay; pray to your God in your own mode; your friends may do the like. My orisons consist in peace and good will, in resignation and hope. Farewell!"

He bowed slightly to the angry disputant who was about to reply; and, turning his horse down Rue Saint Honoré, called on his friends to follow him. He rode slowly, to give time to all to join him at the Barrier, and then issued his orders that those who yielded obedience to him, should rendezvous at Versailles. In the meantime he remained within the walls of Paris, until he had secured the safe retreat of all. In about a fortnight the remainder of the emigrants arrived from England, and they all repaired to Versailles; apartments were prepared for the family of the Protector in the Grand Trianon, and there, after the excitement of these events, we reposed amidst the luxuries of the departed Bourbons.[36]

CHAPTER XXV

AFTER the repose of a few days, we held a council, to decide on our future movements. Our first plan had been to quit our wintry native latitude, and seek for our diminished numbers the luxuries and delights of a southern climate. We had not fixed on any precise spot as the termination of our wanderings; but a vague picture of perpetual spring, fragrant groves, and sparkling streams, floated in our imagination to entice us on. A variety of causes had detained us in England, and we had now arrived at the

---

36 The Grand Trianon is one of two pleasure palaces built by Louis XIV: see
    Journals 1: 133. The Bourbons are the French royal family, including Henry
    IV, Louis XIII, XIV, XV, and XVI (1589-1793) and, after the Revolution and
    the Napoleonic period, Louis XVIII (1815-1824) and Charles X (1824-1830);
    branches of this family held the crowns of Spain, Naples, and Parma.

middle of February; if we pursued our original project, we should find ourselves in a worse situation than before, having exchanged our temperate climate for the intolerable heats of a summer in Egypt or Persia. We were therefore obliged to modify our plan, as the season continued to be inclement; and it was determined that we should await the arrival of spring in our present abode, and so order our future movements as to pass the hot months in the icy vallies of Switzerland, deferring our southern progress until the ensuing autumn, if such a season was ever again to be beheld by us.

The castle and town of Versailles afforded our numbers ample accommodation, and foraging parties took it by turns to supply our wants. There was a strange and appalling motley in the situation of these the last of the race. At first I likened it to a colony, which borne over the far seas, struck root for the first time in a new country. But where was the bustle and industry characteristic of such an assemblage; the rudely constructed dwelling, which was to suffice till a more commodious mansion could be built; the marking out of fields; the attempt at cultivation; the eager curiosity to discover unknown animals and herbs; the excursions for the sake of exploring the country? Our habitations were palaces—our food was ready stored in granaries—there was no need of labour, no inquisitiveness, no restless desire to get on. If we had been assured that we should secure the lives of our present numbers, there would have been more vivacity and hope in our councils. We should have discussed as to the period when the existing produce for man's sustenance would no longer suffice for us, and what mode of life we should then adopt. We should have considered more carefully our future plans, and debated concerning the spot where we should in future dwell. But summer and the plague were near, and we dared not look forward. Every heart sickened at the thought of amusement; if the younger part of our community were ever impelled, by youthful and untamed hilarity, to enter on any dance or song, to cheer the melancholy time, they would suddenly break off, checked by a mournful look or agonizing sigh from any one among them, who was prevented by sorrows and losses from mingling in the festivity. If laughter echoed under our roof, yet the heart was vacant of joy; and, whenever it chanced that I witnessed such attempts at pastime, they encreased instead of diminishing my sense of woe. In the midst of the pleasure-hunting throng, I would close my eyes, and see before me the obscure cavern, where was garnered the mortality of Idris, and the dead lay around, mouldering in hushed repose. When I again became aware of the present hour, softest melody of Lydian flute, or harmonious maze of graceful dance, was but as the demoniac chorus in the Wolf's Glen, and the caperings of the reptiles that surrounded the magic circle.[37]

---

37 MWS refers to the scene in Act 2 of Carl Maria von Weber's opera, *Der Freishütz* ("the free-shooter," 1821), in which the hero, Max, undergoes a

My dearest interval of peace occurred, when, released from the obligation of associating with the crowd, I could repose in the dear home where my children lived. Children I say, for the tenderest emotions of paternity bound me to Clara. She was now fourteen; sorrow, and deep insight into the scenes around her, calmed the restless spirit of girlhood; while the remembrance of her father whom she idolized, and respect for me and Adrian, implanted an high sense of duty in her young heart. Though serious she was not sad; the eager desire that makes us all, when young, plume our wings, and stretch our necks, that we may more swiftly alight tiptoe on the height of maturity, was subdued in her by early experience. All that she could spare of overflowing love from her parents' memory, and attention to her living relatives, was spent upon religion. This was the hidden law of her heart, which she concealed with childish reserve, and cherished the more because it was secret. What faith so entire, what charity so pure, what hope so fervent, as that of early youth? and she, all love, all tenderness and trust, who from infancy had been tossed on the wide sea of passion and misfortune, saw the finger of apparent divinity in all, and her best hope was to make herself acceptable to the power she worshipped. Evelyn was only five years old; his joyous heart was incapable of sorrow, and he enlivened our house with the innocent mirth incident to his years.

The aged Countess of Windsor had fallen from her dream of power, rank and grandeur; she had been suddenly seized with the conviction, that love was the only good of life, virtue the only ennobling distinction and enriching wealth. Such a lesson had been taught her by the dead lips of her neglected daughter; and she devoted herself, with all the fiery violence of her character, to the obtaining the affection of the remnants of her family. In early years the heart of Adrian had been chilled towards her; and, though he observed a due respect, her coldness, mixed with the recollection of disappointment and madness, caused him to feel even pain in her society. She saw this, and yet determined to win his love; the obstacle served the rather to excite her ambition. As Henry, Emperor of Germany, lay in the snow before Pope Leo's gate for three winter days and nights,[38] so did she in humility wait before the icy barriers of his closed heart, till he, the servant of love, and prince of tender courtesy, opened it wide for her admittance, bestowing, with fervency and gratitude, the tribute of fil-

---

supernatural ordeal. The production she saw "two or three times" at the English Opera House (Lyceum) (*Letters* 1: 445, 450) would have been a version called *Der Freishütz; or, The seventh bullet*, which opened 22 July 1824.

38 In 1076 Henry IV of Germany was excommunicated by Pope Gregory VII (not Leo) for denouncing papal authority. Deserted by his supporters, he humbled himself before the pope. Gregory removed the excommunication; but the moral victory of the papacy over the temporal rulers of Europe was strengthened by Henry's capitulation.

ial affection she merited. Her understanding, courage, and presence of mind, became powerful auxiliaries to him in the difficult task of ruling the tumultuous crowd, which were subjected to his control, in truth by a single hair.

The principal circumstances that disturbed our tranquillity during this interval, originated in the vicinity of the impostor-prophet and his followers. They continued to reside at Paris; but missionaries from among them often visited Versailles—and such was the power of assertions, however false, yet vehemently iterated, over the ready credulity of the ignorant and fearful, that they seldom failed in drawing over to their party some from among our numbers. An instance of this nature coming immediately under our notice, we were led to consider the miserable state in which we should leave our countrymen, when we should, at the approach of summer, move on towards Switzerland, and leave a deluded crew behind us in the hands of their miscreant leader. The sense of the smallness of our numbers, and expectation of decrease, pressed upon us; and, while it would be a subject of congratulation to ourselves to add one to our party, it would be doubly gratifying to rescue from the pernicious influence of superstition and unrelenting tyranny, the victims that now, though voluntarily enchained, groaned beneath it. If we had considered the preacher as sincere in a belief of his own denunciations, or only moderately actuated by kind feeling in the exercise of his assumed powers, we should have immediately addressed ourselves to him, and endeavoured with our best arguments to soften and humanize his views. But he was instigated by ambition, he desired to rule over these last stragglers from the fold of death; his projects went so far, as to cause him to calculate that, if, from these crushed remains, a few survived, so that a new race should spring up, he, by holding tight the reins of belief, might be remembered by the post-pestilential race as a patriarch, a prophet, nay a deity; such as of old among the post-diluvians were Jupiter the conqueror, Serapis the lawgiver, and Vishnou the preserver.[39] These ideas made him inflexible in his rule, and violent in his hate of any who presumed to share with him his usurped empire.

It is a strange fact, but incontestible, that the philanthropist, who ardent in his desire to do good, who patient, reasonable and gentle, yet disdains to use other argument than truth, has less influence over men's minds, than he who, grasping and selfish, refuses not to adopt any means, nor awaken any passion, nor diffuse any falsehood, for the advancement

---

39   This triad, which parallels the Christian trinity, is an example of the syncretic mythology that interested the Shelleys. Sir William Jones, "On the Gods of Greece, Italy, and India," offers another version, in which the three roles of Jupiter, "Creator, Preserver, and Destroyer," are expressed by the Hindu triad of Brahma, Vishnu, and Siva (*Works* 3: 348); cf. PBS, "Ode to the West Wind" 14.

of his cause. If this from time immemorial has been the case, the contrast was infinitely greater, now that the one could bring harrowing fears and transcendent hopes into play; while the other had few hopes to hold forth, nor could influence the imagination to diminish the fears which he himself was the first to entertain. The preacher had persuaded his followers, that their escape from the plague, the salvation of their children, and the rise of a new race of men from their seed, depended on their faith in, and their submission to him. They greedily imbibed this belief; and their over-weening credulity even rendered them eager to make converts to the same faith.

How to seduce any individuals from such an alliance of fraud, was a frequent subject of Adrian's meditations and discourse. He formed many plans for the purpose; but his own troop kept him in full occupation to ensure their fidelity and safety; beside which the preacher was as cautious and prudent, as he was cruel. His victims lived under the strictest rules and laws, which either entirely imprisoned them within the Tuileries, or let them out in such numbers, and under such leaders, as precluded the possibility of controversy. There was one among them however whom I resolved to save; she had been known to us in happier days; Idris had loved her; and her excellent nature made it peculiarly lamentable that she should be sacrificed by this merciless cannibal of souls.

This man had between two and three hundred persons enlisted under his banners. More than half of them were women; there were about fifty children of all ages; and not more than eighty men. They were mostly drawn from that which, when such distinctions existed, was denominated the lower rank of society. The exceptions consisted of a few high-born females, who, panic-struck, and tamed by sorrow, had joined him. Among these was one, young, lovely, and enthusiastic, whose very goodness made her a more easy victim. I have mentioned her before: Juliet, the youngest daughter, and now sole relic of the ducal house of L—. There are some beings, whom fate seems to select on whom to pour, in unmeasured portion, the vials of her wrath, and whom she bathes even to the lips in misery. Such a one was the ill-starred Juliet. She had lost her indulgent parents, her brothers and sisters, companions of her youth; in one fell swoop they had been carried off from her. Yet she had again dared to call herself happy; united to her admirer, to him who possessed and filled her whole heart, she yielded to the lethean powers of love, and knew and felt only his life and presence. At the very time when with keen delight she welcomed the tokens of maternity, this sole prop of her life failed, her husband died of the plague. For a time she had been lulled in insanity; the birth of her child restored her to the cruel reality of things, but gave her at the same time an object for whom to preserve at once life and reason. Every friend and relative had died off, and she was reduced to solitude and penury; deep melancholy and angry impatience distorted her judgment, so that she could not persuade herself to disclose her distress to us. When she heard of the plan of universal emigration, she resolved to remain behind with her child, and alone in wide England to live or die, as fate might decree, beside the grave of her beloved. She had hidden herself in one of the many empty habitations of London; it was she who rescued my Idris on the fatal twentieth of November, though my immediate danger, and the subsequent illness of Idris, caused us to forget our hapless friend. This circumstance had however brought her again in contact with her fellow-creatures; a slight illness of her infant, proved to her that she was still bound to humanity by an indestructible tie; to preserve this little creature's life became the object of her being, and she joined the first division of emigrants who went over to Paris.

She became an easy prey to the methodist; her sensibility and acute fears rendered her accessible to every impulse; her love for her child made her eager to cling to the merest straw held out to save him. Her mind, once unstrung, and now tuned by roughest inharmonious hands, made her credulous: beautiful as fabled goddess, with voice of unrivalled sweetness, burning with new lighted enthusiasm, she became a stedfast proselyte, and powerful auxiliary to the leader of the elect. I had remarked her in the crowd, on the day we met on the Place Vendome; and, recollecting suddenly her providential rescue of my lost one, on the night of the twentieth of November, I reproached myself for my neglect and ingratitude, and felt impelled to leave no means that I could adopt untried, to recall her to her better self, and rescue her from the fangs of the hypocrite destroyer.

I will not, at this period of my story, record the artifices I used to penetrate the asylum of the Tuileries, or give what would be a tedious account of my stratagems, disappointments, and perseverance. I at last succeeded in entering these walls, and roamed its halls and corridors in eager hope to find my selected convert. In the evening I contrived to mingle unobserved with the congregation, which assembled in the chapel to listen to the crafty and eloquent harangue of their prophet. I saw Juliet near him. Her dark eyes, fearfully impressed with the restless glare of madness, were fixed on him; she held her infant, not yet a year old, in her arms; and care of it alone could distract her attention from the words to which she eagerly listened. After the sermon was over, the congregation dispersed; all quitted the chapel except she whom I sought; her babe had fallen asleep; so she placed it on a cushion, and sat on the floor beside, watching its tranquil slumber.

I presented myself to her; for a moment natural feeling produced a sentiment of gladness, which disappeared again, when with ardent and affectionate exhortation I besought her to accompany me in flight from this den of superstition and misery. In a moment she relapsed into the delirium of fanaticism, and, but that her gentle nature forbade, would have loaded me with execrations. She conjured me, she commanded me to leave her—"Beware, O beware," she cried, "fly while yet your escape is practicable. Now you are safe; but strange sounds and inspirations come on me at times, and if the Eternal should in awful whisper reveal to me his will, that to save my child you must be sacrificed, I would call in the satellites of him you call the tyrant; they would tear you limb from limb; nor would I hallow the death of him whom Idris loved, by a single tear."

She spoke hurriedly, with tuneless voice, and wild look; her child awoke, and, frightened, began to cry; each sob went to the ill-fated mother's heart, and she mingled the epithets of endearment she addressed to her infant, with angry commands that I should leave her. Had I had the means, I would have risked all, have torn her by force from the murderer's den, and trusted to the healing balm of reason and affection. But I had no choice, no power even of longer struggle; steps were heard along the gallery, and the voice of the preacher drew near. Juliet, straining her child in a close embrace, fled by another passage. Even then I would have followed her; but my foe and his satellites entered; I was surrounded, and taken prisoner.

I remembered the menace of the unhappy Juliet, and expected the full tempest of the man's vengeance, and the awakened wrath of his followers, to fall instantly upon me. I was questioned. My answers were simple and sincere. "His own mouth condemns him," exclaimed the impostor; "he confesses that his intention was to seduce from the way of salvation our well-beloved sister in God; away with him to the dungeon; to-morrow he dies the death; we are manifestly called upon to make an example, tremendous and appalling, to scare the children of sin from our asylum of the saved."

My heart revolted from his hypocritical jargon: but it was unworthy of me to combat in words with the ruffian; and my answer was cool; while, far from being possessed with fear, methought, even at the worst, a man true to himself, courageous and determined, could fight his way, even from the boards of the scaffold, through the herd of these misguided maniacs. "Remember," I said, "who I am; and be well assured that I shall not die unavenged. Your legal magistrate, the Lord Protector, knew of my design, and is aware that I am here; the cry of blood will reach him, and you and your miserable victims will long lament the tragedy you are about to act."

My antagonist did not deign to reply, even by a look;—"You know your duty," he said to his comrades,—"obey."

In a moment I was thrown on the earth, bound, blindfolded, and hurried away—liberty of limb and sight was only restored to me, when, surrounded by dungeon-walls, dark and impervious, I found myself a prisoner and alone.

Such was the result of my attempt to gain over the proselyte of this man of crime; I could not conceive that he would dare put me to death.—Yet I was in his hands; the path of his ambition had ever been dark and cruel; his power was founded upon fear; the one word which might cause me to die, unheard, unseen, in the obscurity of my dungeon, might be easier to speak than the deed of mercy to act. He would not risk probably a public execution; but a private assassination would at once terrify any of my companions from attempting a like feat, at the same time that a cautious line of conduct might enable him to avoid the enquiries and the vengeance of Adrian.

Two months ago, in a vault more obscure than the one I now inhabited, I had revolved the design of quietly laying me down to die; now I shuddered at the approach of fate. My imagination was busied in shaping forth the kind of death he would inflict. Would he allow me to wear out life with famine; or was the food administered to me to be medicined with death? Would he steal on me in my sleep; or should I contend to the last with my murderers, knowing, even while I struggled, that I must be overcome? I lived upon an earth whose diminished population a child's arithmetic might number; I had lived through long months with death stalking close at my side, while at intervals the shadow of his skeleton-shape darkened my path. I had believed that I despised the grim phantom, and laughed his power to scorn.

Any other fate I should have met with courage, nay, have gone out gallantly to encounter. But to be murdered thus at the midnight hour by cold-blooded assassins, no friendly hand to close my eyes, or receive my parting blessing—to die in combat, hate and execration—ah, why, my angel love, didst thou restore me to life, when already I had stepped within the portals of the tomb, now that so soon again I was to be flung back a mangled corpse!

Hours passed—centuries. Could I give words to the many thoughts which occupied me in endless succession during this interval, I should fill volumes. The air was dank, the dungeon-floor mildewed and icy cold; hunger came upon me too, and no sound reached me from without. To-morrow the ruffian had declared that I should die. When would to-morrow come? Was it not already here?

My door was about to be opened. I heard the key turn, and the bars and bolts slowly removed. The opening of intervening passages permitted sounds from the interior of the palace to reach me; and I heard the clock strike one. They come to murder me, I thought; this hour does not befit a public execution. I drew myself up against the wall opposite the entrance; I collected my forces, I rallied my courage, I would not fall a tame prey. Slowly the door receded on its hinges—I was ready to spring forward to seize and grapple with the intruder, till the sight of who it was changed at once the temper of my mind. It was Juliet herself; pale and trembling she stood, a lamp in her hand, on the threshold of the dungeon, looking at me with wistful countenance. But in a moment she re-assumed her self-possession; and her languid eyes recovered their brilliancy. She said, "I am come to save you, Verney."

"And yourself also," I cried: "dearest friend, can we indeed be saved?"

"Not a word," she replied, "follow me!"

I obeyed instantly. We threaded with light steps many corridors, ascended several flights of stairs, and passed through long galleries; at the end of one she unlocked a low portal; a rush of wind extinguished our lamp; but, in lieu of it, we had the blessed moon-beams and the open face of heaven. Then first Juliet spoke:—"You are safe," she said, "God bless you!—farewell!"

I seized her reluctant hand—"Dear friend," I cried, "misguided victim, do you not intend to escape with me? Have you not risked all in facilitating my flight? and do you think, that I will permit you to return, and suffer alone the effects of that miscreant's rage? Never!"

"Do not fear for me," replied the lovely girl mournfully, "and do not imagine that without the consent of our chief you could be without these walls. It is he that has saved you; he assigned to me the part of leading you hither, because I am best acquainted with your motives for coming here, and can best appreciate his mercy in permitting you to depart."

"And are you," I cried, "the dupe of this man? He dreads me alive as an enemy, and dead he fears my avengers. By favouring this clandestine escape he preserves a shew of consistency to his followers; but mercy is far from his heart. Do you forget his artifices, his cruelty, and fraud? As I am free, so are you. Come, Juliet, the mother of our lost Idris will welcome you, the noble Adrian will rejoice to receive you; you will find peace and love, and better hopes than fanaticism can afford. Come, and fear not; long before day we shall be at Versailles; close the door on this abode of crime—come, sweet Juliet, from hypocrisy and guilt to the society of the affectionate and good."

I spoke hurriedly, but with fervour: and while with gentle violence I drew her from the portal, some thought, some recollection of past scenes of youth and happiness, made her listen and yield to me; suddenly she broke away with a piercing shriek:—"My child, my child! he has my child; my darling girl is my hostage."

She darted from me into the passage; the gate closed between us—she was left in the fangs of this man of crime, a prisoner, still to inhale the pestilential atmosphere which adhered to his demoniac nature; the unimpeded breeze played on my cheek, the moon shone graciously upon me, my path was free. Glad to have escaped, yet melancholy in my very joy, I retrod my steps to Versailles.

CHAPTER XXVI

EVENTFUL winter passed; winter, the respite of our ills. By degrees the sun, which with slant beams had before yielded the more extended reign to night, lengthened his diurnal journey, and mounted his highest throne, at once the fosterer of earth's new beauty, and her lover. We who, like flies that congregate upon a dry rock at the ebbing of the tide, had played wantonly with time, allowing our passions, our hopes, and our mad desires to rule us, now heard the approaching roar of the ocean of destruction, and would have fled to some sheltered crevice, before the first wave broke over us. We resolved without delay, to commence our journey to Switzerland; we became eager to leave France. Under the icy vaults of the glaciers, beneath the shadow of the pines, the swinging of whose mighty branches was arrested by a load of snow; beside the streams whose intense cold proclaimed their origin to be from the slow-melting piles of congelated waters, amidst frequent storms which might purify the air, we should find health, if in truth health were not herself diseased.

We began our preparations at first with alacrity. We did not now bid adieu to our native country, to the graves of those we loved, to the flowers, and streams, and trees, which had lived beside us from infancy. Small sorrow would be ours on leaving Paris. A scene of shame, when we remembered our late contentions, and thought that we left behind a flock of miserable, deluded victims, bending under the tyranny of a selfish impostor. Small pangs should we feel in leaving the gardens, woods, and halls of the palaces of the Bourbons at Versailles, which we feared would soon be tainted by the dead, when we looked forward to vallies lovelier than any garden, to mighty forests and halls, built not for mortal majesty, but palaces of nature's own, with the Alp of marmoreal whiteness for their walls, the sky for their roof.

Yet our spirits flagged, as the day drew near which we had fixed for our departure. Dire visions and evil auguries, if such things were, thickened around us, so that in vain might men say—

These are their reasons, they are natural,[40]

we felt them to be ominous, and dreaded the future event enchained to them. That the night owl should screech before the noon-day sun, that the hard-winged bat should wheel around the bed of beauty, that muttering thunder should in early spring startle the cloudless air, that sudden and exterminating blight should fall on the tree and shrub, were unaccustomed, but physical events, less horrible than the mental creations of almighty fear. Some had sight of funeral processions, and faces all begrimed with tears, which flitted through the long avenues of the gardens, and drew aside the curtains of the sleepers at dead of night. Some heard wailing and cries in the air; a mournful chaunt would stream through the dark atmosphere, as if spirits above sang the requiem of the human race.[41] What was there in all this, but that fear created other senses within our frames, making us see, hear, and feel what was not? What was this, but the action of diseased imaginations and childish credulity? So might it be; but what was most real, was the existence of these very

---

40   Shakespeare—Julius Cæsar [MWS's note]; *Julius Caesar* 1.3.30.
41   Cf. Daniel Defoe, *A Journal of the Plague Year*, Appendix C.2.ii.

fears; the staring looks of horror, the faces pale even to ghastliness, the voices struck dumb with harrowing dread, of those among us who saw and heard these things. Of this number was Adrian, who knew the delusion, yet could not cast off the clinging terror. Even ignorant infancy appeared with timorous shrieks and convulsions to acknowledge the presence of unseen powers. We must go: in change of scene, in occupation, and such security as we still hoped to find, we should discover a cure for these gathering horrors.

On mustering our company, we found them to consist of fourteen hundred souls, men, women, and children. Until now therefore, we were undiminished in numbers, except by the desertion of those who had attached themselves to the impostor-prophet, and remained behind in Paris. About fifty French joined us. Our order of march was easily arranged; the ill success which had attended our division, determined Adrian to keep all in one body. I, with an hundred men, went forward first as purveyor, taking the road of the Côte d'Or, through Auxerre, Dijon, Dole, over the Jura to Geneva.[42] I was to make arrangements, at every ten miles, for the accommodation of such numbers as I found the town or village would receive, leaving behind a messenger with a written order, signifying how many were to be quartered there. The remainder of our tribe was then divided into bands of fifty each, every division containing eighteen men, and the remainder, consisting of women and children. Each of these was headed by an officer, who carried the roll of names, by which they were each day to be mustered. If the numbers were divided at night, in the morning those in the van waited for those in the rear. At each of the large towns before mentioned, we were all to assemble; and a conclave of the principal officers would hold council for the general weal. I went first, as I said; Adrian last. His mother, with Clara and Evelyn under her protection, remained also with him. Thus our order being determined, I departed. My plan was to go at first no further than Fontainebleau, where in a few days I should be joined by Adrian, before I took flight again further eastward.[43]

My friend accompanied me a few miles from Versailles. He was sad; and, in a tone of unaccustomed despondency, uttered a prayer for our speedy arrival among the Alps, accompanied with an expression of vain regret that we were not already there. "In that case," I observed, "we can quicken our march; why adhere to a plan whose dilatory proceeding you already disapprove?"

"Nay," replied he, "it is too late now. A month ago, and we were mas-

---

42   This route from the vicinity of Paris across France into Switzerland roughly
     follows the route MWS took in the opposite direction back from Geneva in
     1816; see *Journals* 1: 132-34.
43   Fontainebleau is south of Paris, on the way to Dijon.

ters of ourselves; now,—" he turned his face from me; though gathering twilight had already veiled its expression, he turned it yet more away, as he added—"a man died of the plague last night!"

He spoke in a smothered voice, then suddenly clasping his hands, he exclaimed, "Swiftly, most swiftly advances the last hour for us all; as the stars vanish before the sun, so will his near approach destroy us. I have done my best; with grasping hands and impotent strength, I have hung on the wheel of the chariot of plague; but she drags me along with it, while, like Jaggernaut,[44] she proceeds crushing out the being of all who strew the high road of life. Would that it were over—would that her procession achieved, we had all entered the tomb together!"

Tears streamed from his eyes. "Again and again," he continued, "will the tragedy be acted; again I must hear the groans of the dying, the wailing of the survivors; again witness the pangs, which, consummating all, envelope an eternity in their evanescent existence. Why am I reserved for this? Why the tainted wether of the flock, am I not struck to earth among the first? It is hard, very hard, for one of woman born to endure all that I endure!"

Hitherto, with an undaunted spirit, and an high feeling of duty and worth, Adrian had fulfilled his self-imposed task. I had contemplated him with reverence, and a fruitless desire of imitation. I now offered a few words of encouragement and sympathy. He hid his face in his hands, and while he strove to calm himself, he ejaculated, "For a few months, yet for a few months more, let not, O God, my heart fail, or my courage be bowed down; let not sights of intolerable misery madden this half-crazed brain, or cause this frail heart to beat against its prison-bound, so that it burst. I have believed it to be my destiny to guide and rule the last of the race of man, till death extinguish my government; and to this destiny I submit.

"Pardon me, Verney, I pain you, but I will no longer complain. Now I am myself again, or rather I am better than myself. You have known how from my childhood aspiring thoughts and high desires have warred with inherent disease and overstrained sensitiveness, till the latter became victors. You know how I placed this wasted feeble hand on the abandoned helm of human government. I have been visited at times by intervals of fluctuation; yet, until now, I have felt as if a superior and indefatigable spirit had taken up its abode within me or rather incorporated itself with my weaker being. The holy visitant has for a time slept, perhaps to show me how powerless I am without its inspiration. Yet, stay for a while, O

---

44 Robert Southey, *The Curse of Kehama*, describes a procession of this incarnation of the Hindu god Vishnu: "On Jaga-Naut [the worshippers] call, / The ponderous Car rolls on, and crushes all. / Through flesh and bones it ploughs its dreadful path" (14.5).

Power of goodness and strength; disdain not yet this rent shrine of flesh-
ly mortality, O immortal Capability! While one fellow creature remains to
whom aid can be afforded, stay by and prop your shattered, falling
engine!"

His vehemence, and voice broken by irrepressible sighs, sunk to my
heart; his eyes gleamed in the gloom of night like two earthly stars; and,
his form dilating, his countenance beaming, truly it almost seemed as if at
his eloquent appeal a more than mortal spirit entered his frame, exalting
him above humanity.

He turned quickly towards me, and held out his hand. "Farewell,
Verney," he cried, "brother of my love, farewell; no other weak expression
must cross these lips, I am alive again: to our tasks, to our combats with
our unvanquishable foe, for to the last I will struggle against her."

He grasped my hand, and bent a look on me, more fervent and animated than any smile; then, turning his horse's head, he touched the animal with the spur, and was out of sight in a moment.

A man last night had died of the plague. The quiver was not emptied,
nor the bow unstrung. We stood as marks, while Parthian Pestilence[45]
aimed and shot, insatiated by conquest, unobstructed by the heaps of
slain. A sickness of the soul, contagious even to my physical mechanism,
came over me. My knees knocked together, my teeth chattered, the current of my blood, clotted by sudden cold, painfully forced its way from my
heavy heart. I did not fear for myself, but it was misery to think that we
could not even save this remnant. That those I loved might in a few days
be as clay-cold as Idris in her antique tomb; nor could strength of body or
energy of mind ward off the blow. A sense of degradation came over me.
Did God create man, merely in the end to become dead earth in the midst
of healthful vegetating nature? Was he of no more account to his Maker,
than a field of corn blighted in the ear? Were our proud dreams thus to
fade? Our name was written "a little lower than the angels;"[46] and,
behold, we were no better than ephemera. We had called ourselves the
"paragon of animals," and, lo! we were a "quint-essence of dust."[47] We
repined that the pyramids had outlasted the embalmed body of their
builder. Alas! the mere shepherd's hut of straw we passed on the road,
contained in its structure the principle of greater longevity than the whole
race of man. How reconcile this sad change to our past aspirations, to our
apparent powers!

Sudden an internal voice, articulate and clear, seemed to say:—Thus

---

45   See *Iliad* 1.81 ff.
46   Psalm 8.5; cf. 250n.
47   *Hamlet* 2.2.316-17; the juxtaposition of this passage from *Hamlet* with the quo-
     tation from Psalms that precedes it may have been suggested by Godwin's
     similar juxtaposition in *Of Population* 106.

from eternity, it was decreed: the steeds that bear Time onwards had this hour and this fulfilment enchained to them, since the void brought forth its burthen. Would you read backwards the unchangeable laws of Necessity?[48]

Mother of the world! Servant of the Omnipotent! eternal, changeless Necessity! who with busy fingers sittest ever weaving the indissoluble chain of events!—I will not murmur at thy acts. If my human mind cannot acknowledge that all that is, is right; yet since what is, must be, I will sit amidst the ruins and smile.[49] Truly we were not born to enjoy, but to submit, and to hope.

Will not the reader tire, if I should minutely describe our long-drawn journey from Paris to Geneva? If, day by day, I should record, in the form of a journal, the thronging miseries of our lot, could my hand write, or language afford words to express, the variety of our woe; the hustling and crowding of one deplorable event upon another? Patience, oh reader! whoever thou art, wherever thou dwellest, whether of race spiritual, or, sprung from some surviving pair, thy nature will be human, thy habitation the earth; thou wilt here read of the acts of the extinct race, and wilt ask wonderingly, if they, who suffered what thou findest recorded, were of frail flesh and soft organization like thyself. Most true, they were—weep therefore; for surely, solitary being, thou wilt be of gentle disposition; shed compassionate tears; but the while lend thy attention to the tale, and learn the deeds and sufferings of thy predecessors.

Yet the last events that marked our progress through France were so full of strange horror and gloomy misery, that I dare not pause too long in the narration. If I were to dissect each incident, every small fragment of a second would contain an harrowing tale, whose minutest word would curdle the blood in thy young veins. It is right that I should erect for thy instruction this monument of the foregone race; but not that I should drag thee through the wards of an hospital, nor the secret chambers of the charnel-house. This tale, therefore, shall be rapidly unfolded. Images of destruction, pictures of despair, the procession of the last triumph of

---

48 Cf. PBS, note to *Queen Mab* 6.198: *"Necessity! thou mother of the world!"*: "He who asserts the doctrine of Necessity means that contemplating the events which compose the moral and material universe, he beholds only an immense and uninterrupted chain of causes and effects, no one of which could occupy any other place than it does occupy, or act in other place than it does act."

49 Alexander Pope, *An Essay on Man* 1.294: "spite of pride, in erring reason's spite, / One truth is clear: Whatever IS, is RIGHT." Mary Wollstonecraft quotes this passage to represent Rousseau's view in *Emile*; see *A Vindication of the Rights of Woman*, ed. Carol H. Poston 84. For a less submissive meditation among the ruins, see Volney, *The Ruins*, excerpted below, Appendix D.1.

death,[50] shall be drawn before thee, swift as the rack driven by the north wind along the blotted splendour of the sky.

Weed-grown fields, desolate towns, the wild approach of riderless horses had now become habitual to my eyes; nay, sights far worse, of the unburied dead, and human forms which were strewed on the road side, and on the steps of once frequented habitations, where,

> Through the flesh that wastes away
> Beneath the parching sun, the whitening bones
> Start forth, and moulder in the sable dust.[51]

Sights like these had become—ah, woe the while! so familiar, that we had ceased to shudder, or spur our stung horses to sudden speed, as we passed them. France in its best days, at least that part of France through which we travelled, had been a cultivated desert, and the absence of enclosures, of cottages, and even of peasantry, was saddening to a traveller from sunny Italy, or busy England. Yet the towns were frequent and lively, and the cordial politeness and ready smile of the wooden-shoed peasant restored good humour to the splenetic. Now, the old woman sat no more at the door with her distaff—the lank beggar no longer asked charity in courtier-like phrase; nor on holidays did the peasantry thread with slow grace the mazes of the dance. Silence, melancholy bride of death, went in procession with him from town to town through the spacious region.

We arrived at Fontainebleau, and speedily prepared for the reception of our friends. On mustering our numbers for the night, three were found missing. When I enquired for them, the man to whom I spoke, uttered the word "plague," and fell at my feet in convulsions; he also was infected. There were hard faces around me; for among my troop were sailors who had crossed the line times unnumbered, soldiers who, in Russia and far America, had suffered famine, cold and danger, and men still sterner-featured, once nightly depredators in our over-grown metropolis; men bred from their cradle to see the whole machine of society at work for their destruction. I looked round, and saw upon the faces of all horror and despair written in glaring characters.

We passed four days at Fontainebleau. Several sickened and died, and

---

50 MWS here alludes to the triumphal procession which provides a structure for Petrarch's allegorical "triumphs" of Love, Chastity, Death, Fame, and so on (the *Trionfi*); these in turn influence PBS's *The Triumph of Life*. Cf. the reference to "the Pest's triumphal chariot" in John Wilson, *The City of the Plague* 1.1 (Appendix C.4, line 28).

51 Elton's Translation of Hesiod's "Shield of Hercules" [MWS's note]; from *Remains of Hesiod* (London, 1815): Elton has "their whitening bones."

in the mean time neither Adrian nor any of our friends appeared. My own troop was in commotion; to reach Switzerland, to plunge into rivers of snow, and to dwell in caves of ice, became the mad desire of all. Yet we had promised to wait for the Earl; and he came not. My people demanded to be led forward—rebellion, if so we might call what was the mere casting away of straw-formed shackles, appeared manifestly among them. They would away on the word without a leader. The only chance of safety, the only hope of preservation from every form of indescribable suffering, was our keeping together. I told them this; while the most determined among them answered with sullenness, that they could take care of themselves, and replied to my entreaties with scoffs and menaces.

At length, on the fifth day, a messenger arrived from Adrian, bearing letters, which directed us to proceed to Auxerre, and there await his arrival, which would only be deferred for a few days. Such was the tenor of his public letters. Those privately delivered to me, detailed at length the difficulties of his situation, and left the arrangement of my future plans to my own discretion. His account of the state of affairs at Versailles was brief, but the oral communications of his messenger filled up his omissions, and shewed me that perils of the most frightful nature were gathering around him. At first the re-awakening of the plague had been concealed; but the number of deaths encreasing, the secret was divulged, and the destruction already achieved, was exaggerated by the fears of the survivors. Some emissaries of the enemy of mankind, the accursed Impostors, were among them instilling their doctrine, that safety and life could only be ensured by submission to their chief; and they succeeded so well, that soon, instead of desiring to proceed to Switzerland, the major part of the multitude, weak-minded women, and dastardly men, desired to return to Paris, and, by ranging themselves under the banners of the so called prophet, and by a cowardly worship of the principle of evil, to purchase respite, as they hoped, from impending death. The discord and tumult induced by these conflicting fears and passions, detained Adrian. It required all his ardour in pursuit of an object, and his patience under difficulties, to calm and animate such a number of his followers, as might counterbalance the panic of the rest, and lead them back to the means from which alone safety could be derived. He had hoped immediately to follow me; but, being defeated in this intention, he sent his messenger urging me to secure my own troop at such a distance from Versailles, as to prevent the contagion of rebellion from reaching them; promising, at the same time, to join me the moment a favourable occasion should occur, by means of which he could withdraw the main body of the emigrants from the evil influence at present exercised over them.

I was thrown into a most painful state of uncertainty by these communications. My first impulse was that we should all return to Versailles, there to assist in extricating our chief from his perils. I accordingly assembled my troop, and proposed to them this retrograde movement, instead of the continuation of our journey to Auxerre. With one voice they refused to comply. The notion circulated among them was, that the ravages of the plague alone detained the Protector; they opposed his order to my request; they came to a resolve to proceed without me, should I refuse to accompany them. Argument and adjuration were lost on these dastards. The continual diminution of their own numbers, effected by pestilence, added a sting to their dislike of delay; and my opposition only served to bring their resolution to a crisis. That same evening they departed towards Auxerre. Oaths, as from soldiers to their general, had been taken by them: these they broke. I also had engaged myself not to desert them; it appeared to me inhuman to ground any infraction of my word on theirs. The same spirit that caused them to rebel against me, would impel them to desert each other; and the most dreadful sufferings would be the consequence of their journey in their present unordered and chiefless array. These feelings for a time were paramount; and, in obedience to them, I accompanied the rest towards Auxerre.

We arrived the same night at Villeneuve-la-Guiard, a town at the distance of four posts from Fontainebleau.[52] When my companions had retired to rest, and I was left alone to revolve and ruminate upon the intelligence I received of Adrian's situation, another view of the subject presented itself to me. What was I doing, and what was the object of my present movements? Apparently I was to lead this troop of selfish and lawless men towards Switzerland, leaving behind my family and my selected friend, which, subject as they were hourly to the death that threatened to all, I might never see again. Was it not my first duty to assist the Protector, setting an example of attachment and duty? At a crisis, such as the one I had reached, it is very difficult to balance nicely opposing interests, and that towards which our inclinations lead us, obstinately assumes the appearance of selfishness, even when we meditate a sacrifice. We are easily led at such times to make a compromise of the question; and this was my present resource. I resolved that very night to ride to Versailles; if I found affairs less desperate than I now deemed them, I would return without delay to my troop; I had a vague idea that my arrival at that town, would occasion some sensation more or less strong, of which we might profit, for the purpose of leading forward the vacillating multitude—at least no time was to be lost—I visited the stables, I saddled my favourite horse, and vaulting on his back, without giving myself time for further reflection or hesitation, quitted Villeneuve-la-Guiard on my return to Versailles.

I was glad to escape from my rebellious troop, and to lose sight for a time, of the strife of evil with good, where the former for ever remained triumphant. I was stung almost to madness by my uncertainty concerning the fate of Adrian, and grew reckless of any event, except what might lose

---

52   For Villeneuve-la-Guyard see *Journals* 1: 132. A post is a journey equal to the distance between two relay stations.

or preserve my unequalled friend. With an heavy heart, that sought relief in the rapidity of my course, I rode through the night to Versailles. I spurred my horse, who addressed his free limbs to speed, and tossed his gallant head in pride. The constellations reeled swiftly by, swiftly each tree and stone and landmark fled past my onward career. I bared my head to the rushing wind, which bathed my brow in delightful coolness. As I lost sight of Villeneuve-la-Guiard, I forgot the sad drama of human misery; methought it was happiness enough to live, sensitive the while of the beauty of the verdure-clad earth, the star-bespangled sky, and the tameless wind that lent animation to the whole. My horse grew tired—and I, forgetful of his fatigue, still as he lagged, cheered him with my voice, and urged him with the spur. He was a gallant animal, and I did not wish to exchange him for any chance beast I might light on, leaving him never to be refound. All night we went forward; in the morning he became sensible that we approached Versailles, to reach which as his home, he mustered his flagging strength. The distance we had come was not less than fifty miles, yet he shot down the long Boulevards swift as an arrow; poor fellow, as I dismounted at the gate of the castle, he sunk on his knees, his eyes were covered with a film, he fell on his side, a few gasps inflated his noble chest, and he died. I saw him expire with an anguish, unaccountable even to myself, the spasm was as the wrenching of some limb in agonizing torture, but it was brief as it was intolerable. I forgot him, as I swiftly darted through the open portal, and up the majestic stairs of this castle of victories—heard Adrian's voice—O fool! O woman nurtured, effeminate and contemptible being[53]—I heard his voice, and answered it with convulsive shrieks; I rushed into the Hall of Hercules, where he stood surrounded by a crowd, whose eyes, turned in wonder on me, reminded me that on the stage of the world, a man must repress such girlish extacies. I would have given worlds to have embraced him; I dared not—Half in exhaustion, half voluntarily, I threw myself at my length on the ground—dare I disclose the truth to the gentle offspring of solitude? I did so, that I might kiss the dear and sacred earth he trod.

I found everything in a state of tumult. An emissary of the leader of the elect, had been so worked up by his chief, and by his own fanatical creed, as to make an attempt on the life of the Protector and preserver of lost mankind. His hand was arrested while in the act of poignarding the Earl; this circumstance had caused the clamour I heard on my arrival at the castle, and the confused assembly of persons that I found assembled in the Salle d'Hercule. Although superstition and demoniac fury had crept

---

53 Lionel here reproaches himself for weakness; however, a punctuation error in the first edition (1826) reminds the reader that Lionel supplies only a thin disguise for MWS: "O fool! O woman, nurtured, effeminate and contemptible being."

among the emigrants, yet several adhered with fidelity to their noble chieftain; and many, whose faith and love had been unhinged by fear, felt all their latent affection rekindled by this detestable attempt. A phalanx of faithful breasts closed round him; the wretch, who, although a prisoner and in bonds, vaunted his design, and madly claimed the crown of martyrdom, would have been torn to pieces, had not his intended victim interposed. Adrian, springing forward, shielded him with his own person, and commanded with energy the submission of his infuriate friends—at this moment I had entered.

Discipline and peace were at length restored in the castle; and then Adrian went from house to house, from troop to troop, to soothe the disturbed minds of his followers, and recall them to their ancient obedience. But the fear of immediate death was still rife amongst these survivors of a world's destruction; the horror occasioned by the attempted assassination past away; each eye turned towards Paris. Men love a prop so well, that they will lean on a pointed poisoned spear; and such was he, the impostor, who, with fear of hell for his scourge, most ravenous wolf, played the driver to a credulous flock.

It was a moment of suspense, that shook even the resolution of the unyielding friend of man. Adrian for one moment was about to give in, to cease the struggle, and quit, with a few adherents, the deluded crowd, leaving them a miserable prey to their passions, and to the worse tyrant who excited them. But again, after a brief fluctuation of purpose, he resumed his courage and resolves, sustained by the singleness of his purpose, and the untried spirit of benevolence which animated him. At this moment, as an omen of excellent import, his wretched enemy pulled destruction on his head, destroying with his own hands the dominion he had erected.

His grand hold upon the minds of men, took its rise from the doctrine inculcated by him, that those who believed in, and followed him, were the remnant to be saved, while all the rest of mankind were marked out for death. Now, at the time of the Flood, the omnipotent repented him that he had created man,[54] and as then with water, now with the arrows of pestilence, was about to annihilate all, except those who obeyed his decrees, promulgated by the *ipse dixit*[55] prophet. It is impossible to say on what foundations this man built his hopes of being able to carry on such an imposture. It is likely that he was fully aware of the lie which murderous nature might give to his assertions, and believed it to be the cast of a die, whether he should in future ages be reverenced as an inspired delegate from heaven, or be recognized as an impostor by the present dying

---

54 See Genesis 6.6: "And it repented the Lord that he had made man on the earth, and it grieved him at his heart."

55 Self-styled.

generation. At any rate he resolved to keep up the drama to the last act. When, on the first approach of summer, the fatal disease again made its ravages among the followers of Adrian, the impostor exultingly proclaimed the exemption of his own congregation from the universal calamity. He was believed; his followers, hitherto shut up in Paris, now came to Versailles. Mingling with the coward band there assembled, they reviled their admirable leader, and asserted their own superiority and exemption.

At length the plague, slow-footed, but sure in her noiseless advance, destroyed the illusion, invading the congregation of the elect, and showering promiscuous death among them. Their leader endeavoured to conceal this event; he had a few followers, who, admitted into the arcana of his wickedness, could help him in the execution of his nefarious designs. Those who sickened were immediately and quietly withdrawn, the cord and a midnight-grave disposed of them for ever; while some plausible excuse was given for their absence. At last a female, whose maternal vigilance subdued even the effects of the narcotics administered to her, became a witness of their murderous designs on her only child. Mad with horror, she would have burst among her deluded fellow-victims, and, wildly shrieking, have awaked the dull ear of night with the history of the fiend-like crime; when the Impostor, in his last act of rage and desperation, plunged a poignard in her bosom. Thus wounded to death, her garments dripping with her own life-blood, bearing her strangled infant in her arms, beautiful and young as she was, Juliet, (for it was she) denounced to the host of deceived believers, the wickedness of their leader. He saw the aghast looks of her auditors, changing from horror to fury—the names of those already sacrificed were echoed by their relatives, now assured of their loss. The wretch with that energy of purpose, which had borne him thus far in his guilty career, saw his danger, and resolved to evade the worst forms of it—he rushed on one of the foremost, seized a pistol from his girdle, and his loud laugh of derision mingled with the report of the weapon with which he destroyed himself.

They left his miserable remains even where they lay; they placed the corpse of poor Juliet and her babe upon a bier, and all, with hearts subdued to saddest regret, in long procession walked towards Versailles. They met troops of those who had quitted the kindly protection of Adrian, and were journeying to join the fanatics. The tale of horror was recounted—all turned back; and thus at last, accompanied by the undiminished numbers of surviving humanity, and preceded by the mournful emblem of their recovered reason, they appeared before Adrian, and again and for ever vowed obedience to his commands, and fidelity to his cause.

CHAPTER XXVII

THESE events occupied so much time, that June had numbered more than half its days, before we again commenced our long-protracted journey. The day after my return to Versailles, six men, from among those I had left at Villeneuve-la-Guiard, arrived, with intelligence, that the rest of the troop had already proceeded towards Switzerland. We went forward in the same track.

It is strange, after an interval of time, to look back on a period, which, though short in itself, appeared, when in actual progress, to be drawn out interminably. By the end of July we entered Dijon; by the end of July those hours, days, and weeks had mingled with the ocean of forgotten time, which in their passage teemed with fatal events and agonizing sorrow. By the end of July, little more than a month had gone by, if man's life were measured by the rising and setting of the sun: but, alas! in that interval ardent youth had become grey-haired; furrows deep and uneraseable were trenched in the blooming cheek of the young mother; the elastic limbs of early manhood, paralyzed as by the burthen of years, assumed the decrepitude of age. Nights passed, during whose fatal darkness the sun grew old before it rose; and burning days, to cool whose baleful heat the balmy eve, lingering far in eastern climes, came lagging and ineffectual; days, in which the dial, radiant in its noon-day station, moved not its shadow the space of a little hour, until a whole life of sorrow had brought the sufferer to an untimely grave.

We departed from Versailles fifteen hundred souls. We set out on the eighteenth of June. We made a long procession, in which was contained every dear relationship, or tie of love, that existed in human society. Fathers and husbands, with guardian care, gathered their dear relatives around them; wives and mothers looked for support to the manly form beside them, and then with tender anxiety bent their eyes on the infant troop around. They were sad, but not hopeless. Each thought that some one would be saved; each, with that pertinacious optimism, which to the last characterized our human nature, trusted that their beloved family would be the one preserved.

We passed through France, and found it empty of inhabitants. Some one or two natives survived in the larger towns, which they roamed through like ghosts; we received therefore small encrease to our numbers, and such decrease through death, that at last it became easier to count the scanty list of survivors. As we never deserted any of the sick, until their death permitted us to commit their remains to the shelter of a grave, our journey was long, while every day a frightful gap was made in our troop—they died by tens, by fifties, by hundreds. No mercy was shewn by death; we ceased to expect it, and every day welcomed the sun with the feeling that we might never see it rise again.

The nervous terrors and fearful visions which had scared us during the spring, continued to visit our coward troop during this sad journey. Every evening brought its fresh creation of spectres; a ghost was depicted by every blighted tree; and appalling shapes were manufactured from each shaggy bush. By degrees these common marvels palled on us, and then other wonders were called into being. Once it was confidently asserted, that the sun rose an hour later than its seasonable time; again it was discovered that he grew paler and paler; that shadows took an uncommon appearance. It was impossible to have imagined, during the usual calm routine of life men had before experienced, the terrible effects produced by these extravagant delusions: in truth, of such little worth are our senses, when unsupported by concurring testimony, that it was with the utmost difficulty I kept myself free from the belief in supernatural events, to which the major part of our people readily gave credit. Being one sane amidst a crowd of the mad, I hardly dared assert to my own mind, that the vast luminary had undergone no change—that the shadows of night were unthickened by innumerable shapes of awe and terror; or that the wind, as it sung in the trees, or whistled round an empty building, was not pregnant with sounds of wailing and despair. Sometimes realities took ghostly shapes; and it was impossible for one's blood not to curdle at the perception of an evident mixture of what we knew to be true, with the visionary semblance of all that we feared.

Once, at the dusk of the evening, we saw a figure all in white, apparently of more than human stature, flourishing about the road, now throwing up its arms, now leaping to an astonishing height in the air, then turning round several times successively, then raising itself to its full height and gesticulating violently. Our troop, on the alert to discover and believe in the supernatural, made a halt at some distance from this shape; and, as it became darker, there was something appalling even to the incredulous, in the lonely spectre, whose gambols, if they hardly accorded with spiritual dignity, were beyond human powers. Now it leapt right up in the air, now sheer over a high hedge, and was again the moment after in the road before us. By the time I came up, the fright experienced by the spectators of this ghostly exhibition, began to manifest itself in the flight of some, and the close huddling together of the rest. Our goblin now perceived us; he approached, and, as we drew reverentially back, made a low bow. The sight was irresistibly ludicrous even to our hapless band, and his politeness was hailed by a shout of laughter;—then, again springing up, as a last effort, it sunk to the ground, and became almost invisible through the dusky night. This circumstance again spread silence and fear through the troop; the more courageous at length advanced, and, raising the dying wretch, discovered the tragic explanation of this wild scene. It was an opera-dancer, and had been one of the troop which deserted from Villeneuve-la-Guiard: falling sick, he had been deserted by his companions; in an access of delirium he had fancied himself on the stage, and, poor fellow, his dying sense eagerly accepted the last human applause that could ever be bestowed on his grace and agility.

At another time we were haunted for several days by an apparition, to which our people gave the appellation of the Black Spectre.[56] We never saw it except at evening, when his coal black steed, his mourning dress, and plume of black feathers, had a majestic and awe-striking appearance; his face, one said, who had seen it for a moment, was ashy pale; he had lingered far behind the rest of his troop, and suddenly at a turn in the road, saw the Black Spectre coming towards him; he hid himself in fear, and the horse and his rider slowly past, while the moon-beams fell on the face of the latter, displaying its unearthly hue. Sometimes at dead of night, as we watched the sick, we heard one galloping through the town; it was the Black Spectre come in token of inevitable death. He grew giant tall to vulgar eyes; an icy atmosphere, they said, surrounded him; when he was heard, all animals shuddered, and the dying knew that their last hour was come. It was Death himself, they declared, come visibly to seize on subject earth, and quell at once our decreasing numbers, sole rebels to his law. One day at noon, we saw a dark mass on the road before us, and, coming up, beheld the Black Spectre fallen from his horse, lying in the agonies of disease upon the ground. He did not survive many hours; and his last words disclosed the secret of his mysterious conduct. He was a French noble of distinction, who, from the effects of plague, had been left alone in his district; during many months, he had wandered from town to town, from province to province, seeking some survivor for a companion, and abhorring the loneliness to which he was condemned. When he discovered our troop, fear of contagion conquered his love of society. He dared not join us, yet he could not resolve to lose sight of us, sole human beings who besides himself existed in wide and fertile France; so he accompanied us in the spectral guise I have described, till pestilence gathered him to a larger congregation, even that of Dead Mankind.

It had been well, if such vain terrors could have distracted our thoughts from more tangible evils. But these were too dreadful and too many not to force themselves into every thought, every moment, of our lives. We were obliged to halt at different periods for days together, till another and yet another was consigned as a clod to the vast clod which had been once our living mother. Thus we continued travelling during the hottest season; and it was not till the first of August, that we, the emigrants,—reader, there were just eighty of us in number,—entered the gates of Dijon.

We had expected this moment with eagerness, for now we had accomplished the worst part of our drear journey, and Switzerland was near at hand. Yet how could we congratulate ourselves on any event thus imperfectly fulfilled? Were these miserable beings, who, worn and wretched, passed in sorrowful procession, the sole remnants of the race of man,

---

56   With the figure in white, cf. Defoe, *A Journal of the Plague Year* 350-51, Appendix C.2.iv. The Black Spectre perhaps recalls Raymond on his "coal-black charger" (154) riding into Constantinople (156).

which, like a flood, had once spread over and possessed the whole earth? It had come down clear and unimpeded from its primal mountain source in Ararat,[57] and grew from a puny streamlet to a vast perennial river, generation after generation flowing on ceaselessly. The same, but diversified, it grew, and swept onwards towards the absorbing ocean, whose dim shores we now reached. It had been the mere plaything of nature, when first it crept out of uncreative void into light; but thought brought forth power and knowledge; and, clad with these, the race of man assumed dignity and authority. It was then no longer the mere gardener of earth, or the shepherd of her flocks; "it carried with it an imposing and majestic aspect; it had a pedigree and illustrating ancestors; it had its gallery of portraits, its monumental inscriptions, its records and titles."[58]

This was all over, now that the ocean of death had sucked in the slackening tide, and its source was dried up. We first had bidden adieu to the state of things which having existed many thousand years, seemed eternal; such a state of government, obedience, traffic, and domestic intercourse, as had moulded our hearts and capacities, as far back as memory could reach. Then to patriotic zeal, to the arts, to reputation, to enduring fame, to the name of country, we had bidden farewell. We saw depart all hope of retrieving our ancient state—all expectation, except the feeble one of saving our individual lives from the wreck of the past. To preserve these we had quitted England—England, no more; for without her children, what name could that barren island claim? With tenacious grasp we clung to such rule and order as could best save us; trusting that, if a little colony could be preserved, that would suffice at some remoter period to restore the lost community of mankind.

But the game is up! We must all die; nor leave survivor nor heir to the wide inheritance of earth. We must all die! The species of man must perish; his frame of exquisite workmanship; the wondrous mechanism of his senses; the noble proportion of his godlike limbs; his mind, the throned king of these; must perish. Will the earth still keep her place among the planets; will she still journey with unmarked regularity round the sun; will the seasons change, the trees adorn themselves with leaves, and flowers shed their fragrance, in solitude? Will the mountains remain unmoved, and streams still keep a downward course towards the vast abyss; will the tides rise and fall, and the winds fan universal nature; will beasts pasture,

---

57 After the flood Noah's ark comes to rest "upon the mountains of Ararat" (Genesis 8.4).

58 Burke's Reflections on the French Revolution [MWS's note]; in Edmund Burke's *Reflections on the Revolution in France* (ed. Conor Cruise O'Brien 121), "It" refers to liberty under the British constitution, not (as in *The Last Man*) to "the race of man." The 1826 edition of *The Last Man* reads "illustrating ancestors," as does the "Seventh Edition" of the *Reflections* (1790); "illustrious," preferred by some editors, may be a better reading here.

birds fly, and fishes swim, when man, the lord, possessor, perceiver, and recorder of all these things, has passed away, as though he had never been? O, what mockery is this! Surely death is not death, and humanity is not extinct; but merely passed into other shapes, unsubjected to our perceptions. Death is a vast portal, an high road to life: let us hasten to pass; let us exist no more in this living death, but die that we may live!

We had longed with inexpressible earnestness to reach Dijon, since we had fixed on it, as a kind of station in our progress. But now we entered it with a torpor more painful than acute suffering. We had come slowly but irrevocably to the opinion, that our utmost efforts would not preserve one human being alive. We took our hands therefore away from the long grasped rudder; and the frail vessel on which we floated, seemed, the government over her suspended, to rush, prow foremost, into the dark abyss of the billows. A gush of grief, a wanton profusion of tears, and vain laments, and overflowing tenderness, and passionate but fruitless clinging to the priceless few that remained, was followed by languor and recklessness.

During this disastrous journey we lost all those, not of our own family, to whom we had particularly attached ourselves among the survivors. It were not well to fill these pages with a mere catalogue of losses; yet I cannot refrain from this last mention of those principally dear to us. The little girl whom Adrian had rescued from utter desertion, during our ride through London on the twentieth of November, died at Auxerre. The poor child had attached herself greatly to us; and the suddenness of her death added to our sorrow. In the morning we had seen her apparently in health—in the evening, Lucy, before we retired to rest, visited our quarters to say that she was dead. Poor Lucy herself only survived, till we arrived at Dijon. She had devoted herself throughout to the nursing the sick, and attending the friendless. Her excessive exertions brought on a slow fever, which ended in the dread disease whose approach soon released her from her sufferings. She had throughout been endeared to us by her good qualities, by her ready and cheerful execution of every duty, and mild acquiescence in every turn of adversity. When we consigned her to the tomb, we seemed at the same time to bid a final adieu to those peculiarly feminine virtues conspicuous in her; uneducated and unpretending as she was, she was distinguished for patience, forbearance, and sweetness. These, with all their train of qualities peculiarly English, would never again be revived for us. This type of all that was most worthy of admiration in her class among my countrywomen, was placed under the sod of desert France; and it was as a second separation from our country to have lost sight of her for ever.

The Countess of Windsor died during our abode at Dijon. One morning I was informed that she wished to see me. Her message made me remember, that several days had elapsed since I had last seen her. Such a circumstance had often occurred during our journey, when I remained behind to watch to their close the last moments of some one of our hapless comrades, and the rest of the troop past on before me. But there was something in the manner of her messenger, that made me suspect that all was not right. A caprice of the imagination caused me to conjecture that some ill had occurred to Clara or Evelyn, rather than to this aged lady. Our fears, for ever on the stretch, demanded a nourishment of horror; and it seemed too natural an occurrence, too like past times, for the old to die before the young.

I found the venerable mother of my Idris lying on a couch, her tall emaciated figure stretched out; her face fallen away, from which the nose stood out in sharp profile, and her large dark eyes, hollow and deep, gleamed with such light as may edge a thunder cloud at sun-set. All was shrivelled and dried up, except these lights; her voice too was fearfully changed, as she spoke to me at intervals. "I am afraid," said she, "that it is selfish in me to have asked you to visit the old woman again, before she dies: yet perhaps it would have been a greater shock to suddenly that I was dead, than to see me first thus."

I clasped her shrivelled hand: "Are you indeed so ill?" I asked.

"Do you not perceive death in my face," replied she, "it is strange; I ought to have expected this, and yet I confess it has taken me unaware. I never clung to life, or enjoyed it, till these last months, while among those I senselessly deserted: and it is hard to be snatched immediately away. I am glad, however, that I am not a victim of the plague; probably I should have died at this hour, though the world had continued as it was in my youth."

She spoke with difficulty, and I perceived that she regretted the necessity of death, even more than she cared to confess. Yet she had not to complain of an undue shortening of existence; her faded person shewed that life had naturally spent itself. We had been alone at first; now Clara entered; the Countess turned to her with a smile, and took the hand of this lovely child; her roseate palm and snowy fingers, contrasted with [the] relaxed fibres and yellow hue of those of her aged friend; she bent to kiss her, touching her withered mouth with the warm, full lips of youth. "Verney," said the Countess, "I need not recommend this dear girl to you, for your own sake you will preserve her. Were the world as it was, I should have a thousand sage precautions to impress, that one so sensitive, good, and beauteous, might escape the dangers that used to lurk for the destruction of the fair and excellent. This is all nothing now.

"I commit you, my kind nurse, to your uncle's care; to yours I entrust the dearest relic of my better self. Be to Adrian, sweet one, what you have been to me—enliven his sadness with your sprightly sallies; soothe his anguish by your sober and inspired converse, when he is dying; nurse him as you have done me."

Clara burst into tears; "Kind girl," said the Countess, "do not weep for me. Many dear friends are left to you."

"And yet," cried Clara, "you talk of their dying also. This is indeed cruel—how could I live, if they were gone? If it were possible for my beloved protector to die before me, I could not nurse him; I could only die too."

The venerable lady survived this scene only twenty-four hours. She was the last tie binding us to the ancient state of things. It was impossible to look on her, and not call to mind in their wonted guise, events and persons, as alien to our present situation as the disputes of Themistocles and Aristides, or the wars of the two roses[59] in our native land. The crown of England had pressed her brow; the memory of my father and his misfortunes, the vain struggles of the late king, the images of Raymond, Evadne, and Perdita, who had lived in the world's prime, were brought vividly before us. We consigned her to the oblivious tomb with reluctance; and when I turned from her grave, Janus veiled his retrospective face;[60] that which gazed on future generations had long lost its faculty.

After remaining a week at Dijon, until thirty of our number deserted the vacant ranks of life, we continued our way towards Geneva. At noon on the second day we arrived at the foot of Jura. We halted here during the heat of the day. Here fifty human beings—fifty, the only human beings that survived of the food-teeming earth, assembled to read in the looks of each other ghastly plague, or wasting sorrow, desperation, or worse, carelessness of future or present evil. Here we assembled at the foot of this mighty wall of mountain, under a spreading walnut tree; a brawling stream refreshed the green sward by its sprinkling; and the busy grasshopper chirped among the thyme. We clustered together a groupe of wretched sufferers. A mother cradled in her enfeebled arms the child, last of many, whose glazed eye was about to close for ever. Here beauty, late glowing in youthful lustre and consciousness, now wan and neglected, knelt fanning with uncertain motion the beloved, who lay striving to paint his features, distorted by illness, with a thankful smile. There an hard-featured, weather-worn veteran, having prepared his meal, sat, his head dropped on his breast, the useless knife falling from his grasp, his limbs utterly relaxed, as thought of wife and child, and dearest relative, all lost, passed across his recollection. There sat a man who for forty years had basked in fortune's tranquil sunshine; he held the hand of his last hope, his beloved daughter, who had just attained womanhood; and he gazed on her with anxious eyes, while she tried to rally her fainting spirit to comfort him. Here a servant, faithful to the last, though dying, waited on one, who, though still erect with health, gazed with gasping fear on the variety of woe around.

Adrian stood leaning against a tree; he held a book in his hand, but his

---

59 The conflict between Themistocles and Aristides in Athens led to Aristides' ostracism in 482 BC. The Wars of the Roses, between Yorkist and Lancastrian contenders for the English throne, ended with the accession of Henry VII in 1485.
60 Cf. 172n.

eye wandered from the pages, and sought mine; they mingled a sympathetic glance; his looks confessed that his thoughts had quitted the inanimate print, for pages more pregnant with meaning, more absorbing, spread out before him. By the margin of the stream, apart from all, in a tranquil nook, where the purling brook kissed the green sward gently, Clara and Evelyn were at play, sometimes beating the water with large boughs, sometimes watching the summer-flies that sported upon it. Evelyn now chased a butterfly—now gathered a flower for his cousin; and his laughing cherub-face and clear brow told of the light heart that beat in his bosom. Clara, though she endeavoured to give herself up to his amusement, often forgot him, as she turned to observe Adrian and me. She was now fourteen, and retained her childish appearance, though in height a woman; she acted the part of the tenderest mother to my little orphan boy; to see her playing with him, or attending silently and submissively on our wants, you thought only of her admirable docility and patience; but, in her soft eyes, and the veined curtains that veiled them, in the clearness of her marmoreal brow, and the tender expression of her lips, there was an intelligence and beauty that at once excited admiration and love.

When the sun had sunk towards the precipitate west, and the evening shadows grew long, we prepared to ascend the mountain. The attention that we were obliged to pay to the sick, made our progress slow. The winding road, though steep, presented a confined view of rocky fields and hills, each hiding the other, till our farther ascent disclosed them in succession. We were seldom shaded from the declining sun, whose slant beams were instinct with exhausting heat. There are times when minor difficulties grow gigantic—times, when as the Hebrew poet expressively terms it, "the grasshopper is a burthen;" [61] so was it with our ill fated party this evening. Adrian, usually the first to rally his spirits, and dash foremost into fatigue and hardship, with relaxed limbs and declined head, the reins hanging loosely in his grasp, left the choice of the path to the instinct of his horse, now and then painfully rousing himself, when the steepness of the ascent required that he should keep his seat with better care. Fear and horror encompassed me. Did his languid air attest that he also was struck with contagion? How long, when I look on this matchless specimen of mortality, may I perceive that his thought answers mine? how long will those limbs obey the kindly spirit within? how long will light and life dwell in the eyes of this my sole remaining friend? Thus pacing slowly, each hill surmounted, only presented another to be ascended; each jutting corner only discovered another, sister to the last, endlessly. Sometimes the pressure of sickness in one among us, caused the whole cavalcade to halt; the call for water, the eagerly expressed wish to repose;

---

61 Ecclesiastes 12.5; cf. 255n.

the cry of pain, and suppressed sob of the mourner—such were the sorrowful attendants of our passage of the Jura.

Adrian had gone first. I saw him, while I was detained by the loosening of a girth, struggling with the upward path, seemingly more difficult than any we had yet passed. He reached the top, and the dark outline of his figure stood in relief against the sky. He seemed to behold something unexpected and wonderful; for, pausing, his head stretched out, his arms for a moment extended, he seemed to give an All Hail! to some new vision. Urged by curiosity, I hurried to join him. After battling for many tedious minutes with the precipice, the same scene presented itself to me, which had wrapt him in extatic wonder.

Nature, or nature's favourite, this lovely earth, presented her most unrivalled beauties in resplendent and sudden exhibition. Below, far, far below, even as it were in the yawning abyss of the ponderous globe, lay the placid and azure expanse of lake Leman;[62] vine-covered hills hedged it in, and behind dark mountains in cone-like shape, or irregular cyclopean wall, served for further defence. But beyond, and high above all, as if the spirits of the air had suddenly unveiled their bright abodes, placed in scaleless altitude in the stainless sky, heaven-kissing, companions of the unattainable ether, were the glorious Alps, clothed in dazzling robes of light by the setting sun. And, as if the world's wonders were never to be exhausted, their vast immensities, their jagged crags, and roseate painting, appeared again in the lake below, dipping their proud heights beneath the unruffled waves—palaces for the Naiads of the placid waters. Towns and villages lay scattered at the foot of Jura, which, with dark ravine, and black promontories, stretched its roots into the watery expanse beneath. Carried away by wonder, I forgot the death of man, and the living and beloved friend near me. When I turned, I saw tears streaming from his eyes; his thin hands pressed one against the other, his animated countenance beaming with admiration; "Why," cried he, at last, "Why, oh heart, whisperest thou of grief to me? Drink in the beauty of that scene, and possess delight beyond what a fabled paradise could afford."

By degrees, our whole party surmounting the steep, joined us; not one among them, but gave visible tokens of admiration, surpassing any before experienced. One cried, "God reveals his heaven to us; we may die blessed." Another and another, with broken exclamations, and extravagant phrases, endeavoured to express the intoxicating effect of this wonder of nature. So we remained awhile, lightened of the pressing burthen of fate, forgetful of death, into whose night we were about to plunge; no longer reflecting that our eyes now and for ever were and would be the only ones which might perceive the divine magnificence of this terrestrial exhibition. An enthusiastic transport, akin to happiness, burst, like a

---

sudden ray from the sun, on our darkened life. Precious attribute of woe-worn humanity! that can snatch extatic emotion, even from under the very share and harrow, that ruthlessly ploughs up and lays waste every hope.

This evening was marked by another event. Passing through Ferney in our way to Geneva, unaccustomed sounds of music arose from the rural church which stood embosomed in trees, surrounded by smokeless, vacant cottages. The peal of an organ with rich swell awoke the mute air, lingering along, and mingling with the intense beauty that clothed the rocks and woods, and waves around.

Music—the language of the immortals, disclosed to us as testimony of their existence—music, "silver key of the fountain of tears,"[63] child of love, soother of grief, inspirer of heroism and radiant thoughts, O music, in this our desolation, we had forgotten thee! Nor pipe at eve cheered us, nor harmony of voice, nor linked thrill of string; thou camest upon us now, like the revealing of other forms of being; and transported as we had been by the loveliness of nature, fancying that we beheld the abode of spirits, now we might well imagine that we heard their melodious communings. We paused in such awe as would seize on a pale votarist, visiting some holy shrine at midnight; if she beheld animated and smiling, the image which she worshipped. We all stood mute; many knelt. In a few minutes however, we were recalled to human wonder and sympathy by a familiar strain. The air was Haydn's "New-Created World,"[64] and, old and drooping as humanity had become, the world yet fresh as at creation's day, might still be worthily celebrated by such an hymn of praise. Adrian and I entered the church; the nave was empty, though the smoke of incense rose from the altar, bringing with it the recollection of vast congregations, in once thronged cathedrals; we went into the loft. A blind old man[65] sat at the bellows; his whole soul was ear; and as he sat in the attitude of attentive listening, a bright glow of pleasure was diffused over his countenance; for, though his lack-lustre eye could not reflect the beam, yet his parted lips, and every line of his face and venerable brow spoke delight. A young woman sat at the keys, perhaps twenty years of age. Her auburn hair hung on her neck, and her fair brow shone in its own beauty; but her drooping eyes let fall fast-flowing tears, while the constraint she exercised

---

63 PBS, "A Fragment: To Music" 1 (1817, pub. 1839).

64 MWS's friend Vincent Novello played the organ in a performance of Haydn's "Creation" at the Westminster Abbey Festival in 1823. MWS refers to "the piece, 'A new healed World'—in [Haydn's] Creation" in a letter of December 1823.

65 Cf. the blind father, De Lacey, in *Frankenstein* and the blind father and daughter in PBS's unfinished story, "The Coliseum" (*Works*, ed. Ingpen and Peck 6: 299-306).

to suppress her sobs, and still her trembling, flushed her else pale cheek; she was thin; languor, and alas! sickness, bent her form.

We stood looking at the pair, forgetting what we heard in the absorbing sight; till, the last chord struck, the peal died away in lessening reverberations. The mighty voice, inorganic we might call it, for we could in no way associate it with mechanism of pipe or key, stilled its sonorous tone, and the girl, turning to lend her assistance to her aged companion, at length perceived us.

It was her father; and she, since childhood, had been the guide of his darkened steps. They were Germans from Saxony, and, emigrating thither but a few years before, had formed new ties with the surrounding villagers. About the time that the pestilence had broken out, a young German student had joined them. Their simple history was easily divined. He, a noble, loved the fair daughter of the poor musician, and followed them in their flight from the persecutions of his friends; but soon the mighty leveller came with unblunted scythe to mow, together with the grass, the tall flowers of the field. The youth was an early victim. She preserved herself for her father's sake. His blindness permitted her to continue a delusion, at first the child of accident—and now solitary beings, sole survivors in the land, he remained unacquainted with the change, nor was aware that when he listened to his child's music, the mute mountains, senseless lake, and unconscious trees, were, himself excepted, her sole auditors.

The very day that we arrived she had been attacked by symptomatic illness. She was paralyzed with horror at the idea of leaving her aged, sightless father alone on the empty earth; but she had not courage to disclose the truth, and the very excess of her desperation animated her to surpassing exertions. At the accustomed vesper hour, she led him to the chapel; and, though trembling and weeping on his account, she played, without fault in time, or error in note, the hymn written to celebrate the creation of the adorned earth, soon to be her tomb.

We came to her like visitors from heaven itself; her high-wrought courage; her hardly sustained firmness, fled with the appearance of relief. With a shriek she rushed towards us, embraced the knees of Adrian, and uttering but the words, "O save my father!" with sobs and hysterical cries, opened the long-shut floodgates of her woe.

Poor girl!—she and her father now lie side by side, beneath the high walnut-tree where her lover reposes, and which in her dying moments she had pointed out to us. Her father, at length aware of his daughter's danger, unable to see the changes of her dear countenance, obstinately held her hand, till it was chilled and stiffened by death. Nor did he then move or speak, till, twelve hours after, kindly death took him to his breakless repose. They rest beneath the sod, the tree their monument;—the hallowed spot is distinct in my memory, paled in by craggy Jura, and the far, immeasurable Alps; the spire of the church they frequented still points from out the embosoming trees; and though her hand be cold, still methinks the sounds of divine music which they loved wander about, solacing their gentle ghosts.

CHAPTER XXVIII

WE had now reached Switzerland, so long the final mark and aim of our exertions. We had looked, I know not wherefore, with hope and pleasing expectation on her congregation of hills and snowy crags, and opened our bosoms with renewed spirits to the icy Biz,[66] which even at Midsummer used to come from the northern glacier laden with cold. Yet how could we nourish expectation of relief? Like our native England, and the vast extent of fertile France, this mountain-embowered land was desolate of its inhabitants. Nor bleak mountain-top, nor snow-nourished rivulet; not the ice-laden Biz, nor thunder, the tamer of contagion, had preserved them—why therefore should we claim exemption?

Who was there indeed to save? What troop had we brought fit to stand at bay, and combat with the conqueror? We were a failing remnant, tamed to mere submission to the coming blow. A train half dead, through fear of death—a hopeless, unresisting, almost reckless crew, which, in the tossed bark of life, had given up all pilotage, and resigned themselves to the destructive force of ungoverned winds. Like a few furrows of unreaped corn, which, left standing on a wide field after the rest is gathered to the garner, are swiftly borne down by the winter storm. Like a few straggling swallows, which, remaining after their fellows had, on the first unkind breath of passing autumn, migrated to genial climes, were struck to earth by the first frost of November. Like a stray sheep that wanders over the sleet-beaten hill-side, while the flock is in the pen, and dies before morning-dawn. Like a cloud, like one of many that were spread in inpenetrable woof over the sky, which, when the shepherd north has driven its companions "to drink Antipodean noon,"[67] fades and dissolves in the clear ether—Such were we!

We left the fair margin of the beauteous lake of Geneva, and entered the Alpine ravines; tracing to its source the brawling Arve, through the rock-bound valley of Servox, beside the mighty waterfalls, and under the shadow of the inaccessible mountains, we travelled on; while the luxuriant walnut-tree gave place to the dark pine, whose musical branches swung in the wind, and whose upright forms had braved a thousand storms—till the verdant sod, the flowery dell, and shrubbery hill were

---

66   A cold north or northeast wind blowing down from the Swiss Alps.
67   Thomas Lovell Beddoes, *The Brides' Tragedy* 1.1.6-8: "The wind, their boisterous shepherd, whistling drives them [clouds], / From the drear wilderness of night to drink / Antipodean noon."

exchanged for the sky-piercing, untrodden, seedless rock, "the bones of the world, waiting to be clothed with every thing necessary to give life and beauty."[68] Strange that we should seek shelter here! Surely, if, in those countries where earth was wont, like a tender mother, to nourish her children, we had found her a destroyer, we need not seek it here, where stricken by keen penury she seems to shudder through her stony veins. Nor were we mistaken in our conjecture. We vainly sought the vast and ever moving glaciers of Chamounix, rifts of pendant ice, seas of congelated waters, the leafless groves of tempest-battered pines, dells, mere paths for the loud avalanche, and hill-tops, the resort of thunder-storms. Pestilence reigned paramount even here. By the time that day and night, like twin sisters of equal growth, shared equally their dominion over the hours, one by one, beneath the ice-caves, beside the waters springing from the thawed snows of a thousand winters, another and yet another of the remnant of the race of Man, closed their eyes for ever to the light.

Yet we were not quite wrong in seeking a scene like this, whereon to close the drama. Nature, true to the last, consoled us in the very heart of misery. Sublime grandeur of outward objects soothed our hapless hearts, and were in harmony with our desolation. Many sorrows have befallen man during his chequered course; and many a woe-stricken mourner has found himself sole survivor among many. Our misery took its majestic shape and colouring from the vast ruin, that accompanied and made one with it. Thus, on lovely earth, many a dark ravine contains a brawling stream, shadowed by romantic rocks, threaded by mossy paths—but all, except this, wanted the mighty back-ground, the towering Alps, whose snowy capes, or bared ridges, lifted us from our dull mortal abode, to the palaces of Nature's own.

This solemn harmony of event and situation regulated our feelings, and gave as it were fitting costume to our last act. Majestic gloom and tragic pomp attended the decease of wretched humanity. The funeral procession of monarchs of old, was transcended by our splendid shews. Near the sources of the Arveiron we performed the rites for, four only excepted, the last of the species. Adrian and I, leaving Clara and Evelyn wrapt in peaceful unobserving slumber, carried the body to this desolate spot, and placed it in those caves of ice beneath the glacier, which rive and split with the slightest sound, and bring destruction on those within the clefts—no bird or beast of prey could here profane the frozen form. So, with hushed steps and in silence, we placed the dead on a bier of ice, and then, departing, stood on the rocky platform beside the river springs. All hushed as we had been, the very striking of the air with our persons had sufficed to disturb the repose of this thawless region; and we had hardly left the cavern, before vast blocks of ice, detaching themselves

---

68   Mary Wollstonecraft's Letters from Norway [MWS's note]: see *Letters Written During a Short Residence*, ed. Carol H. Poston, letter 5, 42.

from the roof, fell, and covered the human image we had deposited within. We had chosen a fair moonlight night, but our journey thither had been long, and the crescent sank behind the western heights by the time we had accomplished our purpose. The snowy mountains and blue glaciers shone in their own light. The rugged and abrupt ravine, which formed one side of Mont Anvert, was opposite to us, the glacier at our side; at our feet Arveiron, white and foaming, dashed over the pointed rocks that jutted into it, and, with whirring spray and ceaseless roar, disturbed the stilly night. Yellow lightnings played around the vast dome of Mont Blanc,[69] silent as the snow-clad rock they illuminated; all was bare, wild, and sublime, while the singing of the pines in melodious murmurings added a gentle interest to the rough magnificence. Now the riving and fall of icy rocks clave the air; now the thunder of the avalanche burst on our ears. In countries whose features are of less magnitude, nature betrays her living powers in the foliage of the trees, in the growth of herbage, in the soft purling of meandering streams; here, endowed with giant attributes, the torrent, the thunder-storm, and the flow of massive waters, display her activity. Such the church-yard, such the requiem, such the eternal congregation, that waited on our companion's funeral!

Nor was it the human form alone which we had placed in this eternal sepulchre, whose obsequies we now celebrated. With this last victim Plague vanished from the earth. Death had never wanted weapons wherewith to destroy life, and we, few and weak as we had become, were still exposed to every other shaft with which his full quiver teemed. But pestilence was absent from among them. For seven years it had had full sway upon earth; she had trod every nook of our spacious globe; she had mingled with the atmosphere, which as a cloak enwraps all our fellow-creatures—the inhabitants of native Europe—the luxurious Asiatic—the swarthy African and free American had been vanquished and destroyed by her. Her barbarous tyranny came to its close here in the rocky vale of Chamounix.

Still recurring scenes of misery and pain, the fruits of this distemper, made no more a part of our lives—the word plague no longer rung in our ears—the aspect of plague incarnate in the human countenance no longer appeared before our eyes. From this moment I saw plague no more. She abdicated her throne, and despoiled herself of her imperial sceptre among the ice rocks that surrounded us. She left solitude and silence co-heirs of her kingdom.

My present feelings are so mingled with the past, that I cannot say

---

69   Mont Blanc, near the border between France and northwest Italy, is the site of Frankenstein's first conversation with his creature and the subject of PBS's poem of 1816, "Mont Blanc," published with *History of a Six Weeks' Tour* in 1817. The Shelleys visited the places mentioned here in 1814 and 1816: see *History of a Six Weeks' Tour* (1817).

whether the knowledge of this change visited us, as we stood on this sterile spot. It seems to me that it did; that a cloud seemed to pass from over us, that a weight was taken from the air; that henceforth we breathed more freely, and raised our heads with some portion of former liberty. Yet we did not hope. We were impressed by the sentiment, that our race was run, but that plague would not be our destroyer. The coming time was as a mighty river, down which a charmed boat is driven, whose mortal steersman knows, that the obvious peril is not the one he needs fear, yet that danger is nigh; and who floats awe-struck under beetling precipices, through the dark and turbid waters—seeing in the distance yet stranger and ruder shapes, towards which he is irresistibly impelled. What would become of us? O for some Delphic oracle, or Pythian maid,[70] to utter the secrets of futurity! O for some Œdipus to solve the riddle of the cruel Sphynx![71] Such Œdipus was I to be—not divining a word's juggle, but whose agonizing pangs, and sorrow-tainted life were to be the engines, wherewith to lay bare the secrets of destiny, and reveal the meaning of the enigma, whose explanation closed the history of the human race.

Dim fancies, akin to these, haunted our minds, and instilled feelings not unallied to pleasure, as we stood beside this silent tomb of nature, reared by these lifeless mountains, above her living veins, choking her vital principle. "Thus are we left," said Adrian, "two melancholy blasted trees, where once a forest waved. We are left to mourn, and pine, and die. Yet even now we have our duties, which we must string ourselves to fulfil: the duty of bestowing pleasure where we can, and by force of love, irradiating with rainbow hues the tempest of grief. Nor will I repine if in this extremity we preserve what we now possess. Something tells me, Verney, that we need no longer dread our cruel enemy, and I cling with delight to the oracular voice. Though strange, it will be sweet to mark the growth of your little boy, and the development of Clara's young heart. In the midst of a desert world, we are everything to them; and, if we live, it must be our task to make this new mode of life happy to them. At present this is easy, for their childish ideas do not wander into futurity, and the stinging craving for sympathy, and all of love of which our nature is susceptible, is not yet awake within them: we cannot guess what will happen then, when nature asserts her indefeasible and sacred powers; but, long before that time, we may all be cold, as he who lies in yonder tomb of ice. We need only provide for the present, and endeavour to fill with pleasant images the inexperienced fancy of your lovely niece. The scenes which now surround us, vast and sublime as they are, are not such as can best

---

70   At Apollo's oracle at Delphi, as at Cumae, the Sibyl, or Pythia, uttered
     prophetic words interpreted by priests.
71   To solve the riddle of the Sphinx is to destroy her power, as Oedipus succeed-
     ed in doing; however, for both Oedipus and Lionel Verney, solving the enigma
     is not the end of suffering. See also 179n, above.

contribute to this work. Nature is here like our fortunes, grand, but too destructive, bare, and rude, to be able to afford delight to her young imagination. Let us descend to the sunny plains of Italy. Winter will soon be here, to clothe this wilderness in double desolation; but we will cross the bleak hill-tops, and lead her to scenes of fertility and beauty, where her path will be adorned with flowers, and the cheery atmosphere inspire pleasure and hope."

In pursuance of this plan we quitted Chamounix on the following day. We had no cause to hasten our steps; no event was transacted beyond our actual sphere to enchain our resolves, so we yielded to every idle whim, and deemed our time well spent, when we could behold the passage of the hours without dismay. We loitered along the lovely Vale of Servox; passed long hours on the bridge, which, crossing the ravine of Arve, commands a prospect of its pine-clothed depths, and the snowy mountains that wall it in. We rambled through romantic Switzerland; till, fear of coming winter leading us forward, the first days of October found us in the valley of La Maurienne, which leads to Cenis. I cannot explain the reluctance we felt at leaving this land of mountains; perhaps it was, that we regarded the Alps as boundaries between our former and our future state of existence, and so clung fondly to what of old we had loved. Perhaps, because we had now so few impulses urging to a choice between two modes of action, we were pleased to preserve the existence of one, and preferred the prospect of what we were to do, to the recollection of what had been done. We felt that for this year danger was past; and we believed that, for some months, we were secured to each other. There was a thrilling, agonizing delight in the thought—it filled the eyes with misty tears, it tore the heart with tumultuous heavings; frailer than the "snow fall in the river," [72] were we each and all—but we strove to give life and individuality to the meteoric course of our several existences, and to feel that no moment escaped us unenjoyed. Thus tottering on the dizzy brink, we were happy. Yes! as we sat beneath the toppling rocks, beside the waterfalls, near

—Forests, ancient as the hills,
And folding sunny spots of greenery,[73]

where the chamois grazed, and the timid squirrel laid up its hoard—descanting on the charms of nature, drinking in the while her unalienable beauties—we were, in an empty world, happy.

---

72 Robert Burns, *Tam O'Shanter*: "But pleasures are like poppies spread— / You seize the flow'r, its bloom is shed; / Or like the snow falls in the river— / A moment white—then melts, for ever" (59-62).
73 Coleridge, *Kubla Khan*, 1816 text.

' Yet, O days of joy—days, when eye spoke to eye, and voices, sweeter than the music of the swinging branches of the pines, or rivulet's gentle murmur, answered mine—yet, O days replete with beatitude, days of loved society—days unutterably dear to me forlorn—pass, O pass before me, making me in your memory forget what I am. Behold, how my streaming eyes blot this senseless paper—behold, how my features are convulsed by agonizing throes, at your mere recollection, now that, alone, my tears flow, my lips quiver, my cries fill the air, unseen, unmarked, unheard! Yet, O yet, days of delight! let me dwell on your long-drawn hours!

As the cold increased upon us, we passed the Alps, and descended into Italy. At the uprising of morn, we sat at our repast, and cheated our regrets by gay sallies or learned disquisitions. The live-long day we sauntered on, still keeping in view the end of our journey, but careless of the hour of its completion. As the evening star shone out, and the orange sunset, far in the west, marked the position of the dear land we had for ever left, talk, thought enchaining, made the hours fly—O that we had lived thus for ever and for ever! Of what consequence was it to our four hearts, that they alone were the fountains of life in the wide world? As far as mere individual sentiment was concerned, we had rather be left thus united together, than if, each alone in a populous desert of unknown men, we had wandered truly companionless till life's last term. In this manner, we endeavoured to console each other; in this manner, true philosophy taught us to reason.

It was the delight of Adrian and myself to wait on Clara, naming her the little queen of the world, ourselves her humblest servitors. When we arrived at a town, our first care was to select for her its most choice abode; to make sure that no harrowing relic remained of its former inhabitants; to seek food for her, and minister to her wants with assiduous tenderness. Clara entered into our scheme with childish gaiety. Her chief business was to attend on Evelyn; but it was her sport to array herself in splendid robes, adorn herself with sunny gems, and ape a princely state. Her religion, deep and pure, did not teach her to refuse to blunt thus the keen sting of regret; her youthful vivacity made her enter, heart and soul, into these strange masquerades.

We had resolved to pass the ensuing winter at Milan,[74] which, as being a large and luxurious city, would afford us choice of homes. We had descended the Alps, and left far behind their vast forests and mighty crags. We entered smiling Italy. Mingled grass and corn grew in her plains, the unpruned vines threw their luxuriant branches around the elms. The grapes, overripe, had fallen on the ground, or hung purple, or burnished green, among the red and yellow leaves. The ears of standing corn win-

---

74   In the north of Italy near the border with Switzerland.

nowed to emptiness by the spendthrift winds; the fallen foliage of the trees, the weed-grown brooks, the dusky olive, now spotted with its blackened fruit; the chesnuts, to which the squirrel only was harvest-man; all plenty, and yet, alas! all poverty, painted in wondrous hues and fantastic groupings this land of beauty. In the towns, in the voiceless towns, we visited the churches, adorned by pictures, master-pieces of art, or galleries of statues—while in this genial clime the animals, in new found liberty, rambled through the gorgeous palaces, and hardly feared our forgotten aspect. The dove-coloured oxen turned their full eyes on us, and paced slowly by; a startling throng of silly sheep, with pattering feet, would start up in some chamber, formerly dedicated to the repose of beauty, and rush, huddling past us, down the marble staircase into the street, and again in at the first open door, taking unrebuked possession of hallowed sanctuary, or kingly council-chamber. We no longer started at these occurrences, nor at worse exhibition of change—when the palace had become a mere tomb, pregnant with fetid stench, strewn with the dead; and we could perceive how pestilence and fear had played strange antics, chasing the luxurious dame to the dank fields and bare cottage; gathering, among carpets of Indian woof, and beds of silk, the rough peasant, or the deformed half-human shape of the wretched beggar.

We arrived at Milan, and stationed ourselves in the Vice-Roy's palace.[75] Here we made laws for ourselves, dividing our day, and fixing distinct occupations for each hour. In the morning we rode in the adjoining country, or wandered through the palaces, in search of pictures or antiquities. In the evening we assembled to read or to converse. There were few books that we dared read; few, that did not cruelly deface the painting we bestowed on our solitude, by recalling combinations and emotions never more to be experienced by us. Metaphysical disquisition; fiction, which wandering from all reality, lost itself in self-created errors; poets of times so far gone by, that to read of them was as to read of Atlantis and Utopia;[76] or such as referred to nature only, and the workings of one particular mind; but most of all, talk, varied and ever new, beguiled our hours.

While we paused thus in our onward career towards death, time held on its accustomed course. Still and for ever did the earth roll on, enthroned in her atmospheric car, speeded by the force of the invisible coursers of never-erring necessity. And now, this dew-drop in the sky, this ball, ponderous with mountains, lucent with waves, passing from the short tyranny of watery Pisces and the frigid Ram, entered the radiant

---

75 From 1814 until 1859 Milan was ruled by the Austrian Habsburgs.
76 Atlantis is a mythical island thought to have once existed in the western sea:
see Plato, *Timaeus* and *Critias*; utopia ("no place"), originally an imaginary
island in Sir Thomas More's Utopia (1516), is generally used to describe any
ideal society.

demesne of Taurus and the Twins.[77] There, fanned by vernal airs, the Spirit of Beauty sprung from her cold repose; and, with winnowing wings and soft pacing feet, set a girdle of verdure around the earth, sporting among the violets, hiding within the springing foliage of the trees, tripping lightly down the radiant streams into the sunny deep. "For lo! winter is past, the rain is over and gone; the flowers appear on the earth, the time of the singing of birds is come, and the voice of the turtle is heard in our land; the fig tree putteth forth her green figs, and the vines, with the tender grape, give a good smell."[78] Thus was it in the time of the ancient regal poet; thus was it now.

Yet how could we miserable hail the approach of this delightful season? We hoped indeed that death did not now as heretofore walk in its shadow; yet, left as we were alone to each other, we looked in each other's faces with enquiring eyes, not daring altogether to trust to our presentiments, and endeavouring to divine which would be the hapless survivor to the other three. We were to pass the summer at the lake of Como, and thither we removed as soon as spring grew to her maturity, and the snow disappeared from the hill tops. Ten miles from Como, under the steep heights of the eastern mountains, by the margin of the lake, was a villa called the Pliniana, from its being built on the site of a fountain, whose periodical ebb and flow is described by the younger Pliny in his letters.[79] The house had nearly fallen into ruin, till in the year 2090, an English nobleman had bought it, and fitted it up with every luxury. Two large halls, hung with splendid tapestry, and paved with marble, opened on each side of a court, of whose two other sides one overlooked the deep dark lake, and the other was bounded by a mountain, from whose stony side gushed, with roar and splash, the celebrated fountain. Above, underwood of myrtle and tufts of odorous plants crowned the rock, while the star-pointing giant cypresses reared themselves in the blue air, and the recesses of the hills were adorned with the luxuriant growth of chesnut-trees. Here we fixed our summer residence. We had a lovely skiff, in which we sailed, now stemming the midmost waves, now coasting the over-hanging and craggy banks, thick sown with evergreens, which dipped their shining leaves in the waters, and were mirrored in many a lit-

---

77 Pisces (February-March), followed by Aries or the Ram (March-April), gives way to Taurus or the Bull (April-May) and then to Gemini or the Twins (May-June).

78 Solomon's Song [MWS's note]; Song of Solomon 2.11-13: the "ancient regal poet" is King Solomon, to whom this book is traditionally ascribed.

79 In 1818, the Shelleys made an unsuccessful application to lease a house called Villa Pliniana, on Lake Como near Milan. PBS claimed, as MWS does here, that it was "so called from a fountain which ebbs and flows every three hours described by the younger Pliny which is in the courtyard" (*Letters*, ed. Frederick L. Jones 2: 7).

tle bay and creek of waters of translucent darkness. Here orange plants bloomed, here birds poured forth melodious hymns; and here, during spring, the cold snake emerged from the clefts, and basked on the sunny terraces of rock.

Were we not happy in this paradisiacal retreat? If some kind spirit had whispered forgetfulness to us, methinks we should have been happy here, where the precipitous mountains, nearly pathless, shut from our view the far fields of desolate earth, and with small exertion of the imagination, we might fancy that the cities were still resonant with popular hum, and the peasant still guided his plough through the furrow, and that we, the world's free denizens, enjoyed a voluntary exile, and not a remediless cutting off from our extinct species.

Not one among us enjoyed the beauty of this scenery so much as Clara. Before we quitted Milan, a change had taken place in her habits and manners. She lost her gaiety, she laid aside her sports, and assumed an almost vestal plainness of attire. She shunned us, retiring with Evelyn to some distant chamber or silent nook; nor did she enter into his pastimes with the same zest as she was wont, but would sit and watch him with sadly tender smiles, and eyes bright with tears, yet without a word of complaint. She approached us timidly, avoided our caresses, nor shook off her embarrassment till some serious discussion or lofty theme called her for awhile out of herself. Her beauty grew as a rose, which, opening to the summer wind, discloses leaf after leaf till the sense aches with its excess of loveliness. A slight and variable colour tinged her cheeks, and her motions seemed attuned by some hidden harmony of surpassing sweetness. We redoubled our tenderness and earnest attentions. She received them with grateful smiles, that fled swift as sunny beam from a glittering wave on an April day.

Our only acknowledged point of sympathy with her, appeared to be Evelyn. This dear little fellow was a comforter and delight to us beyond all words. His buoyant spirit, and his innocent ignorance of our vast calamity, were balm to us, whose thoughts and feelings were over-wrought and spun out in the immensity of speculative sorrow. To cherish, to caress, to amuse him was the common task of all. Clara, who felt towards him in some degree like a young mother, gratefully acknowledged our kindness towards him. To me, O! to me, who saw the clear brows and soft eyes of the beloved of my heart, my lost and ever dear Idris, re-born in his gentle face, to me he was dear even to pain; if I pressed him to my heart, methought I clasped a real and living part of her, who had lain there through long years of youthful happiness.

It was the custom of Adrian and myself to go out each day in our skiff to forage in the adjacent country. In these expeditions we were seldom accompanied by Clara or her little charge, but our return was an hour of hilarity. Evelyn ransacked our stores with childish eagerness, and we always brought some new found gift for our fair companion. Then too we made discoveries of lovely scenes or gay palaces, whither in the evening we all proceeded. Our sailing expeditions were most divine, and with a fair wind or transverse course we cut the liquid waves; and, if talk failed under the pressure of thought, I had my clarionet with me, which awoke the echoes, and gave the change to our careful minds. Clara at such times often returned to her former habits of free converse and gay sally; and though our four hearts alone beat in the world, those four hearts were happy.

One day, on our return from the town of Como, with a laden boat, we expected as usual to be met at the port by Clara and Evelyn, and we were somewhat surprised to see the beach vacant. I, as my nature prompted, would not prognosticate evil, but explained it away as a mere casual incident. Not so Adrian. He was seized with sudden trembling and apprehension, and he called to me with vehemence to steer quickly for land, and, when near, leapt from the boat, half falling into the water; and, scrambling up the steep bank, hastened along the narrow strip of garden, the only level space between the lake and the mountain. I followed without delay; the garden and inner court were empty, so was the house, whose every room we visited. Adrian called loudly upon Clara's name, and was about to rush up the near mountain-path, when the door of a summer-house at the end of the garden slowly opened, and Clara appeared, not advancing towards us, but leaning against a column of the building with blanched cheeks, in a posture of utter despondency. Adrian sprang towards her with a cry of joy, and folded her delightedly in his arms. She withdrew from his embrace, and, without a word, again entered the summer-house. Her quivering lips, her despairing heart refused to afford her voice to express our misfortune. Poor little Evelyn had, while playing with her, been seized with sudden fever, and now lay torpid and speechless on a little couch in the summer-house.

For a whole fortnight we unceasingly watched beside the poor child, as his life declined under the ravages of a virulent typhus.[80] His little form and tiny lineaments encaged the embryo of the world-spanning mind of man. Man's nature, brimful of passions and affections, would have had an home in that little heart, whose swift pulsations hurried towards their close. His small hand's fine mechanism, now flaccid and unbent, would in the growth of sinew and muscle, have achieved works of beauty or of strength. His tender rosy feet would have trod in firm manhood the bowers and glades of earth—these reflections were now of little use: he lay, thought and strength suspended, waiting unresisting the final blow.

We watched at his bedside, and when the access of fever was on him, we neither spoke nor looked at each other, marking only his obstructed breath and the mortal glow that tinged his sunken cheek, the heavy death that weighed on his eyelids. It is a trite evasion to say, that words could

---

80 For typhus, see 182n, above.

not express our long drawn agony; yet how can words image sensations, whose tormenting keenness throw us back, as it were, on the deep roots and hidden foundations of our nature, which shake our being with earth-quake-throe, so that we leave to confide in accustomed feelings which like mother-earth support us, and cling to some vain imagination or deceitful hope, which will soon be buried in the ruins occasioned by the final shock. I have called that period a fortnight, which we passed watching the changes of the sweet child's malady—and such it might have been—at night, we wondered to find another day gone, while each particular hour seemed endless. Day and night were exchanged for one another uncounted; we slept hardly at all, nor did we even quit his room, except when a pang of grief seized us, and we retired from each other for a short period to conceal our sobs and tears. We endeavoured in vain to abstract Clara from this deplorable scene. She sat, hour after hour, looking at him, now softly arranging his pillow, and, while he had power to swallow, administered his drink. At length the moment of his death came: the blood paused in its flow—his eyes opened, and then closed again: without convulsion or sigh, the frail tenement was left vacant of its spiritual inhabitant.

I have heard that the sight of the dead has confirmed materialists in their belief. I ever felt otherwise. Was that my child—that moveless decaying inanimation? My child was enraptured by my caresses; his dear voice cloathed with meaning articulations his thoughts, otherwise inaccessible; his smile was a ray of the soul, and the same soul sat upon its throne in his eyes. I turn from this mockery of what he was. Take, O earth, thy debt! freely and for ever I consign to thee the garb thou didst afford. But thou, sweet child, amiable and beloved boy, either thy spirit has sought a fitter dwelling, or, shrined in my heart, thou livest while it lives.

We placed his remains under a cypress, the upright mountain being scooped out to receive them. And then Clara said, "If you wish me to live, take me from hence. There is something in this scene of transcendent beauty, in these trees, and hills and waves, that for ever whisper to me, leave thy cumbrous flesh, and make a part of us. I earnestly entreat you to take me away."

So on the fifteenth of August we bade adieu to our villa, and the embowering shades of this abode of beauty; to calm bay and noisy waterfall; to Evelyn's little grave we bade farewell! and then, with heavy hearts, we departed on our pilgrimage towards Rome.

CHAPTER XXIX

Now—soft awhile—have I arrived so near the end? Yes! it is all over now—a step or two over those new made graves, and the wearisome way is done. Can I accomplish my task? Can I streak my paper with words capacious of the grand conclusion? Arise, black Melancholy! quit thy

Cimmerian solitude![81] Bring with thee murky fogs from hell, which may drink up the day; bring blight and pestiferous exhalations, which, entering the hollow caverns and breathing places of earth, may fill her stony veins with corruption, so that not only herbage may no longer flourish, the trees may rot, and the rivers run with gall—but the everlasting mountains be decomposed, and the mighty deep putrify, and the genial atmosphere which clips the globe, lose all powers of generation and sustenance. Do this, sad visaged power, while I write, while eyes read these pages.

And who will read them? Beware, tender offspring of the re-born world—beware, fair being, with human heart, yet untamed by care, and human brow, yet unploughed by time—beware, lest the cheerful current of thy blood be checked, thy golden locks turn grey, thy sweet dimpling smiles be changed to fixed, harsh wrinkles! Let not day look on these lines, lest garish day waste, turn pale, and die. Seek a cypress grove, whose moaning boughs will be harmony befitting; seek some cave, deep embowered in earth's dark entrails, where no light will penetrate, save that which struggles, red and flickering, through a single fissure, staining thy page with grimmest livery of death.

There is a painful confusion in my brain, which refuses to delineate distinctly succeeding events. Sometimes the irradiation of my friend's gentle smile comes before me; and methinks its light spans and fills eternity—then, again, I feel the gasping throes—

We quitted Como, and in compliance with Adrian's earnest desire, we took Venice in our way to Rome.[82] There was something to the English peculiarly attractive in the idea of this wave-encircled, island-enthroned city. Adrian had never seen it. We went down the Po and the Brenta in a boat; and, the days proving intolerably hot, we rested in the bordering palaces during the day, travelling through the night, when darkness made the bordering banks indistinct, and our solitude less remarkable; when the wandering moon lit the waves that divided before our prow, and the night-wind filled our sails, and the murmuring stream, waving trees, and swelling canvass, accorded in harmonious strain. Clara, long overcome by excessive grief, had to a great degree cast aside her timid, cold reserve, and received our attentions with grateful tenderness. While Adrian with poetic fervour discoursed of the glorious nations of the dead,[83] of the beauteous earth and the fate of man, she crept near him, drinking in his speech with silent pleasure. We banished from our talk, and as much as

---

81 Cf. the beginning of Milton, "L'Allegro," and see also 361. The Cimmerians appear in *Odyssey* 11 as inhabitants of the dark fringes of the world.

82 A rather circuitous route, first to the northeastern coastal city of Venice, then south to Rome; in the first stage of their journey, Lionel and Adrian's party travel by the rivers Po and Brenta, emerging south of Venice.

83 Cf. 160n.

possible from our thoughts, the knowledge of our desolation. And it would be incredible to an inhabitant of cities, to one among a busy throng, to what extent we succeeded. It was as a man confined in a dungeon, whose small and grated rift at first renders the doubtful light more sensibly obscure, till, the visual orb having drunk in the beam, and adapted itself to its scantiness, he finds that clear noon inhabits his cell. So we, a simple triad on empty earth, were multiplied to each other, till we became all in all. We stood like trees, whose roots are loosened by the wind, which support one another, leaning and clinging with encreased fervour while the wintry storms howl.

Thus we floated down the widening stream of the Po, sleeping when the cicale sang, awake with the stars. We entered the narrower banks of the Brenta, and arrived at the shore of the Laguna at sunrise on the sixth of September. The bright orb slowly rose from behind its cupolas and towers, and shed its penetrating light upon the glassy waters. Wrecks of gondolas, and some few uninjured ones, were strewed on the beach at Fusina. We embarked in one of these for the widowed daughter of ocean,[84] who, abandoned and fallen, sat forlorn on her propping isles, looking towards the far mountains of Greece. We rowed lightly over the Laguna, and entered Canale Grande. The tide ebbed sullenly from out the broken portals and violated halls of Venice: sea weed and sea monsters were left on the blackened marble, while the salt ooze defaced the matchless works of art that adorned their walls, and the sea gull flew out from the shattered window. In the midst of this appalling ruin of the monuments of man's power, nature asserted her ascendancy, and shone more beauteous from the contrast. The radiant waters hardly trembled, while the rippling waves made many sided mirrors to the sun; the blue immensity, seen beyond Lido,[85] stretched far, unspecked by boat, so tranquil, so lovely, that it seemed to invite us to quit the land strewn with ruins, and to seek refuge from sorrow and fear on its placid extent.

We saw the ruins of this hapless city from the height of the tower of San Marco, immediately under us, and turned with sickening hearts to the sea, which, though it be a grave, rears no monument, discloses no ruin. Evening had come apace. The sun set in calm majesty behind the misty

---

84 Cf. Byron, *Childe Harold's Pilgrimage* 4.11.91-92: "The spouseless Adriatic mourns her lord; / And annual marriage now no more renewed." Byron alludes to the Ascension Day ceremony (discontinued under the Habsburgs) in which the Doge or ruler of independent Venice had thrown a ring into the sea to symbolize the marriage of city and ocean; MWS reverses gender to make Venice, not the sea, the widow.

85 The lagoon of Venice is protected by the Lido, a long, narrow island that forms a natural breakwater; Fusina is on the coast, south of Venice; the rivers Po and Brenta flow down from the Alps into the Veneto or Venetian plain; the Grand Canal divides Venice into two equal parts.

summits of the Apennines, and its golden and roseate hues painted the mountains of the opposite shore. "That land," said Adrian, "tinged with the last glories of the day, is Greece." Greece! The sound had a responsive chord in the bosom of Clara. She vehemently reminded us that we had promised to take her once again to Greece, to the tomb of her parents. Why go to Rome? what should we do at Rome? We might take one of the many vessels to be found here, embark in it, and steer right for Albania.

I objected the dangers of ocean, and the distance of the mountains we saw, from Athens; a distance which, from the savage uncultivation of the country, was almost impassable. Adrian, who was delighted with Clara's proposal, obviated these objections. The season was favourable; the north-west that blew would take us transversely across the gulph; and then we might find, in some abandoned port, a light Greek caique,[86] adapted for such navigation, and run down the coast of the Morea, and, passing over the Isthmus of Corinth,[87] without much land-travelling or fatigue, find ourselves at Athens. This appeared to me wild talk; but the sea, glowing with a thousand purple hues, looked so brilliant and safe; my beloved companions were so earnest, so determined, that, when Adrian said, "Well, though it is not exactly what you wish, yet consent, to please me"—I could no longer refuse. That evening we selected a vessel, whose size just seemed fitted for our enterprize; we bent the sails and put the rigging in order, and reposing that night in one of the city's thousand palaces, agreed to embark at sunrise the following morning.

When winds that move not its calm surface, sweep
The azure sea, I love the land no more;
The smiles of the serene and tranquil deep
Tempt my unquiet mind—

Thus said Adrian, quoting a translation of Moschus's poem, as in the clear morning light, we rowed over the Laguna, past Lido, into the open sea—I would have added in continuation,

But, when the roar
Of ocean's gray abyss resounds, and foam
Gathers upon the sea, and vast waves burst—[88]

But my friends declared that such verses were evil augury; so in cheerful mood we left the shallow waters, and, when out at sea, unfurled our sails

---

86 A light row-boat or sail-boat used in the eastern Mediterranean.
87 Between Attica and the Peloponnesus.
88 Together, the two passages form a continuous quotation from PBS, translation from Moschus 1-6.

to catch the favourable breeze. The laughing morning air filled them, while sun-light bathed earth, sky and ocean—the placid waves divided to receive our keel, and playfully kissed the dark sides of our little skiff, murmuring a welcome; as land receded, still the blue expanse, most waveless, twin sister to the azure empyrean, afforded smooth conduct to our bark. As the air and waters were tranquil and balmy, so were our minds steeped in quiet. In comparison with the unstained deep, funereal earth appeared a grave, its high rocks and stately mountains were but monuments, its trees the plumes of a hearse, the brooks and rivers brackish with tears for departed man. Farewell to desolate towns—to fields with their savage intermixture of corn and weeds—to ever multiplying relics of our lost species. Ocean, we commit ourselves to thee—even as the patriarch of old[89] floated above the drowned world, let us be saved, as thus we betake ourselves to thy perennial flood.

Adrian sat at the helm; I attended to the rigging, the breeze right aft filled our swelling canvas, and we ran before it over the untroubled deep. The wind died away at noon; its idle breath just permitted us to hold our course. As lazy, fair-weather sailors, careless of the coming hour, we talked gaily of our coasting voyage, of our arrival at Athens. We would make our home of one of the Cyclades,[90] and there in myrtle-groves, amidst perpetual spring, fanned by the wholesome sea-breezes—we would live long years in beatific union—Was there such a thing as death in the world?—

The sun passed its zenith, and lingered down the stainless floor of heaven. Lying in the boat, my face turned up to the sky, I thought I saw on its blue white, marbled streaks, so slight, so immaterial, that now I said—They are there—and now, It is a mere imagination. A sudden fear stung me while I gazed; and, starting up, and running to the prow,—as I stood, my hair was gently lifted on my brow—a dark line of ripples appeared to the east, gaining rapidly on us—my breathless remark to Adrian, was followed by the flapping of the canvas, as the adverse wind struck it, and our boat lurched—swift as speech, the web of the storm thickened over head, the sun went down red, the dark sea was strewed with foam, and our skiff rose and fell in its encreasing furrows.

Behold us now in our frail tenement, hemmed in by hungry, roaring waves, buffeted by winds. In the inky east two vast clouds, sailing contrary ways, met; the lightning leapt forth, and the hoarse thunder muttered. Again in the south, the clouds replied, and the forked stream of fire running along the black sky, shewed us the appalling piles of clouds, now met and obliterated by the heaving waves. Great God! And we alone—we three—alone—alone—sole dwellers on the sea and on the earth, we three must perish! The vast universe, its myriad worlds, and the plains of boundless earth which we had left—the extent of shoreless sea

---

89 Noah.
90 A group of islands in the southern Aegean Sea.

around—contracted to my view—they and all that they contained, shrunk up to one point, even to our tossing bark, freighted with glorious humanity.

A convulsion of despair crossed the love-beaming face of Adrian, while with set teeth he murmured, "Yet they shall be saved!" Clara, visited by an human pang, pale and trembling, crept near him—he looked on her with an encouraging smile—"Do you fear, sweet girl? O, do not fear, we shall soon be on shore!"

The darkness prevented me from seeing the changes of her countenance; but her voice was clear and sweet, as she replied, "Why should I fear? neither sea nor storm can harm us, if mighty destiny or the ruler of destiny does not permit. And then the stinging fear of surviving either of you, is not here—one death will clasp us undivided."

Meanwhile we took in all our sails, save a gib; and, as soon as we might without danger, changed our course, running with the wind for the Italian shore. Dark night mixed everything; we hardly discerned the white crests of the murderous surges, except when lightning made brief noon, and drank the darkness, shewing us our danger, and restoring us to double night. We were all silent, except when Adrian, as steersman, made an encouraging observation. Our little shell obeyed the rudder miraculously well, and ran along on the top of the waves, as if she had been an offspring of the sea, and the angry mother sheltered her endangered child.

I sat at the prow, watching our course; when suddenly I heard the waters break with redoubled fury. We were certainly near the shore—at the same time I cried, "About there!" and a broad lightning filling the concave, shewed us for one moment the level beach a-head, disclosing even the sands, and stunted, ooze-sprinkled beds of reeds, that grew at high water mark. Again it was dark, and we drew in our breath with such content as one may, who, while fragments of volcano-hurled rock darken the air, sees a vast mass ploughing the ground immediately at his feet. What to do we knew not—the breakers here, there, everywhere, encompassed us—they roared, and dashed, and flung their hated spray in our faces. With considerable difficulty and danger we succeeded at length in altering our course, and stretched out from shore. I urged my companions to prepare for the wreck of our little skiff, and to bind themselves to some oar or spar which might suffice to float them. I was myself an excellent swimmer—the very sight of the sea was wont to raise in me such sensations, as a huntsman experiences, when he hears a pack of hounds in full cry; I loved to feel the waves wrap me and strive to overpower me; while I, lord of myself, moved this way or that, in spite of their angry buffetings. Adrian also could swim—but the weakness of his frame prevented him from feeling pleasure in the exercise, or acquiring any great expertness.[91]

---

91   Unlike Byron, PBS was not a swimmer.

But what power could the strongest swimmer oppose to the overpowering violence of ocean in its fury? My efforts to prepare my companions were rendered nearly futile—for the roaring breakers prevented our hearing one another speak, and the waves, that broke continually over our boat, obliged me to exert all my strength in lading the water out, as fast as it came in. The while darkness, palpable and rayless, hemmed us round, dissipated only by the lightning; sometimes we beheld thunderbolts, fiery red, fall into the sea, and at intervals vast spouts stooped from the clouds, churning the wild ocean, which rose to meet them; while the fierce gale bore the rack onwards, and they were lost in the chaotic mingling of sky and sea. Our gunwales had been torn away, our single sail had been rent to ribbands, and borne down the stream of the wind. We had cut away our mast, and lightened the boat of all she contained—Clara attempted to assist me in heaving the water from the hold, and, as she turned her eyes to look on the lightning, I could discern by that momentary gleam, that resignation had conquered every fear. We have a power given us in any worst extremity, which props the else feeble mind of man, and enables us to endure the most savage tortures with a stillness of soul which in hours of happiness we could not have imagined. A calm, more dreadful in truth than the tempest, allayed the wild beatings of my heart—a calm like that of the gamester, the suicide, and the murderer, when the last die is on the point of being cast—while the poisoned cup is at the lips,—as the death-blow is about to be given.

Hours passed thus—hours which might write old age on the face of beardless youth, and grizzle the silky hair of infancy—hours, while the chaotic uproar continued, while each dread gust transcended in fury the one before, and our skiff hung on the breaking wave, and then rushed into the valley below, and trembled and spun between the watery precipices that seemed most to meet above her. For a moment the gale paused, and ocean sank to comparative silence—it was a breathless interval; the wind which, as a practised leaper, had gathered itself up before it sprung, now with terrific roar rushed over the sea, and the waves struck our stern. Adrian exclaimed that the rudder was gone;—"We are lost," cried Clara, "Save yourselves—O save yourselves!" The lightning shewed me the poor girl half buried in the water at the bottom of the boat; as she was sinking in it Adrian caught her up, and sustained her in his arms. We were without a rudder—we rushed prow foremost into the vast billows piled up a-head—they broke over and filled the tiny skiff; one scream I heard—one cry that we were gone, I uttered; I found myself in the waters; darkness was around. When the light of the tempest flashed, I saw the keel of our upset boat close to me—I clung to this, grasping it with clenched hand and nails, while I endeavoured during each flash to discover any appearance of my companions. I thought I saw Adrian at no great distance from me, clinging to an oar; I sprung from my hold, and with energy beyond my human strength, I dashed aside the waters as I strove to lay hold of him. As that hope failed, instinctive love of life animated me, and feelings of contention, as if a hostile will combated with mine. I breasted the surges, and flung them from me, as I would the opposing front and sharpened claws of a lion about to enfang my bosom. When I had been beaten down by one wave, I rose on another, while I felt bitter pride curl my lip.

Ever since the storm had carried us near the shore, we had never attained any great distance from it. With every flash I saw the bordering coast; yet the progress I made was small, while each wave, as it receded, carried me back into ocean's far abysses. At one moment I felt my foot touch the sand, and then again I was in deep water; my arms began to lose their power of motion; my breath failed me under the influence of the strangling waters—a thousand wild and delirious thoughts crossed me: as well as I can now recall them, my chief feeling was, how sweet it would be to lay my head on the quiet earth, where the surges would no longer strike my weakened frame, nor the sound of waters ring in my ears—to attain this repose, not to save my life, I made a last effort—the shelving shore suddenly presented a footing for me. I rose, and was again thrown down by the breakers—a point of rock to which I was enabled to cling, gave me a moment's respite; and then, taking advantage of the ebbing of the waves, I ran forwards—gained the dry sands, and fell senseless on the oozy reeds that sprinkled them.

I must have lain long deprived of life; for when first, with a sickening feeling, I unclosed my eyes, the light of morning met them. Great change had taken place meanwhile: grey dawn dappled the flying clouds, which sped onwards, leaving visible at intervals vast lakes of pure ether. A fountain of light arose in an encreasing stream from the east, behind the waves of the Adriatic, changing the grey to a roseate hue, and then flooding sky and sea with aerial gold.

A kind of stupor followed my fainting; my senses were alive, but memory was extinct. The blessed respite was short—a snake lurked near me to sting me into life—on the first retrospective emotion I would have started up, but my limbs refused to obey me; my knees trembled, the muscles had lost all power. I still believed that I might find one of my beloved companions cast like me, half alive, on the beach; and I strove in every way to restore my frame to the use of its animal functions. I wrung the brine from my hair; and the rays of the risen sun soon visited me with genial warmth. With the restoration of my bodily powers, my mind became in some degree aware of the universe of misery, henceforth to be its dwelling. I ran to the water's edge, calling on the beloved names. Ocean drank in, and absorbed my feeble voice, replying with pitiless roar. I climbed a near tree: the level sands bounded by a pine forest, and the sea clipped round by the horizon, was all that I could discern. In vain I extended my researches along the beach; the mast we had thrown overboard, with tangled cordage, and remnants of a sail, was the sole relic land received of our wreck. Sometimes I stood still, and wrung my hands. I accused earth and sky—the universal machine and the Almighty power that misdirected it. Again I threw myself on the sands, and then the sighing wind, mimicking a human cry, roused me to bitter, fallacious hope. Assuredly if any little bark or smallest canoe had been near, I should have sought the savage plains of ocean, found the dear remains of my lost ones, and clinging round them, have shared their grave.

The day passed thus; each moment contained eternity; although when hour after hour had gone by, I wondered at the quick flight of time. Yet even now I had not drunk the bitter potion to the dregs; I was not yet persuaded of my loss; I did not yet feel in every pulsation, in every nerve, in every thought, that I remained alone of my race,—that I was the LAST MAN.

The day had clouded over, and a drizzling rain set in at sunset. Even the eternal skies weep, I thought; is there any shame then, that mortal man should spend himself in tears? I remembered the ancient fables, in which human beings are described as dissolving away through weeping into ever-gushing fountains. Ah! that so it were; and then my destiny would be in some sort akin to the watery death of Adrian and Clara. Oh! grief is fantastic; it weaves a web on which to trace the history of its woe from every form and change around; it incorporates itself with all living nature; it finds sustenance in every object; as light, it fills all things, and, like light, it gives its own colours to all.

I had wandered in my search to some distance from the spot on which I had been cast, and came to one of those watch-towers, which at stated distances line the Italian shore. I was glad of shelter, glad to find a work of human hands, after I had gazed so long on nature's drear barrenness; so I entered, and ascended the rough winding staircase into the guard-room. So far was fate kind, that no harrowing vestige remained of its former inhabitants; a few planks laid across two iron tressels, and strewed with the dried leaves of Indian corn, was the bed presented to me; and an open chest, containing some half mouldered biscuit, awakened an appetite, which perhaps existed before, but of which, until now, I was not aware. Thirst also, violent and parching, the result of the sea-water I had drank, and of the exhaustion of my frame, tormented me. Kind nature had gifted the supply of these wants with pleasurable sensations, so that I—even I!—was refreshed and calmed, as I ate of this sorry fare, and drank a little of the sour wine which half filled a flask left in this abandoned dwelling. Then I stretched myself on the bed, not to be disdained by the victim of shipwreck. The earthy smell of the dried leaves was balm to my sense after the hateful odour of sea-weed. I forgot my state of loneliness. I neither looked backward nor forward; my senses were hushed to repose; I fell asleep and dreamed of all dear inland scenes, of hay-makers, of the shepherd's whistle to his dog, when he demanded his help to drive the flock to fold; of sights and sounds peculiar to my boyhood's mountain life, which I had long forgotten.

I awoke in a painful agony—for I fancied that ocean, breaking its bounds, carried away the fixed continent and deep rooted mountains, together with the streams I loved, the woods, and the flocks—it raged around, with that continued and dreadful roar which had accompanied the last wreck of surviving humanity. As my waking sense returned, the bare walls of the guard room closed round me, and the rain pattered against the single window. How dreadful it is, to emerge from the oblivion of slumber, and to receive as a good morrow the mute wailing of one's own hapless heart—to return from the land of deceptive dreams, to the heavy knowledge of unchanged disaster!—Thus was it with me, now, and for ever! The sting of other griefs might be blunted by time; and even mine yielded sometimes during the day, to the pleasure inspired by the imagination or the senses; but I never look first upon the morning-light but with my fingers pressed tight on my bursting heart, and my soul deluged with the interminable flood of hopeless misery. Now I awoke for the first time in the dead world—I awoke alone—and the dull dirge of the sea, heard even amidst the rain, recalled me to the reflection of the wretch I had become. The sound came like a reproach, a scoff—like the sting of remorse in the soul—I gasped—the veins and muscles of my throat swelled, suffocating me. I put my fingers to my ears, I buried my head in the leaves of my couch, I would have dived to the centre to lose hearing of that hideous moan.

But another task must be mine—again I visited the detested beach—again I vainly looked far and wide—again I raised my unanswered cry, lifting up the only voice that could ever again force the mute air to syllable the human thought.

What a pitiable, forlorn, disconsolate being I was! My very aspect and garb told the tale of my despair. My hair was matted and wild—my limbs soiled with salt ooze; while at sea, I had thrown off those of my garments that encumbered me, and the rain drenched the thin summer-clothing I had retained—my feet were bare, and the stunted reeds and broken shells made them bleed—the while, I hurried to and fro, now looking earnestly on some distant rock which, islanded in the sands, bore for a moment a deceptive appearance—now with flashing eyes reproaching the murderous ocean for its unutterable cruelty.

For a moment I compared myself to that monarch of the waste—Robinson Crusoe.[92] We had been both thrown companionless—he on the shore of a desolate island: I on that of a desolate world. I was rich in the so called goods of life. If I turned my steps from the near barren scene, and entered any of the earth's million cities, I should find their wealth stored up for my accommodation—clothes, food, books, and a choice of dwelling beyond the command of the princes of former times—every climate was subject to my selection, while he was obliged to toil in the acquirement of every necessary, and was the inhabitant of a

---

92   The shipwrecked hero of Daniel Defoe's *The Life and Adventures of Robinson Crusoe* (1719).

tropical island, against whose heats and storms he could obtain small shelter.—Viewing the question thus, who would not have preferred the Sybarite enjoyments I could command, the philosophic leisure, and ample intellectual resources, to his life of labour and peril? Yet he was far happier than I: for he could hope, nor hope in vain—the destined vessel at last arrived, to bear him to countrymen and kindred, where the events of his solitude became a fire-side tale. To none could I ever relate the story of my adversity; no hope had I. He knew that, beyond the ocean which begirt his lonely island, thousands lived whom the sun enlightened when it shone also on him: beneath the meridian sun and visiting moon, I alone bore human features; I alone could give articulation to thought; and, when I slept, both day and night were unbeheld of any. He had fled from his fellows, and was transported with terror at the print of a human foot. I would have knelt down and worshipped the same. The wild and cruel Caribbee, the merciless Cannibal[93]—or worse than these, the uncouth, brute, and remorseless veteran in the vices of civilization, would have been to me a beloved companion, a treasure dearly prized—his nature would be kin to mine; his form cast in the same mould; human blood would flow in his veins; a human sympathy must link us for ever. It cannot be that I shall never behold a fellow being more! —never!—never!—not in the course of years!—Shall I wake, and speak to none, pass the interminable hours, my soul, islanded in the world, a solitary point, surrounded by vacuum? Will day follow day endlessly thus?—No! no! a God rules the world—providence has not exchanged its golden sceptre for an aspic's sting.[94] Away! let me fly from the ocean-grave, let me depart from this barren nook, paled in, as it is, from access by its own desolateness; let me tread once again the paved towns; step over the threshold of man's dwellings, and most certainly I shall find this thought a horrible vision—a maddening, but evanescent dream.

I entered Ravenna, (the town nearest to the spot whereon I had been cast),[95] before the second sun had set on the empty world; I saw many living creatures; oxen, and horses, and dogs, but there was no man among them; I entered a cottage, it was vacant; I ascended the marble stairs of a palace, the bats and the owls were nestled in the tapestry; I stepped softly, not to awaken the sleeping town: I rebuked a dog, that by yelping disturbed the sacred stillness; I would not believe that all was as it

---

93 A Carib is an aboriginal inhabitant of the southern West Indies; "cannibal" is a corruption of the same word.

94 An aspic is an asp, here signifying death; Cleopatra is supposed to have killed herself by letting asps or poisonous snakes bite her.

95 The boat heads southeast from Venice into the Adriatic and is shipwrecked after having turned back towards the Italian coast. Ravenna is near the coast, south of Venice.

seemed—The world was not dead, but I was mad; I was deprived of sight, hearing, and sense of touch; I was labouring under the force of a spell, which permitted me to behold all sights of earth, except its human inhabitants; they were pursuing their ordinary labours. Every house had its inmate; but I could not perceive them. If I could have deluded myself into a belief of this kind, I should have been far more satisfied. But my brain, tenacious of its reason, refused to lend itself to such imaginations—and though I endeavoured to play the antic to myself, I knew that I, the offspring of man, during long years one among many—now remained sole survivor of my species.

The sun sank behind the western hills; I had fasted since the preceding evening, but, though faint and weary, I loathed food, nor ceased, while yet a ray of light remained, to pace the lonely streets. Night came on, and sent every living creature but me to the bosom of its mate. It was my solace, to blunt my mental agony by personal hardship—of the thousand beds around, I would not seek the luxury of one; I lay down on the pavement,—a cold marble step served me for a pillow—midnight came; and then, though not before, did my wearied lids shut out the sight of the twinkling stars, and their reflex on the pavement near. Thus I passed the second night of my desolation.

CHAPTER XXX

I AWOKE in the morning, just as the higher windows of the lofty houses received the first beams of the rising sun. The birds were chirping, perched on the windows sills and deserted thresholds of the doors. I awoke, and my first thought was, Adrian and Clara are dead. I no longer shall be hailed by their good-morrow—or pass the long day in their society. I shall never see them more. The ocean has robbed me of them—stolen their hearts of love from their breasts, and given over to corruption what was dearer to me than light, or life, or hope.

I was an untaught shepherd-boy, when Adrian deigned to confer on me his friendship. The best years of my life had been passed with him. All I had possessed of this world's goods, of happiness, knowledge, or virtue—I owed to him. He had, in his person, his intellect, and rare qualities, given a glory to my life, which without him it had never known. Beyond all other beings he had taught me, that goodness, pure and single, can be an attribute of man. It was a sight for angels to congregate to behold, to view him lead, govern, and solace, the last days of the human race.

My lovely Clara also was lost to me—she who last of the daughters of man, exhibited all those feminine and maiden virtues, which poets, painters, and sculptors, have in their various languages strove to express. Yet, as far as she was concerned, could I lament that she was removed in early youth from the certain advent of misery? Pure she was of soul, and all her intents were holy. But her heart was the throne of love, and the sensibility her lovely countenance expressed, was the prophet of many woes, not the less deep and drear, because she would have for ever concealed them.

These two wondrously endowed beings had been spared from the universal wreck, to be my companions during the last year of solitude. I had felt, while they were with me, all their worth. I was conscious that every other sentiment, regret, or passion had by degrees merged into a yearning, clinging affection for them. I had not forgotten the sweet partner of my youth, mother of my children, my adored Idris; but I saw at least a part of her spirit alive again in her brother; and after, that by Evelyn's death I had lost what most dearly recalled her to me; I enshrined her memory in Adrian's form, and endeavoured to confound the two dear ideas. I sound the depths of my heart, and try in vain to draw thence the expressions that can typify my love for these remnants of my race. If regret and sorrow came athwart me, as well it might in our solitary and uncertain state, the clear tones of Adrian's voice, and his fervent look, dissipated the gloom; or I was cheered unaware by the mild content and sweet resignation Clara's cloudless brow and deep blue eyes expressed. They were all to me—the suns of my benighted soul—repose in my weariness—slumber in my sleepless woe. Ill, most ill, with disjointed words, bare and weak, have I expressed the feeling with which I clung to them. I would have wound myself like ivy inextricably round them, so that the same blow might destroy us. I would have entered and been a part of them—so that

If the dull substance of my flesh were thought,[96]

even now I had accompanied them to their new and incommunicable abode.

Never shall I see them more. I am bereft of their dear converse—bereft of sight of them. I am a tree rent by lightning; never will the bark close over the bared fibres—never will their quivering life, torn by the winds, receive the opiate of a moment's balm. I am alone in the world—but that expression as yet was less pregnant with misery, than that Adrian and Clara are dead.

The tide of thought and feeling rolls on for ever the same, though the banks and shapes around, which govern its course, and the reflection in the wave, vary. Thus the sentiment of immediate loss in some sort decayed, while that of utter, irremediable loneliness grew on me with time. Three days I wandered through Ravenna—now thinking only of the beloved beings who slept in the oozy caves of ocean—now looking

96   Shakespeare, Sonnet 44, line 1.

forward on the dread blank before me; shuddering to make an onward step—writhing at each change that marked the progress of the hours.

For three days I wandered to and fro in this melancholy town. I passed whole hours in going from house to house, listening whether I could detect some lurking sign of human existence. Sometimes I rang at a bell; it tinkled through the vaulted rooms, and silence succeeded to the sound. I called myself hopeless, yet still I hoped; and still disappointment ushered in the hours, intruding the cold, sharp steel which first pierced me, into the aching festering wound. I fed like a wild beast, which seizes its food only when stung by intolerable hunger. I did not change my garb, or seek the shelter of a roof, during all those days. Burning heats, nervous irritation, a ceaseless, but confused flow of thought, sleepless nights, and days instinct with a frenzy of agitation, possessed me during that time.

As the fever of my blood encreased, a desire of wandering came upon me. I remember, that the sun had set on the fifth day after my wreck, when, without purpose or aim, I quitted the town of Ravenna. I must have been very ill. Had I been possessed by more or less of delirium, that night had surely been my last; for, as I continued to walk on the banks of the Mantone,[97] whose upward course I followed, I looked wistfully on the stream, acknowledging to myself that its pellucid waves could medicine my woes for ever, and was unable to account to myself for my tardiness in seeking their shelter from the poisoned arrows of thought, that were piercing me through and through. I walked a considerable part of the night, and excessive weariness at length conquered my repugnance to the availing myself of the deserted habitations of my species. The waning moon, which had just risen, shewed me a cottage, whose neat entrance and trim garden reminded me of my own England. I lifted up the latch of the door and entered. A kitchen first presented itself, where, guided by the moon beams, I found materials for striking a light. Within this was a bed room; the couch was furnished with sheets of snowy whiteness; the wood piled on the hearth, and an array as for a meal, might almost have deceived me into the dear belief that I had here found what I had so long sought—one survivor, a companion for my loneliness, a solace to my despair. I steeled myself against the delusion; the room itself was vacant: it was only prudent, I repeated to myself, to examine the rest of the house. I fancied that I was proof against the expectation; yet my heart beat audibly, as I laid my hand on the lock of each door, and it sunk again, when I perceived in each the same vacancy. Dark and silent they were as vaults; so I returned to the first chamber, wondering what sightless host had spread the materials for my repast, and my repose. I drew a chair to the table, and examined what the viands were of which I was to partake. In truth it was a death feast! The bread was blue and mouldy; the cheese

---

97   The Montone flows into the Fiumi Uniti and then into the Adriatic south of Ravenna.

lay a heap of dust. I did not dare examine the other dishes; a troop of ants passed in a double line across the table cloth; every utensil was covered with dust, with cobwebs, and myriads of dead flies: these were objects each and all betokening the fallaciousness of my expectations. Tears rushed into my eyes; surely this was a wanton display of the power of the destroyer. What had I done, that each sensitive nerve was thus to be anatomized? Yet why complain more now than ever? This vacant cottage revealed no new sorrow—the world was empty; mankind was dead—I knew it well—why quarrel therefore with an acknowledged and stale truth? Yet, as I said, I had hoped in the very heart of despair, so that every new impression of the hard-cut reality on my soul brought with it a fresh pang, telling me the yet unstudied lesson, that neither change of place nor time could bring alleviation to my misery, but that, as I now was, I must continue, day after day, month after month, year after year, while I lived. I hardly dared conjecture what space of time that expression implied. It is true, I was no longer in the first blush of manhood; neither had I declined far in the vale of years—men have accounted mine the prime of life: I had just entered my thirty-seventh year;[98] every limb was as well knit, every articulation as true, as when I had acted the shepherd on the hills of Cumberland; and with these advantages I was to commence the train of solitary life. Such were the reflections that ushered in my slumber on that night.

The shelter, however, and less disturbed repose which I enjoyed, restored me the following morning to a greater portion of health and strength, than I had experienced since my fatal shipwreck. Among the stores I had discovered on searching the cottage the preceding night, was a quantity of dried grapes; these refreshed me in the morning, as I left my lodging and proceeded towards a town which I discerned at no great distance. As far as I could divine, it must have been Forli.[99] I entered with pleasure its wide and grassy streets. All, it is true, pictured the excess of desolation; yet I loved to find myself in those spots which had been the abode of my fellow creatures. I delighted to traverse street after street, to look up at the tall houses, and repeat to myself, once they contained beings similar to myself—I was not always the wretch I am now. The wide square of Forli, the arcade around it, its light and pleasant aspect cheered me. I was pleased with the idea, that, if the earth should be again peopled, we, the lost race, would, in the relics left behind, present no contemptible exhibition of our powers to the new comers.

I entered one of the palaces, and opened the door of a magnificent saloon. I started—I looked again with renewed wonder. What wild-looking, unkempt, half-naked savage was that before me? The surprise was momentary.

---

98 Like Byron at the time of his death in April 1824.
99 A town southwest of Ravenna.

I perceived that it was I myself whom I beheld in a large mirror at the end of the hall. No wonder that the lover of the princely Idris should fail to recognize himself in the miserable object there pourtrayed. My tattered dress was that in which I had crawled half alive from the tempestuous sea. My long and tangled hair hung in elf locks on my brow—my dark eyes, now hollow and wild, gleamed from under them—my cheeks were discoloured by the jaundice, which (the effect of misery and neglect) suffused my skin, and were half hid by a beard of many days' growth.

Yet why should I not remain thus, I thought; the world is dead, and this squalid attire is a fitter mourning garb than the foppery of a black suit. And thus, methinks, I should have remained, had not hope, without which I do not believe man could exist, whispered to me, that, in such a plight, I should be an object of fear and aversion to the being, preserved I knew not where, but I fondly trusted, at length, to be found by me. Will my readers scorn the vanity, that made me attire myself with some care, for the sake of this visionary being? Or will they forgive the freaks of a half crazed imagination? I can easily forgive myself—for hope, however vague, was so dear to me, and a sentiment of pleasure of so rare occurrence, that I yielded readily to any idea, that cherished the one, or promised any recurrence of the former to my sorrowing heart.

After such occupation, I visited every street, alley, and nook of Forli. These Italian towns presented an appearance of still greater desolation, than those of England or France. Plague had appeared here earlier—it had finished its course, and achieved its work much sooner than with us. Probably the last summer had found no human being alive, in all the track included between the shores of Calabria and the northern Alps. My search was utterly vain, yet I did not despond. Reason methought was on my side; and the chances were by no means contemptible, that there should exist in some part of Italy a survivor like myself—of a wasted, depopulate land. As therefore I rambled through the empty town, I formed my plan for future operations. I would continue to journey on towards Rome. After I should have satisfied myself, by a narrow search, that I left behind no human being in the towns through which I passed, I would write up in a conspicuous part of each, with white paint, in three languages,[100] that "Verney, the last of the race of Englishmen, had taken up his abode in Rome."

In pursuance of this scheme, I entered a painter's shop, and procured myself the paint. It is strange that so trivial an occupation should have consoled, and even enlivened me. But grief renders one childish, despair fantastic. To this simple inscription, I merely added the adjuration, "Friend, come! I wait for thee!—*Deh, vieni! ti aspetto!*"

---

100 Perhaps an allusion to the Rosetta Stone, discovered in 1799, on which an inscription in three languages, Greek, demotic Egyptian, and Egyptian hieroglyphics, allowed scholars to interpret hieroglyphics for the first time.

On the following morning, with something like hope for my companion, I quitted Forli on my way to Rome. Until now, agonizing retrospect, and dreary prospects for the future, had stung me when awake, and cradled me to my repose. Many times I had delivered myself up to the tyranny of anguish—many times I resolved a speedy end to my woes; and death by my own hands was a remedy, whose practicability was even cheering to me. What could I fear in the other world? If there were an hell, and I were doomed to it, I should come an adept to the sufferance of its tortures—the act were easy, the speedy and certain end of my deplorable tragedy. But now these thoughts faded before the new born expectation. I went on my way, not as before, feeling each hour, each minute, to be an age instinct with incalculable pain.

As I wandered along the plain, at the foot of the Appennines—through their vallies, and over their bleak summits, my path led me through a country which had been trodden by heroes, visited and admired by thousands. They had, as a tide, receded, leaving me blank and bare in the midst. But why complain? Did I not hope?—so I schooled myself, even after the enlivening spirit had really deserted me, and thus I was obliged to call up all the fortitude I could command, and that was not much, to prevent a recurrence of that chaotic and intolerable despair, that had succeeded to the miserable shipwreck, that had consummated every fear, and dashed to annihilation every joy.

I rose each day with the morning sun, and left my desolate inn. As my feet strayed through the unpeopled country, my thoughts rambled through the universe, and I was least miserable when I could, absorbed in reverie, forget the passage of the hours. Each evening, in spite of weariness, I detested to enter any dwelling, there to take up my nightly abode—I have sat, hour after hour, at the door of the cottage I had selected, unable to lift the latch, and meet face to face blank desertion within. Many nights, though autumnal mists were spread around, I passed under an ilex—many times I have supped on arbutus berries and chestnuts, making a fire, gypsy-like, on the ground—because wild natural scenery reminded me less acutely of my hopeless state of loneliness. I counted the days, and bore with me a peeled willow-wand, on which, as well as I could remember, I had notched the days that had elapsed since my wreck; and each night I added another unit to the melancholy sum.

I had toiled up a hill which led to Spoleto.[101] Around was spread a plain, encircled by the chesnut-covered Appennines. A dark ravine was on one side, spanned by an aqueduct, whose tall arches were rooted in the dell below, and attested that man had once deigned to bestow labour and thought here, to adorn and civilize nature. Savage, ungrateful nature, which in wild sport defaced his remains, protruding her easily renewed,

---

101 A town in central Italy north of Rome.

and fragile growth of wild flowers and parasite plants around his eternal edifices. I sat on a fragment of rock, and looked round. The sun had bathed in gold the western atmosphere, and in the east the clouds caught the radiance, and budded into transient loveliness. It set on a world that contained me alone for its inhabitant. I took out my wand—I counted the marks. Twenty-five were already traced—twenty-five days had already elapsed, since human voice had gladdened my ears, or human countenance met my gaze. Twenty-five long, weary days, succeeded by dark and lonesome nights, had mingled with foregone years, and had become a part of the past—the never to be recalled—a real, undeniable portion of my life—twenty-five long, long days.

Why this was not a month!—Why talk of days—or weeks—or months—I must grasp years in my imagination, if I would truly picture the future to myself—three, five, ten, twenty, fifty anniversaries of that fatal epoch might elapse—every year containing twelve months, each of more numerous calculation in a diary, than the twenty-five days gone by—Can it be? Will it be?—We had been used to look forward to death tremulously—wherefore, but because its place was obscure? But more terrible, and far more obscure, was the unveiled course of my lone futurity. I broke my wand; I threw it from me. I needed no recorder of the inch and barley-corn growth of my life, while my unquiet thoughts created other divisions, than those ruled over by the planets—and, in looking back on the age that had elapsed since I had been alone, I disdained to give the name of days and hours to the throes of agony which had in truth portioned it out.

I hid my face in my hands. The twitter of the young birds going to rest, and their rustling among the trees, disturbed the still evening-air—the crickets chirped—the aziolo cooed at intervals. My thoughts had been of death—these sounds spoke to me of life. I lifted up my eyes—a bat wheeled round—the sun had sunk behind the jagged line of mountains, and the paly, crescent moon was visible, silver white, amidst the orange sunset, and accompanied by one bright star, prolonged thus the twilight. A herd of cattle passed along in the dell below, untended, towards their watering place—the grass was rustled by a gentle breeze, and the olive-woods, mellowed into soft masses by the moonlight, contrasted their sea-green with the dark chesnut foliage. Yes, this is the earth; there is no change—no ruin—no rent made in her verdurous expanse; she continues to wheel round and round, with alternate night and day, through the sky, though man is not her adorer or inhabitant. Why could I not forget myself like one of those animals, and no longer suffer the wild tumult of misery that I endure? Yet, ah! what a deadly breach yawns between their state and mine! Have not they companions? Have not they each their mate—their cherished young, their home, which, though unexpressed to us, is, I doubt not, endeared and enriched, even in their eyes, by the society which kind nature has created for them? It is I only that am alone—I, on this little hill top, gazing on plain and mountain recess—on sky, and its starry population, listening to every sound of earth, and air, and murmuring wave,—I only cannot express to any companion my many thoughts, nor lay my throbbing head on any loved bosom, nor drink from meeting eyes an intoxicating dew, that transcends the fabulous nectar of the gods. Shall I not then complain? Shall I not curse the murderous engine which has mowed down the children of men, my brethren? Shall I not bestow a malediction on every other of nature's offspring, which dares live and enjoy, while I live and suffer?

Ah, no! I will discipline my sorrowing heart to sympathy in your joys; I will be happy, because ye are so. Live on, ye innocents, nature's selected darlings; I am not much unlike to you. Nerves, pulse, brain, joint, and flesh, of such am I composed, and ye are organized by the same laws. I have something beyond this, but I will call it a defect, not an endowment, if it leads me to misery, while ye are happy. Just then, there emerged from a near copse two goats and a little kid, by the mother's side; they began to browze the herbage of the hill. I approached near to them, without their perceiving me; I gathered a handful of fresh grass, and held it out; the little one nestled close to its mother, while she timidly withdrew. The male stepped forward, fixing his eyes on me: I drew near, still holding out my lure, while he, depressing his head, rushed at me with his horns. I was a very fool; I knew it, yet I yielded to my rage. I snatched up a huge fragment of rock; it would have crushed my rash foe. I poized it—aimed it—then my heart failed me. I hurled it wide of the mark; it rolled clattering among the bushes into dell. My little visitants, all aghast, galloped back into the covert of the wood; while I, my very heart bleeding and torn, rushed down the hill, and by the violence of bodily exertion, sought to escape from my miserable self.

No, no, I will not live among the wild scenes of nature, the enemy of all that lives. I will seek the towns—Rome, the capital of the world, the crown of man's achievements. Among its storied streets, hallowed ruins, and stupendous remains of human exertion, I shall not, as here, find every thing forgetful of man; trampling on his memory, defacing his works, proclaiming from hill to hill, and vale to vale,—by the torrents freed from the boundaries which he imposed—by the vegetation liberated from the laws which he enforced—by his habitation abandoned to mildew and weeds, that his power is lost, his race annihilated for ever.

I hailed the Tiber, for that was as it were an unalienable possession of humanity. I hailed the wild Campagna, for every rood had been trod by man; and its savage uncultivation, of no recent date, only proclaimed more distinctly his power, since he had given an honourable name and sacred title to what else would have been a worthless, barren track. I entered Eternal Rome by the Porta del Popolo, and saluted with awe its time-honoured space. The wide square, the churches near, the long extent of the Corso, the near eminence of Trinita de' Monti appeared like fairy work, they were so silent, so peaceful, and so very fair. It was evening; and the population of animals which still existed in this mighty city, had gone to rest; there was no sound, save the murmur of its many fountains, whose soft monotony was harmony to my soul. The knowledge that I was in Rome, soothed me; that wondrous city, hardly more illustrious for its heroes and sages, than for the power it exercised over the imaginations of men. I went to rest that night; the eternal burning of my heart quenched,—my senses tranquil.

The next morning I eagerly began my rambles in search of oblivion. I ascended the many terraces of the garden of the Colonna Palace, under whose roof I had been sleeping; and passing out from it at its summit, I found myself on Monte Cavallo. The fountain sparkled in the sun; the obelisk above pierced the clear dark-blue air. The statues on each side, the works, as they are inscribed, of Phidias and Praxiteles, stood in undiminished grandeur, representing Castor and Pollux, who with majestic power tamed the rearing animal at their side. If those illustrious artists had in truth chiselled these forms, how many passing generations had their giant proportions outlived![102] and now they were viewed by the last of the species they were sculptured to represent and deify. I had shrunk into insignificance in my own eyes, as I considered the multitudinous beings these stone demigods had outlived, but this after-thought restored me to dignity in my own conception. The sight of the poetry eternized in these statues, took the sting from the thought, arraying it only in poetic ideality.

I repeated to myself,—I am in Rome! I behold, and as it were, familiarly converse with the wonder of the world, sovereign mistress of the imagination, majestic and eternal survivor of millions of generations of extinct men. I endeavoured to quiet the sorrows of my aching heart, by even now taking an interest in what in my youth I had ardently longed to see. Every part of Rome is replete with relics of ancient times. The meanest streets are strewed with truncated columns, broken capitals —Corinthian and Ionic, and sparkling fragments of granite or porphyry. The walls of the most penurious dwellings enclose a fluted pillar or ponderous stone, which once made part of the palace of the Cæsars; and the voice of dead time, in still vibrations, is breathed from these dumb things, animated and glorified as they were by man.

---

102 Lionel is, however, mistaken: the statues of the Dioscuri (Castor and Pollux) at Monte Cavallo were wrongly ascribed by Pope Sixtus V to the ancient Athenian sculptors Phidias and Praxiteles. Rome—which in her fragment, "The Fields of Fancy" (1819), MWS calls "Queen of the World"—is the last of the novel's deserted cities: the Campagna, mentioned at the beginning of the previous paragraph, is the countryside around Rome; the Porta del Populo (gate of the people), Il Corso (Via del Corso, where the Shelleys stayed in 1819), the church of Trinita de' Monti, and the Colonna Palace are all places the Shelleys knew well.

I embraced the vast columns of the temple of Jupiter Stator, which survives in the open space that was the Forum,[103] and leaning my burning cheek against its cold durability, I tried to lose the sense of present misery and present desertion, by recalling to the haunted cell of my brain vivid memories of times gone by. I rejoiced at my success, as I figured Camillus, the Gracchi, Cato, and last the heroes of Tacitus,[104] which shine meteors of surpassing brightness during the murky night of the empire;—as the verses of Horace and Virgil, or the glowing periods of Cicero thronged into the opened gates of my mind, I felt myself exalted by long forgotten enthusiasm. I was delighted to know that I beheld the scene which they beheld—the scene which their wives and mothers, and crowds of the unnamed witnessed, while at the same time they honoured, applauded, or wept for these matchless specimens of humanity. At length, then, I had found a consolation. I had not vainly sought the storied precincts of Rome—I had discovered a medicine for my many and vital wounds.

I sat at the foot of these vast columns. The Coliseum,[105] whose naked ruin is robed by nature in a verdurous and glowing veil, lay in the sunlight on my right. Not far off, to the left, was the Tower of the Capitol. Triumphal arches, the falling walls of many temples, strewed the ground at my feet. I strove, I resolved, to force myself to see the Plebeian multitude and lofty Patrician forms congregated around; and, as the Diorama of ages passed across my subdued fancy, they were replaced by the modern Roman; the Pope, in his white stole, distributing benedictions to the kneeling worshippers; the friar in his cowl; the dark-eyed girl, veiled by her mezzera;[106] the noisy, sun-burnt rustic, leading his herd of buffaloes and oxen to the Campo Vaccino.[107] The romance with which, dipping our pencils in the rainbow hues of sky and transcendent nature, we to a degree gratuitously endow the Italians, replaced the solemn grandeur of

---

103 The remains of the Temple of Jupiter Stator (Jupiter the Stayer, or Jupiter who stands fast) are in the Roman Forum, the market and meeting-place of the ancient city.

104 Plutarch wrote lives of Camillus (Roman statesman and general, fourth century BC), the Gracchi brothers (agrarian reformers, second century BC) and Cato (reformer and orator, 234-149 BC). The heroes of Tacitus include several mentioned in *The Last Man*, including Alexander, Epicharis, Julius Caesar, and Mithridates.

105 The ancient Roman Amphitheatre, completed in AD 80 for gladitorial combat. PBS wrote a fragment of a story called "The Coliseum"; Byron describes the Coliseum in *Childe Harold's Pilgrimage*, adapting Edward Gibbon's quotation from Bede: "As long as the Coliseum stands, Rome shall stand; when the Coliseum falls, Rome will fall; when Rome falls, the world will fall" (*Decline and Fall*, chapter 71; *Childe Harold* 4.145.1297-99).

106 Italian *mesero* or *mesere*, a woman's shawl worn over the head and shoulders.

107 "Cattle pasture"—the fate of the Roman Forum during the middle ages.

antiquity. I remembered the dark monk, and floating figures of "The Italian," [108] and how my boyish blood had thrilled at the description. I called to mind Corinna ascending the Capitol to be crowned,[109] and, passing from the heroine to the author, reflected how the Enchantress Spirit of Rome held sovereign sway over the minds of the imaginative, until it rested on me—sole remaining spectator of its wonders.

I was long wrapt by such ideas; but the soul wearies of a pauseless flight; and, stooping from its wheeling circuits round and round this spot, suddenly it fell ten thousand fathom deep, into the abyss of the present—into self-knowledge—into tenfold sadness. I roused myself—I cast off my waking dreams; and I, who just now could almost hear the shouts of the Roman throng, and was hustled by countless multitudes, now beheld the desart ruins of Rome sleeping under its own blue sky; the shadows lay tranquilly on the ground; sheep were grazing untended on the Palatine, and a buffalo stalked down the Sacred Way that led to the Capitol. I was alone in the Forum; alone in Rome; alone in the world. Would not one living man—one companion in my weary solitude, be worth all the glory and remembered power of this time-honoured city? Double sorrow—sadness, bred in Cimmerian caves, robed my soul in a mourning garb. The generations I had conjured up to my fancy, contrasted more strongly with the end of all—the single point in which, as a pyramid, the mighty fabric of society had ended, while I, on the giddy height, saw vacant space around me.

From such vague laments I turned to the contemplation of the minutiæ of my situation. So far, I had not succeeded in the sole object of my desires, the finding a companion for my desolation. Yet I did not despair. It is true that my inscriptions were set up for the most part, in insignificant towns and villages; yet, even without these memorials, it was possible that the person, who like me should find himself alone in a depopulate land, should, like me, come to Rome. The more slender my expectation was, the more I chose to build on it, and to accommodate my actions to this vague possibility.

It became necessary therefore, that for a time I should domesticate myself at Rome. It became necessary, that I should look my disaster in the

---

108 A novel by Ann Radcliffe (1797), which MWS read in 1814. Radcliffe includes a description of Rome: "At intervals . . . the moon, as the clouds passed away, shewed, for a moment, some of those mighty monuments of Rome's eternal name, those sacred ruins, those gigantic skeletons, which once enclosed a soul, whose energies governed a world!" (ed. Frederick Garber 195).

109 A reference to the climactic scene in Anne-Louise-Germaine de Staël (Mme Necker), *Corinne, ou l'Italie* (1807), a novel whose poet-heroine is based on the Greek Corinna. The Capitoline Hill, the smallest but most famous of Rome's seven hills, was the political and religious centre of the ancient city.

face—not playing the school-boy's part of obedience without submission; enduring life, and yet rebelling against the laws by which I lived.

Yet how could I resign myself? Without love, without sympathy, without communion with any, how could I meet the morning sun, and with it trace its oft repeated journey to the evening shades? Why did I continue to live—why not throw off the weary weight of time, and with my own hand, let out the fluttering prisoner from my agonized breast?—It was not cowardice that withheld me; for the true fortitude was to endure; and death had a soothing sound accompanying it, that would easily entice me to enter its demesne. But this I would not do. I had, from the moment I had reasoned on the subject, instituted myself the subject to fate, and the servant of necessity, the visible laws of the invisible God—I believed that my obedience was the result of sound reasoning, pure feeling, and an exalted sense of the true excellence and nobility of my nature. Could I have seen in this empty earth, in the seasons and their change, the hand of a blind power only, most willingly would I have placed my head on the sod, and closed my eyes on its loveliness for ever. But fate had administered life to me, when the plague had already seized on its prey—she had dragged me by the hair from out the strangling waves—By such miracles she had bought me for her own; I admitted her authority, and bowed to her decrees. If, after mature consideration, such was my resolve, it was doubly necessary that I should not lose the end of life, the improvement of my faculties, and poison its flow by repinings without end. Yet how cease to repine, since there was no hand near to extract the barbed spear that had entered my heart of hearts? I stretched out my hand, and it touched none whose sensations were responsive to mine. I was girded, walled in, vaulted over, by seven-fold barriers of loneliness. Occupation alone, if I could deliver myself up to it, would be capable of affording an opiate to my sleepless sense of woe. Having determined to make Rome my abode, at least for some months, I made arrangements for my accommodation—I selected my home. The Colonna Palace was well adapted for my purpose. Its grandeur—its treasure of paintings, its magnificent halls were objects soothing and even exhilarating.

I found the granaries of Rome well stored with grain, and particularly with Indian corn; this product requiring less art in its preparation for food, I selected as my principal support. I now found the hardships and lawlessness of my youth turn to account. A man cannot throw off the habits of sixteen years. Since that age, it is true, I had lived luxuriously, or at least surrounded by all the conveniences civilization afforded. But before that time, I had been "as uncouth a savage, as the wolf-bred founder of old Rome" [110]—and now, in Rome itself, robber and shepherd propensities, similar to those of its founder, were of advantage to its sole inhabitant. I spent the morning riding and shooting in the Campagna—I passed long

---

110 Lionel Verney quotes his own words on 11, above.

hours in the various galleries—I gazed at each statue, and lost myself in a reverie before many a fair Madonna or beauteous nymph. I haunted the Vatican, and stood surrounded by marble forms of divine beauty. Each stone deity was possessed by sacred gladness, and the eternal fruition of love. They looked on me with unsympathizing complacency, and often in wild accents I reproached them for their supreme indifference—for they were human shapes, the human form divine[111] was manifest in each fairest limb and lineament. The perfect moulding brought with it the idea of colour and motion; often, half in bitter mockery, half in self-delusion, I clasped their icy proportions, and, coming between Cupid and his Psyche's lips,[112] pressed the unconceiving marble.

I endeavoured to read. I visited the libraries of Rome. I selected a volume, and, choosing some sequestered, shady nook, on the banks of the Tiber, or opposite the fair temple in the Borghese Gardens, or under the old pyramid of Cestius,[113] I endeavoured to conceal me from myself, and immerse myself in the subject traced on the pages before me. As if in the same soil you plant nightshade and a myrtle tree, they will each appropriate the mould, moisture, and air administered, for the fostering their several properties—so did my grief find sustenance, and power of existence, and growth, in what else had been divine manna, to feed radiant meditation. Ah! while I streak this paper with the tale of what my so named occupations were—while I shape the skeleton of my days—my hand trembles—my heart pants, and my brain refuses to lend expression, or phrase, or idea, by which to image forth the veil of unutterable woe that clothed these bare realities. O, worn and beating heart, may I dissect thy fibres, and tell how in each unmitigable misery, sadness dire, repinings, and despair, existed? May I record my many ravings—the wild curses I hurled at torturing nature—and how I have passed days shut out from light and food—from all except the burning hell alive in my own bosom?[114]

I was presented, meantime, with one other occupation, the one best fitted to discipline my melancholy thoughts, which strayed backwards,

---

111 Cf. *Paradise Lost* 3.44, which refers to the "human face divine."

112 In Apuleius, *The Metamorphosis, or the Golden Ass*, Cupid, the god of Love, makes love to Psyche by night, forbidding her to discover his identity. Some commentaries read the story as an allegory of the relation between Love and the Soul.

113 The Protestant Cemetery in Rome, burial place of John Keats, PBS, and William Shelley. MWS had visited this spot in November 1818; PBS had described it as "a green slope near the walls, under the pyramidal tomb of Cestius" (PBS to Peacock, *Letters* 2: 59-60; cf. MWS, *Journals* 2: 450-51, and below, Appendix E.1, 407n).

114 Cf. *Paradise Lost* 4.19-22, and MWS's use of this passage in *Frankenstein*, ed. D. L. Macdonald and Kathleen Scherf, 163.

over many a ruin, and through many a flowery glade, even to the mountain recess, from which in early youth I had first emerged.

During one of my rambles through the habitations of Rome, I found writing materials on a table in an author's study. Parts of a manuscript lay scattered about. It contained a learned disquisition on the Italian language; one page an unfinished dedication to posterity, for whose profit the writer had sifted and selected the niceties of this harmonious language—to whose everlasting benefit he bequeathed his labours.

I also will write a book, I cried—for whom to read?—to whom dedicated? And then with silly flourish (what so capricious and childish as despair?) I wrote,

DEDICATION

TO THE ILLUSTRIOUS DEAD.[115]

SHADOWS, ARISE, AND READ YOUR FALL!

BEHOLD THE HISTORY OF THE

LAST MAN.

Yet, will not this world be re-peopled, and the children of a saved pair of lovers, in some to me unknown and unattainable seclusion, wandering to these prodigious relics of the ante-pestilential race, seek to learn how beings so wondrous in their achievements, with imaginations infinite, and powers godlike, had departed from their home to an unknown country?

I will write and leave in this most ancient city, this "world's sole monument,"[116] a record of these things. I will leave a monument of the existence of Verney, the Last Man. At first I thought only to speak of plague, of death, and last, of desertion; but I lingered fondly on my early years, and recorded with sacred zeal the virtues of my companions. They have been with me during the fulfilment of my task. I have brought it to an end—I lift my eyes from my paper—again they are lost to me. Again I feel that I am alone.

A year has passed since I have been thus occupied. The seasons have made their wonted round, and decked this eternal city in a changeful robe of surpassing beauty. A year has passed; and I no longer *guess* at my state or my prospects—loneliness is my familiar, sorrow my inseparable com-

---

115 The phrase "Illustrious Dead" ironically echoes Godwin's scheme to immortalize the dead in *Essays on Sepulchres: or, a Proposal for Erecting Some Memorial of the Illustrious Dead in All Ages on the Spot where their Remains have been Interred* (1809); see Appendix D.8.

116 Spenser, *Ruines of Rome*: "Rome living, was the world's sole ornament, / And dead, is now the world's sole monument" (stanza 29). MWS also quotes these words in her *Journals* (5 March 1819), in her story "Recollections of Italy" (published in the *London Magazine* in January 1824), and in her Preface to the *Posthumous Poems* of PBS (1824).

panion. I have endeavoured to brave the storm—I have endeavoured to school myself to fortitude—I have sought to imbue myself with the lessons of wisdom. It will not do. My hair has become nearly grey—my voice, unused now to utter sound, comes strangely on my ears. My person, with its human powers and features, seem to me a monstrous excrescence of nature. How express in human language a woe human being until this hour never knew! How give intelligible expression to a pang none but I could ever understand!—No one has entered Rome. None will ever come. I smile bitterly at the delusion I have so long nourished, and still more, when I reflect that I have exchanged it for another as delusive, as false, but to which I now cling with the same fond trust.

Winter has come again; and the gardens of Rome have lost their leaves—the sharp air comes over the Campagna, and has driven its brute inhabitants to take up their abode in the many dwellings of the deserted city—frost has suspended the gushing fountains—and Trevi has stilled her eternal music.[117] I had made a rough calculation, aided by the stars, by which I endeavoured to ascertain the first day of the new year. In the old out-worn age, the Sovereign Pontiff was used to go in solemn pomp, and mark the renewal of the year by driving a nail in the gate of the temple of Janus.[118] On that day I ascended St. Peter's, and carved on its topmost stone the æra 2100, last year of the world!

My only companion was a dog, a shaggy fellow, half water and half shepherd's dog, whom I found tending sheep in the Campagna. His master was dead, but nevertheless he continued fulfilling his duties in expectation of his return. If a sheep strayed from the rest, he forced it to return to the flock, and sedulously kept off every intruder. Riding in the Campagna I had come upon his sheep-walk, and for some time observed his repetition of lessons learned from man, now useless, though unforgotten. His delight was excessive when he saw me. He sprung up to my knees; he capered round and round, wagging his tail, with the short, quick bark of pleasure: he left his fold to follow me, and from that day has never neglected to watch by and attend on me, shewing boisterous gratitude whenever I caressed or talked to him. His pattering steps and mine alone were heard, when we entered the magnificent extent of nave and aisle of St. Peter's. We ascended the myriad steps together, when on the summit I achieved my design, and in rough figures noted the date of the last year. I then turned to gaze on the country, and to take leave of Rome. I had long determined to quit it, and I now formed the plan I would adopt for my future career, after I had left this magnificent abode.

A solitary being is by instinct a wanderer, and that I would become. A hope of amelioration always attends on change of place, which would

---

117 That is, the music of the famous fountain.
118 The seat of the Pontifex Maximus or high priest was the Regia, one of the three main areas of the ancient Forum, site of the Temple of Janus.

even lighten the burthen of my life. I had been a fool to remain in Rome all this time: Rome noted for Mal'aria, the famous caterer for death.[119] But it was still possible, that, could I visit the whole extent of earth, I should find in some part of the wide extent a survivor. Methought the sea-side was the most probable retreat to be chosen by such a one. If left alone in an inland district, still they could not continue in the spot where their last hopes had been extinguished; they would journey on, like me, in search of a partner for their solitude, till the watery barrier stopped their further progress.

To that water—cause of my woes, perhaps now to be their cure, I would betake myself. Farewell, Italy!—farewell, thou ornament of the world, matchless Rome, the retreat of the solitary one during long months!—to civilized life—to the settled home and succession of monotonous days, farewell! Peril will now be mine; and I hail her as a friend—death will perpetually cross my path, and I will meet him as a benefactor; hardship, inclement weather, and dangerous tempests will be my sworn mates. Ye spirits of storm, receive me! ye powers of destruction, open wide your arms, and clasp me for ever! if a kinder power have not decreed another end, so that after long endurance I may reap my reward, and again feel my heart beat near the heart of another like to me.

Tiber, the road which is spread by nature's own hand, threading her continent, was at my feet, and many a boat was tethered to the banks. I would with a few books, provisions, and my dog, embark in one of these and float down the current of the stream into the sea; and then, keeping near land, I would coast the beauteous shores and sunny promontories of the blue Mediterranean, pass Naples, along Calabria, and would dare the twin perils of Scylla and Charybdis; then, with fearless aim, (for what had I to lose?) skim ocean's surface towards Malta and the further Cyclades. I would avoid Constantinople, the sight of whose well-known towers and inlets belonged to another state of existence from my present one; I would coast Asia Minor, and Syria, and, passing the seven-mouthed Nile, steer northward again, till losing sight of forgotten Carthage and deserted Lybia, I should reach the pillars of Hercules. And then—no matter where—the oozy caves, and soundless depths of ocean may be my dwelling, before I accomplish this long-drawn voyage, or the arrow of disease find my heart as I float singly on the weltering Mediterranean; or, in some place I touch at, I may find what I seek—a companion; or if this may not be—to endless time, decrepid and grey headed—youth already in the grave with those I love—the lone wanderer will still unfurl his sail, and clasp the tiller—and, still obeying the breezes of heaven, for ever round another and another promontory, anchoring in another and another bay,

---

119 The Shelleys' son, William, died in a malaria (literally "bad air") epidemic at Rome on 7 June 1819; in a letter of 27 June, MWS refers to "the pestilential air of Rome" (*Letters* 1: 100).

still ploughing seedless ocean, leaving behind the verdant land of native Europe, adown the tawny shore of Africa, having weathered the fierce seas of the Cape, I may moor my worn skiff in a creek, shaded by spicy groves of the odorous islands of the far Indian ocean.[120]

These are wild dreams. Yet since, now a week ago, they came on me, as I stood on the height of St. Peter's, they have ruled my imagination. I have chosen my boat, and laid in my scant stores. I have selected a few books; the principal are Homer and Shakespeare—But the libraries of the world are thrown open to me—and in any port I can renew my stock. I form no expectation of alteration for the better; but the monotonous present is intolerable to me. Neither hope nor joy are my pilots—restless despair and fierce desire of change lead me on. I long to grapple with danger, to be excited by fear, to have some task, however slight or voluntary, for each day's fulfilment. I shall witness all the variety of appearance, that the elements can assume—I shall read fair augury in the rainbow—menace in the cloud—some lesson or record dear to my heart in everything. Thus around the shores of deserted earth, while the sun is high, and the moon waxes or wanes, angels, the spirits of the dead, and the ever-open eye of the Supreme, will behold the tiny bark, freighted with Verney—the LAST MAN.

THE END.

---

120 For Lionel's proposed route, see map, 368. Perhaps MWS has in mind Odysseus' journeys, as the reference to Scylla and Charybdis (a monster and a whirlpool in the Straits of Messina, described in *Odyssey* 12) might suggest. If Lionel Verney is her Odysseus, MWS is probably also recalling Dante's account in the *Inferno* (26.90-141) of Ulysses' journey beyond the Pillars of Hercules to his death.

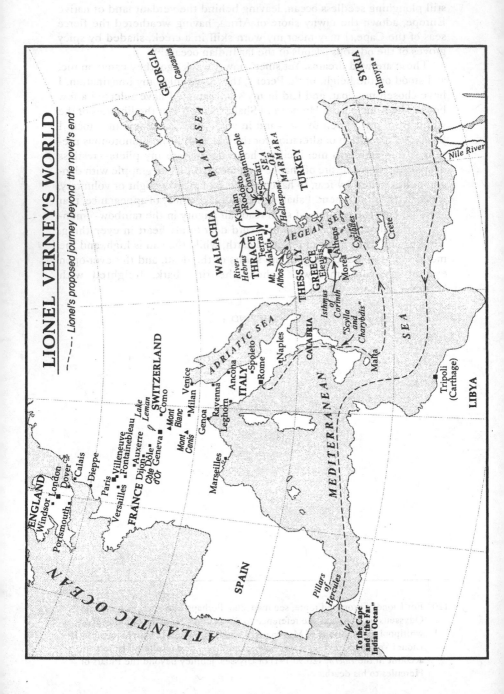

Appendix A: *Some Contemporaries of the Last Man*

For discussion of the last man as a popular literary subject in the early nineteenth century, see Introduction, xiii-xvi. Byron's "Darkness" is not, strictly speaking, about the last man at all; nor is its account of the end of human society much like Mary Shelley's. Its influence is, however, important in shaping the literary context of Shelley's novel. Byron's and Campbell's poems were frequently compared, as in Francis Jeffrey's comment in the *Edinburgh Review* 41.82 (1824-25), part of a review of Campbell's *Theodric*: "Lord Byron's [poem] has more variety of topics, more gloom and terror, and far more daring and misanthropy. Mr Campbell's has more sweetness, more reflection, more considerate loftiness, and more of the spirit of religion" (284).

Thomas Hood's grimly comic last man (1826) owes something to Shelley's, for all the difference of tone. George Dibdin Pitt's last man indicates how familiar the conventional subject had become, even to the kind of non-literary audience his play would have attracted to the Surrey Theatre in 1833. His burlesque recalls the tone of Francis Jeffrey's review of Hood, reprinted in Appendix F.4. Thomas Lovell Beddoes' notes for a projected play about the last man (c. 1837) turn towards the conventions of visionary Shelleyan verse, Goethe's *Faust*, and perhaps also *Omegarus and Syderia*, excerpted below in Appendix B.2.

1. George Gordon, Lord Byron, "Darkness," *The Prisoner of Chillon and Other Poems* (London: Murray, 1816).

I had a dream, which was not all a dream.
The bright sun was extinguish'd, and the stars
Did wander darkling in the eternal space,
Rayless, and pathless, and the icy earth
Swung blind and blackening in the moonless air;   5
Morn came, and went—and came, and brought no day,
And men forgot their passions in the dread
Of this their desolation; and all hearts
Were chill'd into a selfish prayer for light:
And they did live by watchfires—and the thrones,   10
The palaces of crowned kings—the huts,
The habitations of all things which dwell,
Were burnt for beacons; cities were consumed,
And men were gathered round their blazing homes
To look once more into each other's face;   15
Happy were those who dwelt within the eye
Of the volcanos, and their mountain-torch:
A fearful hope was all the world contain'd;
Forests were set on fire—but hour by hour
They fell and faded—and the crackling trunks   20

Extinguish'd with a crash—and all was black.
The brows of men by the despairing light
Wore an unearthly aspect, as by fits
The flashes fell upon them; some lay down
And hid their eyes and wept; and some did rest   25
Their chins upon their clenched hands, and smiled;
And others hurried to and fro, and fed
Their funeral piles with fuel, and looked up
With mad disquietude on the dull sky,
The pall of a past world; and then again   30
With curses cast them down upon the dust,
And gnash'd their teeth and howl'd: the wild birds shriek'd,
And, terrified, did flutter on the ground,
And flap their useless wings; the wildest brutes
Came tame and tremulous; and vipers crawl'd   35
And twined themselves among the multitude,
Hissing, but stingless—they were slain for food:
And War, which for a moment was no more,
Did glut himself again;—a meal was bought
With blood, and each sate sullenly apart   40
Gorging himself in gloom: no love was left;
All earth was but one thought—and that was death,
Immediate and inglorious; and the pang
Of famine fed upon all entrails—men
Died, and their bones were tombless as their flesh;   45
The meagre by the meagre were devoured,
Even dogs assail'd their masters, all save one,
And he was faithful to a corse, and kept
The birds and beasts and famish'd men at bay,
Till hunger clung them, or the dropping dead   50
Lured their lank jaws; himself sought out no food,
But with a piteous and perpetual moan
And a quick desolate cry, licking the hand
Which answered not with a caress—he died.
The crowd was famish'd by degrees; but two   55
Of an enormous city did survive,
And they were enemies; they met beside
The dying embers of an altar-place
Where had been heap'd a mass of holy things
For an unholy usage; they raked up,   60
And shivering scraped with their cold skeleton hands
The feeble ashes, and their feeble breath
Blew for a little life, and made a flame
Which was a mockery; then they lifted up
Their eyes as it grew lighter, and beheld   65
Each other's aspects—saw, and shriek'd, and died—

Even of their mutual hideousness they died,
Unknowing who he was upon whose brow
Famine had written Fiend. The world was void,
The populous and the powerful was a lump,   70
Seasonless, herbless, treeless, manless, lifeless—
A lump of death—a chaos of hard clay.
The rivers, lakes, and ocean all stood still,
And nothing stirred within their silent depths;
Ships sailorless lay rotting on the sea,   75
And their masts fell down piecemeal; as they dropp'd
They slept on the abyss without a surge—
The waves were dead; the tides were in their grave,
The moon their mistress had expired before;
The winds were withered in the stagnant air,   80
And the clouds perish'd; Darkness had no need
Of aid from them—She was the universe.

2. Thomas Campbell, "The Last Man," *New Monthly Magazine* 8 (1823):
272-73.

All worldly shapes shall melt in gloom,
    The Sun himself must die,
Before this mortal shall assume
    Its Immortality!
I saw a vision in my sleep,   5
That gave my spirit strength to sweep
    Adown the gulf of Time!
I saw the last of human mould,
That shall Creation's death behold,
    As Adam saw her prime!   10

The Sun's eye had a sickly glare,
    The Earth with age was wan,
The skeletons of nations were
    Around that lonely man!
Some had expir'd in fight,—the brands   15
Still rusted in their bony hands;
    In plague and famine some!
Earth's cities had no sound nor tread;
And ships were drifting with the dead
    To shores where all was dumb!   20

Yet, prophet like, that lone one stood,
    With dauntless words and high,
That shook the sere leaves from the wood
    As if a storm pass'd by,

Saying, we are twins in death, proud Sun,   25
Thy face is cold, thy race is run,
    'Tis Mercy bids thee go.
For thou ten thousand thousand years
Hast seen the tide of human tears,
    That shall no longer flow.   30

What though beneath thee man put forth
    His pomp, his pride, his skill;
And arts that made fire, flood, and earth,
    The vassals of his will;—
Yet mourn I not thy parted sway,   35
Thou dim discrowned king of day:
    For all those trophied arts
And triumphs that beneath thee sprang,
Heal'd not a passion or a pang
    Entail'd on human hearts.   40

Go, let oblivion's curtain fall
    Upon the stage of men,
Nor with thy rising beams recall
    Life's tragedy again.
Its piteous pageants bring not back,   45
Nor waken flesh, upon the rack
    Of pain anew to writhe;
Stretch'd in disease's shapes abhorr'd,
Or mown in battle by the sword,
    Like grass beneath the scythe.   50

Ev'n I am weary in yon skies
    To watch thy fading fire;
Test of all sumless agonies,
    Behold not me expire.
My lips that speak thy dirge of death—   55
Their rounded gasp and gurgling breath
    To see thou shalt not boast.
The eclipse of Nature spreads my pall,—
The majesty of Darkness shall
    Receive my parting ghost!   60

This spirit shall return to Him
    That gave its heavenly spark;
Yet think not, Sun, it shall be dim
    When thou thyself art dark!
No! it shall live again, and shine   65
In bliss unknown to beams of thine,

By Him recall'd to breath,
Who captive led captivity,
Who robb'd the grave of Victory,—
And took the sting from Death!   70

Go, Sun, while Mercy holds me up
    On Nature's awful waste
To drink this last and bitter cup
    Of grief that man shall taste—
Go, tell the night that hides thy face,   75
Thou saw'st the last of Adam's race,
    On Earth's sepulchral clod,
The dark'ning universe defy
To quench his Immortality,
    Or shake his trust in God!   80

3. Thomas Campbell, to the Editor of the *Edinburgh Review*, 28 February
1825 (in response to the review of *Theodric* quoted in the headnote above,
369, which compares Campbell's poem to Byron's). This letter was published in *The Times*, 24 March 1825.

... You say that my Poem, the Last Man, seems to have been suggested by
Lord Byron's Poem Darkness. Now the truth is, that fifteen, or it may be
more years ago, I called on Lord Byron, who at that time had lodgings
near St. James's-street; and we had a long, and to me, a very memorable
conversation, from which, I have not a doubt, that his Lordship imbibed
those few ideas in the poem, Darkness, which have any resemblance to
mine in the Last Man. I remember my saying to him, that I thought the
idea of a being witnessing the extinction of his species and of the
Creation, and of his looking, under the fading eye of nature, at desolate
cities, ships floating at sea with the dead, would make a striking subject
for a poem. I met those very ideas, many years afterwards, when I read
Lord Byron's poem Darkness. It may be asked why I did not then appeal
to Lord Byron about the originality of those few ideas? As circumstances
have turned out, I now wish that I had done so. Lord Byron's most
attached friend has given me his opinion, that if his Lordship had not forgotten the conversation, and was conscious of using an idea which I had
suggested to him, he did so, prepared to give me credit for the suggestion
whenever I should claim that credit. Had I taken this view of the case,
and had I also then finished my little poem, I should in all probability
have written to Lord B. But I had not written the piece, and at that time
thought I never should write it. Unimportant as the leading idea was, I
was discouraged by its being taken from me. There seemed to me to be
no use in setting on foot a correspondence with Lord Byron, merely to
dun him for an acknowledgement of my right to a stray idea. He might,
or he might not, have recollected our conversation; but if he had forgot-

ten it, his telling me so would have only increased a petty mortification.—Then, as for ascertaining the matter by proofs, after years had past,
how was I to rake up the recollections of those persons, to whom I might
have long ago mentioned the design of my poem?—One might be dead:
a second might be uncertain as to dates; and a third certainly had so
domestic a relation to me, that the evidence was no better than my own.
In reality, I abandoned, for a great many years, the idea of fulfilling my
sketch. But I was provoked to change my mind, when my friend Barry
Cornwall informed me that an acquaintance of his intended to write a
long poem, entitled the *Last Man*.[1]—I thought this hard! The conception
of the Last Man had been mine fifteen years ago; even Lord Byron had
spared the title to me: I therefore wrote my poem so called, and sent it to
the press; for not one idea in which was I indebted to Lord Byron, or to
any other person.

4. Thomas Hood, from "The Last Man," *Whims and Oddities in Prose and
Verse* (1826), 3rd ed. (London: Lupton Relfe, 1828), 31-32. The narrator,
having survived the plague, conducts a trial and then hangs his only
remaining companion, angry "To see him lording so braggart-like / That
was born to his beggar's fare, / And how he had stolen the royal crown /
His betters were meant to wear" (140-43). The poem concludes as follows:

I've buried my babies one by one,
And dug the deep hole for Joan,   200
And covered the faces of kith and kin,
And felt the old churchyard stone
Go cold to my heart, full many a time,
But I never felt so lone!

For the lion and Adam were company,   205
And the tiger him beguil'd;
But the simple kine are foes to my life,
And the household brutes are wild.
If the veriest cur would lick my hand,
I could love it like a child!   210

And the beggar man's ghost besets my dreams,
At night, to make me madder,—
And my wretched conscience, within my breast,
Is like a stinging adder;—
I sigh when I pass the gallows' foot,   215
And look at the rope and ladder!—

---

1   Thomas Lovell Beddoes: see Introduction, xv.

For hanging looks sweet,—but, alas! in vain
My desperate fancy begs,—
I must turn my cup of sorrows quite up,
And drink it to the dregs,—   220
For there is not another man alive,
In the world, to pull my legs!

5. From George Dibdin Pitt (1799-1855), *The Last Man; or, The Miser of
Eltham Green. A Drama in two acts* (New York: Samuel French, n.d.). The
play opened at the Surrey Theatre on 22 July 1833.

Geoffrey Dale (the town miser), to his niece, Lucy:
    I tell thee, child, there are men that are born so lucky as to always catch
the golden moment, and even from misfortune's bitter husk draw forth a
honeyed kernel; while others, by a strange fatality, are always *last* in the
market, *last* in fortune, *last* in every thing—such am I. In childhood's days
my back would frequently smart for being the *last* boy when school bell
rung; when a clerk, the *last* that entered the gloomy office was surely I; I
served in the train band of the city, and on the muster roll Geoffrey Dale
stood *last* again;[2] till on a goodly field-day morn, when all our city youths
had passed the night in active preparation, sleep rocked my brain, and too
late waking, I hurried to the muster ground, found the corps had marched;
and, on the spot, I, the LAST MAN, stood the sneer and mock of all; from
that moment, the nickname stuck to me through life,—I cannot bear to
hear it, have forbid such mention in my house; for I feel here that I am
doomed to live till all the world shall die.

Lucy:
    Dear uncle, what strange idea is this, alike impious and absurd!

Geoffrey:
    Tell me not, Lucy, tell me not,—I know it, I feel it,—it hath been
revealed to me by dream. Listen, Lucy, listen; I dreamed I stood upon a
rock alone, like the fir tree on the blighted hill; all nature seemed as dead;
the sea was calm and still; the sun and clouds moved not, the air was
fixed; the leaf had left the tree, and in yellow heaps bestrewed the forest
and the field; vegetation *died*, and *green* lived but in remembrance of the
eye,—all was dead, and I was left the *Last Man*!!! O! the horror that
thrilled my heart! I called aloud, "Am I the last that's left?" From glen to
glen, from shore to shore, from every clime on earth, an echo came, the
"*last that's left!*" I rushed into the woods; I sought the plain, the town, the
glen; a horrid stillness reigned around, my knees trembled, the scalding

---

2   A trainband is a volunteer militia; a muster roll is a register of troops in a mili-
     tary unit.

tears fell fast and many, a slight sound struck my ear; I looked around—a robin, last of the feathered race, flew towards me, as glad to see a fellow-being left; but 'twas all it could; the burst of joy, its fluttering wing had caused, was quickly drowned in grief; it reached my hand, looked upwards to my face, and tired of life without its kind, drooped its head and gently died. I groaned with agony; my only co-mate in a desolate world was gone—gone, and I left alone forever; my heart, my throat, swelled with agony unutterable, and I awoke, while my prophetic soul did yell prediction to my troubled ear.

6. Thomas Lovell Beddoes, notes for a projected play, to be called *The Last Man* (*The Works of Thomas Lovell Beddoes*, ed. with introd. R.W. Donner [Oxford: Oxford UP, 1935]). Reprinted by permission of Oxford University Press.

i. ACT V. (last man) to open with a chorus from the tombs in a churchyard or catacomb, & Beroe's prophesy of the world's destruction. (520)

ii. Death and the Gods—The last man—to serve Death (whose character is to be new-modelled—see the Devil in Meph.[3]) in some way so that the latter promises not to take his life—After the world is over he goes to heaven and behaves saucily to the Gods—Or make Death a woman and enamoured of Orion the last one &c.[4] Chorus describing the ruins of Olympus & melancholy Jove—And then a dialogue between the sun, moon, and seven stars about the state of the Earth's health. One of the dramatis personae an incarnation of the world's destruction. (c. 1837; 525-26)

---

3   Perhaps a reference to Mephistopheles, the tempting spirit in Goethe's *Faust*, Part 1, 1808, Part 2, 1832.
4   Beddoes seems to be inventing his own story; but cf. Job 9.9, 38.31, and Amos 5.8.

Appendix B: The Sibyl's Cave

1. From Virgil, *Aeneid* 6, trans. James Beresford (London: J. Johnson, 1794), 199-204.

... [G]ood Æneas seeks those lofty tow'rs   11
Where Phœbus holds high rule, and the dark seat,
Stupendous cavern dire, where, dread from far,
The Sibyl dwells; in whom the Delian God[5]
High ecstasies, imaginations grand   15
Inspires, uncovering the dark deeps of Fate.
Now Dian's groves[6] they gain, and golden domes.
Fame tells that Dædalus, when he fled of yore
Minoian realms,[7] dar'd trust him to the skies
On rapid pinions, and sail'd bold along,   20
In journey' untried, to Hyperborean climes,
Then lightly dropp'd, at length, on Chalcis' tow'r.[8]
First in these regions on firm land arriv'd,
Phœbus, he consecrated here to thee
His oary wings, and rear'd a fane sublime.[9]   25
Grav'd on the doors Androgeos' death is seen,[10]
And the Athenian race enjoin'd to pay
With each returning year, condition sad!
Sev'n of their sons, a death-selected band.[11]
Near stands the chanceful urn;[12] in counterview   30
The Gnossian land emerging from the main.[13]
Here was the horrid love to th'bull, and she
Pasiphae, by stealth, led substitute,
And the mix'd race, and Minotaur twin-form'd;—

---

5   Apollo or Phoebus, to whom the Aegean island of Delos was sacred.
6   A wood sacred to Diana (Artemis), sister of Apollo.
7   The realms of Minos, king of Crete.
8   Chalcis is the main city of Euboea, a large island off the northeast coast of Attica from which the original Greek colonists had come to Cumae (on the west coast of Italy, near the modern city of Naples).
9   A fane is a temple.
10 Androgeos was the son of Minos, supposed to have been killed by the Athenians.
11 Sent from Athens to Crete in annual reparation for Androgeos' death.
12 Lots were drawn from an urn to determine which Athenian youths would be sent to Crete.
13 Gnossian should be Cnossian, with reference to Cnossus, the leading city of Crete.

Memorials of abominable lust.[14]   35
And here, beside, the labour'd Labyrinth
Is seen, with its inextricable maze.[15]
But Dædalus, the Princess' ardent love
Viewing compassionate, himself unfolds
The wily windings of th'involved walls,   40
The chief's blind footsteps ruling with a clew.[16]
And, but for sorrow, thou too, Icarus,
Great part in that amazing work hadst borne:[17]
Twice he essay'd to grave thy tale in gold;
Twice dropp'd the Father's hands....   45

Th'Eubœan rock's vast side is hewn to a cave,   56
Whereto conduct an hundred spacious ways,
An hundred mouths, whence rush an hundred sounds,
The Sibyl's answers. At the porch arriv'd,—
The time is now, she cries, to' enquire thy doom: 60
The God! the God!—While by the door she spake,
Sudden no more her aspect, and no more
Her colour was the same; no more her hairs
Hung orderly; but pantings shake her breast,
And frenzied fury swells her labouring heart: 65
Ampler she seems, nor mortal sounds her voice,
Whilst o'er her now th'invading Deity
His rushing effluence breathes....

[Aeneas prays to Phoebus for a new homeland in Latium and for prophetic knowledge of his people's fate.]

Only commit thou not to flitting leaves
Thy songs prophetic; lest, disturb'd, they fly   100
The sport of driving winds: sing, I implore,
With thine own lips thine oracles!—He ceas'd.
But of Apollo not yet patient grown,

---

14 Pasiphae, daughter of the Sun and wife of Minos, fell in love with a bull and
    gave birth to the Minotaur, half human, half bull.
15 Daedalus the artificer built the labyrinth to imprison the Minotaur; within its
    mazes, the monster hunted Athenian prisoners for food.
16 By means of a thread, or clue, Daedalus helped Minos' daughter, Ariadne, to
    rescue the Athenian Theseus, whom she loved.
17 Because of Daedalus' grief, the story of his son Icarus, who fell into the sea
    when his waxen wings melted during the escape from Crete, is not depicted
    on the temple gates.

The Prophet-maid outrageous in the cave
Maddens with Bacchant rage;[18] if from her breast   105
Her strugglings may prevail to shake away
Th'incumbent Godhead: But he tires the more
Her rabid mouth, and potent taming down
Her Lion-heart, coercive moulds her soul.
And now the vault spontaneous opens wide   110
Its hundred monstrous mouths, and sends along
The Prophetess' responses through the air....

... Thus Cuma's Sibyl from the hallow'd cell
Sings her dread mysteries, and in the cave
Loud bellowing, intervolves true in obscure,   135
As Phœbus o'er the raving maid his rein
Shakes, and his goad plies fierce within her breast.
Soon as her frenzy paus'd, and her mad lips
Had rest, then great Æneas thus begins:
To me, O maid! not strange nor unpresag'd   140
Comes any shape of suffering; every woe
Have I forestall'd, and in my lab'ring soul
Exhausted long ere now. One boon I crave,
(Since here the gates of Hell's infernal King,
As fame records, and here that darksome lake,   145
By ebbings fed from th'Acherontic pool,[19])
That thou wouldst lead me longing to the sight
Of my lov'd parent: thither point the way,
And every sacred avenue unclose.

2. From Jean-Baptiste Cousin de Grainville, *The Last Man, or Omegarus and Syderia, A Romance in Futurity*, 2 vols. (London: Dutton, 1806), 1: 1-7.

Near the ruins of Palmyra[20] is a solitary cavern, so much dreaded by the Syrians, that they denominated it the Cavern of Death. No man had ever dared to enter it without instantly receiving the punishment of his temerity. It is said that some intrepid Frenchmen, venturing to penetrate this place with arms in their hands, were all slain, and at the returning dawn their limbs were found scattered about the desert. When the nights are peaceful and serene, dreadful groans and tumultuous shrieks issue from the cavern. Sometimes it vomits forth volumes of flame and smoke, the

---

18 The intoxication of worshippers of Bacchus (Dionysus).
19 Acheron, one of the rivers of the underworld.
20 An ancient city in the desert of Syria, once known as Tadmor: see 2 Chron. 8.4, 269n, and Appendix D.1.

earth shakes, and the ruins of Palmyra are rocked about like the waves of the ocean.

I had travelled over Africa, visited the coasts of the Red Sea, and traversed Palestine. Influenced by some secret and unknown inspiration, I was desirous of beholding that superb city where Zenobia formerly reigned, and more particularly that awful cavern which was supposed to be the abode of Death. I repaired there, attended by several Syrians. Its aspect had nothing terrific: the entrance, shaded over by the thick foliage of the wild vine, invited the traveller to rest himself beneath its cooling shelter. No monster guarded the passage; the terror which it inspired had rendered it inaccessible.

While regarding it attentively, I perceived on the summit a man armed with a torch. His eyes were sharp and piercing, and his majestic brow seemed the seat of peace. From the perfect serenity he appeared to enjoy, it might have been concluded that he had always lived in his present retreat, a stranger to fear and hope. I am ignorant in what manner he communicated his ideas to me, but I understood that he invited me into the cavern, to which I felt myself attracted by a sudden and irresistible impulse; and, notwithstanding the alarm and cries of the Syrians, who were endeavouring to deter me, I sprang into the subterraneous abode.

For a long time I advanced in utter darkness, astonished at my own audacity, for the gloom rather continued to increase, as I advanced into this terrific recess.—Suddenly I lost the use of my external faculties; my feet denied their office, and I became fixed to the ground, like a statue. The air I was inhaling failed, and I felt as if I had been in a void space, where, existing without the power of action, I enjoyed entire repose. A pleasure unknown to human nature, and so exquisite that it surpassed the softest voluptuousness, insensibly overcame me. In an instant after, the thick gloom by which it was enveloped vanished, the pure light of day burst upon my senses, and I beheld the various objects surrounding me.

I found myself in a circus erected with fragments of the hardest rock, opposite a sapphire throne, similar in form to the famous tripod[21] of the priestesses of Apollo. This throne was canopied by gold and azure clouds, which some invisible power held suspended. A volatile flame, free from smoke, sparkled on an infinite number of tapers, and the walls were hung round with magic mirrors, wherein the eye discovered a boundless horizon. On the right, at the foot of an adamantine column, a robust old man was chained down; his shoulders were mutilated, and he looked with an expression of melancholy at the fragments of a broken clock and two bloody wings, lying on the ground.[22]

Then, without the agency of voice, and by means incomprehensible to me, a Spirit who dwelt in the tripod said, "I have punished with death the

---

21   The three-legged seat from which the Sibyl uttered oracles.
22   The old man is an allegorical figure of Time.

rash mortals who, scorning the fear my dwelling almost universally inspires, have fancied their temerity could force its entrance. Fear not the same fate, thou whom I have called into my presence. I am the celestial Spirit to whom eternal futurity is known.—All events are to me as if they were passed. Here Time is loaded with chains, and his empire destroyed.—In me behold the father of pre-science and dreams: I dictate oracles, and inspire celebrated politicians. The moment that a mortal has stained his hands with crimes, I place before his sight the preparations of that chastisement which human justice has in store for the guilty, and, as an augmentation of his torment, I make him prophecy of his punishment and death.

"If I have conducted thy steps to this cavern, it was for the particular purpose of raising before thee the veil which conceals dark futurity from man, and to make thee a spectator of the scenes that will terminate the destinies of the universe.—In the magic mirrors thou beholdest around, the last man will stand revealed to thy sight. There, as on a stage, where the actors represent heroes who are no more, thou shalt hear him converse with the most illustrious personages of the last ages of the world, read in his soul his most secret thoughts, and be the witness and judge of his last actions.

"Think not that I intend by this spectacle merely to gratify the wishes of thy curiosity;—a nobler design actuates me. The last man will not have any posterity to know and admire him. I wish before his birth that he may live in memory: I desire to celebrate his struggles and victories over himself,—to tell what pains he will undergo to shorten those of human kind, to terminate the reign of time, and to hasten the day of everlasting recompence which the just have to expect; I wish to reveal to men this history, so deserving of their attention.... But attend! The great representation now commences, and will pass rapidly before thee!"

Appendix C: Versions of Plague

Mary Shelley's plague starts in Constantinople and spreads to Athens, two cities famous for actual outbreaks of plague. Gibbon's account of the plague at Constantinople in AD 542, the first excerpt below, is concerned with some of the same questions that Mary Shelley treats: is the plague contagious? how does it spread? Citing Procopius, whose *History of the Wars* recounts the wars of the emperor Justinian in the sixth century AD, Gibbon graphically describes the symptoms of bubonic plague, the disease that periodically ravaged Europe throughout the Middle Ages (especially in the Black Death of the fourteenth century, the backdrop to Boccaccio's *Decameron*). Gibbon's account concludes with a statement that plague can permanently reduce the population of an affected region, a claim which is challenged by Thomas Robert Malthus's view, expressed in the excerpt from *An Essay on Population* (1798) in Appendix D.3.ii.

The Great Plague of 1665, fictionalized in Daniel Defoe's *A Journal of the Plague Year* (1722), is an acknowledged source, along with Charles Brockden Brown's *Arthur Mervyn* (1799-1800), for Mary Shelley's descriptions of plague. Brown, however, describes not the bubonic plague of Defoe's and Gibbon's accounts but yellow fever or "malignant fever": "plague" or "pestilence" (from Latin *pestis*, plague) need not refer to a single disease. Similarly, the plague at Athens in the fifth century BC, described by Thucydides, was probably not bubonic plague. According to a modern scholar, J.S. Rusten, "Attempts are regularly made to identify the disease .... But no candidate (among them smallpox, bubonic plague, measles, typhus, typhoid fever or a combination of two diseases) has yet found general acceptance."[23] *The Last Man* refers to a range of illnesses and symptoms, including yellow fever, scarlet fever, malaria, and typhus. Although Shelley never specifically mentions bubonic plague, she seems to be aware of contemporary debates about whether or not plague was contagious, and to be alluding to them quite directly in Chapter XVI of *The Last Man*. The final excerpts in Appendix C.5 are from a long review article on this subject published in 1825 in the *Westminster Review*.

1. From Edward Gibbon, *The History of the Decline and Fall of the Roman Empire*, 6 vols. (London: Strahan and Cadell, 1776-88), 4: 327-31. At the end of chapter 43, Gibbon is describing the famous plague at Constantinople in AD 542.

---

23. Thucydides, *History of the Peloponnesian War*, Book 2, ed. J.S. Rusten (Cambridge: Cambridge UP, 1989) 182-83. Thucydides' account was a source for accounts of plague in Lucretius, *The Nature of Things* 6, and Ovid, *Metamorphoses* 7.

Æthiopia and Egypt have been stigmatised in every age, as the original source and seminary of the plague. In a damp, hot, stagnating air, this African fever is generated from the putrefaction of animal substances, and especially from the swarms of locusts, not less destructive to mankind in their death than in their lives. The fatal disease which depopulated the earth in the time of Justinian and his successors, first appeared in the neighbourhood of Pelusium, between the Serbonian bog and the eastern channel of the Nile.[24] From thence, tracing as it were a double path, it spread to the East, over Syria, Persia, and the Indies, and penetrated to the West, along the coast of Africa, and over the continent of Europe. In the spring of the second year, Constantinople, during three or four months, was visited by the pestilence: and Procopius, who observed its progress and symptoms with the eyes of a physician, has emulated the skill and diligence of Thucydides in the description of the plague of Athens.[25] The infection was sometimes announced by the visions of a distempered fancy, and the victim despaired as soon as he had heard the menace and felt the stroke of an invisible spectre. But the greater number, in their beds, in the streets, in their usual occupation, were surprised by a slight fever; so slight indeed, that neither the pulse nor the colour of the patient gave any signs of the approaching danger. The same, the next, or the succeeding day, it was declared by the swelling of the glands, particularly those of the groin, of the arm-pits, and under the ear; and when these bubos or tumours were opened, they were found to contain a *coal*, or black substance, of the size of a lentil. If they came to a just swelling and suppuration, the patient was saved by this kind and natural discharge of the morbid humour. But, if they continued hard and dry, a mortification quickly ensued, and the fifth day was commonly the term of his life. The fever was often accompanied with lethargy or delirium; the bodies of the sick were covered with black pustules or carbuncles, the symptoms of immediate death; and, in the constitutions too feeble to produce an eruption, the vomiting of blood was followed by a mortification of the bowels. To pregnant women the plague was generally mortal: yet one infant was drawn alive from his dead mother, and three mothers survived the loss of their infected fœtus. Youth was the most perilous season; and the female sex was less susceptible than the male: but every rank and profession was attacked with indiscriminate rage, and many of those who were escaped were deprived of the use of their speech, without being secure from a return of the disorder. The physicians of Constantinople were zealous and skilful: but their art was baffled by the various symptoms and pertinacious vehe-

---

24 Pelusium forms a bridge between Egypt to the west and Palestine to the northeast.

25 Procopius tells about the plague at Byzantium (Constantinople) in the time of Justinian in his *History of the Wars* 2.22 (trans. H. B. Dewing 1: 451-65); for Thucydides, see above, 383n, and headnote to Appendix C.

mence of the disease: the same remedies were productive of contrary effects, and the event capriciously disappointed their prognostics of death or recovery. The order of funerals, and the right of sepulchres, were confounded; those who were left without friends or servants, lay unburied in the streets or in their desolate houses; and a magistrate was authorised to collect the promiscuous heaps of dead bodies, to transport them by land or water, and to inter them in deep pits beyond the precincts of the city. Their own danger, and the prospect of public distress, awakened some remorse in the minds of the most vicious of mankind: the confidence of health again revived their passions and habits; but philosophy must disdain the observation of Procopius that the lives of such men were guarded by the peculiar favour of fortune or providence. He forgot, or perhaps he secretly recollected, that the plague had touched the person of Justinian himself: but the abstemious diet of the emperor may suggest, as in the case of Socrates, a more rational and honourable cause for his recovery. During his sickness, the public consternation was expressed in the habits of the citizens; and their idleness and despondence occasioned a general scarcity in the capital of the East.

Contagion is the inseparable symptom of the plague; which, by mutual respiration, is transfused from the infected persons to the lungs and stomach of those who approach them. While philosophers believe and tremble, it is singular, that the existence of a real danger should have been denied by a people most prone to vain and imaginary terrors. Yet the fellow-citizens of Procopius were satisfied, by some short and partial experience, that the infection could not be gained by the closest conversation;[26] and this persuasion might support the assiduity of friends or physicians in the care of the sick, whom inhuman prudence would have condemned to solitude and despair. But the fatal security, like the predestination of the Turks,[27] must have aided the progress of the contagion; and those salutary precautions to which Europe is indebted for her safety, were unknown to the government of Justinian. No restraints were imposed on the free and frequent intercourse of the Roman provinces: from Persia to France, the nations were mingled and infected by wars and emigrations; and the pestilential odour which lurks for years in a bale of cotton, was imported, by the abuse of trade, into the most distant regions.[28] The mode of its propagation is explained by the remark of Procopius himself, that it always spread from the sea-coast to the inland country: the most sequestered islands and mountains were successively visited; the places which had escaped the fury of its first passage, were alone exposed to the

---

26 Cf. below, Appendix C.5.iii.

27 In Moslem countries the Turkish word *kismet*, from Arabic *qisma*, is used in this sense.

28 A recurring fear, which some governments tried to meet by trade restrictions; see Introduction xxx-xxxi.

contagion of the ensuing year. The winds might diffuse that subtle venom; but unless the atmosphere be previously disposed for its reception, the plague would soon expire in the cold or temperate climates of the earth. Such was the universal corruption of the air, that the pestilence which burst forth in the fifteenth year of Justinian was not checked or alleviated by any difference of the seasons. In time, its first malignity was abated and dispersed; the disease alternately languished and revived; but it was not till the end of a calamitous period of fifty-two years, that mankind recovered their health, or the air resumed its pure and salubrious quality. No facts have been preserved to sustain an account, or even a conjecture, of the numbers that perished in this extraordinary mortality. I only find, that during three months, five, and at length ten, thousand persons died each day at Constantinople; that many cities of the East were left vacant, and that in several districts of Italy the harvest and the vintage withered on the ground. The triple scourge of war, pestilence, and famine, afflicted the subjects of Justinian, and his reign is disgraced by a visible decrease of the human species, which has never been repaired in some of the fairest countries of the globe.

2. From Daniel Defoe, *The History of the Great Plague in London, in the Year 1665 ... by a citizen* [*A Journal of the Plague Year*, 1722] (London: John Offor, 1819).

i. In the first place, a blazing star or comet appeared for several months before the Plague, as there did the year after another, a little before the fire; the old women, and the phlegmatic hypochondriac part of the other sex, whom I could almost call old women too, remarked (especially afterward, though not till both those judgments were over,) that those two Comets passed directly over the city, and that so very near the houses, that it was plain they imported something peculiar to the city alone; that the Comet before the pestilence was of a faint, dull, languid colour, and its motion very heavy, solemn, and slow: but that the Comet before the fire was bright and sparkling, or, as others said, flaming, and its motion swift and furious; and that accordingly, one foretold a heavy judgment, slow, but severe, terrible, and frightful, as was the Plague; but the other foretold a stroke, sudden, swift, and fiery, as the conflagration; nay, so particular some people were that, as they looked upon that Comet preceding the fire, they fancied that they not only saw it pass swiftly and fiercely, and could perceive the motion with their eye, but even they heard it; that it made a rushing mighty noise, fierce, and terrible, though at a distance, and but just perceivable.

I saw both these stars, and I must confess, had so much of the common notion of such things in my head, that I was apt to look upon them as the forerunners and warnings of God's judgments; and especially when, after the Plague had followed the first, I yet saw another of the like kind, I could not but say, God had not yet sufficiently scourged the city. (40-42)

ii. Next ... were the dreams of old women, or, I should say, the interpretation of old women upon other people's dreams; and these put abundance of people even out of their wits: some heard voices warning them to be gone, for that there would be such a Plague in London so that the living would not be able to bury the dead: others saw apparitions in the air; and I must be allowed to say of both, I hope without breach of charity, that they heard voices that never spake, and saw sights that never appeared; but the imagination of the people was really turned wayward and possessed: and no wonder if they who were poring continually at the clouds saw shapes and figures, representations and appearances, which had nothing in them but air and vapour.... One time, before the Plague was begun, ... I think it was in March, seeing a crowd of people in the street, I joined with them to satisfy my curiosity, and found them all staring up into the air, to see what a woman told them appeared plain to her, which was an Angel clothed in white, with a fiery sword in his hand, waving it, or brandishing it over his head: she described every part of the figure to the life; shewed them the motion, and the form; and the poor people came into it so eagerly, and with so much readiness. "Yes, I see it all plainly," says one; "there is the sword as plain as can be." Another saw the Angel. One saw his very face, and cried out, "what a glorious creature he was!" One saw one thing, and one, another. I looked as earnestly as the rest, but, perhaps, not with so much willingness to be imposed upon; and I said, indeed, that I could see nothing but a white cloud, bright on one side, by the shining of the sun upon the other part. (45-47)

iii. I cannot omit taking notice what a desolate place the city was at that time: the great street I lived in, which is known to be one of the broadest of all the streets of London, I mean of the suburbs, as well as the liberties; all the side where the butchers lived, especially without the bars, was more like a green field than a paved street, and the people generally went in the middle with the horses and carts: it is true, that the farthest end, towards Whitechapel church, was not all paved, but even the part that was paved was full of grass also; but this need not seem strange, since the great streets within the city, such as Leadenhall-street, Bishopsgate-street, Cornhill, and even the Exchange itself, had grass growing in them in several places; neither cart or coach were seen in the streets from morning to evening, except some country carts, to bring roots and beans, or pease, hay and straw to the market, and those but very few, compared to what was usual; as for coaches, they were scarce used, but to carry sick people to the pest-house,[29] and to other hospitals, and some few to carry physicians to such places as they thought fit to venture to visit; for really coaches were dangerous things, and people did not care to venture into them, because they did not know who might have been carried in them

---

29 Hospital for plague victims.

last; and sick infected people were, as I have said, ordinarily carried in them to the pest-houses, and sometimes people expired in them as they went along. (204-05)

iv. But I must still speak of the Plague, as in its height, raging even to desolation, and the people under the most dreadful consternation, even, as I have said, to despair. It is hardly credible to what excesses the passions of men carried them in this extremity of the distemper; and this part, I think, was as moving as the rest. What could affect a man in his full power of reflection; and what could make deeper impressions on the soul than to see a man, almost naked, and got out of his house, or perhaps out of his bed into the street, come out of Harrow-alley, a populous conjunction or collection of alleys, courts, and passages in the Butcher-row, in Whitechapel! I say, what could be more affecting, than to see this poor man come out into the open street, run dancing and singing, and making a thousand antic gestures, with five or six women and children running after him, crying and calling upon him, for the Lord's sake to come back, and entreating the help of others to bring him back, but all in vain, nobody daring to lay a hand upon him, or to come near him. (350-51)

3. From Charles Brockden Brown, *Arthur Mervyn, or Memoirs of the Year 1793* [1799-1800], 2 vols. Philadelphia: D. McKay, 1887.

i. [During the yellow-fever epidemic in Philadelphia, Arthur Mervyn, the narrator, is searching for Wallace in Thetford's house by night.]

I mounted the stair. As I approached the door of which I was in search, a vapour, infectious and deadly, assailed my senses. It resembled nothing of which I had ever before been sensible. Many odours had been met with, even since my arrival in the city, less supportable than this. I seemed not so much to smell as to taste the element that now encompassed me. I felt as if I had inhaled a poisonous and subtle fluid, whose power instantly bereft my stomach of all vigour. Some fatal influence appeared to seize upon my vitals, and the work of corrosion and decomposition to be busily begun.

... Whether my case would be lenient or malignant, whether I should recover or perish, was to be left to the decision of the future. This incident, instead of appalling me, tended rather to invigorate my courage. The danger which I feared had come. I might enter with indifference on this theatre of pestilence. I might execute, without faltering, the duties that my circumstances might create. My state was no longer hazardous; and my destiny would be totally uninfluenced by my future conduct.

The pang with which I was first seized, and the momentary inclination to vomit, which it produced, presently subsided. My wholesome feelings, indeed, did not revisit me, but strength to proceed was restored to me.

The effluvia became more sensible as I approached the door of the chamber. The door was ajar; and the light within was perceived. My belief that those within were dead was presently confuted by sound, which I first supposed to be that of steps moving quickly and timorously across the floor. This ceased, and was succeeded by sounds of different but inexplicable import.

Having entered the apartment, I saw a candle on the hearth. A table was covered with vials and other apparatus of a sick-chamber. A bed stood on one side, the curtain of which was dropped at the foot, so as to conceal any one within. I fixed my eyes upon this object. There were sufficient tokens that some one lay upon the bed. Breath, drawn at long intervals; mutterings scarcely audible; and a tremendous motion in the bedstead, were fearful and intelligible indication. (1: 144-46)

ii. [The dying man was not Wallace. Mervyn, already sick with the fever, eventually finds his friend and hears about the horrors of the pestilence-hospital.]

"I have no perfect recollection of what passed till my arrival at the hospital [Wallace tells Mervyn]. My passions combined with my disease to make me frantic and wild. In a state like mine, the slightest motion could not be endured without agony. What then must I have felt, scorched and dazzled by the sun, sustained by hard boards, and borne for miles over a rugged pavement?

"I cannot make you comprehend the anguish of my feelings. To be disjointed and torn piecemeal by the rack was a torment inexpressibly inferior to this. Nothing excites my wonder but that I did not expire before the cart had moved three paces.

"I knew not how, or by whom, I was moved from this vehicle. Insensibility came at length to my relief. After a time I opened my eyes, and slowly gained some knowledge of my situation. I lay upon a mattress, whose condition proved that a half-decayed corpse had recently been dragged from it. The room was large, but it was covered with beds like my own. Between each, there was scarcely the interval of three feet. Each sustained a wretch, whose groans and distortions bespoke the desperateness of his condition.

"The atmosphere was loaded by mortal stenches. A vapour, suffocating and malignant, scarcely allowed me to breathe. No suitable receptacle was provided for the evacuations produced by medicine or disease. My nearest neighbour was struggling with death, and my bed, casually extended, was moist with the detestable matter which had flowed from his stomach.

"You will scarcely believe that, in this scene of horrors, the sound of laughter should be overheard. While the upper rooms of this building are filled with the sick and the dying, the lower apartments are the scene of carousels and mirth. The wretches who are hired, at enormous wages, to tend the sick and convey away the dead, neglect their duty, and consume the cordials which are provided for the patients, in debauchery and riot.

"A female visage, bloated with malignity and drunkenness, occasionally looked in. Dying eyes were cast upon her, invoking the boon, perhaps, of a drop of cold water, or her assistance to change a posture which compelled him to behold the ghastly writhings or deathful *smile* of his neighbour...." (1: 172-73)

4. From John Wilson, *The City of the Plague and Other Poems* (Edinburgh: Constable, 1816), I.i.

[An Old Man with an infant in his arms is talking to Frankfort and Wilmot, two naval officers newly arrived in plague-stricken London.]

Old Man. Know ye what you will meet with in the city?
    Together will ye walk, through long, long streets,
    All standing silent as a midnight church.
    You will hear nothing but the brown red grass
    Rustling beneath your feet; the very beating   5
    Of your own hearts will awe you; the small voice
    Of that vain bauble, idly counting time,
    Will speak a solemn language in the desert.
    Look up to heaven, and there the sultry clouds,
    Still threatening thunder, lower with grim delight,   10
    As if the Spirit of the plague dwelt there,
    Darkening the city with the shadows of death.
    Know ye that hideous hubbub? Hark, far off
    A tumult like an echo! on it comes,
    Weeping and wailing, shrieks and groaning prayer;   15
    And louder than all outrageous blasphemy.
    The passing storm hath left the silent streets.
    But are these houses near you tenantless?
    Over your heads from a window, suddenly
    A ghastly face is thrust, and yells of death   20
    With voice not human. Who is he that flies,
    As if a demon dogg'd him on his path?
    With ragged hair, white face, and bloodshot eyes,
    Raving, he rushes past you; till he falls,
    As if struck by lightning, down upon the stones,   25
    Or, in blind madness, dash'd against the wall,
    Sinks backward into stillness. Stand aloof,
    And let the Pest's triumphal chariot
    Have open way advancing to the tomb.
    See how he mocks the pomp and pageantry   30
    Of earthly kings! A miserable cart,

Heap'd up with human bodies; dragg'd along
By pale steeds, skeleton-anatomies!
And onwards urged by a wan meagre wretch,
Doom'd never to return from the foul pit,   35
Whither, with oaths he drives his load of horror.

5. From "Contagion and Sanitary Laws," *Westminster Review* 3 (1825): 134-67. This is a long review of several books and reports taking different sides in a current debate about whether plague was contagious (transmitted from one person to another by contact and body fluids) or whether it was epidemic (transmitted through "a certain condition of the air" [135]). The reviewer takes the latter position.

i. In assigning certain conditions of the air as the cause of epidemic diseases, we are able to advance one step. The air, it is certain, is often charged with noxious exhalations arising from the putrefaction of animal and vegetable matter. These exhalations are generated in marshy situations, or where stagnant water contains dead vegetable matter; and their production is greatly promoted by heat. Their precise nature is not known, for they have never been obtained in a separate state; but it is ascertained that they are suspended in the air; that, naturally, they do not extend far beyond the place where they are generated; that, by currents of wind, they are capable of being conveyed to a great distance; that they exert a powerful agency in producing some of the most malignant fevers; and that a long-continued exposure to them, wonderfully shortens the duration of human life.... It is certain that these exhalations exert a most important agency in the production of epidemic diseases; it is equally true, that often-times their influence cannot be traced, and that in the most terrible pestilences which, there is reason to believe, depend entirely on the condition of the air, it is impossible to attribute to such exhalations any share in producing its morbid state. (142)

ii. Like other epidemics, the plague begins and ceases at periods surprisingly regular; these periods correspond exactly to the usual epidemic seasons; thus, in Asia Minor, it prevails from April to July; at Smyrna, from February to June; at Constantinople, from July to December; in Europe, in the same Autumnal months. (158)

iii. The disease obeys every law of an epidemic; it does not obey a single law of a contagious disease; it is not communicated by wearing clothes impregnated with the sweat, pus, and ichorous matter from the bodies of those who have died of the malady; it is not communicated by coming into the closest possible contact with their living body; it is not communicated by sleeping in the same bed with them; the husband who dies in the arms of his wife communicates it not to her; sister communicates it not to sister; the child deriving sustenance from the breast of its mother, who is perishing, and who does perish by it, receives it not; the sick who fly for succour to a purer air, impart it not to the inhabitants of these more favoured places; whole armies continue in unrestrained and constant intercourse, with affected towns and villages, without receiving it in a single instance; again, then, we demand what proof is it possible to imagine, that this malady is not contagious, which we do not actually possess? (166-67)

Appendix D: "The Web of Mind"

The following passages can introduce only some of the intellectual and literary contexts of Mary Shelley's novel. In the passage from Volney's *Les ruines* (1791), translated into English as *The Ruins*, the narrator, guided by Nature and Reason, reflects on the folly responsible for human misery. This connects a particular mood of late eighteenth-century literature, elegiac and contemplative, with the radical political creed adopted by Shelley's parents, William Godwin and Mary Wollstonecraft. Passages from Godwin's *Political Justice* (1793) and Thomas Robert Malthus's *Essay on Population* (1798; revised 1803) set the optimism of the first (based on his belief in human perfectibility) against the pessimism of the second (based on Malthus's conviction that food supply, increasing arithmetically, could never be adequate to a geometric increase in population). Other passages from *Political Justice* record Godwin's theory of necessity and his speculations about the future of humankind in a world without children and without death.

Mary Wollstonecraft's account of the French Revolution, based on personal observation in 1792-94, retains Godwinian optimism in the long-term effects of democratic institutions but deplores "the despotism of licentious freedom." Her vivid images of loss, rationalized from a pro-revolutionary perspective tempered by the experience of life in Paris, may contribute to her daughter's novel, especially to the descriptions of Versailles and to the episode which ends with Lionel Verney glimpsing his own image in the mirror of a palace (354-55).

In his *Letter to a Noble Lord* (1796), Edmund Burke uses the discourse of speculative astronomy figuratively to make an anti-revolutionary point. The passage from Percy Bysshe Shelley's Notes to *Queen Mab* (1813), a philosophical and visionary poem celebrating republicanism, atheism, and free love, uses a similar discourse to serve a very different political purpose. This passage implies something about the complexity of characterization in *The Last Man*: while the idealized Adrian may represent Percy Shelley, so does Merrival the astronomer, whose futile speculations recall some of the crankier aspects of such poems as *Queen Mab*. Other passages from Wollstonecraft, Burke, and Percy Shelley show how disease can be used as a political metaphor. P. B. Shelley's account of the poet's education (in his Preface to *The Revolt of Islam*) is to some degree a model for Lionel Verney's; the interests he describes recall Adrian's.

The final passage, from Godwin's *Essay on Sepulchres*, is a good example of the kind of optimism that Mary Shelley's novel subverts: in *The Last Man*, the "illustrious dead" could never be recalled by such simple means as Godwin here describes. In a sense, Mary Shelley's novel is a version, perhaps parodic, of Godwin's map of illustrious graves.

1. From Constantin François de Chasseboeuf, comte de Volney, *The Ruins, or A Survey of the Revolutions of Empires* [French text 1791] (London: A. Seale, n.d.)

i. SOLITARY ruins, sacred tombs, ye mouldering and silent walls, all hail! To you I address my Invocation. While the vulgar shrink from your aspect with secret terror, my heart finds in the contemplation a thousand delicious sentiments, a thousand admirable recollections. Pregnant, I may truly call you, with useful lessons, with pathetic and irresistible advice to the man who knows how to consult you. A while ago the whole world bowed the neck in silence before the tyrants that oppressed it; and yet in that hopeless moment you already proclaimed the truths that tyrants hold in abhorrence: mixing the dust of the proudest kings with that of the meanest slaves, you called upon us to contemplate this example of EQUALITY. From your caverns, whither the musing and anxious love of LIBERTY led me, I saw escape its venerable shade, and with unexpected felicity direct its flight and marshal my steps the way to renovated France.

Tombs, what virtues and potency do you exhibit! Tyrants tremble at your aspect; you poison with secret alarm their impious pleasures; they turn from you with impatience, and, coward like, endeavour to forget you amid the sumptuousness of their palaces. It is you that bring home the rod of justice to the powerful oppressor; it is you that wrest the ill gotten gold from the merciless extortioner, and avenge the cause of him that has none to help; you compensate the narrow enjoyments of the poor, by dashing with care the goblet of the rich; to the unfortunate you offer a last and inviolable asylum; in fine,[30] you give to the soul that just equilibrium of strength and tenderness which constitutes the wisdom of the sage and the science of life. The wise man looks towards you, and scorns to amass vain grandeur and useless riches with which he must soon part: you check his lawless flights, without disarming his adventure and his courage; he feels the necessity of passing through the period assigned him, and he gives employment to his hours, and makes use of the goods that fortune has assigned him. Thus do you reign in [i.e. rein in] the wild sallies of cupidity, calm the fever of tumultuous enjoyment, free the mind from the anarchy of the passions and raise it above those little interests which torment the mass of mankind. We ascend the eminence you afford us, and, viewing with one glance the limits of nations and the succession of ages, are incapable of any affections but such as are sublime, and entertain no ideas but those of virtue and glory. Alas! when this uncertain dream of life shall be over, what then will avail all our busy passions, unless they have left behind them the footsteps of utility.[31]

---

30 Finally, in the end.
31 See above, 115n.

Ye ruins, I will turn once more to attend your lessons! I will resume my place in the midst of your wide spreading solitude. I will leave the tragic scene of the passions, will love my species rather from recollection than actual survey, will employ my activity in promoting their happiness, and compose my own happiness of the pleasing remembrance that I have hastened theirs. (xi-xiv)

ii. [The narrator goes on to describe a journey in the year 1784 through parts of Egypt and Syria.]

Directing all my attention to what concerns the happiness of mankind in a state of society, I entered cities, and studied the manners of their inhabitants; I gained admission into palaces, and observed the conduct of those who govern; I wandered over the country, and examined the condition of the peasants: and no where perceiving [a]ught but robbery and devastation, tyranny and wretchedness, my heart was oppressed with sorrow and indignation.

Every day I found in my route fields abandoned by the plough, villages deserted, and cities in ruins. Frequently I met with antique monuments; wrecks of temples, palaces, and fortifications; pillars, aqueducts, sepulchres. By these objects my thoughts were directed to past ages, and my mind absorbed in serious and profound meditation.

Arrived at Hamsa on the borders of the Orontes,[32] and being at no great distance from the city of Palmyra, situated in the desert, I resolved to examine for myself its boasted monuments. After three days travel in barren solitude, and having passed through a valley filled with grottos and tombs, my eyes were suddenly struck, on leaving this valley and entering a plain, with a most astonishing scene of ruins. It consisted of a countless multitude of superb columns standing erect, and which, like the avenues of our parks, extended in regular files farther than the eye could reach. Among these columns magnificent edifices were observable, some entire, others in a state half demolished. The ground was covered on all sides with fragments of similar buildings, cornices, capitals, shafts, entablatures, and pilasters, all constructed of a marble of admirable whiteness and exquisite workmanship. After a walk of three quarters of an hour along these ruins, I entered the inclosure of a vast edifice which had formerly been a temple dedicated to the sun; and I accepted the hospitality of some poor Arabian peasants, who had established their huts in the very area of the temple. Here I resolved for some days to remain, that I might contemplate, at leisure, the beauty of so many stupendous works.

Every day I visited some of the monuments which covered the plain; and one evening that, my mind lost in reflection, I had advanced as far as the *Valley of Sepulchres*, I ascended the heights that bound it, and from

---

32   Orontes is the ancient name of the chief river in Syria.

which the eye commands at once the whole of the ruins and the immensity of the desert.—The sun had just sunk below the horizon; a streak of red still marked the place of his descent, behind the distant mountains of Syria: the full moon appearing with brightness upon a ground of deep blue, rose in the east from the smooth banks of the Euphrates: the sky was unclouded; the air calm and serene; the expiring light of day served to soften the horror of approaching darkness; the refreshing breeze of the night gratefully relieved the intolerable sultriness of the day that had preceded it; the shepherds had led the camels to their stalls; the grey firmament bounded the silent landscape; through the whole desert every thing was marked with stillness, undisturbed but by the mournful cries of the bird of night, and of some *chacals*[33]—The dusk increased, and already I could distinguish nothing more than the pale phantoms of walls and columns—The solitariness of the situation, the serenity of evening, and the grandeur of the scene, impressed my mind with religious thoughtfulness. The view of an illustrious city deserted, the remembrance of past times, their comparison with the present state of things, all combined to raise my heart to a strain of sublime meditations. I sat down on the base of a column; and there, my elbow on my knee, and my head resting on my hand, sometimes turning my eyes towards the desert; and sometimes fixing them on the ruins, I fell into profound reverie. (2-5)

2. From William Godwin, *An Enquiry Concerning Political Justice, and its Influence on General Virtue and Happiness*, 2 vols. (London: Robinson, 1793).

i. If government be a subject, which, like mathematics, natural philosophy and morals, admits of argument and demonstration, then may we reasonably hope that men shall some time or other agree respecting it. If it comprehend every thing that is most important and interesting to man, it is probable that, when the theory is greatly advanced, the practice will not be wholly neglected. Men may one day feel that they are partakers of a common nature, and that true freedom and perfect equity, like food and air, are pregnant with benefit to every constitution. If there be the faintest hope that this shall be the final result, then certainly no subject can inspire to a sound mind such generous enthusiasm, such enlightened ardour and such invincible perseverance.

The probability of this improvement will be sufficiently established, if we consider, FIRST, that the moral characters of men are the result of their perceptions: and, SECONDLY, that of all the modes of operating upon mind government is the most considerable. In addition to these arguments it will be found, THIRDLY, that the good and ill effects of political institu-

---

33 An animal considerably like the Fox, but less cunning, and of a frightful aspect. It lives upon dead bodies, and rocks and ruins are the places of its habitation [Volney's note]; the jackal.

tions are not less conspicuous in detail than in principle; and, FOURTHLY, that perfectibility is one of the most unequivocal characteristics of the human species, so that the political, as well as the intellectual state of man, may be presumed to be in a course of progressive improvement. (1: 10-11)

ii. A ... consequence of the doctrine of necessity[34] is its tendency to make us survey all events with a tranquil and placid temper, and approve and disapprove without impeachment to our self possession. It is true, that events may be contingent as to any knowledge we possess respecting them, however certain they are in themselves. Thus the advocate of liberty knows that his relation was either lost or saved in the great storm that happened two months ago; he regards this event as past and certain, and yet he does not fail to be anxious about it. But it is not less true, that all anxiety and perturbation imply an imperfect sense of contingency, and a feeling as if our efforts could make some alteration in the event. When the person recollects with clearness that the event is over, his mind grows composed; but presently he feels as if it were in the power of God or man to alter it, and his distress is renewed. All that is more than this is the impatience of curiosity; but philosophy and reason have an evident tendency to prevent an useless curiosity from disturbing our peace. He therefore who regards all things past, present and to come as links of an indissoluble chain, will, as often as he recollects this comprehensive view, be superior to the tumult of passion; and will reflect upon the moral concerns of mankind with the same clearness of perception, the same unalterable firmness of judgment, and the same tranquillity as we are accustomed to do upon the truths of geometry. (1: 316-17)

iii. The men ... who exist when the earth shall refuse itself to a more extended population, will cease to propagate, for they will no longer have any motive, either of error or duty, to induce them. In addition to this they will perhaps be immortal. The whole will be a people of men, and not of children. Generation will not succeed generation, nor truth have in a certain degree to recommence her career at the end of every thirty years. There will be no war, no crimes, no administration of justice as it is called, and no government. These latter articles are at no great distance; and it is not impossible that some of the present race of men may live to see them in part accomplished. But beside this, there will be no disease, no anguish, no melancholy and no resentment. Every man will seek with ineffable ardour the good of all. Mind will be active and eager, yet never disappointed. Men will see the progressive advancement of virtue and good, and feel that, if things occasionally happen contrary to their hopes, the miscarriage itself was a necessary part of that progress. They will

---

34   See above, 312n.

know, that they are members of the chain, that each has his several utility, and they will not feel indifferent to that utility. They will be eager to enquire into the good that already exists, the means by which it was produced, and the greater good that is yet in store. They will never want motives for exertion; for that benefit which a man thoroughly understands and earnestly loves, he cannot refrain from endeavouring to promote. (2: 871-72)

3. From Thomas Malthus, *An Essay on the Principle of Population as it affects the Future Improvement of Society* (London: J. Johnson, 1798).

i. [P]opulation increases exactly in the proportion, that the two great checks to it, misery and vice, are removed; and ... there is not a truer criterion of the happiness and innocence of a people, than the rapidity of their increase. The unwholesomeness of towns, to which some persons are necessarily driven, from the nature of their trades, must be considered as a species of misery; and every the slightest check to marriage, from a prospect of the difficulty of maintaining a family, may be fairly classed under the same head. In short, it is difficult to conceive any check to population, which does not come under the description of some species of misery or vice. (107-08)

ii. ... The fertile province of Flanders, which has been so often the seat of the most destructive wars, after a respite of a few years, has appeared always as fruitful and as populous as ever. Even the Palatinate lifted up its head again after the execrable ravages of Lewis the Fourteenth.[35] The effects of the dreadful plague in London in 1666, were not perceptible 15 or 20 years afterwards. The traces of the most destructive famines in China and Indostan, are by all accounts very soon obliterated. It may even be doubted whether Turkey and Egypt are upon an average much less populous, for the plagues that periodically lay them waste. If the number of people which they contain be less now than formerly, it is, probably, rather to be attributed to the tyranny and oppression of the government under which they groan, and the consequent discouragements to agriculture, than to the loss which they sustain by the plague. The most tremendous convulsions of nature, such as volcanic eruptions and earthquakes, if they do not happen so frequently as to drive away the inhabitants, or to destroy their spirit of industry, have but a trifling effect on the average population of any state. Naples, and the country under Vesuvius, are still very populous, notwithstanding the repeated eruptions of that mountain.

---

35   From 1673 to 1679, Louis XIV of France (1638-1715) attacked and devastated the Palatinate, a district of Germany.

And Lisbon and Lima are now, probably, nearly in the same state with regard to population, as they were before the last earthquakes.[36] (110-12)

iii. The great error under which Mr. Godwin labours throughout his whole work [*Political Justice*], is, the attributing almost all the vices and misery that are seen in civil society to human institutions. Political regulations, and the established administration of property, are with him the fruitful sources of all evil, the hotbeds of all the crimes that degrade mankind. Were this really a true state of the case, it would not seem a hopeless task to remove evil completely from the world; and reason seems to be the proper and adequate instrument for effecting so great a purpose. But the truth is, that though human institutions appear to be the obvious and obtrusive causes of much mischief to mankind; yet, in reality, they are light and superficial, they are mere feathers that float on the surface, in comparison with those deeper seated causes of impurity that corrupt the springs, and render turbid the whole stream of human life. (176-77)

4. From Mary Wollstonecraft, *An Historical and Moral View of the Origin and Progress of the French Revolution; and the Effect it has Produced in Europe* (London: J. Johnson, 1794).

i. How silent is now Versailles!—The solitary foot, that mounts the sumptuous stair-case, rests on each landing-place, whilst the eye traverses the void, almost expecting to see the strong images of fancy burst into life.—The train of the Louises, like the posterity of the Banquoes,[37] pass in solemn sadness, pointing at the nothingness of grandeur, fading away on the cold canvass, which covers the nakedness of the spacious walls—whilst the gloominess of the atmosphere gives a deeper shade to the gigantic figures, that seem to be sinking into the embraces of death.

Warily entering the endless apartments, half shut up, the fleeting shadow of the pensive wanderer, reflected in long glasses, that vainly gleam in every direction, slacken the nerves, without appalling the heart; though lascivious pictures, in which grace varnishes voluptuousness, no longer seductive, strike continually home to the bosom the melancholy moral, that anticipates the frozen lesson of experience. The very air is chill, seeming to clog the breath; and the wasting dampness of destruction appears to be stealing into the vast pile, on every side.

The oppressed heart seeks for relief in the garden; but even there the same images glide along the wide neglected walks—all is fearfully still; and, if a little rill creeping through the gathering moss down the cascade,

---

36 Most of Lisbon was destroyed by earthquake, tidal wave, and fire in November 1755; the great earthquake at Lima destroyed its cathedral in 1746.

37 See *Macbeth* 3.4.

over which it used to rush, bring to mind the description of the grand water works, it is only to excite a languid smile at the futile attempt to equal nature.

Lo! this was the palace of the great king!—the abode of magnificence! Who has broken the charm?—Why does it now inspire only pity?— Why;—because nature, smiling around, presents to the imagination materials to build farms, and hospitable mansions, where, without raising idle admiration, that gladness will reign, which opens the heart to benevolence, and that industry, which renders innocent pleasure sweet.

Weeping—scarcely conscious that I weep, O France! over the vestiges of thy former oppression; which, separating man from man with a fence of iron, sophisticated all, and made many completely wretched; I tremble, lest I should meet some unfortunate being, fleeing from the despotism of licentious freedom, hearing the snap of the *guillotine* at his heels; merely because he was once noble, or has afforded an asylum to those, whose only crime is their name—and, if my pen almost bound with eagerness to record the day, that levelled the Bastille with the dust, making the towers of despair tremble to their base;[38] the recollection, that still the abbey is appropriated to hold the victims of revenge and suspicion, palsies the hand that would fain do justice to the assault, which tumbled into heaps of ruins walls that seemed to mock the resistless force of time.—Down fell the temple of despotism; but—despotism has not been buried in it's ruins!—Unhappy country!—when will thy children cease to tear thy bosom?—When will a change of opinion, producing a change of morals, render thee truly free?—When will truth give life to real magnanimity, and justice place equality on a stable seat?—When will thy sons trust, because they deserve to be trusted; and private virtue become the guarantee of patriotism? Ah!—when will thy government become the most perfect, because thy citizens are the most virtuous! (161-64)

ii. Thus had France grown up, and sickened on the corruption of a state diseased. But, as in medicine there is a species of complaint in the bowels which works it's own cure, and, leaving the body healthy, gives an invigorated tone to the system, so there is in politics: and whilst the agitation of it's regeneration continues, the excrementitious humours exuding from the contaminated body will excite a general dislike and contempt for the nation; and it is only the philosophical eye, which looks into the nature and weighs the consequences of human actions, that will be able to discern the cause, which has produced so many dreadful effects. (522)

---

38   The fall of the Bastille in July 1789 was the symbolic focus of revolutionary hopes throughout Europe.

5. From Edmund Burke, *Letter ... to a Noble Lord, on the attacks made upon him and his pension, in the House of Lords* [1796], The Cabinet Library of Scarce and Celebrated Tracts, No. 8 (Edinburgh: Clark, 1837).

i. Astronomers have supposed that if a certain comet, whose path intersected the ecliptic, had met the earth, in some (I forget what) sign, it would have whirled us along with it, in its eccentric course, into God knows what regions of heat and cold.[39] Had the portentous comet of the rights of man, (which "from its horrid hair shakes pestilence, and war," and, "with fear of change perplexes monarchs,"[40]) had that comet crossed upon us in that internal state of England, nothing human could have prevented our being irresistibly hurried, out of the highway of heaven, into all the vices, crimes, horrors and miseries of the French revolution. (9-10)

ii. ... My merit has been in resisting the power and pride of France, under any form of its rule; but in opposing it with the greatest zeal and earnestness, when that rule appeared in the worst form it could assume; the worst indeed which the prime cause and principle of all evil could possibly give it. It was my endeavour by every means to excite a spirit in the house, where I had the honour of a seat, for carrying on with early vigour and decision, the most clearly just and necessary war, that this or any nation ever carried on; in order to save my country from the iron yoke of its power, and from the more dreadful contagion of its principles; to preserve while they can be preserved pure and untainted, the ancient, inbred integrity, piety, good nature, and good humour of the people of England, from the dreadful pestilence which beginning in France, threatens to lay waste the whole moral, and in a great degree the whole physical world, having done both in the focus of its most intense malignity.... (29-30)

6. From P. B. Shelley, Notes to *Queen Mab, The Poetical Works of Percy Bysshe Shelley*, ed. Mary Wollstonecraft Shelley, 4 vols. (London: Edward Moxon, 1839), vol. 1. The speaker in this part of the poem is the Spirit of Ianthe, responding to instruction by Mab, the Fairy Queen, on the follies and cruelties of society. In his notes, Shelley quotes only the italicized lines.

---

39 The ecliptic is either the great circle of the celestial sphere which is the apparent orbit of the sun, or (as here) the great circle on the terrestrial sphere which at any given moment lies in the plane of the celestial ecliptic; an eccentric orbit is one that is neither circular nor dependent on a fixed centre.

40 From *Paradise Lost* 1: 598-99, part of a description of the eclipsed sun, and 2.707-11: "on th'other side / Incens't with indignation *Satan* stood / Unterrifi'd, and like a Comet burn'd, / That ... from his horrid hair / Shakes Pestilence and War."

How sweet a scene will earth become!
Of purest spirits a pure dwelling-place,
Symphonious with the planetary spheres;
When man, with changeless Nature coalescing,
Will undertake regeneration's work,
When its ungenial poles no longer point
　To the red and baleful sun
　That faintly twinkles there. [6.39-46]

The north polar star, to which the axis of the earth, in its present state of obliquity, points. It is exceedingly probable, from many considerations, that this obliquity will gradually diminish, until the equator coincides with the ecliptic: the nights and days will then become equal on the earth throughout the year, and probably the seasons also. There is no great extravagance in presuming that the progress of the perpendicularity of the poles may be as rapid as the progress of intellect; or that there should be a perfect identity between the moral and physical improvement of the human species. It is certain that wisdom is not compatible with disease, and that, in the present state of the climates of the earth, health, in the true and comprehensive sense of the word, is out of the reach of civilised man. Astronomy teaches us that the earth is now in its progress, and that the poles are every year becoming more and more perpendicular to the ecliptic. The strong evidence afforded by the history of mythology and geological researches, that some event of this nature has taken place already, affords a strong presumption that this progress is not merely an oscillation, as has been surmised by some late astronomers.[41] (1: 81)

7. From P. B. Shelley, Preface to *The Revolt of Islam, Poetical Works*, ed. Mary Wollstonecraft Shelley, 4 vols. (London: Edward Moxon, 1839).

i. ... The panic which, like an epidemic transport, seized upon all classes of men during the excesses consequent upon the French Revolution, is gradually giving place to sanity. It has ceased to be believed that whole generations of mankind ought to consign themselves to a hopeless inheritance of ignorance and misery, because a nation of men who had been dupes and slaves for centuries were incapable of conducting themselves

---

41　Laplace, Système du Monde [PBS's note]; cf. 226n. PBS's note offers a pseudo-scientific basis for the return of the Golden Age. Unlike Laplace, who demonstrated an oscillation of the earth's axis without diminished obliquity, Percy Shelley's modern editor, Neville Rogers, explains that "[PBS] wrongly concluded that the obliquity of the ecliptic would decrease, instead of oscillating about the mean value, near 23 1/2 degrees, according to which hypothesis the seasons would become identical and seasonal change be replaced, he hoped, by universal mildness" (1: 393).

with the wisdom and tranquillity of freemen so soon as some of their fetters were partially loosened. That their conduct could not have been marked by any other characters than ferocity and thoughtlessness is the historical fact from which liberty derives all its recommendations, and falsehood the worst features of its deformity. There is a reflux in the tide of human things which bears the shipwrecked hopes of men into a secure haven after the storms are past. Methinks, those who now live have survived an age of despair. (1: 146-47)

ii. There is an education peculiarly fitted for a Poet, without which genius and sensibility can hardly fill the circle of their capacities.... I have been familiar from boyhood with mountains and lake, and the sea, and the solitude of forests: Danger, which sports upon the brink of precipices, has been my playmate. I have trodden the glaciers of the Alps, and lived under the eye of Mont Blanc. I have been a wanderer among distant fields. I have sailed down mighty rivers. and seen the sun rise and set, and the stars come forth, whilst I have sailed night and day down a rapid stream among mountains. I have seen populous cities, and have watched the passions which rise and spread, and sink and change, amongst assembled multitudes of men. I have seen the theatre of the more visible ravages of tyranny and war; cities and villages reduced to scattered groups of black and roofless houses, and the naked inhabitants sitting famished upon their desolated thresholds. I have conversed with living men of genius. The poetry of ancient Greece and Rome, and modern Italy, and our own country, has been to me, like external nature, a passion and an enjoyment. Such are the sources from which the materials for the imagery of my Poem have been drawn. (1: 149)

8. From Godwin, *Essay on Sepulchres: or, A Proposal for Erecting Some Memorial of the Illustrious Dead in All Ages on the Spot where their Remains have been Interred* (London: W. Miller, 1809). Godwin's scheme is briefly stated in his title; his memorials are simple wooden crosses, replaced as necessary, to honour mainly literary achievements.

One observation more. If it should be thought that such a scheme as is here suggested, would, from the mere fluctuation and uncertainty of human affairs, be too precarious in its operation, one further security might be employed. I spoke a while ago of maps, in which the scenes of famous battles were distinguished with a peculiar mark. Why might not something of this kind be introduced in the subject before us? It might be called, the Atlas of those who Have Lived, for the Use of Men Hereafter to be Born. It might be plentifully marked with meridian lines and circles of latitude, "with centric and eccentric scribbled o'er,"[42] so as

---

42 *Paradise Lost* 8.83.

to ascertain with incredible minuteness where the monuments of eminent men had been, and where their ashes continue to repose. If this were done, nothing more would be necessary in times of the greatest calamity and devastation, than to preserve one copy of this precious depository of the records of past ages. Though cities were demolished, and empires overthrown, though the ploughshares were passed over the site of populous streets, and the soil they once occupied were "sown with salt,"[43] the materials would thus be preserved, by means of which, at the greatest distance of time, every thing that was most sacred might be restored, and the calamity which had swallowed up whole generations of men, might be obliterated as if it had never been. (111-14)

---

43   See Judges 9.45.

Appendix E: Mary Shelley's poems

From Mary Shelley's *Journals*, ed. Paula R. Feldman and Diana Scott-Kilvert (Oxford: Clarendon, 1987), 2: 490-95, reprinted by permission of Oxford University Press.

1. "The Choice" [44]

My Choice! My choice—alas was had & gone
With the red gleam of the last summer's sun—
Lost in the deep in which he bathed his head,
My choice, my life, my hope together fled:—
A wanderer—here, no more I seek an home   5
The sky a vault—& Italy a tomb!
Yet as some days a pilgrim I remain
Linked to my orphan child by duty's chain;
And since I have a faith that I must earn
By suffering & by patience, a return   10
Of that companionship & love, which first
Upon my young life's cloud, like sunlight burst,
And now has left me dark as when its beams,
Quench[e]d by the might of dreadful ocean streams,
Leave that one cloud, a gloomy speck on high,   15
Beside one star in the else darkened sky;—
Since I must live, how would I pass the day,
How meet with fewest tears the morning's ray
How sleep with calmest dreams, how find delights
—As fire:flies gleam through interlunar nights!   20

First, let me call on thee, lost as thou art
Thy name aye fills my sense, thy love my heart—
Oh! Gentle Spirit, thou has often sung
How fall'n on evil days thy heart was wrung;
Now fierce remorse and unreplying death   25
Waken a chord within my heart, whose breath,
Thrilling and keen, in accents audible,
A tale of unrequited love doth tell.
It was not anger—while thy earthly dress
Encompassed still thy soul's rare loveliness,   30
All anger was attoned by many a kind
Caress or tear that spoke the softened mind:—

---

44 In form and title MWS's poem echoes Leigh Hunt's poem in *The Liberal* 2
(1823): 265-79, which commemorates PBS and alludes in turn to John
Pomfret's earlier poem, "The Choice," 1700.

It speaks of cold neglect, averted eyes
That blindly crushed thy heart's fond sacrifice:—
My heart was all thine own—but yet a shell   35
Closed in its core, which seemed impenetrable,
Till sharp:toothed Misery tore the husk in twain
Which gaping lies nor may unite again—
Forgive me! let thy love descend in dew
Of soft repentance and regret most true;—   40
In a strange guise thou dost descend—or how
Could love soothe fell remorse?—as it does now!—
—By this remorse and love—and by the years
Through which we shared our common hopes & fears,
By all our best companionship, I dare   45
Call on thy sacred name without a fear
And thus I pray to thee, my Friend; my Heart,
That in thy new abode thou'lt bear a part
In soothing thy poor Mary's heavy [pain],
As link by link she weaves her heavy chain!   50
And thou, strange Star! ascendant at my birth
Which rained, they said, kind influence on the earth,
So from great parents sprung I dared to boast
Fortune my friend, till set, thy beams were lost!
And thou—Inscrutable! by whose decree   55
Has burst this hideous storm of misery!
Here let me cling, here to these solitudes,
These myrtle shaded streams and chesnut woods;
Tear me not hence—here let me live & die,
In my adopted land, my country, Italy!   60

In happy Mother first I saw its sun—
Beneath her sky my race of joy was run—
First my sweet girl—whose face resembled His,
Slept on bleak Lido, near Venetian seas.[45]—
Yet still my eldest born, my loveliest, dearest—   65
Clung to my side—most joyful then when nearest—
An English home had given this angel birth—
Near those royal towers[46]—where the glass:clad earth
Is shadowed o'er my England's loftiest trees:—
Then our companion o'er the swift-passed seas   70
Had dwelt beside the Alps—or gently slept
Rocked by the waves, o'er which our vessel swept,

---

45 Clara Shelley died at Venice in 1818.
46 William Shelley was born at Bishopsgate, near Windsor Castle, in January
    1816.

Beside his father—nurst upon my breast,
While Leman's waters[47] tost with fierce unrest
His fairest limbs had bathed in Serchio's stream,[48]   75
His eyes had watched Italian lightnings gleam;
His childish voice had with its loudest call,
The echoes waked of Este's Castle wall;[49]
Had paced Pompeii's Roman market Place
Had gazed with infant wonder on the grace   80
Of stone wrought deities and pictured saints
In Rome's high palaces—there were no taints
Of ruin on his cheek—all shadowless
Grim death approached—the boy met his caress—
And while his glowing limbs with life's warmth shone,   85
Around those limbs his icy arms were thrown—
His spoils were strewed beneath the land of Rome
Whose flowers now star the dark earth near his tomb[50]—
Its airs & plants received the mortal part,
His spirit beats within his Mother's heart!   90
Infant immortal! Chosen of the sky!
No grief upon thy brows young purity
Entrenched sad lines, or blotted with its might
The sunshine of thy smile's celestial light—
The image shattered—thy bright spirit fled,   95
Thou shin'st the evening star among the dead.
And thou his playmate—whose deep lucid eyes
Were a reflection of these bluest skies;
Child of our hearts, divided in ill hour,
We could not watch the bud's expanding flower,   100
Now thou art gone, one lovely victim more
To the black death which rules this sunny shore[51]

Companion of my griefs! thy sinking frame
Had often drooped—& then erect again

---

47 The Lake of Geneva.
48 A river in Tuscany. The Shelleys returned there after William's death: in May
    1821 PBS and Edward Williams took the boat trip recorded in "The Boat on
    the Serchio."
49 In the summer of 1818 the Shelleys stayed at Byron's villa at Este, about 40
    miles from Venice.
50 See above, 363n and MWS's description in her Preface to PBS's *Adonais* of the
    Protestant Cemetery in Rome, burial-place of John Keats, William Shelley,
    and PBS.
51 The Shelley's niece, Allegra, died in April 1822. Here, "black death" associ-
    ates the idea of plague with any cause of early, unforeseen death.

With shews of health had mocked forebodings dark;   105
Watching the changes of that quivering spark
I feared and hoped—and dared to trust at length
Thy very weakness was my tower of strength—
Methought thou wert a spirit from the sky,
Which struggled with its chains, yet could not die,   110
And that destruction had no power to win,
From out those limbs the soul that burnt within.
Tell me, ye ancient walls, and weed:grown towers,
Ye Roman airs, and brightly painted flowers,
Does not his spirit visit that recess   115
Which built by love, enshrines his earthly dress?
—No more! No more! What tho' that form be fled
My trembling hands shall never write thee—dead—
Thou liv'st in Nature—love—my Memory,
With deathless faith for aye adoring thee—   120
The wife of time no more—I wed Eternity—

'Tis thus the past on which my spirit leans,
Makes dearest to my soul Italian scenes.—
In Tuscan fields, the winds in odours steeped
From flowers and cypresses—when skies have wept,   125
Shall like the notes of music—once most dear,
Which brings the unstrung voice upon my ear
Of one beloved, to memory display
Past scenes—past joys—past hopes, in long array.
The Serchio's stream upon whose banks he stood—   130
The pools reflecting Pisa's old pine wood,
The fire:flies beam—the aziolo's cry—[52]
All breath his spirit, which shall never die.—
Such memories have linked these hills & caves,
These woodland paths, & streams—& knelling waves   135
Fast to each sad pulsation of my breast
And made their melancholy arms the haven of my rest

Here will I live within a little dell,
Which but a month ago I saw full well;
A dream then pictured forth the solitude,   140
Deep in the shelter of a lovely wood:—
A voice then whispered a strange prophesy—
My dearest widowed friend[53]—that thou and I—

---

52 See 139n, above.
53 Jane Williams, whose husband, Edward, was drowned with Shelley.

Should there together pass the livelong day
As we have done before in Spezia's bay[54]   145

2. "On Reading Wordsworth's Lines on Peel Castle"[55]—

It is with me, as erst with you,
    O Poet, Nature's Chronicler,
The summer seas have lost their hue
    And storm sits brooding every where.—

The gentlest rustlings of the deep   5
    Aye sings the dirge of him I lost,
And when the furious billows leap
    And mighty ships in wreck are tost,—

A voice I hear upon the wind—
    Which bids me haste to join him there,   10
And woo the tempest's horrors kind
    Which gives to me a kindred bier.—

And when all smooth are ocean's plains,
    And sails afar are glittering,
The fairest skiff his form contains   15
    To my poor heart's mad picturing.

Then wildly to the beach I rush,
    And fain would seize the frailest boat,
And from dull earth the pinnace push
    On dancing waves towards him to float.   20

"Nor may I e'er again behold
    "The sea, and be as I have been
"My bitter grief will ne'er grow old—
    "Nor say I this with mind serene"[56]—

---

54   At the Casa Magni on the Bay of Spezia, where the Shelleys moved at the end
     of April 1822.
55   Wordsworth's poem, "Elegiac Stanzas Suggested by a Picture of Peele Castle,
     in a storm, painted by Sir George Beaumont," is about the poet's feelings after
     the death of his brother, John, in 1805.
56   A paraphrase of Wordsworth, "Elegiac Stanzas," 37-40: "Not for a moment
     could I now behold / A smiling sea, and be what I have been: / The feeling of
     my loss will ne'er be old; / This, which I know, I speak with mind serene."

For oft I weep in solitude
    And shed so many bitter tears,
While on past joys I vainly brood,
    And shrink in fear from coming years.

3. "To Jane— (with the 'Last Man')"

Tribute for thee dear solace of my life
    Reject not thou thy Mary's offering,
A tale of woe, with many sorrows rife,
    Tribute unmeet, with cypress bound, I bring—

It is the echo, sweet

[Four leaves have been cut out of the manuscript.]

Appendix F: Contemporary Comments on and Reviews of The Last Man

1. From *The Literary Magnet or Monthly Journal of the Belles Lettres*, ns 1 (January 1826): 56.

Mrs. Shelley, the authoress of that monstrous literary abortion, Franken-stein or the modern Prometheus, is, we understand, about to produce another Raw-head-and-bloody-bones, called 'The Last Man.' There is, we believe a novel already published, entitled Omegarius [sic], or the Last Man, a bantling of the Leadenhall press;[57] a fact which might have spared Mr. Campbell the trouble of writing his long letter to the editor of the Edinburgh Review, on the subject of the originality of the conception of *his* Last Man.

2. From *The Literary Gazette, and Journal of the Belles Letters*, 474 (Saturday 18 Feb. 1826): 103-05.

[After some negative general comments on *The Last Man*, the reviewer goes on to quote extensively from the novel. Having quoted the first para-graph of volume 1, chapter 5 ([1: 46-47] above), he continues as follows.]

Were this not written by a woman, it would be sad, vapid imperti-nence: as it is written by a woman, we male critics do not know what it is. We wish we did! Who will teach us?
... When we repeat that these volumes are the production of a female pen, and that we have not ceased to consider Mrs. Shelley as a woman and a widow, we shall have given the clue to our abstinence from remarks upon them. That we must deem the tale altogether to be an instance of the strange misapplication of considerable talent, is most true. After the first volume, it is a sickening repetition of horrors, and a struggle after the display of morbid feelings which could not exist under the circumstances, nor even in the world as it now exists, with good and evil, joys and woes, mingled together. To hear a *last man* talking of having his "sensitive nerves anatomised"[58] by any thing, is sheer nonsense: by the time a man had outlived his kind, Mrs. Shelley might be assured that the nervous sys-tem too was pretty nearly abolished. Then there is no keeping in any of the parts. In spite of the perfection of ballooning, people ride, and drive, and sail, as in the olden days, when aerial travelling was not so agreeable,

---

57 R. Dutton, publisher of *Omegarus and Syderia*, had an office at 45 Gracechurch St., which adjoins Leadenhall St. in the City of London.
58 Sitting down before a mouldy feast near the end of *The Last Man*, Lionel Verney asks himself, "What had I done, that each sensitive nerve was thus to be anatomized?" (354).

when the remnant few of the world are all equal, of course—still, the principal characters hire chaises, have attendants, escorts, postilions! Really these are sad doings. We confess that we cannot get so seriously through the world in its last convulsions as we could wish; but there may be readers who can enter into the spirit of the thing, and to them the perusal of Mrs. Shelley's book may afford gratification. We will add, that there are some strong imaginings in it; and not the least cruel of these flights appears to us to be, the author's making the last human being an unfortunate gentleman. Why not the last Woman? she would have known better how to paint her distress at having nobody left to talk to: we are sure the tale would have been more interesting.

3. From the *Monthly Review* 1 (1826): 333-35.

MRS. Shelley, true to the genius of her family, has found this breathing world and the operations and scenes which enliven it, so little worthy of her soaring fancy, that she once more ventures to create a world of her own, to people it with beings modelled by her own hand, and to govern it by laws drawn from the visionary theories which she has been so long taught to admire as the perfection of wisdom. She seems herself to belong to a sphere different from that with which we are conversant. Her imagination appears to delight in inventions which have no foundation in ordinary occurrences, and no charm for the common sympathies of mankind. We praise our most successful authors for the fidelity with which they paint the human character, for the simplicity which marks their representations of the living drama of life, and for the air of probability which they are sedulous to observe, even when they borrow most abundantly from the resources of imagination. If Mrs. Shelly [sic] is to be set down amongst our popular writers, she will owe her good fortune to the boldness of her departure from all the acknowledged canons of inventive literature; for the whole course of her ambition has been to pourtray monsters which could have existed only in her own conception, and to involve them in scenes and events which are wholly unparalleled by any thing that the world has yet witnessed.

... There is nothing in the conduct, in the characters, in the incidents, or in the descriptive matter of this work, to which we feel any pleasure in referring. The whole appears to us to be the offspring of a diseased imagination, and of a most polluted taste. We must observe, however, that the powers of composition displayed in this production, are by no means of an ordinary character. They are indeed uncontrolled by any of the rules of good writing; but they certainly bear the impress of genius, though perverted and spoiled by morbid affectation. Mrs. Shelley frequently attempts to give her style a rythmical [sic] conciseness, and a poetical colouring, which we take to have been the main causes of the bombast that disfigures almost every chapter of this unamiable romance.

The descriptions of the operations of the pestilence are particularly objectionable for their minuteness. It is not a picture which she gives us, but a lecture in anatomy, in which every part of the human frame is laid bare to the eye, in its most putrid state of corruption. In this part of her subject, as indeed in every other, she amplifies beyond all the bounds of moderation. We are reluctantly obliged to pronounce the work a decided failure.

4. From [John Wilson,] "[review of Hood's] Whims and Oddities," *Blackwood's* 21 (1827): 54.

It will never be known till the last day, whether my Lord Byron or Mister Thomas Campbell was the first to select as a subject of poesie, the Last Man. It is most melancholy, even to a disposition naturally cheerful, to think on the huge mass of unmixed nonsense under which the said poor ill-used Last Man has been buried. Mr. Hood, alive to the ludicrous, has viewed the Last Man in his proper light; and had the verses been published two years ago, they surely would have saved Mrs Shelley from the perpetration of her stupid cruelties. Let that lady, or Mr Campbell, set fire to a sheet of paper, and observe the way in which sparks go out—

There goes the squire, a most illustrious spark,
And there, scarce less illustrious, goes the clerk;

but no one poor unhappy devil of a spark continues scintillating for hours by himself among the ashes, as if he would never go out—but require three volumes of Memoirs to elucidate his character—under the title of the Last Spark. The idea is most pitiful, and unimaginative—and you might as well prove pathetic at a gooseberry bush, over the fate of that last small black hairy grosset.[59] There is no such thing as the Last Man, or the Last Grosset, or the Last Dew-drop, or the Last Rose of Summer, or the Last Kick to a Cockney, or the Last Pot of Porter, or the Last Long Sermon,—but the class of objects to which they one and all do severally belong, goes off after quite another fashion,—men, grossets, dew-drops, sparks, roses, kicks, and sermons, all perish, not by a consecutive series of deaths, but by simultaneous extinction....

A genuine poem, so far from being degraded in our imagination by a successful parody, rises up more beautiful beside its caricatured Eidolon.[60] What the worse has the "Elegy in the Country Church-yard"[61] been of the many thousand parodies that its unparalleled popularity has provoked? Not a whit. On the contrary, it triumphs over them all; either

59 The *OED* gives "groset" or "grossart," a gooseberry.
60 Phantom, image.
61 "Elegy Written in a Country Church-yard," a popular poem by Thomas Gray published in 1751.

sending them into utter oblivion, or embalming them, by means of some portion of its own immortal spirit transfused into the otherwise perishable materials. But a counterfeit poem cannot endure the test of parody, and falls to pieces at once. Its hollowness is exposed—its glitter is seen not to be gold—and the parodist appearing a much clever artist than his original, his original is dished for life. Mr Campbell is a poet of a very high order; and Mr Hood's Last Man is not a parody, it is true, of Mr Campbell's Last Man; but the whole conception of such a person as a Last Man is with great power burlesqued, and that is the same thing in our present argument. Had there been anything really sublime, or striking, or terrible, in the idea of a Last Man, Mr Hood's poem would have left it unimpaired in our imaginations; but the very idea being in itself absurd, and contrary to the very nature and constitution of things, not even to be dreamt on a supper of pork-chops, Mr Hood's poem has exposed its absurdity: and the Last Man of Mr Campbell drifting along in a ship to shores where all are dumb,[62] is just as grotesque a Christian, as Mr Hood's Last Man, perched and puffing on the gallows-tree, with a pound of pigtail in each pocket of his trowsers, and a half-chewed quid in the envelope of his jacket-sleeve, and a club of hair, tufted like a tot's tail, hanging down to his hurdies.[63]

---

62   See Thomas Campbell, "The Last Man" 19-20, Appendix A.2.
63   Pigtail is tobacco twisted into a thin rope; a quid is a piece of chewing tobacco; hurdies are buttocks.

Appendix G: Postscript

From Mary Shelley, *Rambles in Germany and Italy, in 1840, 1842, and 1843*, 2 vols. (London: Edward Moxon, 1844).

Can it, indeed, be true, that I am about to revisit Italy? How many years are gone since I quitted that country! There I left the mortal remains of those beloved—my husband and my children, whose loss changed my whole existence, substituting, for happy peace and the interchange of deep-rooted affections, years of desolate solitude, and a hard struggle with the world; which only now, as my son is growing up, is brightening into a better day. The name of Italy has magic in its very syllables. The hope of seeing it again recalls vividly to my memory that time, when misfortune seemed an empty word, and my habitation on earth a secure abode, which no evil could shake. Graves have opened in my path since then; and, instead of the cheerful voices of the living, I have dwelt among the early tombs of those I loved. Now a new generation has sprung up; and, at the name of Italy, I grow young again in their enjoyments, and gladly prepare to share them. You know, also, how grievously my health has been shaken; a nervous illness interrupts my usual occupations, and disturbs the ordinary tenor of my life. Travelling will cure all: my busy, brooding thoughts will be scattered abroad; and, to use a figure of speech, my mind will, amidst novel and various scenes, renew the outworn and tattered garments in which it has long been clothed, and array itself in a vesture all gay in fresh and glossy hues, when we are beyond the Alps.

Works Cited/Recommended Reading

1. Works by Mary Shelley

The following list is limited to first editions of the novels and standard modern editions of short fiction and other prose.

Mounseer Montongpaw: a new version. London: Juvenile Library, 1808.

History of a Six Weeks' Tour. London: T. Hookham and C. and J. Ollier, 1817; rpt. Oxford: Woodstock, 1989.

Frankenstein, or The Modern Prometheus. 3 vols. London: Lackington, Hughes, Harding, Mayor and Jones, 1818.

Valperga: or, the Life and Adventures of Castruccio, Prince of Lucca. 3 vols. London: G. and W. B. Whittaker, 1823.

Posthumous Poems of Percy Bysshe Shelley. [Ed. Mary Wollstonecraft Shelley] London: Hunt, 1824.

The Last Man. 3 vols. London: Colburn, 1826.

The Fortunes of Perkin Warbeck, a romance. 3 vols. London: Colburn and Bentley, 1830.

Frankenstein, or The Modern Prometheus. Rev. 3rd ed. London: Colburn and Bentley, 1831.

Lodore. 3 vols. London: R. Bentley, 1835.

Falkner, a novel. 3 vols. in 1. London: Saunders and Bentley, 1837.

Eminent Literary and Scientific Men of Italy, Spain, and Portugal. The Cabinet Cyclopaedia, conducted by the Rev. Dionysus Lardner ... assisted by Eminent Literary and Scientific Men. 3 vols. London: Longman, Orme, Brown, Green, and Longmans, 1835-37.

Lives of the Most Eminent Literary and Scientific Men of France. Lardner's Cabinet Cyclopaedia. 2 vols. London: Longman, 1838-39.

The Poetical Works of Percy Bysshe Shelley. Ed. Mary Wollstonecraft Shelley. 4 vols. London: Edward Moxon, 1839.

Rambles in Germany and Italy, in 1840, 1842, and 1843. 2 vols. London: Edward Moxon, 1844.

Proserpine and Midas: two unpublished mythological dramas. Ed. with introd. A. Koszul. London: H. Milford, 1922.

Mathilda [with "The Fields of Fancy"]. Ed. Elizabeth Nitchie. Chapel Hill: U of North Carolina P, [1959].

The Letters of Mary Wollstonecraft Shelley. Ed. Betty T. Bennett. 3 vols. Baltimore: Johns Hopkins UP, 1980.

The Journals of Mary Shelley. Ed. Paula R. Feldman and Diana Scott-Kilvert. 2 vols. Oxford: Clarendon, 1987.

Collected Tales and Stories. Ed. Charles E. Robinson. Baltimore: Johns Hopkins UP, 1990.

2. Some Contemporaries of Mary Shelley's Last Man

Beddoes, Thomas Lovell. "The Last Man" [fragments]. *The Works of Thomas Lovell Beddoes*. Ed. with introd. R. W. Donner. Oxford: Oxford UP, 1935. 520, 525-26.

Byron, George Gordon, Lord. "Darkness." *The Prisoner of Chillon and Other Poems*. London: Murray, 1816.

—. *The Prisoner of Chillon and Other Poems*. Vol. 2 of *Lord Byrons Werke in Kritischen Texten mit Einleitungen und Anmerkungen*. Ed. Eugen Kölbing. Weimar: Emil Felber, 1896.

Campbell, Thomas. "The Last Man." *New Monthly Magazine* 8 (1823): 272-73.

Grainville, Jean-Baptiste Cousin de. *Le dernier homme*. Trans. as *The Last Man, or Omegarus and Syderia: A Romance in Futurity*. 2 vols. London: Dutton, 1806.

Hood, Thomas. "The Last Man." *Whims and Oddities in Prose and Verse* [1826]. 3rd ed. London: Lupton Relfe, 1828. 31-32

Ouseley, P. J. "The Last Man, a fragment." *A Vision of Death's Destruction and Other Poems*. London: 1839. 69-74. Rpt. Byron, ed. Kölbing 224-26.

Pitt, George Dibdin. *The Last Man; or, The Miser of Eltham Green. A Drama in two acts*. New York and London: French, n.d.

"Proteus Harlequin." "The World's End." *Political Miscellanies*. 1825; rpt. Byron, ed. Kölbing.

Reade, John Edmund. "The Last Plague." *Poetical Works*. 2 vols. London: Chapman, 1852. 1: 382-86. Rpt. (1829 text, entitled "Darkness") in Byron, ed. Kölbing 234-38.

"The City of the Dead." *New Monthly* 16 (1826): 404-05.

"The Dance of Death." *Blackwood's* 31 (February 1832): 328-52.

"The Death of the World." *European Magazine* ns 2 (1826): 351-53. Rpt. Byron, ed. Kölbing 208-11.

"The Last Man." *Blackwood's* 19 (March 1826): 284-86.

3. Other Sources, References and Intertexts

Apuleius. *The Transformations of Lucius, otherwise known as The Golden Ass*. Trans. Robert Graves. Harmondsworth: Penguin, 1950.

Ariosto. *Orlando Furioso*. Trans. with introd. Barbara Reynolds. 2 vols. Harmondsworth: Penguin, 1975.

Bacon, Francis. *Essays*. Introd. Oliphant Smeaton. London: Dent, 1906.

—. *Sylva Sylvarum: or a Natural History. The Works of Francis Bacon*. Ed. J. Spedding, R. L. Ellis, and D. D. Heath. London: Longman, 1859. 2: 331-672.

Baughman, Ernest W. *Type and Motif-Index of the Folktales of England and North America*. The Hague: Mouton, 1966.

Beaumont, Francis, and John Fletcher. *The Maid's Tragedy*. Ed. Howard B. Norland. Lincoln: U of Nebraska P, 1968.

Beckford, William. *Vathek*. Ed. with introd. Roger Lonsdale. London: Oxford UP, 1970.

Beddoes, Thomas Lovell. *Works*. See 2. above.

Blackburn, Simon, *Oxford History of Philosophy*. New York: Oxford UP, 1994.

Boccaccio, Giovanni. *The Decameron*. Trans. J. M. Rigg. Introd. Edward Hutton. 2 vols. in 1. London: Dent, 1978.

Browne, Sir Thomas. *Hydriotaphia. The Works of Sir Thomas Browne*. Ed. Sir Geoffrey Keynes. 4 vols. London: Faber, 1964. 1: 129-72.

Brown, Charles Brockden. *Arthur Mervyn, or Memoirs of the Year 1793*. 2 vols. Philadelphia: D. McKay, 1887.

Burke, Edmund. *A Letter to a Noble Lord. The Writings and Speeches of Edmund Burke*. Ed. R. B. McDowell. Gen. ed. Paul Langford. Textual ed. William B. Todd. 9 vols. Oxford: Clarendon, 1991. 9: 145-87.

—. *Letter ... to a Noble Lord, on the attacks made upon him and his pension, in the House of Lords*. The Cabinet Library of Scarce and Celebrated Tracts, No. 8. Edinburgh: Clark, 1837.

—. *A Philosophical Inquiry into the Origin of our Ideas Concerning the Sublime and Beautiful*. Ed. with introd. Adam Phillips. Oxford: Oxford UP, 1990.

—. *Reflections on the Revolution in France*. Ed. Conor Cruise O'Brien. Harmondsworth: Penguin, 1986.

Burns, Robert. *Poems and Songs*. Ed. James Kinsley. 3 vols. Oxford: Clarendon, 1968.

Byron, George Gordon, Lord. *Byron's Letters and Journals*. Ed. Leslie A. Marchand. 12 vols. London: Murray; Cambridge, Mass.: Bellknap, 1973-1982.

—. *The Complete Poetical Works*. Ed. Jerome J. McGann. 7 vols. Oxford: Clarendon, 1980-93.

Calderón de la Barca. *El Príncipe Constante*. Madrid: Espasa-Calpe, 1975.

—. *La Vida es Sueño*. Ed. Enrique Rull. Madrid: Clasicos Taurus, 1992.

Cameron, Kenneth Neill. *The Young Shelley: Genesis of a Radical*. New York: Collier, 1950.

Cameron, Kenneth Neil, and Donald H. Reiman, eds. *Shelley and his Circle, 1773-1822*. Cambridge, Mass.: Harvard UP, 1961-67.

Campbell, Thomas. To the Editor of the *Edinburgh Review*, 28 February 1825. *Times*, 24 March 1825.

Clairmont, Claire. *The Journals of Claire Clairmont*. Ed. Marion Kingston Stocking. Cambridge, Mass.: Harvard UP, 1968.

The Clairmont Correspondence: Letters of Claire Clairmont, Charles Clairmont, and Fanny Imlay Godwin. Ed. Marion Kingston Stocking. 2 vols. Baltimore: Johns Hopkins, 1995.

Cleveland, John. *Poems by J[ohn] C[leveland] with Additions, never before Printed*. London, 1653.

Coleridge, Samuel Taylor. *The Poems of Samuel Taylor Coleridge*. Ed. Ernest Hartley Coleridge. London: Oxford UP, 1912.

"Contagion and Sanitary Laws." *Westminster Review* 3 (1825): 134-67.

Dante Alighieri. *The Divine Comedy, Vol. 1: Inferno.* Trans. with introd. and notes Mark Musa. Harmondsworth: Penguin, 1984.

Defoe, Daniel. *The History of the Great Plague in London, in the Year 1665 ... by a citizen.* [A Journal of the Plague Year.] London: John Offor, 1819.

———. *A Journal of the Plague Year.* Ed. Anthony Burgess and Christopher Bristow. Introd. Anthony Burgess. Harmondsworth: Penguin, 1970.

———. *The Life and Adventures of Robinson Crusoe.* 1719. Ed. with introd. Angus Ross. Harmondsworth: Penguin, 1965.

Elton, Charles Abraham, ed. *Remains of Hesiod.* See Hesiod.

———. *Specimens of the classic poets, in a chronological series from Homer to Tryphiodorus.* Translated into English verse ... by Charles Abraham Elton. 3 vols. London: Baldwin, 1814.

Euripides. *The Suppliant Women.* Trans. Rosanna Warren and Stephen Scully. New York: Oxford UP, 1995.

Fisher, Lois H. *A Literary Gazeteer of England.* New York: McGraw-Hill, 1980.

Genest, John. *Some Account of the English Stage from the Restoration in 1660 to 1830.* 10 vols. Bath: Carrington, 1832.

Gibbon, Edward. *The History of the Decline and Fall of the Roman Empire.* 6 vols. London: Strahan and Cadell, 1776-88.

Godwin, William. *Caleb Williams, or Things As They Are.* Ed. with introd. David McCracken. London: Oxford UP, 1970.

———. *An Enquiry Concerning Political Justice, and its Influence on General Virtue and Happiness.* 2 vols. London: Robinson, 1793.

———. *Essay on Sepulchres: or, A Proposal for Erecting Some Memorial of the Illustrious Dead in All Ages on the Spot where their Remains have been Interred.* London: W. Miller, 1809.

———. *Fables, ancient and modern.* 2 vols. London: Juvenile Library, [1805].

———. *History of the Commonwealth of England. From its Commencement, to the Restoration of Charles the Second.* 4 vols. London: Colburn, 1824.

———. *Of Population; an enquiry concerning the power of increase in the numbers of mankind, being an answer to Mr. Malthus's essay on that subject.* London: Longman, Hurst, Rees, Orme and Brown, 1820.

Goethe, Johann Wolfgang von. *Goethe's Faust.* Trans. Barker Fairley. Toronto: U of Toronto P, 1970.

———. *The Sorrows of Young Werther and Selected Writings.* Trans. Catherine Hutter. Foreword Hermann J. Weigand. New York: Signet, 1962.

Hazlitt, William. "My First Acquaintance with Poets." *The Liberal* 2 (1823): 23-46.

Hesiod. *Remains of Hesiod.* Trans. Charles Abraham Elton. 2nd ed. London, 1815.

Holmes, Richard. *Shelley: The Pursuit.* New York: Dutton, 1975.

Homer. *The Iliad.* Trans. with introd. Richmond Lattimore. Chicago: Phoenix, 1961.

———. *The Odyssey.* Trans. E. V. Rieu. Harmondsworth: Penguin, 1946.

Hunt, Leigh. *The Poetical Works of Leigh Hunt*. Ed. H. S. Milford. 1923. New York: AMS, 1978.

Jeffrey, Francis. Review of Thomas Campbell's *Theodric*. *Edinburgh Review* 41.82 (1824-25): 271-87.

Jones, Sir William. *The Works of Sir William Jones with a Life of the Author by Lord Teignmouth*. 6 vols. 1799; rpt. Delhi: Agam Prakashan, 1977.

Keats, John. *The Poems of John Keats*. Ed. Jack Stillinger. Cambridge, Mass.: Harvard UP, 1978.

Lewis, Matthew Gregory. *The Monk*. Ed. Howard Anderson. Oxford: Oxford UP, 1980.

Lucretius. *The Nature of Things*. Trans. Frank O. Copley. New York: Norton, 1977.

Lyles, W. H. *Mary Shelley: An Annotated Bibliography*. New York: Garland, 1975.

Mackey, Sampson Arnold. *Mythological Astronomy of the Ancients Demonstrated by Restoring to the Fables and Symbols their Original Meanings*. 1822-23. Minneapolis: Wizards' Bookshelf, 1973.

Malthus, Thomas Robert. *An Essay on the Principle of Population, as it affects the Future Improvement of Society*. London: J. Johnson, 1798.

Marvell, Andrew. *Selected Poetry*. Ed. Frank Kermode. New York: New American Library, 1967.

Milton, John. *Complete Poems and Major Prose*. Ed. Merritt Y. Hughes. Indianapolis: Bobbs-Merrill, 1957.

Montagu, Lady Mary Wortley. *Letters from the Levant during the Embassy to Constantinople, 1716-18*. With a preliminary discourse and notes ... by J. A. St. John, Esq. London: Joseph Rickerby, 1839.

Moore, Thomas. *The Poetical Works*. New York: Lovell, n.d.

Nitchie, Elizabeth. *Mary Shelley*. New Brunswick: Rutgers UP, 1953.

Ovid. *The Art of Love, and Other Poems*. With trans. J. H. Mozley. Cambridge, Mass.: Harvard UP, 1939.

——. *Metamorphoses*. With trans. by Frank Justus Miller. 3rd ed. 2 vols. London: Heinemann, 1977.

Owenson, Sydney, Lady Morgan. *The Missionary: an Indian Tale*. 3 vols. London: Stockdale, 1811.

Paine, Thomas. *Rights of Man*. Introd. Eric Foner. Notes by Henry Collins. Harmondsworth: Penguin, 1985.

Paquin, Marie Thérèse, trans. *Don Giovanni* [libretto]. Montreal: Les Presses de l'Université de Montréal, 1974.

Peacock, Thomas Love. *Rhododaphne: or The Thessalian Spell. A Poem*. London: Hookham, 1818.

——. *Palmyra, and Other Poems*. London: Richardson, 1806.

Petrarch (Francesco Petrarca). *Petrarch's Lyric Poems: The "Rime sparsa" and Other Lyrics*. Trans. and ed. Robert M. Durling. Cambridge, Mass.: Harvard UP, 1976.

"Plague—Typhus Fever—Quarantine." *Westminster Review*, 3 (1825): 499-530.

Plato. *The Collected Dialogues*. Ed. Edith Hamilton and Huntington Cairns. Bollingen Series 71. Princeton: Princeton UP, 1963.

—. *The Symposium* ["The Banquet of Plato"]. Trans. P. B. Shelley. *Complete Works*. Ed. Roger Ingpen and Walter E. Peck. 7: 165-220.

Pliny. *Natural History*. With trans. by H. Rackham. 10 vols. London: Heinemann, 1956.

Plutarch. "The Dialogue on Love." *Moralia*. With trans. Edwin L. Minar, F. H. Sandbach, and W. C. Helmbold. 15 vols. London: Heinemann, 1961. 9: 303-441.

Pope, Alexander. *The Poems of Alexander Pope*. Ed. John Butt. London: Methuen, 1963.

Prior, Matthew. *Literary Works*. Ed. H. Bunker Wright and Monroe K. Spears. 2 vols. Oxford: Clarendon, 1959.

Procopius. *History of the Wars*. [Works.] With trans. by H. B. Dewing. 6 vols. London: Heinemann, 1914. Vol. 1.

Radcliffe, Ann. *The Italian*. Ed. Frederick Garber. Oxford: Oxford UP, 1981.

Rev. of *The Last Man*. *The Literary Magnet or Monthly Journal of the Belles Lettres*, ns 1 (January 1826): 56.

Rev. of *The Last Man*. *The Literary Gazette, and Journal of the Belles Letters* 474 (Saturday 18 February 1826): 103-05.

Rev. of *The Last Man*. *Monthly Review* 1 (1826): 333-35.

Schiller, Friedrich. *The Death of Wallenstein*. Trans. S. T. Coleridge. London: Longman and Rees, 1800.

Schoep, Arthur, and Daniel Harris. *Word-by-Word Translations of Songs and Arias, Part 2—Italian*. Metuchen, New Jersey: Scarecrow, 1972.

Shakespeare, William. *Complete Works*. Ed. Peter Alexander. London: Collins, 1951.

Sheil, Richard. *Evadne, or, The Statue*. New York and London: French, n.d.

Shelley, Mary. *Frankenstein; or, The Modern Prometheus*. The 1818 version. Ed. D. L. Macdonald and Kathleen Scherf. Peterborough: Broadview, 1994.

—. *The Last Man*. Ed. Hugh J. Luke, Jr. 1965. Introd. Anne K. Mellor. Lincoln: U of Nebraska P, 1993.

—. *The Last Man*. Ed. with introd. Morton D. Paley. Oxford: Oxford UP, 1994.

Shelley, Percy Bysshe. *The Complete Poetical Works of Percy Bysshe Shelley*. Ed. Neville Rogers. 4 vols. Oxford: Clarendon, 1972-.

—. *Complete Works*. Ed. Roger Ingpen and Walter E. Peck. 10 vols. New York: Gordian, 1965.

—. *The Letters of Percy Bysshe Shelley*. Ed. Frederick L. Jones. 3 vols. Oxford: Clarendon, 1964.

—. *The Poetical Works of Percy Bysshe Shelley*. Ed. Thomas Hutchinson. Corrected by G. M. Matthew. Oxford: Oxford UP, 1970.

Smith, Charlotte. *Desmond, A Novel*. 3 vols. London: Robinson, 1792.

Sophocles. *Oedipus the King, Oedipus at Colonus, Antigone.* Trans. David Grene, Robert Fitzgerald, Elizabeth Wyckoff. New York: Washington Square, 1967.

Southey, Robert. *Poems.* Ed. Maurice H. Fitzgerald. London: Frowde, 1909.

Spenser, Edmund. *Poetical Works.* Ed. J. C. Smith and E. De Selincourt. London: Oxford UP, 1969.

Staël, Anne-Louise-Germaine de. *Corinne, or, Italy.* Trans. with introd. Avriel H. Goldberger. New Brunswick, N.J.: Rutgers UP, 1987.

St Clair, William. *The Godwins and the Shelleys: The Biography of a Family.* New York: Norton, 1989.

Swift, Jonathan. *Gulliver's Travels. The Writings of Jonathan Swift.* Ed. Robert A. Greenberg and William B. Piper. New York: Norton, 1973.

Tacitus. *Histories; The Annals.* 4 vols. Cambridge, Mass.: Harvard UP, 1925.

Thucydides. *History of the Peloponnesian War,* Book 2. Ed. J. S. Rusten. Cambridge: Cambridge UP, 1989.

—. *The Plague of Athens, Which ha[p]pened in the Second Year of the Peloponnesian War.* Trans. Thomas Sprat. London: H. Hills, 1709.

Virgil. *The Aeneid.* Trans. James Beresford. London: J. Johnson, 1794.

—. *Eclogues, Georgics, Aeneid.* With trans. by H. Rushton Fairclough. 2 vols. London: Heinemann, 1974.

—. *P. Vergilis Maronis Aeneidos Liber Sextus.* Commentary by R.G. Austin. Oxford: Clarendon, 1977.

Volney, Constantin François de Chasseboeuf, comte de. *The Ruins, or A Survey of the Revolutions of Empires.* London: A. Seale, n.d.

Wasserman, Earl. *Shelley: A Critical Reading.* Baltimore and London: Johns Hopkins, 1971.

[Wilson, John.] "[Review of Thomas Hood's] Whims and Oddities." *Blackwood's* 21 (1827): 54.

—. *The City of the Plague and Other Poems.* Edinburgh: Constable, 1816. Rpt. *Oxford Prize Poems and The City of the Plague.* Introd. Donald H. Reiman. New York and London: Garland, 1979.

Wollstonecraft, Mary. *A Vindication of the Rights of Woman.* 1792. Ed. Carol H. Poston. 2nd ed. New York: Norton, 1988.

—. *A Vindication of the Rights of Men. Political Writings.* Ed. Janet Todd. Toronto: U of Toronto P, 1993. 1-65.

—. *An Historical and Moral View of the Origin and Progress of the French Revolution; and the effect it has produced in Europe.* Vol. 1 [of only one completed]. London: J. Johnson, 1794.

—. *Letters Written during a Short Residence in Sweden, Norway, and Denmark.* Ed. with introd. Carol H. Poston. Lincoln: U of Nebraska P, 1976.

Wordsworth, William. *Poetical Works.* Ed. with introd. Thomas Hutchinson. Rev. Ernest de Selincourt. London: Oxford UP, 1950.

Young, Edward. *The Complete Works, Poetry and Prose.* Ed. James Nichols. 1854; rpt. Hildesheim: Georg Olms, 1968.

4. Further Reading on Mary Shelley's *The Last Man*

Aaron, Jane. "The Return of the Repressed: Reading Mary Shelley's The Last Man." *Feminist Criticism: Theory and Practice.* Ed. Susan Seller. Toronto: U of Toronto P, 1991. 9-21.

Bloom, Harold, ed. *Mary Shelley.* New York: Chelsea House, 1985.

Ellis, Kate Ferguson. "Subversive Surfaces: The Limits of Domestic Affection in Mary Shelley's Later Fiction." Fisch, Mellor, and Schor 220-34.

Fisch, Audrey A. "Plaguing Politics: AIDS, Deconstruction, and *The Last Man.*" Fisch, Mellor, and Schor 267-86.

Fisch, Audrey A., Anne K. Mellor, and Esther H. Schor, eds. *The Other Mary Shelley: Beyond "Frankenstein."* New York: Oxford UP, 1993.

Franci, Giovanni. "A Mirror of the Future: Vision and Apocalypse in Mary Shelley's *The Last Man.*" Bloom 181-91.

Goldsmith, Steven. "Of Gender, Plague, and Apocalypse: Mary Shelley's *Last Man.*" *Yale Journal of Criticism,* 4.1 (1990): 129-73.

Johnson, Barbara. "The Last Man." Trans. from French in Fisch, Mellor, and Schor 258-66.

Lovell, Ernest J., Jr. "Byron and the Byronic Hero in the Novels of Mary Shelley," *University of Texas Studies in English* 30 (1951): 158-83.

Luke, Hugh M., Jr. "The Last Man: Mary Shelley's Myth of the Solitary." *Prairie Schooner* 39 (1965-66): 316-27.

—. Introduction to *The Last Man.* Ed. Hugh J. Luke, Jr. Lincoln: U of Nebraska P, 1965.

Majewski, Henry F. "Grainville's *Le Dernier Homme.*" *Symposium* 17.2 (1963): 114-22.

Mellor, Anne K. *Mary Shelley: Her Life, Her Fiction, Her Monsters.* New York: Routledge, 1988.

—. "On Feminist Utopias." *Women's Studies* 9 (1982): 241-62.

Miller, Arthur McA. *The Last Man: A Study of the Eschatological Theme in English Poetry and Fiction from 1806 through 1839.* Ph.D. diss. Duke University, 1966.

Palacio, Jean de. "Mary Shelley and *The Last Man*: A Minor Romantic Theme." *Revue de Littérature Comparée* 42 (1968): 37-49.

Paley, Morton D. "*Le dernier homme*: The French Revolution as the Failure of Typology." *Mosaic: A Journal for the Interdisciplinary Study of Literature* 24.1 (1991): 67-76.

—. *The Last Man*: Apocalypse without Millennium." Fisch, Mellor, and Schor 107-23.

—. Introduction to *The Last Man.* Ed. Morton D. Paley.

Peck, Walter E. "The Biographical Element in the Novels of Mary Wollstonecraft Shelley." *PMLA* 38 (1923): 196-219.

Poovey, Mary. *The Proper Lady and the Woman Writer: Ideology as Style in the Works of Mary Wollstonecraft, Mary Shelley, and Jane Austen.* Chicago: U of Chicago P, 1984.

Sambrook, A. J. "A Romantic Theme: The Last Man." *Forum for Modern Language Studies* 2 (1966): 25-33.

Snyder, Robert Lance. "Apocalypse and Indeterminacy in Mary Shelley's *The Last Man*." *Studies in Romanticism* 17 (1978): 435-52.

Spatt, Hartley S. "Mary Shelley's Last Men: The Truth of Dreams." *Studies in the Novel* 7 (1975): 526-37.

Sterrenburg, Lee. "*The Last Man*: Anatomy of Failed Revolutions." *Nineteenth-Century Fiction* 33 (1978): 324-47.

Zimmerman, Phyllis. "Some Lines of Italian Poetry in the Introduction to *The Last Man*." *Notes and Queries* 235 (1990): 31-32.

From the Publisher

A name never says it all, but the word "Broadview" expresses a good deal of the philosophy behind our company. We are open to a broad range of academic approaches and political viewpoints. We pay attention to the broad impact book publishing and book printing has in the wider world; for some years now we have used 100% recycled paper for most titles. Our publishing program is internationally oriented and broad-ranging. Our individual titles often appeal to a broad readership too; many are of interest as much to general readers as to academics and students.

Founded in 1985, Broadview remains a fully independent company owned by its shareholders—not an imprint or subsidiary of a larger multinational.

For the most accurate information on our books (including information on pricing, editions, and formats) please visit our website at www.broadviewpress.com. Our print books and ebooks are also available for sale on our site.

broadview press
www.broadviewpress.com

The interior of this book is printed on 100% recycled paper.

100%

TCF

BIO·GAS
ENERGY

PERMANENT